Acclaim for the
"top-notch romantic suspense"
(Booklist) of
Karen Robards

TO TRUST A STRANGER

"Vintage Robards. . . . [A] choice romantic thriller."
—*Romantic Times* (A *Romantic Times* Top Pick)

"[A] tough, sensual romantic mystery from the prolific and popular Robards."   —*Kirkus Reviews*

"Seduction, corruption, and bone-chilling suspense. . . . A really good edge-of-your-seat, humorous, and sexy romantic suspense novel that all can enjoy."
—*The Sullivan County Democrat*

"[A] taut thriller . . . that never slows down."
—*The Midwest Book Review*

"You'll be snagged on the first page. . . ."
—*The Pilot* (Southern Pines, NC)

WHISPERS AT MIDNIGHT

"Southern gothic, suspense, and rough-and-tumble romance. . . . Robards is a lively storyteller."
—*Publishers Weekly*

"One of [her] best. . . . If you're looking for love, get out the fan: This one is hot."   —*The Columbus Dispatch*

"Robards has perfected a knack for blending intrigue and romance. . . . Fun. . . . Keeps you turning the pages."
—Knight Ridder/Tribune News Service

KAREN ROBARDS

To Trust A Stranger

Whispers At Midnight

POCKET BOOKS

New York London Toronto Sydney

POCKET BOOKS, a division of Simon & Schuster, Inc.
1230 Avenue of the Americas, New York, NY 10020

This book is a work of fiction. Names, characters, places and incidents are products of the author's imagination or are used fictitiously. Any resemblance to actual events or locales or persons, living or dead, is entirely coincidental.

ISBN-13: 978-1-4165-0738-3
ISBN-10:   1-4165-0738-8

First Pocket Books trade paperback edition January 2005

10 9 8 7 6 5 4 3

POCKET and colophon are registered trademarks of Simon & Schuster, Inc.

Manufactured in the United States of America

For information regarding special discounts for bulk purchases, please contact Simon & Schuster Special Sales at 1-800-456-6798 or business@simonandschuster.com.

To Trust A Stranger

This book is dedicated to my new niece, Catherine Spicer, and my new nephew, Hunter Johnson. It is also dedicated to Samantha Spicer, Bradley, Blake and Chase Johnson, Austin and Trevor Johnson, Jason Wearren, Justin Kennady and Rachel Rose. And of course, as always, it is dedicated to my husband, Doug, and my three sons, Peter, Christopher and Jack, with much love.

PROLOGUE

1987

"Please. Please don't do this." Kelly Carlson's voice broke. Tears flowed as she looked beseechingly over her shoulder at the man prodding her forward. The wet tracks sliding down her pale cheeks shone silver in the moonlight.

"Walk down to the end of the car." The gun aimed at her back never wavered. The eyes of the man holding it were as cold and soulless as the dark waters of South Carolina's Lake Moultrie, which spread out like a black-tinted mirror before them, reflecting in its rippling surface the cold blue glitter of the stars overhead. The brand-new champagne-colored Cougar was parked on a twelve-foot-high wooded cliff overlooking the lake. It was a popular spot for family picnics in the summer. Tonight, with the temperature hovering at around forty degrees and the time well past two A.M., it was deserted except for the desperate little tableau being played out around the car.

"I'm begging you. Please." Kelly obediently stumbled forward, her gait unsteady, her boots crunching through drifts of fallen leaves. Her voice was high-pitched, near hysteria. Daniel McQuarry could have told her that begging for her life was a waste of time. He would have told her, if the duct tape covering his mouth had allowed him to say anything at all.

Woozy from the just-ended beating that had left him bruised and bloodied, sick at his stomach with the pain of what he judged to be roughly half a dozen cracked or broken ribs, he could barely keep her in focus as he leaned against the cool smooth curve of the driver's door, his hands cuffed behind his back, a gun grinding into his spine. Blinking the blood that poured from a cut on his forehead from his eyes, he watched her stumbling progress, mentally apologizing to her for not having recognized the danger earlier, in time to save them both from this. He'd been stupid, cocky, sure of his ability to follow the devil down to hell and come back out again smelling like a rose.

It was the story of his life, and now it was going to get him—and Kelly, pretty blond twenty-two-year-old Kelly, who'd made the mistake of trusting him with both the deadly secret she'd uncovered and her safety—killed.

Terror swamped the pain, causing his heart to race. He was twenty-five years old. He had a lot of living left to do. He didn't want to die.

Tough titty, as his grandma was fond of saying. Unless something went his way pretty damned fast, he was going to.

He moved, and the hideous stabbing pain cutting like hot knives through his chest drove out the terror. Nostrils shuddering with the effort of drawing in air through his battered nose, able to take only the shortest, shallowest breaths because of his damaged ribs, he fought to keep from passing out. If he did, they didn't have a chance.

Who was he trying to kid? They didn't have a chance anyway. All his highly specialized training not withstanding, there was no way that he could see out of this.

One of the four men—he knew them all, had worked and played with them as friends even while doing the job the government paid him to do—surrounding the vehicle popped the trunk. It rose, pale and ominous as Marley's ghost, above the black, gaping mouth that he realized with sudden icy certainty was intended to be his and Kelly's tomb.

He knew how they worked, and how they worked wasn't pretty. Violence came as naturally to them as breathing, and anyone who posed a threat to them ended up dead. They'd beaten the information they'd needed out of him—or at least, so they thought—and now that they had it, he was just so much garbage to be disposed of. Kelly too, despite the fact that she was the wife of the boss's son.

"Daniel, do something." Kelly's eyes were wide and terrified as she looked around at him. Her narrow shoulders in the black leather blazer she wore over jeans were visibly shaking. "Can't you *do* something? They're going to kill us. Please don't let them kill us." She started to sob, terrible wrenching sobs that hurt him to hear, and turned toward the man behind her. "Don't kill us. I'm so scared. Oh, God, I'll do anything. Anything. . . ."

"You shouldn't've done what you did." Her captor grabbed her shoulder to stop her, turn her back around. "Get in the trunk."

"No! Oh, please. . . ." Gasping and crying hysterically, Kelly shook free and bolted, taking everyone by surprise. She bounded away from the Cougar and fled toward the road, toward the empty ribbon of black asphalt some quarter of a mile away that would have offered her no succor even if she had had a prayer of reaching it, which she didn't. Her high, keening screams rent the darkness as she ran. Daniel's blood ran cold. A memory flashed into his mind of a pig he had heard once as it was being hung for slaughter.

"Get her!" They all, with the exception of the man behind him, raced after Kelly.

It was his last, best chance to make his move. Summoning superhuman strength, Daniel gritted his teeth against bodily weakness and the torture his ribs were inflicting on him and whirled, kicking out with his leg. The movement was slow and feeble compared with his usual highly trained ferocity, but it caught his captor by surprise.

He went down with an oath.

Daniel sprang away, heading for the beckoning line of trees some three hundred yards to the left. If he could reach the woods he had the merest sliver of a chance. But even as he frantically lurched forward, bent like an old crone and in agonizing pain that increased a thousandfold with every step, he knew that it was futile, knew that he wasn't going to make it.

In the distance he heard a shot and a gurgling scream: Kelly. His heart leaped, and tears—he hadn't cried since he was seven—began to ooze from his eyes.

When the bullet caught him, it was almost a relief. It hit him like a kick from a mule, knocking him forward, sending him sprawling on his face on the hard, cold ground. Instead of hurting, though, the explosion blasted away his pain. Senses dimming, he realized that his spinal cord had probably been severed, and that there was a great pumping hole in his chest. Blood was gushing out around him like water from a hose. Within seconds he was lying in a dark gleaming pool of it.

The good news was, he didn't feel pain any longer. He didn't feel afraid. What he felt was—cold.

The bad news was, he wasn't going to make it. He

wasn't going to see his grandma or mother or brother or anyone or anything else he loved ever again in this life.

More tears leaked from his eyes at the thought.

But by the time they came for him, two of them, lifting him up by his armpits and his knees, carrying him back toward the car, he was able to look up at the star-studded sky with a little smile on his lips. When they shoved him into the trunk beside Kelly—poor dead Kelly, her eyes stared at him glassily—and shut the lid, closing him into darkness forever, he was able to hold that image in his mind.

He was still seeing that beautiful spangled sky as he died.

1

Fifteen years later

W*AKE UP.*

Julie Carlson's eyes blinked open. For a moment she lay still, heart racing, staring groggily into the darkness, not sure what had awakened her or why she felt so frightened. It took only a moment or so for her to realize that she was lying in her own bed, in her own bedroom, listening to the familiar hum of the air conditioner as it kept the sweltering heat of the July night at bay and smelling the comforting aroma of her own smooth clean sheets. Her potbellied teddy bear, a poignant memento of her late father, sat stolidly in its accustomed spot on the bedside table. She could just see the comforting shape of it by the faint glow of the alarm clock.

She must have had a nightmare. That would explain why she was curled up in a tight little ball under the bedclothes when she usually slept sprawled on her stomach; it would account for the now-slowing thud of her heart; it would explain her sense of—there was no other word for it—dread.

Something's wrong.

Although the words were distinct, the urgent whisper was in her head. She was all alone in her bedroom, all alone in the whole huge upstairs of her house. Sid, the dog, was obviously spending another night in the guest room.

At the thought, Julie felt her stomach knot. She had gone downstairs around eleven, to find her husband sitting on the couch in the den watching TV.

"I'll be up after the news," he'd said. Not wanting to start a fight—all they did lately was fight—she'd crossed her fingers and gone back upstairs to bed without uttering so much as a cross or demanding word. But here it was—she focused on the clock—at two minutes after midnight, and she was still alone in their bed.

Maybe—maybe he was still coming. Maybe he was watching Letterman. Maybe tonight Leno had an especially fascinating guest.

Get real, she told herself, uncurling her arms and legs as anger edged out fear. And maybe the Pope was a Protestant, too.

Listen.

Her attention immediately refocused. Trying not to be creeped out, Julie put out a hand, groping for the switch to the bedside lamp.

Then she heard it, and froze.

The distant sound—vibration really—of the garage door going up made her eyes widen and her fists clench.

Her heart gave an odd little leap. Her stomach heaved. She forced herself to take a pair of deep, calming breaths.

Despite all her hopes, all her prayers, it was happening again.

Oh, God, what should she do?

Julie Carlson didn't know it, but she had less than an hour left to live.

Other than a single light in a downstairs room, her house was dark. It was a big house in an exclusive gated community just west of Charleston, and, if all went according to plan, in a few minutes she was going to be all alone in it.

Then he would emerge from the shadows beneath the rustling palmettos in her side yard, break in through her back door, and creep up the stairs to the first door on the left. That door opened into the master bedroom, where she should already—it was a few minutes after midnight—be sound asleep.

Surprise, surprise.

Roger Basta allowed himself a small smile. This was going to be fun. The thought of what he was going to do to Julie Carlson made his breathing quicken. He'd been watching her for weeks, getting the household schedule down, making his plans, anticipating. Tonight he got to enjoy the fruits of all that labor.

Sometimes, and this was one, he loved what he did for a living.

The light went out downstairs. The house was now totally dark.

Just a few minutes more.

He fingered the snapshot in his pocket. It was too dark for him to be able to see it, but he was nearly as familiar with the image on it as he was with his own face in the mirror. Julie Carlson in a white bikini, slim and tanned and laughing, poised to dive into the swimming pool in her own backyard.

He'd taken it himself three days before.

One of the quartet of garage doors that faced his position rose, and seconds later a big black Mercedes purred silently down the driveway. The husband was leaving, right on schedule.

The garage door closed again. The Mercedes turned left at the end of the driveway, and drove away toward the interstate some five miles distant. The house was once again dark and quiet.

Everything was going down as expected.

The burglar alarm would be off, which made his job just that much easier. He had a window of maybe three and a quarter hours to get in and out before the husband returned. He would need far less.

Although he might want to linger over this one. Remembering the picture, he smiled. He definitely wanted to linger over this one.

Julie Carlson was a babe.

His instructions had been to make the hit look like anything but the professional, targeted job it was.

His reply had been, Can do.

Crouching, Basta set the small black satchel he carried on the carpet of golf-course-quality grass that covered the lawn and unzipped it. The steamy July heat, complete with swarms of hungry mosquitoes and a faint fruity scent, wrapped uncomfortably around him. It reminded him that he was wearing long pants and a cotton turtle-neck, both black, on a night that cried out for shorts and not much else. A quick rummage through the contents reassured him that everything he might need was in the bag: burglary tools, duct tape, a small flashlight, a thin nylon cord and a pencil to use as a garrote, a box of surgi-cal gloves, another of condoms. He touched his knit cap, making sure it fit tightly around his head and over his eyebrows. He'd shaved his body completely so as not to leave telltale hairs at the scene, but shaving his head and eyebrows would, he feared, make him too memorable to those who might be questioned in the aftermath of the crime. The last thing he wanted was to be memorable.

Besides, his thinning gray hair gave him an innocuous look, he felt. Countless people usually saw him in the days before a hit—neighbors, passersby, convenience-store clerks, trash collectors—but nobody ever remembered him, because he looked like a fifty-something Joe Average. DNA notwithstanding, the cap worked. The first two hadn't had time to dislodge it before he'd had them duct-taped into immobility, and Julie Carlson wouldn't either.

He was that good.

Sliding the flashlight into his pocket, he rezipped the bag, picked up his pistol, stood up and headed around to the back of the house. The swimming pool sparkled in the moonlight. Lush pots of tropical flowers gave off a heady scent. Cicadas and crickets and tree frogs sang.

South Carolina would be one of his favorite states, he thought, if only it wasn't so damned hot and humid in the summer.

The back door, the sliding one opening onto the stone patio and the swimming pool, was his target.

In a matter of minutes he'd be inside.

Piece of cake. The alarm was off, the locks were laughable, the woman was alone, and they didn't even own a dog. Might as well hang out a sign: *Come and get me.*

A light came on downstairs.

Basta froze in his tracks in the act of reaching for the doorknob, frowning at the window that was suddenly glowing warmly from within. This was unexpected. He retreated a few stealthy paces to the concealing shadow of an enormous magnolia, his senses on high alert. He'd been casing the house for three weeks, and she'd never once turned on a light after her husband was gone. Was she sick? Did they have company? No, he couldn't have missed that.

What gave?

The light went off as suddenly as it had come on, and

the house was dark and still once more. He stared meditatively at the looming facade, the shiny black windows, the
two doors that he could see, probing the darkness for her
with every instinct he possessed. He was so attuned to her
now as predator to victim that he fancied he could almost
hear her breathing through the brick walls.

Where was she?

A sound made him turn his head sharply. It came from
the side of the house where he'd waited until just
moments before. Alert as a dog on the hunt, taking care to
stay deep in the shadows, he retraced his steps until he
once more stood beneath the palmettos. His eyes widened
as he saw that another of the garage doors was open now.

His pistol came up, but there was no way he could use it.

He could do nothing but watch as Julie Carlson's silver
Jaguar nosed out of the garage, gathered speed going
down the driveway, then turned left at the street and vanished like a bat into the night.

Just as quick as that.

He was left to look blankly back at an empty house as,
with a barely audible thump, the garage door closed
again.

She was gone. It took a minute or so for that incontro-
vertible fact to sink in. When it did, he felt empty,
cheated. A surging anger at having his careful plans dis-
rupted threatened to swamp his previously good mood.

Could she have somehow known he was there? Basta
looked quickly around, wary of a trap. Given the group he
worked for, a double-cross was never beyond the realm of
possibility.

Then good sense reasserted itself. There was no trap;
he was too valuable to the organization for that. And she
could not possibly have known he was there unless she
was psychic.

The most logical explanation was that some sort of emergency had arisen. What, he didn't know, but then, he didn't need to know. The pertinent thing was that, sooner or later, she would be back.

And he would be waiting.

The certainty of that was calming. Glitches of this sort happened even to consummate professionals such as himself.

Acknowledging that, Basta felt better. Circling back around behind the house, he even began to hum. When he realized what the song was, he felt a spurt of amusement at the sheer appropriateness of it.

"Ti-i-ime is on my side. . . ."

2

"I DON'T WANT TO HURT YOUR FEELINGS or anything, McQuarry, but you sure are one ugly-ass woman."

Mac shot his partner a withering look. Hinkle, walking beside him, was snickering openly. It was a suffocatingly hot Friday night in July, and the two of them had just met up in the parking lot of the Pink Pussycat, one of Charleston's most notorious gay bars.

"Hey, I feel pretty, all right? Back off."

"*I* wouldn't date you, that's for sure."

"You are dating me, so shut the hell up." Mac's spike heel caught on a crack in the pavement and he stumbled, nearly twisting his ankle. Grabbing Hinkle's arm, he recovered his balance with no harm done beyond a warning twinge. "Shit. How women walk in these things beats the hell out of me. My feet hurt already. I'll be a cripple before the night's over."

Chortling, Hinkle pulled his arm free. "You better be keeping them hands to yourself, homes. Rawanda's the jealous type. She'll kick your ass, she catches you molesting me."

"You're just lucky the guy's fucking prejudiced. Otherwise your black ass'd be in this getup."

"I'd be lookin' good, too, unlike some people I could

name. Hey, man, you can't go scratchin' yourself if you're gonna hang with me. It's not ladylike."

"I'm not scratching myself, I'm pulling up my fricking panty hose." Mac gave the waistband, which seemed more determined to head south than General William Tecumseh Sherman on his Civil War–era march to the sea, another savage tug. "Shut up, here we go."

They joined the throng on the sidewalk in front of the bar.

Located in the middle of a run-down area taken over long since by girlie bars and porn shops, the Pink Pussycat was a three-story cinderblock building painted flaming flamingo with a giant, reclining neon cat swilling a martini affixed to the front wall. The small curtained windows were outfitted with black iron bars like a prison. A bouncer checking IDs stood just outside the door. It was near midnight, and there was a line. At least half the patrons, Mac was relieved to see, looked as freaky as he felt. He was six-one barefoot, maybe six-four or six-five in the damned spindly heeled shoes, which meant that at the moment he towered over the crowd. Oh, well, at least being able to see over everybody's head would make it easier to spot their target.

According to his sources, Clinton Edwards had a thing for buxom blond drag queens. And since Edwards' wife was paying through the nose so she could nail him good in their divorce, Mac was willing to turn himself into a buxom blond drag queen, wired for pictures and sound, to get the dirt. He hated domestic cases, hated them with a passion, and this one was even slimier than most, but McQuarry and Hinkle, Private Investigators, were not successful enough to be particular about the jobs they took.

In other words, if it paid, he sashayed.

"That'll be ten bucks." The bald, multi-earringed

bouncer looked them over without interest. In the spirit of getting into his role, Mac almost batted his heavily mascaraed eyelashes at him. But nah, the guy was shorter than he was but stocky, one of those weight-lifter types, and who knew, he might get into it. Fending off a two-hundred-pound-plus lovestruck fruit was not on tonight's agenda.

Well, it was, maybe, but in any case not this particular lovestruck fruit. Edwards weighed somewhere north of two-fifty, according to his bio, but he was sixty years old and all lard.

Yum-yum, Mac thought with an inward sigh. Just his type.

The things he did to earn a living.

Hinkle paid, and they walked inside. It was dark and smoky and smelled of beer and BO. Plastic palm trees adorned the corners, and the DJ was playing "Margaritaville." Couples, some male-male, some female-female, some who-knew-what, swayed on the tiny dance floor in the middle of the room. Up on the stage, a blonde with boobs the size of basketballs stripped in time to the music. She was peeling off her gold lamé panties before Mac realized to his horror that she wasn't a woman. Averting his gaze, he forced his mind back to business and scanned the room for their quarry.

Somebody grabbed his ass.

"Yow!" Mac was so surprised he jumped a foot straight up in the air. Landing on his spike heels, he wobbled, tottered, and nearly went down. Catching himself on a table, he got his ankles straightened out and turned around. It was all he could do to stop himself from reaching for his Glock, which was conveniently holstered in his eighteen-hour bra.

"Hey, now, don't you be grabbin' my bitch." Hinkle's

grin as he warned the bespectacled accountant type who was looking Mac up and down with clearly lascivious intent made Mac long to pop him one.

"Sorry, man, I didn't realize she was with somebody." The accountant held up both hands in a gesture of peace, leaned back in his chair, and picked up his beer. Over the mug's rim, his eyes met Mac's with an unmistakable message. Seeing that Hinkle's attention was briefly elsewhere, his lips pursed in a silent kiss.

Mac's eyes widened. Then he gritted his teeth and managed a saccharine smile.

"See you around," the accountant said.

"Yeah, see ya." It was his best falsetto. Careful to keep his assets out of reach, Mac turned and minced toward the bar. Christ, now both ankles were giving him trouble. He had to remind himself again just how much Mrs. Edwards was paying them. If he hadn't, he would have turned tail there and then and gotten the hell out of Dodge.

"From now on, you watch my back," he growled over his shoulder at Hinkle. But Hinkle wasn't looking at him. He was staring across the room, an arrested expression on his face.

"Shit, there he is."

"Where?" Alert now too, Mac followed his gaze. Sure enough, Edwards was seated with a gorgeous-looking blonde—Mac had to remind himself that the babe was a *guy*—at a little round table in the corner. As he watched, the blonde stood up, smiled flirtatiously at Edwards, then headed across the room. She disappeared inside a door adorned with a neon sign that read LADIES.

Jesus.

"Looks like you're on, boss," Hinkle said under his breath.

Mac looked at that door, looked back at Hinkle, and

resigned himself to the inevitable. Sometimes a man had to do what a man had to do.

"You know," he said in his creaky falsetto, "I think I have to go tinkle."

With Hinkle laughing like a juiced-up hyena behind him, Mac teetered off to make a girlfriend of the blonde. If she could be persuaded to invite him and Hinkle to join her and Edwards at their table, his life was suddenly made a whole lot easier. If not, he was going to have to go to Plan B. He didn't even want to think about Plan B. It involved getting friendlier with Edwards than he ever wanted to be with someone who didn't have two X chromosomes.

Either way, he thought as he pushed through the door into the soft pink lighting of the little girls' room, it was going to be a long night.

He should have listened to his grandma and become a lawyer.

Julie turned another corner, took a quick look around, and, for the third time in five minutes, pressed the button that secured all four car doors just to make sure they really were locked. All right, so driving a shiny silver Jaguar deep into Charleston's bustling red-light district in the middle of a Friday night was probably not the smartest thing she had ever done. But then, when she'd left the house, she hadn't known where she was headed, so she really couldn't be convicted of total stupidity. Lying in bed listening to the distant hum of the garage door closing, she'd made up her mind, and lit out after Sid. She'd followed him blindly, desperate to know where he went when he snuck out of their house after he thought she was asleep, and she'd ended up here. Not exactly a positive reflection on their marriage, was it?

All up and down the street, neon signs blinked GIRLS! LIVE! ONSTAGE! and ADULT MOVIES and XXX. Acknowledging their import, Julie felt the knot that seemed to have lodged permanently in the pit of her stomach twist itself several degrees tighter.

Sid was forty years old and healthy as a horse as far as she knew. She was twenty-nine, with a slim curvaceous figure she worked hard to keep, great legs if she did say so herself, long black hair that waved naturally in the sauna-like heat, and a face that had taken her far from her wrong-side-of-the-track roots. She was clean, sweet-smelling, bought her lingerie at Victoria's Secret. In other words, there was absolutely nothing about her that might turn a husband off.

She and Sid hadn't had sex in more than eight months. And it certainly wasn't from lack of interest or effort on her part. But trying to entice her own husband into bed without success was ego-busting, to say the least.

Especially for someone who had once been called the prettiest girl in South Carolina.

Sid's excuse, when she confronted him about their dead sex life, was that he was under a lot of stress at work, so he'd appreciate it if she would just let him the hell alone. He was a contractor who, in partnership with his now-retired father, owned a very successful business, All-American Builders, which made tons of money developing subdivisions and building luxury homes across the state. She had no doubt that he *was* under a significant amount of stress.

But enough stress to keep him from having sex? Uh-uh. No way.

It had taken a while for the other shoe to drop, but finally it did when she'd found diamond-shaped blue Viagra pills mixed in with some vitamins in his medicine cabinet. At first hope had flared, and she waited with anticipation, sure he'd decided to see a doctor to fix their little problem. But nothing had happened. There'd been eight pills when she'd discovered the cache on Monday. By this evening—Friday—when she'd checked again, only six were left.

So she'd dressed for the night in her sexy best, even going downstairs to make sure he saw her in it, then lay in bed waiting for the jackass to come to her.

The rest, as they say, was history. What was going on became suddenly clear.

Sid was having sex, all right—just not with her.

At least he'd apparently been telling the truth about stress impairing his sexual functioning.

Ever since she'd awakened to the sound of the garage door going up, she'd been sick to her stomach. It was hard to admit that her Cinderella, rags-to-riches, fairy-tale marriage had about as much life left in it as yesterday's road-kill. To make matters worse, her whole family was now dependent on Sid: her mother and stepfather lived in a house he owned; her sister's husband worked as a vice-president at his company, a job that paid Kenny perhaps three times what he was worth, enough for Becky to stay home with their two girls.

Divorce was such an ugly word. But Julie had a sinking feeling that she was looking it right in the face.

Until just a little while ago, when she'd finally had enough sense to add two and two and get four, she hadn't allowed herself to seriously consider ending her marriage. Maybe, she kept telling herself, things would get better. Maybe work stress really was the reason Sid wasn't inter-ested in her sexually anymore. Maybe there was also a perfectly reasonable explanation for why he was so cold and brusque to her most of the time, and why he slept in the spare bedroom, and why he snuck out at night after she had gone upstairs to bed.

Yeah, and maybe there was an Easter bunny, too.

She'd asked him about all those things, nicely and at the top of her lungs and every other way in between. His response had been that the stress of keeping her in the style to which she was definitely not accustomed had both robbed him of his manhood and given him insomnia, he slept in the spare bedroom because he didn't want his insomnia to keep her awake, and when he couldn't sleep, he sometimes went out driving around his subdivisions. Looking at houses he'd built relaxed him.

Her response was, Uh-*huh*.

But still, coward that she was, she had wanted to believe. A stable home, a stable marriage, were precious to her. As a child, she and her mother and sister Becky had been so poor they'd sometimes lived in homeless shelters. Hunger wasn't some abstract concept involving starving children in Africa—from experience, she knew exactly how it felt. Her looks had gotten her and her family out of that hell and had won her Sid, the handsome millionaire ultimate prize she'd been dreaming of all her life. She'd fallen wildly in love with him when she was barely twenty, and he, in turn, had seemed to adore her. But somehow, over the course of eight years of marriage, it had all gone wrong.

The love had disappeared from their marriage like air escaping from a tiny hole in a balloon: the loss was so gradual no one noticed until the thing went flat.

So here she was, at quarter to one, caught in a snarl of traffic on this X-rated street just around the corner from the Citadel, spying on her husband. Who had certainly not built a home anywhere in the vicinity that she knew of.

She should just turn around and go home, Julie told

herself. Sid would kill her if he caught her following him—and she'd lost him anyway. She'd seen his big black Mercedes turn onto this street and that was it.

When she had turned the same corner just a few minutes later, nothing. At least, no Sid.

Plenty of people who made her think that driving the Jaguar had been a bad idea, though. Like the promenading hookers eyeing her wheels from the sidewalk with dollar signs in their eyes. And the sleazy john-types who cast furtive glances her way before disappearing into the XXX doorways. And the shirtless, tattooed bald guy who crossed the street right in front of her, thumping a fist on the hood and waggling his metal-studded tongue suggestively at her as he passed.

That was it. Abort mission. She was going home. She who turns and runs away lives to follow her husband another day.

Julie hung a right into the nearest parking lot, swung the Jag around—and frowned to find her exit blocked by a beat-up blue pickup that pulled in behind her.

Her frown deepened when the doors opened and a pair of muscle-bound skinheads in sagging jeans and wifebeater undershirts got out. As they approached the Jag, Julie's eyes widened. A quick glance around told her that there was no place to go. Parked cars ringed the lot on all sides. There was only one exit—and the pickup loomed between her and it.

Instinctively she punched the lock button again. It clicked vainly. The doors were already locked. The windows were up. The punks kept coming. What else could she do? Her cell phone was in her purse. Julie grabbed her shoulder bag, ripped open the zipper, thrust her hand inside, and rooted frantically around. A hairbrush—makeup—a jumble of miscellaneous junk—where oh where was that phone?

Just as her fingers closed around it, knuckles rapped on her window. Julie looked up to find an Eminem clone grinning through the glass at her.

"Hey, open up."

His tone was almost friendly, but the gun in his hand was not.

Julie's heart began to pound. Oh, God, she was about to be mugged, or carjacked, or worse. What was she going to do? What *could* she do? He was armed with a gun. She was armed with a cell phone.

If it came down to a duel, she was willing to bet that he could shoot her before she could punch in 911.

Whichever way it worked out, there would be no keeping this a secret. Sid was bound to find out. And if her husband discovered that she'd followed him into Charleston, he would kill her.

Always assuming that she was still alive to be killed, of course. The thought of Sid knowing what she'd done was scary, but the delinquent at her window was a more immediate threat.

"I said open the god-damned door, bitch."

Her assailant didn't sound friendly at all this time. He'd just been kind of holding the gun at waist level before. Now he was leveling it at her.

Julie imagined a bullet shattering the glass and tearing into her flesh.

Her heart sped up until it could have run a four-minute mile. Her mouth went dry. Her fight-or-flight impulse kicked in, and it didn't come down on the side of fighting. Slamming the transmission into reverse, she stomped the gas and rammed the heel of her hand down on the horn at the same time. The Jag shot backward. The horn blared. The thugs cursed and gave chase.

And the Jag crashed into the side of a black Chevy

Blazer that was just at that moment backing out of a parking space.

The impact threw her forward, and brought the Jag to a shuddering stop. At about the same time her window shattered, showering her with glass. Her head whipped around in time to see the punk who had knocked on her window thrust his arm into the car and pull up the lock. Before she could do anything but gasp, her door swung open, the punk leaned across her cool as a Popsicle to unfasten her seat belt, and she was yanked from her seat.

Her butt and elbows hit the pavement hard and she cried out. The punks jumped into the car. She barely had time to roll out of the way before her Jag and the pickup that had blocked it peeled rubber out of the parking lot.

The bad news was, her Jag had been stolen. The good news was, she was relatively unharmed.

The plaintive lament of a slide guitar and voices, both reaching her ears from a little distance, brought her out of her first shocked immobility. Her phone, she discovered, making a quick inventory, was still in her hand. She'd lost her car, but she still had her phone. Frantically she punched in 9, then paused, recovering enough wit to think the situation through. She was sprawled out in the parking lot of some girlie joint deep in the heart of Charleston, lying on pavement that was hot enough to toast bread even so long after sundown, wearing nothing but her hubby-come-hither sleeping attire of hot pink satin tap pants and a skimpy matching top, along with a pair of Nikes. Her butt was bruised, her elbows stung—and her car was gone. How was she ever going to explain this to Sid?

Oh, God, what if it hit the papers?

Maybe calling 911 was not the best idea, she thought with her finger poised above the button. But what else was she going to do?

"Have a fight with your boyfriend?"

The voice was masculine. The vision that filled her eyes as she glanced up in response was anything but. Pointy-toed black patent stilettos big enough to swim in. Muscular calves in opaque black panty hose. A red sequined skirt that stopped several inches above a pair of athletic-looking knees. A shiny black blouse with a deep décolletage that was filled in with a red and black polka-dot scarf. Breasts the size and shape of traffic cones. Long platinum blond hair. A lean hard chin and manly features whose gender was given the lie by garish makeup ladled on thick. All this on a broad-shouldered, narrow-hipped frame that stood easily six and a half feet tall. The overall effect was Dolly Parton morphed with the Terminator.

She must have been gaping, because the question was repeated with a hint of impatience. It recalled her to the full dimensions of her dilemma, and the oddity of her questioner was forgotten.

"They stole my car! Those two punks—they stole my car."

Julie peeled herself off the pavement and scrambled to her feet. Stabs of pain from her butt and elbows were ignored as she stared helplessly in the direction in which her car had disappeared. The street and sidewalks were still clogged with traffic, vehicular and otherwise, but her car was no longer in sight. Neither was the pickup. There was an intersection just half a block away. They could have turned left—or right.

Her legs went rubbery, and she swayed a little before she could lock her knees into place. A surprisingly masculine-feeling hand closed around her upper arm, steadying her.

"Are you drunk?" The voice was surprisingly masculine, too, given the appearance of its owner, and faintly disapproving. Glancing up, Julie confronted the full glory of twin arches of sky blue eye shadow above sea blue eyes and gleaming scarlet lips above a strong chin with the faintest hint of five-o'clock shadow, and knew despair. There was no help to be had here.

"No!" Impatient, she jerked her arm free, raised the phone, and added a 1 to the 9. Then she paused. Sid . . .

"You know, you banged into my car pretty good. You have a license? Insurance?"

"What?" She was so busy performing a fast mental search through the pros and cons of a variety of actions that she had pretty much blocked out everything else.

"License? Insurance? You know, the kind of information most people exchange when they've had a wreck?"

Julie took a deep breath, and tried to focus on what was being said to her. One problem at a time. Arnold and Dolly's bastard offspring was obviously afraid that he—she—oh, whatever—was going to be stuck for the damage to his car. A glance beyond him told her that it was pretty substantial. The dent extended from the middle of the right rear door to past the wheel well.

"Yes. Yes, of course I have a license and insurance. Oh, my purse is in the car. *They stole my car.* I have to get it back." Her finger shot to the final 1 and then she paused again, glancing despairingly toward the intersection. No doubt about it: the Jag was long gone. There was no way to keep this secret from Sid. She might as well go on and bite the bullet and call the police and be done with it.

Still she hesitated, racking her brain to come up with an—any—alternative. She glanced up appealingly, only to find that he was giving her the once-over. Julie was almost sure of it. She had been on the receiving end of enough of those looks to recognize it for what it was.

A bubble of near-hysterical laughter rose in her throat.

How much worse could this night get? Her probably cheating husband had snuck out of their home after she'd gone up to bed. She'd chased him onto a block that looked like vice cops should be swarming all over it. There she'd had a wreck and been assaulted and her Jaguar had been stolen. Now she was standing in her skimpy satin husband-bait in the parking lot of some sort of sex bar with a drag queen checking her out.

About to call the cops.

Life didn't get much better than that.

He finished his perusal of her body, glanced up, and their gazes met and held. Hers was indignant, challenging. She was *not* in the mood to be sexually harassed by what looked like the humongous hooker from hell. His had something she thought she recognized as being very male in it. After the briefest of pregnant moments he broke off eye contact, and his gaze dropped down her body again. Blatantly this time.

Julie bristled and opened her mouth to slay him with a few choice words.

He beat her to it.

"Girlfriend, you really should be wearing heels with an outfit like that," he said in a slow, faintly disapproving drawl.

He'd been checking out her *shoes?* Julie felt insane laughter bubbling up her throat. She swallowed it along with the blast she'd been getting ready to flatten him with, took a deep, calming breath, and glanced around.

People had entered the parking lot since she'd jumped to her feet: an entwined couple and an extravagantly dressed woman, walking separately, heading for their cars. It said a lot for the standards of the area that they didn't even give her in her sexy pj's and Amazonia in all her jaw-dropping glory a second glance.

Not that it mattered. The only thing that mattered was getting her car back and getting home before Sid. The problem was, how was she supposed to do that?

"Damn Sid anyway," she muttered aloud. This entire disaster was every bit his fault.

"Miz Carlson?" Amazonia asked then, on a faintly disbelieving note. Julie's eyes widened and shot to his face. Her previous conviction to the contrary, the night had suddenly gotten much, much worse. Whoever or whatever this—this person was, he knew her name.

Julie's heart began to slam against her breastbone. She met his gaze wide-eyed. A denial trembled on her lips, but she realized almost at once that it would only make her look foolish, and the situation even more questionable. There was no hope of concealing anything now. Might as well just punch in the final 1 and get it over with.

"Y—yes."

There was the tiniest pause as the heavily made-up eyes narrowed and the bright red lips thinned. "Well, now," he said as his gaze ran over her once more, with an entirely different expression. "If that just don't absolutely beat all."

Julie wasn't sure what he meant by that, but she was sure she didn't like the sound of it.

"Hey, Deb-*bie,*" a slurred voice interrupted. Julie glanced around. The couple—an overweight, obviously drunken man in a rumpled suit and a beautiful blonde in an elegant black cocktail dress who clung possessively to his arm— came up behind them and paused, the woman obviously supporting the man, who was a little unsteady on his feet. The scent of booze emanating from the man was unpleasantly strong. Wrinkling her nose in instinctive protest, Julie realized that the greeting, uttered by the man, had been addressed to Amazonia. Debbie? Julie shot him a glance.

The name seemed far too ordinary for such an extraordinary individual.

"You still got the address? It's gonna be a hell of a good time." The man's gaze shifted from Debbie to Julie, and moved over her in a way that creeped her out. "Your pretty friend here's welcome, too."

"Oh, Clint, you know I wouldn't miss it for the world." Debbie smiled and spoke in a mincing falsetto that in no way resembled the growling masculine tone he'd used with her. "You and Lana go on ahead, sugar. I'll be along shortly."

"Remember, we've got lots of blow. All you need to bring is maybe your little friend, and we'll party all night. There's plenty of fun to be had by all." Clint gave Julie a leering smile. Julie recoiled. As Lana pulled Clint away, she glanced back over her shoulder at Julie.

"You stay away, bitch," she mouthed. Then, waggling her fingers at Debbie, she added aloud, "See you later, sweet cheeks."

Sweet cheeks? Debbie? It hit Julie with the force of a blow: Lana was a man. She gaped after the pair as they resumed their unsteady journey toward the far end of the parking lot. The beautiful, shapely blonde swaying so sexily in four-inch heels was a *man*.

"She thinks *I'm* a man!" Julie exclaimed as revelation struck.

She caught Debbie's eye just then, and discovered that he was grinning.

"Close your mouth, Miz Carlson, you'll catch flies," he chided in his masculine voice, and gently tapped her slack jaw with a forefinger. Her teeth clamped together with an audible click. "You should feel flattered. You made Lana jealous. You notice she's not jealous of *me*."

For a moment Julie felt something like Alice after she

fell down the rabbit hole. This was definitely a parallel universe. Then she remembered the mess she was in, and everything else was wiped from her mind.

"My car," she groaned, and started to punch in the final 1 before hesitating once more.

"You gonna call the police or not? I got places to go and things to do here. And we're going to need that police report for the insurance."

When a six-and-a-half-foot-tall transvestite crosses his arms over his eye-popping chest, gives you an impatient look, and starts tapping his pointed patent-leather toe, the effect is galvanizing, Julie discovered. She clutched the phone tighter, but could not quite bring herself to punch in that last 1.

If she did, all hell would break loose the minute she got home.

"Look, I've got a problem, okay? I don't want my husband to find out I was out tonight," she confessed, her shoulders slumping in defeat as she lowered the phone. Debbie knew who she was and therefore almost certainly knew Sid in some way or another, although her mind boggled at picturing mucho macho Sid having an acquaintance with a drag queen. But Debbie was such a bizarre figure that it seemed all right to confide, a little, in him. He would have his share of secrets, too. Besides, she'd wrecked his car, he wanted to call the police, and she was just now fully beginning to comprehend what a really bad idea that was. She was willing to bet good money that every cop in South Carolina knew or knew of her husband, and once she called them she might just as well take out an ad in the paper describing the night's debacle and be done with. If telling Debbie a little of the truth would win her enough sympathy to give her time to think, Julie was all for that.

"Oh, yeah?" Debbie sounded interested rather than sympathetic, but interested worked too. More people were coming into the parking lot now, and a candy-red Corvette drove past them on the way to the exit. It honked, and a manicured hand tipped in long, bright red nails waved gaily out the driver's window. Lana and Clint.

"If you know who I am, then you must know I'm good for the damages to your car," Julie said. "But I really don't want to call the police."

"Is that right?" Debbie was looking at her speculatively. "Suppose we get in my car where we can have a little bit of privacy and you tell me all about it. Maybe I can help you out here."

Debbie's very masculine-feeling hand curled around her upper arm again before Julie could answer, urging her toward his damaged vehicle. Julie glanced up, registered once again the mind-boggling dichotomy of platinum curls bouncing against breasts roughly the size of the Himalayas on a linebacker's broad-shouldered frame, then allowed herself to be persuaded. Turning to a flamboyant, gender-bending stranger for help was probably only a little less stupid than chasing after Sid in the first place, but under the circumstances none of the other options she could think of were any more appealing.

Debbie opened the Blazer door for her, and Julie slid into the black leather seat. It was only as he shut the door behind her and walked around the hood to get in himself that it occurred to her that maybe getting into a car with a strange man in women's clothes might not be the smartest thing she had ever done.

3

JULIE CARLSON WAS EVERY BIT AS HOT as Mac remembered. Great tits, great ass, great legs, skin the color of honey, long, tousled black hair that would look fantastic spread out over a man's pillow, kissable lips, big brown eyes. He'd first seen her at her wedding. At the time he'd been a cop, hired for the occasion to provide security, and while he'd been full of admiration for the sexy young bride he'd been busy thinking about other things, and she had never so much as glanced his way. Her eyes had been all for her groom: John Sidney Carlson IV, born with a silver spoon in his mouth that Mac had never stopped wanting to cram up his ass instead. Back then Sid made a splash with everything he did, and his wedding—his second wedding—was no exception. There'd been a thousand guests, including the governor and more big names than you could shake a stick at, TV and newspaper coverage, and Julie Ann Williams, one month out of her reign as Miss South Carolina, for a bride.

That was eight years ago. A lot of water had gone under the bridge since then, including his own firing from the Charleston PD, which Sid, the corrupt bastard, had almost certainly orchestrated. But that was just a tiny part of his beef with Sid. The major part, the part that

Mac could never forget, concerned his brother. Daniel, who had been eight years his senior, had vanished some fifteen years before. And Mac had grown increasingly convinced that Sid, Daniel's friend from childhood, at the very least knew what had happened to him.

At first, they—his mother, his grandmother, and himself, Daniel's family—thought Daniel had simply taken off somewhere. He'd been twenty-five years old at the time, after all, and a free spirit if there ever was one. Then, when months passed without a word, they began to wonder if perhaps he'd gotten in some kind of a jam and was lying low. As months turned into years, they had entertained theories ranging from a foreign prison to amnesia. Mac's mother had died ten years ago, still uncertain about her older son's fate and grieving at his absence. Mac had promised her on her deathbed that he would find his brother. So far he hadn't been able to make good on that promise.

The last time he had talked to Daniel had been during a hurried telephone call. His brother had begged out of a basketball game he'd promised to take then seventeen-year-old Mac to because of a job he had to do for Richie. Richie—as in Richie Rich—was their private nickname for Sid, because Sid lived a life that seemed dazzlingly opulent to two working-class sons of a dead-in-the-line-of-duty cop. Something in Daniel's tone had made Mac think that whatever the "job" was, it was not the nine-to-five variety, but Mac hadn't asked and Daniel hadn't been any more specific than that. Once he'd become a cop himself, Mac had, quietly and on his own time, started searching for his brother, and checking Sid out had been right there at the top of his to-do list. He hadn't really expected to find much on Richie Rich, but what he'd turned up had surprised him. Sid's first wife, for example, had walked out on their marriage at about the same time that Daniel had disappeared. Interestingly enough, she couldn't be found. And word on the street was that Sid was involved in the drug trade. Given Daniel's apparently comfortable finances, his lack of a steady job after leaving the military, and his renewed involvement with childhood friend Sid, Mac had come to suspect that Daniel's "job" for Sid and his subsequent disappearance could both be linked to a drug operation Sid was running. But he couldn't prove it. Nobody in authority seemed at all interested in taking up the investigation. The Carlsons were VIPs in South Carolina, after all, with friends in high places, and nobody wanted to call the wrath of the powers that be down upon his own head. The consensus had been shut up, get over your brother, and find something else to do. It didn't help that Daniel had spent years flirting with the wrong side of the law. It also didn't help that the ex-wife was from California, that home of all things degenerate, where she'd presumably returned before dropping out of sight.

In the end, as was none too gently pointed out to him, all he had on Sid was basically gossip. When he'd persevered, trying to get proof of illegal activity, he'd ended up getting his ass kicked off the force.

Now, through the kind of twist of fate that Mac had almost quit believing in, he was being given a second chance to get at some answers: Sid's beauty-queen bride was sitting in his car with him, looking sexy as hell in an itty-bitty pink satin getup that played up all her best points, in a jam and scared of her husband and turning to him for help.

Suddenly the gods were smiling on him.

He fished his cell phone out of his cleavage—it was lodged in there right along with the wad of athletic socks that served as his right tit, while his Glock nestled securely under the wad on the left—punched a button, and started the car, all at approximately the same time. The AC blasted out hot air. He turned it down and rolled down the windows until the interior could reach a decent temperature. Street sounds formed a steady background noise not unlike the buzz of a giant insect.

"Uh, wait a minute." Julie Carlson sounded uneasy. The look she sent him was wary. God, she was a pretty thing. Sid had always been about a million times luckier than he deserved, and his wife was no exception.

"Sit tight," he said to her with a quick, meant-to-be-reassuring smile that he had no idea struck its recipient as downright scary, framed as it was in scarlet lipstick and platinum curls. He put the Blazer in reverse before she could say anything else and then spoke into the phone as Hinkle answered. "Yo. Change of plan. Get over to 85 Dumesnil Street and get some pictures. Edwards is having a party and I want an album."

"Me?" Hinkle squawked, his disembodied voice making his displeasure clear. "What about you? You seemed to be getting along with him real good. You turnin' tail now that the going's getting tough, you chicken shit?"

"Somebody hit my car, and I've got to sort it out. It's going to take a while. Get those pictures." He drove toward the exit. Now that they were moving, there was a breeze, which made the temperature inside the car almost bearable. Beside him, his passenger was looking more uneasy than ever. Mac smiled at her again. Sid's wife falling into his lap like this was the most promising thing that had happened to him in a long time, and he meant to make the most of it.

"Edwards doesn't know me from crap," Hinkle said. "How'm I supposed to get in?"

"Take a pizza. Pretend you're delivering. Hell, just walk

in. Nobody'll notice. Edwards is drunk off his ass, and apparently there's going to be quite a crowd." There was a break in the traffic. Mac pulled out behind a big white Caddy and headed south. If the thieves were pros—and they almost certainly were—the Jaguar was long gone. But it was always possible she'd been robbed by a couple of kids out for a joyride, in which case the car might have been abandoned somewhere nearby.

"I don't think this is such a good idea," Julie Carlson said. "Would you take me back to the parking lot, please?"

Mac caught her eye, held up one finger—*wait a minute*—and gave her another of those reassuring smiles. He watched her glance down at the cell phone in her hand and hesitate, and then he tracked her other hand as it crept up the door toward the handle. Was she thinking about jumping out? Not unless she had a death wish. The street was jammed with cars, and at this time of night it was a good bet that most of the drivers were feeling no pain. If he'd still been a cop, he could have done a month's worth of busts right here, knocking on windows and hauling the over-the-limit ones in.

"Yeah, like nobody's gonna notice a straight black man taking pictures at a gay white guy's orgy. I'm gonna get my ass kicked." Hinkle's gloomy-sounding voice spoke in his ear. "Shit. This always happens. Every damned time."

"Got to go," Mac said as he stopped at a traffic light, saw Julie Carlson's fingers curl around the door handle, and broke the connection.

"What was that all about?" She was looking at him apprehensively.

"I was supposed to take some pictures at a party, and now, thanks to you, I can't make it. A friend's going instead." Mac shot her a quick, assessing glance as he folded the phone and dropped it back down inside his blouse.

There wasn't much positive he could say about the size-42DD Maidenform that was even now threatening to cut him in two, except that it made a hell of a holster for phone and pistol alike. That elastic was strong stuff. If NASA hadn't discovered it, somebody should clue them in.

He looked pointedly at her hand on the door handle. "You planning on getting out?"

"N-no." She looked guilty as hell. Her hand dropped back down into her lap.

"Because if you did, it could be dangerous."

She blanched.

Frowning, he spelled it out. "You could get hit by a car."

The light changed, and Mac went through the inter-section, heading down toward the Battery, which in his estimation was the most likely place to discover an abandoned car. The air coming out of the vents now was cool, and Mac rolled the windows up with a touch of a button. She sucked in her breath.

"Um, where are we going?" she asked, real polite. Her hands were in her lap now, clasped around the cell phone, and she was chewing on her lower lip. She looked sexy as hell doing that. Mac noticed, and wished he hadn't. Getting turned on by Sid's sex-kitten wife was no part of his plan.

"You worried you're being kidnapped?" Realization dawned. There was amusement in his tone.

She stopped chewing on her lip, thank God, and her eyes shot to his face.

"Maybe. Am I?"

He had to give her this: she was no shrinking violet. There was challenge in the question, and in the look she gave him. His estimation of Sid's wife scooted a notch higher, even though it meant awarding Sid points for good taste.

"Nah. You're as safe with me as you would be with your own mama, I promise," he said soothingly, and turned right, onto an even more run-down street than the one they had left. Drunks and whores and people looking for trouble roamed the sidewalks here, ducking into seedy bars, keeping to the shadows away from the streetlights. Like cockroaches, most of these folks did their scuttling at night. Unlike cockroaches, some of them could be deadly. Fortunately, Mac knew the score.

"Look, Debbie, now that I've had time to think it over I think I'll just call the police." She lifted her cell phone ostentatiously; her forefinger hovered over the keypad without touching the buttons.

Debbie? For a moment Mac was at a loss. Then he remembered his new persona, and grinned. Debbie—his ex-wife's name, conjured up out of the blue when he'd glanced into the mirror in the ladies' room at the Pink Pussycat and noticed that, except for the height and shoulders, he kind of resembled her—definitely was not a normal-looking person. No wonder she was nervous.

"I thought you didn't want your husband to know you're out."

She started chewing her lower lip again. Mac, noticing, forced himself to concentrate on scanning the street for her stolen car. The hand holding the cell phone wavered.

"I don't." Her voice was low. "But . . ."

"So how about if we see if we can't find your car?"

She sucked in her breath, and her gaze flew to his face. "Do you think that's even remotely possible?"

Mac felt a stab of compunction. Being married to Sid was obviously no picnic, and she was looking to him for help. But he *was* going to help her, he quieted his nascent knight-in-shining-armor, even if there was an ulterior motive to his assistance. At least, he was going to do what he could to get her car back for her. After that, he made no promises.

He'd been gunning for Sid for too long to let a little thing like a flare of sympathy for his wife hold him back.

"Maybe. Sounds like somebody put in an order for a Jaguar of the same make and model as yours. Either for parts, or somebody wants to acquire one on the cheap. I'm betting on parts, though."

"Somebody put in an order?" Her tone was disbelieving, but she dropped the cell phone back to her lap.

He turned onto Bay Street and sped up to pass one of the horse-drawn carriages that took tourists on sightseeing rides at all hours of the day and night and were a menace to traffic all over the city. In the distance, the bay looked black as oil except for an occasional string of lights that signified a boat. A foghorn gave its lonely call.

"Happens all the time, especially with a high-end car like yours."

Her thighs were pressed tightly together, he noticed, her long, slim, and shapely thighs that were bare beneath the crotch-high hem of the pink satin shorts she wore. Glancing down at them—he couldn't help himself—he found himself wondering if her skin tasted as much like honey as it looked. Annoyed at the direction his thoughts were taking, he shifted his gaze back out to the street where it belonged and picked up his phone.

"License-plate number?" he asked crisply, confining his gaze to her face now as he punched in some numbers. She told him, and he nodded.

"Yeah?" The grumpy-sounding voice on the other end of the phone belonged to Mother Jones. Mother was the go-to man for all the local car thieves; as a gung-ho rookie police officer Mac had arrested him twice in his first two months on the job, been first infuriated and then chagrined to discover that Mother was back on the streets within twenty-four hours each time, and then got clued in to the program before any real harm was done to Mother's operation or his own career. Fortunately, Mother was not one to bear grudges, and what with one thing and another, they'd ended up developing a mutual respect that had turned into almost a friendship over the years. If anybody could get information on a just-pinched Jaguar in south Charleston, Mother was the man.

"What you interested in it for?" Mother asked cautiously, when Mac gave him the particulars. At times like this, Mother tended to remember that Mac had once been on the other side.

"Lady who owns it is a friend of mine. Her husband's gonna go ape-shit when he finds out she let it get stolen, and she's sitting here beside me right now crying her eyes out, afraid she's gonna get beat up when she goes home."

Julie Carlson stiffened and looked at him indignantly. Mac shook his head at her, warning her to silence.

"Shee-it." Mother tut-tutted under his breath, and Mac knew he had punched the right buttons. Mother was a devoted family man with six daughters. "Ain't no call for that kind of shit, you know? Man who'd rough up his woman, he ought to have his ass kicked."

"Yeah," Mac said, agreeing. "Can you help us out here?"

There was a pause. "If I can, you know it gonna cost you."

"No problem." He figured Julie Carlson was good for it. Hell, Sid was rich enough.

A grunt. "I'll make some calls, see what I can do. I'll let you know. What's the number?"

Mac gave him his cell-phone number, disconnected, and glanced at his frowning passenger.

"It's going to cost you to get your car back. Probably about a couple of thousand. If it can be done."

"I heard." She sounded disgusted. "I can't believe I have to pay to get my own car back."

"You don't want to, I'll call Mother back and tell him to forget it."

"No." There was a sudden note of panic in her voice, and her hands tightened on her phone. "No, I want it."

Mac's lips compressed. She was definitely afraid of Sid. Under the circumstances, feeling sorry for her was a mistake, but feel sorry for her he did.

"Mother's going to want the money on delivery. If we're lucky, and he can find your car."

She looked worried. "I can write him a check. That is, if he brings back my purse, too. It was in the car."

A check. Mac sighed. "Darlin', he's going to want cash."

Now she was looking really worried. "I only have about fifty dollars in my purse. I can go to an ATM machine when I get it back, but I think the limit for withdrawals is two hundred dollars."

Mac thought of the cash advance Elizabeth Edwards had given him only hours earlier. It was stashed in the safe at his house, ready to be deposited in the bank bright and early in the morning. He pictured Hinkle's reaction if he knew what Mac was about to do, made up his mind, and mentally flipped Hinkle the bird. "I got it covered. As long as you're good for it. You are good for it, right?"

Sid's wife was definitely not a credit risk, and obviously she had an urgent reason to keep Sid from finding out what she had been up to tonight. The satin thingy she was wearing told its own story. She wouldn't stiff him.

"Yes. Oh, yes. Thank you."

"You're welcome." His voice was dry. The idea of Julie Carlson cavorting with a boyfriend was cheering, considering who she was married to, but unfortunately it got his thoughts going where they shouldn't again. She was hot stuff, no doubt about it—but, he reminded himself sternly, she wasn't bed material. Not for him.

What she was, if the gods continued in their current good mood, might just be the inside source he needed to finally get the goods on Sid. He would help her out of her present difficulty, and in the process pump her for all the information he could get.

Mac smiled as he turned down his street, a quiet row of small, single-story, tile-roofed homes that were reasonably well maintained but had seen better days, and parked at the curb. A motley collection of other cars had done likewise all up and down the street.

"Where are we?" She was sounding nervous again.

"My house. I happen to have some cash on hand. Besides, Mother finds your car, we're going to have to meet with him to get it back. It'd be better for my reputation if he doesn't see me like this." He made a gesture encompassing his finery.

"Oh." She looked him up and down, and her expression turned faintly sympathetic as her gaze met his. "He doesn't—know?"

"No," Mac said, refusing to acknowledge how sweet she sounded. He shut off the ignition. "He doesn't know. You coming in? You can wait in the car if it makes you feel safer."

She took another look around at the dark street, which was deserted except for old Mr. Leiferman down at the corner waiting under the streetlight for his Boston terrier to do his business, and shook her head.

"I'll come in with you, if you don't mind," she said, just as he'd been pretty sure she would.

She opened the door and slid out. He pulled the wig

off, tossed it into the backseat, and scratched his head vig-orously. Then he got out himself, locked the car, and headed for his front door. He could hear the delicate swish of her satin shorts as she walked beside him, and tried to shut his ears to the sound.

Reaching the porch, he unlocked the door and stood back to let her precede him inside.

As she stepped over the threshold into the pitch-dark house, a wry smile curved his lips.

Something Daniel used to delight in saying to him on the few occasions when little brother was invited into his room popped into Mac's head. It was so appropriate it was downright eerie.

Come into my parlor, said the spider to the fly. . . .

4

THE TINY WHITE POODLE that greeted their arrival with a series of ecstatic yaps and jumps reassured Julie *almost* completely. The dog was adorable, right down to her pink, rhinestone-studded collar and the small pink bow tied over each ear.

No straight man, much less a homicidal sex fiend, had ever possessed a dog like that.

"Hi, sweetheart." Julie crouched down, offering her fingers for the excited poodle's approval while Debbie flipped on a lamp. A quick sniff, and then the dog had both front paws on Julie's bare knee, begging for attention and wagging her tail so hard her whole body shook as she tried to lick Julie's face. It was a puffball of doggy lovableness that immediately sent Julie's opinion of Debbie skyrocketing. The clothes might be over the top, the wig might be too kitschy for words, but the poodle was perfect.

"Is she yours?" Just so there was no mistake.

"Yep. Meet Josephine." There was a dryness to Debbie's voice that caused Julie to glance up at him. He'd lost the wig, she registered with surprise, and his hair stood up all over his head in sweaty-looking dark blond spikes. Which, given his heavy makeup, made him look just as bizarre as before, only in a different way: Debbie as Boy George. The narrow-eyed look he gave his pet distracted her from his appearance. From it, Julie surmised that Josephine must be in the doghouse, figuratively speaking. Well, as Sid was always pointing out to her, that was the trouble with dogs: they barked, they had fleas, and they messed the floor. But, Debbie's tone notwithstanding, it was clear that he loved the animal: Josephine was exquisitely groomed, right down to her gyrating pom-pom of a tail and little pink-painted toenails, and displayed the kind of innocent exuberance that was only ever seen in a cherished pet.

"She's a doll," Julie said sincerely.

"Yeah, well. This morning she ate one of my shoes." Debbie gave the poodle a dark look, and gestured at the living room in which they stood. "Make yourself at home. I'll be right back."

He clumped off toward the back of the house in his enormous high heels, turning lights on as he went. Julie was left to stand up and look around her.

It was a narrow, one-story, shotgun-style house, like many of the older dwellings in the eclectic mix of single-family homes, apartments, condo complexes, and cheap hotels that had been shoehorned into the area known as North of Broad. The room she was in, the living room, had white plaster walls, bare wooden floors, gold drapes pulled tight across the large single window that looked out onto the street, an enormous gold tweed couch with a rectangular oak coffee table in front of it, and a brown velour recliner. The TV took pride of place against one wall. Magazines and newspapers lay in a haphazard pile beside the recliner. Various nondescript prints of land-scapes adorned the walls.

Debbie was clearly not an inspired decorator. It was kind of disappointing, given his flamboyant taste in clothes.

Julie sat down on the couch. Josephine jumped up

beside her, her small head edging beneath Julie's arm. Patting the wiry tuft on top of Josephine's head, Julie realized that the dog smelled faintly of some floral perfume. How cute, she thought, charmed, and with relief dismissed the last vestiges of a lurking suspicion that she might have fallen into the hands of a rapist-murderer. Well, almost the last vestiges. He could still be a really kinky rapist-murderer, but the poodle made her far more inclined than before to give him the benefit of the doubt.

With her mind all but relieved of that particular worry, Julie immediately focused on another and looked around for a clock. As the saying went, time was of the essence.

Sid was usually home no later than three-fifteen. She had stayed awake enough nights listening for him to know. Which meant, if her spy project was to go undetected, she had to be home by three, complete with Jaguar.

What were the chances?

There was no clock anywhere that she could see. Too nervous to sit any longer, Julie stood and moved toward the kitchen, which was next to the living room. Josephine followed, trotting daintily at her heels, her nails clicking on the floor. The narrow, L-shaped kitchen was as aesthetically uninspired as the living room. The end of the L, obviously intended as an eating area, had been converted into a small home office. There was a metal desk with a computer on it, a chair, a pair of file cabinets—and a clock on the wall.

1:58. She had just over an hour to retrieve her car and get home before her absence was discovered.

Nibbling anxiously at a fingernail, she stepped back into the hall and glanced toward the back room, the bedroom, where her host had disappeared. At that moment Debbie himself stepped into view, emerging into the bedroom from an adjoining room, a bathroom presumably, because he was holding a towel to his head with both hands, rubbing briskly.

He was wearing jeans, but his chest was bare.

It was a very masculine-looking chest: wide beneath broad shoulders, tanned, muscular, adorned with a thick wedge of dark brown hair. His biceps were tanned too, and thick with muscle, and his forearms were sinewy and appropriately hairy. The jeans were old, hanging low on his hipbones to reveal a washboard stomach and part of an innie naval before hugging long, powerful-looking legs.

Anyone who looked less like a Debbie would have been difficult to imagine. Julie blinked at him in surprise.

He must have felt her gaze on him, because at that moment he lowered the towel and their eyes met. The makeup was gone. His hair no longer stood up from his scalp in sweaty spikes. Looking as if it had been just washed and towel-dried, it was sandy blond now and slightly tousled. His face was lean, hard-jawed, handsome. Without the distorting effect of the eye shadow, his eyes, which were a light, almost translucent blue beneath thick brown brows, were to die for. His nose was straight, his mouth long and firm and well cut, his chin square.

In short, in his masculine incarnation, Debbie was gorgeous.

Julie stared at him for a moment while all kinds of inappropriate thoughts chased themselves around her brain.

"You *are* gay, right?" The question just popped out, and she could have bitten off her tongue the moment it did. His gaze held hers for a long, uncomfortable moment as his jaw tightened and his eyes narrowed.

"Does it matter?" The look he gave her was cool, shuttered, a little wary. Had she committed some unforgivable faux pas by asking? Probably. Her knowledge of drag-queen etiquette was admittedly a bit rusty.

"No. No, of course it doesn't," she assured him hurriedly. "I think that all people should have the right to be exactly who they are. Free to be you and me, and all that."

She truly *didn't* care if he was gay, except that, from a purely female point of view, it seemed such a waste. In fact, though, now that she thought about it, it was probably better that he was. Otherwise he was too mouthwatering for her peace of mind, especially given her hanging-by-a-thread marriage and her sexually deprived state. Anyway, she felt more at ease with him if she thought of him as a girlfriend. She could admire his physical attributes without the smallest risk of succumbing to them, which was kind of nice.

Her girlfriend the hunk. The thought made her smile.

"Whatever." He gave her a narrow-eyed glance as if to assess her sincerity, then stepped out of her line of vision, moving on into the bedroom. Moments later he reappeared, pulling a faded, faintly ragged-looking black T-shirt over his head.

Coors, it said on the front.

What your well-dressed drag queen wore on his downtime this season? Her brow wrinkled. She wouldn't have guessed it, but then, what did she know?

As she was lately learning, not much about not much.

"I really need to get home," she said, her surprise at the new Debbie ebbing in the face of the urgency of the situation. "How long do you think this is going to take?"

His expression relaxed.

"Not long. Mother will call when he has something. You want me to go ahead and take you home, and then call you about your car?"

"No. No." Julie chewed her lower lip, thinking aloud.

"Sid will notice the Jaguar is gone as soon as he pulls in. I've got to have the car. And I've got to be home by three."

"You're scared of this guy, aren't you?" There was a faintly harsh note to his voice. Julie looked at him in surprise.

"Sid? No!" She recovered, and shook her head vigorously. Too vigorously? she asked herself, then answered: Yeah. The lady doth protest too much.

"Not usually," she amended with a grimace. "It's just— Sid's not going to like it if he gets home and finds me gone."

And that was the understatement of the year.

"Miz Carlson, you out running around on your husband?" The question was gentle. The glance that slid over her was speculative, and at the same time more masculine than she would have expected, given that it came from Debbie. Of course, the last time he had given her one of those looks, he'd been checking out her shoes. Still, it made Julie remember all over again what she was wearing—or, rather, what she was not wearing, like panties or a bra. Or any semblance of normal clothes. She was suddenly acutely conscious that her nipples were plainly visible through the slithery camisole and that her long tanned legs were bare to the very tops of her thighs.

Now that Debbie had morphed into a hot-looking guy it didn't seem right somehow to be wearing part of her collection of man-bait in his presence. But of course, she reminded herself, he was *Debbie,* and they were fast becoming girlfriends, sort of, and anyway the outfit covered her better than a bathing suit, even a one-piece. She certainly had never expected it to be seen by anyone, because she'd never meant to put so much as a toe outside her car. So if he was giving her that look because he thought she was some kind of an exhibitionist, he could just quit. Anyway, speaking of sartorial deficiencies, until just a few minutes ago *he* had looked like Steroid Barbie, all tarted up and headed downtown.

So there.

"Wearing this?" She glanced down at herself derisively. "I don't think so."

"You look pretty good to me."

Her eyes flew to his, and for a moment their gazes held. That masculine look was back in his eyes—wasn't it? Or was it her imagination? Before she could quite sort the matter out, his expression changed, and he shook his head at her. "What you look like, girlfriend, is a woman who just rolled out of somebody's bed."

Her spine stiffened and her chin came up. "I did. Mine. I rolled out of bed, shoved my feet into my shoes, and jumped into my car. Where I stayed until it got stolen."

"If you say so." He sounded politely skeptical.

"I do."

"Fine by me." He shrugged. "Want something to drink? I got water, orange juice, beer. . . ."

He moved toward the kitchen, which brought him close—too close. Having him invade her personal space was unsettling—he was a surprisingly big man, and he *looked* so very male—so Julie felt compelled to move too, backward out of his path, and nearly tripped over Josephine in the process. Josephine yelped and shot toward the living room and safety, Julie stumbled, and Debbie grabbed her arm to steady her. Julie was just recovering her balance when Debbie let go suddenly and looked down at his hand.

"You're bleeding."

Julie's brow knit. There were, indeed, smears of blood on his palm. Twisting her arm around and craning her neck, she looked down and discovered a nasty skinned place about the size of a half dollar on her elbow. Blood oozed to the surface even as she watched. Until that moment she hadn't even been aware of the injury. Now that she was, she could feel it burning.

"Let me see." His hand encircled her wrist, and he shifted her arm so that he could look at her elbow.

"It's no big deal. Just a little scrape."

"Tough guy, huh?" He glanced up, met her gaze, and grinned. At close quarters, Julie reflected, those blue eyes could be quite dazzling. "Well, you're going to have to humor me. I get all light-headed at the sight of blood, see, so we're going to have to fix it. Come on."

She had to smile at the sheer absurdity of it. "Wuss."

But she didn't resist as, his hand still gripping her wrist, he pulled her after him toward the bathroom. Passing through, Julie caught just a glimpse of an untidy bedroom—chest against one wall, unmade queen-sized bed, Debbie's discarded clothing flung over a bentwood rocker in the corner so that one stretched-out black panty-hose leg trailed from the pile toward the barge-sized pumps on the floor—before she found herself in a small, green-tiled bathroom that had obviously not been updated in decades. The toilet and tub/shower combination were, like the sink, white and strictly utilitarian. The room smelled of soap. Droplets of water still clung to the clear plastic shower curtain. A jar of cold cream with the lid off was on the counter; a big scoop was missing from its shiny white contents. Obviously Debbie had just used the cold cream as a makeup remover.

"Let's get you cleaned up."

He turned on the sink taps, pumped liquid soap onto his fingers from a dispenser beside the sink, then rubbed it, none too gently in her opinion, into the open wound on her elbow.

"Ow! That stings!" Julie jumped as the soap hit her raw flesh, and would have jerked her arm free, but he held on. He was behind her in the confined space, his body keeping her in place as he maneuvered her elbow under the gushing water.

"Thought you were a tough guy." He met her gaze through the mirror. A teasing smile just turned up the corners of his mouth as the water did its work and vanquished the soap. Unfortunately, having the soap flushed away by a stream so strong it could have come out of a fire hose didn't feel much better than having the injury assaulted with soap. She wrinkled her nose at him through the mirror. His expression changed. The smile vanished, and his eyes were suddenly unreadable.

"How old are you, anyway?" The question was abrupt.

"Twenty-nine. What about you?" She pushed back against him in a vain attempt to win free of his ministrations, then suddenly stopped. His body felt hard and masculine, and having it pressed so close to hers sent currents of electricity shooting along her nerve endings. Whatever he was or wasn't, he *felt* like a guy. Her instantaneous physical reaction to that fact both unnerved her and reminded her far too forcefully of the sorry state of her love life.

It was, she reflected wryly, a sad day when she found herself getting turned on by someone named Debbie.

"Thirty-two. There, I'm done."

He stepped to the side, suddenly no longer touching her anywhere at all, which, she told herself, was a relief. She watched his face through the mirror while he directed his attention to the faucets, turning them off with quick twists of his wrists. If he was aware of the effect he was having on her, he gave no indication of it. Of course, he probably had no idea that he'd given her a thrill. Under the circumstances, she could hardly expect that she would float his boat.

"How old's your husband?"

Instead of making a move on her, which in her confused state she might even have welcomed, he handed her a towel.

"Forty." She patted her elbow dry.

"A little old for you, isn't he? You must be the second wife."

She put down the towel. He passed her a tube of ointment and laid a Band-Aid on the sink in front of her.

"Yes, I am. So what?" She gave him a quick want-to-make-something-of-it look, then started to apply the ointment because the scrape was really beginning to sting.

"So what happened to wifey number one? Did he dump her for you?" He tore open the Band-Aid and handed it to her.

"They were divorced years ago." She accepted the Band-Aid, positioning it carefully over the scrape.

"Have you ever met her? Or talked to her, or anything?"

"No, I haven't. She's been completely out of the picture since long before I came into it." Having finished with the Band-Aid, she lowered her arm and looked up at him with a sudden frown. "What is this, twenty questions?"

He shrugged. "Just curious about how the other half conducts their love lives."

"Oh." That made sense, in a way. "Thanks for the Band-Aid."

"No problem."

Julie met his gaze, made a mental note of her own sudden vulnerability to sheer masculine good looks, and turned and headed toward the living room again.

He followed her. Josephine, who'd been an interested observer all this time, trotted on ahead and beat Julie to the couch. Julie sank down beside the poodle and was rewarded by a cold nose prodding her arm. Gathering Josephine onto her lap, she gave her a hug.

Debbie stopped a few feet away, folding his arms over his chest and regarding her with a thoughtful expression.

"Okay, let me see if I've got this straight: You rolled out of bed, stuck your feet in your shoes, jumped in your car, and drove into Charleston. In the middle of the night. Care to explain why?" He took up the conversation—or was it an interrogation?—where they had left off earlier without missing a beat.

Josephine licked her arm. Julie accepted the only affection on offer and cuddled her close. Just having the dog near was comforting. She had always wanted a pet of her own. Maybe, she thought with a glimmer of gallows humor, she should try to think of what was happening less as a catastrophic marriage breakdown and more as a golden opportunity to trade Sid in for her very own dog.

At the moment, she was about ready to go with the dog.

"Maybe I just felt like going for a midnight drive."

His expression said *yeah, right,* and Julie sighed.

"Look, I'm sorry about your car, I'm grateful for all your help, and if you can somehow get my car back for me I'll kiss the ground you walk on, but I really don't want to go into every little detail of my personal life, okay?"

"So you *are* cheating on your husband."

"No, I am *not.*"

At the outrage in her tone, he lifted his hands, palms up, in a placating gesture. "Okay, okay. Hey, if you don't want to tell me what's going on, fine. It just seems to me like if you're rolling out of bed in the middle of the night to drive downtown in your underwear, then are scared to death your husband is going to find out, something is wrong in your life and—maybe you need a friend."

His voice gentled on that last, and the smile he gave her was disarmingly charming. So charming, in fact, that it caused a pang in the region of her heart. God, he was good-looking—and she wanted to trust him, she really did. He was right, at the moment she could use a friend.

"I'm wearing pajamas, not underwear," she said for the record.

"My mistake."

"How do you know my name?" There was a wary note to that, because she was busy reminding herself that it was better to be safe than sorry. Impossible as it seemed, he *might* have some sort of connection with Sid. Of course, she realized with a sick feeling in the pit of her stomach, in that case the trick would be to keep him quiet about what he already knew.

Debbie shrugged, and stuck his hands into the front pockets of his jeans. "I've seen you around. You own a dress shop out in Summerville, don't you? Flashy evening gowns, sequins, feathers, that kind of thing?" He grinned. "Nothing in my size, though. You might want to rethink that. Us larger gals like to look pretty, too."

Julie smiled involuntarily at the idea of him trying to squeeze into one of her gorgeous gowns, none of which came in a size larger than 8. If he did somehow manage to get one on, and then actually wore it out, he would ruin her reputation forever.

"I'll keep it in mind," she said. Actually, she designed and made gowns and other wardrobe essentials for beauty pageants, and her shop was strictly for contestants and their handlers, but there was no point in going into all that.

The clock was still ticking. That thought left her unable to sit still a moment longer.

"Oh, God, what time is it?"

She put Josephine on the floor and stood up, moving toward the kitchen to check. Debbie stopped her with a hand on her arm. Too nervous now to be more than peripherally conscious of the hard warmth of that hand as it curled around her upper arm, Julie glanced up at him.

"Two-twelve." He was looking past her shoulder at the VCR atop the TV. Following his gaze, Julie realized that there'd been a little digital time readout in the room with her all along.

"I've got to get home." She pulled free of his hand to pace the long wall that separated the living room from the kitchen.

"I'm no friend of your husband's, you know," he said, watching her. "Nothing you tell me will get back to him, I promise. And you never know, maybe I can help you get whatever this is sorted out."

The ensuing pause as she stopped pacing and their gazes met lasted perhaps a couple of heartbeats.

"I think Sid is cheating on me." Julie blurted it out. She hadn't really made a conscious decision to confide in Debbie, the words had just sort of come out on their own, but the minute they left her lips she experienced an overwhelming sense of relief. She had needed to tell someone, she realized. Needed someone to listen to her suspicions and tell her that she was being an idiot—or not.

"Ah," Debbie said, the single syllable drawn out. "And what makes you think that?"

"He's been sneaking out at night after I've gone to bed," she said. "Tonight I followed him. I heard him leave the house and I jumped out of bed and followed him. I lost him on the street where I hit your car. I was turning around in the parking lot when those punks stole the Jag."

Julie took a deep, shaken breath and folded her arms

over her chest. It felt—cleansing, somehow, to utter her suspicions aloud. No more pretending that Sid was the perfect husband, or that hers was the perfect marriage. Telling the truth was cathartic.

"Let me get this straight," Debbie said after the briefest of pauses, rocking back on his heels and giving her a severe look. "You were tailing your husband in your own car? A *Jaguar*? You ever think he might just possibly have glanced in his rearview mirror and noticed you behind him?"

Julie's eyes widened as the terrible possibility sank in.

"I never thought about that. I just jumped in my car and took off after him." Coming close to panicking at the idea, she mentally reviewed the drive.

"Girl, you're not safe to be let out." He shook his head in disgust.

Julie ignored that, reached the end of her cogitations, and felt relieved. "If he'd seen me, I would have known it. Sid's not subtle. Believe me, I would have known it."

Debbie looked thoughtful.

"It ever occur to you that maybe he's just going out for a late-night snack or something?"

Julie grimaced. "And winding up on a street with triple-X bars and strip joints? I wish I could think so, but I don't. Besides, we—I have other reasons to think he's having an affair."

"Oh, yeah?" He eyed her with interest. "Like what?"

"On Monday I found eight Viagra pills in his medicine cabinet," she confessed. "By tonight there were only six. And . . . and . . ."

"You weren't the lucky beneficiary, hmm?" Her expression must have told the tale, because he grinned. "Okay, I get the picture. So hubby's been sneaking out at night, has he? Every night? About what time?"

"Two or three nights a week for the last month. A weekend night, usually, and one or two others. It varies. I usually go to bed around eleven, and he's out by midnight."

"You ever followed him before?"

"No."

"So . . ."

He was interrupted by a muffled ringing sound. Digging his cell phone out of the front pocket of his jeans, he opened it and spoke into it. "Yeah?"

Julie held her breath as the voice on the other end said something she could not quite hear. Then Debbie grimaced. "Shit."

The expletive scared her. He wouldn't say that if things were going according to plan, would he?

"Okay, you do that. Yeah. Catch you later."

He broke the connection, then returned the phone to his pocket. His gaze as it met hers was rueful.

"What?" she asked faintly.

"Well, the good news is they found your car."

"They did?" Hope springs eternal.

"Too late. It's been stripped. Engine, tires, even the stereo. All gone."

5

"Oh, no." Julie felt limp suddenly, as though all the rigidity had suddenly evaporated from her bones. Her knees threatened to give way, and she swayed as the room did a slow revolution around her.

"Whoa!" Debbie reached out and snagged her elbows, stopping her spineless wilt before she ended up in a puddle on the floor. Mindlessly she tilted toward him, and he pulled her against his chest. He felt very strong, very solid, very safe—a rock to lean on. She snagged handfuls of his T-shirt for support and breathed.

"Okay, don't panic. We can still figure out something to get you off the hook." He rubbed her back reassuringly. Julie allowed herself the pure luxury of being comforted. He was warm, and strong, and he smelled faintly of soap and cold cream, and his wide, well-muscled chest was the perfect pillow for her head. It felt so good to be in a man's arms again that she snuggled close. Her cheek rested on a firm pec, and she could hear the slow, steady beat of his heart beneath her ear. He must have sensed her need for comfort, because his arms wrapped around her, holding her close.

She'd missed this: being held by a man. Even in this nonsexual context, it felt so amazingly good.

"Like what?" Her voice sounded despairing to her own ears. She closed her eyes, and tightened her grip on his T-shirt. Her next words were tragicomic. "I might as well just go ahead and kill myself and save Sid the trouble."

"That might be a little drastic, don't you think?"

From his voice, it sounded like he was smiling. Her eyes opened, and a swift upward glance confirmed it: he *was* smiling. Well, she supposed she was glad someone could.

"Not really." Her voice was glum.

"You know, most people in your situation would probably just get a divorce."

Debbie's dry observation so exactly meshed with her thoughts that Julie glanced up again, startled.

"I'm thinking about it," she admitted. To actually express the thought aloud was liberating somehow. "But, to me, divorce is kind of a big deal."

Just watching her mother change marriage partners had probably traumatized her for life. As a little girl, she'd promised herself that when *she* got married, it would be forever.

"People do it every day."

"*I* don't." She took a deep breath and, much as she hated to do it, pulled herself out of Debbie's arms. Wonderful as it felt to be cuddled and comforted, it was over. Time to face the music. "I suppose I might as well go ahead and call the police. I'm going to have to report the Jaguar stolen now. Sid's going to have to know."

The thought made her stomach churn. With fear? She didn't know how else to describe what she was feeling.

Oh, God, when had she become afraid of Sid?

Debbie frowned at her.

"How about if I take you home, and you go on upstairs to bed just like you've never been out at all, and then I break into your garage? When your husband gets home, he'll discover your car missing and call the police. They'll find signs of a break-in and assume the Jaguar was stolen right out of your garage. Doesn't make any difference where the car goes missing from, you know."

Julie stared at him as hope did its eternal thing again.

"Isn't lying to the police a crime?"

He shrugged. "Hey, crime happens. Spitting on the sidewalk's a crime. So is murder. It's all a matter of degree. This particular one won't cause so much as a ripple. The question is, would you rather tell the police you've been in bed asleep all night or tell your husband exactly how you came to lose your Jaguar?"

Julie shuddered. It wasn't even close. "Okay, so I'll lie to the police."

He grinned at her. "Attagirl."

Another problem reared its thorny head. "My purse was stolen too. Oh, I guess I can say I left it in the Jaguar. Which is true. I *did* leave it in the Jaguar, so that part won't be a lie. Exactly."

"Don't think of it as lying. Think of it as telling carefully selected facts." His grin broadened. "Welcome to the dark side, Luke Skywalker."

She made a face, then stiffened as a hideous possibility occurred to her. "What if the police find the punks who stole my car and they tell where they got it?"

"They won't find them."

"How can you be so sure?"

"I just am. Believe me. Mother and his pals run a tight ship, no violence, not hurting anybody, and the cops mostly look the other way."

Julie took a deep breath, and glanced over her shoulder. The clock read 2:15. She was out of time. And, she realized, despite countless objections raised by her basically cautious, law-abiding nature, out of options. The decision had been made: she was going to go with his suggestion.

"I need to get home. Sid's usually back by three."

"No problem. Let's go. Let me grab some gloves."

"Gloves?"

"I don't want to leave fingerprints all over your garage when I break in." He was already heading toward the bedroom again.

"Oh." Her voice was small. She couldn't believe that she was actually going to take part in a crime. The thought was scary. She'd never even so much as filched a quarter from the collection plate at church before.

He was back in a moment, stuffing a pair of black knit gloves into the pocket of his jeans. "All set?"

Julie nodded and turned toward the door. As she did, she saw Josephine, almost hidden behind the recliner, happily worrying a magazine that she held between her front paws. That corner of the room was strewn with shredded strips of newsprint and glossy magazine pages. Julie remembered the pile of reading material that had earlier waited beside the chair, and her eyes widened. There was nothing left but confetti.

Apparently following her gaze, Debbie saw the same thing.

"Damn it, Josephine!"

Josephine looked up at that, bright-eyed, tail wagging, the picture of innocence—if it hadn't been for the strips of shredded magazine dangling from her mouth.

"Hold on a minute," he said with a sigh, and swooped down on the offender. Josephine was scooped up without protest, and borne off toward the back of the house, her adorable pom-pom of a tail still wagging furiously.

"What did you do with her?" Julie asked with some trepidation when Debbie returned, minus the poodle.

"Locked her in the bathroom. There's not much she can get into in there, I don't think." He opened the door, then stood back to let her precede him outside.

The steamy heat felt good, Julie thought, and realized that she had been cold, from nerves or his air-conditioning, she couldn't be sure which. The jasmine-laden night air wrapped around her like a lover's caress, and she welcomed it.

"Even if she did chew up your magazines, you're lucky to have her. I've wanted a dog for years. Sid won't hear of it," she told him over her shoulder as she walked down the short front sidewalk toward his car. The street was deserted now, except for the insects that fluttered around the streetlight on the corner. Lights were on in the upstairs windows of two of the houses; a few night owls were apparently still up. Overhead, a pale sickle moon and thousands of pinprick stars gleamed ghostly white. All in all, and in spite of the fact that she was sick with some weird combination of betrayal and fear, it was a beautiful night.

"Sid's smart." There was a sour note to Debbie's voice that made Julie frown reproachfully at him.

"How can you say that? Josephine is adorable."

A grunt was the only reply. He walked around the car to unlock her door for her, opened it, then waited for her to get settled inside before closing it again. Julie made a face as it occurred to her that, had the slight impediment of his sexual preference not stood in the way, Debbie would have been the kind of guy that women drooled over.

Herself included.

"I am so incredibly nervous about this," she said as he got in beside her.

"About what? Deceiving your husband or lying to the police?" His sideways glance was teasing as he started the car and pulled away from the curb.

She frowned at him. "You're not helping."

He drove to the corner and then turned right. "As long as you stick to the story that you went to bed at the usual time, heard nothing, and have no idea what happened to your car, you'll be fine. With your husband and the police."

Julie grimaced. "Easy for you to say. You don't have to do it."

"You can always change your mind."

Julie thought about that, considered the consequences, and shuddered. "No. I'll lie."

"That's the spirit. Hang tough."

He turned up the ramp onto the expressway, heading northwest. The streetlights glared yellow, completely outshining the moon. A few cars whizzed past, but not many. It was too late—or early, depending upon one's point of view—for the kind of heavy traffic that usually poured into and around Charleston in the summer, courtesy of clueless tourists who didn't know that summer was the worst possible time to visit, thanks to the humidity and swarms of biting insects.

A thought occurred to Julie. "Hey, wait a minute. How did you know which way to go? You don't know where I live. Do you?"

The glance he gave her was unreadable in the shadowy interior of the car. "I assumed you lived out in Summerville near your shop. Am I wrong?"

"No-o, you're right. We live in Summerville." She eyed him doubtfully. His reply had been just a shade too casual—hadn't it? Or was she being paranoid again?

It's not paranoid if they're really after you. The saying popped into her head uninvited. Under the circumstances, it seemed appropriate.

But Debbie had fallen into her life purely by chance,

and since then he had put himself out to help her. More, he had proved to be kind and caring, a friend.

And she badly needed a friend.

"Just tell me where to turn off." He sounded cheerfully unconcerned, and, because she really had no basis for them, she let her suspicions go.

"The first Summerville exit."

"Same as the shop. What's it called?"

"Carolina Belle."

"Maybe I'll stop in again sometime. If you start carrying larger sizes, that is." A crooked smile accompanied his sideways glance.

"Actually, I only sell to the trade." Julie smiled too at the sudden irresistible picture of Debbie in one of her gowns, and was grateful for the resulting easing of the tension that had her hands curled into fists in her lap. "Pageant contestants, that is. And their handlers."

"Are you telling me that you've got to be in a beauty contest to buy clothes at your shop?"

He sounded so affronted that Julie's smile broadened. "Basically."

As a former Miss South Carolina, a veteran of pageants from the age of two on, and the wife of a rich and prominent businessman, her credentials for running a shop that sold custom-designed and fitted evening gowns, swimsuits, and costumes for use on the state and national pageant circuit were impeccable. Carolina Belle was, in fact, quite successful, and she made a decent little income from it. Divorcing Sid would be bad for business, she thought, and with that gloomy reflection felt her muscles start to tense all over again. Every other girl in South Carolina entered beauty pageants; it was almost a sport, like football or something. All the ones she took on liked to think that if they faithfully dieted and exercised and waxed and tanned and bleached and curled, they would end up just like Julie: Cinderella after the ball and the wedding to the prince. An acrimonious divorce wasn't part of that dream.

Glancing down, she saw that her hands were once again curled into fists in her lap.

"Life's a bitch," Debbie said.

Julie suddenly, totally agreed. "Amen."

There was a pause as he sped up to pass a lumbering semi. Then he glanced at her.

"Listen, next time you feel like following your husband on one of his nocturnal adventures, don't. You want him followed, call a professional."

If he was trying to distract her from her own gloomy thoughts, he succeeded.

"A professional?" She almost hooted. "A professional what? Husband follower?"

"Private investigator. You hire one, he gets the goods on your husband for you. It's a lot less messy than doing it yourself, believe me. And a lot less dangerous for you."

"A private investigator?" Julie wrinkled up her nose doubtfully. "I wouldn't know how to go about finding one. It seems kind of risky just to look one up in the yellow pages. And—well, you know how things are around here. Everybody's related to everybody, or knows everybody, or something. Word would get out. There'd be gossip. Sid would find out." Julie shuddered.

"Not if you got somebody you could trust."

"There's nobody I trust. Not when it comes to Sid." It was so true that there was a tinge of bitterness in her voice. Sid was a Carlson, and a Sidney, and in South Carolina the Carlsons and the Sidneys, along with the Pughs and the Pettigrews and the Hughleys, were God. He was related, by blood or marriage, to half the population.

The other half, like her own less-than-pedigreed family, just didn't count.

"You can trust me."

"You?" She glanced at him in surprise.

"I'm the McQuarry half of McQuarry and Hinkle, Private Investigators." He said it almost apologetically. Julie's eyes widened.

"*You're* a private investigator? Are you serious?"

"Serious as a grave."

"I never would have guessed." Julie realized she still sounded incredulous. Debbie—a private investigator? Turning the notion over in her mind, Julie realized that it was no more mind-boggling than picturing him as a bank clerk. In fact, less. Everybody had to have a job. "Do people actually hire you to spy on their husbands?"

"All the time." The skin around his eyes crinkled as he smiled. "Wives, too. You'd be amazed at how many spouses cheat. Sometimes I think most of 'em do. What you're going through isn't anything out of the ordinary, believe me."

That was so depressing that Julie was momentarily silenced. She didn't say anything more until a big green sign just a few hundred yards ahead jolted her back to reality.

"This is the exit!"

She thought he was going to miss it—she'd given the warning way too late—but he was already pulling into the appropriate lane as she spoke. Of course, she'd told him the first Summerville exit. Good thing he'd remembered.

The Blazer rolled down the ramp, paused at the red light at the bottom, then headed into the sleepy bedroom community of Summerville.

The tiny, picturesque town had an old-resort feel to it. The streets were wide and perpetually shady, lined with huge bearded live oaks and masses of azaleas. The historic district consisted of gracious antebellum structures complete with soaring Greek columns, some of which had been converted into shops and hotels and others of which remained private residences, nestled cozily side by side. Carolina Belle was located in an area of newer development a little to the north. At Julie's direction they turned the other way, heading toward the Ashley River, where some of the finest new houses in the area had been built, many of them by All-American Builders. As they drove along the deserted streets, she checked the time again: 2:50. They were going to be cutting it close.

Butterflies took wing in her stomach. Returning to her house suddenly seemed about as appealing as a convict might find returning to prison. She was going to have to face Sid and lie, face the police and lie. . . .

She really, truly, positively didn't want to go home. She had to struggle with herself not to ask him to turn the car around and floor it in the opposite direction.

"How long is it going to take you to break into the garage, do you think?" she asked, careful to keep her voice even.

"Not long. A couple of minutes."

"Is that all?" It seemed a ridiculously short amount of time to circumvent metal garage doors and deadbolt locks. "The house is new, you know. The locks are pretty sturdy. Oh, and what about the alarm system?"

If it went off, the police would come right away. He could be caught in the act.

"Was the alarm set? Did Sid set it when he left? Did you?"

Julie thought. She'd been in such a hurry not to lose Sid. . . .

"Sid usually sets it before he goes to sleep. But it wasn't

set when I left—it would have gone off—and I never touched it. So it's off."

If Sid had set it before he left, he would have had to turn it off when he got back home. And whenever it was turned off, the alarm beeped a loud warning in their bedroom.

If she'd been asleep, she would almost certainly have woken up. And Sid, knowing that, would have taken the safer route of not turning the alarm on at all. After all, there was no real risk. Crime in Summerville was practically nonexistent.

"Then we're in business."

Julie pointed out her house, an eight-thousand-square-foot Greek Revival mansion that Sid had designed and built himself, and the Blazer stopped in front of it. The tall iron gates were still open—they stayed that way most of the time because it was a pain to wait for them to open electronically—but he didn't pull up the driveway.

"It'd be better if we walk up. That way, the neighbors won't see a strange car pulling into your driveway in the middle of the night," he said, answering her unspoken question.

"Good idea." Although the neighbors were in all likelihood sound asleep. At least the other houses—she could see only three from where she stood, the Macalasters', the DeForests', and the Cranes'—were all dark. Like her house, they had been designed and built by Sid's company to similarly tasteful specifications, although of course the facades were all different. Sutherland Estates was Sid's showcase development, which was why they had a house in it. Whichever development was his baby of the moment was where they lived.

Since their marriage, they'd had no permanent home. Sid's father—his mother had died when Sid was young—

was living with his girlfriend in the family's moldy Civil War–era mansion in Charleston's historic district, which Sid, as the only child, expected to inherit one day. Given that circumstance, he'd seen no compelling reason to establish a real, true home of his own. At first, when Julie had hoped to fill the many rooms of the various big houses with children, she'd planned to go to the mat with Sid about settling down permanently as soon as she got pregnant. But Sid basically felt about children the way he felt about dogs, and he'd kept putting her off about having any of their own. She'd let the matter slide, and now she guessed that she wouldn't be going to the mat about living in this house permanently, either.

It was starting to look like she wouldn't be living in any house permanently. At least, not with Sid.

She and Debbie were both out of the vehicle now, and Julie was walking around it to join him. He was wearing the gloves, she saw as she reached him, and carrying a crowbar in one hand. Her stomach turned over at the thought of what they were about to do, but there was no help for it. She was just going to have to lie as convincingly as she could and hope for the best.

Too nervous to talk, she walked silently beside him up the driveway. It was paved in brick, and pink and white creeping petunias bloomed in bright profusion along the edges. Night reduced their colors to no more than shadowy patches of dark and light, but their perfume scented the air. Julie reached under a loose stone and grabbed the spare house key. The katydids were busy, adding their distinctive chorus to the soft chirp of the crickets and the piping of the tree frogs. The strategic stand of palmettos that, along with a brick privacy fence, provided protection from the Macalasters next door rustled faintly as some nocturnal animal moved about among the branches. The sound certainly didn't result from a breeze. There wasn't any. The air could only be described as sultry.

They reached the garage, a long, single-story brick rectangle angled away from the street with a quartet of identical white car doors set into it, and paused.

"Which one?" he asked.

Julie indicated the second door from the left.

He glanced at it. "Piece of cake."

"You've been great," she said, the words heartfelt, looking up at him through the shadowy darkness. "I don't know what I would have done without you tonight."

"I try." He smiled at her, a slow, charmingly crooked smile that did something funny to her insides. Reaching into his rear pocket, he pulled out his wallet, thumbed through the contents, and withdrew a white business card, which he handed to her. "My number's on this. Next time you get the urge to go chasing after your husband in the middle of the night, call me instead."

"Will do." She glanced down at the card. It was impossible to read anything in the darkness. "And I'll call you tomorrow about the damage to your car."

"Sounds good."

She needed to make a move. Seconds were ticking swiftly past, and seconds added up to minutes, and minutes were all she had. Still, she hated to walk away.

She didn't want to go in. She wanted to stay out here in this heavy perfumed darkness forever with this stranger who had somehow morphed into her new best friend.

So he happened to be a guy named Debbie: it didn't matter. It occurred to her that whoever he was, whatever he was, she felt safe with him. She'd gotten more comfort from him tonight than she had from her own husband in years. Once she walked away from him, she was on her own. Her problems were strictly hers to deal with.

"I've got to go in now."

"Yeah." He was hefting the crowbar in his gloved hands, his expression unreadable in the darkness.

She summoned a smile. "If you hear about me being arrested on the morning news, you'll know just how bad a liar I am," she said. Then she impulsively laid a hand on his arm, and rose up to press a quick kiss on his warm, sandpapery cheek.

"Thank you," she said. "You were right: Tonight I really needed a friend."

"No problem."

She gave him one last smile, turned her back, and walked away.

Even before she rounded the corner of the garage, she could hear the grating of iron on metal.

He was doing his part by breaking in. Now all she had to do was go to bed, wait, and lie through her teeth when Sid started screaming.

Mac watched her go, and realized that he felt like the biggest criminal left unhanged. She was sweet, unbelievably sweet considering who she was married to, and more vulnerable than she knew. It had become obvious to him over the course of the last hour or so that, when it came to Sid, she didn't have a clue.

But even if he told her, even if he shared all he knew with her, she almost certainly wouldn't believe him. Besides, whether she did or not, knowing so much might put her in a bad situation. He wasn't one hundred percent sure Sid was dangerous, at least as far as she was concerned, but he strongly suspected that he could be.

The best course of action was probably just to keep his mouth shut and let the situation play itself out. Hang loose and wait to see what developed. As long as she stayed clueless, she was probably perfectly safe. She could get her divorce and get off the stage before anything bad happened to anyone.

Thus there was really no reason at all for him to feel like he was crouched on a deer stand waiting to take pot-shots at Bambi. But, Mac realized as he wedged the end of the crowbar beneath the metal door and gave a mighty heave, telling himself that wasn't much help. He could rationalize all he wanted. He still felt guilty as hell.

6

Basta had just reached the foot of the wide, curving front staircase when he heard the unmistakable sounds of someone entering the house.

He froze, his senses on high alert, then clicked off his small Mag-lite and slipped silently into the nearest room: the den. Earlier he'd prowled through it, just like he'd gone through the rest of the house. Getting the lay of the land, so to speak, so tonight wouldn't be a dead loss.

Just in case his quarry didn't return before he had to leave. But, it seemed, she had. Who else could this be?

Waiting just inside the den's doorway, careful to stand to the side so, should someone decide to flip on the chandelier in the cavernous entry hall, he wouldn't be caught in its light, he kept his eyes trained on the darkness beyond the door and listened intently. Soft footsteps were heading his way, barely audible at first as they came through the kitchen but a little louder as they reached the cool black and white marble of the hall. Whoever it was was in a hurry, and feeling secretive, too—so far, no light had been turned on anywhere in the house.

Basta inhaled, then smiled. After so many years in

this business his senses were nearly as acute as a dog's. And what he smelled was—the soft, sweet scent of a woman.

It was Julie Carlson all right.

A moment later she stepped into view. Moonlight from the glass sidelights on either side of the front door bathed the hall in twin shafts of soft silvery light. They glinted on the shiny pink thing she was almost wearing: nice, was his verdict. She passed out of his line of vision, and he moved to keep her in view, visually catching up with her again as she began to climb the stairs. She was moving quickly, and her long, slim legs flashing in the moonlight were even nicer than her outfit.

Watching her, he smiled. They were all alone, the house was dark and quiet, and she was his for the taking. There wasn't much time left—it had been nearly three when he'd started down the steps—but then he didn't need much. Five minutes, if that was all he had, would be enough. Although it seemed a shame to rush, he was professional enough to do it if circumstances dictated.

And right now it seemed they did.

Silently he stepped out of the den and began to follow her up the stairs, keeping a tight grip on his bag. She wouldn't have time to make a phone call and there was no gun anywhere in the house, so it didn't matter if she heard him. Might even add to the fun if they had to play chase, although he couldn't toy with her for long because they were out of time.

He didn't want to cut it too close. It was his nature to be careful.

She didn't hear him. He was certain of that. She reached the top of the stairs and disappeared into the enveloping blackness of the upstairs hall. Heading for her bedroom, no doubt: a big, fancy affair with a marble Jacuzzi in each of the two adjoining bathrooms and a leopard-print throw on the enormous bed. His hand tightened on the cool wrought-iron railing as he regretted that he was not going to have time to do everything he wanted to her on that bed.

In just a minute or so he would have her bound and helpless. Then he would strip her naked and do her fast and squeeze the life out of her.

Tomorrow he would collect what was still owing on his fee and get back to his regular life. For starters, there was a fishing boat out there with his name on it.

As he neared the top of the stairs, he fancied he could hear her getting into bed: a soft rustle of bedclothes and a creak as she settled down, and over all the surprisingly hurried in and out of her breathing.

He smiled. He'd soon have her breathing faster yet.

Behind him, his sharpened senses picked up something less pleasing: sounds coming from the garage.

He frowned, pausing with one foot on the top step as he listened. Yes, he could definitely hear something he wished he could not.

The husband must be home. Some five, ten minutes early.

For a moment Basta hesitated, irresolute. Julie Carlson lay tantalizingly defenseless maybe thirty feet from where he stood. He could hear her breathing, smell her scent, practically taste her. She was his. He vibrated with longing to do what he'd come here to do.

He would do it, he promised himself. But not tonight.

His lips pursed as he faced the inevitability of that. With the sounds from the garage, the window of opportunity had just slammed shut.

He had to get out of the house.

Turning, he ran silently down the stairs, then with long swift strides headed for the door he had entered by.

Julie Carlson didn't know how lucky she was, he reflected as he let himself out the door, then slipped away through the shadows.

She got to live for one more day.

7

SID WAS CHEATING ON HER. Julie knew it as well as she knew her own name, and the knowledge hurt more than she had ever imagined it would. It felt like a boa constrictor curled around her chest, crushing it so that she could hardly breathe.

Last night he had come running up the stairs at seventeen minutes past three, according to the bedside clock. The mere fact that he was coming upstairs at all at such an hour—to say nothing of the hurry he'd been in at the time—told her that he'd missed the Jaguar as soon as he had arrived home, just as she had known he would. She'd pretended to be asleep, although it was hard to keep her breathing slow and rhythmic when her heart was racing like a NASCAR winner's engine. She'd been curled on her side, the covers pulled high over her shoulders, her eyes shut, when he'd reached the bedroom door. For a moment he'd loomed there, both hands resting on opposite sides of the jamb, breathing hard and just staring at her as she lay in bed. He was wearing a dark suit—Sid always wore a dark suit, even in the dead of summer, because he didn't believe in relaxing standards even in the heat—and his wire-rimmed glasses had been askew, which they never were, because Sid was nothing if not meticulous. He was a

hair shy of six feet tall and thin—Sid watched his diet reli-
giously—but even so he had looked almost . . . *menacing*
standing there.

Which was ridiculous. Sid was many things—Julie
could think of more than a few choice epithets now that
she turned her mind to it—but menacing wasn't one of
them.

At least, it never had been.

She'd held her breath, waiting for the inevitable explosion, waiting for Sid to totally lose it like he did more and
more often when he was mad, until she remembered that
she was supposed to be asleep.

Breathe, baby, breathe.

So she breathed, in and out, real rhythmic—and after a
minute or two Sid had exhaled slowly through his teeth
and gone away.

Just like that.

Without uttering a word about her missing car. In fact,
he'd said nothing whatsoever to her until this morning,
shortly before nine A.M., the time when he usually left for
work and she was usually just getting back from her
morning run, which she had skipped this morning
because she didn't want to be the one to notice the car
was gone. He'd "discovered" the Jaguar was missing when
he started to leave for work. He came roaring into the
house and dragged her downstairs to view the broken
door and empty garage bay and stomped and cursed and
carried on just like she'd known he would—only about
four hours too late.

Give the man an Oscar, she thought with a cynicism
that was new to her.

And give her one, too. Because she pretended to be
surprised and bewildered and absolutely without a clue
as to what could have become of her car. In fact, she'd

been so disingenuous about it she'd reminded herself of the *Home Alone* kid clapping his hands to the sides of his face.

My car's been stolen, oh, my!

And all the while she had professed ignorance and tried to calm Sid down she had been dealing with the fact that her marriage was dead. Because if his little midnight excursion had been innocent, he would have had his hissy fit the minute he got home at seventeen after three.

Gotcha, she thought, gazing steadily at Sid, but the knowledge gave her no satisfaction. She didn't want to *get* Sid. She wanted to live happily ever after with him, just like they'd been doing for the past eight years.

Only apparently he hadn't been so happy. And neither, she realized, had she.

All the while he ranted and raved, she watched him as objectively as she might have a strange animal in a zoo. Who was this man, with his thinning dark hair, his cold gray eyes, his narrow, clever face? Julie realized that she didn't know him anymore.

Maybe she never had. Maybe, with her infinite capacity for mentally spinning straw into gold, she'd made him into the man she wanted him to be, and he'd never really been that man at all.

To add insult to injury, he threw temper tantrums like a thwarted two-year-old. A grown man beating walls with his fists and stomping his Italian-shod feet on the kitchen floor was not a pretty sight.

Her reaction to his histrionics must not have been all he'd hoped for, because he turned on her as they waited in the kitchen for the police to arrive.

"You seem pretty damned unconcerned about the whole thing," he snarled at her as she sliced a banana into the blender to complete the healthy shake he liked for a pick-me-up. He was dressed in a fresh dark suit, and she was wrapped in a robe.

"It's only a car, Sid." Icy calm, she pressed the blender button and looked at him. As he digested her reply, his face, she noticed with the detached interest that seemed to be the only emotion she could summon at the moment, turned almost the color of the trio of bright red tomatoes ripening on the windowsill behind him.

"Only a car! Only a car! It's a fucking Jaguar, you stupid . . . ! Of course you don't appreciate it. You don't appreciate any damned thing I've done for you. You don't appreciate your fifty-thousand-dollar car, or your million-dollar house, or this whole lifestyle I've given you that is light-years beyond anything you ever had in your life, you with your trailer-trash family!"

Two police officers arrived just then, which was probably a good thing because she was on the verge of abandoning her icy calm in favor of braining him with the blender. The good news was, she was so furious by that time that lying to the cop was much easier than she had anticipated—*no, officer, I didn't hear anything*—because she was thinking about how much she wanted to kill Sid all the while. The bad news was, she no longer even much wanted to try to save her marriage.

On second thought, maybe that was good news, too.

Sid and the cops ended up leaving at the same time, which meant that she'd been left home alone with a whole bellyful of nasty things to say and no one to say them to.

Which was probably just as well. Before she took a baseball bat to Sid's head, as she badly wanted to do, she needed to take a deep breath and *think,* she told herself sternly. There was still a chance, no matter how remote, that she was wrong about what Sid had been up to the night before. So he'd lied about cruising his houses. Maybe he was doing something totally innocent that he didn't want her to know anything about.

Like planning a marvelous surprise for her thirtieth birthday? Gee, that wasn't until November. Volunteering to work the twelve-to-three shift in a homeless shelter? She'd had no idea Sid was so altruistic. Screwing some babe whose husband worked the night shift? Bingo! Give the lady a cigar.

In any case, she told herself, breathing deeply again, there was a right and a wrong way to end a marriage, or a smart and a dumb way, however you wanted to look at it. If hers had to end, she was going to do it the right, smart way.

Which meant no going off the deep end. She ordered herself to chill, then got dressed and headed out for the shop. If her life was disintegrating around her she was going to have to deal with it later. She had an appointment with a client at ten-thirty, which meant she was pushing it, time-wise. And she still had to deal with the fallout of having her purse stolen: canceling her credit cards, replacing her driver's license. . . .

It was only as she reached the garage that Julie remembered about her missing Jaguar. Her life was going to hell on a greased slide, and she didn't even have a car. Gritting her teeth, she turned on her elegant stacked heel, marched back into the house, and called a cab.

It was just like Sid not to remember, or care, that she would need a ride to work.

Sid was all about Sid. He always had been, but she hadn't realized it until just recently because for a long time she'd been all about Sid, too.

No more. Julie was important, too.

Whatever happened, she was going to face it with dignity. She was going to hold her head up and smile.

Evidently her smile was less than a success, though, because when she pushed through the glass-and-steel front door of her shop and stepped into the pristine white showroom, Meredith Haney, one of her two assistants, turned from the rack of competition gowns she was straightening to greet her and broke off in mid-hello.

"What's up with you?" Meredith asked, her hand falling away from the sparkly blue gown she'd been rehanging. A short, perky twenty-four-year-old blonde, Meredith was a former Miss Marion County.

Clearly there was no point in trying to pretend nothing was amiss. Best go for the obvious cause.

"My car was stolen last night," Julie said as she headed toward her elegantly appointed office. Then, over her shoulder, "Is the ten-thirty here yet?"

"The *Jaguar?*" Meredith breathed, ignoring her question even as she abandoned her task to follow Julie into the back. "Oh, my God, were you *car-jacked?* Or . . ."

"It was stolen out of my garage." Julie tucked her purse—a cream-colored straw that felt strangely light because there was so little in it—under her desk in her private office and opened the top left-hand drawer of the desk. There it was, right where she always kept it in case of emergencies. . . .

"Oh, my God!" Meredith said again, stopping in the doorway and staring at her wide-eyed. The sleeveless denim jumpsuit she was wearing—out of *Carolina Belle's* daywear stock—was, Julie noted absently, both chic and becoming. "Are you just *sick?*"

"Yes. I'm sick. Absolutely sick." She had never said anything more true in her life. Abruptly she changed the subject. "Is everything ready for the ten-thirty? And where's Amber?"

Amber O'Connell was her other assistant, a twenty-year-old brunette former Miss Angel of Beauty. Julie's tone was brusque because she so badly needed to get rid of Meredith. All she required was about two minutes alone to get her fix, and she'd feel a hundred percent better.

"She called to say she's running a little late. She had a problem with her car." Meredith paused, and grinned. "Nothing like yours, though. Hers just had a flat tire. Anyway, everything's set for the ten-thirty. It's Carlene Squabb, by the way."

Carlene Squabb. Of course, it would be. Her day just kept getting better and better. Now she *really* needed Meredith to go away.

"Why don't you . . ." she began, only to be interrupted by the tinkling little bell that announced that someone had entered the premises.

"That'll be Carlene," Meredith said, sounding as cheered by the prospect as Julie felt. She turned and headed toward the showroom, and at long last Julie was left alone. She snatched the Hershey bar out of the drawer, unwrapped it, broke off a piece, and popped it into her mouth.

As it melted, bathing her tongue in chocolate, she closed her eyes in the closest she'd come lately to ecstasy.

"Julie Ann Williams, are you eating *candy?*" Her mother's scandalized voice caused Julie's eyes to pop open. For an instant she stared guiltily at the comfortably plump, shockingly redheaded woman in the doorway. Then she swallowed.

"Yes, Mama, I am," she said, and defiantly popped another of the succulent rectangles into her mouth right where her mother could see. Her mother didn't really resemble her in looks even if you didn't count the red hair, which you couldn't because it was dyed. Her jaw was wider, her features were less regular, and her artfully made-up eyes were hazel. Julie, as her mother always said wistfully, looked like her father. For all his faults—and they were numerous—Mike Williams had been one good-looking man.

"A moment on the lips, forever on the hips."

"Mama, my hips are a size six."

"See what I mean."

"Mo-*ther*."

"They were a size two when you won the title."

"That was eight years ago!"

"So are you planning to go up two sizes every eight years? I'm just asking because that's exactly what happened to me, you know. A little here, a little there, and bingo, I'm a size twelve."

Her mother, as Julie well knew, was actually more of a size sixteen. Dixie Clay lied about everything from her weight to her age to her shoe size to how many times she'd been married. It didn't matter. Julie could feel the sugar hitting her bloodstream at about the same time the guilt hit her brain. Her mother, blast her, was right. The cost of wallowing in chocolate was high, especially for a woman who might soon be single again. Julie slid the drawer shut—discreetly—and narrowed her eyes at her sole surviving parent.

"Did you want something?"

"I heard your car got stolen." Her mother came on into the office and stopped in front of the desk, planting hands tipped with bright tangerine nails on the black acrylic surface, looking Julie over with a critical eye. Julie braced herself for criticism of her simple white linen sheath: her mother preferred bright colors. Whatever else might have changed over the years, Dixie's taste in fashion had remained exactly the same: bold and eye-catching, just like Dixie herself. She was dressed today in snug white capri pants, a vividly patterned purple, orange, and white tunic-length silk blouse, and high-heeled white mules. With her fire-engine red hair in an Ivana-style upsweep, bejeweled sunglasses dangling from a gold chain around her neck, and beaded earrings the size of chandeliers just brushing her shoulders, she was a sight to turn heads.

Just like she'd always been. Ever since she was a little girl, Julie could remember people staring at her mother. Dixie might never have been a conventional beauty, as she would be the first to admit, but she'd certainly had something that made people want to look at her.

Sid said she was tacky, tacky, tacky. Which, Julie reflected with a quick stab of angry pain, was just one more reason to get rid of Sid.

"Last night." Julie nodded in wry confirmation, relieved not to have to defend her clothing choice. The urge to tell her mother everything was suddenly strong, but if she did there would be no putting the genie back in the bottle. Her mother would be horrified. She would dissect the subject to death, then call Becky and dissect the subject to death with her, and then, as there was not a subtle bone in her body, probably be all for confronting Sid.

Which was something Julie wasn't ready for. Not yet. Not until she had some answers herself.

Instead Julie asked, "How did you find out? It's only been about an hour since I reported it to the police."

"Kenny told Becky, and she called me."

"Oh." Kenny was Becky's husband. Most days, as one of the company's two vice-presidents, he worked directly with Sid. Sid would have arrived at work livid about the stolen car. Kenny would have called Becky pronto, and her mother, the next to be alerted, would have instantly been on her way to check on her younger daughter for herself. That was how the family's jungle-drum system worked.

"They stole it right out of your *garage*? You didn't see anything?"

Julie repressed a sigh. "I was asleep."

"I hear Sid had a cow." There was concern in Dixie's voice. Julie met her mother's frowning gaze, and wavered. Again the urge to confide in her was strong.

The little tinkle that announced someone's arrival sounded again. Saved by the bell, Julie thought.

"I've got to get to work."

Meredith appeared in the doorway. "Carlene Squabb, Julie."

It was all Julie could do to suppress a grimace. The urge for chocolate was suddenly strong again. She was having a really bad day, it was only ten-thirty, and one more little bite wouldn't condemn her to a lifetime of plus sizes—would it?

"Take her on in, Meredith. I'll be right there."

Meredith nodded and disappeared. Her voice mingled with Carlene's in the distance. Julie stood up. Her fingers inched toward the drawer, and she clenched them into a fist as she looked at her mother. "Mama . . ."

"Don't forget you're supposed to be at Becky's at two," Dixie said. "Did you remember to get a gift?"

"Malibu Barbie." It was Kelly's birthday. Kelly, age four today, was Becky's baby. Becky was having a party for her, the little girl's first real birthday party, and Julie had volunteered to help out.

"She'll like that. Is Sid coming?"

Julie shook her head. The mere mention of Sid made her stomach twist into a knot. Oh, God, if she divorced Sid, Sid would fire Kenny, and Becky and Kelly and six-year-old Erin would have their comfortable lives ruined. "I don't think so. He's busy."

"Seems like he's always busy these days." Her mother

looked her up and down, frowning, then held out her hand imperiously. "Julie."

Julie met her unyielding gaze, and realized she was busted. Which was probably just as well. Swallowing hard, she opened the desk drawer, picked up the candy bar, and reluctantly handed it over.

"See you at two," Dixie said, satisfied, tucking the candy bar into her purse, and turned to leave. "Oh, and by the way, you should add a scarf or some beads or something to that dress. It needs a little color."

"Yes, Mama." Julie had long since learned the futility of arguing with her mother. As a general rule, she pretty much agreed with whatever Dixie said, then she did as she pleased. She walked her to the door, said good-bye, then after she was gone just stood staring for a moment out at the bright and busy street. With the world ablaze with heat and light outside, how was it possible that her glass-fronted shop could feel so cold and dark? Julie closed her eyes, then determinedly opened them again. Enough of that. She refused to wallow. Wallowing was for sissies.

Pushing all thoughts of Sid and corollary images of chocolate from her mind, Julie headed for the largest of the fitting rooms, where she knew she would find Meredith and Carlene. Sure enough, as she entered, Meredith was in the act of easing a glittering scarlet ball dress over Carlene's raven head.

"God, I need a cigarette! Could you please hurry up?" Carlene said as her head popped out of the dress. All four walls were mirrored, and as a result about eight images of Carlene stared at Julie as she entered.

Julie greeted Carlene, nodded wordlessly at Meredith, and took over. The dress was her own design, lovingly conceived and executed because Carlene, however trying

Julie might personally find her, was a strong candidate to win the Miss Southern Beauty pageant to be held the following Saturday night. If Carlene won Miss Southern Beauty, then she would go on to the Miss American Beauty contest. If she was victorious there—and Carlene, if she kept her mouth shut and her bitchy tendencies in check, was lovely enough to make it a possibility—she would compete for Miss World Beauty. All providing wonderful exposure for Carolina Belle, of course. And exposure for Carolina Belle took on a whole new level of importance if she was contemplating divorcing Sid.

"This will just take a minute," Julie said, carefully zipping up the back of the gown. It was a truly gorgeous creation, if she did say so herself. One of her most inspired. Both Carlene and Mabel Purcell, Carlene's handler, had gone gaga over it when they'd seen the sketches. "I don't anticipate having to make any changes. It . . ."

Julie's voice broke off as the zipper stopped halfway up Carlene's back. Frowning, she looked more closely at the elegant folded edges of scarlet silk concealing the zipper and the inches of smooth tanned back that still remained between them.

It was clear at a glance: the dress, custom made to Carlene's measure, was not going to zip.

Julie stared disbelievingly at the gap in the back, then looked at the dress—and Carlene in the dress—through the mirror. Everything was just as it should have been—full skirt aswirl with hand beading, boned, lined, fitted to the millimeter, strapless bodice, breasts round and firm as oranges swelling coyly over the top. . . . Julie's gaze fixed on those breasts. Instead of oranges, she was looking at cantaloupes.

"You got implants!" Julie couldn't help it. She was aghast, and sounded it.

Carlene nodded complacently. "I had it done last Friday. Don't they look great?"

She turned this way and that, thrusting her newly eye-popping chest out as she surveyed herself with satisfaction in the mirror.

"The pageant starts on Thursday. That's only four days." It wasn't just the gown. There was the swimsuit, too, and the conservative black suit for the interview with the judges and the kicky little sundress for the opening break-fast with the press. . . . "Your whole wardrobe will have to be refitted!"

"Is that a problem?" Carlene asked with a little frown, meeting Julie's gaze through the mirror. Julie thought of the size of the order, of Carlene's chances of winning, of the small pageant world that would hear within the hour if Julie totally lost it and wrapped her fingers around her most promising client's neck. She thought briefly, fleetingly, longingly, of the calming effects of the confiscated bar of chocolate. Then she summoned up her most professional manner, and even managed to smile. Admittedly, it was a rather grim smile, but it was a smile nonetheless.

"Well, it certainly can be done, but it's going to take some doing. To begin with, you need to try everything on again and . . ."

"Julie, you're wanted on the phone. Mr. Carlson." Amber, now well over an hour and a half late, appeared in the dressing-room doorway with the message. It was an indication of how badly the day was going that Amber's lateness was the least of Julie's concerns.

"Thank you, Amber." She massaged her temple dis-creetly. "Meredith, remeasure Carlene's bust, would you, and mark the gown? Then let's go to the swimsuit. Amber will help you."

"How long is this going to take?" Carlene reached for

her cigarettes, which were lying atop her purse on a nearby chair.

"I'm sorry, but Carolina Belle has a no-smoking policy, remember? Because the smoke makes the gowns smell, and the judges don't like that," Julie said, as Meredith took over with a quick, discreet roll of her eyes.

"Fuck," Carlene said, straightening away from the chair.

With that elegant reply echoing in her ears, Julie escaped to her office with a soothing "I'll be right back."

Oh, God, she didn't want to talk to Sid now, she thought, staring at the phone as if it were a snake coiled to strike. In fact, she didn't want to talk to him at all, ever again in her life. But there was no help for it. The glowing yellow light that signified a caller on line one would not be denied. Picking up the receiver, Julie punched the button and said hello.

"You remember to get my cleaning?" Sid asked. She knew his voice so well, and yet today it was almost like listening to a stranger. A lying, cheating, louse of a stranger.

" 'Fraid not. It's kind of hard to stop by the cleaner's when I don't have a car." Her voice was brittle. He didn't seem to notice.

"Well, try to get it before you come home, would you? We've got that charity auction at the country club tonight, remember. Dad and Pamela will be there."

Julie remembered, and groaned. The last thing she needed at the moment was to have to act the part of Sid's loving wife before his father and his father's girlfriend.

"I called the insurance company about your car, by the way. They'll be sending a loaner over to the shop before noon." Sid's tone was suddenly friendlier. Julie suspected, from certain background sounds, that he was no longer alone. Then Sid said "Thanks, Heidi,"—Heidi Benton was

his administrative assistant—as he was apparently handed
something, and her suspicion was confirmed.

"Fantastic." Her reply was flat.

"You're mad, aren't you?" He sighed. Julie could still
hear Heidi moving around in the background. "Because of
this morning. I yelled at you, and I shouldn't have."

"No, you certainly shouldn't have," Julie agreed, giving
him a big crocodile smile that he couldn't see. He was
being nice for Heidi's benefit, she knew. "And thanks for
giving me a ride to work, by the way."

"I'm sorry, okay? I was upset about the car." His voice
dropped. "I love you, Julie."

Julie's eyes widened. The remark was so totally out of
character for Sid that she could only assume that either he
wanted Heidi to hear it or he was trying to ease his own
guilt about cheating by throwing a little verbal affection
her way. Before she could reply, Sid hung up. Which was a
good thing, Julie thought. She wouldn't have known what
to say. Sid hadn't said he loved her for so long she couldn't
remember the last time, and he *never* apologized.

Maybe she was totally paranoid, totally unhinged, but
this was almost more suspicious than the missing Viagra.

Julie realized that she had to know, one way or another,
finally and for sure and without any doubt, what Sid was
up to. If he was a true and faithful husband with nothing
more than anger issues, sexual dysfunction, and a bad
case of insomnia—well, she could work with that. She
would kick herself for her suspicions and invest in even
more sexy lingerie and try her best to make her marriage
work.

But if he wasn't, he was marital toast.

With her stomach twisting itself into a pretzel at what
she was about to do, she dragged her purse out from
under the desk and dug for the business card she had

dropped inside it that morning. This time she would let a professional do the spying for her.

Punching in the number on the card, she listened to the phone ring once, twice.

"McQuarry and Hinkle, Private Investigators." It was a woman's voice.

Julie took a deep breath. "May I speak to Debbie, please?"

8

"Debbie?" Rawanda asked, sounding blank.

Mac had been standing in front of his desk shuffling through the papers on top hunting for receipts when Rawanda, sitting behind the desk and engaged in the same task, answered the phone. He glanced up, alerted by the name she uttered. Rawanda was short and round in all the right places and pretty, with face-framing black curls and eyes the color of caramels. She'd been working for McQuarry and Hinkle for almost a year, answering the phone and filing and doing word processing, hired because they'd gotten a subsidy to cover her salary through a state program that paid to put former convicts to work. Rawanda had done six months for check kiting, but insisted she was now completely reformed. During the time she'd worked for them she'd managed to get her well-manicured nails firmly into Hinkle's vulnerable hide. Now the subsidy was just about up, and they were going to have to scrounge up the money to keep her on at their own expense, because, as Hinkle put it, *I ain't lettin' this bitch go.* Mac pretty much agreed with that, although for a different reason: Rawanda was flat-out good at her job. At the moment she was frowning into the phone, her head shaking from side to side.

"Ain't no Debbie here, ma'am. You must've dialed the wrong number."

Even as Mac realized who must be on the other end of the line, Rawanda was looking at him with widening eyes.

"Debbie *McQuarry?*" She blinked at Mac. "You sure?"

"Give that to me," Mac said, and took the phone away from Rawanda before she dropped it. All too conscious of two curious pairs of eyes and ears suddenly focused on him with all the subtlety of a pair of Rottweilers spotting a kitten—Hinkle was sitting on the couch at the far side of the room, where he had been going through some pictures from the night before—Mac spoke into the receiver.

"McQuarry here."

"Debbie?" Julie Carlson's voice sounded a little uncertain. But he would have recognized it anywhere, regardless.

"Out here in the workaday world, I generally go by Mac."

"Oh." There was a tiny pause. "I hope I didn't say the wrong thing to whoever answered the phone. I mean, I didn't mean to cause you any trouble or anything. I never thought—it never occurred to me that you wouldn't go by Debbie at work as well."

Mac couldn't help himself. Even with Rawanda and Hinkle watching avidly, he had to smile. "Don't worry about it. You haven't exactly outed me. What can I do for you?"

"Well, I need to make arrangements to pay for the damage to your car—" There was another of those tiny pauses—he could almost picture her chewing her lower lip—and then the rest of the words came out in a rush. "And—and I want to hire you to follow my husband."

Her voice had dropped so low as to be almost inaudible as she finished. But Mac heard, and understood.

"Smart call." His tone was brisk. If this was as difficult for her as it seemed to be, he wanted to make it sound like business as usual for him. He'd been expecting her to call this morning about the damages to his car if nothing else, but for her to hire him to tail Sid was on the order of life handing him a little present. Now that he'd been put on the scent, he'd had every intention of tailing Sid anyway. If the scumbag was merely cheating on his wife, that was one thing; but if he was up to something else, Mac meant to move heaven and earth to find out what it was. Getting paid for his efforts was pure gravy.

Paybacks are a bitch, he said to his mental image of Sid, then returned his attention to Sid's wife, who was still talking.

"I don't have any idea how to go about this. What do I need to do? Is there somebody in your office I need to make arrangements with or—you understand I want to keep this completely confidential."

She sounded nervous, skittish, as though she was ready to abandon the whole idea at the least hint of a problem. Mac blocked out of his mind a sudden vivid image of the way she had kissed his cheek the night before—no need to get the guilt thing going again—and set himself to reassuring her.

"I'll handle it myself, don't worry. And nobody else has to know. I'll need a little more information, though. Could we meet? Where are you now?" If the idea of seeing Julie Carlson again had a certain appeal above and beyond his desire to learn everything she knew about her husband, he wasn't admitting it even to himself.

"At my shop." He got the impression she was growing increasingly nervous. "I can't come to you. I don't have a car, remember? And you can't come here. Sid might find out. I . . ."

"Okay," Mac interrupted soothingly, before she could spook herself into canceling the whole thing. "I understand. Isn't there a Kroger across the street from you? How about if I drive over there and wait for you in the parking lot? You won't have any trouble recognizing the Blazer"— his voice took on a humorous note meant to reassure her—"it's the one with the big dent in the side, remember? All you have to do is hop in. I'll be parked in the row right behind the Taco Bell. Just give me a time."

He heard her sucking in air. His muscles tensed in anticipation of a hang-up. But she didn't.

"It's Saturday, so Carolina Belle closes at noon. I suppose I could meet you at about a quarter after. Oh, gosh, I can't believe I'm doing this. If Sid finds out . . ."

"He won't," Mac said. "Not unless you want him to, that is. You're doing the smart thing here. Just keep reminding yourself of that, and try not to worry. I'll see you in the Kroger parking lot at quarter past twelve. Okay?"

Not for nothing had he worked selling yellow page ads to pay the bills during his freshman year at USC. If nothing else, he knew how to close a sale.

"Okay."

Asking for the order still worked. But she didn't sound happy.

"I'll be there waiting. Twelve-fifteen in the Kroger parking lot."

"Okay," she said again. He heard someone calling her— another woman—and she drew in her breath.

"I've got to go," she said into the phone, and hung up.

Mac hung up too, slowly, lost for the moment in thought. She had sounded scared to death, not that he was particularly surprised. Taking on Sid Carlson was scary work, as he knew himself to his cost. The consequences of losing could be devastating. Sid cornered was a scorched-earth kind of guy.

Grimacing at the memories that reflection brought with it, Mac looked up to find both Hinkle and Rawanda staring at him.

"Debbie?" Rawanda's questioning gaze slid over as much of him as she could see with his big oak desk standing between them.

"Who was that?" Hinkle demanded at almost exactly the same moment.

Mac shrugged, and returned to rifling through the remaining papers as though the call had been nothing more or less than business as usual. Somewhere in the pile there had to be a receipt for a hundred twenty-three dollars for new tires, to replace two of his that had been slashed on a stakeout at the beginning of the month, and eighty-nine dollars for the motel room required to listen in on the adulterous tryst taking place on the other side of the wall. No receipts, no reimbursement. He had instituted the rule himself, but that didn't help when Rawanda, who now handled petty cash, applied it to him.

"A new client. I promised her total confidentiality. So don't ask." This case he didn't mean to share with anyone. Even if Julie Carlson hadn't insisted on confidentiality, he would have kept quiet about it. Hinkle, who, having gotten busted out of the police force right along with Mac and having subsequently been let in on the whole thing about Daniel, was now as wary of Sid as a bird was of a snake. He would have tried his damndest to talk Mac out of getting involved with the Carlsons in any way, shape, or form.

Actually, Hinkle probably would have had a point, but with this tantalizing new opportunity falling into his lap like a gift from the gods, Mac wouldn't have listened. No way in hell was he walking away from this thing now.

"Debbie?" Rawanda sounded even more incredulous than before. She glanced at Hinkle. "That woman on the phone was asking for *Debbie* McQuarry. I didn't know the boss here sometimes went by Debbie."

Mac sent her an aren't-you-funny glance, but otherwise ignored her as he continued to shuffle through the papers. Hinkle grinned at Rawanda, then looked at Mac.

"This is someone you met last night, right? At the Pink Pussycat?" In response to Rawanda's increasingly agog expression, Hinkle added for her benefit: "Mac was in drag for the Edwards case. He was calling himself Debbie." A grin split his face. "He was looking pretty hot, too."

"Damn, and I missed it!" Rawanda met Mac's gaze, looked him up and down with exaggerated lasciviousness, hooted with laughter, and stood up. Her black spandex mini hugged her butt and made a virtue of plump but curvaceous legs lengthened by her platform pumps. Her low-cut white tee revealed a great deal of her other ample assets. "I just love this detecting business. How come you guys never take me along on none of your cases? I bet I could detect real good."

" 'Cause you're way too fine to go poking your nose into trouble." Hinkle stood up, slid the photos he'd been looking at back into a manila envelope, and crossed the well-worn linoleum floor to hand the envelope to Mac. The three of them shared a basic two-room suite outfitted with a single telephone line, a black vinyl couch, and a trio of ancient wooden desks, one of which was positioned in the small reception area and belonged to Rawanda. It was located on the second floor of a World War II–era office building not far from Mac's house. The building wasn't exactly Trump Tower, but it was affordable even when private-eye pickings were slim, as they usually were in the summer, when all sensible residents left

Charleston for cooler environs and the city was aswarm with tourists. Considering the uncertain nature of the business, affordable, in Mac's opinion, was key.

"You going to take these over to Mrs. Edwards today?" Hinkle asked, nodding at the envelope.

Rawanda came around the desk to slip her arms around Hinkle's waist, and he reciprocated. They made a good-looking pair, Mac observed absently, with Hinkle tall and slim and dapper in a pale seersucker suit and Rawanda all curvy and sexy in her poured-on clothes, but their association, which he had not foreseen when he had hired Rawanda, was probably not going to be good for business in the long term. When the breakup came, as it inevitably would—he was readier to believe in the tooth fairy than in the long-term success of male-female couplings—the fall-out was going to be bad. Rawanda, he had already learned, did not do things by halves.

Ah, well, that was a worry to be saved for another day, along with a host of others.

"Monday. Mrs. Edwards is out of town for the week-end."

Mac walked around his desk and stowed the envelope in the bottom drawer, which he locked, pocketing the key. Josephine, who'd been stretched out in the knee space beneath the desk, turned onto her back, waving her tiny paws at him. He eyed her askance. He had already learned that Josephine, like most females, tended to smile the sweetest right before she bit him in the ass. Figuratively speaking, of course.

"She should be real happy. We got the goods on Edwards. Big time." Hinkle was smiling down at Rawanda as he spoke.

Rawanda batted her eyelashes at him. "You-all ever thought about trying to sell them pictures back to Mr.

Edwards? If I were him, I'd sure-nuff pay to keep anyone from seeing me down on my hands and knees with . . ."

"That's called blackmail, sugar," Hinkle interrupted. "It's a crime."

"Oh." Rawanda batted her lashes some more. "We sure don't want to commit no crime."

Mac, mentally rolling his eyes, interrupted before the billing and cooing made him lose the doughnut he'd eaten for breakfast.

"Okay, gang, I'm out of here. Hinkle, don't forget you're on the third shift at that Hanes warehouse down in the Battery tonight. You be sure and keep your eye out for anybody pilfering panties."

Hinkle groaned. "Like I said before: How come *I* get all the shitty jobs?"

"Hey, last night I was the one who got my ass grabbed, remember? Rawanda, as of right now you're on doggy duty. Actually, I'll probably need you to keep Josephine all night."

Rawanda pulled away from Hinkle to plant both fists on her hips, shaking her head vigorously at Mac.

"Uh-uh! I ain't keepin' that dog for you no more. Last time you left her with me, here at the office, she went crazy. Attacked my purse like one of them pit bulls and wouldn't let go for nothin'. My cell phone was in there, ringing like there was no tomorrow, and she wouldn't even let me get to it. I missed a call from my parole officer, which ain't no good thing, let me tell you. She chewed the strap clean off it before I managed to pull it away. I already took the money out of petty cash to pay for my purse—thirty-two bucks, which I cannot afford—but I ain't takin' no chances with her going crazy on me again. And I sure ain't takin' her home with me. Anyway, this is Saturday. After twelve o'clock, I am *o-fic-ially* off duty for the weekend. You're the one whose granny sweet-talked him into taking her dog. In my book, that makes her your problem."

"I'm meeting a client this afternoon. Tonight I'll probably be on stakeout."

"Well, boo-hoo, sing me another sad song."

Hinkle was grinning. He loved Rawanda's sass. Mac glared at Rawanda, opened his mouth to continue the discussion, and gave it up. He could tell by looking at Rawanda that there was going to be no winning this one short of firing her, which he wasn't going to do. And they both knew it.

"Fine. I'll take her with me. Josephine." Mac snapped his fingers authoritatively. Nothing happened. He tried again. Still nothing.

In the sudden silence he became aware of an ominous grinding sound.

He looked under his desk. Josephine the ever-obedient was going after the right front leg like a beaver in a building frenzy.

"*Josephine.*" He would have cursed if he'd been alone. Josephine never even glanced around.

"Hey, boss, looks like your dog's eating your desk." Rawanda was chortling as she looked under the desk with him. "Must be hungry. Whole leg's just about gone."

Shit.

"I needed a new one anyway," Mac said with as much equanimity as he could muster, and hauled the culprit out, brushing the crumbs of his admittedly old but perfectly serviceable desk from around her mouth as he straightened with her in his arms. Her tail went wild, and she gave him a look of pure doggy devotion and licked his cheek. Mac tucked the dog under his arm football-style without succumbing to the now-familiar urge to wring her neck, waved, and got the hell out of his office before his guffawing companions drove him to murder. He loved Grandma Henderson devotedly, but why he had let her talk him into taking her dog when she moved into a retirement home was beyond him.

But he had, and now he was stuck. His grandma loved the thrice-damned animal, and he loved his grandma. He even took the pooch to visit her once a week, which entailed a visit to the doggy beauty parlor beforehand so Grandma would see Josephine looking nice. You couldn't get much more devoted than that.

But so far—and he'd been the proud possessor of the purebred toy poodle for approximately three weeks— Josephine had been the canine equivalent of the bad seed. Despite her deceptively angelic looks, she had chewed up an armchair, a briefcase, a plastic trash can, a lamp cord, a bed pillow, a rug, and enough wood products to qualify for the termite hall of fame. When he'd walked back into his house last night after driving Julie Carlson home, he'd found his shower curtain in shreds, which was why Josephine was at the office with him today: he was scared to leave her alone in his house. Now she'd started in on his desk. He was starting to wonder if the dog was part devil. The bad part.

"Bad dog," he said dispiritedly. He'd already learned that those words were not, apparently, part of her doggy lexicon. Sure enough, she licked his hand in response.

"No lick," he said. She apparently didn't understand that either, because she did it again.

Shit. Tromping down the stairs—the ancient elevator had been broken for a week, and given its recent history he felt safer with the stairs anyway—Mac headed toward where his car was parked behind the building. He was a low-country boy born and bred, and the truly oppressive heat didn't bother him. In fact, he kind of liked it.

What he didn't like was truly oppressive heat coupled with perfumed dog frizz. The combination made him itch.

He dropped Josephine into the backseat—which was useless, as she jumped into the front before he was even all the way inside—and started the car, thinking longingly of doggy shelters all the while.

The air conditioner shot out a blast of air hotter than anything ever produced by any furnace. The radio blared. Even as he offed the radio with a savage forefinger jab, Josephine planted her front paws on his shoulder and licked his ear.

"No lick," he said, jerking his head away, then gave it up. He had already discovered that there was just no reasoning with Josephine. Popping open the glove box, he fished a dog biscuit out of the bag he had learned to keep in there and handed it to her, then peeled rubber out of the parking lot as, satisfied, she settled herself down on the passenger seat for a quick snack. As he headed out toward Summerville to the sound of crunching and the certainty of crumbs, he forced himself to mentally tally the poodle's good points before the idea of doggy shelters took unshakable possession of his mind.

The problem was, the only good point he could attribute to Josephine at the moment was that merely being in possession of her made him look gay.

Which, as far as he was concerned, was only a good point when Julie Carlson was around.

Probably letting her think he was gay was not exactly ethical, Mac reflected as he blew past most of the light traffic headed away from the beaches. But twice, once after he'd just kind of instinctively checked her out there in the parking lot of the Pink Pussycat and again after he'd shed his Debbie regalia, he'd seen a look on her face that warned him that if she realized he was straight her comfort level with him was going to go way down.

And he wanted her to be comfortable with him. She represented a tantalizing new link to Sid. What with being fired, getting divorced, and all the hassles involved with establishing a new business, his hunt for Daniel had been kind of on the back burner for the past five years. But he hadn't forgotten. He would never forget.

Anyway, if, between the dress and the wig and the poodle, she had chosen to assume he was gay, he could not really be blamed, he told himself. After all, he had not actually lied.

When she'd asked him if he was gay, he'd asked if it mattered. And *that* was not lying.

Exactly.

But it occurred to him, as he took the Summerville exit and then drove the few blocks to the Kroger, that he did not particularly like the idea that Julie Carlson thought he was gay.

And even less did he like the idea that he did not like the idea.

The whys and wherefores of that did not become clear to him until he had been parked behind the Taco Bell for some minutes and at last saw Julie Carlson herself come walking across the steaming asphalt toward him.

Even through the rising veil of heat she looked cool and tempting as vanilla ice cream in a slim white dress that somehow managed to be both classy and sexy at the same time. Her hair was pulled back from her face to hang in a shining black waterfall down her back. She was frowning slightly, one hand raised to block the sun from her eyes, as she scanned the parked cars. Her long tanned legs flashed beneath the hem of her dress as she moved. He was willing to bet dollars to doughnuts that they were bare, and to his dismay just thinking about Julie Carlson's bare legs made him hotter than the asphalt.

Unbidden, lightning snapshots from the night before flashed through his mind: the sweet-smelling suppleness of her in his arms; her breasts, firm and round as oranges with pert little nipples that seemed to beg for attention, pressing into his chest; her truly world-class ass all slithery in satin as it rubbed up against his definitely noticing crotch; the silky texture of her hair; the creamy smoothness of her skin; the soft warmth of her lips as she kissed his cheek.

The truth hit him like a hammer over the head: He had a galloping case of the hots for his newest client, who was not incidentally his oldest enemy's wife.

He was walking into quicksand here, and if he had the sense God gave a gnat he'd turn around and walk back out again before he wound up floundering over his head.

9

DEBBIE—NO, THAT WASN'T RIGHT, hadn't he told her
that he went by Mac on the job?—didn't look particularly
happy to see her, Julie thought as she slid into the Blazer
beside him. Which made them even, because she wasn't
all that thrilled to see him, either. Having made up her
mind that hiring a private investigator was the smartest
thing she could do, she was now suffering a major attack
of buyer's remorse. If he hadn't shown up, she wouldn't
have been altogether sorry.

But she would have been on her own. And the thought
of that made her shiver despite the heat.

"Hi," she offered as she closed the door, then smiled
with genuine delight as Josephine jumped into her lap
from the backseat. "Hi, Josephine."

"Hey." He sounded about as glad to see her as he
looked. Scratching an ecstatic Josephine behind the ears,
Julie frowned at him. "Careful, she'll lick you to death."

"I don't mind." Her frown deepened as Josephine
licked her chin. There was something about his expression . . . "Is something wrong?"

Their gazes met and held for the space of a couple
of heartbeats. Then one corner of his mouth quirked
up wryly.

"What could be wrong?" He reached past her, opened the glove compartment, and extracted what looked like a dried-up brownie from a paper bag. "Josephine." When the poodle looked at him, he tossed the brownie into the backseat. "Go get it."

With an eager yap, Josephine leaped into the back. He put the Blazer into reverse, and pulled out of the parking space. Julie absently watched the play of light and shadow over his classic profile and then, as he turned his head, the chiseled planes and angles of his face. As she'd lain awake into the dawn, his had been one of the many images that had chased themselves endlessly through her mind. Remembering her physical response to him in his male incarnation had both stimulated her sex-deprived senses and, by extension, depressed her even more than she was already. He was, she was less than delighted to discover, just as attractive by the glaring light of day. He was wearing jeans, sneakers, and a white T-shirt with a blindingly bright Hawaiian shirt open over it, and he looked good enough to eat.

Good thing there was no chance of him being on the menu. Her life was messed up enough right now without adding another potentially explosive element to the mix.

"Where are we going?" Unlike last night, she didn't feel particularly nervous about the answer, Julie realized. Whatever her feelings might be about hiring a private investigator—and they were so tangled that it would probably take years if she tried to sort them out—she no longer had any qualms about the man beside her. He was, quite simply, a friend.

"We'll attract less attention if we drive around as we talk. Put your seat belt on."

He pulled out onto the street as she complied, and turned left, heading away from the business district. Traffic was fairly heavy, and there was a good possibility that she had at least a passing acquaintance with most of the people in the surrounding cars. Flipping her visor down to provide some degree of cover, she sought to make herself as invisible as possible.

"You can quit trying to hide. The windows are tinted." He glanced at her. "So how's your elbow?"

"Fine. Nobody even noticed the Band-Aid."

"What happened after you went in last night?"

Julie grimaced. "Sid came in at the same time he always does—and didn't say anything about the car being missing until nine this morning."

"Oh, yeah?" Clearly he understood the implication of that.

"Yeah." Her tone was glum.

"Actually, I saw him go into the house. I decided to hang around for a while in case . . ." The words trailed off.

"In case what?"

He glanced at her again, his expression unreadable. "In case you needed me. In case your husband lost it when he found out the Jaguar was gone, and started roughing you up or something."

Touched, Julie smiled at him. "That was sweet. Thank you."

His eyes held hers for the space of a heartbeat, and his mouth did its wry thing again. "Sweet's my middle name."

His attention returned to the road.

"For your information, Sid doesn't rough me up. He's not the violent type. Anyway, I don't see how you would have known if he did."

He grinned, and the atmosphere lightened. "Hey, I'm a professional. I have ways. So what happened at nine this morning when he supposedly made the big discovery?"

"He threw a tantrum. And called the police."

"Oh, yeah? You have any trouble there?"

"By the time they got to the house I was so mad at Sid I didn't even care if I *was* lying to the police."

He laughed. "That works."

Turning down East Doty, where Civil War–era relics were crammed doric-columned porch to doric-columned porch, he turned serious again. "Calling me was a smart thing to do. Following your husband around yourself would only have gotten you into trouble."

"I found that out last night."

"There are worse things than getting your car stolen." The Blazer stopped at a light, and his gaze met hers. "Look, I've got to tell you: I've never worked on one of these cheating-spouse cases where the party who hired me was wrong about what was going on."

Julie took a deep breath, and her hands clenched in her lap. "I'm prepared for that. And I don't think I'm wrong. But I have to be sure."

"You will be. Either way."

Josephine jumped back into the front seat and landed in Julie's lap.

"Good girl, Josephine." Julie hugged the little dog.

"I think she likes you."

"What's not to like?" Julie sent a teasing glance his way as Josephine curled up in her lap like a cat.

"Nothing that I can see." His response was barely audible. But the tone of it seemed so infused with purely heterosexual meaning that Julie frowned. He met her eyes for the briefest of pregnant moments, then slid his gaze along the bare length of her legs, his expression openly covetous. Julie's eyes widened. Then he added: "I have to tell you, girlfriend, those are absolutely to-die-for shoes. Are they Manolos?"

So much for her sudden suspicion that he was behaving in a very *male* way. She should have remembered: Debbie had a thing for shoes. He'd recommended heels with last night's lingerie, after all.

"Jimmy Choo."

"Ah." He nodded. "Nice. Too bad they don't make 'em in a size twelve."

Julie grinned. "I doubt there's much market for Jimmy Choo sandals in a man's size twelve."

"You'd be surprised, Miz Carlson. You'd be surprised."

"Julie, please."

"Julie, then. And I'm Mac. It's kind of hard to get taken seriously in a business setting when you're a man and then someone goes and calls you Debbie." He braked at a traffic light.

"Did I cause a problem for you at work? I'm sorry."

"Lucky I own sixty percent of the business. With a more conservative boss, you could have gotten me fired."

Julie laughed. Then she sobered as she got down to business. "You'll have to tell me how this private-investigator thing works, because I don't have a clue. Do you have a daily rate or something? Do you take checks? Credit cards?"

"In your situation you're better off paying me cash." He was suddenly all business, too. "That way nothing can be traced back to you if your husband should somehow get suspicious and start looking into things. You should know that can happen. Domestic cases have a way of getting real nasty sometimes."

Julie had no doubt of that. As soon as Sid found out she was thinking divorce the proverbial excrement was going to hit the proverbial fan.

"I'll bill you for my hours," he added. "It'll probably end up being two or three thousand dollars by the time everything's said and done. If I think it's going to go over that, I'll get your approval first."

Julie nodded. "Okay. And you'll let me know how much your car is to fix, won't you?"

"I'll add it to the tab. If you're not careful, you're going to wind up owing me your firstborn child."

The words were meant to be humorous, but they caused a tiny pang in the region of Julie's heart. If the divorce happened, the children she wanted and that Sid had resisted would never become reality. And at twenty-nine, her biological clock was already starting to tick loud and clear.

"So tell me about your marriage. For example, when did you and your husband first meet?"

Julie was glad to be distracted. "I met Sid the night after I was crowned Miss South Carolina. There was a big reception at the governor's mansion and he was there. I was talking to the governor, so thrilled to be there that I was pretty much on cloud nine anyway, and then Sid came up and that was that. He swept me off my feet. We dated for the year of my reign, and then married a month after it was over."

Instead of being moved by her story, Mac frowned as he listened. Which, considering how her marriage looked like it was turning out, was probably a more appropriate response anyway.

"What were you, twenty when you met him? Didn't your family have any objections to you getting involved with a man so much older?"

"Eleven years isn't that much," Julie said. "And no, my family didn't object. Are you kidding? There were just the three of us—my mother and my sister Becky and me—and we were so poor that eating at McDonald's was like going to a fancy restaurant. Sid was rich. He was handsome. He was charming. And I was in love with him. My family—my mother especially—was over the moon."

His lips tightened. "What happened to your father?"

Julie hesitated a moment before replying. Talking about the father who had never been there was still, after all these years, a little painful.

"He and my mother divorced when I was little. I used to see him periodically—a couple of times a year. Then he went away somewhere. I just saw him once more, and then he drowned a couple of weeks later."

A lump—stupid, stupid lump—rose in her throat, and she swallowed hard to get rid of it.

"Sounds like you had a tough life." There was a certain rough sympathy to his tone. His gaze slid in her direction, and Julie saw that he was looking—what?—a little annoyed? Or maybe that was just how he looked when he felt sorry for someone.

Julie's chin came up. She wasn't much into sympathy, at least not when it was directed at her. All her sympathy went to people who were in the same boat she had once been in. She did her best to reach out a hand to them, teaching a regular class on makeup and grooming to the ever-changing residents of the local women's shelter, donating clothes and fittings to poor women who had nothing to wear to job interviews, and generally doing what she could to help others along the path. But she no longer wanted or needed sympathy for herself. She had pulled herself out of poverty by her bootstraps—or, to be more accurate, by her high heels. And if she had to, she could do it again.

Her response was, therefore, deliberately light. "It was interesting."

At that moment Josephine stood up on her lap and gave an imperious-sounding yap. All attention immediately focused on her.

"What?" Mac said to Josephine, sounding exasperated. Her tail wagged madly, and she yapped again.

"She's got to go to the bathroom," he translated for Julie's benefit, and glanced around. They were approaching the Azalea Park and Bird Sanctuary, which was a magnet for tourists, although the locals, being blasé about so familiar a site, rarely visited. Pushcarts offering all manner of foodstuffs, vendors hawking balloons, and a juggler tossing china plates in the air prowled the area in front of the gates. Visitors streamed along the footpaths leading into the park.

Mac found a parking place near the gates and pulled in. Julie looked around nervously. She really didn't want to be spotted in his company—she could hear the questions about her companion's identity now—but that didn't seem very likely. The chance of someone she knew being at this particular tourist trap at just past noon on a steamy Saturday in July was so slim as to be negligible.

He reached into the backseat and came up with a leash. It was pink leather and rhinestones, like Josephine's collar.

Josephine wriggled excitedly when she saw it. His expression was something less than excited as he clipped it to her collar.

"Want to walk for a few minutes, or would you rather wait in the car?" His gaze met hers.

"I'll walk."

He turned off the engine, pocketed the keys, and got out of the car. Julie got out, too, and waited on the sidewalk for him to come around. The sun blazed down, the heat was oppressive, and the tourists were, for the most part, elderly folk decked out in plaid Bermuda shorts and crushable hats. Still, Julie felt happier than she had all day. Josephine squatted and relieved herself the moment she hit grass. Then Mac, his expression faintly martyred, and Josephine, wreathed in doggy smiles, headed toward her. Looking from one to the other—the tall, broad-shouldered, athletically built man with his surfer-god looks and the prancing white puffball of a very feminine poodle, linked by a rhinestone studded pink leash— brought a smile to her face. Julie was suddenly very glad that she was not facing this situation with Sid alone. Debbie and dog might be unlikely allies, but they were allies nonetheless.

"Still feel like walking?" He smiled wryly at her. Josephine wagged her tail.

"Sure." Julie turned toward the gates. Mac and Josephine fell into step beside her. Josephine, being adorable, attracted her fair share of glances. Those glances inevitably shifted from the tiny prancing dog to Mac at the other end of the leash and tended to end with surprised expressions. Mac smiled in answer to the smiles directed at him, but Julie noticed that he didn't look particularly happy to be the focus of so much attention.

Just before they stepped inside the park, Mac signaled to one of the ice-cream vendors, who responded by pushing his cart their way. A pair of elderly women walked by, birding glasses in hand, casting covert glances at Mac and Josephine as they passed.

"Tell you what, I'll buy you an ice cream if you hold the leash," Mac said.

Julie laughed and took the proffered leash as the ice-cream vendor reached them. Mac ordered a DoveBar, then glanced inquiringly at Julie.

"None for me, thanks."

"You sure?"

She nodded, and he shrugged and paid. The ice-cream vendor moved on, and they headed inside the park. Now that Julie held the leash, the attention Josephine attracted was unambiguously positive.

"You don't like ice cream?" Mac took a bite out of one

corner. Julie watched enviously as he crunched through the crisp chocolate shell to expose the creamy white goodness within.

"I love ice cream. I just don't eat it."

"Why not?"

"A moment on the lips, forever on the hips." God, she sounded like her mother.

His gaze ran over her body. "You don't look like you need to worry."

"If I didn't worry, I *would* need to. Just eat your ice cream, okay? It's not like I'm starving or anything."

Her stomach growled just then, giving the lie to her words. Julie's eyes widened, then flew to meet his. He grinned at her.

"It's lunchtime, and I haven't eaten yet." She felt compelled to explain away her body's embarrassing gaffe.

"So take a bite of ice cream." He held the DoveBar out to her. Julie eyed the unbitten corner covetously. She *loved* DoveBars. They were right up there with Hershey bars on her forbidden list. "One bite won't make you fat."

One bite. One piece of chocolate. It was a slippery slope, as her mother had pointed out earlier, and Julie knew it. But still—she surrendered to temptation, and sank her teeth into the treat held so tantalizingly close.

Oh, it was good. It was *so-o* good. Smooth milk chocolate wrapped around sweet vanilla ice cream—she could just die.

"Thank you," she said, when the treat had left her mouth in search of her hips and she was able to talk.

"My pleasure." He held the DoveBar out to her again, but this time she shook her head. Firmly. He shrugged, took another bite, then passed the rest to Josephine, who, apparently unconcerned with her girlish figure, downed it greedily. When she was finished she looked up, clearly hoping for more. She had a ring of chocolate around her mouth and looked so comically expectant that Julie had to chuckle.

"Don't laugh. You're not in much better shape." Mac grinned at her. They had stopped in the shade of an enormous magnolia while Josephine wolfed her treat, and the scent of the waxy white blossoms wafted around them. The path underfoot was crunchy gravel, and birdsong filled the air. The only tourists in sight were busy exclaiming about a yellow-throated bullfinch or some such creature apparently perched high in a bearded oak some twenty yards away.

"I have chocolate on my mouth?" Julie's fingers rose to her mouth self-consciously. Tracing the perimeter, she shook her head at him. "I do not."

"Yes you do. Just there." Still grinning, he touched the center of her lower lip with his forefinger, then rubbed his finger back and forth along the line where her lips joined. Her response to the playful gesture shocked her. Her lips parted, and heat shot from where his finger touched clear down to her toes, awakening every single nerve ending in between. She had to stop herself from touching that hard warm finger with her tongue, or drawing it into her mouth and biting down, or . . .

Oh, God, was she pathetic or what? Even as she gritted her teeth and pressed her lips together to stave off the impulse, her gaze flew to his face. Surely he must be experiencing this surge of mind-blowing electricity too? It was impossible that such sizzling heat could be affecting her alone.

But if he was battling a sudden fierce attack of sexual desire, he showed no sign of it. He was looking down at Josephine, his expression perfectly peaceful, and his hand was already dropping away from her mouth. The dismal truth hit her like a splash of cold water in the face: her body was at full boil, and his hadn't even hit simmer.

Of course it hadn't. He wasn't interested in her that way. Good thing, too.

Grimly reminding herself of all the reasons *why* that was a good thing, Julie took a deep and, she hoped, unnoticed breath.

"Do you need anything else from me? I have to be getting back." Her voice sounded perfectly normal, she was pleased to discover.

"Numbers where you can be reached, including cell phone. As much as you know about your husband's daily schedule and usual associates. The kind of car he drives, including license-plate number. Anything else I can get later." He glanced up, met her gaze, and smiled. Those beautiful blue eyes, she was both chagrined and relieved to discover, showed no awareness of her as a woman. "And one dollar."

"One dollar?" Julie asked, surprised. Then, realizing that she had left her purse in the car, she shook her head. "I don't have any money on me."

Mac sighed, pulled out his wallet, extracted a dollar bill, and handed it to her.

"Now give it back to me."

"What?" Julie was smiling at the sheer silliness of it as she obeyed. "Why?"

"Retainer. Congratulations, ma'am: You've just officially hired yourself a private investigator."

And that was *all*, Julie told herself sternly as they retraced their steps to the Blazer, and tried to feel happy about it.

"From here on out you want to be careful. When you're with your husband, behave as normally as possible. Whatever you do, don't get in a fight with him and tell him you're having him investigated. You could wind up getting hurt," he warned some ten minutes later, as, with the information Julie had scribbled in a notepad for him tucked safely away in the glove compartment, he stopped in the Kroger parking lot.

"I told you, Sid isn't violent." Julie opened the door and got out. The bright heat of the parking lot was almost disorienting after the air-conditioned protection of the Blazer. Josephine, dislodged from her comfortable perch on Julie's lap, stood on the seat wagging her tail in doggy good-bye. Mac gave Julie a skeptical look.

"Emotions tend to run high in this kind of case. People do all sorts of unlikely things. So you mind what I say." His tone was cautionary.

Julie smiled. "I will."

Promising that was easy. Whether Sid was apt to turn violent or not, she wasn't about to tell him what she had done. He would be livid if he found out. She started to shut the door, then hesitated, glancing in at him again. "When will you start?"

"Right now. There's some preliminary work I can do, and tonight I'll be parked out in front of your house, waiting for the midnight ride of Paul Revere Carlson."

"Funny." It was lame, but it made her smile again, and smiling, as she had discovered earlier, boosted her spirits. Actually, *he* boosted her spirits. He and Josephine.

"Mac. Thanks."

Their gazes met, and the skin around his eyes crinkled as he returned her smile with, she thought, a touch of ruefulness.

"You're welcome. Julie."

10

"AUNT JULIE! AUNT JULIE!"

Erin and Kelly both came tearing into the hall as Julie stepped through the door of her sister's house. Although it was nowhere near as big and fine as Julie's, it was a comfortable, two-story brick house in a nice neighborhood. Becky and Kenny had moved in when the former construction worker had been offered a job by Sid shortly before Erin was born, and they seemed prepared to spend the rest of their lives there.

If Kenny didn't lose his job as collateral damage in her possible divorce, that is.

"Erin. Kelly." Echoing the girls' boisterous greeting, Julie set her packages down on the blue slate floor and opened her arms to them. They reached her at the same time, and she was giving them both a big hug when her sister walked into the hall, looking harried.

"Hey, Jules. You're just in the nick of time. In five minutes we'll be knee-deep in preschoolers and Mama's decided that this is the moment to start drawing smiley faces on four dozen balloons." Becky rolled her eyes. "What I need is someone to finish filling the party bags. That means you."

"Hey, Beck." Julie grinned at her sister over the girls' heads. Becky was three years her senior, and was in appearance pretty much a younger version of their mother, minus about thirty pounds and the red hair, of course. She had mink brown hair cut sensibly short, and a round, cheerful face. Her body was sturdy rather than slender, and she looked very much the suburban mom in belted khaki shorts and a white camp shirt.

"Julie, is that you?" Dixie yelled from the kitchen. "Get in here. I need help."

"Hi, Mama," Julie hollered back. Then, to Becky, "My car got stolen last night," as Kelly, the birthday girl, began jumping up and down with excitement, loudly begging to know if the gaily wrapped packages on the floor were for her.

"I know *that*," Becky said, turning a well-practiced deaf ear to her daughter. "What I want to know is, how mad was Sid?"

"Mad." Julie switched her gaze to her not-to-be-denied niece. "One for you, and one for Erin."

She handed a package to each girl. Kelly immediately began tearing at the wrapping paper on hers, eager to get at the gift.

"But it's not my birthday," Erin objected, hesitating even as she accepted hers. Erin looked much like Becky, although she had her father's gray eyes. She was a sweet, earnest child and Julie loved her dearly.

"Ith *my* birthday, Aunt Julie," Kelly lisped importantly, looking up from her struggle to tug the ribbon off. Kelly's build was far more delicate than her sister's, and her hair was darker, mahogany rather than mink, and wildly curly. She was a pretty, lively child, and Julie loved her dearly, too. "I'm five now."

"Wow, five. That's a big girl." Julie smiled at Kelly, and then at Erin. "I thought you needed a present to help celebrate your sister turning five."

"Was he mad at *you?*" There was concern in Becky's voice. Julie wondered, as she had once or twice before, if perhaps Becky suspected that all was not shining in Camelot, but she shook her head and said, "He was just mad," as Erin, reassured, started unwrapping her gift, carefully separating the edges of the paper instead of ripping it off with abandon as Kelly was doing. Telling Becky the truth was even less an option than confiding in her mother. Becky would worry, and if she was worried, Kenny would know and badger her until he found out why, and then Kenny would run immediately to Sid. Kenny was fine as a brother-in-law, he loved her sister and the kids, but he knew which side his bread was buttered on. And in this case, Sid was the man with the butter.

"Barbie!" Kelly shrieked gleefully, having finally succeeded in getting the wrappings off, and headed at a dead run for the kitchen, brandishing her gift. "Nana, look, Aunt Julie got me Barbie!"

"I got Barbie too!" Erin yelled after her sister, having unwrapped enough of the present to identify the contents, and took off in hot pursuit.

"What do you *say?*" Becky called after her daughters as she and Julie trailed them into the kitchen, which was a big square space decorated in cheery yellow. A taped-up HAPPY BIRTHDAY banner formed a swag over the top of the window that looked out into the neat backyard.

Dozens of brightly colored balloons with a rainbow of ribbons attached bobbed against the ceiling. Dixie, holding a balloon with two circle eyes but no mouth drawn on it in one hand and a permanent marker in the other, bent over her granddaughters, admiring their gifts.

"Thank you, Aunt Julie," the girls chorused as their mother prompted them again. Then, still clutching the dolls, they tore off in the direction of their bedrooms.

"Here, Jules, finish filling these. They each get a Fruit Roll-Up, a package of SweeTarts, three stickers, a barrette, and a pencil." Looking harassed again, Becky pushed Julie toward the kitchen table, which was cluttered with Powerpuff Girl–decorated party bags, about two-thirds of which were filled, and a jumble of the aforementioned goodies. Julie went to work as Becky turned to the birthday cake on the counter and started sticking small blue candles into the white icing.

"Kelly and Erin remind me so much of you two at their age," Dixie said with a hint of nostalgia as she drew a smiling mouth to complete the balloon, then reached for another one. "If Becky weren't so silly about entering the girls in pageants, I bet Kelly could win as many titles as you did, Julie."

"No," Becky responded sharply. Dixie pursed her lips at her older daughter, but before she could argue the doorbell pealed. With a quelling look at her mother, Becky went to answer it to the accompaniment of wild whoops from her daughters, who skidded past in an effort to beat her to the door.

"Can you believe she's that way? You winning all those pageants was the best thing that ever happened to us, her included." Dixie's gaze shifted to Julie in a transparent appeal for support. From as far back as Julie could remember, Dixie had entered her in every beauty contest that came along, worrying over her hair and makeup and strategizing over how to come up with eye-catching costumes on their dollar-store budget, which had actually been a good thing, because Julie had learned how to design and make the most beautiful clothes out of nothing, which in turn had led to Carolina Belle. Julie's looks would be their ticket, Dixie had prophesied time and time again, and so it had proved.

"Sometimes I think Becky's downright ashamed of where she came from," Dixie continued in a hurt tone that she was careful to keep low so that Becky would not overhear.

In her mind, Julie heard Sid calling them *trailer trash,* and could not find it in her heart to blame her sister, although she would never say as much to their mother. Much as she hated to admit it, *trailer trash* was putting a positive spin on their childhood. Lots of times, between Dixie's tumultuous love life and complete lack of marketable skills, they hadn't even had so much as a trailer to live in. When Dixie was in between husbands and boyfriends, there'd been cheap motel rooms and women's shelters and even a memorable month spent living in a tent in a campground just like Girl Scouts, as Dixie had bracingly described the demoralizing regimen of public showers and toilets and sleeping on blankets on the ground, while Julie and Becky tried to go to school and pretend their lives were just like everyone else's. Always, for Julie, there'd been beauty pageants, the winning of which was often accompanied by a little prize money or some gift certificates or something to buoy them along. When she'd turned thirteen and Becky was sixteen, they'd ganged up together to put their dual feet down about their mother's love life, absolutely refusing to move in with her boyfriend du jour and insisting they get a place of their own. That's when they'd become trailer trash, which had been a wonderful thing because that rented double-wide was the first permanent home she and Becky had ever known. After that, Dixie had forsworn men, and all three of them had waited tables and cleaned houses and weeded flower beds and baby-sat and did whatever else they could find to do just to afford to eat and pay rent on their treasured new home. Then Julie had won a big one, Miss Teenage South Carolina Peach, when she was fifteen, and modeling gigs had started coming her way, and what with those and some local television commercials and a few more titles that came with scholarships attached, their lives had become almost normal and she'd even been able to go to college. Becky, with whom she had shared her winnings as much as she could, had opted for a job at a rent-a-car place, and Dixie had met and fallen in love with Hiram Clay. Then Becky met Kenny, Dixie married Hiram, and Julie won Miss South Carolina and met Sid, all in the same year.

And so here the three of them were, eight years later, living out their happily-ever-afters. Each of them had gotten what she'd always wanted, and each dream had a flaw. Dixie's husband had been disabled in a car crash four years after the wedding; Becky's wholehearted embrace of her role as the Perfect Suburban Mom had a kind of compulsive quality to it that Julie suspected was the result of their tumultuous childhood; and in her own case, the sad truth was that the stable home and loving marriage that she'd craved all her life—were not.

So much for the idea of happily-ever-after. Julie was pretty sure that, in reality, happily-ever-after simply didn't exist.

"I don't think it's so much that Becky's ashamed," Julie said. "But that was then and this is now, Mama. I can see why she thinks that putting Kelly in beauty pageants probably isn't a good idea. For one thing, it might make Erin feel bad."

Dixie said, *"Julie,"* as though Julie had deeply wounded her. Then, bristling slightly, she added, "Are you saying that you think Becky felt bad when you were winning all those pageants?"

Julie suppressed a sigh. "I don't know, Mama. But . . ."

Erin and Kelly came running back into the kitchen with two of their friends at their heels just then, and any thought of continuing the conversation was forgotten. The birthday party was under way.

When it was over, Julie just had time to pick up the cleaning and get home before Sid did. Julie was in the shower when he came upstairs to get his clothes out of his part of the huge his-and-her walk-in closets, dressing areas, and bathrooms that adjoined the master suite on either side, so she missed seeing him. By the time she came downstairs, dressed and ready to go, he was already standing in the living room waiting for her.

He was wearing a classic black tux, which became him. With his dark hair brushed back to hide the bald spot at his crown and his wire-rimmed glasses firmly in place on the bridge of his long, thin nose he looked both elegant and distinguished. Looking at him as she paused in the arched doorway, Julie was reminded of why she had married him in the first place, and her heart ached.

How could he do this to her? To them? The questions quivered on the tip of her tongue. It was all she could do not to ask Sid outright, but she remembered Mac's warning in time to bite the words back. Sid would only deny everything anyway, so what was the point?

"You're not going to wear *that,* are you?" Sid asked, snapping the cell phone on which he'd been talking closed and looking her over with a critical eye. Feeling immediately defensive, Julie glanced down at herself. Her cocktail dress was fuchsia silk, short and sleeveless, with a flirty ruffle around the hem. Until that moment, she'd thought that it looked great. That *she* looked great.

"What's wrong with it?" Her throat felt tight.

"It makes you look hippy. Every bit of the weight you've

gained lately seems to have gone right to your butt, have you noticed? Well, too late now. We'll be late if you go change." His gaze ran over her again, mildly disdainful as only Sid could be, and then he took her arm and practically propelled her out the door in front of him. Moments later Julie was buckled into the front seat of the Mercedes, where she rode in tight-lipped silence to the country club. Once there, she plastered a big smile on her face and settled in for an evening spent hiding her mega-butt and pretending her marriage was wonderful while guilty visions of Hershey squares and DoveBars molding themselves to her rear danced through her head.

"Here's the big guy." Wreathed in smiles, Sid stood up as his father, John Sidney Carlson III, known as John, threaded his way through the crowded room toward them. He was heavier than Sid, obviously decades older, and bald except for a white fringe above his ears, but there could be no doubt that the two were father and son. They exchanged a back-clapping embrace as Julie greeted his girlfriend du jour with a smile and an air kiss. Pamela Tipton was a couple of years younger than she was—John was seventy-one—and lovely. She had a short, silvery-blond pixie cut, enormous blue eyes, and a size-two body. Complete with a very small, very toned tush.

"And how's my favorite daughter-in-law?" John asked, turning to her. Smiling gamely at this old joke—she was his only daughter-in-law—Julie lifted her cheek for his kiss and then sat down again to feign interest in the ensuing conversation. Sipping at a glass of iced tea, she barely picked at a salad and concentrated on looking happy when she was feeling anything but.

If she had only herself to consider, she thought as she exchanged friendly chitchat with Mary Bishop, the lieutenant governor's wife—the couple shared their table along with Sid's partner Raymond Campbell and his wife Lisa and Circuit Court Judge Jimmy Morris and his wife Tricia—maybe getting Sid out of her life might not be such a bad thing.

In fact, she was beginning to cotton to the idea of telling Sid to take a hike. A permanent hike. As in, take this marriage and shove it.

On the way home, Julie was surprised at how much she longed to fling both her suspicions and her private investigator in Sid's face. With the supreme density that she had come to expect from him, he seemed to have no idea that she was angry. Reminding herself that discretion was the better part of valor, she bit her tongue as he made a few general comments about the evening. Fortunately, his cell phone rang before she succumbed to the temptation to do more than nod in reply. He started talking to someone about some problem that had to do with the supply of bricks. Julie stopped listening, entertaining herself by looking out the window instead.

It was a beautiful starlit night like the one before, but its beauty merely served to underline her own unhappiness. After a few minutes in which her mind wandered hither and yon, she found herself thinking about Mac, and as soon as she did, some of her inner turmoil eased. She'd had fun with him under the unlikeliest of circumstances, he was the hottest-looking guy she'd met in forever, his dog was an absolute darling, and—he was gay. Oh, well. In this case, three out of four was probably a good thing.

As the Mercedes drove up their street she oh-so-casually glanced around but saw no sign of Mac or his Blazer. Of course, he could be anywhere—or nowhere. As dark as it was under the overhanging oaks that lined the street, it was almost impossible to be sure that he was—or wasn't—there.

Once inside the house, Sid—naturally—headed for the den while she went directly upstairs and stripped off the fuchsia dress. She knew herself well enough to know that she would never wear it again.

She was as afraid of looking hippy as a little child might be of a monster hiding under the bed.

Which Sid knew, of course. He'd said that to make her feel bad. He was good at that, making little needling remarks that stung forever. She knew she should ignore them, but she couldn't.

He knew what buttons to push, and he pushed them with cruel glee.

Kicking off her shoes, Julie peeled off her panty hose, then headed into the bathroom in her bra and panties to turn on the taps. She would take a long, hot bath, put on the ugliest, most unsexy nightwear she could find, and go to sleep. No more humiliating trips to the den to see when—if—he was coming to bed. No more worrying about what there was about her person that turned him off. No more wondering if he was cheating.

Finding out what Sid was up to was Mac's problem now. The knowledge was a tremendous relief.

Still, while the water ran she could not help going into Sid's bathroom and just peeking in his medicine cabinet. There, on the third shelf, was the bottle of vitamins. Pouring the contents into her palm, she took a quick inventory: mixed in with the businesslike yellow-and-white capsules were six—count 'em, six—blue diamond-shaped pills.

Sid must be staying home tonight.

Lip curling at the thought, Julie returned to her bathroom, turned off the taps, and walked thoughtfully back into the bedroom. Flipping off the light so that the room was plunged into darkness, she crossed to the window and edged the heavy silk drape aside so that she could look out. Moonlight filtered across the lawn, overlaying the silvery velvet of the grass with black chiffon shadows from the trees that shifted and swayed as if to music she couldn't hear. Beyond the low brick wall that fronted the lawn, the street was a solid impenetrable black. Was Mac's Blazer parked down there somewhere? Maybe. He'd said he would be waiting. But she had no way of knowing for sure.

How long she stood there, lost in thought, she couldn't have said. What brought her out of her reverie was, from downstairs, the faint but unmistakable sound of the door between the kitchen and the garage opening and then closing again.

Sid had either left something in the car or, Viagra notwithstanding, he *was* going out.

Julie's whole body stiffened at the thought. All of a sudden she knew, *knew,* that she wasn't going to be able to bear just waiting around for Mac's report.

She certainly wasn't going to be able to calmly have her bath and go to sleep.

She wanted to see what Sid was up to with her own eyes. She *needed* to see what Sid was up to with her own eyes.

That would be closure. And for her to finally, once and for all, end her marriage in her own mind and heart, closure was what she needed.

She heard a low, vibrating hum. She knew that sound, too: the garage door was going up.

Galvanized, Julie ran for her closet, yanked on the first dress that came to hand—a red mini styled like a polo shirt—grabbed a reasonable pair of shoes—slides with tiny shaped heels—and, shoes in hand, sprinted barefoot for the stairs.

If Mac was out there, she was going with him. If he wasn't, she would follow Sid herself.

Flying through the hall, she yanked open the front door, leaped down the white stone steps, and sped across the soft, cushiony grass toward the small iron gate at the far corner of the yard.

Bright beacons lit the driveway, stretching toward the street like reaching arms. Sid's car rolled in near silence out of the garage, heading down the driveway. Would he see her? Julie's heart began to slam against her breastbone as she glanced over her shoulder at the moving car. No. She was far enough away that she was pretty sure he couldn't. But she was going to be too late. . . .

The Mercedes turned left at the street exactly as it had the night before. Julie was forced to hold up just as she reached the gate, ducking behind the brick wall, drawing in great gulps of air as she listened to chorusing katydids and caroling crickets and waited for the big car to pass. She heard the purr of the expensive engine, the swish of tires on pavement, and then Sid was gone.

Bursting through the gate, she bolted onto the still-warm pavement just as the Mercedes reached the corner. Its taillights glowed bright red as it paused at the stop sign.

Oh, God, where was Mac?

She looked wildly around. There, in front of the Cranes', a vehicle was parked. In the dark it was impossible to be certain, but it might be the Blazer.

Or it might not.

Taking a deep breath, she sprinted toward it just as its headlights came on, pinning her in their glare.

11

MAC COULDN'T BELIEVE HIS EYES when Julie darted into his headlight beams like a startled deer. Before he could do more than slam on his brakes—running over a client was not something that was generally conducive to repeat business—she was yanking open the passenger door and flinging herself into the seat beside him.

"Go, go, go," she said urgently, slamming her door. "You'll lose him."

Sid's Mercedes was, indeed, disappearing around the corner.

"Damn it . . ." Mac began, then gave it up as he realized he had a choice: he could sit there and reason with Julie or lose the man he wanted in the worst way to follow.

With one narrow-eyed look at her, he took his foot off the brake and headed out in pursuit. She fastened her seat belt and settled in.

"This was not part of the plan," he said as he reached the intersection.

"Screw the plan." Julie sounded breathless. "He's my husband, I'm paying to have him followed, and that means that I get to go along if I want to."

The Mercedes was perhaps three blocks away, easing through Summerville's side streets toward the expressway.

Mac kept it in sight, but was careful to stay far enough back to not attract Sid's attention.

"Oh yeah? Just what surveillance handbook did you read?"

"He didn't notice me the last time. *And* I was in my Jaguar."

"You got lucky." His mouth was grim. She was wearing some kind of perfume—every time he breathed he got a whiff of it, soft and tantalizing. Her hair, black as the night, hung in loose waves around her face. Her eyes were huge with excitement, glinting at him in the faint light from the dash. Her lips—those lush, beautiful lips that he had been fool enough to touch earlier in the day; the warm, soft lips that had kissed his cheek—were parted as she breathed. The dress she was almost wearing stopped at approximately mid-thigh, and clung to every delectable curve on the way down. And he was willing to bet every dollar he possessed that her long tanned legs were bare again.

This he did not need. It was distracting, to say the least. *She* was distracting.

"I'll stay out of your way, I promise. You won't even know I'm here."

Mac almost laughed at the impossibility of that. Up ahead, Sid hit Summerville's main drag and turned, as expected, for the expressway. Mac followed, keeping well back.

"This is stupid." He turned up the long ramp onto the expressway in Sid's wake, and glanced at her. "This is not happening again. *I* follow your husband. *You* stay home. *I* bring you a full report and pictures, if warranted. *You* pay me. Got it?"

"If I'm paying, I get to do it any way I want."

"Not if you're paying *me.*"

"If you don't like it, you can quit. Just turn around,

take me back home, and quit. I can always follow Sid myself."

She had him there. No way in hell was he going to quit. He'd wanted to get the goods on Sid too badly for too long—and now there was Julie's well-being to consider, too.

Although thinking about Julie as anything other than Sid's wife was a truly dumb idea.

"You pull this again, and I will quit," he said, although he knew that by his not immediately turning around the threat lost most of its teeth.

A small smile curved her mouth as she realized she'd won.

"I won't be any trouble, you'll see," she said.

Mac had to fight not to roll his eyes.

"Where's Josephine?" She glanced into the backseat.

"The only creature that could possibly be more in the way than you on a job like this is Josephine. I left her at home." In the bathroom, actually. This time he'd taken care to tie the (new) shower curtain out of reach. With the rug stuffed into the cabinet under the sink along with the toilet paper, and all toiletries plus his razor stashed in the medicine cabinet, there was no possible damage she could do. He didn't think.

Julie leaned forward suddenly. "He's changing lanes. He must be getting ready to get off. There—see?"

They had reached Charleston, and the Mercedes was, indeed, pulling into the far right lane. Traffic was fairly heavy—it was a Saturday night in July, after all, and tourists were as ubiquitous as fire ants—so Mac didn't much worry about being spotted. Yet. It was when he had to get out of the Blazer and follow Sid with Sid's extremely noticeable wife in tow that the situation was going to deteriorate into farce.

"I see," he said, and pulled into that lane too. It was only as they passed into an area of figure-eight ramps lit up bright as day by the huge overhead lights that he noticed the color of her dress. "Did you *have* to wear red? Why not just stick a flashing light on your head and be done with it?"

She glanced down at herself. "It wasn't intentional. I just grabbed the first thing I could reach and pulled it on."

"I guess I should thank my lucky stars that tonight you bothered to get dressed."

"Don't be bitchy, Mac." She smiled at him, a sweet and coaxing smile that made his blood heat. God help him, but he was a sucker for her kind of smile, for her kind of dark, sultry looks—oh, face the facts, a sucker for her.

Also just a sucker in general, he told himself sourly, for letting what should have been a fairly simple thing—get more information on Sid, check it out, see if it led anywhere he might be interested in following—get so involved. If he had an ounce of sense, he'd turn around right this minute, take her back home, give her the name of a couple of other private investigators she could contact, and wash his hands of her.

But even as he had the thought Mac knew he wasn't going to do it, so he gave up thinking for the moment and concentrated on keeping the Mercedes in sight as they left the expressway and made their way through Charleston's crowded warren of streets.

"He's going to the same place. I knew it." Julie leaned forward again.

"If he's meeting someone, they probably have a regular place to be together." Mac glanced at her and sighed. "Look, why don't you let me take you home? I'll follow him—*alone*—the next time he goes out. One thing I don't need—and you don't need either, if you just had the sense to know it—is you creating some huge scene when we catch up to Sid and his cutie."

Julie looked at him then, and he was surprised at the sudden glint in her eyes.

"I'm not going to make a scene," she said. "I just have to know. Sid and I have been married eight years. That means something to me. I don't even think I love him anymore, but the fact that we are married *means* something to me. I just can't walk out without seeing with my own two eyes that he's cheating. Can you understand that?"

Meeting her gaze, Mac found a new reason to want to stick it to Sid. A man who could cheat on a wife like his didn't deserve to keep her—but then, that was Sid. He always had been sure he could have his cake and eat it, too.

"What I understand is that I'm nuts for not turning around right now and driving you home," he said shortly, and she made a face at him.

He turned a corner to find himself on the street where he had met Julie the night before. The Pink Pussycat was three blocks down on the left. Would Clinton Edwards be there again, blissfully ignorant that he had been busted by his wife? Probably. It had been his experience that people stayed true to their patterns. There were approximately four dozen bars, strip joints, massage parlors, and porn shops crowded into a six-block square. When he had been a cop, this area had been known as no-man's-land. Robberies, rapes, shootings, assaults, and various other crimes happened down here in multiple numbers every single weekend night when the weather was good. And in Charleston the weather was almost always good.

"I can't see him." Julie had one leg beneath her now, peering through the windshield at the press of cars. The street was congested with traffic; the sidewalks were thick with pedestrians looking for a walk on the wild side as part of their vacation.

"I can." No need to add that, if he lost sight of the Mercedes, he could always follow its progress on the handy-dandy little device stored at the moment in the console between the seats. That, plus the tiny transmitter he'd had the forethought to slip under the Mercedes' bumper not long after he'd dropped Julie off at her store earlier, made this particular part of tonight's surveillance not a problem.

"What's he doing?" Julie's voice was urgent.

"Parking. Sit tight. I would pull in right behind him, but no point in letting him spot us first thing."

That bit of sarcasm earned him a withering look. Mac finally allowed himself to smile as he drove on past the lot where the Mercedes had turned in.

Truth was, he'd made up his mind: as far as keeping Sid under surveillance was concerned, tonight he was going to have to write off as a dead loss. The situation, if it played out the way it very well could, had the potential to get explosive, and nobody needed that, least of all his wrongheaded client. The thing to do was to take Julie on a nice tour of some of the area's establishments—not the hole-in-the-wall dives where perversions of almost unimaginable varieties gave the term "performance art" a whole new meaning, but the more mainstream bars—proclaim Sid lost, and return her home again safe and sound with the clear understanding that he would do the job on his own another day.

Or else.

An alley up the street led to an out-of-the-way parking lot that was used mainly by clients of the rent-a-room-by-the-hour hookers that worked over the adult bookstore on the building's main floor. The lot was dark, its patrons were as bent on secrecy as he was, and the chances of encountering Sid in it were, he calculated, near zero.

"He'll be long gone by the time we get back to where he parked," Julie said, throwing him an impatient look that said *some private eye you are.* Mac didn't grin, but didn't miss it by much. Now that the evening's agenda had changed, he was starting to enjoy himself.

"I have an idea where he's headed." Actually, he didn't—this whole area seemed out of character for Sid— but he did have a good idea of where Sid *wasn't* headed, and under the circumstances that worked just as well.

"You do?" She sounded impressed, he noted as he parked the car.

"Ma'am, that's what us PIs do." His voice was suitably modest.

Clearly she was in no mood to appreciate subtle humor. She was already reaching for the door handle as he turned off the ignition. He grabbed her arm—and in the process registered that it was slender, firm, with warm silky skin— before she could bolt off in pursuit of Sid. "Whoa. Slow down a minute."

"What?" She glanced around at him. Impatience came through loud and clear.

"We're going to have to make some adjustments here. Unless your husband's a blind man." There was always the possibility, however remote, that they might encounter Sid in the street.

"What kind of adjustments?"

Mac let go of her arm and reached into the back. He groped around the footwell behind her seat, and came up with the prize he sought: his Debbie wig, right where it had landed the night before. He handed it to her.

"What . . . ?" She looked down at the hunk of hair in her hand as if she thought it might bite her.

"Don't you want to find out for yourself if blondes really do have more fun?" He grinned. She didn't.

Her eyes met his. "You're kidding, right?"

"Nope. Put it on."

Julie looked revolted, but after one more glance at the wig she flipped down the visor and did as she was told, twisting her own hair around her head and smoothing the long platinum strands down over it.

"I look like Jennifer Lopez disguised as Britney Spears." She sounded appalled.

"Just as long as you don't look like Julie Carlson, we're in business." He flipped her visor closed, and leaned across her to open her door. "Let's go."

The temperature had cooled off considerably from the steam-room conditions that had existed that afternoon, but it was still hot and humid, he noted as he got out of the car. Street noises, indistinguishable voices, and throbbing strains of music provided a background for the closer sounds of Julie shutting her door and walking around the Blazer toward him. Actually, he thought, appraising her almost unwillingly as she rounded his front bumper, she looked pretty good as a blonde. Then he permitted himself a wry inner smile. Might as well face the truth: With that killer bod and those yard-long legs, she could dye her hair neon green and still knock men dead at forty paces.

"Yo, man, it cost you twenty dollah to park here." A hulking kid in a wifebeater and homeboy jeans appeared out of the shadows, walking forward with his hand out and an insolent swagger that told Mac he'd gotten lucky with this scam before.

"You collecting for Fitch now?" He turned to face the kid, keeping his posture relaxed—he wasn't expecting trouble, but you never knew—and Julie came up on his left side. Her hand curled around his arm just above the elbow as she stepped close, facing the kid too, pressing against his side as if for protection, and her perfume wafted up to his nostrils. The whole I-didn't-inhale thing was crapola in this case, there was no way he could resist it, and the scent of her plus the gentle slide of her fingers against his skin sent his libido into overdrive. He gritted his teeth in sheer self-defense.

"You know Fitch?" Luckily—with Julie disordering his senses, he wasn't in any shape for the situation to get aggressive—this gave the kid pause.

"Yeah."

"Oh. Sorry, man." Easy as that, the kid melted back into the shadows. Beside him, he heard Julie let out a sigh of relief. Her hand slid down his arm and over his wrist, trailing fire every millimeter of the way, to nestle into his. His fingers closed around hers automatically. Still holding her hand, because he found that he was absolutely incapable of not holding it once presented with the temptation, he started walking down the alley toward the main drag with her tap-tapping on those sexy little heels right beside him.

"The punks who stole my car looked just like that." She was sticking close. He could feel her arm brushing his, generating a heat that radiated throughout his body.

"They all look just like that."

He was feeling tense, and it had absolutely nothing to do with the thought that the kid or others even worse might be lurking in the shadows waiting to pounce.

"Is Fitch the owner of the parking lot? And do you really know him?"

"Yes. To both." His replies were terse. He realized that, but bending his mind around more eloquent conversation was beyond him at the moment. The mind-over-body thing he prided himself on was taking a couple of minutes to work.

"You know some interesting people."

They reached the street before he had to reply. Stepping onto the sidewalk, they were immediately caught up in a river of people sweeping along porn central. Having Julie go up on tiptoe and crane her neck both ways brought them a great deal of unwelcome attention as the current was forced to part around them.

"I don't see Sid anywhere." She was keeping her balance by resting the hand that wasn't clutching his flat in the center of his chest. He could almost feel the outline of her fingers like a brand through his shirt.

"I know where to look." The reminder that she was not free was timely. This was not some hot little honey that he would be getting better acquainted with between the sheets later. This was Julie Carlson, his client, Sid's wife.

Too bad the part of him that most needed to know that didn't seem to have much of a brain.

"Come on." He removed her hand from his chest and started walking. Her fingers were entwined with his now, and, short of wresting his hand free, which with the best will in the world he couldn't seem to discover within himself an inclination to do, he appeared to be stuck with that. Not even bothering to look for Sid—if they ran across him it would be pure bad luck—he headed toward Sweetwater's, one of the more mainstream of the girlie bars on the strip.

Everybody and his daddy ended up at Sweetwater's sooner or later. If Sid was meeting a lady on the sly, Sweetwater's was the one place he wouldn't go. It was both too raunchy and too public for a lying, cheating, fornicating pseudo family man and pillar of the community like Sid.

"You really think he's here?" Julie asked after Mac had paid their cover and they were ushered inside. The question, which should have been hushed, had to be almost shouted to be heard over the pounding music.

"Maybe."

The warehouse-sized front room was aglow with a disorienting purple light. The reflecting walls were the silver of aluminum foil. Pairs of women, naked except for swirls of glitter paint decorating their already decorative bodies, danced back to back in Plexiglas cages about seven feet above the floor. Couples—basically fully dressed men and half-naked women, except for the few female tourists who were as easy to spot as skunks on snow—shook their booties with enthusiasm. The hostess, a fine-looking redhead in a silver thong and glow-in-the-dark pasties, met them at the door and led them toward a purple leather banquette that stretched most of the length of one wall. Small rectangular tables stood in front of the banquette at approximately four-foot intervals, leaving just enough room for a couple behind each table. There were about half a dozen couples sitting there now like ducks in a row. Mac took a closer look at some of the action going on behind those tables and amended that to, like depraved ducks in a row.

Two lap dances, one spanking, one woman busy beneath the table, and one titty grope were in progress as they approached. The hostess indicated their table—a lap dance to the left, the titty grope to the right—and he stood back to let Julie slide in before him. Her eyes were as big as saucers as she glanced around, and he felt a momentary stab of compunction at exposing such an obvious neophyte to the seamier side of Charleston's nightlife.

He appeased it with the reflection that, given the area, this was one of the more mainstream places he could have taken her.

"What can I get you?" When they were both seated a silver-thonged waitress appeared, smiled at him rather than Julie, and bent deliberately close as she waited for his answer. The resulting view was well worth looking at, but considering his company he refrained. Fortunately, this far from the car-sized speakers it was possible to hear and be heard without being right in the waitress's—uh—face.

"Heineken." He glanced at Julie.

"White wine."

The waitress smirked, gave Julie a pitying glance, and turned on her heel. And yes, she was wearing heels. Spikes. Silver. And they and the minuscule silver strip snaking between her cheeks were it. Whatever other faults Sweetwater's had, he mused as he reflexively eyeballed her retreating form, at least the scenery was good.

"Oh my God, there's Sid!"

What? Mac didn't say it aloud, but his head whipped around in the direction Julie was looking so fast he was surprised his neck didn't snap.

There was Sid all right, dark suit, slicked-back hair, wire-rimmed glasses, the ultimate preppy sleazeball, headed straight toward them with the redheaded hostess all smiles as she said something to him over her shoulder and two women, both lookers in thongs just like the redhead, hanging one on either arm.

It was all Mac could do to keep his jaw from dropping in amazement. Christ, had the prescient SOB somehow gotten the drop on *them?*

"Oh my God," Julie said again, a hand flying to her mouth.

Shit.

But Sid didn't appear to have any idea that anybody who shouldn't be was present—and Mac meant to keep it that way. He reached for Julie—her eyes were now big as *flying* saucers and locked on Sid—and slid both arms around her waist. Time for damage control. Fast.

Clearly startled, she met his gaze.

"Climb up on my lap."

He blocked her view of Sid—and Sid's of the pair of them—with his back as he spoke. Julie's face was just inches away now, so close he could see the creamy texture of her skin, the little veins of gold in her eyes, each separate velvety black eyelash. Her eyes were wide and shocked and her lips were soft and curved, and to make bad worse she felt warm and supple and sexy as hell in his arms. He willed himself to ignore his body's immediate response, to cool out, to respond to this unforeseen emergency like the professional he was.

Then Julie did as he told her and climbed onto his lap, straddling him in a remarkably good imitation of the base position of the undulating lap dancer on her left. Her slim, tanned legs pressed tight on either side of his—and yes, he discovered as he automatically grasped warm, taut-muscled, satin-skinned thighs to settle her into position, her legs were bare.

His self-control did a kamikaze dive as suddenly Sid's presence became the least of his problems. He had to instantly remind himself of just what had happened to those suicidal Japanese pilots and pull up while he still could.

Saved from fiery self-immolation by the narrowest of margins, he took a deep breath and assessed the situation.

She was facing him now, instead of Sid, which was good.

And her sweet little twat in the silky black panties that he'd gotten just a glimpse of as she'd swung astride was nestled against the big, dumb part of him which had already proved conclusively that it lacked a brain.

Which was bad.

12

Hanging on to Mac's shoulders for balance, Julie perched atop his lap and glared at Sid through the reflecting silver wall. Her suspicions were right on, she realized, and felt her stomach clench. She'd known it, of course, all along. Sid was with a woman—two women. Two nearly naked women who were on him like white on paper and seemed to know him pretty damned well.

Although the pounding music made it impossible to be sure, she was almost positive she'd heard one call him *Sid* in a squeaky baby voice that sounded like Marilyn Monroe on helium.

Her cheating husband was no more than ten feet behind her now, and if it hadn't been for Mac's restraining hands on her legs she would have dismounted and walked over to him and punched the no-good dirty rotten lying cheater right in the nose.

Can you spell "history," Sid? she thought, watching him pull one of the Minnie Mouse–voiced silicone queens close to his side and nuzzle her neck. 'Cause that's what you're getting ready to be.

Sid must have sensed something, or maybe felt the force of her gaze, because just then he glanced her way. To her horror, his eyes fixed on her as she sat astride Mac's lap, sliding down her back in an appraising kind of way, then glancing into the mirror-like wall in an attempt to see her face. Julie panicked, then realized that her image, like his, was faintly distorted by the silver panel, and the blond wig was probably enough to throw him off. Still . . .

She dived for cover. Figuratively speaking, of course.

Pulse racing, she ducked without, she hoped, seeming to do so, by the simple method of bending her head and pressing her mouth to Mac's. Desperate situations called for desperate measures, after all. She wasn't ready to confront Sid yet: she wanted to sort this out in her head *and* with a really hardball-playing lawyer before Sid realized she was on to him. Plus, she was still just a little afraid of Sid's reaction if he should discover that she was following him, although what he might actually do, she didn't quite know. Keeping quiet was the result of a gut feeling, not justified by anything except a kind of sixth sense.

But that sixth sense was giving her as shrill and urgent a warning as a smoke alarm in a house on fire.

So she shook her false hair forward to hide her face and kissed Mac, knowing that, as her partner in this emergency, he would understand why she was doing it and play along.

His lips were dry, warm, and firm, and, she discovered, she quite liked kissing them, his sexual orientation notwithstanding. He didn't seem to have any problems with the kiss either. At least, he did not push her away or recoil in disgust. In fact, after one pregnant instant in which their gazes met, he even seemed to get into it. His lids closed and his hands slid up her thighs with a carnality that made her still-open eyes widen.

He took over the kiss, handling it like a pro, slanting his mouth over hers and licking between her lips until, just from instinct, her eyes closed and her lips parted to let his tongue inside. Then his tongue filled her mouth, and he was kissing her so expertly and so thoroughly that it was clear he'd had some experience somewhere. His arms went around her, hard and strong as steel bands, and his hands splayed over her back, so hot they burned her skin even through her dress. He pulled her close against him, flattening her breasts against the solid wall of his chest.

She loved it.

The same sizzle of electricity that had afflicted her when he'd touched her mouth at the bird sanctuary shot through her again times about a trillion, and she went all soft and shivery inside.

The warm, wet invasion of her mouth thrilled her clear down to her toes. Which, she discovered as they curled in ecstatic response, were now bare, her shoes having apparently slid unnoticed from her feet sometime within the last couple of seconds. Totally swept away, she wrapped her arms around Mac's neck and put her tongue in his mouth and kissed him back.

"That'll be ten dollars," the waitress said.

What could have been seconds or lifetimes later, Julie registered the words and their meaning and pulled her mouth from his. The way she felt gave dazed and confused a whole new meaning, she thought as she lifted her lids to stare at him in dazzled surprise. His eyes met hers. Julie saw that his pupils had dilated to the point where his irises looked almost black. A dark flush rode high on his cheekbones, and his lips were still parted from their kiss. He was breathing hard. She could feel the rapid rise and fall of his chest against her breasts.

"Mac," she said, alerting him to the waitress's presence. His mouth tightened, and his eyes as they met hers had a hot, sexy gleam in them that made her catch her breath.

Oh God, he was gorgeous, she thought, her gaze drinking him in.

"Got it." His gaze flicked to the waitress. One hand dropped away from her back to dig in the rear pocket of his jeans for his wallet. The other joined it seconds later as, his arms still around her but loosely now, he opened his wallet and extracted a bill. He handed the bill to the waitress, of whom Julie was now only peripherally aware. All her senses were suddenly too full of Mac again to allow anything else to really register. His crotch was pushing into hers, and there was a hard and urgent mound beneath his jeans. It felt so incredibly good pressing against her that she sucked in her breath and pressed back.

"Keep the change." Mac was speaking to the waitress, but his voice was thick and his eyes were on Julie again. The waitress said something—probably *thanks,* although Julie couldn't be sure—and disappeared. Mac shoved the wallet back into his pocket, shifting beneath her in the process. Julie felt the nudge of that jeans-covered bulge against the most sensitive part of her and suddenly knew what it meant to truly crave something.

Forget chocolate: what she wanted with every greedy nerve ending was sex. With Mac.

Her throat went dry, her loins tightened and began to radiate heat. She shivered, conscious of an almost overwhelming urge to rip off her panties and have her way with him there and then.

Then it hit her like a baseball bat over the head that this was Debbie—*Debbie*—and he had a giant—really, truly, enormous—hard-on. For her.

She blinked in befuddled, passion-clouded surprise. What was the deal with that?

"Do you—do you go both ways?" Her voice was soft and faintly unsteady. Puzzled, she frowned into his eyes, but even as she tried to make sense of the whole thing she snuggled closer against him, her arms tightening around his neck, loving the hot prickly feel of her nipples as they pressed against the solid warmth of his chest, loving the silky slide of her panties over the hardness in his jeans, particularly loving the throbbing deep inside her panties, too turned on at the moment to do more than wonder vaguely about the fine points of his sexual wiring.

He stared at her, seemingly uncomprehending, for the space of a couple of heartbeats. Then she saw a flicker in his eyes as comprehension dawned, and he grimaced.

"No," he said, and slid a hand around her nape beneath the heavy flow of artificial hair, pulling her mouth back down to his. Then he kissed her again.

Oh, God, if she had ever been so hot for someone in her life she didn't remember it. His kiss was hard and hungry and yet gentle at the same time, and she was completely bowled over by the warm wet urgency of it. He explored her mouth with an expertise that made her dizzy while she kissed him back and pressed her breasts against his chest and moved sensuously against the tangible evidence that he was experiencing at least this one heterosexual urge. His hands were under her dress now, both of them, cupping her bottom, squeezing her cheeks through the silky panties, and she melted inside like microwaved plastic.

Oh, God, a little more of this and she was going to come. . . .

Somebody lurched into their table. There was a tinkling crash, and Julie felt a cool rain of liquid on her bare instep even as she dragged her mouth from Mac's and glanced around.

"Sorry." The man who'd been enjoying the lap dancer was on his feet trying to get out between the tables.

Obviously drunk, his attention focused on the near-naked woman who was pulling him by the hand, he'd stumbled into their table, causing her wineglass to topple onto its side, break, and disgorge its contents. Wine trickled over the edge of the table onto her foot. With no more than an impatient look at the cause of the distraction, Julie shifted positions to escape the stream and turned back to Mac.

What they were doing felt too good to interrupt for a spilled glass of wine.

"No problem," Mac said to the man, looking past her.

"Can I get you some more wine?" The waitress appeared with a handful of napkins and started mopping. Julie, impatient, leaned forward to nibble Mac's ear, just to keep him from losing focus until they could get back to business. The lobe was soft and tender and tasted faintly salty. But she was starting to sense some resistance from Mac.

"No thanks," Mac said to the waitress, sounding as if he was talking through clenched teeth. He was still turned on, she could tell—among other obvious signs, his instant stiffening when she twirled her tongue in his ear was a dead giveaway—but distraction was taking its toll. Then, not particularly to Julie's surprise, his hands closed over her hipbones and he lifted her bodily off him.

"Mac!" She wanted to weep.

Despite her plaintive protest and clinging hands he managed to slide out from under her, slippery as a fish wriggling off the hook, and as her bottom hit leather his hands were busy tugging her arms from around his neck. The waitress, finished with her mopping, loaded the broken glass onto her tray and moved away. Defeated, Julie slumped down onto the banquette, Mac's hands gripping her wrists.

"Sid's gone into the back room. We need to get out of here while we can."

Sid. Glancing around, Julie realized that Mac was right: Sid was nowhere in sight. She also realized that, in the heat of the last few steamy minutes, she had completely forgotten about her cheating spouse. Unbelievable—but the cause was leaning toward her, looking a million times better than chocolate ever had as he held her wrists in an unbreakable grip, and the situation was extreme when even the size and warmth of his hands keeping her away from him struck her as sexy.

Meeting his gaze, she realized that while his eyes still held a trace of that superheated gleam, his lips were set in an obstinate line and his jaw was hard. Clearly, Romeo had left the building. Meanwhile, she felt as if she'd been poleaxed. The intensity of the voltage that had leaped between her and Mac had robbed her of any outside awareness as thoroughly as if she'd been unwary enough to press her lips to a stun gun.

"Come on, move it."

Apparently not subject to extended postmortem ruminations of his own, Mac slid out from behind the table, picked up his beer and took a quick swig, then pulled her out after him, one hand wrapped around her wrist as if he was afraid she'd try to escape. Still feeling vaguely dazed, Julie fell in with the program. At the same time she tried to figure out what, exactly, had just happened. Her mind reeled as she considered. She'd caught Sid with his hand in the cookie jar, and kissed and been kissed by Mac cum Debbie, all within the space of maybe ten minutes. The unsettling thing was, the events seemed to be assuming almost equal importance in her mind. When she stumbled, glanced down to see what had tripped her up, and discovered that the offending object was one of her own tan leather slides, she wasn't even surprised to find that she had been on the verge of leaving in her bare feet without even realizing it.

Now that was dazed and confused.

"What's the holdup?"

As she stopped, Mac looked around at her with a frown.

"My shoes."

She tried to right her shoe with her toes so that she could slide her foot inside, but she couldn't do it because, she thought, all her blood was still busy rushing somewhere more interesting than her brain. Watching, Mac made an impatient sound and swooped on the shoes, scooping them both up in his free hand. Hanging on to them, he headed purposefully toward the door, towing her barefoot behind him.

Stepping out of the chilly purple gloom of Sweetwater's into the dark, crowded bustle of the street was disorienting. The heat enfolded her, welcome as a blanket on a winter's night, and Julie realized that the nightclub had been downright cold. She simply hadn't noticed after the first few minutes because she had been wrapped in Mac's arms.

Which in spite of the overenthusiastic air-conditioning had made her hot enough to want to get naked. Right there. Right then.

With Mac.

The realization was mind-boggling.

"Here."

Mac stopped just past the line waiting to get in, handing her her shoes. She leaned against the smooth painted brick of Sweetwater's outer wall to slip them on while what seemed to be the entire population of several states went by around them and he created a jostle-free zone for her with his body. As she stood on first one foot and then the other, he watched without saying a word. When she straightened, shoes in place, his gaze met hers.

The sizzle in his eyes was as tangible as the heat in the bricks she leaned against.

Hmm. Something here was not right.

Mac broke off eye contact then and started walking, hauling her after him, plowing through the throng on the sidewalk like a wide receiver with the football tucked under his arm and the goalposts in sight. Julie followed in the wake he created, entertaining a variety of thoughts in quick succession as, with dispassionate assessment, she eyed his retreating back.

He had nice shoulders, broad and muscular in a navy tee that equally showed off equally nice arms. He had a nice butt, small and tight and sexy in well-worn jeans. He was tall, athletically built, handsome.

Any woman would salivate.

So it wasn't surprising that she wanted him. In fact, it would have been surprising if she didn't. She was a normal, red-blooded American female, after all, and he was a hunky guy. To say nothing of the fact that she was in a marriage so dead rigor mortis was about to set in and, to clench matters, was extremely sexually deprived.

But he wanted her, too. She wasn't mistaken about that, and that was where the question lay. Her thoughts curled around boat-sized high heels and blond wigs and mountainous boobs and pink leashes and Josephine. And she tried to recall just what he'd said when she'd asked him point-blank if he was gay.

She couldn't remember exactly. But the short answer, as recorded by her brain, had been *yes*.

Just a little while ago, when she'd asked him if he went both ways, he'd said no. And punctuated that by kissing her until her brain was practically fried.

So where did that leave her? Julie wasn't sure, but "frustrated" came to mind.

"Hold on just one minute," she said, digging in her heels.

They were in the alley now, headed toward the lot where the Blazer was parked. It was dark and shadowy and smelled of booze and garbage and should have been scary as all get-out, but Julie scarcely noticed. Her attention was all for the man pulling her along after him as if she'd been a recalcitrant Josephine.

No, probably he would have shown more consideration for the poodle.

When she balked, he stopped, turning to face her.

"What now?"

The various lights from the establishments they'd left behind created a reddish glow at the mouth of the alley that allowed her to see his expression. He looked almost—wary.

"What did you mean, no?" She narrowed her eyes at him. In the shadows along one wall, something stirred. Seeing the movement out of the corner of her eye, she jumped about a foot in the air and skittered toward Mac. He released her wrist to wrap an arm around her waist and pull her against his side, his gaze focused on the threat. They both watched as, not ten feet away, a man got to his feet and, with no more than a single glance at them, staggered toward the street.

The smell of booze was suddenly overpowering. Julie realized that they had disturbed a sleeping drunk.

"You want to have a conversation, wait till we get to the car."

With that curt response Mac was off again, pulling her behind him, not pausing until they reached the Blazer.

With more haste than courtesy he bundled her inside, slammed the door behind her, and got in himself.

Then, without a word, without so much as a glance at her, he started the car. He was reaching for the button that controlled the lights when she turned off the ignition.

"What the . . ." As he glanced at her in surprise, she curled one leg beneath her, leaned across the console, and pressed her lips to his mouth.

13

His RESPONSE WAS INSTANTANEOUS and unmistakable. His lips molded themselves to hers and the blaze of heat that flared between them told Julie everything she needed to know. He tasted faintly of beer. His kiss was hungry, insistent, arousing. An instant memory of his hands, hot as they slid up under her dress, making her hot as they cupped and caressed her bottom, threatened to make her forget her purpose. She wanted him—*God, she wanted him.*

And he wanted her, too. No doubt at all remained about that.

Shaken but satisfied at the result of her impromptu research, Julie lifted her mouth from his before she could completely lose her head, breaking off the kiss even as he pulled her across the console and into his lap.

"You're not gay." If her voice was faintly breathless—all right, a lot breathless—it was also accusing. His hands still gripped her waist; hers rested on his shoulders. She was half lying, half sitting, with her back cradled by his arm and her breasts just brushing his chest. He curved over her, his wide shoulders blocking out her view of the rest of the front seat. Their faces were just inches apart. She could feel the warmth of his breath feathering across her lips. Unfortunately, it was too dark to read his expression. But she imagined it—he was no doubt looking guilty as hell.

"You—are—not—gay." She said it again, with emphasis, as if to drive the point home to herself as well as him.

That seemed to make an impression. He took a deep breath and straightened, pulling her up with him and then lifting her back over the console into her own seat. Once there, she gave a tug to her skirt to make sure she was decent, folded her arms over her chest, and glared at him.

"I never said I was." His voice was cool as a glass of lemonade.

To her annoyance, as he spoke, he restarted the car as though nothing at all out of the ordinary had happened. The lights came on, bouncing off the wall in front of them to reflect on his face. He did *not* look guilty, she noticed with increasing ire. He looked—he looked as calm if they were discussing the vagaries of the weather.

"You did too." Once again she searched her mind for his exact words. "When I asked you before you said . . . you said . . ."

"I asked you if it mattered." He pulled out of the parking lot and turned down the alley. The beams illuminated graffiti-adorned brick walls, a Dumpster with a partially open lid, piles of litter. He glanced her way. "If I remember correctly, you said it didn't."

Julie narrowed her eyes at him."Well, *now,*" she said with more than a hint of bite, "it does."

"So I'm not gay." He slid her another of those so-calm-she-wanted-to-kill-him looks before edging out into the still heavy traffic. "Put on your seat belt."

Julie's lips compressed. Mentally counting to ten, she put on her seat belt. Her temper was heading toward slow boil, but she decided to suspend judgment until she was sure she had the full picture. Maybe there was something she was missing here.

"Are you a cross-dresser?"

He gave a grunt that might have been laughter. "Only when I have to be. As far as I'm concerned, panty hose could have been invented by the Spanish Inquisition. How women wear those things is beyond me. And bras are a bitch, too. But the shoes were killer. I was really starting to get into the shoes. Yours especially." He switched into his Debbie voice. "Girlfriend, I gotta tell you, those little heels you're wearing are the bomb."

He leered at her slides.

Julie glowered at him. "You'll notice I'm not laughing." In fact, she was starting to feel like a fool for ever believing he was gay in the first place. There had been so many signs—how could she have been so blind? "Let me make sure I understand this time: You're straight, right?"

"Yeah, pretty much."

"Pretty much?"

"Well, actually, about a hundred percent."

"You *lied* to me." There was a definite sizzle in her tone.

He threw a quick glance her way. "I didn't lie. You made assumptions, and I just didn't correct them."

"Oh, that makes it all better."

"Look, if you'd known from the beginning I was straight, would you have let me help you?"

Julie sneered. "Are you actually attempting to claim that you lied to me for my own good?"

"That's pretty much it in a nutshell." He sounded almost pleased at being presented with such a tidy summing-up.

"Yeah, right." Julie took a deep, calming breath. "So, you want to explain the whole Debbie thing to me?"

"I was working. Undercover, you might say. The guy I was tailing—you met him in the parking lot last night—is into drag queens. Ergo, Debbie." He shrugged, looking unrepentant, and his eyes twinkled at her infuriatingly. "Hey, babe, a PI's got to do what a PI's got to do."

"Maybe I should point out here that I am *so* not finding this amusing."

There was a pause as they reached the expressway and he pulled on and accelerated, quickly leaving the worst of the traffic behind. Julie used it to take a firm, two-handed grip on her temper before she could lose it completely.

"What about Josephine? Is she even yours? Or were you just using her as a prop?" Her voice was sharp with growing outrage.

"Until three weeks ago, Josephine belonged to my grandmother. Then Grandma moved into a retirement home and I inherited her dog, complete with collar, leash, and a weekly appointment with the groomer."

Julie looked at him suspiciously. Imagining him with a grandmother—a grandmother he cared enough about to adopt her tiny fluffball of a poodle—was a stretch. A big stretch.

"Is that the truth?"

"Yes." A smile touched his mouth as he glanced at her. "Cross my heart."

Julie snorted. "That certainly clenches it for me."

"I don't know why you're mad. You liked Debbie."

"Not to make out with!" As soon as she said it, she could have kicked herself. The dignified thing to have done would have been to ignore those breath-stealing kisses completely. Too late now.

"Ah. Good point."

He gave her a look that made her hot all over again—

until she remembered that he had deliberately deceived her. Debbie, indeed.

Talk about your wolf in sheep's clothing—what she had here was a hound in poodle-wear.

She glared at him.

He continued in a semi-apologetic tone, "At the time, making out with you didn't seem to be an option."

"It's not an option now, either." Her voice was tart. She felt like a fool, and she didn't like the feeling—or, for that matter, at the moment at least, its cause. "What happened back there was strictly a one-time thing that was entirely dictated by unfortunate circumstances. So don't start thinking you're about to get lucky, because you're not."

"I swear, if you hadn't just now put the idea in my head, such a thought never would have crossed my mind." He shook his head virtuously. When Julie responded with a *yeah, right* look, he grinned. Julie realized that she was being teased. "But in the interests of full disclosure, I think I ought to mention that we have a strict company policy against 'getting lucky' with clients. Of course, being that I'm the boss, I guess I could make an exception if you asked me real nice."

"Not a chance." She gave him a smile that was scarcely more than a baring of her teeth. "I'll give you credit, though: pretending to be Debbie as a come-on technique is original, if nothing else. Although actually, from a woman's point of view, I have to tell you that being lied to about something like that pretty much sucks."

"Just for the record, I think I should point out here that you're the one who came on to me. You kissed me first back there, not the other way around, remember? And if I'd been trying to get you into bed, you'd have known it a whole hell of a lot sooner." A beat went by. "Besides, I never actually lied."

"Okay, that's it. You lied and you know it. And if you want my opinion, deceiving me like that was a pretty rotten thing to do."

"Darlin', you're losing sight of the big picture here. Who I choose to sleep with doesn't matter. What matters is that here in the down-and-dirty divorce wars I'm on your side."

"What matters is that you lied."

A swaying eighteen-wheeler whizzing around them so fast it made the car shake distracted their attention before the conversation could deteriorate further. Then they were at the Summerville exit and the Blazer was easing off the expressway into the dark, deserted hush of the town.

A glance at the dashboard clock told Julie that it was 1:43, and sent her thoughts careening back to her larger problem: Sid. Tonight she had plenty of time: a good hour and a half before her cheating husband snuck back in the house. Should she pack and leave before he even got home? Or wait with folded arms like a wife in a comic strip until he got in and let him have it with both barrels? Or should she bite her tongue, bide her time, and see a lawyer before she walked out? The idea of even having to set eyes on Sid again, much less spend a few more nights under the same roof with him, made her sick to her stomach and almost made the decision for her. But she'd been cool so far and, she thought, had made all the right moves. She didn't want to lose what advantage knowledge gave her now.

Sid would be ruthless about finances, ruthless about everything. She'd seen him in operation on the golf course, the tennis court, and in business deals when things got sticky: always, he played to win.

He would play to win in their divorce, too.

Glancing at the man beside her, she pushed thoughts of Sid and their divorce to the back burner. All she could deal with was one problem at a time, and her personal private investigator was another one. Mac had deliberately deceived her over the Debbie thing, but he'd also been a strong shoulder for her to lean on when she'd needed one. He had made her laugh and made her hot at a time when she hadn't thought either was possible, and for that she was grateful. The idea that she wouldn't be seeing him again cost her a pang, much as she hated to admit it even to herself. Still, his job was done. Thanks to him, tonight she had seen what Sid was up to with her very own eyes. As for anything else—such as a quick hop in the sack, maybe, just because she wanted to more than she had wanted anything in forever—well, the cold hard truth was that she needed another man in her life right now like she needed a bad case of poison ivy.

Especially another *lying* man.

"Okay, you're right, I guess it doesn't really matter that you lied." Her voice had lost its angry edge; instead it was faintly frosty. "You did what you were hired to do, and I recognize that. Seeing as how this whole thing got resolved so quickly, I'll understand if you want to impose some kind of minimum charge for your time." Their gazes met as he glanced at her with a gathering frown. "Add the cost of fixing your car, of course. If you'll let me know how much it all is, I'll see that you get your money right away."

"Whoa, wait a minute. Not so fast, Miss America."

The tone of that made her frown at him. "What?"

"I don't think this whole thing *is* resolved. A rich, prominent man like Sid doesn't cheat on his wife by going someplace like Sweetwater's and hooking up with the girls there. He was way, way too visible, almost like he wanted to be seen. A man cheating on his wife hides out in a hotel or an out-of-the-way apartment or meets his honey on a business trip. Trust me, I know. I investigate this kind of thing for a living."

Julie's frown deepened. "So what are you saying?"

"I'm saying something doesn't make sense. I don't know what Sid was doing in Sweetwater's, but I don't think he was hooking up with his honey."

A sudden memory made Julie's eyes widen.

"He didn't take any Viagra tonight. There were still six pills mixed in with his vitamins. I counted when we got home from the club, and he never came upstairs again."

A half-smile quirked up one corner of Mac's mouth. "Well, there you go. Proof positive."

"Do you think it's possible that Sid's *not* cheating?" Funny, the idea didn't bring any upsurge of happiness with it. Probably because she knew, deep down inside, that it just wasn't true. But also, she thought, because the marriage was over where it counted, in her heart. It had taken a combination of Sid's behavior tonight and her sizzling reaction to Mac's kiss to make her realize that. Her attraction to Mac might be a phase—in fact, it probably was, a rebound kind of thing as she came to terms with the end of her marriage—but still she wanted more in a personal sense than Sid could give her, had ever given her. She *deserved* more.

It was Julie time.

"Possible? Anything's possible. But I don't think so. If he's taking Viagra and you're not getting any, I'd say it's a pretty sure bet he's cheating. But you haven't caught him at it yet. He had another reason for going to Sweetwater's tonight. I just haven't figured out what it is." He sounded thoughtful.

Outside the Blazer, the whole world seemed to be asleep. They were driving along familiar residential streets now; the houses were dark and the streets themselves were deserted. Julie was still digesting his words when he glanced at her again.

Why don't you let me keep looking into this for a few more days?"

If I did, I could keep seeing you for a few more days. The thought caught Julie unaware. Its implications annoyed her. He was a phase, she told herself. *A phase.* She watched *Oprah;* she knew. The death of a marriage, like any other death, brought on various psychological states as the individual tried to cope. Mindless promiscuity probably came right after discovering your husband was cheating for everybody. *She* was not going to fall into that trap. She was going to keep herself on an even keel, or die in the attempt.

She shook her head. "I don't think so. That would require being civil to Sid and acting as if everything between us is hunky-dory for a few more days, and I just don't think I can do that. Besides, you lied to me."

They had reached her street now. A glance told Julie that it was as dark and quiet as the rest of the town.

"You want me to apologize for Debbie? All right, I apologize. Next time I run across a beautiful damsel in distress while I'm dressed like one myself, I'll jump her bones immediately just so there's no mistake."

Julie glared at him. Then the sheer absurdity of the image he'd painted made her smile, albeit reluctantly. If he had come on to her while dressed as Debbie, she would have run screaming for miles.

Seeing her smile, he smiled too. "That's better." His smile turned coaxing. "Don't you want to know who the lucky recipient of all that Viagra is?"

Julie hadn't thought of that. Oh, God, did she want to

know? The possibilities were endless, now that she considered them. Was it one of the women who worked for him? Heidi, his administrative assistant, came immediately to mind. She was young, pretty, and appeared to think Sid hung the moon. Or maybe it was one of their friends. In that category there were endless possibilities. Or a neighbor. Or—or anyone. It could be anyone at all. Just thinking about it made her feel sick, but Julie realized to her own surprise that she needed to know. If she didn't, she would wonder forever. The idea that a woman she *knew,* maybe even one she considered a friend, was having an affair with her husband behind her back was almost like a kind of mental poison. Unless she learned the truth, she would never be able to look at any of them in quite the same way again. She would always wonder, Was it you?

"How long do you think it would take?" Her smile had vanished, and her mouth was suddenly dry. She swallowed to try to wet it again.

"Probably no more than a week."

Oh, God, could she bear living with this burden—and Sid—for a week more? She'd been so in love with Sid once. Now she just wanted to walk away and never have to see him again—but of course nothing in life was ever that easy.

Nothing in her life, anyway.

"I could use that time to find a lawyer." She chewed on her lower lip. It was important that she think about Becky and her mother, as well as her own financial security. Knowing Sid, he would do his best to see that they all ended up back in the double-wide if he could. He would love that.

"Good idea." Mac pulled up in front of her house, doused the lights and engine, then looked at her. "You realize that once Sid finds out you're filing for divorce, he's going to play to win. You need to make sure your lawyer is someone you can trust."

Julie gave a ghost of a laugh as the near impossibility of that occurred to her. "All the lawyers I know are Sid's friends."

Mac grimaced. "That's a problem. Want me to check around, see if I can find somebody who's up to taking on Sid?"

"Would you?"

"With pleasure."

Julie felt the last of her hostility over the discovery that Debbie was a fraud waft away. Mac was still a shoulder to lean on, and she was glad, really, really, glad, that he wasn't walking out of her life just yet. Still, if he was going to be staying on for a while, she wasn't going to let him off the hook so easily.

She shot him a severe look which he didn't see. He was staring out through the windshield, apparently lost in thought.

"You did your best to deliberately deceive me. Admit it."

The look he shot her was almost startled. "I did?"

"About Debbie."

"Oh." A beat went by. "Maybe I was a little bit deceptive."

"Admit it. You lied."

"Fine. You want to hear me say it? I lied."

"That's better. Don't do it again."

He grinned at her. "But I wasn't kidding about the shoes. I've got a real thing for your shoes."

Julie shot him a withering look. Then she realized that at some point after he'd parked the car, he'd picked up her hand. Or maybe she'd picked up his. Since she couldn't remember them coming together, she couldn't be sure.

But they were joined now, her smooth slender fingers laced with his long capable ones. She felt the strength of his hand clasping hers, felt the heat radiating from his palm to hers, and her pulse rate shot to double time. Which might feel nice, but probably wasn't a good thing. Her life was chock-full of man trouble already; more she definitely did not need.

She glanced up at him.

"I'm not going to sleep with you, you know," she said. Best to lay it on the line—for herself as well as for him—even if she did feel a little prickle of regret at turning her back on what she was pretty sure would be really phenomenal sex. By saying it aloud, she fixed the ban firmly in her own mind; also, he was put on notice that there was no quid pro quo beyond a reasonable sum of money for his efforts on her behalf.

His lips compressed. His hand tightened on hers. Their gazes met. His thoughts were impossible to read in the darkness, but the hard grip of his fingers said a lot.

"It's usually considered good manners to wait till you're asked."

"I just want to make sure we have everything clear."

"Clear as crystal."

He released her hand, but she could feel the lingering warmth of his grip even as she pulled her hand back to the neutral territory of her lap.

"Okay. Good. I'm going in now."

She opened the door. The interior light came on. A glance over her shoulder told her that he was watching her get out. His eyes were narrowed and his mouth was a thin firm line. His expression was hard to decipher, but it certainly couldn't have been described as warm and friendly. Or anything close.

"I'll be in touch. You've got my number if you need me," he said as he met her gaze.

His voice was definitely businesslike. Her warning had set the right, necessary tone.

To her own annoyance, Julie found herself regretting that she had ever opened her mouth on the subject as she headed inside.

14

SOMETHING WAS WRONG. Julie Carlson was off schedule. She was supposed to be at home, in bed, asleep. For the second night in a row, she was not. Where the hell was she? If he didn't get the job done tonight, there was going to be hell to pay.

The phone call from the Big Boss had made that clear.

"You get it done tonight, you understand? *No more screwups.* Do I make myself clear?"

So clear Basta broke out in a sweat just remembering the conversation. Now he was here to get the job done.

Basta had already prowled around inside her house, looking for some kind of clue as to what was going on. There were no phone messages, he'd discovered as he disabled the phone. No notes on the refrigerator to let her hubby know where she had gone. The car the insurance company had provided her with was still in the garage; the only vehicle missing was the husband's Mercedes. That meant that either she was out walking around the streets—so unlikely at this hour that he didn't even bother to go looking—or somebody had picked her up.

Maybe all of a sudden she had something going on the side. Basta frowned as he pondered that. The thought did not bother him particularly. Except for its effect on his plans, he did not care if she slept with the entire male population of nearby Fort Jackson. But he was a businessman, and time was money. He was running out of time.

And the Big Boss was running out of patience. In his line of work, it was never a good idea to tee off the boss.

If he missed her again tonight—and it looked like he might well be going to—there was going to be a problem.

He'd looked in the closets, under the beds, even in the damned refrigerator, on the off chance that she had somehow heard him come in and decided to hide. Nothing. Of course there was nothing.

She would never have heard him. She was not in the house.

He could almost smell the balmy breezes of Key West. That's where he should be right now, sitting out on a starlit hotel balcony, a rum and Coke in his hand, enjoying his reward for a job well done.

Not kicked back in a leather armchair in his intended victim's cave-dark den, playing Donkey Kong with the sound turned off on a Game Boy he'd found while searching the spare bedrooms, waiting with growing frustration for said victim to get home where she belonged.

This time, if she so much as stuck a toe in the door while he was still there, he was taking care of business regardless. It was getting to him, this waiting. Especially this waiting under the fulminating eye of the boss.

As it happened, he was so busy hammering the stupid little alligator things that were part of the game that he didn't even hear her come in.

A burst of light as the enormous chandelier in the front hall was flipped on nearly gave him a heart attack. For a split second, from pure astonishment, he sat as if turned to stone, his thumbs frozen on the game controls, his gaze snapping to the open doorway, trapped in a flood of illumination. Then instinct kicked in and he dove over the side of the chair, placing its bulk between himself and the door, sheltering behind it as he peered cautiously over the arm like a kid playing hide-and-seek.

Luckily he managed to hang on to the Game Boy. If he had dropped it, the sound might have been enough to alert his prey.

Because it was her. Even as his heart resumed its normal steady beat, he was reaching out into the hall with every sense he possessed.

Several light footsteps, a sigh, the merest flicker of a shadow across the square of light that was all he could see of the hall—it was enough. Julie Carlson was home. He knew it as well as if he'd gotten a full, 360-degree view of her.

A quick glance at his watch brought a smile to his face. Tonight there would be plenty of time.

The ensuing wave of relief left him feeling buoyant in its wake. As his mother had always told him, all things come to he who waits.

The light went out in the hall as suddenly as it had come on. Basta listened to her footsteps moving lightly up the stairs. When she reached the top, he stopped concentrating on her to carefully unzip his bag and place the Game Boy inside. He couldn't leave it. It had his fingerprints all over it, he'd had to take his gloves off to operate the tiny controls, and besides, he wasn't finished with the game. He waited for a little while, ten minutes or so, to give her enough time to get really settled in and comfy. Then he pulled on his gloves, rolled the ski mask down over his face, and fished his Sig Sauer semi-automatic out of the bottom of the bag. Time for the fun to begin.

* * *

Go back.

Julie listened to the little voice in her head and made a face at herself in her bathroom mirror.

"I'd love to," she answered it aloud. "But sleeping with him is a really dumb idea."

It occurred to her that when people started talking back to the little voices that they heard, that's when they knew they were really in trouble.

So she wasn't going to listen to the little voice anymore, much less talk to it. Even if she really, really wanted to do what it suggested. Her inner self obviously had no idea of how complicated things could get if she gave in to its urging.

That thing with Mac tonight was the closest she had come to having an orgasm in months, Julie thought as she turned her attention back to her own reflection and anxiously examined what looked to be a wrinkle forming between her eyebrows. Actually, years, now that she came to think about it. Sid's lovemaking had been perfunctory for some time before he'd finally given up the ghost altogether. Call her difficult, but she just wasn't able to get off in the five minutes tops it usually took Sid from the first peck on her lips until he rolled over and went to sleep.

Yet one more reason to get rid of Sid: He was lousy in bed. At least, she thought he was. She didn't really have much to compare him with—which brought her thoughts back full circle to Mac.

She would love a chance to compare Sid with Mac.

Julie glared at the tiny line between her brows as ferociously as if it were the source of her wayward thoughts, and scooped Mudd out of a jar, slapping some over the wrinkle before slathering it lavishly over the rest of her just-washed face.

Go back outside.

She was *not* going to let the fact that she was staring divorce in the face get her down, she told herself determinedly. She was not going to start hearing voices. She was not going to have a nervous breakdown. She was not going to sleep with Mac. She was not going to crack a baseball bat over Sid's head. And she was definitely *not* going to gain a hundred pounds or so. Perish the thought.

Get thee behind me, chocolate, she thought, glancing over her shoulder in some regret as the last of the Hershey's Kisses she kept in her lingerie chest for emergencies swirled down the toilet, where just minutes ago she'd gathered the willpower to dump them. Then, in a hasty mental aside just in case some listening spirit took that too seriously, she amended that to *Get thee gone, chocolate.* She certainly didn't want the rejected calories ending up on her already substantial enough behind.

In any case, she was going to get her stress release in a less destructive way from now on.

And *no,* not from a Mac-induced Big O. Although she was really starting to regret not having gone for it while she had the chance, she comforted herself with the knowledge that she had done the right thing.

Aromatherapy might not be as much fun, but it came with a lot fewer drawbacks. The most important of which was, a man wasn't involved. The smell of the chamomile bath salts was soothing, just as the printing on the packet had promised. Julie breathed deeply, filling her lungs with the aroma as steam filled the bathroom. As soon as the bath was ready, she would slide down into the hot water, immerse herself in the calming scent, and press the button that would activate the Jacuzzi.

Bliss. Or at least, as close to bliss as she could get under the circumstances.

Go outside now.

Take that, stress, she thought, pretending the little voice was not there as she inhaled again with grim determination. The steam was sweet smelling but—unsuccessful. So far, anyway. She resolutely refused even to think about checking out her lingerie chest just to make sure that no Hershey's Kisses had been left behind. Instead, she returned her attention to the task at hand. She was not going to lose her looks over this, and not losing her looks involved taking care of her skin. The last of the Mudd she slathered down the middle of her nose like peanut butter on bread.

Rinsing her fingers, she looked at herself in the mirror again. With her hair swept up into a ponytail high on the top of her head and the mask covering every bit of her face now except for white circles around her mouth and eyes, she looked like Pebbles Flintstone doing *The Creature from the Black Lagoon.*

It took a lot of ugly to make a woman beautiful. Good thing all anyone ever saw was the end result.

Was it Cindy Crawford who'd said looking good was the best revenge?

No matter. It was now her mantra. Every time she even started to think of Sid and his extracurricular activities she was going to do something positive for herself.

Like treat her skin to a mask. Or scrub her teeth with super-whitening paste. Or wax her legs.

Or take a really hot, relaxing bath foaming with calming herbs, and go to bed. Where she was going to go right to sleep and not, not, *not* dream of men.

Not Sid the Jerk. Or Mac the Hunk. Or anyone remotely male.

Give her a society that was man-free, and what a happy world it would be.

Go now.

She hadn't even heard that, she told herself with a final glance in the mirror. The mask was already starting to harden. It was crisping around the edges, and cracks were starting to appear in her cheeks. A few more minutes and she would rinse it off, slather on moisturizer, wax her legs, and get in the tub. After that, she would go to bed, and *sleep.*

She was not going to end up a withered, embittered old woman with wrinkles and bad teeth and hairy legs and a rear end the size of a schoolbus just because she'd had the bad judgment to marry a cheating no-good asshole.

So there.

Upon entering her bedroom some ten minutes before, she'd flipped on the light, stripped off her clothes, and grabbed a nightgown out of the lingerie chest. The nightgown was more husband-bait, a short, silky leopard-print thing with black lace trim and spaghetti straps, but there was no help for it, so, beyond deciding that a shopping spree for oversized T-shirts and cotton panties was definitely in order, she had resolved not to obsess about it. Sliding the newly despised garment over her head, she had flipped off the light and crossed to the window, pulling the curtains apart to see if she could see Mac's car.

Too dark.

Just as well anyway, she told herself as memories of that steamy interlude at Sweetwater's intruded, making her loins ache and tighten in reflexive response. Julie watched her eyelids droop and her lips part in her fuzzy reflection in the window glass, recognized the look for the sexual yearning it was, and sighed. Clearly she was destined to stay chronically hungry in more ways than one.

A moment or two later she had shut the curtain, turned her back on the window, and retreated to her bathroom, scooping up the Hershey's Kisses on the way. Sex, as usual, remained tantalizingly out of reach. But tonight, chocolate was at hand.

Once inside the bathroom, with the help of her reflection in a three-way mirror, a critical look at her much-maligned butt, and a little hard-won self-control, she'd dredged up enough unexpected strength of character to flush the chocolate before it could add to the landmass that seemed to be following her around, and resolved there and then that even if her life went to hell, her looks weren't going with it.

GO NOW.

Don't shout, she almost answered aloud, but remembered that talking back to the voice was bad. A glance showed her that the tub was almost to the brim. In full Creature mode, Julie walked barefoot across the cool white tile, bent to turn off the taps, rescued the floating jar of leg wax that had been warming in the water, inhaled deeply of the aromatic steam that didn't seem to be doing crap about her stress as far as she could tell, straightened and turned back toward the sink, jar in hand. She would rinse the mask off her face, wax her legs, and get in the tub, where the stress-reducing part of the chamomile would surely kick in.

She took a single step and stopped dead.

A man was staring at her through the bathroom mirror.

A man with his back pressed flat against the bedroom wall outside her bathroom door. A man with a black ski mask pulled down over his face so that she could see nothing of him except for the dark glint of his eyes through the round holes. A man who was at that very moment watching her watch him.

Every tiny hair on her body catapulted upright as Julie met his gaze in horror.

The little voice screamed. Julie was too dumbstruck to follow suit.

Then he stepped into the doorway, filling it, blocking all hope of escape.

Her breath escaped from her body in an audible hiss.

"Hello, Julie," he said as she stood frozen to the spot. The caressing note in his voice and the gloating way he looked her over sent chills racing along her spine. In that split second she realized that she was facing every woman's worst nightmare come true: a rapist, maybe even a killer. At the same time she registered with the tiny part of her mind that was not absolutely numb with terror that he was big, not so much tall but burly, and dressed all in black and carrying a gun which he held negligently in one surgical-gloved hand.

Oh, God, a gun to use on her.

He started to lift it, to point it at her. Her heart freed itself from its state of shock-induced suspended animation to give a great leap in her chest. She sucked in a huge gulp of air, found her voice, and screamed like a siren, all in a single instant. Then, acting purely on instinct, she hurled the jar of leg wax at his head.

It was a heavy jar, dark blue glass filled with warmed wax, and it hit him square in the middle of the forehead with a sound like a cork popping out of a champagne bottle.

"Son of a *bitch!*" he yelled, staggering backward and clapping a hand to his forehead as the jar spun away to crash against the wall and drop to the tile with a clatter. He disappeared through the doorway. For a split second after he was no longer in sight, Julie remained frozen in place. She knew he was still there, heard breathing and cursing and movements that told her he was just beyond the door.

Run.

No duh, was her inner response to the little voice as, with terror giving wings to her feet, she flew toward the door, knowing that this was, very possibly, her only chance to get away.

Exploding from the bathroom like a sprinter on speed, she saw in a single petrified glance that he was only a couple of feet away, a big dark shape with one hand still clapped to his forehead as he bent over to pick up the gun he had apparently dropped. She leaped past him even as he looked up.

"Son of a bitch!" Abandoning the gun, he lunged for her, trying to grab her with both arms.

"No!" Dodging, gasping for breath, her heart pounding so hard that she could hear nothing beyond the drumming of her own blood in her ears, she fled toward her bedroom door and the hall and the stairs and the outside door below, screaming her lungs out all the way.

Oh, God, oh, God, oh, God, he was chasing her, surprisingly nimble and fast on his feet considering his size. He was going to catch her. She knew he was; it was just a matter of minutes, seconds. . . .

Frantically she tried to recall some basics from the self-defense class she had taken once. Its mantra had been, if attacked, SING. S-I-N-G. The only problem was, now in her time of extremis she couldn't remember what the S stood for.

The only S word she could call to mind that seemed at all appropriate was *scream.*

And she was already screaming like a steam whistle and it didn't seem to be doing much good, unless deafening him as well as herself was part of the plan.

"Help! Help!"

He was right behind her as she reached the top of the

stairs, lunging and grabbing and *closing his fist over the flying banner of her hair.*

Julie shrieked loud enough to shatter glass in Columbia as her head was jerked backward so hard she was surprised her neck didn't snap. Then his arm wrapped around her waist, yanking her against him, and his gloved hand clamped down over her mouth and nose, silencing her, suffocating her. She was enveloped by the heat of his body and the smell of talc from the glove and sweat from the man.

"You shouldn't've hit me," he growled in her ear. She smelled onions on his breath.

Her stomach heaved. Lack of oxygen and terror made her head swim. Her heart pounded. Her skin crawled everywhere his rubberized fingers touched as if ants were running amok over her flesh. Still she fought as he dragged her back toward the bedroom, tearing at his gloved hand with her nails, kicking at his shins with her bare feet, twisting and writhing and struggling with every ounce of strength she possessed, with every atom of knowledge the streetwise little girl she had once been had had to learn to survive, knowing even as she fought that it was probably futile, that she was not going to be able to save herself, that, at maybe a hundred twenty pounds soaking wet, she was no match for a brute who was easily twice her weight.

He dragged her back over the threshold of her bedroom, back into the room with the tasteful white carpet and taupe walls and huge black-lacquered bed. Understated, all of it, right down to the white summer linens on the bed. A room for quiet contemplation and restful sleep, not unspeakable acts and violence and death.

Oh, please don't let him kill me.

The prayer shot skyward even as she managed to grab

his mask and pull it off over his head, and he picked her up and threw her down on her back on the bed.

She landed with a bounce. He was on top of her before she could move, pinning her with his weight, forcing her deep into the mattress even as she tried and failed to knee him in the groin, tried and failed to roll free. Her nightgown was twisting toward her waist, she could feel the rough abrasion of his clothes against her tender skin, feel the heat and weight of him with a revulsion that was like nothing she had ever experienced in her life. She knew what he intended to do, knew it and screamed her terror into his face and thrashed and kicked and fought, all to no avail.

"Shut up, bitch." One hand wrapped around her throat, cutting her scream off in midblast, brutal in its intent to cause pain, squeezing so that she gagged and choked and squealed like a small animal caught in a trap. Her gaze caught on her teddy bear sitting Buddha-like on the bedside table, and she realized with a sense of horrified disbelief that it might be the last thing she saw before she died. He was crushing her throat, cutting off her voice, her air. Her blood seemed to spike in her ears. All she could do was claw frantically at his hand and wheeze.

"Shut up," he said again. She nodded jerkily, so grateful for the chance to live that she would do anything, and he loosened his grip enough so that she could once again breathe. He let go of her throat and grabbed her wrists, lifting them over her head as she lay unresisting, intent on drawing in blessed air. The weight of his body pinned her as he transferred both her captured wrists to one huge meaty hand. Then, with a ripping noise more terrifying than anything she had ever heard, he began to bind her wrists together with a roll of duct tape that had somehow appeared in his hand.

The tape wrapping her wrists felt sticky and tight and full of doom. She struggled weakly, trying to pull free of it. She couldn't break it, couldn't free her hands.

One hand returned to grip her throat punishingly.

"Give me any more trouble, and I'll crush your throat and be done with it," he said, then used his teeth to tear the tape from the roll. As he patted the strip down, his face was so close his oniony breath made her gag. His body, huge and smothering and ripe with BO, lay over hers, effectively rendering her helpless. Her heart pounded so hard she was surprised it didn't burst through her chest. She panted with terror; her bruised throat was pulsing in and out like gills on a fish.

Except for the light streaming from the open bathroom door the bedroom was dark, and his features were lost in shadows. But she could see the gleam in the eyes just inches from her own, the flash of his teeth against parted lips, the dark jut of his nose. . . .

His nose.

Savage as a cornered animal, Julie lunged upward and fastened her teeth on his nose and clamped down.

She heard a crunch. Blood, warm and salty, spurted into her mouth.

He howled, punching her viciously in the temple and throwing himself off her as her teeth were jarred loose by the stunning blow. Her head was knocked sideways. The room spun and she saw stars.

It didn't matter. Her fight-or-flight response was operating at full throttle now, and this time it screamed flight. She felt his weight shift and, spinning room and stars and all, she was off that bed as if propelled by industrial-strength springs, off the bed and bounding toward the door, running like Death himself was after her as she very much feared he was. She flew over the carpet and across the hardwood floor of the hall and down the slippery marble steps so fast that her feet barely touched ground, breathing in great ragged gasps that hurt her throat, her heart beating like the wings of a trapped bird, screaming like a thousand lost souls on their way to hell.

"Bitch! Bitch! Bitch!"

Oh, God, please let him not have his gun.

Her shoulders scrunched in terrified expectation of a bullet in the back as she leaped down the last few stairs.

"Come back here!"

He was gaining on her, getting close, so close, grabbing for her, exuding so much fury and menace and evil that she could feel them like some huge trio of hounds snapping at her heels. Cold sweat poured from her body as it seemed to her that she was running in slow motion with the front door drawing ever farther away. The smell of him, oniony and rank, surrounded her. The rasp of his breathing filled her ears. The floor seemed to vibrate beneath her feet as he lumbered like some enormous, death-dealing monster in her wake.

"Julie!"

Mac's voice shouting her name was the most welcome sound Julie had ever heard. It came from the direction of the kitchen. Screaming, Julie veered that way, scant inches ahead of the man behind her, her bare feet slipping and sliding over the cool slick marble of the entry hall, her bound hands stretching out in front of her, her fingers clawing at the darkness as if it was something tangible she could grasp and pull. She bolted through the dining room's arched doorway, then raced across freshly waxed hardwood toward the kitchen.

"Julie!"

"Help! Help me!"

As her feet hit the cool stone of the kitchen floor, the

overhead light came on, all but blinding her. Unable in that split second to see, she careened into the corner of the glass-topped kitchen table and bounced off and kept going, not even feeling the pain as the sharp corner thrust into her tender abdomen.

Then—thank God, thank God—she saw Mac, standing in the doorway between the kitchen and the family room, one hand on the light switch. Her first glimpse of him seemed to catch him in midmotion, and then he saw her, too, and stopped dead, looking tall and strong and out of breath and nearly as terrified as she felt.

"Mac!"

She launched herself at him from maybe six feet away, sobbing and gasping and trying to warn him of the monster coming behind her in a hysterical screech that was all but incomprehensible to her own ears. Two things registered in the same instant: one, Mac—Mac!—was holding a gun; and two, she couldn't hear the monster behind her anymore.

Oh, God, where was he?

"What the hell . . ."

Mac caught her as she landed against him, wrapping a hard arm around her waist, pulling her close to his chest as she screamed her warning. He held her one-armed while he shifted in a quick dance step that brought his back up against the nearest wall. His grip on the gun stayed firm and sure, and he aimed it toward the door through which she had come.

"Julie. Julie. It's okay, I've got you safe." He spoke over the noise she made, and she collapsed gasping and shuddering against his chest. His body was tense, ready for action; she got the sense that he was balanced on the balls of his feet. Clearly he knew his way around a gun. He exuded controlled power, and she was suddenly possessed of absolute faith in his ability to protect her. Accordingly, she clung to him as to a rock in a murderous sea. "Stay right here, and I'll . . ."

"No!" She clutched his shirtfront with both her bound hands, her hold a death grip that she never meant to release. "He's got a gun."

Then her ears started to ring, and the world was once again spinning madly. Her knees gave way and the floor seemed to rise up to meet her. If he hadn't caught her, she would have slithered right down the front of his body to expire in a quivering puddle of spineless terror on the floor.

15

"Julie! Christ, Julie!"

She had fainted in his arms.

At least, he hoped it was a faint. Any other possibility scared the hell out of him.

Mac supported her dead weight with one arm, running a quick, anxious glance over her at the same time as he tried to keep an eye on both doors that opened into the huge, gleaming, stainless-steel and white kitchen. The silky thing she was almost wearing made it hard to keep his grip on her. The brown crust that covered most of her face appeared, at closer glance, to be some kind of cosmetic rather than any of the more horrific possibilities, like blood or burns, that had flashed into his mind when he had first spotted her flying toward him. Her wrists were bound tightly together with silver duct tape. Her throat was a deep, ugly red that gave promise of turning purple later. But there was no blood that he could see, and no other obvious sign of injury.

Had she been raped?

Fear for her joined forces with a deep, atavistic fury that made him want to go after whoever had done this to her and rip him apart with his bare hands, or, at the very least, empty a magazine into him.

The perp was still in the house. Mac knew it with the kind of sixth sense that had, long ago, made him such an effective cop.

He could not leave Julie alone to go after the bastard.

That much coolheadedness he retained. If the perp by some unlucky chance managed to get him first, the way would be clear for the sick bastard to finish what he'd started with Julie.

The graphic mental images that accompanied the thought made him feel murderous all over again.

Cool out, he warned himself. His first objective had to be to get Julie to safety.

With a low growl of frustration he bent and heaved her over his shoulder. Her arms and head hung sack-of-potatoes-style down his back. The silky animal-print stuff of her nightgown was cool against his ear and cheek. The lace that hemmed it tickled his jaw whenever he moved his head. She was not heavy but she was awkward to carry, to no small degree because her slithery gown made her deadweight keep wanting to slide off his shoulder. He had to hold her tight, with his arm locked across her thighs. Her position might very well have left her something less than decently covered, but he was too preoccupied with getting them both out of there to register the occasional glimpse of a sweetly curved cheek more than peripherally. He did notice, because he couldn't help it, that the backs of her thighs felt smooth and firm and silky—as well as surprisingly cold to the touch. From shock or the air-conditioning, he couldn't be sure, but he was betting on shock.

She'd said her attacker had a gun. The chances were good that the guy would run for it, but criminals were not known for their reliability and Mac wasn't taking any chances. What he was doing was hauling ass.

A single set of keys dangling from a hook near the door caught his eye. Thinking fast, juggling Julie and his pistol and praying that he wasn't about to be jumped from behind, he snagged them, fairly sure that they were the keys to the white Infiniti in the garage. It was a loaner from her insurance company; that much he knew. That made it, in effect, her car.

He was taking her straight to the nearest hospital. Sid would get home sooner or later, the police would do their thing, and what had happened in the Carlson house tonight would be the talk of Summerville tomorrow. In the interests of keeping Julie's retention of a private investigator confidential, it would be better if he took her in her car. After he made sure she was safe and in good hands he could fade into the scenery, and, when the time came for her to give a statement, she could claim that she had escaped on her own and driven herself in.

Always provided that she was conscious and talking by then.

Mac dismissed the thought as useless and distracting, and backed warily out through the heavy panel door leading into the garage.

Except for the light from the open kitchen door, it was dark in the garage. It was far warmer than the air-conditioned house, and smelled faintly of freshly cut grass and 10-W-40. Mac was jumpy as a squirrel in a cat's backyard and moving fast as he rounded the Infiniti's hood and tried its rear door, knowing that they could come under fire at any second. To put her in the car required both hands. Cursing a blue streak under his breath, he placed the Glock on the roof. Unarmed now and feeling hideously vulnerable, he did a clumsy juggling maneuver with her inert body that by the grace of God somehow ended with her lying, knees bent, on her side in the backseat.

Good enough. Mac shoved her feet all the way inside, closed the door, grabbed the Glock, and leaped for the garage door that he had broken into on his previous visit to the house. It had not yet been fixed; he knew, because he'd entered through it. Keeping a wary eye on the bright rectangle of light, he heaved the door up, wincing at the telltale rattle it made, then jumped behind the wheel of the car, placing the Glock within easy reach on the front passenger seat. The key fit, the engine turned over, Mac slammed the car into drive, and they were out of there.

Thank God. Until he hung a left at the end of the driveway and felt the tension leave his shoulders, Mac didn't realize just how scared he'd been.

He had left the Blazer parked across the street. Pulling up behind it, he stopped, sprinted to the driver's-side door, opened it, retrieved his cell phone, and locked the door again. Jumping back in the Infiniti, he saw that Julie had not stirred. She was still breathing; her breasts rose and fell rhythmically beneath the flimsy nightgown, and her truly world-class legs shifted restlessly as he watched.

Alarm at her state made his movements jerky and his foot heavier than usual on the accelerator. Peeling out around the Blazer, he dialed 911 and reported a break-in in progress at Julie's address. At least that would get some uniforms on the scene, though he doubted that it would do much good.

Unless the intruder had shit for brains, he was already long gone. Mac gritted his teeth at the thought. It went way against the grain with him to just let the son of a bitch escape, but under the circumstances there seemed to be no help for it.

It occurred to him then that the degree of his fear and anger was way out of proportion, considering Julie Carlson's role in his life. He should be feeling a decent amount of concern, a little chagrin that the attack had happened right under his nose, but nothing like the combination of grinding fear and murderous rage that was at that very moment churning through his guts.

Mac didn't think he'd ever been so petrified in his entire adult life as he had been when he'd first heard Julie scream.

Speeding through the stop sign at the corner with scarcely more than a pause and a glance, he went cold all over again as he remembered.

After she had left him, he had settled down in the Blazer to wait for Sid to get home, turning his spy ears on so that he could listen to what was going on in the house but not hearing anything because there was nothing to hear. Julie was alone. The time to really listen was after Sid was inside the house. If anything was going to happen, it would happen then.

Julie had said Sid wasn't violent, but Mac had his own reasons for knowing better than that. The thing was, Sid apparently wasn't violent to Julie. Of course, that could be because she'd never given him cause.

Having him followed as a prelude to divorcing him might well, in Sid's book, constitute cause.

In any case, Mac wasn't inclined to bet the farm that it wouldn't. If Sid had made them at Sweetwater's—and he didn't think Sid had, but it never paid to take things like that for granted—Julie might just discover a whole new side to her husband that she apparently had no idea existed.

If that were to happen, Mac meant to be on hand. Over the last twenty-four hours, watching out for Julie seemed to have become his mission in life.

Besides, knowing what time Sid got home and what he did after he got there could be important in figuring out exactly what was going down. Maybe Sid would make a phone call. Maybe he'd go out for a walk. Maybe he'd simply go to bed.

Although not, Mac was glad to remember, with Julie. Mac didn't think he could listen to that. No, he knew he couldn't listen to that and stay sane.

Which was a bad sign. A really bad sign. Julie Carlson was his client, for God's sake, and his link to Sid, and that was all. He had no interest in her beyond that.

Yeah, and his real name was Debbie, too.

Mac grimaced as he realized that the situation was starting to get way out of hand.

She kissed him like she was dying to take him to bed, then twenty minutes later told him she wasn't going to sleep with him. Well, that was fine by him, because he wasn't planning to sleep with her either. Sleeping with her would be the equivalent of a last fatal step into quicksand.

Unfortunately, he couldn't help recalling some saying about what happened to even the best-laid plans of—was it mice and men? He couldn't remember how it went exactly, but the upshot was that the plans went to hell, and the mice and men that made them pretty much wound up being roadkill.

Under the circumstances, though, keeping his eye on the ball wasn't all that easy. When he'd been sitting in the Blazer in the dark, growing old waiting for Sid's Mercedes to pull up the driveway, pretty much all he had found to do was breathe and think about Julie. He had tried not thinking about her, but that didn't work, so at last he gave up and allowed his memory—and his fantasies—free rein.

Having to take a leak was almost a welcome interruption.

He'd gotten out, taken care of business, then set off on a leisurely stroll around the Carlson McMansion just for something to do. Standing at the edge of the stone patio, looking at the moonlight glinting off the kidney-shaped swimming pool, he had acknowledged that there just might be a real solid reason why Julie wanted to hang on to her marriage.

Yo, little bro, big bucks buy babes.

He could almost hear Daniel saying it, all those years ago, and a wry, faintly tender smile touched his mouth at the memory. As a cocky sixteen-year-old he'd confronted his big brother, who at the time had no steady employment that he knew of, about the illegality of his newest money-making venture, demanding to know how he could have done something so damned stupid as to fly a buttload of marijuana into the country from Mexico in the small plane he'd somehow managed to buy.

Daniel had grinned that big, shit-eating grin that had driven girls wild and made his more serious-minded little brother increasingly want to pop him in the nose, and said he did it because there were big bucks in it, and yo, little bro, big bucks buy babes.

Julie Carlson was definitely a babe. Had big bucks bought her? Looking around ye olde McMansion, there didn't seem to be much doubt.

"Mac?" Julie's voice was faint, but it snapped Mac's attention back to the present as effectively as a shout. Glancing over his shoulder as the Infiniti scooted through yet another stop sign, he saw that her beautiful brown eyes were open at last and she was struggling to sit up.

"Yeah," he said. "Don't move. We're on our way to the hospital."

"Oh, God, Mac, he—I . . ." Her reply ended in a wordless quaver.

That quaver went through him like a knife.

"It's okay," he said, his voice gruffer than usual because

he wasn't sure he was ready to hear the details of what had happened. He figured, while he was driving, it might be better that he not know. If the answers were bad, talking about it might further traumatize her, too. "You're safe now."

"I—must have blacked out." She sounded faintly woozy still, and she kept trying to sit up, although her bound wrists seemed to be making sitting up more difficult than it should be. Or maybe she had some injury he hadn't spotted, and it was hindering her. The thought turned him cold.

"No shit," he said. Then, with another glance at her over his shoulder that nearly caused him to sideswipe a mailbox, he added, in the hard, cop voice he hadn't used in years, "Did you recognize him? Was it someone you know?"

"No. I don't know. I don't think so. God, he—he knew my name." She shuddered, and he cursed under his breath. Easy, he reminded himself, take it easy.

He deliberately gentled his tone. "Can you describe him? What did he look like?"

She shook her head, and took a deep, shaking breath. "He was wearing a mask, at first. And then—I didn't get that good of a look."

"Are you hurt anywhere? Any pain or anything like that?"

"My head hurts," she said after letting a beat pass in which Mac realized his palms were starting to sweat. "He punched me in the head. And my neck. He was going to strangle me, I think. After—after . . ."

Her voice broke. Mac ground his teeth. He took the safer tack of glancing at her through the mirror. She was sitting up now. Her head rested limply back against the tan leather upholstery. Her hair in that ridiculous cascading ponytail still nearly reached her shoulders. Her face was covered with a cracked and flaking layer of something brown.

"And my hands are numb," she continued more strongly, as if rallying.

Mac sucked a calming breath in through his teeth. The idea that some bastard had wrapped her wrists with duct tape made him want to start breaking faces. To say nothing of the rest of what had been done to her.

"I'll get the tape off for you when we get to the hospital. Just a few more minutes." His tone was soothing.

"The hospital?"

"That's where we're going." Clearly she hadn't registered what he'd said the first time. That worried him. Just how hard had she been hit? He stepped on the accelerator, glanced in the mirror again—and went straight through a stop sign. Jesus. He hadn't even seen it. Good thing the traffic in Summerville at three in the morning was so light as to be almost nonexistent.

"Mac. Pull over." There was a sudden urgency to her voice.

"What? Why?" He glanced in the mirror again.

"I think I'm going to throw up."

Mac groaned, and pulled the Infiniti over to the side of the road.

Julie was already fumbling at the handle when he got her door open.

"Hold still." He had his pocketknife out and ready. Hooking his fingers beneath the edge of the tape, he sliced through the sticky layers with relative ease, then pulled the tape off with one quick yank and felt a twinge of guilt as she winced. He imagined the sensation was something akin to having a mega-Band-Aid removed the quick way. In short, not pleasant.

"Mac, *move*." The order was urgent, and then she pressed her lips tightly together as if she was afraid of what might follow the words. Even as she flexed her fingers and shook out her hands, she swung her legs out of the car and scooted forward. Her bare feet were pale against the dark bristle of the grass as she tried to stand. Her legs were long and slim and luscious beneath the hem of that unbelievably sexy nightgown. From the neck down, she was every teenage boy's wet dream; from the neck up, she was every grown man's fear of what he would end up sleeping with for the next fifty years once the honeymoon was over.

The bad part was, even with a silly ponytail and a face full of muck, she still looked beautiful. And with that thought, Mac realized to his dismay that he was already smack in the middle of the quicksand, and it was closing over his head.

She was about halfway out the door when she swayed and sank back. Mac, standing a little to one side to give her room, saw that she needed help and bravely put himself directly in the line of fire. Grabbing her by both elbows, he hauled her out. With an arm wrapped around her waist he supported her as she stumbled about six feet away from the car.

He then stood over her feeling helpless while she dropped to her knees at the side of the road.

16

Her head swam, her stomach heaved, but in the end she managed to keep herself from vomiting by sheer force of will. After a moment in which the issue hung in the balance, Julie sank back on her heels and flopped forward so that her head rested on her thighs and her arms lay limply on the grass beside her folded legs, too dizzy and exhausted to even sit up. Her stomach settled, but her head throbbed mercilessly, her throat ached, and her newly freed hands tingled and burned. Julie looked at the marks the tape had made on her wrists and shuddered.

"Julie?" Mac crouched beside her and put a hand, warm and large, on her back. For once the muggy heat was welcome; she felt cold to the bone. The scent of fresh-cut grass was all around her. The grass itself felt cool and faintly damp beneath her.

Julie turned her head toward him, registered the gilt-edged outline of his head against the star-dusted sky, registered the broad-shouldered power of his build, registered his sheer masculine beauty, and felt comforted. No matter if he had deceived her in the matter of Debbie, Mac could be counted on to keep her safe.

"I'm glad you're not gay," she said.

"Me too." His voice was dry. He was looking her over

carefully. She smiled at him. If it hadn't been for Mac—well, she wasn't going to think about that. Not now. If she thought about what might have happened, she feared she would totally lose it, which would not help the situation in any way that she could see.

"How are you feeling?"

"I'm okay," she said.

"I can tell." The dryness took on a grim edge. She watched as he glanced away from her, then back. "There's a water fountain over there. Feel like a drink?"

It was only then that she realized they were at the edge of Sawyer Park, a children's play area consisting of a grassy acre chock-full of swings and slides and sandboxes and other assorted kiddie paraphernalia. She knew it well, thanks to countless afternoons spent playing in it with Erin and Kelly.

"Sounds good."

Before she could make more than a feeble attempt to rise, he made a sound under his breath and scooped her up in his arms. He straightened as easily as if she weighed nothing at all, and started walking with her toward the small silver monolith of a drinking fountain that gleamed in the moonlight some hundred yards away.

Julie didn't even think about protesting, but curled close against his chest and looped her arms around his neck, content to be right where she was. Her knees felt rubbery, her head swam, and she had a funny feeling that she wasn't quite hitting on all her usual mental cylinders. She wasn't sure she could have walked to the water fountain even if she'd wanted to. But she didn't want to. She loved being in Mac's arms. They were hard and strong beneath her knees and around her back. His chest was firm and solid, and his whole body was so *warm*. She realized that what she was experiencing was probably a trauma-induced primitive female reaction to his superior male strength, mentally deplored the retro-ness of her own response, and settled down to savor it anyway. She let her head rest on his wide shoulder, closed her eyes, and tightened her hold on his neck.

"Okay, I'll bite," Mac said a beat or so later, sounding slightly grumpy. She opened her eyes to find that they were closing on their goal fast: his long strides were eating up the ground. "Want to tell me what the heck that stuff is on your face?"

For a moment Julie couldn't think what he was talking about. Then she remembered the Mudd, and surprised herself by smiling. Here she was, enjoying a little escapist romantic fantasy about being borne away into the darkness by a truly hot guy, and all the while she looked like a refugee from an *I Love Lucy* episode. Was that the way life worked or what? At least, her life.

"Mudd."

"You usually sleep with mud on your face?" He sounded politely interested.

"Mudd. M-U-double dee. It's a mask. For your skin. I was going to take a bath before I went to bed, and I put Mudd on my face first. Then I saw *him* in the mirror before I could get in the tub."

She shuddered, and his grip tightened. The instant when she had seen her attacker in the mirror was vivid—too horribly vivid to be borne. She tried to dismiss it from her mind; it was impossible. Out of nowhere came the memory of her little voice. Goose bumps prickled to life all over her as she realized that the voice had been warning her. It must have been some kind of sixth sense. On some level, she must have realized that there was someone in the house.

That thought was scary, too. She didn't much like the idea that she knew things she didn't know she knew.

"How did you know I was in trouble?" Maybe he'd had a sixth sense experience, too.

"Darlin', you have a scream like a banshee. I was standing outside by your pool when you let loose. Hearing you took about twenty years off my life, by the way." He took a deep breath. "Then I saw that someone had already broken in. It wasn't the best moment I've ever had, let me tell you."

For a moment neither of them said anything more. His feet moving over the grass and the chirping chorus of the usual insects were the only sounds. Moonlight bathed the playground in a ghostly glow. The playthings took on a whole different ambience in the dead of night, Julie discovered. A sinister ambience.

She felt a chill race down her spine and realized that the sheer terror of being attacked in her own home was still with her, hiding deep within her body's cells to reemerge at will like a particularly nasty virus. Never again, she feared, would she feel totally safe. If it could happen there, it could happen anywhere, even in this innocuous little playground. "Assume the worst" seemed to be her body's new rule of thumb, and she was correspondingly anxious. Thank God Mac was with her. She would have been spooked out of her mind otherwise.

No, if Mac hadn't been with her, she wouldn't have been here in this cheerful-by-day, eerie-by-night playground to be creeped out by ghostly toys.

Maybe she wouldn't have been anywhere. The thought sent a whole series of chills chasing after the first. He must have felt her shiver, because his arms tightened around her, cuddling her closer.

"Mac. Thank you."

"For?" He slanted a glance down at her. His face was very close.

"I think you probably saved my life."

He grunted. "Not a problem."

"What if he comes after us here?" Her voice was low. The terror was bubbling up again, sparked by their isolation, by the darkness, by the sense that anything could lurk in the shadows. She glanced fearfully around.

"I'll keep you safe whatever happens, I promise. But you don't need to worry: he won't come. He's long gone, believe me."

"You have a gun, don't you?"

"Yup."

"You know how to use it, right?"

His mouth twitched. "I used to be a cop. Before that, Navy SEAL. That make you feel better?"

"A little. No, actually, a lot." She felt dizzy, and rested her head against his shoulder again. He looked down at her.

"You okay?"

"Yes. Why aren't you a cop anymore?"

His jaw tightened. She felt a sudden tension in his body. For a moment she thought he wasn't going to answer, and she lifted her head and looked at him inquiringly. His gaze met hers and held for the briefest of moments. Then he glanced away.

"I got fired."

"You got *fired?*" Getting fired from the police force was the last thing she would ever expect to happen to Mac, Julie realized with some surprise. The Debbie thing notwithstanding, he was just about the most solidly reliable person she had ever met in her life. "Why?"

He sighed. "Because drugs went missing from the evidence room and were found in my possession. A boatload of people were willing to swear I'd been dealing. I got fired. I would have been prosecuted, but the department didn't want the publicity."

"You were innocent." It wasn't a question.

"Yeah, I was. The guy I was investigating at the time got to me before I could get him."

They reached the fountain then and he set her on her feet, keeping both hands on her waist and standing behind her, bracing her body with his. Julie rinsed her mouth several times then sluiced her face and throat, which felt bruised on the outside but didn't hurt particularly when she swallowed. No internal damage then, she judged, and felt thankful. The water was more lukewarm than cold, but it rinsed the Mudd away and made her feel better nonetheless. After several splashes she felt almost normal. When she was finished, she looked around at Mac, blinking as she wiped the water from her cheeks with her fingers.

"Here." He turned her around with his hands on her hipbones and wiped her face dry with the hem of his shirt.

"Now your shirt's wet." She steadied herself by grabbing onto his waist. It was narrow and hard beneath his T-shirt. His muscles flexed beneath her fingers as he moved.

"I'll survive."

He reached out and tugged at the scrunchie that held her hair up. Her hair was falling out of its high ponytail anyway, with tendrils straggling around her ears and down the back of her neck and tickling her cheeks. The bulk of it tumbled around her face as he pulled the scrunchie free. Julie instinctively shook her head to restore what order she could to her errant locks, then winced at the resultant stab of pain. He handed her the scrunchie and she slid it onto her arm.

"Better," he said, looking her over. "Not that you didn't look good with that mud stuff all over your face and your hair done up like a mop, of course."

Julie smiled. "Lying's going to get you in big trouble one of these days."

For a moment he simply looked down at her without saying anything. His hands rested on her upper arms. Their heat burned her skin. He was standing very close. Her breasts were just inches from his chest, her pelvis just inches from the zippered front of his jeans. A sudden, sensual hunger sprang to life inside her. She shivered a little, remembering the way he had kissed her earlier, welcoming the memory because it crowded out all the horrible memories that had come later. He made a slight, restive movement and she glanced up. Her gaze collided with his. He was frowning down at her, and the air between them was suddenly charged. Her lips parted. Her breathing quickened. His fingers tightened on her arms.

She felt positively light-headed—and she didn't think it was because of the blow to her head.

"We need to get going. You up to walking, do you think?" His abrupt words belied the heat in his eyes.

She smiled dreamily up at him. The alternative, of course, was for him to sweep her up in his arms again and carry her away into the night. Every atom of her being practically drooled at the prospect. In some small part of her mind, Julie recognized that weakness and fear had rendered her vulnerable, and mentally girded her loins. She *wanted* to be in his arms, but, she reminded herself sternly, a little wanting of that nature could be a dangerous thing.

"I can walk." Her voice sounded far more robust than she felt.

He let go of her arms, and she was both glad and sorry to be taken at her word. Instead of sweeping her up, he slid a hand around her elbow with all the decorousness he might have shown a maiden aunt, and urged her forward.

Setting her jaw determinedly, Julie started walking, breathing deep of the heavy night air that was, she discovered, the opposite of revivifying. She made it about half a dozen paces. Then her knees dissolved from rubbery straight to pure liquid, and she folded like an accordion. Mac grabbed her around the waist in the nick of time, barely saving her from ending up flat on her face in the grass.

"To hell with it," he said, sounding angry, and scooped her up again. Try though she might, Julie couldn't summon up so much as a smidgen of regret. Her head swam and her limbs felt as limp as cooked noodles—but not limp enough to prevent her from wrapping her arms around his neck. It was then that she faced the awful truth: Dangerous or not, Mac's arms felt like home to her now.

For the length of a couple of strides neither of them said anything. Julie breathed in the slightly beery, slightly musky scent of him and snuggled as close as she could get. He basically walked and breathed.

Then Mac gave a disgusted grunt. His hands—one on her bare thigh just above her knee, one just below her right breast—tightened.

"Just for the record, are you wearing anything at all under that nightgown?"

Julie looked up at him, admiring the clean, classical lines of his jaw and chin and noting with some interest that blond men were perfectly capable of sprouting a considerable amount of five-o'clock shadow given the right circumstances.

"No. Not a thing."

"That's what I thought."

He was sweating, she noticed, observing small beads of moisture on his forehead with interest, although she didn't think it was from effort. After all, he had carried her from the car to the drinking fountain without any trouble. And, hippy or no, she didn't weigh all that much.

"So what's your point?" she prodded when he didn't say anything else.

"No point."

They reached the car. Keeping a steadying arm around her waist, Mac set her on her feet to open the front passenger door. Tugging the hem of her nightgown down—it had ridden up to the point of indecency as she slid down his body—she leaned contentedly against him, her bare shoulder butting into his chest, her silk-clad hipbone nudging his abdomen. She shifted position a little and her hip brushed the front of his jeans. There was a palpable hardness there. Julie registered it, and her lips curved into a small, purely feminine smile.

"Don't you like my nightgown?" There, she was flirting with him, openly, unmistakably flirting, pounding head, bruised throat and all. Julie realized that she hadn't flirted in years; flirting, she rediscovered, was fun.

Mac looked down at her with a considering expression. The now-open door waited beside her like an eager mouth, but she wasn't ready to be swallowed up by it just yet.

"That depends." He sounded cautious as he studied her face. Then he seemed to make up his mind about something. His jaw tightened, his lips compressed, and he added in a firmer tone, "Now be a good girl and get in."

When she didn't move but just stood there smiling beatifically at him, he grimaced and bundled her inside with ruthless efficiency, lifting her legs in when she was slow to do so, pulling her seat belt down and leaning across her to fasten it.

"Depends on what?" Voice sultry, she slid her hand up inside his T-shirt as he leaned across her, enjoying the feel of his warm, satiny skin, the hard smoothness of his stomach, the brawny width of his chest. He froze at her touch, and as her fingers traveled upward, burrowing into the soft mat of hair she discovered, his gaze met hers. Their faces were so close she could feel the warmth of his breath on her skin.

His eyes were hot; his mouth was—sexy as hell. She couldn't stop looking at it. Her hand stilled on his chest, palm flattening, fingers spreading luxuriantly in the silky hair. She could feel the steady beat of his heart against her palm.

"On whether you meant what you said earlier about not sleeping with me."

There was a huskiness to his voice that made her breathing quicken. Her lips parted. Instinctively she lifted them toward his.

His eyes narrowed; his lips compressed; his head pulled back. Then his hand caught hers and pulled it out from under his shirt despite her sound of protest.

"Mac!"

He hesitated, his hand tightening on hers, and their eyes met again. Electricity leaped between them, so strong it practically ignited the air. Then he muttered something that sounded like *damn* under his breath, leaned forward and kissed her, his mouth slanting across hers with a hungry urgency that made her dizzier than she already was. Julie's eyes closed. Her lips parted. His kiss was hot, and fierce, and tasted faintly of beer, and she responded to it with mindless pleasure. Her loins tightened and began to throb. Her breasts swelled greedily toward his chest. Her fingers curled around his, claiming his hand for her own. Head reeling, she licked into his mouth and pressed the hand that was joined to hers palm-down over her breast. It rested there, radiating heat through the thin layer of silk, hard and heavy and crazy-making on the soft fullness of her. His hand on her breast felt so wonderfully, unbelievably good. . . .

For a moment, as she held his hand to her breast and her nipple pebbled against his palm, she thought he wasn't going to respond. Then he made a sound deep in his throat, the kiss seemed to burst into flame, and his hand got with the program, tightening and squeezing with an almost compulsive need. Her heart pounded; her loins throbbed; her toes curled. His kiss drove her wild. His hand caressed her breast, cupped it; his thumb ran knowingly back and forth across her nipple. She moved enticingly, straining upward against the constraint of her seat belt, her hand sliding behind his neck to pull him closer yet; a delicious tightening sensation began deep inside her body. She moaned, arching her back—and then he was pulling away, lifting his mouth from hers, removing his hand from her breast, putting inches of space between them when all she wanted to do was get closer to him than his own underwear.

She opened her eyes and gave him a look that said *do me right now or die* as clearly as if she'd shouted it. Although, of course, verbally she would never be that crude. Instead she fluttered her lashes and gave him a sexy little murmur of encouragement.

"Mac . . ."

His eyes narrowed at her.

"Don't mess with me, Julie, or I'm liable to forget you're operating with a bad case of scrambled brains here."

And with that he pulled his hand from hers and withdrew, just like that, shutting her door and walking around the hood to get in himself.

"I do not," she said with what dignity she could muster, crossing her arms over her still tingly chest and scowling at him as he put the key in the ignition, "have scrambled brains."

"Tell me that after a doctor's looked at you." He started the car.

"Maybe I'm just rethinking my position." She uncrossed her arms, and trailed a teasing finger down the sinewy arm closest to her. "After all, why shouldn't I sleep with you?"

"Because it's a bad idea." He dodged to escape her touch. Julie let her hand drop.

They were moving now. The car slid through the night with a whisper of tires, leaving the playground behind. In seconds they were once again cruising past dark houses with sleeping families tucked cozily inside.

"Why is it a bad idea? Don't you want to sleep with me?" She hunched her shoulders petulantly, casting him a sidelong look.

He laughed. They were moving into the commercial district now, and by the light of 7-Elevens and Dunkin' Donuts and streetlamps she was able to see him quite clearly. He looked—better than a chocolate-glazed. And also faintly rueful.

"Does that mean yes or no?" There was an edge to her voice.

"I'd say definitely yes."

She rested her head on the seat back and glared at him, exasperated. "So what's your problem?"

His eyes cut to her. "My problem is that we need to have this conversation when you're not a couple of french fries short of a Happy Meal." He sounded way too patient for her liking.

"That's ridiculous."

He shrugged. "Maybe."

She made a face at him. "Chicken."

"Damn right," he said, and made clucking sounds. "And here we are."

To her annoyance, he sounded relieved.

He parked in the lot to the left of the emergency-room entrance and turned off the car. Then he sat for a moment with his hands resting on the steering wheel, staring out through the windshield at the nearly full lot with a gathering frown on his face. The yellowish glow of the tall lamps that illuminated the area allowed her to see him clearly. His mouth and jaw were taut; his eyes were hard.

"What?" Julie asked when he didn't say anything.

"Okay." The word was abrupt. His gaze slashed toward her. "I need to know. Were you raped?" His fingers curled around the steering wheel as he spoke, then tightened so that his knuckles showed white.

"No. *No.*" Julie swallowed as the brutality of the attack came back to her in a sudden sickening wave. "He—I think that's what he had in mind, but it didn't happen."

"Why not?" He looked fully at her then, and his tone was milder. The tension in his body eased. Even his grip on the steering wheel relaxed to a degree.

"I bit his nose. Then I ran."

A beat passed. *"You bit his nose?"*

Julie nodded.

"Hard," she said with relish, remembering. "It was bleeding. I heard it crunch. Then he screamed and rolled off me, and I jumped up and ran downstairs."

He stared at her for a moment as if he couldn't believe his ears. Then his face relaxed and a hint of a smile turned up one corner of his mouth. "That would work." The smile widened into a grin. "You're something, you know that? Really something."

"So sleep with me." Julie's tone was deliberately, flirtatiously seductive. Her gaze locked with his.

"Later," he said. "Maybe."

He pulled the keys from the ignition and got out of the car. Julie watched as he came around to open her door. She was starting to feel really bad again, she realized, light-headed and sick at her stomach, and it occurred to her that maybe Mac was right—maybe she was short a few vital french fries. Or maybe she felt so ill because talking about it so graphically had brought the reality of the attack back to her with a vengeance. Before, when she'd been flirting with Mac, the whole nightmarish sequence of events had seemed far away, long ago, and almost as if had happened to someone else.

That kind of distancing was, she realized, probably some sort of defense mechanism kicking in. Whatever, its protective effect was gone now, and she felt *bad*.

Mac opened her door and reached across her to unfasten her belt. This time she didn't move, just lay limply back against the seat with her hands in her lap, battling a renewed urge to heave. When the latch released, he eased the seat belt away from her and took a quick, assessing look at her face.

"Hang on a few more minutes, tough guy," he said, his voice both rough and surprisingly tender at the same time, and slid his arms around her to scoop her out.

Julie didn't answer. She was too busy trying to keep all her cookies on board. Instead, she curled her arms around his neck and burrowed her head into the hollow between his neck and shoulder and closed her eyes, trusting him to take care of everything, to take care of her.

It was amazing to consider how much, in such a short span of time, she had grown to trust Mac.

"When we get inside," he said, striding toward the

emergency room doors with her in his arms, "here's what I need you to do. . . ."

Later, after the police had arrived along with a frantic-seeming Sid and, some ten minutes after that, Julie's even more frantic-seeming mother and sister, Mac slid out from behind the potted ficus and the newspapers that had served as his cover and left the hospital. The circus was in full swing inside. He didn't want any part of that. And Julie didn't need him anymore. At least, not at this end.

Dawn was just beginning to outline the eastern horizon in glowing orange. Not that the early hour made any difference to his plans. He slid into the taxi that waited, and made a second phone call as it pulled away from the curb.

When Mother answered, clearly peeved at having his beauty sleep disturbed, Mac cut him off with a few well-chosen words.

"I need some information."

17

By Tuesday morning Julie was back at work. She'd spent Sunday night in the hospital for observation and Monday night at her mother's. Although to everyone else she insisted that she was fine, to herself she acknowledged that she was still not mentally over the attack. Or physically over it either, for that matter. As Mac had suspected, she had suffered a slight concussion—or, as he'd so descriptively put it, scrambled brains. She had a baseball-sized bruise on her temple, three more in the approximate shape of ladyfingers on her throat, and one small crescent-shaped one just to the left of her belly button. All were an ugly shade of purple, and the ones on her face and throat were all but impervious to attempts to hide them with makeup. In their honor, she wore a petal-pink sleeveless sweater dress with a high, concealing turtleneck that she would have ordinarily deemed too hot for the weather, and accessorized it with a narrow purple belt and a pair of sinfully expensive purple sandals.

At least, she thought with a glimmer of humor, eyeing herself in one of the mirrored walls of her shop, no one could say she wasn't color-coordinated.

They could say plenty of other things, though. She was starting to feel like a one-woman sideshow. She'd been badgered for details by everyone from the police to Sid to her mother and Becky to friends and neighbors to people she didn't remember ever meeting in her life. Only Sid's combined cajoling and threatening of the publisher had kept the story out of the local newspaper. The consensus was that the attack was probably related to the theft of her car: either the thief had come across her picture in her purse—on her driver's license, maybe—and been moved by it to attack, or the attack had been part of the original plan, which had been aborted for some reason, and the criminal had come back to finish the job.

After all, what were the chances of two unconnected crimes occurring at the same address within two days?

Not to worry, though: The police assured her that (a) they would solve the case; and (b) it was unlikely that the criminal would return.

Given what they knew, Julie supposed that both were reasonable assumptions. She was not convinced of either point, however: look how easy they were to fool. She *was* sure that the man who had attacked her was not one of the punks who had stolen her car. No way, no how. Number one, the punks who stole her car had her keys, a fact of which the police were not aware and which she could find no way of letting them in on that did not involve admitting her lie; they would not have needed to jimmy the back door, which her attacker had done. For obvious reasons, she discussed that small glitch in the official theory with no one but Mac. He had called her twice, once at the hospital and once at her mother's, and they'd spoken briefly and guardedly, but she had not seen him since he'd left her in the emergency room.

To her own dismay, she caught herself missing him. A lot.

It was an unusually busy morning, both because

Monday's appointments had been blended with Tuesday's and because of the looming start of the Miss Southern Beauty pageant. Besides Carlene, Julie was dressing seven other contestants. All had come in for final fittings, and finding herself knee-deep in adjusting built-in padded bras and waist-whittling spandex dress liners was cathartic. Life was, more or less, back to normal, and Julie was grateful for that. She never in her life wanted to go through another weekend like the one she had just spent.

When the phone rang around one, Julie was on her knees putting the last few stitches in a client's competition evening gown. Her mouth was full of the pins she had removed from the aqua silk-satin creation as she worked her way around the hem, tacking it up.

"Julie, you have a phone call," Meredith said, entering the dressing room and looking down at her. "Someone named Debbie."

Julie almost swallowed the pins. In the interests of personal health and safety, she spit them out in her hand.

"Thanks." She motioned Meredith over to continue the task, and stood up, smiling at her red-haired client through the mirror. "Excuse me. I'll be right back."

This one—Tara Lumley—was sweet, as most of them were. Her handler sat quietly in a corner thumbing through a magazine. Absolute dolls, both of them. Too bad that, in Julie's expert opinion, Tara didn't have a prayer of defeating Carlene. Julie was all for someone, anyone, defeating Carlene.

Julie deposited the pins in a crystal container on her desk, and picked up the phone.

"Hi," she said, her voice far huskier and more intimate than it would have been if she truly had been addressing a Debbie whose name and gender matched.

"Hi, yourself." The sound of Mac's voice made her heartbeat quicken and her hand tighten on the receiver. Julie recognized her response as a bad thing, and enjoyed it anyway. "You got any plans for lunch?"

"I've already eaten." Two carrots and some crackers, just before noon. Oh, God, she wanted to see him. So much it scared her.

"Me too. So's how about you heading across the street to the Taco Bell anyway? I need to talk to you."

"About what?"

"Tell you when you get here."

Julie hesitated, thinking of Tara. Amber had gone to lunch, which meant that Meredith would have to handle everything alone. But Amber would be back within the hour, and Meredith was perfectly capable of dealing with anything that came up, as long as Julie was back by three. That's when Carlene was scheduled for her next fitting. Thinking of Carlene, Julie groaned inwardly and made up her mind. She deserved a break today.

"Be right there," she said, and put down the phone. Catching a glimpse of herself in the mirrored wall across the room, Julie frowned. Suddenly pink and purple to match her bruises didn't seem like such a good idea—and the clingy skirt seemed to make her butt look enormous. Frowning, she walked into the showroom and rifled through the racks until she found the square-necked lilac sundress she sought. It was short, slim-cut, and far more chic than the pink sweater dress, and had the added advantage of working well with her sandals. Hurrying back into her office, she changed, hanging her discarded dress on the rack with some of the newly arrived stock that had yet to be put on display. With the addition of a four-strand pearl choker to hide the worst of the bruises on her throat, and pearl earrings, also from stock, she was ready. Observing herself in another of the ubiquitous mir-

rors as she left, she smiled. With her black hair and
tanned skin providing a nice contrast to the lilac linen and
pearls, she looked good. Very Jackie O, but good.

Butterflies took flight in her stomach at the idea that
Mac was waiting for her right across the street, and she
shook her head at herself. She was reacting like a teenager
in the throes of her first crush. And over Debbie! The
thought made her smile.

After calling Meredith aside and telling her that she
had to run a quick errand, Julie walked across the street
to the Taco Bell. She said a cheery *good afternoon* to one
of the clerks from the candle shop next door, who was
outside smoking a cigarette and stared at the still faintly
visible, despite her best efforts with makeup, bruise on
her temple with unabashed curiosity. The sun was blinding as it bounced off the pavement, the heat hung like
a translucent veil in the air, and the passing cars were
no more than shooting flashes of color and carbon
monoxide.

Traffic was heavy as usual at midday as shoppers
patronized both the strip mall where Carolina Belle was
located and the larger shopping center directly across the
street. Julie was careful as she hurried across the road,
shielding her eyes with her hand and looking both ways.
Jaywalking was officially illegal, but everyone did it,
including the tourists. Summerville was that kind of town.

The Taco Bell was busy. A line of cars crept toward the
drive-through window, and through the plate glass Julie
could see that the restaurant was full. She was just about
to head inside when a short, sharp whistle drew her attention. Glancing around, she spotted Mac, and her pulse
rate immediately increased. He was near the back of the
parking lot, leaning against the Blazer with his arms
crossed over his chest, dressed in jeans and a white T-shirt

under a Hawaiian shirt so bright it rivaled the sun. A pair of Oakleys were wrapped around his face. It was clear from the smile just touching the corners of his mouth that he was watching her, but the sunglasses kept her from seeing his eyes.

God, he was gorgeous, was the thought that immediately sprang into her mind. Then, with an inner groan: Why did he have to be gorgeous?

Even as the thought hit her, Julie felt an answering smile curve her lips quite of its own volition. Gorgeous or not, she was glad to see him. Really, *really* glad to see him.

And a little embarrassed, too, she realized, which wasn't surprising when she thought about it. After all, this was the man she had kissed shamelessly the last time she'd set eyes on him. The man whose lap she had straddled and whose hand she had boldly pressed to her breast. The man she had all but begged to make love to her.

The man who had said no.

She didn't know whether to be mad at him or grateful for that.

"Yo," Mac said by way of a greeting as she got closer. His arms uncrossed, his hands dropped, and Julie realized that he was holding one end of a leash. A black leather leash. Eyes widening, she followed it down past the front of the Blazer just in time to see Josephine emerge from behind one of the small, scruffy bushes that grew in the grassy strip that separated the Taco Bell parking lot from the Kroger parking lot next door: Josephine, minus her pink hair bows and nail polish, sporting a black leather collar with silver studs.

Spotting Julie in turn, Josephine gave a sharp little yap of recognition and danced to meet her.

"Hi, Josephine." Julie squatted to pet her. Josephine

waxed ecstatic, wagging her tail so hard her whole body shook, licking Julie's chin and her hand and in every doggy way possible giving Julie to understand that she was delighted to see her.

"What did you *do?*" Julie glanced up at Mac accusingly. He had straightened away from the car, she saw as her gaze traveled up the lean, hard length of him with appreciation, and was at that moment in the act of removing his sunglasses.

"What? Oh, you mean the collar? I got her a new one. The pink was doing bad things to my self-esteem."

"She looks like dominatrix poodle." Julie gurgled with laughter as she stood up.

"She does not." Tucking the Oakleys away in his shirt pocket, he looked at Josephine, who was balanced on her haunches in front of Julie with her front paws waving in the air in an obvious bid for more attention. "Damn, she does."

"Yes, I know. He has *no* taste," Julie said to Josephine in a commiserating tone as she picked the poodle up. "You can tell from his shirts. But don't worry, I'll talk to him about getting your collar back, I promise."

"You got a problem with my shirts?" Mac sounded affronted. He was also grinning.

"Not at all. Except that a person needs sunglasses to look at them."

"They make me look like a tourist. I'm trying to blend in."

"I'm sorry to be the one to break the news, but I don't think it's working."

Julie was smiling as she glanced up from petting Josephine. Her eyes met Mac's and held. The memory of the last time they were together quivered in the air between them, as intangible but indisputably there as the heat, and

Julie felt her body quicken in instinctive response. Then, from the security of Julie's arms, Josephine wriggled and whined, drawing Julie's attention away from Mac to her doggy self, as was, no doubt, her intent. Which was probably a good thing, Julie thought as, acting as Josephine's surrogate, she unfastened the offending collar and handed it, leash still attached, to Mac with an audible sniff, while Josephine shook her head in obvious pleasure at being liberated. She was still a married woman in the first throes of a divorce, after all, and Mac was still, hard as it was to accept the *Oprah*-certified truth, probably no more and no less than a predictable phase she was going through.

A hunky predictable phase.

A hunky predictable phase who had saved her life.

A hunky predictable phase who had saved her life and whose mere presence made her day.

"Just like two females to stick together. For your information, Mr. Blackwell, she's lucky to be alive to get a new collar," Mac said, shooting Josephine a dark look as he unlocked the passenger door. "While you and I were out having fun the other night, she ate my bathroom wall. Chewed a hole in it the size of a basketball."

"Oh, dear." Julie couldn't help it. She laughed. "She must have been bored."

"She must have been something. Like suicidal." Mac opened the door and waited for Julie to get in. As she passed him, his gaze touched on her bruised temple and the corners of his eyes tightened in obvious concern. "How are you feeling?"

His tone had gentled.

"Better than I look."

"Not possible," he said, and closed the door before she could reply.

Julie sat there with her arms around Josephine and her

heart skipping like a little lamb in springtime while he came around the front of the car to slide in behind the wheel. He's a phase, she reminded herself sternly once again as he tossed the collar and leash in the back and she got a good look at an athlete's muscled arms and torso in motion. Just a phase.

"So what do you want to talk to me about?" she asked in as businesslike a tone as she could muster as he started the car. Josephine wriggled out of her hold, then stretched her length across her lap and closed her eyes. The warm weight of the little dog was soothing. Absently, Julie stroked Josephine's frizzy coat.

"Word on the street is that nobody local did this." His gaze touched meaningfully on the bruise on her temple. The Blazer headed for the street. "At least, if it's someone local, he's not one of the usual cast of criminals and perverts."

Julie felt her stomach tense as she tried to ward off memories of the attack.

"What does that mean?"

"It could mean a lot of things. A burglar escalating things to a whole new level. Somebody just moved in from out of town, whose MO's still off the radar. I'm not sure yet. Which is one reason I wanted to talk to you. I want permission to search your house."

Julie stared at him. A blue Corvette just outside her window kept pace with the Blazer, and Julie realized that they had reached the street and were moving with the flow of traffic. The wizened little man driving it, natty in a linen sport coat and striped shirt, had to be at least eighty. You go, guy, she thought with a tiny inner smile, and returned her attention with some difficulty to the topic at hand.

"The police have already searched the house." Her voice

was constricted. She did better if she just flatly refused to think about the attack.

Something in Mac's expression made Julie feel like there was a drop of ice water trickling slowly down her spine. Looking at him, she gave an involuntary little shiver. Josephine, apparently feeling the movement, looked up from her nap with big, questioning eyes. Julie rubbed her ears, and found some relief in doing so.

"I know," Mac said. Julie was starting to recognize that impassive face. It meant there was something he wasn't sharing with her. "But you've got to understand that the police are busy. They've got lots of crimes to investigate—and your husband made it clear to the powers that be that he wants to minimize this one. Any clue why he'd want to brush a brutal assault on his wife under the rug?"

Julie gave a bitter little laugh, and burrowed her fingers deep in Josephine's coat. "That's easy. The subdivision. Sid's company developed it, you know. It might hurt property values if people started thinking that women were being attacked in their own homes there. And Sid is really, really against anything that might hurt property values."

Josephine responded to the attention with an enormous yawn. Her lids drooped, and her head returned to her paws. Julie wished that she could rid herself of her own worries that easily.

"Property values are important." Mac's tone was dry.

"I thought you were supposed to be finding out who my husband bought the Viagra for." Julie deliberately tried for a lighter note. Having her stomach tie itself in knots was not a pleasant sensation, and she was getting tired of it.

Mac grinned, glancing at her, and the atmosphere did indeed lighten. "Hey, what can I say? I'm a full-service investigator."

Julie made a face at him, relieved that the knot in her stomach was easing. "For your information, Mr. Full Service Investigator, Sid's going to Atlanta this afternoon. He'll be gone for three days. So what are you doing about it?"

"I know that. You think I don't know that? That's another reason I wanted to talk to you. Ordinarily, I'd follow him, because cheaters tend to hook up with their honeys on out-of-town trips. But under the circumstances I think it's better if I stay here. I don't like the idea of leaving you on your own." A serious note entered his voice as he said that last.

"You think the guy's coming back, don't you?" This time her spine was assaulted by an icy river instead of an icy drop. Julie shivered again, more violently this time.

"Slow down." He saw her shiver and shook his head. "I don't necessarily think he's coming back. What I think is, it pays to be careful. Whatever happens, I'll make sure you're safe until we get this all sorted out. Trust me."

Julie took a deep, steadying breath. "I do."

The smile he gave her then was slow and sweet, and sexy as hell. "That's my girl."

His girl. God, what she wouldn't give to be. Phase or no.

The Blazer stopped, and Julie realized that they were pulling onto the grass verge in front of the DeForests' big brick house, which was across the street and catty-corner to her own.

"What are you doing?"

"I told you, I want to search the house. Now's the best time, because none of your neighbors are home during the day, and Sid's headed out of town. What I'd like you to do is come in with me, show me around, maybe walk me through what happened Saturday night. Are you up to it?" He put the car in park and looked at her steadily. Julie's every instinct quailed at the prospect. She had not entered the house since Mac had carried her out of it; Sid had spent the last two nights in it alone. Left to her own devices, she was more likely to fly to the moon than walk inside that house again. Even thinking about it made her start to hyperventilate.

But if Mac thought this guy would be coming back . . .

She took a deep, calming breath, clenched her fists so that her nails dug into her palms, and nodded. Josephine, sensing her unease, looked up again.

"I'll be right with you every step of the way." A smile crinkled the corners of his eyes as he glanced down at Josephine, who was getting to her feet in Julie's lap and arching her back in a luxurious stretch like a cat. "And hey, you've even got a guard dog on duty. What could be safer than that?"

It was hard to picture Josephine as a guard dog, Julie reflected, but she smiled gamely nonetheless. And, paradoxically, smiling made her feel better. And braver.

She still had her *I'm so brave* smile firmly in place when she walked around the front of the Blazer, Josephine cradled in her arms, to discover Mac affixing a large, white, magnetic sign to the driver's door.

LAWN-PRO LAWN AND LANDSCAPING, it said, above a local telephone number. Reading it, Julie's eyes widened.

"I keep it in the back for occasions such as this," Mac explained, in response to Julie's look. "Nobody ever gives me a second glance with this thing on the door. You'd be surprised how many of these services operate in neighborhoods like this during the day."

Indeed, now that she thought about it, Julie could hear the muted roar of a lawn mower in the distance. A glance around showed her a man sitting atop an orange commercial mower several yards over, paying them not the least attention as he merrily did his thing. Ordinarily, she never would have noticed him.

"It's called hiding in plain sight," Mac said as if he could read her mind. Curling a hand around her upper arm, he practically towed her up her own driveway.

The contrast between the relentless sun and baking heat outside and the cool, dim hush of the house couldn't have been more unsettling as, using her key, Mac opened the front door and they stepped inside.

He closed the door behind them. Julie's heart raced as gloom enveloped them, and her stomach felt like it was playing Twister. Her breathing quickened; sure enough, she was going to hyperventilate.

Stop it, she ordered herself as she took several hesitant steps inside her own front hall. Carefully she regulated her breathing: in and out, slow and steady.

At least, she thought, there were no words of warning from her little voice. If she ever heard that puppy again, she was listening up big time.

Josephine, lying contentedly in her arms, was a godsend. The little dog gave her something to concentrate on besides her fear. She was no heavier than Kelly or Erin on the day they'd been born, and her woolly coat reminded Julie of a fleece the girls had slept on as babies. Holding the dog closer, she grew calm enough to look around. There was no visible reminder of her ordeal, she was relieved to see: no footprints, no drops of blood, nothing. The house was pristine, and smelled faintly of Murphy's Oil. Of course, the cleaning service came every Tuesday and Thursday morning; that also accounted for the fresh sheen on the marble floor and the gleam on the just-polished furniture. Strange that the house should be exactly as it had always been, unchanged by what had happened within its walls, while she felt as if the attack had altered her inner landscape forever. Fear was now part of her internal language, which it never had been before.

Her glance fell on the imposing staircase with its wrought-iron railing, and her breathing quickened again as images of herself fleeing for her life down those steps scrolled unbidden through her mind. She could almost feel the hideous yank of a fist closing on her hair. . . .

"You okay?" Mac's hands dropped onto her shoulders, making her start. He was behind her, solid and strong and infinitely reliable, and it was this knowledge that calmed her down and enabled her to breathe normally again. She nodded, clutched Josephine closer, and, taking a tight mental grip on her courage, walked on toward the staircase, determined not to give in to the fear that threatened to engulf her.

Despite her determination, speaking was an effort; she swallowed, realizing her throat was dry.

"The cleaning people came today. If the police missed any kind of evidence, it's probably gone now."

Mac muttered something short and probably profane under his breath. Julie was almost at the foot of the stairs now, and he was a few paces behind her, looking around with weighing eyes. The marble floor, the crystal chandelier, the staircase that was designed to impress—the whole house that was designed to impress—would be new to him.

"I was in my bathroom . . ." Julie began, looking up the stairs. Then memory assailed her again, and she shivered and shook her head. "Mac, I don't think I can go up there."

"You don't have to do anything you're not ready for." He was right behind her again, and his hand just brushed over her bare arm in a comforting caress. "We'll stay downstairs, if you want." His eyes shifted past her to fix on the open door that led into the den. "Is that some sort of office?"

Julie followed his gaze, and nodded. "Sid's desk is in there, and his computer. He does quite a bit of work at home."

"Mind if I check it out?" he asked, already heading that way.

"Go ahead." She was talking to his back. Trailing him, she stood in the doorway of the den and watched as he conducted a quick search of the desk, opening the drawers and rifling through the contents, then turned on the computer.

"What are you looking for?" She was feeling better. Steadier, less jumpy. Having her back to the staircase helped, she thought, but she also knew that one day— one day soon—she would be able to climb those stairs. The knowledge eased something that had been twisted tight inside her. Coming back inside her house had been a necessary step in reclaiming her life, she realized.

Mac shrugged noncommittally. "I don't suppose you know the password to any of these files, by any chance?" He was staring intently at the screen, typing as he spoke.

Julie shook her head. "No clue."

Mac grunted unsurprised acknowledgment as he continued to point and click, then peck away at the keyboard, apparently trying words at random.

"Ah," he said moments later with obvious satisfaction, watching as text popped into view.

Julie did a double-take. She was just about to ask how he'd done that—clearly he had either figured out the password to one of the files or somehow bypassed the system's security—when an unexpected sound from somewhere behind her made the hair on the back of her neck stand on end. She spun around. In her arms, Josephine stiffened. The little dog's eyes stared alertly toward the kitchen.

Because there was no possibility of mistake: someone was entering the house through the garage door.

18

TERRIFYING MEMORIES CAME BACK IN A RUSH, threatening to swamp every last vestige of calm that remained to her. Julie's pulse raced, and her breathing grew choppy. Cold sweat broke out on her forehead and her palms.

"I'm right here."

Mac had obviously heard the sounds too. He was behind her before she could break and run, his voice low, one hand wrapping around Josephine's muzzle. Even as he spoke he drew Julie back inside the den. A glance told Julie that the computer was now dark and still; Mac must have turned it off.

"Keep Josephine quiet," he breathed in her ear, closing her hand around the poodle's muzzle as he removed his own. Julie obediently held Josephine's mouth shut, but to the dog's credit she showed no inclination to bark. Still, she seemed almost as petrified as Julie felt, and Julie wondered with the part of her mind that was still capable of entertaining such speculations if the dog was somehow able to pick up on her emotions. Josephine's slight body was stiff in Julie's arms, and her eyes bugged out, as shiny and round as black marbles in a nest of white frizz. Like Julie, she was breathing fast, and her heart was thudding.

Julie could feel it pounding in double-quick counterpart to her own.

"Shh." Mac's arm slid around Julie as they reached one of the two long windows overlooking the manicured back lawn and the pool. He pulled her with him behind the drapes that hung from ceiling to floor, letting the heavy taupe velvet and the whisper-soft sheer beneath wrap around them, hiding them from sight. Enveloped by the sickly-sweet aroma of the rose-scented air freshener that clung to the curtains, shrouded now in shadow, Julie discovered that she was trembling; fear washed over her in waves. Trying to keep her breathing under control, she leaned against Mac, her cheek resting against his chest, listening to the steady drum of his heart. Josephine remained stiffly alert in her arms. Julie prayed that the dog would remain silent and they would not be discovered. She didn't think she could live through another terrifying encounter, not even with Mac and Josephine the would-be guard dog for protection. Confronted, she would die of a heart attack on the spot.

Mac held her close, an arm hard around her waist. The sheer size of him was reassuring. She tended to forget what a big man he was until she was in his arms. A sideways glance told her that he had produced a gun from somewhere on his person, which he now held in his hand. It was the black, businesslike weapon she had seen before, when he had appeared like a guardian angel in her kitchen, when the monster had been hard on her heels and she'd been running for her life.

The world spun as she remembered, and for a hideous, horrible moment Julie feared she might faint. Mac's arm tightened as if he sensed her sudden weakness. She closed her eyes and rested heavily against him and counted to ten and forced the dizziness away by sheer force of will. Then Josephine whimpered, the slightest sound, and tried to pull away from Julie's hand. Julie realized that she was holding the dog's muzzle too tight even as the murmur of approaching voices made her shudder. Forcing herself to remain in the present, to remain focused, she loosened her grip on Josephine and apologetically cuddled her closer, drawn back from the precipice just in time. She could not, would not, let fear overwhelm her. If she succumbed to the mindless terror that hovered near, she might very well make some sound or do something that would reveal their presence, thereby endangering Mac and Josephine as well as herself.

But once she was in control enough to really listen, she realized that this was not the monster returned. At least one of the voices was all too familiar. This was—Sid. Sid and a woman.

Julie's spine stiffened. Her head rose like that of a doe's scenting danger.

"It's Sid," she whispered.

"Don't move, and don't make a sound." Mac's voice was scarcely louder than a breath. His arm around her hardened into an unbreakable band as though he feared she might pull away from him, might dart out and confront her husband there and then. Mac shifted position without loosening his hold on her, maneuvering so that her back was against the wall and he was in front of her, as if to both shield her and keep her in place. Julie once again got a good look at the gun in his hand. He had not lowered it, or relaxed in any way. His attention seemed to be divided equally between her and the newcomers who were now talking unconcernedly in the hall just a few yards away.

Julie realized that Mac considered Sid's presence a threat.

Before she could get all the implications of that sorted out in her head, her husband's voice came to her clearly.

". . . plenty of time," he said in a jocular tone.

"I guess I can tell her I had to run an errand, but I absolutely, positively have to be back by three." The woman's voice was young, giggly—and almost as familiar as Sid's. Julie froze, poleaxed.

"If you're in a hurry, we could always do it right here on the steps."

"Oh, Sid." A high-pitched giggle. Rapturous silence. Then, from a little bit farther away, as though they were climbing the stairs: "What time does your plane leave?"

"Four. God, you've got such a nice, tight little butt. . . ."

Even as Julie registered that bit of insult that had just been added to injury, the voices faded into indistinctness. Or, at least, Julie could no longer hear them distinctly, which worked just as well. There was another, muffled giggle, followed by distant footsteps and the sound of a door closing. She realized, with the kind of distant clarity that was a hallmark of certain dire situations, that Sid and another woman were in her bedroom. She felt as if, like Lot's wife, she'd witnessed something she wasn't supposed to witness and had been turned into a pillar of salt where she stood as a result.

She would never breathe, never move, never feel anything again.

"Come on, we're getting out of here." Mac's voice was a growl in her ear. Pillar of salt or not, he was moving her, thrusting his gun down the back of his jeans and taking Josephine from her and wrapping his hand around her wrist and literally dragging her from their hiding place.

With no will to resist, Julie allowed herself to be dragged: through the hall, the dining room, the kitchen, the garage, while visions of what she was leaving behind swirled through her head. Sid's Mercedes was parked in the garage. The big, black Mercedes that he drove so proudly as a symbol of his success.

"Wait," she said hoarsely, and freed her wrist from Mac's hold with a sudden yank. Before he could stop her, she was back inside the house, in the cool hush of her own kitchen, quick and quiet as a cat as she snatched what she needed from the pantry cabinet. Mac was already coming across the kitchen after her as she brushed by him again on her way back down into the garage, illusive as a drop of mercury as he reached for her, silent and focused and totally intent on her task.

With a flip of her hand and two quick turns of her wrist, she had the Mercedes' gas cap off. Then she upended the five-pound bag of sugar she carried, and, carefully using one corner as a funnel, poured the contents down the tank.

"What the hell . . . ?" Encumbered by Josephine, Mac wasn't fast enough to stop her. He came to a halt a pace away, looking at her like she'd suddenly sprouted horns and a tail.

"Sid loves this car," Julie said with savage satisfaction, screwing the lid back on and closing the little door. Only a small amount of sugar had spilled on the floor. She kicked it under the car with her toe so that no telltale sign remained.

"Remind me never to tick you off." A quick smile just touched his mouth as Mac grabbed her wrist again and pulled her out of the garage. Julie crumpled the sugar bag into a tight little ball as she was hauled bodily down the driveway.

"Get in," Mac ordered when they reached the Blazer, jerking open the door. He took the sugar-bag ball from her and tossed it into the backseat. A quick glance back at her house told Julie that the curtains had been drawn across the master bedroom's windows. A stab of some fierce emotion—fury, she thought, more than pain—made her grit her teeth.

"That was Amber," she said through her teeth, looking at Mac. "The no-good dirty rotten bastard is doing Amber in my bedroom. *On my bed.*"

The thought made her so mad she wanted to spit.

"Get in," Mac said again, practically pushing her inside. This time she complied—she really had no choice—and he dumped Josephine in on top of her and closed her door. Seconds later he slid behind the wheel, tossing the white lawn-service sign into the backseat where the sugar bag and Josephine's rejected collar and leash and no telling what else already took up space.

Josephine stood on her lap, wagging her tail and staring up into Julie's face, her expression worried, as if she somehow sensed that a crisis was occurring around her. Mac leaned across, opened the glove compartment, extracted a doggy brownie from it, and tossed it into the backseat.

"Go get it," he said.

Josephine, way ahead of him, had looked around at the first stretch of his hand toward the glove compartment and was already springing like a mini-kangaroo over the seat as he spoke.

"So who's Amber?" With another quick, frowning glance at Julie, Mac got the car under way. Julie was barely aware of the changing scenery that meant they were moving. She felt numb, the kind of numb that signified deep psychic shock.

And why not? The life she had known for the last eight years had just been blasted into oblivion.

"She works for me. She and Meredith. At Carolina Belle. I don't believe this." Julie began to laugh, the sound high-pitched and unnatural to her own ears. "No wonder Sid needed Viagra—to keep up with her! She's only twenty—the same age I was when Sid met me. She's a brunette, like me. And last year she won Miss Angel of Beauty. He's replacing me with me."

"Men do that a lot." Mac's voice was even. The glance he sent her way was stark with concern. "There's a certain type they like, and they go back to it again and again."

"Oh, so now I'm a type." Julie bared her teeth at him in a feral travesty of a smile. "Thanks a lot."

"Hey, it could be worse. At least you're a beautiful, sexy type."

This attempt to make her feel better, if that was what it was, failed miserably. Her fists clenched. "I hate him so much I want to kill him. I want to do him harm."

A flicker of a smile lightened his expression. "That sugar in the gas tank thing was a pretty good start. You know, that car cost about eighty grand."

"Yeah." There was a wealth of pleasure in Julie's voice. Then it faded. "Of course, insurance will cover it. He'll just get another one."

"Look, I know you're hurting, I know you're upset, but you need to focus on the big picture here. You got him right where you want him. He just handed you his head on a plate." Mac fished his cell phone out of the console and punched a button. "Hang on a minute. I want to make sure Sid's walk on the wild side gets recorded for posterity."

Before Julie could reply to that, someone on the other end of the phone answered. The voice was distant and faintly muffled, but she could hear every word.

"Mac, man, where you at? Rawanda's been looking for you—seems Ed Barundi came stomping in, all hot because his girlfriend found out about the background check we ran on her and dumped him—and she said you're not answering your cell."

"Yeah, well, never mind that now." Mac frowned, and hung a left that had them heading back toward downtown. "You're working on the Laura Simmons thing, right?" There was an affirmative sound on the other end. "That puts you about five minutes from here. I need you to come on into Summerville as quick as you can and get as much audio and visual as possible on a couple shacked up in the upstairs front bedroom at 451 Magnolia in the Sutherland Estates subdivision. You got that?" He repeated the address.

"Who you got in there?" The voice sounded interested.

"Just do what I tell you," Mac growled. Then, before the sputter at the other end could resolve itself into words, he added: "Catch you later."

Then he disconnected.

Julie frowned at him. "Who was that?"

The phone rang shrilly before he could reply. He glanced at it, grimaced, apparently at the number that was displayed on the caller I.D. readout, hit the power off button, and dropped the phone back down into the console. "My partner. That was him calling back, too. Sometimes he wants more information than is good for him. Don't worry about it. We need proof that Sid's shacked up with your employee in the marital home so that it doesn't deteriorate into just a he-said, she-said kind of situation. Even if it's just the two of them leaving the house together. Whoever said a picture is worth a thousand words knew what he was talking about, at least in court."

"I'm going to have to fire Amber," Julie said numbly, losing focus as some of the ramifications of what she had just seen started to occur to her. "How does this sound? She walks in from her long lunch and I meet her at the door and say, *You're fired for screwing my husband.* She's worked for me for over a year. I liked her."

"Probably you shouldn't go back to work right now. Give the worst of the shock time to wear off."

"Take two aspirin, and fire her in the morning?" Julie smiled without humor, then frowned, thinking back. As far as she'd known, Sid had only ever met Amber casually, on the very few occasions when he had stopped by the shop. If there had been signs of what was going on, she had missed them. "She's probably been sleeping with Sid for most of the time she's been working for me. I had no idea. I can't believe I had no idea."

"That's how it usually works." There was a certain rough sympathy in his voice.

"How it usually works *stinks.*"

"Yeah."

Julie was outraged; she was sick at her stomach; she was frightened and sad and angry and a thousand other emotions all at the same time. Then yet another unwanted ramification popped into her head.

"I'm going to have to tell my mother I'm getting a divorce." It was a groan.

Mac smiled faintly. "You say that like it's the worst thing in the world. What, do you have one of those mothers from hell?"

Julie tipped her head back against the seat, closed her eyes and shook her head. "My mother is wonderful. She's super, fantastic, one of a kind. I love her. But—my being married to Sid means a lot to her. Sort of like I won the ultimate prize. When she finds out I'm getting a divorce, she's going to just die. She'll probably try to get us into counseling or something. And she'll definitely drag my sister into it. Then Kenny—my sister's husband; he works for Sid—will get dragged into it, too, and when I still insist on getting a divorce everybody will have to choose sides and Kenny'll lose his job and the girls—my nieces—will be destitute and . . ."

"Whoa," Mac said. "It won't be as bad as all that."

Julie straightened in the seat, clenched her fists and looked at him. "Yes, it will. It will be just that bad." A lump rose in her throat and she swallowed painfully. "How could Sid *do* this? When we got married, I thought we would be married forever. I was so *happy.*"

Her voice broke.

Mac's lips compressed. The glance he shot her was unreadable. "You'll be happy again. Think of this as a pothole in the road of life. You'll come out on the other side as good as new."

Julie made a disbelieving sound. "How do you know? Were you ever married?" A hideous thought occurred to her, and the lump was forgotten as her eyes widened. Another blow was more than she could bear. "You're not married now, are you?"

Mac shook his head, and Julie found that she could breathe again.

"Not now. For about nine months five years or so ago."

"You're divorced?"

Mac nodded.

"What happened?" Her voice was hushed, as if she was asking for the details of some dreadful accident.

Mac shrugged. "When I got fired from being a cop, my wife decided that she couldn't deal with a husband who was not only an embarrassment but couldn't pay the bills. She left me. Best thing that could have happened to me. Of course, I didn't think so at the time."

His insouciant attitude hid a world of remembered pain, Julie was sure. She reached out and laid a consoling hand on his jeans-clad thigh.

"She must have been insane."

Mac gave her another of those inscrutable looks, and covered her hand with his. His hand was far bigger than hers, long-fingered, broad through the palm, bronzed, utterly masculine. And warm. Very, very warm. Just like the muscled thigh beneath the jeans. Lately, it seemed, she had craved warm.

"Funny, I was just thinking the same thing about Sid."

It took a couple of seconds for that to sink in. When it did, Julie felt her heart skip a beat. She drew in a deep, cleansing breath.

There were two ways to look at what had just happened, she thought. One: Sid had betrayed her. Or, two: Sid had set her free.

It was Julie time, she told herself as she had once before. Only now, there was nothing and no one, not even her own conscience, to stand in the way of her going after what she wanted.

She looked at Mac.

"What are your plans for the afternoon? Do you have any, or are you free?" Her tone was politeness itself.

But something in her voice or expression must have been off kilter, because he looked at her carefully.

"I'm as free as I want to be. Why?"

Julie smiled.

"Because I want you to take me somewhere where we can be alone and take off all my clothes and fuck me until I scream."

19

"W*HAT?*" M*AC* *COULDN'T* *BELIEVE* *HIS* *EARS*. He had a
sudden mental vision of a small gray mouse with a head
full of careful plans looking to the left, looking to the
right, stepping cautiously into the road—and being flattened from behind by an eighteen-wheeler. His bodily
response was so sudden and enthusiastic that it was
painful. His mental response was less clear-cut. "Darlin',
you want to be careful what you say. Somebody just might
take you up on that kind of offer one of these days."

"I want you to take me up on it right now. I want you
to take me somewhere we can be alone and take off my
clothes and . . ."

"I heard you the first time," Mac interrupted hastily, not
sure he could live through the exquisite agony of hearing
it again.

Julie smiled, unfastened her seat belt, curled both long,
slim, tanned and utterly bare legs beneath her on the
black leather seat—did the woman never wear stockings?
he wondered testily—and leaned forward to put a hand
on his shoulder and her tongue in his ear.

"Jesus," Mac said, and drove off the road. Gravel from
the shoulder flew every which way before he got the car
straightened out and all four wheels once again on the

pavement. By then Julie was back in her seat, her seat belt refastened, smiling at him like a cat with its eye on a nice, plump canary.

He had a feeling that he was earmarked for the role of canary.

"Don't you want to?" Julie asked, giving him a look that would have melted a glacier.

His instant, instinctive answer was, more than he had ever wanted anything in his life. He would gladly have surrendered one or more body parts for the privilege. But there were other important considerations to keep in mind, not the least of which was that his original objective here was not nailing Sid's wife, but nailing Sid. Sid was the key to finding Daniel. He was more sure of that with every passing day. He'd just had a major break: he'd managed to access All-American Builders' files from Sid's home computer.

Hard to believe Sid couldn't come up with a better password for his business files than Vader, as in Darth Vader of *Star Wars* fame. Sid used to use that name on a vanity plate on the front of his black Porsche when he was a teenager. The car, license plate and all, had made a big impression on the little kid Mac had been then. The moniker was still as appropriate as ever. In fact, more so. It fit Sid to a T, just as it always had. Like Vader, Sid was corrupt almost all the way through.

Of course, most people probably didn't know that once upon a time—Mac had no idea if he still was—Sid had been a big *Star Wars* fan. Daniel had been, too. Mac, as little brother, had soaked it all up.

And it had just paid off.

Thanks to the finger-sized memory chip he carried on his key chain for just such emergencies, the contents of those files were dangling from the Blazer's ignition at that very moment. As soon as he'd accessed the information, he'd pulled the business end of the memory key from his ring, plugged it into an open USB port, and downloaded. The whole operation had taken perhaps a minute. When he got home, he would transfer what he'd captured to his own computer and examine it at his leisure. If what he hoped was on there somewhere actually turned up, all he would have to do was make a few calls to set in motion the ultimate payback.

Of course, sleeping with Sid's wife would be a pretty good advance payment on that payback. The trouble was, he didn't want to sleep with Sid's wife. He wanted to sleep with Julie. Beautiful, feisty, sexy Julie. Julie the temptress. Julie the enchantress. Julie the siren of his dreams.

Not Julie Carlson. Just Julie.

And that was a complication. A huge complication that he would never in a million years have foreseen.

For almost half his life, his goal had been to find out what had happened to his brother. He was as certain as it was possible to be without actually knowing it for a fact that Daniel was dead, and was almost certain that, whatever had happened, Sid was involved. If so, he meant to see that Sid got everything that was coming to him. The difference now was that he was equally determined to keep Julie safe while he did it. She was an innocent caught up in a dirty little war she didn't even know existed. She deserved better than to be a pawn in Sid's game.

Hell, she deserved better than to be a pawn in his game, too.

Looking at her, all big eyes and lush lips and sexy curves that hid an inner sweetness that was almost more attractive to him than her very attractive outer package, Mac could almost find it in himself to forget the past; he

could almost walk away, taking Julie with him as payment, and call it even.

Almost.

He wanted her so much that under any other circumstances in the world he would have gladly jogged barefoot
over hot coals to get to her. And here she was, his for the
taking, begging him to carry her off to bed. But no matter
how much he wanted to, he discovered to his own disgust
that he couldn't just turn his back on the past. Daniel's little brother was still bound by unbreakable ties of love and
loyalty, even after all these years.

There was Julie to consider, too. To take her when she
trusted him, when she thought he was no more than some
stray PI who had stumbled into her life by accident then
stayed to help her just because she needed help, would be
wrong. In its own way, it would be a betrayal almost as
bad as any of Sid's.

If there truly was such a thing as cosmic retribution,
this time it seemed to be directed right at him. If he'd been
in a laughing mood it would have been almost funny:
after all, the cosmic joke was now on him. But he found
that under the circumstances he couldn't summon even so
much as an ironic smile.

He wanted Julie too much. And, in good conscience,
he wasn't going to be able to take what he wanted.

"Hell-o-o."

Julie's tone brought Mac back to the present as suddenly as if she'd snapped his arm with a rubber band. He
realized that he'd been lost for far too long in the
labyrinthine corridors of his own private hell.

"Remember me?" She waggled her fingers at him in a
smart-alecky little wave as he blinked at her. With her
legs still tucked up under her and her truly inspiring
body turned sideways to face him and her black hair

flowing loose over her shoulders and her big brown eyes fixed on his face, she looked like the embodiment of every sexy dream he'd ever had. "I just asked you to sleep with me."

God give him strength. He was going to need it.

"I heard you," he said with commendable coolness. "You might want to slow down and think about what you're saying for a minute. What you're suggesting here is basically a revenge fuck. And believe me, darlin', if you go through with it you'll hate yourself in the morning."

"No, I won't," she said, those eyes going all heavy-lidded and sultry on him. If Mac hadn't been driving, he would have closed his own eyes to block out the sight. "I've got my life back, and from now on I'm going to do exactly what I want. And right now what I want to do is you."

Jesus H. Christ. If she made him any hotter he'd self-immolate right where he sat.

"You're a head case, you know that?" He shot her a grim look. If he slept with her, it would be even more of a revenge fuck than she knew, although it was growing harder with each passing second to keep that firmly fixed in his mind. "And you're turning me into one, too."

Julie stared at him for a moment without saying anything.

"You don't want to? Fine."

She uncoiled her legs, shifted position so that she was facing forward, crossed her arms over her chest and flopped her head back against the seat. Then she closed her eyes. Silence ensued. Finally able to focus on what he was doing, Mac took a deep breath, glanced around and realized that he had turned onto the expressway and gotten almost halfway back to Charleston with no awareness whatsoever of what he was doing. He was heading toward his house, he realized, and at the same time realized why.

Take me somewhere where we can be alone. . . .

Such was the power of suggestion—especially when he wanted what she was suggesting so much that he was going nuts trying not to think about it.

"Feel like going for a walk?" he asked, searching for an alternative—public—destination fast. "I think we need to walk. And talk. Yeah, some talking is definitely what we need to do here."

She opened her eyes and shot him a look. Forget sultry. Now she looked mad.

"I don't want to walk. Or talk. If you want to play psychiatrist, fine. Just not with me. Forget I said anything, okay? Just take me back to the shop."

Great. Now she sounded—and looked—downright militant. She'd done nothing but surprise him since she'd slammed into his car in the Pink Pussycat's parking lot. There was plenty of piss and vinegar mixed in with that innate sweetness, enough to keep any man hopping. He thought about the sugar down the gas tank, and succumbed to an involuntary inner smile even as he had the unsettling feeling that in her current state of upset she might be capable of any degree of mayhem. The best thing to do was give her time to cool off. No matter what she said, he was not letting her out of his sight. Not until he was sure she was not going to go off the deep end in some hideously self-destructive way.

Forget the gas tank. Uneasy visions of her finding somebody else to join her in her revenge fuck danced through his head.

"Did you hear me? I want to go back to the shop."

He'd just passed one of those clover-shaped exits where he could have done an easy one-eighty and headed back toward Summerville, and she had obviously noticed. Mac made a face at the windshield and kept on trucking down the expressway toward Charleston.

A more specific destination would no doubt occur to him when he got there. Maybe the beach. . . .

"Are you *ignoring* me?"

Now she was mad at *him.* Mac did a mental—at least he hoped it was mental, because if she saw such a thing he knew from experience that he was liable to get bopped upside the head—eye roll. God save him from women when they were being irrational.

God save him from women, period.

He tried a placating tone. "Julie . . ."

"Don't you *Julie* me. You take me back to my shop. Right now." She crossed her arms over her chest, and punctuated her words with a killing glare.

He strove for patience, and even tried to inject a note of humor into the situation. "You wouldn't want me to make a U-turn in the middle of the expressway, would you?"

"If that's what it takes."

Irrational didn't begin to cover it. Mac's patience was starting to fray around the edges.

"You got a death wish, that's your problem. Fortunately for us both, I don't."

"I want you to turn this car around right now."

Mac discovered that his teeth were clenched. He drew in air through them as he tried once again to think the situation through. The problem was, it was difficult to think clearly when his dick was roughly the size and shape of the Washington Monument.

Especially when his brain seemed to be in cahoots with his dick.

"Too bad," he said, perfectly pleasantly.

She stiffened like someone had just shoved a poker up her sweet little ass, and gave him the kind of glare that would have reduced a lesser man to blubbering idiocy on the spot.

"You know what?" She smiled at him. It didn't take more than the briefest of sideways glances to recognize it for the crocodile smile it was. "You don't get to make the decisions here. I do. Me, employ*er*. You, employ*ee*."

Mac's patience snapped.

"No, it's more like, me, sane. You, temporarily nuts. Until that changes, you're not getting out of my sight. So live with it."

The exit he always took to get home was next, and Mac found himself pulling over into the appropriate lane automatically. Why not? he thought, and took it. There were many public places he could drive to from there. If not the beach, which was sure to be thick with tourists about now, then the Battery. . . .

"Don't you take that line with me, you—you *man*." Julie's fists were clenched and her eyes snapped. "Is that why you think you can tell me what to do? Because you're a man? Well, I've got news for you: So what? All that means is that your brains are zipped up inside your pants ninety percent of the time. Men make me sick. I *hate* men. All men. You included."

Mac had to admit, in all honesty and in light of his own situation, that there was at least a grain of truth in what she said. But in the interests of retaining what was left of his cool and keeping a lid on the situation, he didn't reply. Instead, he watched from the corner of his eye as Josephine, obviously having finished her dog biscuit, hopped up on the console from the backseat. Long strips of what looked like noodles hung from her mouth. White plastic noodles . . .

Mac's jaw dropped.

"She ate my sign!"

"Red light!" Julie yelled.

Glancing around, Mac saw that she was right and stood on the brake. The Blazer stopped with a lurch and a squeal of tires. Mac took a deep breath, looking at the rush of traffic charging past. During the day, this was one of the busiest intersections in Charleston—he knew, because his house and the office of McQuarry and Hinkle were approximately three blocks to the north and he had to fight through this mess every day—and, if it hadn't been for Julie, he would have plunged right into the middle of it.

The consequences wouldn't have been good.

Damn dog, he thought, giving Josephine an evil look. If he'd been into crediting animals with humanlike emotions, he would have sworn she smiled at him, plastic noodles and all.

Then his attention was abruptly, forcibly refocused. There, at the corner of a four-way intersection refereed by a posse of traffic lights, with cars lined up impatiently on two sides and rushing bumper to bumper across the middle in an impenetrable line, Julie simply opened the door and got out.

For a moment Mac couldn't believe it. One second she was making outraged noises in the seat beside him, and the next she was out the door, slamming it behind her so hard the car shook, then stalking with her back ramrod straight and her head held high between two idling cars as she headed toward the sidewalk.

"May God damn all female creatures to hell for all eternity," Mac said bitterly to Josephine, who didn't seem impressed. Then he shoved the car into park and got out.

Feeling like the biggest fool alive, furious enough to twist nails into pretzels with his bare hands if he'd been handed any, Mac went after her.

When he caught up to her, after making an end run

around throngs of tourists and shoppers and what seemed to be a whole bus full of kids on a field trip, most of whom were armed with drippy ice-cream bars, she was still marching along at a pretty good clip.

"Just hold it right there," he said through his teeth, grabbing her arm.

She stopped dead, and whirled to face him.

Her whole body was quivering with temper. Her head was high. Her eyes were enormous and shooting sparks.

And tears were tracing bright paths down her cheeks.

"Fuck," Mac said, and meant it.

"Fuck *you,*" she snapped, trying without success to pull her arm from his grasp. She then ruined the whole touch-me-and-die thing she had going on by sniffling. He stared down at her, feeling as if he had just taken a punch to the stomach. She looked furious and pathetic and so gorgeous that she stole his breath, all at the same time. When he didn't say anything more, her eyes flashed dangerously, and she opened her mouth to yell at him—he could tell that was what she had in mind, her eyes telegraphed her intention and she was still bristling with rage—so he did the only thing any sane man faced with such circumstances could do.

He pulled her into his arms and kissed her.

And even as he did it realized that he had just done a swan dive out of the frying pan straight into the sizzling heart of the fire.

20

T HE SOUND OF BLARING HORNS penetrated Julie's consciousness slowly. Before she had quite registered exactly what she was hearing, Mac lifted his head and seemed much struck by the cacophonous sounds.

"Fuck," he said again, glancing around, then focused on her. Those beautiful blue eyes narrowed with some emotion she couldn't quite put a name to as they ran over her face. His mouth compressed into a thin hard line. She was in his arms, her body plastered to his, her hands locked behind his neck, her face tilted toward his, blinking up at him with some bemusement. The cause of her tears—indeed, the tears themselves—was forgotten for the moment. The sun reflected blindingly off the shopwindows and the roofs of cars cruising past, the smell of exhaust hung heavy in the muggy air, and Mac felt hard and strong and absolutely right against her.

Julie realized that once again she was just exactly where she wanted to be. Except, of course, for the blaring horns.

Mac had to raise his voice to be heard over them. "Look, I apologize, okay? Anything I said to upset you, I take it back." But, she thought, frowning, he didn't sound too happy about it. "Now, could we please get back in the car before the police show up?"

Comprehension caused Julie's eyes to widen. The honking, the shouts—Mac had abandoned the Blazer in the middle of the street. Before she had time to say anything, or even to fully surface from that soul-shaking kiss, he stepped back from the embrace, locked a hand around her wrist and strode back toward the car with her in tow, apparently taking her assent for granted.

Julie sniffed and wiped what was left of the moisture from her cheeks as she practically ran in her high-heeled sandals in his wake, not sure how she felt about being treated so cavalierly. The only thing she was sure of was, she wasn't ready to walk away from Mac again just yet.

This was getting interesting.

"Lady, do you need any help?" A paunchy man in a business suit turned to watch as she was hustled past. Julie realized that she and Mac were the cynosure of all eyes. Even preteens with their faces full of ice cream were staring with interest.

"I'm fine, thanks," she called back with a wave. Mac threw her an assessing glance over his shoulder as he pulled her after him into the street. The deafening honking had died down some. Julie realized that traffic on their side of the light was stopped again, and that at least one and possibly more traffic cycles had passed since she had gotten out of the Blazer. Cars were out of alignment in both lanes as those vehicles behind the Blazer that had tried to maneuver around it had been frozen in awkward place by the changing of the light.

Everybody inside every car that Julie could see looked mad as hornets. She waved at them feebly. More horns blared.

For his part, Mac ignored them all, heading straight toward the marooned Blazer. Just as he reached it, a woman popped up on the driver's side. Obviously a tourist, in a neon-green floral blouse and a big straw hat, she waggled a finger at Mac across the hood.

"Don't you know better than to leave a dog in a car?" she said in a scolding tone. "Especially on a hot day like this?"

Mac groaned, jerked open Julie's door, thrust her inside, and said something like *give me a break* to the woman as he shut the door again. Julie, tenderly wiping the remnants of Mac's sign from Josephine's mouth as the poodle settled down in her lap, missed the rest of the conversation, but Mac looked thoroughly teed off as he slid behind the wheel.

The woman, mouth still working, bent down to look in Mac's window. He ignored her, except to shoot her a scowl as she tapped imperatively on it. The light changed. The Blazer moved into the intersection, where they took a left. As quick as that they were anonymous again, for which Julie was thankful.

"So, you want to tell me why you were crying?"

Julie's chin lifted defiantly. That she had succumbed to tears embarrassed her—but she hadn't expected him to see them, and, hey, she was having a really bad day.

"It's my divorce. I can cry if I want to."

"Good point."

"If we're playing twenty questions, why did you kiss me?"

"Because I'm as nuts as you are?"

Julie bristled anew. "I am not nuts."

Mac opened his mouth as if to reply, seemed to think better of what he'd been going to say, and shot her an exasperated look.

"Do me a favor: Just sit there and don't say or do anything until we get out of the car, okay?"

"Fine." Julie settled back in the seat, not too unhappily, content to wait on events. That searing kiss had said volumes, even if he was inexplicably grumpy now.

The Blazer turned down a residential street, then another. The houses in this neighborhood were nothing like her own, Julie thought. These houses were older, small, with neat green postage-stamp yards punctuated by the occasional palmetto. Julie realized that this particular street was familiar just as Mac pulled to the curb and stopped.

She glanced around and began to smile. The last time she'd been here it had been the middle of the night, but she didn't think she was mistaken: Mac had brought her to his house.

Life was looking up.

Josephine apparently realized where she was, too, because she stood up in Julie's lap and yapped excitedly. Mac eyed the two of them with disfavor as he pulled the key from the ignition. When he opened his door, Josephine scrambled across his lap and hopped out.

"She doesn't have a collar on," Julie said, alarmed, grabbing for the dog and missing.

"Josephine has her faults, God knows she does, but she's not totally stupid. *She* knows enough not to go running off on her own."

There was so much not-so-hidden meaning in his tone that Julie stiffened. But he slid out of the car before she could reply. She opened her door and got out too, forestalling him in the act of coming around to fetch her.

"Was that some sort of dig at me?" Her tone was almost too polite as she walked around the hood of the Blazer toward him. He stopped where he was, on the curb, waiting, arms crossed over his chest, Oakleys once again in place. She couldn't see his eyes, but his stance and general attitude made it clear enough: he might have succumbed enough to bring her to his house, but he wasn't happy about it.

"You realize you just about caused a riot back there?" His usually drawling voice was clipped.

Julie stopped walking and glared at him, her fists on her hips. "Me? You're the one who abandoned the car in the middle of the street."

"Because you were childish enough to get out and take off. What did you think I was going to do, just drive away and let you go stomping off to God knows where all by yourself?"

"Believe it or not, I think I just about have sense enough to call a cab to take me where I want to go, which at the time was back to my shop."

"I *don't* believe it." Mac muttered this half under his breath, but Julie heard. She was just opening her mouth to verbally flatten him when a woman's voice called out.

"Mac! Mac! Have you seen Gus?"

Mac swung around in the direction of the voice. Shading her eyes, Julie discovered a wizened little woman in a faded floral housedress waving at them from a concrete stoop two houses down.

"No, I haven't, Miz Leiferman," Mac called back politely.

"Can you believe that man? I send him to take out the trash and he disappears. What do you bet he snuck around the block to have a smoke?"

"I wouldn't be a bit surprised." Mac cast a quick glance at Julie. Lips compressing, he caught her hand and started walking toward the house, pulling her behind him. "You take care, Miz Leiferman."

Mrs. Leiferman waved in answer, and turned to look searchingly up and down the street.

"She's a friend of my grandmother's, and the biggest

gossip in Charleston," Mac said under his breath as he unlocked his door. "She probably came outside just to get a look at you. Next time I go see Grandma, I guarantee you I'll get the third degree."

He whistled for Josephine, who true to his prediction came trotting up, then herded Julie and Josephine inside. Mrs. Leiferman was still on her porch, Julie saw, and she was once again looking their way.

"The neighbors spy on you for your grandmother?" The notion was so irresistibly charming that Julie gave up on being annoyed at him and smiled.

"She used to live in this house, and they used to be *her* neighbors. I bought it from her five years ago when she decided to move in with her sister and I got divorced. I haven't done much to it, except get rid of some bric-brac. My grandfather's old '55 Chevy is still parked in the garage. Anyway, Aunt Rose sold her house just a few weeks ago— that's when I got custody of Josephine—and she and Grandma moved into a retirement home together, but she still keeps in touch with the neighbors."

"I think that's sweet."

The house was just as she remembered it, Julie thought as she walked inside: cool and dark and pleasantly shabby. The curtains were drawn to keep out the worst of the after-noon sun. The couch and chair and TV were just where they had been before. The big difference was that newspa-pers and magazines no longer cluttered the floor by the chair. Looking closer, Julie discovered a pile of reading material stacked high on top of the TV, and her smile widened. Pet training seemed to be working: Josephine had obviously taught Mac to keep things off the floor.

"Yeah, well, you don't have to live with it." Sounding more disgruntled than ever, Mac closed the door behind them, shutting out Mrs. Leiferman and the street, then took off his sunglasses, placing them on a nearby end table. His gun, extracted from somewhere behind his back, followed the sunglasses. Meanwhile, Josephine looked up at Julie, wagged her tail as if in a doggy version of *excuse me,* and disappeared in the direction of the kitchen.

"By the way, you can forget about trying to pick a fight with me," Julie said to Mac over her shoulder. "It's not going to work."

"Darlin', I don't know what you're talking about."

Mac came up behind her. Julie was just opening her mouth to say something—she could never afterwards remember exactly what—when his arms slid around her waist from behind and his hands covered her breasts.

Sheer surprise caused her to stiffen and glance down even as the sight and feel of his hands flattening over her breasts sent fiery pinwheels of desire tumbling through her veins.

"Okay," he said, his breath stirring her hair, his body big and hard and swoon-making as it pressed against hers. "You got what you wanted. We're all alone. If you're still bound and determined on that revenge fuck, I'm your man."

Something about his tone—to say nothing of his approach—told her that he hoped to anger or shock her into declining. And, Julie reflected as she stood motionless for a moment while his hands tightened and squeezed provocatively, if she hadn't figured him out well enough by this time to realize exactly what he was doing, he might just have succeeded.

But she had.

She turned in his arms, slid her own arms around his neck, and took a moment to assess the situation. Her bare arms looked tanned and slender and graceful draped over the gaudy, parrot-filled palm trees growing up his rayon shirt. His tee looked very white indeed against the bronze of his throat. The breadth of his shoulders and the solid feel of his chest against her already sensitized breasts dazzled her. Even though she was wearing heels, the top of her head didn't quite reach his nose, and again she was reminded of the sheer size of him. He was frowning as he looked down at her, his brows drawn closer together than usual, his mouth still a little grim.

In Mac's case, Julie decided that grim was sexy. Actually, Mac was sexy, no matter what mode he was in. If grim was all she could get, she would take grim.

"So start taking off my clothes," she said, a tiny smile curving her mouth as her gaze locked with his. "And, later, don't forget the part about making me scream."

His eyes flared. Then his arms, which had been curved loosely around her, shifted so that his hands were gripping her hipbones. She got the sense that he was getting ready to put some space between them, and tightened her arms around his neck.

"Damn it, Julie," he began, his frown deepening so that his brows all but met over his nose.

"You're cute when you're grumpy," she said.

"Cute?" He sounded revolted, and she had to grin. Then she did her best to forestall further conversation by the simple act of going up on tiptoe and pressing her mouth to his. Kissing him like this just because she wanted to was such a luxury, she thought as her lips made the first butterfly contact with his. It signified that their relationship had taken a whole new turn. Above and beyond the blazing sexual attraction that was making her toes curl, there was an easy intimacy between them, a friendship, a caring, that she suddenly treasured. Being with Mac like this marked the beginning of a whole new chapter in her life, she realized with a feeling very close to wonder as her lips molded themselves coaxingly to the warm firmness of his and her tongue slid inside to beg his to come out and play. Even under the circumstances, doing this with just anybody wouldn't have been a possibility for her; he could call it a revenge fuck if he wanted to, but the truth was that the only man she wanted to sleep with was Mac.

Just like the only man she wanted to kiss was Mac, and kiss him she did. His tongue was soft and hot but resistant at first as she touched it with her own. Her tongue prodded his, stroked it, and finally managed to draw it into her mouth. She nibbled the tip, sucked on it, and suddenly his fingers dug into her hipbones so hard they hurt and his tongue woke up and filled her mouth, taking the play into her court with a vengeance. She'd meant the kiss to be brief, no more than the merest tease, but with his response a wildfire ignited between them and the kiss took on a life of its own.

When she finally pulled her lips from his because she absolutely had to breathe, she looked up at him to gauge the kiss's effect. There were unmistakable signs that it had been a rousing success: his jaw was set, a flush had risen to stain his cheekbones, and his eyes were smoldering as they met hers.

"Julie." His suddenly hoarse voice bore no relation to his usual drawl. His fingers still gripped her hipbones hard. "This is a mistake."

Not what she had expected. Julie narrowed her eyes at him.

"What are you, a reluctant virgin?" She gave him another of those tiny smiles, pressing closer against him so that her soft curves were flattened against the solid, tantalizing length of him, and threaded her fingers through the short crisp strands of hair that covered the back of his skull. She looked up at him through her lashes—being a former beauty queen had its practical uses, she actually knew how to do things like that—and fluttered them at him flirtatiously. "Don't worry, I'll be gentle."

"I'm serious here." He sounded grimmer than ever, but his voice was thick, and Julie realized that the war was won even as he fought conceding. For whatever murky reason—professional ethics? gentlemanly scruples? a truly commendable distaste for getting involved with a woman who wasn't yet divorced?—he was trying to resist what he badly wanted to do. Fortunately, from her point of view, he was failing. His gaze was hot as molten steel on her face as, belying his words, his hands abandoned the beach head of her hipbones to slide slowly around her waist. His arms tightened, pulling her so close that she could feel every hard contour of his body. Even through the layers of their clothes, the heat and brawny strength of him made her tingle.

To say nothing of the impossible-to-miss erection that prodded her abdomen just below her navel.

"I'm serious, too," she said softly, her parted lips reaching toward his again. "Make love to me, Mac."

His pupils dilated, turning his eyes almost black. He inhaled, then made a little hissing sound as he released air through his teeth. His face tightened, throwing the chiseled planes and angles into sharp relief. Then his head bent, moving so slowly that her parted lips trembled in anticipation. His warm breath feathered across her skin. Her breathing quickened. Her lids closed. Her heart gave a great, shuddering leap. She wanted him so much she felt woozy from just thinking about it, and, she realized, such intense wanting felt wonderful. It had been a long time since she had wanted anything this much—so long she couldn't remember when.

Then his lips found hers, and she quit thinking altogether as he kissed her.

Julie sighed into his mouth, tightening her arms around his neck, and kissed him back for all she was worth. He owned this kiss, controlled it, and she reveled in the hungry fierceness of it. His mouth slanted over hers, hard and hot and demanding, as his tongue claimed her mouth. One of his hands slid down her back, tracing the curve of her spine. Julie felt a tug, heard a faint but distinctive sound, and realized with the tiny part of her brain that was still capable of registering anything outside of that blistering kiss that he was lowering her zipper.

Her knees went weak.

Cool air touched the bare skin of her back in the wake of his hand, and she shivered. He must have felt the slight tremor. Even as his hand came to rest at the base of her zipper, flattening on the small of her back and pressing her closer yet to the urgent evidence of his desire, he lifted his head to look at her. His eyes were ablaze with passion, and his breathing was uneven. Her body was plastered to his, so close she could feel every long muscle and bone and sinew of his body—and every telltale thump of his heart. It was beating fast, like a runner's, and she realized that hers was racing, too. Straining against the unyielding wall of his chest, her breasts felt heavy and swollen; her nipples puckered against the suddenly too-confining fabric of her bra. A hot quickening in her loins seemed to spiral through her body, turning her blood to liquid fire as it spread.

He simply stared down at her for a moment without speaking, his eyes heavy-lidded and so hot they made her tremble as they moved over her face. She knew her skin was flushed, knew her eyes were wide and slumberous, knew her lips were parted and damp and clearly eager for more. There was no hiding how turned on she was, and anyway, she didn't want to hide it.

This was Julie time, she reminded herself. From now on, what Julie wanted, Julie was going to do her best to get. And what Julie wanted most in the whole wide world right now was—

"Mac." His name emerged scarcely louder than a breath.

"Last chance to change your mind." He sounded as if he was having to work to keep his voice steady. His hand was already sliding inside her open zipper. Her gaze fluttered over his lean jaw with its faint suggestion of bristle, touched on the sensuous curve of his mouth, admired the classic lines of his cheeks, the straight nose, the blue eyes, the blond hair.

"Not on your life." She shook her head, shivering as the pads of his fingers stroked warmly along her spine. Her knees had been weak before; now they were pure Jell-O.

Their eyes locked. His were hard and restless and nearly black with wanting her. One hand caressed her bare back possessively; the other still lay flat on the lilac linen at the base of her spine. She could feel it just above the flare of her bottom, pressing her close. Julie moved, tilting her pelvis against him instinctively, then caught her breath as his body responded with a sexy move that sent undulating waves of desire rippling down her thighs.

"Remember you said that." There was a warning note to his voice.

Then she completely lost the thread of the conversation as he dipped his head. His mouth was hot and wet as it found the sensitive skin of her shoulder, then moved lower and crawled across her collarbone, nudging aside the loosened bodice of her dress. Goose bumps sprang up in its wake, and she moved against him again. Without warning his head came up, and he reached up to grasp her wrists and pull her hands from around his neck. He kissed first one palm and then the other, his eyes gleaming at her over her hands, then let go of her wrists and reached for her. Julie held on to his waist for balance and watched his face as he slid her dress off her shoulders. His gaze had shifted to the skin he uncovered, and he looked intent as the handkerchief-fine cloth slid down her arms. Before he could bare more than her shoulders and the upper slopes of her breasts, though, Julie stopped him by pressing one hand flat against the sliding front of her bodice.

"Wait." She shook her head at him.

He looked up then, meeting her gaze with a frown. She took a deep breath, martialed her wits and her knees, and stepped back out of his hold. He let her go without protest, although his mouth tightened as if to do so was an effort. His hands dropped to his sides, where they curled into fists as if he would prevent himself from reaching for her.

Julie smiled at him.

"Let me," she said.

At that his eyes flickered and flared and then seemed to ignite, but he didn't say anything. Taking silence for assent, she let go of the front of her dress and gave a provocative little shimmy. The fragile linen dropped with the faintest of rustling sounds to the floor. Then, still watching his face, she stepped out of the lilac puddle and nudged it aside with her foot.

For a moment she simply let him look, shaking the heavy black mane of her hair back from her face, keeping her back straight and her chin high. Her lips were parted as she breathed through them, and her hands rested lightly, sensuously on her bare thighs.

At least her husband-bait wasn't a dead loss, she reflected as his eyes seemed to scorch her. In fact, from the look on his face it had been worth every penny she had spent on it after all.

She knew how she must appear to him: slender and tanned and curved in all the right places, with a collar of creamy pearls around her throat and more pearls in her ears, her high full breasts with their puckered brown nipples swelling against the filmy, nearly translucent cups of her pale pink strapless bra and her stomach flat and smooth above tiny matching panties so sheer that the sable triangle of her sex was merely lightly veiled rather than concealed. She knew she had nice legs, long and elegant like the stems of hothouse roses, and she knew too that they should be looking extra enticing because her high-heeled sandals were designed for the sole purpose of emphasizing their loveliness.

In short, she knew she was nearly naked and looking hot. And just the idea that Mac was looking at her when she was nearly naked and looking hot made her want to jump his bones without further ado.

"Tell me something." Mac's eyes flickered up to meet hers, and his voice had a croaky quality to it that pleased her a lot. "Do you *own* any lingerie that isn't sexy as hell?"

Julie shook her head. "Do you mind?"

He gave a grunt of what might have been laughter. "It's a hard burden to bear, but I guess I can stand it."

Then his gaze dropped again. Julie's tongue came out to wet her lips because her mouth was suddenly dry. His eyes were all over her, hard and hot and hungry, sending delicious shivers of anticipation racing over her skin everywhere they touched. She watched his fists open, then clench, tighter than before, so tight his knuckles showed white, before opening again. Then he looked up, and his eyes met hers. The diamond-hard glint in his was enough to curl her toes.

"You are the most beautiful thing I have ever seen in my life, and I want you so much I am going out of my mind."

He moved even as he said it, so fast that she didn't even realize what he meant to do until he swept her off her feet and up into his arms and carried her off toward his bedroom, kissing her with a torrid eroticism that sent her senses spinning wildly out of control as he went.

21

L IKE THE REST OF THE HOUSE, the bedroom was dark, with the curtains drawn tightly over the windows, and faintly chilly from the air-conditioning. Mac carried her over to the bed, laid her down, and came down with her, his mouth moving from her mouth to her breast even as her back hit the mattress. The bed was unmade and smelled faintly of fabric softener, with what seemed to be a quilt and a single top sheet kicked to the bottom and spilling off one corner. The mattress was firm, and the sheet—she had some hazy awareness that it was dark blue—was cool and smooth against her back. But it was his mouth on her breast that riveted her attention.

Hot and wet and open, it rested against the tip of her breast, scalding her sensitive skin even through the barely-there layer of her bra. His tongue flicked over her nipple, causing it to instantly pucker into a tiny hard point that cried out for more attention. Then he did it again. Moaning, Julie dug her nails into his nape and arched her back.

"Mac . . ."

"Julie."

For the moment there seemed to be nothing more to say, for either of them. He shifted his attention to her other breast, kissing and licking her nipple until it, too, was hot and wet and throbbing. His jean-clad thigh slid between hers, pressing against the juncture of her legs, abrading the tender skin of her inner thighs and doing unbelievable things to the part of her that was already damp with readiness for him. The sheer pleasure generated by even that limited contact was unbelievable, and Julie tightened her thighs around his in instinctive response. He pressed harder into the center of her, and a mind-bending jolt of electricity shot through what was suddenly her body's focal point.

Julie gasped as a series of tiny, intense contractions followed, then went still in an effort to counteract the effect. It had been way too long since she had done this, she thought frantically as she relaxed her grip on his thigh and concentrated on drawing regular, steady breaths. He didn't even have her naked yet, and she was on the verge of coming like a house on fire.

Slow down, she told herself. She wanted to enjoy this. It had been so long—too long.

He lifted his head and flicked a glance at her. His thigh, solid and warm, shifted, rubbing against her sensuously as he moved. Julie felt her lips part, and, if the way she was feeling was any indication, her eyes glaze over. God, his leg moving against her there felt so-o good. . . .

"Let's see, what came next? Oh, yeah, you wanted me to take off all your clothes." A smile just touched one corner of his mouth; belying it, his voice was husky and his eyes were ablaze.

Julie took a deep breath, unable to do anything but curl her nails into his shoulders by way of a reply as he propped himself on an elbow and reached behind her. Deftly he unfastened her bra and pulled it off, tossing it to one side. He looked down at the breasts he'd bared while her gaze fastened on his face. His jaw was set and his eyes glittered like jewels.

He cupped her breast in his hand as if to gauge its size and shape, then ran his thumb over the nipple that was already distended and glistening wetly from his mouth.

"Oh, God, Mac." At the exquisite sensation she gritted her teeth and curled her toes and tried to remember to breathe.

"They're beautiful," he said, guttural now, meeting her gaze, then covered her breast with his hand and kissed her mouth.

Julie wrapped her arms around his neck and kissed him back as devouringly as he was kissing her, loving the musky taste of his mouth, the unmistakably masculine warmth of his hand caressing her breast, the hard pressure of his thigh pressing between hers, the weight and friction of his still-clothed body lying on top of her nearly naked one. She wanted him naked, wanted to be naked with him, more than she had ever wanted anything in her life. Her hands slid along his broad shoulders, over the slippery rayon covering his back until she reached his waist. Then she burrowed beneath the fabric to touch his skin. It was warm and faintly damp and smooth; the muscles beneath, she discovered as she slid her hands up his back, were tensile and resilient. He shuddered beneath her touch, and lifted his head.

"Take off your shirt," she said.

He met her gaze, then reached down to pull off both shirts in a single supple over-the-head move. Before the garments were even all the way off, Julie stared, entranced, at the magnificent flesh he'd bared. She had forgotten just how breathtaking his naked torso was. His shoulders were bronzed and broad and thickly muscled; his chest was wide and tapered and covered with a thick wedge of ash brown hair through which she could see his flat male nipples. His abdomen was the weight lifter's six-pack, ridged with muscle, looking impossibly hard and enticing above the waistband of his jeans. The jeans themselves rode low on his hipbones, revealing his navel and a tantalizing arrow of hair that disappeared beneath them.

Julie realized that she was looking at the human equivalent of Godiva chocolate, the thing she had always lusted after most in all the world.

Now, the thing she lusted after *second* most. Mac had just claimed a hard-won first place.

"God, you're gorgeous." She unconsciously put into words what she'd thought since she'd gotten her first look at him sans Debbie gear.

"I think that's my line," he said, and bent his head to kiss her. Even as she kissed him back she ran her hands over his chest, intoxicated by the feel of the crisp hair that covered all his muscles like a particularly erotic frosting. Her nails gently scored his nipples and he groaned and came down on top of her, stretching out at full length. He was heavy, but she barely noticed, and didn't care. Sliding her hands over his shoulders and around his neck, she absorbed the hard weight of his body pressing hers down into the mattress with a sensation bordering on delight. The feel of his hair-roughened chest, so warm and powerfully muscled, against her breasts was unbelievably erotic. She moved sensuously against him, enjoying the heat and pressure, the delicious friction, of his body on hers.

When he lifted his head again at last, breathing deeply and looking down into her eyes, she cradled his head in her hands and wordlessly guided his mouth to her nipple, arching her back as she offered herself up to him.

This time, when his mouth closed on her breast, there wasn't even a thin layer of cloth between them.

If she had died in that instant, she would have died happy, Julie thought, closing her eyes and shivering at the sheer pleasure of it. The feel of his hot mouth fastening on her nipple, suckling it, laving it with his tongue, was exquisite. She moaned and moved and pressed his head to her breasts with a complete abandonment of what few inhibitions she had left to her. Her hands were buried in his hair; her legs were wrapped around his like ribbons around a maypole. He was lying between her thighs now, and her knees came up instinctively to accommodate him. This shift in position brought his jean-clad pelvis hard against the part of her that ached and burned and wept for his possession. He rocked against her, the movement deliberate, and she cried out. No longer able to resist what she knew was coming, she began to surge upward in urgent answer to his rhythmic movements.

"Easy." His head lifted, and the mind-blowing pressure between her legs disappeared as he eased himself away from Ground Zero just that moment too soon, lifting himself deftly off her. Even as she reached for him, aghast at being abandoned at such a crucial juncture, he caught her hands and pinned them to the mattress beside her head, then knelt over her, his thighs on either side of her legs now, trapping them together.

"Mac." Julie wriggled in protest, which, given that he was now touching nothing vital, didn't do the slightest bit of good. She bit her lower lip in frustration, scowling up at him as he looked her over with obvious appreciation. What he'd just done gave a whole new meaning to the phrase *so near, and yet so far.*

"Let's take this slow."

"I don't want to take it slow."

"Yes, you do. You just don't know it."

Against logic like that, what could she say? Anyway,

her heart was pounding so hard and she was breathing so fast that any kind of sustained, sensible talk—much less an argument on the merits of when to actually do the deed—was beyond her. He seemed maddeningly cool until she really looked at him. Then she realized that his eyes were heavy-lidded and burning hot and his lips were clamped into a thin line and his jaw was set as if he was having to work hard to maintain control. She watched him look at her, watched as the flush in his cheekbones spread to suffuse his whole face, and felt the worst of her frustration fade.

Then he appeased her even more by releasing her wrists to embark on a discovery mission, caressing each breast in turn, stroking over her stomach with an extra, comforting caress for the V-shaped bruise, dipping into her navel, trailing fire wherever he touched. His hands had a fine tremor to them now, she saw, and his muscled torso flexed with his every movement. Both circumstances were almost as potent an aphrodisiac as the way he was touching her.

"Pretty," he said softly, his fingers tracing the outline of her panties from hipbone to hipbone and over the filmy triangle between. Julie felt the tantalizing whisper-touch burn like a brand through the cloth to the soft nest of curls, then sucked in her breath as he hooked his fingers over the elastic and tugged her panties down her legs.

At last, she thought, and felt her body clench. He moved, kneeling beside her as he pulled her panties all the way down to her ankles. Watching dry-mouthed, feeling like her insides had suddenly been reduced to the quivery consistency of a jellyfish, Julie realized with a prickle of surprise that she was still wearing her shoes.

Mac picked up each foot and carefully eased her

panties over the delicate high heels. Then he tossed the wisp of pink gauze in the same general direction as her bra.

Nails curling into the mattress from the sheer effort of maintaining some semblance of control, Julie looked down at herself, at the brown-tipped globes of her breasts still glistening from the attentions of his mouth, at the delicate curves of her waist and hips, at the satin-smooth plane of her stomach, at the sable triangle between her thighs. Her eyes slid down the long-limbed grace of her own legs, separated now to an indecent degree as he held a slender, daintily shod foot with one supremely masculine looking hand wrapped around her ankle.

The sight of herself, naked except for a high collar of pearls and strappy purple sandals with delicate high heels, spread out before Mac like a feast, was the most erotic thing she had ever seen in her life.

"Great shoes." He still held her right foot in his hand, and as he spoke he turned his head and pressed his open mouth to the delicate bone of her ankle, which was circled by a skinny purple strap. Heart pounding, Julie felt streamers of delight ripple up her leg from the place where his tongue caressed her skin; her breath caught as she watched his fingers working at the tiny buckle. "I especially like 'em when they're all you're wearing."

Even as he spoke, Mac got the buckle unfastened and slid the shoe from her foot. He picked up the other one, and did the same thing.

Then he kissed that ankle, and suddenly his mouth was crawling up the inside of her leg.

As she realized where he was headed, Julie began to shake.

When he reached the velvety delta between her legs, she closed her eyes. He kissed her there, his mouth scalding. His tongue touched the tiny bud that quivered and ached for attention, and she cried out.

"You like that?" It was a rough whisper.

Julie nodded without opening her eyes.

"Thought you would."

Any other time, the smug masculine overtone of that might have caused her to bristle. But the pleasure she was experiencing was too exquisite to allow her to focus on anything else. She felt as if all her bones had turned to water and her insides to fire. Breathing in fast little pants now, clutching the sheet for dear life, she lay supine, her head thrown back, her body pulsing with tremors as he pressed his mouth to her needy flesh. His hands slid beneath her, closing on her firm round cheeks to lift her and hold her in place, and as his mouth worked its magic she thought she had died and gone to some place far more marvelous than heaven.

Her body burned and clutched and trembled; she bucked and squirmed under his ministrations like a worm on a hook. Her orgasm was there, right there, rising on the horizon like a blazing summer sun, blinding her with its promised brilliance, searing her with its building heat. . . .

And then he stopped what he was doing, stopped just like that, pulled his mouth back and heaved himself up and away from her and right off the bed.

"Mac!" Her eyes flew open. He was standing beside the bed, looking down at her, his eyes flaming, his hair mussed, shucking his jeans. She saw what he was doing, knew what was coming, but still felt indignant—and bereft. She lay there naked, watching him, trembling, weak with longing, so hot and hungry for him, her body so burning and empty and needy, that she couldn't even stay still. Her breasts rose and fell as she drew in quick panting breaths. Her legs and hips moved restlessly. Then his jeans dropped, and his shorts with them. She saw that he was enormous and *hung,* and she reached out for him because she just couldn't help herself.

He was already climbing back onto the bed when her hands found him. His shaft was burning hot velvet over steel and as her fingers closed around him he groaned and seemed at last to lose control. His eyes flashed at her, his jaw hardened, and every mouthwatering muscle she could see seemed to go taut as a bowstring. Then he was moving, pushing her down and coming on top of her, and she wrapped her legs around his waist and clung to his shoulders and arched up to meet him.

With one quick thrust he was inside her. He felt so unbelievably good, filling her to capacity and then some, that she cried out. Then he was taking her, hard and fast, plunging into her until Julie was so caught up in the pounding rhythm that she lost all sense of time and place in the fiery maelstrom of her response. Only dimly did she register that it was she who cried out again and again and again. When he kissed her, she tasted herself on his lips and shuddered. While she was shuddering he drove inside her with a shattering series of fierce, deep thrusts and she came, just like that, so violently that her body convulsed and she dug into his back with her nails and screamed his name, "Mac, Mac, Mac, Mac, *Mac!*"

"Julie," he groaned in answer, burying his mouth in the tender hollow between her neck and shoulder, and found his own release, grinding himself into her shaking body, then, finally, shuddering and going limp.

Afterward, she lay there, totally replete. Her eyes were closed and her body was motionless except for the random tremors that still racked it. Mac lay on top of her, sweaty, hot, his deadweight about as heavy as a truckload of wet cement. About as responsive, too. His face was buried in the curve of her neck, and his breathing was stertorous and growing louder.

She wondered if he had fallen asleep. From the feel of him, and the sound of his breathing, probably.

God, were all men alike that way?

For the first time since she had said I do, she had slept with a man besides Sid.

Could anybody say, adultery?

Julie opened her eyes. A wide bronzed shoulder blocked her view of most of the room. When she shifted her gaze to the right, a fair-sized section of close-cropped blond hair, an ear, the hard curve of his jaw, part of his cheek, and a glimpse of his parted lips—if the breathing that fluttered them wasn't snoring, she didn't know what it was—came into view.

Looking the other way, she saw a single window with floor-length blue drapes closed over it, an unadorned white wall—and his hand still curved possessively around her breast.

Julie felt a stab of squirm-inducing guilt. What had she done?

Her marriage was over, she reminded herself, averting her eyes from the sight of those long bronzed fingers cupping her so intimately, in every way but the legal. She had nothing to feel guilty about. Indeed, she had done just what Oprah had said most women do on the demise of a marriage—fall into bed with the first presentable guy who asks.

Only Mac hadn't exactly done the asking.

And he was a little bit more than presentable. All right, a lot more.

And she didn't regret it. Exactly.

How could she? The sex had been phenomenal. She'd definitely felt the earth move. She now *owned* the Big O.

But lying here with him like this, naked and sweaty and listening to him snore, felt—weird. Like she wasn't herself any longer. What she really wanted to do was get up and go home and take some time to just sort this whole thing out. But, she remembered forlornly, she had no home to go to. No home that felt like home, anyway. Not anymore.

First she'd been viciously attacked there. Then Sid had brought a woman—girl—child—*Amber*—into her house.

Julie realized that she was feeling sorry for herself, and took a deep breath. Instead of looking back with regret, she was going to look forward with anticipation. She was going to face her problems head-on, and deal with them one at a time. That's what she had always done, ever since she was a little girl. For too long now, her whole identity had been wrapped up in being Sid's wife. She was going to reclaim her life.

Phase One of her recovery was already over: she'd had down-and-dirty sex with a really hot guy.

Phase Two involved confronting Sid, firing Amber, contacting a lawyer, telling her mother, filing for divorce—in other words, blowing her life as she knew it off the map.

Okay, so the prospect was enough to give her hives. Get over it, she told herself. Phase One might have been more fun, but she was going to make it through Phase Two as well. The secret was, as she'd learned many times over, to just keeping trudging ahead one step at a time.

Her life might have been reduced to rubble, but she was going to survive. She was going to leave the shambles behind and move on.

And the first step in moving on was to get off this bed.

Some things—including the direction any future involvement with Mac might take—required perspective before any rational decision could be made, and in this particular case perspective required distance.

Stealthily, not wanting to wake him until she had come up with a mature and sophisticated response to the current situation, Julie pushed his hand off her breast. She would just wriggle out from beneath him and get dressed. . . .

He stirred, lifted his head, and looked at her. Julie felt her stomach clench as she met his eyes head-on.

So much for distance.

Feeling trapped and a little panicky, Julie held his gaze. With his hair all tousled and his eyes sleepy-looking and a small smile curving his lips, he looked like a man who was content with the world. Which of course he should be. She had just given him her all.

At the thought, Julie winced.

He must have seen, because his smile vanished, to be replaced by a searching look, and then a touch of wryness around his mouth. The hand that curved around her rib cage—the one she had just pushed off her breast—tightened. Its warmth and size felt uncomfortably intimate against her skin.

Feeling more trapped than ever, Julie tensed.

"So, was it as good for you as it was for me?" There was a slightly ironic note to his voice that told her that he was aware that she was not exactly planning to wrap her arms around his neck and beg for more.

Thank God he wasn't going all kissy-face on her, was Julie's predominant coherent thought as she registered his tone. She might be naked and he might be on top of her, but Mac was still being Mac, and she could deal with that. Kisses and cuddles she couldn't have faced. Not until she had her own feelings sorted out.

"It was good. Thank you very much. Now, would you

please get off me?" Her tone was polite: the kind of tone she had used frequently in the past to thank the hostess of a dinner party for a well-prepared meal.

Apparently he didn't appreciate it. His eyes narrowed at her.

"So now we're on to the hating yourself in the morning part, are we? Jesus Christ, Julie, how predictable is that?"

22

Mac DIDN'T KNOW WHY he felt as if he'd just found the winning lottery ticket in a jumble of papers in his wallet only to discover minutes later that the damned thing had expired the previous week. He had a beautiful, naked girl in his bed. A beautiful, naked girl he'd just shown a hell of a good time. A beautiful, naked girl he'd had a hard-on for since he'd first laid eyes on her.

What was there to get bent out of shape about in that?

"I don't hate myself, it isn't morning, and I believe I asked you to get off me. Please."

If she used that ultra-polite tone on him much more, he was going to lose it, Mac thought, rolling onto his side but keeping his arm around her so that she couldn't just spring up and take off. A fleeting mental picture of her hightailing it naked down the street with him equally naked in hot pursuit had a certain appeal, but he didn't think there was much chance of that actually happening and, anyway, if it did Mrs. Leiferman would have a field day and he'd hear about it later in spades.

"You ever hear of pillow talk?" He didn't know why her clear desire to put the steamy little interlude they'd just shared behind her bugged him so: he would have bet dollars to doughnuts on her having just that reaction. Her skin was silky and supple beneath his hand, and he had to fight an urge to stroke it, which he had a feeling would not, just at present, be well received. Her entire right side was pressed up against him, soft and warm, and she smelled totally delectable. The elusive fragrance of the perfume she habitually wore, mixed with the scent of her skin and the unmistakable aroma of sex, was the most potent aphrodisiac ever to assault his nostrils. Probably the scent was what was playing games with his head. While he was inhaling it, he couldn't think straight. "Something on the order of, *Oh, Mac, that was just wonderful?*"

"What do you want, a blow-by-blow?"

It was her snippy attitude, he decided, that annoyed him so, as well as a few other things. Her hands were covering her breasts now, he noticed, as if to hide them from his view. The truly delectable leg closest to him was raised and bent at the knee and tilted inward over her body, which pretty much kept him from seeing any other salient body part, too. She seemed to be forgetting that he'd just done a whole hell of a lot more than look at just about every square millimeter of her. By default, his gaze returned to her face. Then he wished it hadn't. Her eyes were big and brown and shooting off sparks at him. Her cheeks were flushed a rosy pink. Her hair was a mass of shiny black waves spread out like a halo around her head. Mac frowned. Even with her lipstick all kissed off and her nose shiny and her expression peeved, she was so beautiful she grabbed at his heart.

Then she drew her lower lip into her mouth and started to chew on it, and he felt himself start to get hard all over again.

Hell. What was happening to him here was not a good thing.

"Hey," he said. "Give the attitude a rest, okay? You had a good time. You came."

She quit chewing on her lower lip and glared at him. "Let me up."

He lifted his arm obligingly, and was rewarded for good behavior by an excellent view of her shapely butt and legs as she scrambled off the bed and stood up with her back to him. Propping himself on his elbow, he rather grudgingly admired creamy shoulder blades and the delicate curve of her spine and a truly bodacious set of butt cheeks before she crouched down out of sight to retrieve the top sheet from the floor. He craned his neck instinctively, but it was no use: she was already wrapping herself in yards of dark blue cotton. As she straightened, pulling the cloth modestly around her legs and tucking one end in between her breasts, he happened to glance down at himself. What he saw sent him grabbing for the edge of the sheet—only the fitted bottom one was available, and persuading it to part company with the mattress required a vicious tug—which he dragged across his waist to hide the fact that he was now at full mast.

Once she was swathed from armpits to ankles in voluminous folds of cloth, she seemed to consider herself girded for battle. Shaking her hair back from her face, taking a deep breath, she glared at him.

"Could you get up and get dressed, please? I've got to get back to the shop. I've got an important client coming in at three."

Mac glanced at his watch and smiled at her. Admittedly, it was not a nice smile. More on the nasty side. But hey, sweetness and light was beyond him for the moment.

"I'd say you're shit out of luck, Miss America. It's four-fifteen. And I thought we agreed that you weren't going back to work today."

"Oh, no! It was Carlene Squabb." Her face was a study in consternation. Then her gaze fixed on him, and darkened stormily. "And if you want to talk about attitudes, *yours* could use some major work. I don't know what you're so grumpy about. You got what you wanted."

"*Me?*" Mac's gaze slid over her from the tip of her tousled black head to her delicate pink-painted toes, which he could just see peeking out from under the layers of sheet, and he felt his sense of disgruntlement increase right along with other sensitive meters of his state of mind. "I don't *think* so. It wasn't *me* who said"—here he assumed his Debbie falsetto—"*take me somewhere where we can be alone and take off all my clothes and fuck me until I scream. All I did was oblige. And darlin', you did scream.*"

Julie's lips tightened and her eyes shot twin beams of pure fire at him. Then she seemed to make an effort to grab hold of her temper before she lost it entirely. Her fists clenched, her eyes closed—Mac imagined her mentally counting to ten—and she took a deep breath.

When she opened her eyes again the look she gave him was far cooler. Maddeningly so, Mac discovered. He'd rather by far fight with her than have her distance herself from him.

"Look, I'm not blaming you for this, okay? You're right, I wanted it, and nothing that happened here is your fault. I realize now that I'm in kind of an emotional state about ending my marriage, and having sex with you was a stage I had to go through to start really getting over it. If we could just put this whole thing behind us and forget it ever happened, that would be good."

A beat passed while that sank in. So he was a phase, was he? Mac found that he liked that less than anything that had come out of her mouth since she'd started talking—and that was saying a whole hell of a lot.

"Not a problem." Mac rolled off the other side of the bed and stood up, keeping a firm grip on the sheet as he went.

No point in letting her in on the fact that he was ready, willing, and able to go on to Round Two. He watched her gather up her bra and panties and realized that he was really, truly, royally pissed off. Which was stupid, he told himself. She'd offered him every guy's wet dream on a platter—a mind-blowing sex session with a hot babe without any of the usual female icky-poo aftermath—and it was making him mad?

What the hell was the matter with him?

The obvious answer, of course, was that she was enough to try the patience of a saint, and he wasn't planning to put in for canonization any time soon.

"Do you mind if I take a shower?" She was back in polite mode, which, he supposed, was no more or less irritating than anything else she'd done since she gotten her rocks off. He was fifty kinds of a fool to let her attitude get under his skin.

But he couldn't seem to help it.

"Help yourself." He gestured toward the bathroom, as polite as she was now, and awarded himself mental kudos for the poker-worthy cool front he was maintaining. As she headed toward the bathroom, she flicked him a sideways glance and one of her little Mona Lisa smiles. Then he was left to stare at his own bathroom door as it was firmly closed in his face.

Shit, he thought. That was just what he felt like, too: shit. Never in his life would he have imagined he could feel so crummy after such truly great sex.

What had just happened here?

Mac was still trying to figure it out as he rounded up his clothes from the floor, pulled them on, ran his fingers through his hair and headed toward the kitchen. The phone began to ring, but he ignored it. He had a pretty good idea of who it was, but he wasn't in the mood to talk to Hinkle just yet. He'd grab a beer, then maybe, if Julie was still in the shower—in his experience, women could drag a shower that should take them five minutes out for days—take a minute or so to upload the contents of Sid's files into his computer. After all, that was what this was all about, really. Not doing Julie. Getting Sid.

The sound of the shower followed him into the kitchen. Not imagining Julie standing naked under the spray required more effort than he was capable of at the moment. The ringing had stopped, he realized as he grabbed a beer from the refrigerator and moodily unscrewed the cap. Taking a swig, he headed on into the living room, only to stop dead on the threshold.

Josephine had the telephone cord in her mouth. The instrument lay on the floor, on its side, the receiver belly-up like a dead goldfish.

"Damn it, Josephine!" he barked. The poodle, not being stupid, jumped to her feet and bolted for the bed-room, still clutching the cord in her mouth, the severed receiver bumping after her across the hardwood.

Mac said a whole string of cuss words as he picked up the decapitated phone. There was nothing to do, he acknowledged, turning what was left of it over in his hand, except toss it. The thing was definitely dead.

Fortunately the extension in the bedroom could take over until this one was replaced. He unplugged the corpse from the wall outlet, and placed it on the end table beside his gun to await a decent burial in the garbage.

Chalk the death of his phone up as just one more in a series of things, large and small, that had not gone his way today.

Mac yanked open the curtains, hoping that an infusion of sunshine would improve his mood. The room was immediately flooded with light, which made him blink and revealed his every housekeeping deficiency from the cobwebs in the corners to the dust on the coffee table. Great. He sank down on the couch, propped his stocking feet up on the coffee table, and took another swig of beer. His gaze fell on Julie's discarded dress, crumpled into a pale purple heap near the wall. If he was not a gentleman, he would just sit here and wait until she emerged from the bathroom to fetch it. If he was, he'd pick it up, shake it out, carry it back to the bathroom, knock on the door, and yell that he was leaving her dress on the doorknob for her when she was ready.

The decision wasn't hard. He stayed where he was, watching swirling dust motes joust in the sunlight and chugging his beer.

There was a knock at his front door. Mac frowned, and cast a glance over his shoulder out the front window. He and Julie had been inside for well over an hour. Mrs. Leiferman must be about to expire of curiosity by now. It wasn't her usual MO—his activities were usually only fair game when he was outside the house—but it was possible that the old lady couldn't take the suspense and had come up with the bright idea of coming over to borrow a cup of sugar or something of the sort.

But the tailored white pants leg he could see on his stoop did not belong to Mrs. Leiferman. It was definitely a male leg. It didn't take a genius to guess whose.

He got up and went to answer the door.

"What the fuck is the matter with you?" Hinkle demanded in a furious tone the moment he opened the door, pushing past him into the house before Mac could say a word. "You got a spark plug loose, gettin' mixed up with that shit again? You got your panties in a twist about Sid Carlson, that's your business. But I'm not getting involved, you hear? That dude is *bad,* and you know it."

"Hey to you too," Mac said mildly, closing the door. Natty as always in a white suit with a black shirt and tie, Hinkle stood in the middle of the living room, arms akimbo, glaring at him. Mac walked over, picked up his beer from the coffee table, drained the last mouthful, and gestured at Hinkle with the bottle. "Want a beer?"

"Hell, no, I don't want a beer. I want to know what the hell you think you're doing nosing around Carlson again. Soon as I figured out who I was taking pictures of, I about crapped my pants. I tried to call you, but you're not answering your damned cell phone—again!—and when you picked up here, you didn't say a damned word. So here I am, asking you to your face: What the fuck are you *doing?*"

Mac thought about explaining that it had been Josephine who picked up, not he, but it didn't seem worth the effort. Instead, he asked, "Did you get the pictures?"

"Did I get the—" Hinkle looked like he was about to blow a gasket. "It doesn't matter whether or not I got the pictures. We aren't going to use them. You hear me? Are N-O-T *not.* Remember the last time you tried taking him on? Remember that we were cops, back then? Remember things were going pretty good for both of us? And what did you do? You got a burr up your ass about Sid Carlson. You went after him, and he nailed your ass to the wall—and mine too. I'm not making that mistake twice, and neither are you, if I can help it. Face the facts, Mac: You aren't going to take Sid Carlson down. If you keep trying, he'll be the one taking you down, and this time I . . ."

He broke off, looking at something beyond Mac's shoulder, his eyes widening. Mac felt a premonition of disaster, and glanced around. Sure enough, there stood Julie, barefoot, his white bathrobe, so big on her that she looked like she was swimming in it, knotted around her waist. Her hair was twisted into a loose and fetching knot on the top of her head, her beautiful face was scrubbed clean, and her big brown eyes were questioning as they swung from him to Hinkle and back.

"Julie, meet my partner, George Hinkle." There didn't seem to be much else to do, under the circumstances, but make the necessary introductions. To a certain degree, anyway. No need to reveal Julie's full identity, because if Hinkle knew exactly who she was he would freak for sure. The urgent question was, how much had she heard? Mac looked at her hard, but couldn't tell.

"Julie—*Carlson?*" Hinkle choked, staring at her as if she'd been a six-foot-tall spitting cobra instead of a ravishing babe in a bathrobe.

So much for keeping her identity to himself, Mac thought, grimacing. He was surprised his partner had recognized her at all, much less so fast. But then, the light was good in the room now, and Hinkle had just been taking pictures of Sid, so he would naturally have Carlson on the brain. Plus, he'd been working security at her wedding, too, and a looker like Julie could be counted on to be remembered by any male between ten and ninety. And he could have seen her umpteen times since, for all Mac knew. After all, he also had a vested interest in keeping tabs on Sid, if for no other reason than to stay as far away from him as possible.

"Julie's a client," Mac said, which was perfectly true even if it was obvious to the most casual observer that Julie was far more than that. After all, how many clients came strolling into his living room clad in nothing but his bathrobe, obviously fresh from his shower? None that he could think of.

"Hello," Julie offered. She was unsmiling, but Mac still could not judge whether she'd heard more than she should.

"Shit," Hinkle said, turning incredulous eyes on him. Mac met that dumbstruck look impassively. Recollecting himself, Hinkle swung his gaze back to Julie. "Meaning no disrespect, ma'am."

Then his gaze moved to something on the floor, and his expression changed again. Following the direction of that appalled glance, Mac realized that his partner had just spotted Julie's dress. Julie apparently realized it, too, because she stepped forward and, with praiseworthy dignity, retrieved the garment, which she folded over her arm.

"You were at my house earlier, weren't you?" she asked Hinkle, her manner both direct and composed. Mac had to give her credit for not letting Hinkle—or him—see the embarrassment she had to be feeling. "I heard you talking to Mac over the phone. Did you—were you able to get pictures of my husband with his girlfriend?"

Hinkle gulped. "Uh—uh. . . ." His gaze shot to Mac. "Could I speak to you in private for just one minute?"

"He got them," Mac said to Julie, who met his gaze with absolutely nothing that he could decipher in her eyes.

"I'll just go get dressed." She turned to head back into the bedroom, then glanced over her shoulder. "Nice meeting you, Mr. Hinkle."

Hinkle gave her a sickly smile. "You, too, Mrs.—uh—Carlson."

Julie's very lack of expression made Mac apprehensive. Either she'd heard something she shouldn't, or she was still wallowing in her après-sex snit. Silence reigned in the living room until it was interrupted by the barely audible click of the bedroom door closing.

Then Hinkle, looking nearly apoplectic, turned on him with a vengeance.

"What the fuck are you *doing?*" he demanded in a fierce whisper. "You're fucking Sid Carlson's *wife,* you dumbass. Are you out of your tiny mind?"

Denying it would clearly be a waste of time. Mac put the beer bottle down on the coffee table, stuck his hands in the front pockets of his jeans, rocked back on his heels, and regarded Hinkle meditatively.

"Like I said, Julie's a client. She hired me—us—to find out if her husband's cheating on her. As you saw, he is."

"You're fucking sleeping with her." Hinkle did the best under-his-breath yell Mac had ever heard. It wasn't loud, but it was forceful. "And there's no *us* in this. Uh-uh. This is you on your damn fool own."

Mac pursed his lips. "Fine. I'll consider her a private client. That make you feel better?"

"No. No, it doesn't make me feel better. Who's going to *know* she's your private client, that's what I want to know? What are you gonna do, hang a sign around her neck? If Carlson gets wind that we're spying on him, we got a shit-load of trouble. If he finds out you're also making it with his wife"—Hinkle visibly shuddered—"which he will do when lawyers get involved, you mark my words—he'll come after us—not you, *us*—with everything he's got." Hinkle shook his head. "Been there, done that. I don't know about you, but nothing in that experience made me want to go down that road again."

Mac said nothing for a moment. Everything Hinkle said was true. The last time he'd gone after Sid, Sid's retaliation had been stunning in its swiftness. Days after Mac had briefed his superiors on what he was doing and—he'd thought—set up a sting that would bring Sid crashing down, drugs missing from the evidence room had been found in Mac's locker. In the ensuing investigation, half a dozen witnesses had come forward willing to swear that

Mac had sold them everything from coke to smack to LSD while on the job. The sting against Sid had come up empty—how ironic was that?—and in the end Mac, not Sid, had been the one to come crashing down. And Hinkle, who'd been tarred with the same brush just because he'd had the misfortune to be Mac's partner, had crashed with him. Mac had gone to Greg Rice, his captain and immediate superior as well as, he'd thought, a friend, in an attempt to at least save Hinkle's job, but Rice had said there was nothing he could do. The word had come down from on high: he and Hinkle were gone.

Mac's eyes had been opened by that fiasco: the tentacles of the beast he was hunting reached everywhere. Even his fellow cops had turned on him when the shit started hitting the fan, and he had never been sure just who had been motivated by genuine belief in his guilt and who Sid had gotten to.

In the end, it hadn't mattered. Although no criminal charges were ever officially filed, he and Hinkle had been fired from the department, and both their lives had pretty much gone to hell. Not much more than casual acquaintances when it had happened, they'd stuck together afterward—Hinkle had said it was because nobody else would have either of them—and built McQuarry and Hinkle up over the intervening years.

Looking at it that way, Mac could definitely see Hinkle's point: It had only been in the last year or two that they'd actually started making decent money, and now, by going after Sid again, he was risking everything they'd built up.

"I can't just walk away," Mac said quietly. "I'm too close to getting him this time. But I'll keep you out of it from here on out. In fact, if you want to buy me out, I'll understand. I'm pretty sure Don Hadley at the bank will give you a loan. That would keep you out of it as much as anything could."

"I don't want to buy you out." Hinkle groaned. "Would you be smart for once in your life and leave this alone?"

Mac started to say something, then heard the bedroom door open again and shook his head at Hinkle, warning him without words to shut up.

Hinkle looked like someone had just forced him to swallow a mouthful of vinegar, but he was silent as Julie appeared in the doorway, looking so beautiful that Mac was suddenly uncomfortable in a most particular way, as if the front of his jeans had all of a sudden grown too tight. It probably had something to do with the whisper-soft purple dress, he thought, or maybe the sexy shoes. He had a clear mental vision of how each garment had come off. . . .

"If you're busy"—Julie's gaze flicked to Hinkle, who offered her a nervous-looking smile—"I can call a taxi. I need to get back to work."

"I'm not busy." Mac picked up his gun and shoved it down inside the back of his waistband, then grabbed his sunglasses and his keys. His gaze slid to Hinkle. "I'll give you a buzz."

"Yeah," Hinkle said, looking as nervous as a beetle in an aviary, and headed for the door.

Josephine appeared—of course she did, she could see everybody was leaving, and she wanted to go too—and Julie glanced down at her.

"Do you want to take her, or . . . ?"

Mac gave Josephine a sour look. "Take her. There's less she can chew up in the car."

Julie was already gathering Josephine up.

"I'm going back to the office," Hinkle said to him, holding the door for Julie. His gaze flicked to her. "Pleasure making your acquaintance, Mrs. Carlson."

"Good-bye, Mr. Hinkle." Julie was already walking down the steps toward the Blazer. With another speaking glance at Mac, Hinkle headed for his car. Mac followed Julie, glad to see that Mrs. Leiferman was nowhere in sight. Finally, at least one thing today was going his way. Maybe, if he was lucky, it would be the start of a trend.

Julie didn't say anything until he had the Blazer started and, hot air blasting, they were heading down the street. Then she fixed him with a gaze that made alarm bells go off in his head.

"So," she said. "Is there something I'm missing here?"

23

SITTING IN A PARKED CAR on a blazing hot day ranked right up there with hitting himself in the head with a hammer as one of his favorite things to do, Roger Basta reflected sourly. But the Big Boss had made it clear that he had just this one last chance to take care of Julie Carlson. If he failed, he wasn't likely to get another. People did not fail the boss. Not and live to tell the tale.

He'd been watching for her, waiting for her to come out of her dress store. When she did, he was going to get the business over with once and for all. No more elaborate schemes. No more worries about DNA or misdirecting the cops. "Keep it simple, stupid" was his new motto. Just do the deed and have done. With her out of the way, he could get back to his real life.

At least, until the Big Boss called again.

Maybe it was time he started thinking about retirement. He was fifty-five, not old really, but old for this business. He was getting tired. He was getting scared.

This hit on Julie Carlson was the first time he had ever failed. It was making him doubt his abilities. It was making the boss doubt his abilities.

If there was one thing he had learned over the course

of his career, it was don't mess with the boss. People who did ended up dead.

For the first time ever, it occurred to him that he might not come out of this business with a nice little nest egg and a lot of years left to spend it. He might come out of this business dead. He knew where a hell of a lot of bodies were buried. Literally.

It might not pay for the boss to let him just retire and walk away.

Damn Julie Carlson anyway. He hadn't borne her any ill will at first; the hit on her had been just another job. Now it was more than that. Number one, she'd marked him. Very few of his victims had ever marked him, and those who had hadn't lived to tell the tale. Number two, she was making him look less than competent. Looking less than competent was bad for business. It was also dangerous.

As soon as she put in an appearance, he was going to kill her stone cold dead. Give him three minutes, and it would be all over.

It must have been well over a hundred degrees inside the car. He'd deliberately stolen one with tinted windows so no one could see him inside. If he ran the engine, and thus the air-conditioner, he might attract attention, and so he refrained. When one was sitting in a stolen car with murder on one's mind, attention was bad.

It was nearly five o'clock. The sun was dipping toward the horizon. Its rays poured through the windshield, both cooking and half blinding him. He was hungry, he had a headache from the sun, and he was all out of the Gatorade he'd been chugging to keep from sweating to death. To add insult to injury, his nose throbbed. He tried to assuage the pain with the melting ice pack he'd brought along, but all he really succeeded in doing was getting his shirt wet.

The nose made it personal. He was going to make her pay for that.

If she ever stepped outside. He'd watched her go into her store that morning, then scouted the area for the best place to wait and watch. He knew her work schedule: she closed up shop at five. He figured if he showed up at three, there would be no way he could miss her, even if she decided to leave early.

He couldn't afford to miss her again.

So he was prepared to sit out here and roast alive for as long as it took.

Then he was heading for Key West and a nice little vacation, before he returned to his regular job. He could retire from it, too, in a few years.

It was time he started making plans for his future. Serious plans.

24

"I THOUGHT WE AGREED that it would be best if you didn't go back to work." Mac stopped at the stop sign, then turned the corner as he spoke. "What with one thing and another, you've had an eventful day."

That was such an understatement that under other circumstances Julie would have snorted. But she didn't, because she was busy watching Mac's face. She'd come to know him well, she realized. The fact that he was avoiding her question spoke volumes.

"I have to go back to work. I called the shop from your bedroom to check on things, and Meredith—my other assistant—told me that my three o'clock is still there and things are not going well. Besides, I have to face Amber sometime. Better at the end of the day today than early in the morning tomorrow." Julie paused, her gaze keen on his face. "Now, do you want to tell me what was going on back there with your partner?"

Mac glanced at her, hesitated, then grimaced as if in resignation. "Remember I told you that there was a company policy against sleeping with clients? Hinkle was upset that I violated it."

Julie regarded him with a degree of suspicion. She hadn't been able to hear what was being said between the two men, but that Hinkle was extremely upset with Mac was obvious. Too upset for Mac's explanation to account for it?

"Is that the truth?"

His mouth twisted in a wry smile. "Absolutely." He glanced her way again. "What are your plans for the evening? After you fire your assistant, I mean."

"I guess I'll go to my mother's. I'm certainly not going back to my house." She shuddered at the thought.

"I could take you to dinner." It was said casually, in almost throwaway fashion. They were on the expressway now, and traffic was heavy. That might account for his unusual attention to the road, but Julie didn't think so.

"Mac . . ." Julie hesitated. He was handsome, he was sexy, he was great in the sack. He was funny. He was dependable. He had an adorable dog. Just looking at him made her heart go pitter-pat; thinking about what they'd done in bed made her burn—with a certain degree of embarrassment when she mentally replayed all the details, and with a slowly building desire to do it all again. But she was particularly vulnerable right now, she knew, and she was growing dangerously used to relying on him for comfort and support. Add explosive sex to the mix, and the result could be bad. Her heart was bruised and battered enough from her marriage; a failed romance with Mac might break it entirely. "I'm not sure I'm ready for a relationship right now."

A beat passed.

"Darlin', who's talking about a relationship here? Not me. What I'm talking about is dinner—and lots of casual sex." He threw her a quick grin, and Julie, despite her mixed-up emotions, had to smile back. "Or not. That part's up to you. But I think you could still use a friend. And you have to eat."

Another beat as she mulled that over.

"Did you have any particular place in mind?" A smile played around Julie's lips as she looked at him. It was capitulation—to dinner only—and they both knew it. Suddenly the decision felt very right. Maybe getting involved with Mac right now was dangerous, but then, life was dangerous. Josephine was lying contentedly across her thighs, and Julie stroked the poodle's springy coat. Being with Mac was like having Josephine in her lap: something that made her feel happy.

And from now on she was going to grab all the happiness she could with both hands.

"You choose. Any place you want."

Julie thought. "Considering that we have Josephine with us, how about O'Connell's?" O'Connell's was casual, with expansive decks and patios that many of the patrons preferred to the large indoor dining room. Sid had never liked the simple dishes and breezy service; it was the kind of place she went to with Becky and her girls. Josephine would be fine at one of the patio tables.

"I can see you're going to be a cheap date." He smiled at her as he pulled off the expressway into Summerville. The sun was starting its downward trajectory, Julie noticed as they headed right toward it and the bright rays all but blinded her. It would be evening soon—and she would be having dinner with Mac.

Suddenly she was really, really glad about that. It was the proverbial spoonful of sugar in the bitter medicine that was currently her life.

"Mac," she said, "I'm sorry if I was a little—um, out of sorts earlier."

His expression told her that he knew what she meant: a little out of sorts after sex.

"That's okay," he said, his voice as grave as hers had

been. Then he grinned at her. "You can be out of sorts with me any time—especially if it's from the same cause."

She laughed, and as she did felt a little more of the damage to her heart heal. It was going to take some time, she thought, but she was going to be okay.

He pulled into the Kroger lot and parked. It was nearly full at this time of day as people stopped by the grocery and the pharmacy and the other stores in the shopping center on their way home from work. The street in front of them was no less busy, with cars whizzing along it as their drivers hurried to beat the coming rush hour. Across the street, Carolina Belle's plate-glass windows were inpenetrable. All she could see in them was a reflection of the still-blazing sun.

Oh, God, now there was Amber to deal with, and Carlene. Back to real life.

"Want me to come in with you?" Mac had been watching her face. His eyes met hers; he was no longer smiling. She realized that he understood just how much she was having to steel herself to face what lay ahead, and thought, This is nice. She couldn't remember Sid ever particularly caring about what was going on in her mind—or her life—apart from him. "This could get unpleasant, you realize."

Simply knowing that Mac was on her side, that there was somebody else with her in this boat that she was pushing out into uncharted seas, strengthened her.

Julie shook her head. "No, thanks. I can do this. Then I'll close up and meet you back here at—six?"

"I'll wait for you. Come whenever you're ready. If you need me beforehand, call me." He tapped his cell phone.

"I will. But I shouldn't need you. Unless Amber decides to pull an Amy Fisher on me." Julie smiled to indicate that she was being facetious, lifted Josephine off her lap and slid out of the car, then glanced back in at Mac. "I won't be any longer than I can help."

"I'll be here."

Julie shut the Blazer's door and started walking, conscious of Mac's eyes on her back. Strictly for his benefit, she put a little extra sway in her walk and smiled to herself as she imagined what he thought of it. She hoped it turned him on.

To her surprise, pleasure, and slight dismay, she found that she was getting turned on thinking about him getting turned on.

Sex as an antidote to the divorce blues. She thought about that for a moment and concluded, works for me.

The heat hugged her like an overly effusive friend. People's voices, the rattle of shopping carts, and the whoosh of traffic speeding past on the street in front of her joined with the smell of melting asphalt and car exhaust to form a backdrop that was both exhausting and familiar. It was good to know that Mac would be waiting when she came out, she thought as she headed toward her shop.

It made her feel stronger, braver, safer. It made her feel as if her life wasn't ending, but beginning.

She stepped over the scraggly little bushes that separated the Kroger from the Taco Bell, feeling the tingle of pleasure she'd gotten from thinking of turning Mac on fade as she mentally rehearsed what she was going to say to Amber. *You're fired, bimbette* didn't seem to quite cut it, but she couldn't think of anything more dignified that conveyed her sentiments in quite the same way.

The shadow of the Taco Bell had just blocked out the worst of the sun when a green Lexus pulled up behind her and stopped. Julie glanced over her shoulder at it because its front bumper was close, but she kept walking, not paying any attention to it beyond that first instinctive glance. Vaguely she registered the sound of a car door opening and closing.

Seconds later a hard hand clamped around her arm. Julie was so startled that she jumped a foot straight up in the air. She whirled, heart pounding, to find herself face-to-face with Sid.

"What the hell did you do? Huh? What did you do?"

Dressed in a charcoal suit and crisp white shirt despite the heat, red-faced and scowling with his glasses slipping down his nose and his red silk tie askew, he looked furious. It was so unlike Sid to be anything less than completely dapper that she knew that he must be really enraged. His nostrils were distended, he was breathing hard, and his fingers were really hurting as they dug into her arm. For a moment, the briefest, flickering moment, she felt her stomach clench. She had always hated to make Sid mad, and the visceral reaction was still there—until she remembered all the reasons why she didn't have to put up with his temper anymore. The thought that had occurred to her earlier replayed in her head: He had set her free. He no longer had any claim on her. He had severed the tie that bound her to him by his own actions. From the time of their marriage she had been less a person to him than an accessory he used to flaunt his success, like his Italian leather shoes or his expensive silk tie. She realized that she'd been tired of being an accessory for a long time.

Their marriage had been over in all but name long before Amber had come on the scene.

Amber had simply awakened her to the truth.

Suddenly Julie realized that she was being given a second chance. She was Julie again, not Julie Carlson anymore but Julie her own true self. It was that Julie who reacted as Sid's good little wife never would have, that Julie who glared at Sid and jerked her arm from his hold.

"I don't know what you're talking about." Her voice was icy. "And keep your hands off me."

Surprise flickered in his eyes for the briefest of moments. Then his face darkened. He seemed to vibrate with temper as he took a step closer, looming over her almost threateningly, his eyes hard and angry as they bored into hers.

"You know what I'm talking about, all right. You were in the house, weren't you? Were you spying on me? You were, weren't you, you sneaky little . . . What the hell did you do to my car? I missed my plane! Do you know how important that meeting was? Because of you, I missed it!"

Despite her own rising fury, Julie was, for just a moment, rendered speechless. She could do nothing more than glare at him. The emotion that was uppermost in the maelstrom of her feelings, she decided, was total disbelief. Instead of apologizing, explaining, or even attempting to make some excuse for being caught red-handed in her house with her twenty-year-old employee, he was yelling at *her* for finding him out and damaging his car.

There was something wrong with this picture, but for-tunately, Julie thought, she didn't have to stick around any longer to try to figure out exactly what it was.

"Hell-o-o? I found your Viagra. I saw you in my house with Amber. I know what you did. So you know what? I don't care if you missed your plane. I don't care if you missed your meeting. And I'll let you figure out what I did to your car. And just so you know, I think you're a total dickhead; a horse's ass; a mean, conceited, pompous, impo-tent bastard. Our marriage is over: I'm getting a divorce."

For a moment he simply stared at her, looking as stunned as if a kitten had suddenly morphed into a tiger and bitten him, while his face grew redder and redder until it was the approximate color of a tomato and his eyes bulged out at her.

"The hell you are." He grabbed her by the arm again and started dragging her toward the Lexus, his fingers digging hurtfully into the soft flesh above her elbow. He was breathing hard now, and his features were contorted in an ugly snarl. Julie dug her heels into the heat-softened pavement and resisted, and he turned on her ferociously. "You'll get a divorce when I say you can get a divorce and not before, you got that? You trashy little bitch, anybody would go looking for something with a little more class—and a little less ass—if they were married to you."

He gave a vicious yank, and despite her best efforts at resistance she stumbled forward. He was dragging her again, toward the Lexus, and she couldn't seem to get away. Julie felt a tiny spurt of fear mix with her rage. She had never, she realized, pushed Sid to the limit before. Always she had pretty much done whatever he wanted. Now that she was no longer his to command, how far would he go?

She discovered that she didn't want to find out.

"Let me go!"

This time his grip was unbreakable. She glanced wildly around even as she fought being pulled the last couple of feet toward the car. They were in the shadow of the Taco Bell still, back near the Dumpster, which of course happened to be the one fairly empty area in the whole vast asphalt sea. No one seemed to be paying the least attention to her and Sid; it was up to her to save herself.

She could scream, she realized. But the last small part of her that was still Sid Carlson's wife shuddered at the thought of creating such a scene.

On the other hand, she was damned if she'd let herself

be manhandled into that Lexus by her furious soon-to-be ex-husband. Nothing good could come of that.

"Get your hands off her, Sid."

Mac's voice stopped Julie in the act of preparing to kick Sid as hard as she could in the shins. She glanced around again to see him looming behind her, reaching for her, his gaze fixed on Sid. Sid, for his part, stopped dead and stared at Mac as if he were seeing a ghost. His grip on her arm slackened from, she thought, sheer surprise. Mac caught her arm and pulled her away from Sid's hold. Freed, she moved instinctively to Mac's side. Standing in his protective shadow, she wrapped her arms over her chest and glared at Sid.

It would be a long time before she would forget or forgive that little pang of fear.

"Well, if it isn't Mac McQuarry." Sid's lips stretched into a mocking smile, but his eyes were suddenly alert and cold. He was no longer looking at her. His focus was all on Mac. "I thought you got run out of town a few years back. Something about being a dirty cop, wasn't it?"

Mac smiled, too, with as little humor as Sid, and their gazes clashed like rapiers. Julie could feel the enmity crackling between the two like an electrical charge. Her glance moved from one to the other: Sid shorter, leaner, older, looking like the successful businessman he was but still a little out of place on this blazing hot day in his expensive dark suit; Mac taller, broader, younger, handsomer, a blond surfer-god in his Hawaiian shirt and jeans and tennis shoes—and, surprisingly, with the grim set to his jaw and the hard glint in his eye, the more formidable looking of the two. It hit her with the force of a two-by-four over the head that there was some kind of history—unpleasant history—between the two.

Mac replied in a deadly voice that was like nothing

Julie had ever heard come out of his mouth before: "Don't tell me you've forgotten the details. I haven't. For a long time now I've been meaning to drop by and congratulate you on doing such a good job."

"Is that supposed to be some kind of a threat?" Sid looked ready to explode. Then, suddenly, his expression changed, and he glanced at her and then back at Mac. "What the hell are you doing with my wife?"

"Looks to me like I'm keeping her safe from you, asshole."

Mac's snarling response reinforced what Julie had already sensed: the tension between the two was long-standing in nature. Mac had never mentioned that he knew Sid. . . .

"I hired him," she said, pushing her confusion to the back burner until Sid was dealt with. "He's a private investigator. He's got pictures of you with Amber. I'm going to fire her, by the way, just as soon as I see her. And, like I said, I'm going to divorce you."

Sid stared at her. Then he looked at Mac. Then, to Julie's complete and utter stupefaction, he began to laugh, jeering laughter that set her teeth on edge. Julie frowned at him. Of all the reactions she would have expected from Sid, this was not one. Beside her, she felt Mac stiffen. Glancing up at him, she saw that his face had gone utterly still, utterly blank.

"You stupid little bitch," Sid said, drawing her attention once more. "Don't you know when you're being used? He's been pumping you for all kinds of information about me, hasn't he? And you fed him everything you know."

Julie must have looked as shocked as she felt, because he shook his head contemptuously at her. "You didn't have a clue, did you? Sometimes I think your bra size is bigger than your IQ. This guy's been after me for years, and now he's using you to try to get to me. What did you tell him?"

Feeling suddenly cold despite the blazing heat, Julie ignored Sid to glance up at Mac. "Is that true?"

He looked down at her. His eyes as they met hers told her everything she needed to know: Sid was telling the truth.

"Julie . . ."

"It is true, isn't it?" There was a ringing in her ears as she faced the hideous knowledge that Mac had betrayed her, too.

"I can explain. . . ."

Sid cut him off with another of those jeering little laughs that brought Julie's gaze swiveling back around to him. "What did you do, go waltzing into his office and ask him to investigate me? He must have thought it was his lucky day. He didn't even tell you he knew me, did he?" Her face must have answered for her because he laughed again. "Like I said, he's been using you."

He moved, walking the few steps back to the Lexus and opening the passenger door, then jerked his head at her commandingly. "Now get in the car. We'll go someplace private and talk this through."

Julie's gaze locked with Mac's. She felt as if she'd just been punched in the stomach. She could hardly breathe. To her surprise, and burgeoning horror, this betrayal hurt far more than discovering Sid with Amber.

"Julie, listen. . . ." Mac focused on her now, ignoring Sid completely. His voice was low, his eyes pained. She cut him off with a curt shake of her head.

"It was a rotten thing to do." Her voice was scarcely louder than a whisper.

"Don't tell me you had something going on the side with him?"

Something in their attitude toward each other must have alerted Sid. He sounded so outraged that Julie almost wanted to laugh. Her gaze swung around to him.

"Actually, I slept with him this afternoon." Her voice was strong again, thank goodness. She swallowed, battling back the growing lump in her throat that she was afraid might, if she let it, turn into tears. "If you have anything to say to me after this, you can call my lawyer. I'll call the office tomorrow and leave his name and number with Heidi." As Sid sputtered furiously, she looked at Mac. "As for you, I never want to see you again as long as I live."

"Julie . . ." Mac said again, reaching for her, his voice hoarse, his eyes desperate. "Give me a chance to explain."

Julie eluded him with a deft sideways step.

"Go to hell," she said to him. His eyes darkened as if at a blow and his arms dropped to his sides. Her gaze swung back to Sid. "You go to hell, too."

Head high and back straight, she pivoted and started walking away.

"You cheating little slut, you get your ass back here," Sid roared. No sooner had the words left his mouth than Julie heard a flurry of movement, followed by the sharp crack of a blow. Glancing back, she saw Sid flying backward while Mac, fists still clenched, body poised for more, watched with a look of savage satisfaction. Julie saw that the scene was finally starting to attract onlookers, and kept walking. Behind her she heard rapid footsteps, and increased her own pace until she was nearly running. A hand grabbed her arm. She didn't even have to look back to know it belonged to Mac.

"Julie, please. I know it sounds bad, but . . ." He pulled her around to face him.

"Sounds bad? Is that what it does?" Hurt and anger and a sense of terrible betrayal made her voice unsteady. She jerked her arm from his hold and bared her teeth at him savagely. "Go away! Leave me alone! I don't want to listen to anything you have to say. Send me a bill and I'll pay it, and other than that stay the hell out of my life. Understand?"

It was only as she saw several passersby glance her way that she realized that she was yelling. From the corner of her eye, she saw that Sid, face red, fists clenched, was headed their way. A woman shopper complete with loaded grocery cart was punching numbers into her cell phone even as she kept looking at them, wide-eyed. Julie guessed that she was calling 911.

Julie could only pray that both men ended up in jail.

"You have to listen to me," Mac said.

"No, I don't," she bit out. Then, grabbing the shreds of her dignity with both hands, she turned her back on him and stalked toward the sidewalk. A movement across the street in front of Carolina Belle caught her eye. As she identified its source, her lips pursed. Carlene Squabb had emerged from the shop and was coming her way, obviously having spotted her through the glass, an annoyed expression that Julie knew all too well on her face. Julie almost turned on her heel and headed in the opposite direction. Of all the things she didn't need right now, listening to Carlene bitch about how Julie was neglecting her was right up there at the top of the list.

"Julie, please. Just give me a minute."

Mac caught her arm again, pulling her around to face him just as she reached the edge of the parking lot. Sid was closing fast, his nose bleeding, murder in his eye, but Mac didn't seem to notice, or care if he did. From the corner of her eye, Julie saw Carlene look both ways and step off the curb. It was only then that she realized that Carlene was wearing the pink sweater dress she herself had discarded earlier. Why on earth . . . ?

A sudden blur of movement on the street caught Julie's attention. Seemingly from out of nowhere a mid-size blue car hurtled toward Carlene. Carlene saw it coming: Julie could see horror in her widening eyes, her opening mouth.

Carlene tried to get out of the way, but there was no time. The car hit her with a sickening thump. She flew up in the air, twisting feet over head, limp as a rag doll as she seemed to cartwheel over the car.

Julie screamed, and, screaming, rushed toward where Carlene now lay limp and bleeding in the street.

25

CARLENE WAS DEAD. Julie could hardly believe it. Numb with shock, she walked out of the hospital at shortly after ten into the welcoming arms of the night. It was still hot, stickily humid, with a sprinkling of stars overhead and a beautiful crescent moon. Shivering at the cruel irony of such serene beauty on a night that had witnessed a terrible, brutal death, Julie was nevertheless grateful for the embracing heat. She was so cold that she felt as if she'd been turned to ice from the inside out; so cold that she felt like she would never be warm again.

Sitting there in that impersonal lounge with Carlene's family as they waited for news had been one of the most wrenching experiences of her life.

Carlene had been the victim of a hit-and-run. The police were investigating, of course. They'd talked to Meredith and they'd talked to Julie, and they'd talked to scores of other people as well. There'd been dozens of witnesses, a few of whom had actually had the presence of mind to get at least part of the license-plate number. Neither the car nor the driver had yet been found, but the police seemed confident that they would be. Julie prayed it would be soon. She found the accident horrifying in more ways than one.

She could not get past the fact that Carlene had been

wearing Julie's own discarded dress when she was hit. Julie pointed that out to the officer who had interviewed her, and he had dutifully written it down, but she had a feeling that the information had not made much of an impression and would wind up buried in a file some-where.

The consensus was, Carlene had probably been the unfortunate victim of a driver who was drunk, or high, or elderly, or a kid, who had then panicked. The police were confident that both car and driver would be found, and then all questions would be answered.

When Julie had asked her, Meredith had said that Carlene, annoyed at being left to the tender mercies of a mere assistant, had been chain-smoking in the dressing room. She had dropped ashes on her own dress, which had burned a tiny hole in a particularly unfortunate spot on the bodice. Carlene had pitched a fit, blamed the whole fiasco on Meredith, and insisted that she could not possibly step outside the store in a dress with a hole in the tit. Meredith, not knowing what else to do, had invited her to take her pick from Carolina Belle's stock. Unfortunately, with her new implants, the only other gar-ment in the store that would fit Carlene was Julie's stretchy sweater dress. So Meredith let her wear it.

And Carlene had died in it.

"You ever think that maybe walking alone through a parking lot at night might not be a good idea?"

The voice, coming from behind her as she headed toward her car, made Julie jump even as she recognized it. She was edgy, she realized, nervous, and didn't have to delve far to find the reason why: Carlene dying in her dress had scared the pants off her. She was just now fully realizing it.

"Go away." She didn't even bother to glance over her

shoulder. Maddeningly, just knowing that Mac was behind her and she was, therefore, physically safe made her nerves relax. It also made her heart ache, and her temper heat.

"I know you're mad. I'm even willing to admit that you have a right to be. But I can explain."

Having fished her keys out of her purse as she walked, Julie pressed the unlock button just as she reached the white Infiniti. Then she turned on him. Every muscle in her body hummed with tension; her eyes were blazing.

"Exactly what part of *go away* don't you understand?"

The moonlight turned his hair to molten silver. It was reflected in his eyes, turning them silvery, too. It cast deep shadows beneath his high cheekbones, his straight nose, his firm chin. He looked tall and broad and achingly handsome standing there regarding her so gravely, and Julie hated him.

It scared her to realize that she hated him. Hate was too strong an emotion to feel for this sexy near-stranger who had slept with and betrayed her. She didn't even hate Sid anymore. She'd gotten over hating him long since.

No matter what he had done, Mac was a tiny, unimportant chapter in her life. A phase. She should have been mad, but she shouldn't have been hating him.

Mac grimaced, and stuck his hands in the front pockets of his jeans. "Look, Sid and I go way back, okay? When I stumbled across you, I admit that my first thought was that I could maybe get some information from you about him. But . . ."

"Forget it," Julie said through her teeth. "You're wasting your breath. At this point, if you told me the sun rises in the east I'd get a second opinion. Now leave me alone."

She turned on her heel, presenting him with her back as she opened her car door.

"It ever occur to you that Sid might be trying to kill you?"

"What?" The question was so unexpected—and yet so in sync with her own uneasy feelings—that she stiffened and turned to face him again.

"Oh, not Sid himself. He's not the type to get his hands dirty. What he might do is hire somebody—a professional. A hit man. Think about it: The girl who got killed today—she was wearing your dress, wasn't she? And coming out of your shop? Maybe somebody thought she was you. Maybe the same somebody who attacked you in your house. And maybe he's still out there. You've escaped him twice now. Maybe he's going to try again."

Julie's heart leaped in her chest. Goose bumps prickled into life all over her skin. What he was suggesting was ridiculous, of course. Sid would never hire someone to kill her—would he? It was the stuff of bad movies.

She could barely keep herself from glancing all around, fearfully probing the shadows. If Mac hadn't been standing right in front of her, watching her narrowly to, she thought, judge her reaction, she would have done just that. But she refused to give him the satisfaction of knowing that he had succeeded in scaring her.

Even though he had.

"If you really believe that, you need to go to the police." Julie was proud of how cool her voice sounded. She slid into her car, and prepared to close the door. His hand closing on the top of the window frame prevented her.

"They don't listen to me anymore—especially when it comes to Sid. Remember I told you that I got fired because the guy I was investigating set me up? That would be Sid."

Julie's eyes widened. She stopped in the act of inserting her key into the ignition.

"You were investigating *Sid?*" Her throat felt suddenly dry. "Why?"

"Drugs." His eyes bored into hers. "At the time I thought he was running a drug operation, big time. Among other things."

For a moment Julie simply gaped at him. Then the sheer absurdity of the accusation hit her. Her brows snapped together, and she jerked the door away from him, closing and locking it before he could react. He stood there with his fists on his hips scowling at her through the glass. Julie started the car, then, unable to resist, rolled her window down the merest crack.

"You need professional help, you know that? If I were you, I'd run, not walk, to the nearest treatment facility. Now good-bye."

She rolled up the window and shifted into reverse at the same time, leaving him standing there in the shadowy parking lot glaring after her. Thank goodness he'd finally strayed into the realm of the ridiculous, Julie told herself as she drove away. For a minute there, he'd really had her going. But imagining Sid—meticulous, blue-blooded Sid with his golf games and his business meetings and his fussy insistence on order and punctuality—as a drug dealer was too much. Even in the throes of divorcing him, she couldn't go that far.

It was Mac's suggestion that someone was trying to kill her that had made her listen to him at all.

For some reason, his words had seemed to strike a chord. They took on a resonance inside her that would not be dismissed no matter how far-fetched the rest of his suggestions might be.

Julie realized that his warning echoed her own fears.

Turning off the main drag into the labyrinth of narrow

dark streets that led to her mother's house—it would be a cold day in hell before she stepped foot inside her own again; she supposed she was going to have to hire movers to retrieve her things, and beg Becky to supervise—she became conscious of one particular set of headlights that stayed a consistent half a block back, making all the turns she made, slowing down when she slowed, speeding up when she hit the gas.

She was being followed. The knowledge broke over her like a cold wave. Julie's breathing quickened, and she reached in a panic for her cell phone.

Then she realized who it almost had to be: Mac.

Slowly she put her phone down. If she was wrong, if this really was a hit man on a mission, she was going to feel dumb as a rock before she died. But she didn't think she was wrong.

Just to be sure, she watched carefully in her rearview mirror as the black Blazer passed beneath the only street-light on the route. And it *was* a black Blazer.

Mac was following her.

That infuriated her so much that she was parked in front of her mother's modest brick ranch house waiting when he got there. By the time he pulled up behind her, she was already out of her car and advancing on him, cell phone in hand.

He got out of the Blazer just as she reached it, shutting the door but leaving the motor running. For Josephine, Julie guessed in passing. She could see the poodle's fluffy white head peering at her through the window. The sight of Josephine cost her a pang. She realized that somehow, over the course of this nightmare, she had fallen in love—with Josephine.

Certainly not with the jackass leaning against the

side of the Blazer with his arms crossed over his chest.

"If you don't leave me alone, I'm going to call the police," she threatened, waving her cell phone at him.

He ignored that. He was, Julie thought furiously, good at ignoring things.

"You remember I asked you about Sid's first wife? You said she was completely out of the picture before you came into it. That's more true than you know: after an evening spent at a party with Sid, she was never seen again. Just walked off the face of the earth. I've been searching for her for years without turning up so much as a trace. Her name was Kelly. She was only twenty-two."

"Are you trying to make me believe that Sid killed her?" Her voice quivered with outrage—and, if she was honest, just the tiniest, most infuriating smidgen of fear.

Mac shrugged. "I think it's more likely that he had her killed."

"You're insane." Julie took a deep breath. "If you really believe that, why don't you go to the police?"

"I *was* the police, remember? Once upon a time. I was a cop when I first noticed that Kelly Carlson was nowhere to be found, but the bottom line is, no witnesses, no bodies, no crime. The story was that the first Mrs. Carlson went home to her family in California. The powers that be at the department were fine with that—even though there was no family in California for her to go home to. Although she was from California originally, her parents had died before she married Sid. I can find no record of her anywhere on this planet after she left him. Now the department doesn't even want to talk to me. They might listen to you, if you went to them and told them that you think your husband's trying to kill you, but then again, they might not. There's no proof: not yet. And Sid and his family have some powerful friends."

"You're trying to scare me!" And he was succeeding too; put together the right way, everything that had happened could be interpreted in such a way that it was possible to conclude that Sid had hired someone to kill her. But how unlikely was that? Sid was many unpleasant things, but she couldn't picture him as a cold-blooded killer. It was far more likely that Mac was adding two and two and getting five—or lying again for some nefarious purpose of his own. Remembering how he had already lied to her infuriated her all over again. She turned on her heel, meaning to walk away.

"I'm trying to keep you alive." He came away from the Blazer then, catching her arm and pulling her around to face him. "I've been doing my homework lately, darlin', and I don't like what I'm learning. Did you know that Sweetwater's—remember Sweetwater's, Sid's after-hours hang-out?—is owned by Rand Corporation, which also owns All-American Builders? Yeah, Sid's company. Apparently Sweetwater's is a happening place: cash goes through there by the truckload. Word on the street is that it's used for money laundering by the mob. And Rand Corporation is owned by—want to guess who?—John Sidney Carlson the Third. In other words, Sid's dad. John Sidney Carlson the Second—Sid's grandfather—was chairman emeritus up until he died."

"You think Sid's father and grandfather are involved in money laundering? For the *mob?*" Julie stared up at him incredulously. Imagining Sid and his family as a southern-fried version of the Sopranos was mind-boggling. "That's ridiculous."

Mac shook his head. "No, it isn't. I don't have all the i's dotted and t's crossed yet. I haven't had time. But I think Rand Corporation and its offshoots—in other words, Sid and his father and grandfather, going back I don't know how many generations—are fronts for organized crime. I think they're into drug smuggling, gun running, gambling, protection rackets, money laundering, the whole bit. And I think anyone who gets in their way ends up dead."

"Are you saying that I'm in their way?"

"Did you know that there has never been a divorce in the Carlson family?"

Julie blinked at the non sequitur. "That's a sign of organized crime?"

"That's a sign of real bad luck for women who marry into the Carlson family. There's never been a divorce, but there've been lots of remarriages. The Carlsons' wives tend to die."

Julie gaped at him. Then, as she thought about it, her heart started to thud. The eerie truth of it hit her like a brick. John had been married twice before he'd apparently decided to limit himself to girlfriends. Sid had said his mother had been hit by a car when he was three; John's second wife had drowned.

Another equally scary idea flashed into her mind. Carlene had been hit by a car. Her own father had drowned. Julie's blood ran cold. It was a coincidence. It had to be. But—

"When I was a little girl, my father would sometimes do work for a company called Rand Corporation." Her voice was constricted.

Mac stared down at her with a slowly gathering frown. "He did? When?"

"I don't know—when I was seven or eight, maybe. He and my mother were divorced by then, but he would come by sometimes and give her his paycheck to pay for things for Becky and me. The checks were drawn on the Rand Corporation. I remember the name, because Becky and I were greedy to know everything we could about him. He didn't come around much."

She didn't think her tone revealed her pain, but something must have given her away, because his lips compressed. His eyes darkened on her face. He was holding both her arms now, and his grip tightened as if he would draw her closer.

"Julie . . ."

"Oh no you don't!" Julie remembered the old saying *Fool me once, shame on you, fool me twice, shame on me* with some force, and pulled out of his arms. Maybe his warning had merit and maybe it didn't, but she wasn't going to just take his word for anything anymore. "You've lied to me since I first met you. Why the hell should I start believing you now?"

He started to reply, but before he could say anything a light on the small porch of her mother's house blinked on. Her mother stepped out onto the porch.

"Julie! Julie, is that you?" She peered toward where Julie stood talking to Mac at the edge of the front yard just beyond the reach of the light. Her red hair was twisted onto pink foam curlers in preparation for bed, and she wore a knee-length flowered robe and slippers.

"Yes, Mama," she called. Her mother came to the edge of the porch, shading her eyes from the light with her hand.

"Are you all right?"

"I'm fine."

"Who's that with you?"

"Nobody, Mama." Then, to Mac, Julie said in a much quieter voice that was nevertheless strong with conviction, "I *don't* believe you. Not a single word. I don't know what you're up to, but whatever it is I don't want any part of it. Go away and leave me alone. I mean it."

"Julie, for God's sake . . ." Mac began, only to be drowned out by Dixie, who was coming down the steps.

"That is too somebody. Land sakes, Julie, it's not the man who punched Sid in the nose, is it?"

Julie almost groaned aloud. Trust the family's jungle drums. "Who told you that?"

Not waiting for an answer, she started walking quickly across the front yard toward her mother, and at the same time hissed at Mac over her shoulder. "Leave. Now."

"Becky told me. Kenny told her. Sid's secretary—Heidi whosit—told Kenny. She knew because she had to meet Sid at the airport with a fresh shirt because the one he was wearing had blood all over it and he told her that you had a lover who attacked him." Dixie's voice grew shrill with indignation on that last part. " 'Course, I didn't believe *that.*"

"Oh, did Sid go ahead and go to Atlanta after all?" Julie felt a degree of relief at the idea that at least one of her problems was out of the way for a few days.

"I guess he did, but that's not the point. The point is he's going around saying you have a *lover.*"

Dixie was quivering with indignation as they met at the foot of the steps. Putting an arm around her mother's shoulders, Julie determinedly steered her back up them. A quick glance back at Mac told her that he was still standing beside the Blazer watching them, making no attempt to go away. Gritting her teeth, she tried to push him and his crazy-making warnings from her mind.

"Mama, there's no easy way to say this." As they reached the level surface of the porch, she took a deep breath and decided to go for it. "I'm getting a divorce."

If she'd been looking for something to distract her mother from Mac's presence—and she had—she couldn't have found a better topic.

Her mother gave a little gasp. Both hands flew up to cover her mouth.

"Oh, my God, Julie! Why? *Why?*" There was the tiniest pause, while Dixie's eyes fixed on Julie's face with growing horror. "Was Sid telling the truth? I can't believe it! Never say you really do have a lover?"

"Have you ever thought that maybe she takes after you, Mama?" Becky opened the screen door to admit them, fixing their mother with a stern look. "How many lovers have you had? I bet you've lost count. Julie's allowed to have *one.*"

"Thanks, Beck," Julie said dispiritedly, realizing that her truly horrible day was about to keep on keeping on. She didn't know why she was surprised at Becky's presence—her mother was a great believer in double-teaming. If she'd been thinking straight, she would have *known* that Becky would be at her mother's house waiting for her. "Is Kenny watching the girls?"

"Yeah. He's pretty upset. Says this could cost him his job." Becky grinned teasingly at her. "Whoever would have thunk it—my perfect little sister with a lover. Way to go, Jules—you're making me look good."

"Shut up, Becky."

"Listen to me, Julie Ann." Dixie pulled her the rest of the way inside the house and shut the door. "Just because you have a lover doesn't mean you have to get a divorce. With a little work, I just know you and Sid can patch this up. . . ."

Julie sighed, allowed herself to be drawn into the kitchen where all their family powwows seemed to take place, and resigned herself: It was going to be a long night.

26

AFTER HOURS SPENT *NOT* SLEEPING in the increasingly cramped front seat of his SUV, Mac was beyond grumpy. All through the night, he'd kept watch over the house where Julie slept; via his cell phone, he'd sent Hinkle and Rawanda and Mother and just about everyone else he knew scurrying to round up information fast; and he'd done everything from taking Josephine on brisk walks around the property's perimeter to jumping jacks to remain alert. The night had passed undisturbed, except for the poodle's maddeningly frequent urge to pee and her determined destruction of a motley assortment of items he'd stored for possible later use in the backseat. What he needed most by dawn's early light was a shower and a cup of coffee, not necessarily in that order. What he got, instead, was the sight of Julie emerging from her mother's house, dressed in bicycle shorts and an oversized pink T-shirt with some kind of cartoon character on it, her hair in a ponytail and sneakers on her feet.

The mere sight of her made his heart speed up. And not just from the dazzling effect of her beauty on all his salient male parts, although that was there in the mix, too. What really got his heart going was pure, unadulterated fear.

She was, obviously, going for a run. Alone. From the spot behind the overgrown honeysuckle hedge where he had resituated the Blazer after she'd gone inside with her mother, Mac watched with utter disbelief as she ran down the steps and across the yard, then set off down the sidewalk at a brisk pace. Either the woman hadn't believed a single word he'd said, or she had a death wish.

Or both.

He said a few choice words under his breath as he sprang out of the Blazer, glanced at Josephine, who was stretched out sound asleep on her back, paws flapping in the air, amid the destruction in the backseat, obviously exhausted by her active night, and set off after Julie. The neighborhood was semi-rural, a quiet enclave of ranch-style homes on well-tended half-acre lots about five miles to the north of Summerville proper. He knew the area fairly well: it was a nice enough one, inhabited mostly by retirees and empty-nesters looking to downsize. A glance at his watch told him that it was twenty-six minutes after seven A.M. Most of these people—the intelligent ones, anyway—would still be in bed. One old lady came out on her porch to retrieve her newspaper as Mac jogged past. He waved at her. She scowled at him suspiciously.

He already knew that they didn't cotton much to strangers around these parts. He'd once done a background check on the daughter of a woman who lived in the area, and it had been like pulling hen's teeth to get the neighbors to talk to him.

It would be an ideal place for a hit. Few witnesses. Easy access to the expressway. Just pull up beside her and *blam,* blow her away.

Mac's blood ran cold at the thought.

Up ahead, Julie turned the corner, still running at a steady pace and sticking to the sidewalk. He eyed her slender figure with growing wrath. She hadn't betrayed the least awareness of him, and as he got a good view of her profile—delicate features, swinging ponytail, bouncing breasts, long, limber legs—he saw why: She was wearing a Walkman.

An army division could have been running behind her in full combat gear and she wouldn't have heard. To a professional killer with a job to finish, taking her out would be a piece of cake.

Disgusted, he decided to show her just how vulnerable to a surprise attack she was. He increased his pace until he was right behind her and gave her ponytail a tug.

She spun, screeching, and thrust her hand in his direction as she danced backward. Before he realized what was happening, he found himself on the business end of a can of—was it Mace?

It was. Before he could react, the mist hit his eyes like a flamethrower. The instant burning made him think of hellfire. He bellowed in surprise and pain, clawing at his face, his eyes, bending double, scrubbing at his face with the end of his shirt, all to no avail.

He was going to be burned, scarred, blinded for life. At least, that was how it felt. He knew, *knew,* that Mace hurt like hell but left no permanent aftereffects. There was faint comfort in the knowledge when his face felt like it was melting and his eyes felt like someone had stuck hot pokers deep in the sockets.

"Damn it, Julie!" It was a groan of agony.

"Mac! Oh, Mac! Oh, Mac!" Her hand was on his shoulder, the top of his head, his arm. He got the impression that she was bending over him, peering into his face, but he couldn't be sure because he couldn't see. "I'm so sorry! I thought you were the hit man."

Then the horror in her voice gave way to—was it a giggle? Yes, it was. A whole infuriating string of them. Seconds later she was talking through them to someone— he couldn't quite make out what was being said, or who the newcomer was, although the voice sounded male. Still bent almost double, staggering around like a blind, drunken hunchback, Mac felt stark fear override even the pain. She had rendered him—her supposed protector— all but helpless, and now, right at the worst possible moment, here came some unknown guy. Was it the hit man? Not likely. If it had been, she would have been dead by now, and so probably would he. Professional killers didn't usually hang about exchanging conversation with their giggling victims. Desperate to see who had accosted her, Mac scrubbed at his face with a different portion of his shirt, and managed to open his swollen, burning eyes a slit.

Just in time to get hit in the face with a burst of cold water so strong it could have been shot from a cannon. Julie had found a hose, complete with water and a little old man who had apparently brought it to her, and turned it on him.

"Oh, Jesus!" Stumbling backward, Mac tried to protect his face as the water caused the burning to intensify exponentially.

"Here, you do it," Julie said, thrusting the hose into his hand. "I want to finish my run."

"You stay right here. Do you hear me?" It was a barked order, uttered as his fingers closed blindly around the pulsing rubber tube. He grabbed for her with his free hand, but couldn't find her. But at least she was nearby. He could hear her still chuckling at his plight. Did she have no clue as to how much danger she was in? Obviously not. If he could just get the stuff out of his eyes, he thought frantically, they'd be all right. Remembering his police training on Mace—no matter how much it hurt, water was the preferred vehicle for flushing it from the eyes—he tried angling the hose up so that the onslaught would not be as extreme and pulling his lids apart with his free hand at the same time so that the falling water could run into them, and groaned as he succeeded. Cold torrent or no, his eyes burned like be-damned.

"I saw how this fellow was chasing you before you squirted him. You want I should call the police?" The old guy was brandishing a cell phone and talking to Julie, and from his tone Mac supposed he should consider himself lucky the guy didn't have his own can of Mace.

Mac managed another look to find that the man, who appeared to be about as old as Methuselah, was wearing belted, baggy shorts that ended just above his knobby knees, a striped, tucked-in sport shirt, black socks, and dress shoes. He was standing shoulder to shoulder with Julie, phone at the ready. Both of them were watching Mac's suffering without a trace of sympathy that he could detect, although his vision was admittedly still pretty blurry.

"No. Oh, no." Julie laughed again—thus dispelling Mac's last hope that maybe there was some sympathy there he just was not picking up on—as Mac soaked the end of his shirt and scrubbed it one more time over his burning face. "I'm sure he's learned his lesson. Thanks for your help."

Then, to Mac's combined horror and disbelief, she turned on her heel and took off again, continuing her run with the same blithe disregard for her continued existence that had caused the whole fiasco in the first place.

"Damn it, Julie, come back here!" he yelled after her, blinking and squinting at her retreating figure, knowing that he was in no condition to follow. But, except for an airy wave that was scarcely more than a blur to his traumatized eyes, she paid no attention at all. Instead, she restored the headphones to their previous position over her ears and picked up the pace until she turned another corner and disappeared from sight.

"Damn it to *hell*." But there was no help for it. He couldn't see well enough to go chasing after her. She was on her own.

By the time he made it back to the Blazer some fifteen minutes later, he was having waking nightmares about what might have befallen her. To add to the fun, his face and eyes felt like they'd been stung by about a thousand jellyfish, his clothes were dripping wet and icy cold, and he was being harangued from behind by Julie's would-be protector, who had followed him suspiciously all the way back to the car. As a consequence, he was mad as hell.

He was also just in time to watch Julie sprint up the steps of her mother's house and disappear safely inside. At that point, he didn't know whether to be glad or sorry. If the hit man had taken her out, at least he would have been saved the trouble of later wringing her neck.

The old man's cell phone started ringing, distracting him from his determined pursuit. Mac took advantage of the opportunity to jerk open the driver's door, meaning to collapse on the front seat and close and lock the door before the old guy could start in on him again. To his amazement, a snarling Josephine leaped past him like a fuzzy white missile and proceeded to commit felonious assault upon the now screaming old gentleman's bare, bony shin.

It cost him five hundred dollars, a look at Josephine's license—thank God the pink collar to which it was attached was still in the backseat—and a couple of Band-Aids from the glove compartment to make *that* go away.

Hanging grimly on to Josephine, wondering if she was (a) rabid despite having been vaccinated, or (b) just plain insane, Mac at last got rid of the now-raving old man and sank down in the Blazer's front seat for a badly needed period of R and R.

"What were you *thinking?*" This he addressed to Josephine, who was now sitting in the passenger seat beside him, once again daintily feminine in her favorite pink-and-rhinestone collar. She wagged her tail and looked innocent, clearly hoping to convince the unwary that she hadn't just tried to chew off a helpless old man's leg. Mac thanked God that she was a seven-pound poodle instead of a rottweiler, realized that he was talking to the dog as if she could understand him and, furthermore, reply, and dropped his head back against the seat in despair. He was the one who was losing his marbles, he decided. No, not losing. Had lost.

Out of the corner of his eye, Mac saw a white blur drive past. A horn honked. A hand waved.

Julie.

He sat up in time to watch the white Infiniti disappear around the corner.

Swearing a blue streak, he started the Blazer, did a one-eighty, and took off after her, despite a sudden, fleeting temptation just to leave her to the tender mercies of the hit man he was pretty damn sure was out there.

Not much to his surprise, she drove into Summerville and pulled up in the parking lot behind the strip mall that housed her shop. The one in which people who were not trying to keep their presence in her life a secret generally parked.

To hell with it. He figured that cat was out of the bag with a vengeance now anyway. As he slammed to a halt beside the Infiniti, he watched her walk across the parking lot toward one of the brown metal doors set into the back of the low brick building. She looked cool and beautiful—hell, when did she ever not?—in a snug black T-shirt and a teensy white skirt with her hair falling loose around her shoulders. There were a few other people in the lot—a man heading toward another of the metal doors, a woman carrying a garbage bag toward the Dumpster—but to all intents and purposes she was alone.

If he were a hit man, she'd be toast.

Fortunately for her, he was not. He grabbed Josephine—it was already too hot to leave her in the car with the motor turned off—tucked her football-style under his arm, and sprinted across the parking lot after Julie.

He reached her just as she was inserting her key into the lock of the metal door. The tension in her stance told him that she'd seen him coming. The tilt of her head told him that she didn't like it.

"What are you, a slow learner?" She gave him an evil look that was mitigated somewhat by the sheer beauty of those long-lashed Bambi eyes. "Leave me alone." Her gaze flicked down to the poodle, which was wriggling with pleasure at seeing her. "Hello, Josephine."

Josephine yapped excitedly and tried beating him to death with her tail.

"You two *should* be buddies," Mac said sourly. "You're both major pains in the ass. Now that you've had your fun for the morning, you feel like listening to my side of the story?"

"Take a hike." She got the door open, stepped inside, and tried closing it in his face. He snorted and strong-armed his way through.

"Okay, forget it. I lied to you and I used you. If that's going to be the bottom line for you, it's fine by me."

He was standing in an office, he discovered as he set

Josephine down on the carpeted floor, that was dark and pleasant-smelling and approximately as cold as Antartica in winter. Julie's face tightened as she looked at him, but she seemed to realize, rightly, that ordering him out would be a waste of breath because she closed and locked the door again, then turned to glare at him.

"Good. Then we're both happy. Or at least, I would be if you'd get the hell out of my shop."

"Not happening."

Mac walked a couple of paces into the room, casting wary looks around. Mirrors everywhere. A shiny black desk with nothing on it except a desk set and a telephone. A silver rack half-full of dresses. A gray flannel couch.

"It's freezing in here."

"If you're cold, it's probably because you're all wet." Her tone gave that a double meaning which she obviously relished.

He returned from a quick inspection of the bathroom that opened off the office to look at her.

"And I would be all wet because somebody Maced me."

Julie gave an unrepentant laugh as she crossed to her desk. "You shouldn't have scared me."

"Listen, Miss America, can you say hit man?" Her cavalier attitude was really beginning to irk him.

"No, but I can say bullshit." She straightened up from tucking her purse under the desk and gave him a great big go-to-hell smile. "And that's what I do say: bullshit, bullshit, bullshit."

"You willing to bet your life you're right?" Now that her office had been awarded the all-clear, Mac glanced around for the thermostat. If he didn't get that air-conditioner shut off soon, it was going to kill him. "Remember the guy who broke into your house? Remember the girl who got hit by a car while wearing *your* dress in front of *your* store last night? What are they, figments of my imagination?"

There was a pause. Julie stared at him without speaking. Then her lips pursed, and she glanced away.

Hah, Mac thought. He was finally getting through. He spotted the thermostat on the wall nearby and stepped over to it, turning the little knob until the blast of arctic air abruptly stopped.

"Leave the air-conditioning alone," Julie said, coming up behind him and smacking his hand away from the control, then turning the knob the other way again so that refrigerator-caliber air once again blasted from the vents. "I have clients coming. If you're cold, I have a simple remedy for you: leave."

"Keep sweet-talking me like that, and you may never get rid of me." He abandoned his surreptitious repeat attack on the knob to grab her around the waist and swing her back behind him when she would have walked out into the main area of the store. "Hold it right there."

"Let go of me! What do you think you're doing?" She glared at him as she whisked herself free of his hold.

"Besides forming icicles?" Drawing his gun from its berth in the small of his back—which was, thankfully, one of the few remaining dry areas on his body—he moved into the large, elegant room ahead of her, scanning it for any sign of disturbance or unauthorized occupancy, checking behind racks of dresses and a large potted palm and a pair of gray flannel chairs for an intruder. "Doing my best to keep you alive. Without any noticeable help from you, I might add. Is that front door locked?"

"Of course it's locked. I haven't opened up yet."

"Keep it that way. Only open it to people you know."

A beat passed during which she just looked at him.

"You're being ridiculous."

Without answering, he headed toward the back rooms—

fitting rooms, he discovered, three of them, large and elegantly appointed and paneled in floor-to-ceiling mirrors. Julie, with Josephine at her heels, followed. Both watched his efforts with heads cocked in a way that was purely feminine.

"No hit man?" Julie's voice was sardonic as he emerged from the last of the fitting rooms.

"Not so far."

"I can't tell you how much that relieves my mind." She glared at him. "Now that you've made sure there's no bogeyman under the bed, you can get out of my shop. I have a business to run here, and you are in the way."

"What I can't understand," Mac said, ignoring that last speech entirely as he moved back into the main room where the blast from the air-conditioning was at least distributed over a larger area, somewhat lessening its effect, "is why you're here today at all. Shouldn't you close up shop for a while as a sign of respect to the dearly departed?"

Julie's brow wrinkled, and a flash of pain darkened her eyes. "I thought about closing, but I talked to the Miss Southern Beauty officials last night. The pageant will go ahead as scheduled. They mean to have a moment of silence during the opening ceremony tomorrow to honor Carlene, but otherwise there's no change. And I'm dressing seven other girls. Five of them are scheduled to come in for final wardrobe fittings today. If the pageant's on, I have no choice but to be here."

"I don't believe this." Trying not to shiver, Mac shook his head in complete and total frustration. "I'm talking about somebody trying to kill you here, and you're talking about a beauty pageant. Let's try to get a handle on our priorities, shall we? What we need to do is get you the hell out of Dodge. Lie low somewhere out of state, maybe, until we get some answers. Forget the damned beauty pageant."

"No," Julie said, fists on hips as she scowled at him. "I won't forget it. This is my business. And those girls are counting on me. Anyway, please explain to me exactly why I need you, because I don't have a clue. Let's just say, for a moment, that you're right about this hit-man thing. If I really thought I was in danger, I'd run to the police so fast you wouldn't see me for the blur."

"And they'd be real polite, and write up a nice little report, and that would be that." Mac's voice was flat. "Until you were dead. *Then* they might start an investigation. But, oopsy, too late for you."

Julie's eyes shot sparks at that. Mac supposed that his words hadn't been all that tactful, but he was tired and wet and cold and his eyes burned and her attitude was not only driving him totally around the bend, it was dangerous. For her.

And it bothered him a whole hell of a lot to realize that anything that was dangerous for her scared the socks off him.

"You know what?" she said with that little clenched-teeth smile he was beginning to know way better than he wanted to. "I'm prepared to take my chances. So you can just go away. You know, leave. Vamoose. Scram. Shoo. Whichever one of those works for you."

He returned her unflinching stare for unflinching stare, then took a calming minute to return his gun to its accustomed position inside his waistband. She could lose her temper all she wanted to, he told himself. He was going to keep his.

Then at least one of them would be operating with a

full order of french fries. "Give it up, Julie," he said tiredly. "I'm not going anywhere. At least, not without you. You want to know why you need me? Because, whether you believe it or not, I'm pretty sure your life is in danger here. Which means you need somebody watching out for you, and from where I'm standing, darlin', it looks like I'm all you've got."

27

BY SEVEN P.M., JULIE WAS SO TIRED her eyes felt grainy. Tara Lumley was the last of her clients, and her handler had wanted some eleventh-hour beading added to her aqua evening gown. With Carlene out of the picture—a fact every single girl had bemoaned, right down to the shedding of tears, even while they schemed how best to take advantage of the loss of the widely acknowledged favorite—the pageant had been blown wide open. It was a free-for-all, and Tara wanted to do everything she could to catch the judges' eyes. They all did.

In consequence, Julie sewed and stuffed and whittled and trimmed as she never had before in her life.

"You'll be there tomorrow night, won't you, Julie?" Tara asked anxiously as Julie let her and Linda Wheeler, her handler, out the front door, which, to pacify Mac, she'd kept locked at the cost of great inconvenience to clients and staff alike all day.

"I'll be there for the duration. Don't worry, you're going to do great." She hugged Tara, and Linda, then watched them walk out into the still-bright evening.

"Like hell you will," Mac said, appearing in the doorway between the showroom and the office, where he had spent most of the day alternately talking on the phone and using her computer, just as she walked past it. He was wearing a fresh pair of jeans and a plain black T-shirt that he'd had his assistant, Rawanda, bring him early that morning, and he looked so handsome that the girls had fluttered at the sight of him. Several had asked her covertly who he was when he had disappeared back into her office again after the cursory visual check he subjected all arrivals and departures to. Julie had told them that he was a visiting dress designer who went by the name of Debbie, and had taken perverse satisfaction in watching their faces fall.

"What?" Julie stopped and glared at him. She was getting tired of this master-of-the-universe thing he'd had going on all day.

"I said, you're not going to that beauty pageant." Mac returned her glare with stony-eyed determination. His eyes were bloodshot, and there were lines she'd never noticed before around them and his mouth. In addition, his disposition had been deteriorating steadily all day. "Everybody and his mother expects you to be there. Let's try to at least make the guy who's trying to kill you work hard to earn his money, okay?"

Julie simmered. "I've got a news flash for you, bubba: You don't tell me what to do. Anyway, I've been thinking: Exactly *why* is Sid supposed to want to kill me? It can't be over money: I signed a prenup. It can't be because I made the colossal mistake of sleeping with you: He didn't know about that until just a couple of minutes before that car hit Carlene. Are you suggesting he wants to kill me just so he won't have to endure the trauma of divorce? Sorry, I don't buy it. So what's your rationale here?"

Mac's lips compressed. "I don't know exactly yet."

Julie made a derisive sound. "That's what I thought."

"Julie, what time do you want me in the morning?" Meredith emerged from the dressing room where she'd been tidying up. She couldn't have heard their conversation—it had been conducted in little more than hissed whispers—but she must have sensed the atmosphere between them, because she stopped in the doorway and looked self-consciously from Julie to Mac and back. "Oh, sorry, I didn't mean to interrupt."

"You're not interrupting," Julie said with a sigh, pointedly turning her back on Mac to smile at Meredith. Her head ached from doing so much close work with her needle—those bugle beads were tiny, and the design Tara had wanted had required hundreds—and she massaged the area just above her nose with a forefinger. "There are no appointments tomorrow, so why don't you just plan to meet me in the auditorium tomorrow night? Be a little early, in case any of the girls' gowns need work."

Meredith smiled. "I'm so excited. I've never been to the governor's mansion before."

"It should be fun."

Mac still stood in the doorway, silently smoldering, and Julie glared at him while Meredith went to retrieve her purse.

"I'm going now," Meredith said, returning with her purse tucked under her arm. Julie wasn't sure how much Meredith actually knew about what was going on, but obviously she knew that Amber was no longer there—Julie had left a message on Amber's answering machine firing her when she didn't come in again that morning—and something major was up. If nothing else, Sid had called twice and both times Julie had refused to take his calls, which she never did; and Mac's largely silent but impossible to overlook presence all day was a dead giveaway. But she hadn't asked any questions, and Julie appreciated that.

Now Meredith glanced from Julie to Mac and back, then seemed to hesitate. "Uh, Julie—do you need me to stay? Are you going to be all right?"

"I'll be fine. You go on," Julie said, while Mac, obviously knowing when he was being insulted, however subtly, leaned one shoulder against the jamb, crossed his arms over his chest, and looked sardonic.

"See you tomorrow night, then," Meredith said.

"Thanks for all your hard work today." Julie walked her to the door and smiled at her as she left. She was glad to see that Meredith was looking slightly reassured as she set off down the sidewalk.

"You will not," Mac said, scowling, as Julie locked the door and turned back into the room, "see her tomorrow night."

"Want to bet?" Julie smiled sweetly as she walked toward him.

"Oh, yeah."

"Excuse me." The words were pointed, because he still blocked the doorway to her office as she reached it. He didn't move, and she had perforce to stop, glaring at him. He met her gaze with a meditative expression.

"Know what I've been doing today?"

"Besides being a total jackass and guzzling enough coffee to float the ark?" Julie asked. "No clue."

"I've been checking payroll records for Rand Corporation."

"What? How?"

Mac held up his hand. His key ring dangled from a finger.

"With this." He touched a black spark-plug-looking thing that hung on the ring with the keys. "I used it to download files off your computer yesterday. Sid's business records make interesting reading."

"Aren't you the sneaky one!" Julie marveled, punching him none-too-gently in the stomach and then, as he stepped back with an *ooph* and rubbed his belly in reaction, shoving past him into her office. "But I must say that it's a nice change to hear you actually *admitting* that you used me to get information on Sid."

"I am not admitting . . ."

Julie interrupted ruthlessly. "Know what? I don't care."

Silenced, Mac eyed her in exasperation as she retrieved her purse from under the desk. Josephine, who was stretched out beside Julie's purse, looked up and wagged her tail inquiringly. The poodle was once again wearing her sparkly pink collar, and looked adorable. Like Mac, she had been a big hit with the girls.

"Time to go home," Julie said to her, straightening, purse in hand.

"Your father received a steady paycheck from the Rand Corporation until fifteen years ago. Then it stopped. The same month as Kelly Carlson disappeared. The same month as . . ."

"Will you stop?" Julie headed for the door. "Enough with the conspiracy theories already. I'm tired, I'm hungry, and I've got a headache. For your information, I believe that Lee Harvey Oswald acted alone. I believe that Princess Diana's car crash was an accident. And I believe that you've gone totally out of your mind."

She jerked open the door and looked pointedly at him. "And now, would you please walk out this door so I can lock up?"

Mac gave her a narrow-eyed look, then snapped his fingers for Josephine. The poodle appeared, stretching and yawning luxuriously, and Mac scooped her up.

"Too bad you're not more like your dog," Julie said as Mac walked past her into the soft bright warmth of the summer evening. *"She's* a sweetheart. You're a sweetheart, Josephine."

Josephine wagged her tail.

"So what do you want for dinner?" Mac asked as she finished locking the door and turned to find him waiting.

"Are you suggesting that you and I might be going to have a mutual dinner? Not a chance." After taking a careful look around—not that she really, truly *believed* Mac's nonsense, mind you, but it had raised just enough doubt in her mind to make her slightly paranoid and, anyway, she couldn't get Carlene's awful fate out of her mind—Julie headed toward her car.

Mac and Josephine fell in beside her. "If you don't feel like eating, fine. You can watch me."

"I'm having dinner with my mother. She's cooking. She's still very upset because I'm getting a divorce. She needs to vent." Just the thought made Julie feel gloomy. She was going to hear about the folly of divorcing Sid for approximately the next hundred years.

"Call her and tell her you have other plans."

Mac obviously had never dealt with her mother.

"No." But the idea was tempting. Oh, so tempting. She was so not in the mood to be harangued.

Julie reached the protection of the Infiniti's back end and stopped between it and the Blazer. If there did happen to be more to Mac's hit-man theory than hot air, at least she wasn't going to get run over if she could help it.

The image of Carlene somersaulting over the roof of the car that killed her had replayed itself in her mind every time she had closed her eyes. As a result, she'd been awake most of the night. If Mac was right, that should have been her. The thought made her shiver. Maybe she *should* go to the police. Only Mac had said they wouldn't be able to keep her safe. . . .

"Okay, here's the . . ." *deal,* she started to say, but broke off as Mac handed her Josephine then dropped to his hands and knees on the pavement. While she watched, astonished, he peered underneath the Blazer.

"What are you doing?"

He took his sweet time looking, then rose lithely to his feet, dusting off his hands and knees and retrieving Josephine from her. "Checking for bombs."

"Oh, my God." Julie rolled her eyes.

That was it. This was getting bizarre. And scary. She hated to admit it, but it was also getting very scary. She didn't know which part was scarier, though: the idea that Mac was insane, or the idea that he wasn't. In any case, she was going to the police—right after she had dinner with her mother.

"If you're planning to follow me out to my mother's again tonight, you can just forget it." Her voice was tart. She scowled at him.

"You don't have to worry. I'm not."

He opened the Blazer's back door and deposited Josephine inside. Closing that door, he opened the front passenger door and did something to the inner panel. Then he looked at her.

"Get in."

"*What?* No."

Julie turned to the Infiniti. Before she could punch the button that unlocked the door, he gave an unamused sounding laugh and scooped her up from behind.

"What are you doing? Put me down!"

She kicked wildly. She would have punched him, but her arms were trapped by his.

Without replying, he stuffed her into the front seat of the Blazer with practiced efficiency and shut the door on her. As he walked around to the other side, Julie immediately tried to get out. The door wouldn't open. She realized with a burst of fury that he had depressed the tiny button on the inner panel of the door that activated the childproof locks.

"What the hell do you think you're doing?" Snarling, she turned on him with clenched fists as he slid inside. "You let me out!"

"Put your seat belt on," he said, and started the car, backing up in a smooth arc.

"I am not going anywhere with you! Nowhere, do you hear? I knew it all along: you're a dangerous lunatic! This is kidnapping, you no-good, lying . . ." Left groping for words bad enough to describe him, she grabbed for the keys, which were dangling from the ignition, instead.

"Oh no you don't." He caught her hand, slamming on the brake at the same time. The Blazer screeched to a halt in the middle of the parking lot. Removing her hand from the keys but keeping his hold on it, Mac turned on her. His expression was grim.

"Just so there's no mistake," he said in a lethal drawl that left her in no doubt that he teetered on the brink of losing his temper, too, "I think you should know that I'm having a bad day here. I didn't get any sleep last night. I got Maced this morning. I got soaked with a hose. I'm starving. I may be suffering from an overdose of caffeine. This damned case is a riddle, and I've got a pounding headache from trying to solve it. I think I'm catching a cold, thanks to your air-conditioning. I've spent the entire day in a dress shop listening to a gaggle of women think up ways to fool us poor men about the size of every female body part under the sun. And I've had to put up with your piss-poor attitude throughout. Tonight I have a ton of work I have to do, and I also need food and sleep. None of these things can happen while I'm chasing around the countryside after you. Which means that you're coming with me. And I don't want to hear another word about it. Am I making myself clear here?"

"If I don't show up for supper, my mother will call the police," Julie said, snatching her hand from his.

"Told her about Sid's take on *till death do us part,* did you?"

He took his foot off the brake. The Blazer was moving once more.

"If by that you mean, did I tell her about your ridiculous idea that Sid's hired a hit man to kill me, no, I did not. I didn't want to worry her."

They were on the street now, moving toward the expressway. Glowering at Mac, Julie pulled on her seat belt. It would be stupid to die in an accident just to prove she could.

"Did you ever think that you might be endangering your family by being with them? Whoever our hit man is, he's obviously not all that careful about who he kills. If they're with you when he comes for you, he might get your mother or sister too—or instead."

The thought was so appalling that Julie was left with nothing to say.

"Give me your phone." Her voice was sulky.

He passed it to her. She shot him a look chock-full of loathing. Then she punched in the number.

"Mama? It's Julie. I'm not going to make it home for supper. I'll talk to you later. Love you. Bye." She punched the disconnect button and puffed out her cheeks in a relieved sigh. "I got the answering machine, thank goodness."

"Does your mother scare you that much?" Mac sounded amused.

"She'll scare you too," Julie said with relish. "She blames

you for ruining my marriage, and nothing I say can convince her otherwise. She wants to meet you."

"She sounds about as amenable to reason as you."

Josephine chose that moment to climb into Julie's lap. Distracted, Julie scratched behind her ears, then stroked her coat as she settled down with obvious contentment. Thank God for Josephine. Josephine was better for the nerves than Valium.

"So, what do you want for dinner?" Mac asked with a half-smile after a moment.

Julie scowled at him. "My mother's tuna casserole."

"Great. I feel like pizza, too. That way I can eat while I work."

He picked up his cell phone and punched in some numbers.

"McQuarry and Hinkle." Julie had heard that voice before. She realized that it belonged to Rawanda, Mac's assistant.

"Order pizza. One with everything, and one with—" Mac glanced at Julie inquiringly.

"Vegetarian," she said, only because she was really hungry and feared what she would be forced to eat if she didn't. Pizza was way too fattening to be one of her diet staples. Pizza was also right up there with chocolate as one of her true loves.

"Veggies only," he repeated into the phone, and hung up.

They were on the expressway now, heading toward Charleston. Traffic was moderate. In the distance, a mountain of purple clouds rolling in over the bay promised rain later. Rain was a good thing, because it would usually cool things off for a few hours. It was also a bad thing, because after the initial relief the humidity would only get worse.

Julie said nothing for the duration of the drive, and Mac, after a glance at her face, didn't say anything either.

When he finally parked, it was in an alley that ran through the middle of a block of small, not especially prosperous-looking office buildings.

"Now be nice," he said. "These people are putting themselves at risk to help keep you safe."

Julie glared at him. "I'm always nice. Unless I'm lied to. Or lied to and used. I have to admit, that tends to take away from my nice."

Mac laughed, and got out of the car.

When he came around to her side, Julie, holding Josephine, got out too. She didn't seem to have much choice.

"Let her down for a minute," he said, scrounging in the back and coming up with Josephine's leash, which he clipped to her collar. "It seemed like she had to go every five minutes last night, and I'd just as soon not have a repeat."

Julie obediently put Josephine on the ground. She held on to the leash and Mac held on to her with a hand wrapped around her wrist as if he was afraid she might take off running.

"Where are we going, anyway?"

"To my office. I've had people working on this since yesterday. I need to check in, see what they've found out."

Mac steered her back to the street, around a corner, and across a parking lot toward the third in a row of four nondescript buildings.

"Why didn't you just park in the lot?" Her high-heeled slides weren't meant for lengthy hikes.

"I thought you might feel like getting some exercise." He grinned at the look on her face. "Actually, I parked back there so that no one could tell we're inside from just driving by. Rest easy, though: By the time we're ready to leave, there will be a vehicle waiting for us right out front.

Mother's dropping us off some new wheels. The Blazer's history for the duration."

"How convenient to know a car thief."

"It is, isn't it?"

Mac's office was on the second floor, behind a wooden door with a frosted-glass insert on which was painted in bold black script MCQUARRY AND HINKLE, PRIVATE INVESTIGATORS. The door opened as they reached it, and, glancing inside, Julie realized that its windows overlooked the parking lot and they must have been seen arriving.

"Did you time that right or what? Pizza just got here." Rawanda, looking plumply pretty in tight orange jeans and a purple T-shirt, greeted them at the door. "Whoa, boss, you lookin' rough. What you been doin' to him, honey?"

"For one thing, she kept me up all night," Mac replied as he ushered Julie inside, then grinned in response to Julie's outraged look. George Hinkle, neatly casual in a white polo shirt and dark slacks, looked up from where he was working at a computer on a desk near the door and nodded at her.

"Hey, Mac. Mrs. Carlson." There was a fair amount of reserve in his tone as he greeted her, and Julie remembered that he'd been upset about Mac's association with her. He didn't look any happier about it tonight. Which was fine with her. She wasn't sure how happy she was about it herself.

"Please call me Julie," she said, then made a wry face. "I'm about to lose the Carlson, anyway. I'm getting a divorce."

"We heard that," Rawanda said, shaking her head in commiseration. "Divorce is a bitch. I've done had two. Didn't make me a dime out of either one, either."

"You didn't tell me you'd had *two*." Hinkle frowned at

Rawanda, who looked self-conscious. Clearly there was a relationship between them—of which Mac, who was moving toward the pizza boxes a step ahead of Josephine, seemed to disapprove, if his expression was anything to go by.

"Uh, I might just have forgotten to mention one." Rawanda's gaze swung to Julie. "You want some pizza? No need to let the boss hog it all."

"Um, just one slice," Julie said, following Rawanda as the other woman headed toward where Mac was opening the pizza boxes. A heavenly smell reached Julie's nostrils, making her stomach growl. She realized that, between stress and the press of work, she hadn't eaten anything all day except a glass of orange juice at her mother's that morning and a pair of stray Hershey's Kisses found at the bottom of her work basket at the shop.

"Here." Mac put a slice of vegetarian pizza on a napkin and passed it to her. A six-pack of Coke had obviously come with the pizza, and he handed her a can. It wasn't diet, which was what she usually drank, but it would do. The whole supremely unhealthy meal would do. Oh, yes, she thought, biting off the tip of her slice and savoring the wonderful flavor, it would definitely do.

"You get that Simmons thing done?" Mac, sitting on a corner of the desk and biting into his own well-laden slice, asked his partner. Hinkle was on his feet now, helping himself to pizza.

"Yeah." He glanced at Julie, then back at Mac. "You want those pictures, they're on your desk."

Sinking down on the couch to savor her treat, Julie interpreted the glance that Hinkle had thrown her way to mean that the pictures were the ones he had taken of Sid and Amber.

The thought didn't even hurt.

Mac nodded. "Thanks." He took another bite. "So what have you got for me?"

Rawanda, her mouth full of pizza, shook her head and said, "Ooh, boy."

Hinkle took a bite out of his own pizza slice, then slid a sideways glance at Julie before replying. "The Rand Corporation is the parent company for all kinds of business enterprises. Some of them seem legitimate, or at least they perform real services, like All-American Builders or Sweetwater's. Others appear to be dummy companies used to move assets and money around, kind of like a shell game. Bottom line is, Rand Corporation is definitely mob-affiliated, if not mob-controlled. Julie's father, Mike Williams, drew a steady paycheck from the Rand Corporation for eleven years, ending in January 1987. He was listed as a transportation specialist, which I interpreted as a truck driver. Most of the personnel records have some sort of notation about the reason employment with the company ended—retirement, resignation, termination. His paychecks simply stopped being issued. No reason given."

"The same month Daniel and Kelly Carlson disappeared," Mac said. "All right, what's the connection?"

"That I don't know," Hinkle said. "At least, not yet."

Mac looked thoughtful. "Mike Williams stopped working for Rand Corporation in January 1987, but he was still alive. He was seen again after that date."

"He didn't die until 1992," Hinkle said, confirming Mac's words.

Mac's gaze moved to Julie. "Didn't you say that you saw your father off and on until you were fourteen, and then he dropped out of your life for a few years? When did you see him again?"

Julie took a swallow of Coke. Even after all these years,

she didn't much like talking about the father who'd been pretty much a nonpresence in her life.

"I was nineteen. It was right before I won Miss South Carolina."

Mac got an arrested expression on his face. "Didn't you say you met Sid right after you won that?"

Julie nodded.

"I need you to tell me everything you can remember about your father, all the way up to your last meeting with him. Can you do that?"

28

JULIE JUST LOOKED AT MAC for a moment without reply-ing. Suddenly the slice of pizza she had just polished off felt heavy as lead in her stomach. She wished, vainly, that she hadn't eaten it.

"I think Mr. Hinkle—"

"George," George interjected.

"George, then. I think George was right. I think my father was a truck driver. At least, there was a time when he was always saying he'd do this or that with us—Becky and me—when he got off the road. And he was on the road a lot." She paused, her eyes meeting Mac's as she took a deep, and, she hoped, unobtrusive breath. "I really don't know that much about him. He and my mother divorced when I was two. He was her second husband. She had four others after him. Men are—they used to be—kind of dis-posable for her. He never came around much, although Mama would call him sometimes—" Telling this was hard, she discovered, harder even than she had expected: it was way too personal; if Mac had not held her gaze, giving her a lifeline to grab on to, she would never have gotten so much out. "—when she needed money. When he had it, he would give it to her. I got the impression he didn't have it a lot."

"He dropped out of your life entirely when you were fourteen?"

Julie nodded, and swallowed. Mac got up from the desk and came to crouch in front of her, taking her hands. Julie's fingers tightened around his almost convulsively.

"Can you tell me about the last time you saw him? I think it might be important."

It was clear from his expression that he realized this was a difficult subject for her. His silent support strengthened her. She forgot that he had lied to her, had used her, and that there had been an ulterior motive to his friendship from the beginning. All she knew was that every time, when she had needed him, he'd been there for her—just as he was there for her now. She looked into his eyes, locked her gaze on his, and, reluctantly, cast her mind back ten years.

"Mama and Becky were both gone somewhere—I don't remember where now, but I do remember I was alone. It was just getting dark, and I was sitting in the living room of our trailer—we lived in a trailer, Mama and Becky and me—hemming a dress I meant to wear in the Miss South Carolina pageant and watching something on TV, and there was a knock on the door. I got up to answer it, and there stood Daddy, just as big as Ike. I hadn't seen him in about five years, and we just looked at each other for a minute, and then he said *howdy, Becky* and I kind of laughed and said *I'm Julie* and he said *oh, of course* and *how you doing* and that sort of thing. He came on in, but he seemed real uncomfortable—well, I was uncomfortable, too, because I didn't know him very well, even if he was my father, and he didn't even know me well enough to tell me apart from Becky. Anyway, we visited for a little while—I can't really remember what we talked about, but nothing very much. Like I said, it was kind of awkward, and he seemed kind of on edge, like he was anxious to go."

Julie paused, and swallowed again, and her eyes dropped from Mac's eyes to his mouth. It was a truly beautiful mouth, even if it was a man's mouth and "beautiful" probably wasn't the right word for it. She stared at it and thought how beautiful it was because she didn't want to think about anything else.

"Julie?"

Unwillingly, her eyes met his again. God, she didn't want to go back there. These memories belonged to another lifetime—another Julie. A far too vulnerable Julie.

"Then he left. He walked out the door, and I walked to the door too, and watched him walk to his truck—it was a beat-up old truck—and then he turned around and looked right at me and I waved, and he said *I love you, Becky.*" Julie swallowed. "Then he got in the truck and drove away. I never saw him again until I went to his funeral. The whole time I was there at that funeral I just kept thinking, He was my daddy and he couldn't even get my name straight. How pathetic is that?"

All of a sudden she couldn't talk any more because her throat ached too much. She blinked because her eyes stung. She felt moisture spill over her lower lids and slide down her cheeks and realized she was crying. Embarrassed, she closed her eyes and pulled her hands free of Mac's and covered her face and willed the tears to stop.

"Julie," Mac said, and stood up and gathered her up in his arms and sat back down on the couch with her on his lap. Julie took a deep breath and lowered her hands and blinked at him, hoping the worst of her loss of control was over. After all, it was stupid—*stupid*—to cry over something that was so far in the past. Mac was all blurry, she discovered as she tried to focus him. The tears wouldn't stop no matter how she tried to hold them back, and as she took a deep, meant-to-be-calming breath, it turned without warning into a sob.

Mac's face tightened, and his arms tightened, and he said something that she didn't understand. Knowing that he cared made the tears flow faster despite her best efforts to contain them. She couldn't bear it, she thought, couldn't stand facing the fact that her father had never loved her enough to even make sure of her name, couldn't deal with the welling resurgence of the sense of loss and abandonment that had stayed with her all her life, and she closed her eyes, trying to block the world out along with the pain.

"Oh, God, I'm sorry." It was all she could do to choke the words out. "I'm making a total fool out of myself, I know."

"It's all right to cry." Mac's voice was very soft, and it was her final undoing. He felt so safe and solid and comforting, and she realized that she had needed safe and solid and comforting for years without even realizing it. The thought brought more tears with it, and she gave up the fight to contain them, melting bonelessly against him, wrapping her arms around his neck and burying her face on his shoulder and crying as if her heart would break.

There were vague sounds of movement in the room behind her, but Julie barely noticed. She clung to Mac like a fly to sticky paper and wept as if from a well of sorrow that would never go dry.

"We'll just go now," George said, presumably to Mac. "Call if you need anything."

"Yeah, we're gonna go," Rawanda echoed.

Julie had all but forgotten their presence until they spoke. It was as if she and Mac had been all alone in a bubble, and now, with the realization that others were present, the bubble had popped. She felt a fresh sting of embarrassment, and tried to at least stop the tears now and sit up and show them that, though she might have succumbed to temporary weakness, she had gotten it all out of her system now, and she was far from the crybaby they must think her.

But it was too late: she heard the sound of the door opening and closing and they were gone. Anyway, though she tried hard, really, really hard, she couldn't stop, she discovered to her horror. Now that the tap that led to her deepest, most long-buried emotions had been opened, she couldn't turn it off again any more than she could stop her heart from beating. It was as if she had to cry, just like she had to breathe, to live. The pain had been building up too long, and it had to get out. She hadn't cried, she realized, since her father's final visit, when she'd wept bitterly after he'd left because she'd been secretly wanting her father for years and when he had finally come he couldn't even tell her from her sister. She hadn't even cried at his funeral, and she hadn't cried—not one time—since.

It was almost funny that she was just at this moment realizing that. Was she in touch with her feelings, or what?

The thought brought a little giggle with it that came out sounding more like a gasping sob, and then Mac was kissing her cheek, her ear, her jaw—whatever he could reach—and rocking her back and forth in his arms as if she were a baby and murmuring soothing things to her, and she was acting like a baby and crying as though her heart would break.

Finally, when the tears ended and the sobs quieted into no more than an occasional long shivery sigh, she rested in his arms, spent. Her head was buried in the curve between his shoulder and neck, and she kept it there for a long time because lying against him like that was just exactly what she craved, and anyway she was too drained and too ashamed to look up.

Finally she did. She didn't sit up, but she lifted her head and looked at him. His blue eyes were grave and beautiful as they met hers, and his hand stroked her back through her thin cotton T-shirt almost absently. Her legs, bare to the tops of her thighs because her skirt was short anyway and had ridden up, were bent at the knees and curved around his torso. Her breasts were nestled against his chest and her arms were draped around his neck. He felt warm and firm and so good, so right, holding her that it scared her. She gritted her teeth and lifted her chin because she knew she'd made an absolute fool of herself, and then she gave him a wary frown capped by a prosaic little sniff.

He smiled at her, slowly, and his eyes turned tender.

"Hey," he said. "You're breaking my heart here, you know."

Then he slid his hand up her back to her nape and bent his head and kissed her.

At the touch of his mouth, Julie caught fire. She was suddenly desperate for his warmth, for his tenderness, for the solid comfort of touching him. She pushed her tongue into his mouth, and at the touch of her tongue against his, Mac seemed to detonate. The kiss exploded. Suddenly they were both clinging together, desperate for each other, consumed with passion. His tongue was scalding hot as it thrust deep into her mouth. His mouth was hard and fierce, his arms around her as tight as steel bands. She was plastered so closely against him that she could feel the thud of his heart against her breasts. His hands, as they stroked down her back and pulled the hem of her T-shirt free of her skirt to slide, warm and faintly rough, up her rib cage, were shaking. Julie shivered in response, tightening her arms around her neck and kissing him as if she would die if she didn't. One hard warm hand found her breast, and she made a little sound deep in her throat and was lost, totally lost, to the licking flames of desire.

"Oh, God, Julie." The words were more growl than groan. Mac pressed her backward, and Julie felt the cool slide of leather against her back. Then he was looming over her, yanking her T-shirt over her head, unfastening her skirt and pulling it off, and she was helping him, pulling at his clothes too, until he was bare to the waist and she was tugging his jeans down his legs. He kicked off his sneakers, shucked his briefs, and then he was coming back down to her and she was spreading her knees for him and tugging at his shoulders to bring him closer. His thighs were hard and hot and rough with hair, and unbearably exciting against the silky smoothness of hers. His chest was wide and well muscled, with just the right amount of hair, and it made her mouth go dry just looking at it. His shoulders were broad and firm and slightly damp with sweat beneath her palms.

She wanted him with an intensity that made her dizzy.

But he paused, still keeping his weight from her with his knees and his hands, his gaze sweeping over her.

"Nice," he said, in apparent reference to the lacey white bra and panties she still wore but possibly also to what was inside them. His voice was thick and his eyes burned, and Julie moved sensuously beneath his searing regard. Her hand moved up to cup the back of his head, and she pulled his mouth down to hers. The kiss, which she had meant to be soft and leisurely, was fierce and deep and dazzling instead. When he lifted his head she murmured a protest, sliding her lips down his neck, her mouth open and shaking, as he pulled a little away.

With quick, deft movements he slid his hands behind

her to unfasten her bra and pull it off, then bent his head to capture one of the full, creamy breasts he had exposed. Julie closed her eyes, moaning, and pressed his head closer as his mouth closed over her nipple. His mouth was hot and wet and unbelievably arousing as he suckled first one breast, then the other. Julie arched her back, offering him her breasts with abandon, clutching his head with both hands now as he kissed and sucked and played. She moved with mindless longing beneath him, stroking her hands down his back, over his buttocks, around the tops of his thighs.

He was hard and enormous, she discovered as her hands found him, and she wanted him so much she thought she would die if she had to wait another minute. He groaned as her hand closed around him, and lifted his head from her breasts to watch her face with glittering eyes. Breathless, aching for him, she guided him to her, only to come up against a barrier and be reminded at the last minute that she still wore her tiny lace panties.

She moaned in frustration as he pushed against the barrier of the fragile cloth, ready to rip the offending garment off with her bare hands if she had to to get what she wanted. But his hand was already between them, between her legs, touching her through her panties, rubbing her, making her gasp. Then his hand moved inside one leg opening to slide inside her, in and out, hard and fast, while at the same time he bent his head to kiss her breasts.

"Mac. Oh, Mac." Head flung back against the leather couch, hair spilling toward the floor, Julie reacted like a wild thing, squirming shamelessly beneath him, clutching his shoulders, lifting her hips in wordless supplication, feeling the heat and tension build inside her until she was shaking with it, until she was so hot she thought she would die if he didn't come into her right then.

"Love me, Mac," she whispered, her eyes opening. For a moment he loomed above her, looking down at her, his face hard and fierce, his eyes almost black with wanting her, his fingers still inside her.

"I do," he said then in a low, shaken voice. "God help me, Julie, I do."

Then he yanked her panties down her legs and kissed her and came inside her hard, all so fast that Julie could do nothing but cling and wrap her legs around his waist and cry out his name. He stretched her, filled her, bringing her to the brink of fulfillment just by that one single act of possession. Even as she cried out her pleasure and surged against him in response he moved again, withdrawing and then thrusting with the desperate urgency of a man now bent on his own release. She was with him with every movement, burning hotter and higher until she was consumed by the inferno, sobbing her ecstasy into his mouth, coming with a fierce frenzy that made her world explode into a million brightly colored starbursts of passion.

"Mac! Oh, Mac!"

Groaning in response, he found his own release, grinding himself deep into her shaking body and finally going still.

When Julie had spent sufficient time blissed out in sexual nirvana, she gradually started to become aware of her surroundings again. Her breathing was still faintly ragged but it was getting back to normal, she found, and her body was more or less functional. At least, she could wiggle her fingers and toes.

The rest of her was being crushed by a large, hot and sweaty male body.

At that moment Mac lifted his head and looked at her. Searchingly.

Julie met his gaze. "It was really, really good for me," she said gravely.

A smile stretched his mouth and eyes. "You're learning, Miss America. That's the kind of pillow talk I like to hear."

"You know, I kind of guessed that." Lying naked and sweaty on a leather couch was not nearly as erotic as it sounded, Julie discovered. It was like lying naked on a bed of tape: moving was all but impossible. Mac must have seen her discomfort in her eyes, because he shifted, rolling between her and the back of the couch, then pulling her over so that she lay on top of him.

For a minute she simply savored her new position. Then she folded her arms on his chest, rested her chin on her hands, and looked at him thoughtfully.

"Mac."

"Hmm?" His hands were shaping her bottom, and one particular part of him on which she was lying seemed to be recuperating from its recent exertions with amazing speed. She wriggled a little in instinctive response, and his hands tightened and squeezed.

"Did you say you loved me, just now?" Her voice was faintly breathless from his attentions.

He winced, and his hands stilled. "Paying attention, were you?"

"Yes."

He studied her face for a moment without speaking, then gave her a wry little smile.

"I'm so in love with you it scares me. Ever since I met you, it's like the sun has come out on my life. You walk into view, and I feel the earth move. You smile, and I go weak at the knees. You cry, and my heart breaks. Does that answer your question?"

Julie's eyes widened. "That's beautiful."

"I try."

"Is it true?" There was the tiniest note of suspicion in her voice.

He laughed. "Yeah."

Still sprawled naked on his chest, with her chin resting on her folded hands, she eyed him broodingly.

"Okay. You have one chance. Explain to me how you lied to me and used me to get information about Sid in a way that doesn't make me want to kill you."

He met her gaze, and sighed. "I bare my heart and soul to you—to say nothing of my body—and you still don't trust me? I'm wounded."

"You certainly could be if you don't start talking." The look she gave him was minatory.

He grinned. "Okay. Like I said before, originally Debbie had nothing to do with you. I . . ."

There was a knock at the door. Josephine erupted from under a desk, charging the door with a cacophony of shrill yaps. Mac and Julie exchanged glances. Frowning, Mac slid out from beneath her, getting to his feet and grabbing for his clothes. Julie scrambled to follow suit.

There was another knock, louder and more peremptory than before. Alarmed, Julie looked at Mac. Did hit men knock on doors? Surely not.

Mac was frowning. He had his jeans on, and was pulling on his shirt.

"Who is it?" he called, casting her a quick, assessing glance as he scooped up his gun from a table near the end of the couch; Julie hadn't seen him discard it, but she supposed he must have put it there when he was stripping off his clothes. She was on her feet, fastening her skirt—she already had on her bra and panties—as he moved toward the door, his arm stiff, his gun at his side and pointed down. Josephine was barking her head off; Julie realized that her own heart was racing.

"Open up! Police!"

Julie's eyes widened. That was a good thing, right? Maybe not, from the look on Mac's face. Hastily she pulled on her T-shirt, then looked around for her shoes.

"That you, Dorsey?"

"Yeah, it's me. Open up, McQuarry."

Mac looked around at her. She was dressed now, complete to her shoes, clutching her purse in one hand as she ran a quick brush through her hair.

After all, she didn't want to look like she'd just been engaged in what she'd been engaged in.

"It's okay. I know this guy. He's a prick, but he's an honest prick."

Julie nodded, breathing a little easier. Mac stuck his gun inside the back of his jeans, pulled his shirt down over it, and opened the door. Two uniformed cops stood there, looking stolid and unthreatening, their gazes touching on Mac, then moving past him to find Julie, who had just scooped Josephine up. Now that she was safe in someone's arms, Josephine was once again quiet.

"What can I do for you?" Mac didn't sound particularly friendly.

The beefier of the two cops grimaced.

"You're under arrest, McQuarry."

29

"You've got to be kidding me."

Mac stared at Dorsey disbelievingly. The other man, a career patrol cop who'd been on the force when Mac was there, shook his head.

"Nope. You carrying? Sure you are. Want to make this easy, and give me your piece?" Dorsey stepped into the room and held out his hand. Behind him, the other cop drew his gun.

"You can't arrest me. For what?"

"Assault. We got a warrant. You . . ."

"*What?*"

". . . got the right to remain silent. If you . . ."

"I know my rights. Damn it, Dorsey, I'm on a job here. See that lady?" He jerked his head at Julie, who was watching the proceedings wide-eyed. "There's a hit out on her. Somebody's trying to kill her. I'm working as her bodyguard, and I'm all that's keeping her alive."

"Yeah, yeah." Dorsey drew out his cuffs, and locked one around Mac's wrist before Mac was more than peripherally aware of what was headed his way. The cold metal bracelet brought the reality of this preposterous situation home like nothing else could have. Dorsey was turning him around, reaching for his other hand, finishing off with his rights, and the other cop had him shoved up against a desk and was starting to pat him down.

"Don't hurt him." Julie took a step toward him, Josephine clutched close to her breast.

"Ma'am, we're not hurting him. Please stay out of this," said the other cop, the one Mac didn't know. Mac got a glimpse of Julie's whitening face even as he pulled his uncuffed hand out of Dorsey's hold.

"Damn it, McQuarry. . . ." Dorsey grabbed his hand again as the other cop relieved him of his Glock.

"Mac, should I call somebody? Who should I call?" Julie sounded frightened now.

"Hinkle," he said, and told her the number, playing keep-away with his hand all the while.

"Can't you just make this easy on everybody, McQuarry?" Dorsey said with a sigh, then shoved his knee into the small of Mac's back, making him grunt with pain. While Mac was busy reacting, Dorsey grabbed his hand.

"You *are* hurting him!" Julie was standing by his desk now, her eyes huge and dark, her face pale. She held the telephone receiver to her ear. "Mac, he's not home. The answering machine picked up."

"Tell him what's happening. Tell him to haul ass down to the Seventy-third Precinct."

If he sounded desperate, it was because he was. Dorsey didn't have enough brain wattage to power a flashlight. It was going to be impossible to talk him out of this, and if he didn't talk him out of it, Julie was going to be left at the mercy of whoever was hunting her. Julie was still talking into the phone when, without warning, Dorsey jerked his arm up behind his back. The pain was sharp and intense. Mac made a sound, and twisted instinctively to ease it. The second bracelet clicked into place. His hands were cuffed behind his back.

Shit, this was going down. Right now.

They were already pushing him toward the door. "Julie, stay with me. Dorsey, you can take her down to the station with us, can't you?"

"No can do." His voice grew a tad more polite as he added, over his shoulder as they hustled Mac along the hall, "Sorry, ma'am."

"Julie."

"I'm here, Mac. Officers, you can't . . ."

One on either side, they shoved him into the elevator, and the closing door cut off her words. For a moment Mac stared at the dingy metal panels in stupefaction as the elevator lurched into motion.

"Julie!" he roared, only to be rewarded for his pains by Dorsey twisting his arms up behind his back again, both of them this time, and harder than before.

Mac groaned.

"You yell like that again and I'm gonna break your head for you."

His arms were released.

"Dorsey, you stupid shit. If anything happens to her, I'm going to take you apart limb from limb."

Mac was sweating buckets. The elevator clanked slowly down. Meanwhile, Julie was left behind on the second floor, alone except for Josephine.

"You hear that, Nichols? Sounds like terroristic threatening to me."

Mac took a deep breath. If he lost his cool, if he provoked Dorsey into doing something drastic, Julie would be left defenseless. If the hit man was in the vicinity, and Mac was growing more convinced with every passing second that he was—Dorsey was an honest if brutish cop, but this arrest coming when it had was too pat, somebody was behind it, and Mac's blood ran cold as he guessed who—Julie would die. At the thought, a burst of fear went through him like a wintry blast. He remembered the girl hit by the car in front of her store; he remembered the way Julie had been attacked before. Fear turned into stark terror. He had to force it back. Giving into it was the worst thing he could do.

He emptied his mind, channeling calm, readying himself, as the elevator finally, finally, reached the ground floor.

30

WITH JOSEPHINE TUCKED UNDER ONE ARM and her purse under the other, Julie was left gaping as the elevator doors closed in her face. Just like that, Mac was gone.

All she could see was herself, reflected in the dull silver surface. Staring blankly at her own image, she saw that her lips were slightly swollen from Mac's kisses, her cheeks were rosy with color, and her eyes shone. Even her hair seemed to have developed extra bounce.

She looked like—a woman in love.

Mac had said he was in love with her.

Despite the exigencies of her present situation, Julie was suddenly suffused with warmth. The corners of her mouth turned up in a little smile.

Get out of here.

The words in her head came out of nowhere, and the smile vanished from her face as if it had been drawn on a blackboard and then wiped clean in a single swipe.

Realizing that, Julie forgot about being a woman in love and went back to being a woman in fear for her life. The hair rose on the back of her neck; her pulse raced. She stood stock-still, electrified, her eyes darting fearfully around.

If she had learned nothing else in the course of this

nightmare, she had learned that the little voice meant big trouble.

Hurry.

Oh, yeah. She was out of there. Like the wind.

The elevator was too slow. The stairs she and Mac had used earlier were to her left. Hanging on to Josephine for dear life—thank God for Josephine, Julie thought, she would have died of fright on the spot without her—she ran for the door, only to stop in her tracks as she heard— something. A sound just beyond it, in the stairwell.

It could be anything, she told herself as she strained to hear over the pounding of her own blood in her ears. A cat. A bum. A hit man.

Great going, Julie. Way to be calm.

All right, forget calm. Scared half to death would have to do. Her heart was thudding in her chest like a race-horse galloping toward the finish line. She was suddenly terrified to venture as much as one step farther—but she was equally terrified not to.

There were only two choices: the elevator or the stairs. And the elevator door remained stubbornly closed.

All she had to do was go down one measly flight of stairs, and she would be safe in the company of Mac and two burly cops.

Hide.

Even as she registered the word, the door opened. Just like that, with no more warning at all. Julie's blood ran cold. Icy dread froze her in place.

"Hello, Julie."

Julie's heart gave a great, panic-stricken leap in her chest.

She didn't know what terrified her more: the gun that was pointed at her, or the fact that it was being held by a man with a swollen, discolored nose.

* * *

They were armed, he was not. There were two of them to one of him. His hands were cuffed behind his back.

The only chance he had was to take them on in this confined space.

There was no talking sense to these guys. If he didn't win free, he was going to jail. And Julie would die.

The elevator stopped with a little ping, distracting their attention. The doors started to open. Mac called on every bit of training he had ever had as a SEAL, and pivoted on one leg, spinning like a top and slashing out with his raised leg with the force and fury of a tornado.

"Ahhhh!" Dorsey screamed as he went flying into Nichols, who smacked into the wall. Their guns somersaulted into the air, they went down in a heap, and Mac leaped on them ruthlessly, kicking Dorsey under the chin as he tried to rise, stomping on Nichols' back. Dorsey crashed backward, his eyes rolling back in his head as he collapsed. Cursing, Nichols got his hands under him and tried to lever himself up, but Dorsey's legs were sprawled across his butt, slowing him just enough for Mac to kick him in the side of the jaw. Nichols collapsed like a house of cards. Then it was over. The whole thing had taken perhaps a minute. Both men were sprawled on the floor, unconscious and bleeding, but alive. His training had taught him to kill, but he'd tried his best to avoid that negative outcome. Even so, beating cops to a pulp was a major no-no, and Mac realized that he had bought himself a boatload of trouble. It was something to worry about later. Right now he had to get to Julie, and get both of them as far away as possible as fast as he could.

Moving quickly, he crouched and stepped through the loop formed by his cuffed hands. With his hands in front of him now, he grabbed his Glock from Nichols' belt, sticking it down inside the front of his jeans, then fished in Dorsey's pocket for the keys to the cuffs. Dorsey's breathing was shallow, and blood trickled from a corner of his mouth. Mac grimaced as his fingers closed around the keys. Sorry, asshole, he thought, and maneuvered the small silver key into the lock. It clicked open. He pulled the cuffs off, then checked the pulse of both men: strong and steady. They would live to make him rue the day. A quick glance around confirmed what he already knew: he was in what was essentially a metal box. There was nothing to cuff them to. Thinking fast, he snapped a cuff around one of Dorsey's wrists, knotted the chain around Nichols' ankle, then fastened the second cuff around Dorsey's other wrist.

That would slow them down.

Smiling faintly, he stepped out of the elevator, shoving Dorsey's legs in so that the door would close, then hit the button for the fourth and top floor.

The way that elevator worked, even if they were awake and aware, he would have just bought himself and Julie a good five minutes to get away.

Casting a quick glance around to make sure she wasn't somewhere behind him—no, she wasn't, and neither was anyone else; fortunately, the building pretty much emptied out at five—Mac drew his gun, turned, and sprinted for the stairs.

He went up them two at a time, practically running as he shoved through the heavy metal door that opened onto the second floor. The hall was deserted. She must have gone back to his office to wait.

Mac tried to ignore the little tendrils of fear that started to curl through his stomach as it occurred to him that Julie *should* have been on the first floor waiting for them to get off the elevator. She should have been on the stairs.

Returning to his office didn't seem like something she would do.

Reaching the door, he opened it and stepped inside, some instinct causing him to automatically assume combat stance.

"Julie," he called, doing a fast visual survey of the room. Everything was just as it had been left: lights on, computer on, pizza boxes still sitting atop Rawanda's desk.

But no Julie.

"Julie!"

His blood raced through his veins. His heart pounded like a trip-hammer. He did a quick search of the office, knowing already that she wasn't there.

In the few minutes that they'd been separated, Sid's hireling had gotten to her. He knew it in his gut.

"Oh, God, Julie."

The anguish in his own voice sobered him. Giving into emotion would get her killed faster than anything he could do. He had already made one mistake by bringing her to his office at all. He'd thought she'd be safe, with him right beside her, never letting her out of his sight.

He'd been wrong. He couldn't afford to be wrong again. His being wrong could very well get her killed.

He should have taken her and run while he had the chance. To hell with everything else: Julie was what mattered.

God help him, what was he going to do?

Her purse. Where was her purse? He looked around on the floor by the couch, where she had set it down. It wasn't there. It wasn't anywhere he could see.

She'd been carrying it as she'd followed him down the hall. He remembered now. Please God she was still hanging on to it. Please, please God.

He'd put a button-sized homing device in her purse that morning, just in case she got it into her head to try to elude him at some point during the day.

In his experience, women rarely went anywhere without their purses. That quirk of female nature might very well save her life.

He left his office, leaped down the stairs without sparing so much as a thought for the men he'd left in the elevator, and ran like a madman for the Blazer, cursing himself with each step for parking so far away. Finally reaching it, he jumped inside, and fished frantically around in the back for the global positioning unit the homing device worked with. Turning it on, he waited with bated breath for the screen to warm up.

Then—there it was. Or rather, there she was: a tiny green dot moving at a fast pace through the maze of streets laid out like a map on the dark screen. If she and her purse were still keeping company, that is. He wasn't ordinarily a religious man, but he was getting religion fast. He prayed that she was hanging on to that purse as he had never prayed for anything in his life.

Starting the Blazer, he stepped on the gas, meaning to peel rubber out of the lot. A small white shape bounding toward him through the darkness caught his eye. He stared, frowned, and stood on the brake, then swung open his door.

"Get in," he yelled at Josephine.

31

"How does it feel to know that you're going to die tonight, Julie?" Sid's voice was eerily conversational. Julie felt her stomach cramp. She was so frightened that her body seemed to be drawing in on itself, with all her organs squeezing painfully together. He had been waiting for her in a dark-colored car that she had never seen before when the man with the bitten nose—Sid called him Basta—had brought her out of the building. He was driving now, heading north on a narrow, dark country road, with her sitting beside him and Basta—terrifying Basta, who smiled at her with the coldest eyes she'd ever seen—silent in the backseat. Sid and his hit man: Mac had been right all along.

"You don't want to kill me, Sid. Remember how we loved each other? There's still something left of that."

Not screaming and clawing at the door in a frantic attempt to escape required almost Herculean control on her part. Any minute now she expected to feel Basta's hands slide around her neck, or his gun nudge the back of her head. Then he would squeeze, or pull the trigger—and she would be dead.

Oh, God, would it hurt?

Sid laughed. "I never loved you, you trashy little slut. I

may have thought I did, once upon a time, but all I really wanted was to fuck you, and now I don't even want to do that."

The words did not carry the sting he obviously intended them to have. The rose-colored lenses with which she had once regarded Sid had already been ripped from her eyes, and she was easily able to see him for the cruel, self-centered man he was. As much as she wanted to tell him so, though, now was definitely not the time. What she needed to do, what she had to do if she was to survive, was to reestablish their relationship, to somehow reconnect with him, at least in his mind.

It would be easier without Sid's hired killer watching her from the backseat like a vicious dog eyeing a rabbit. The knowledge that he was there made the hairs prickle on the back of her neck. She did her best to block him out, but it was hard: she could see his massive shadow from the corner of her eye, and she could hear his raspy breathing.

She could almost, even, smell onions. . . . But she wouldn't think of that. She wouldn't remember that night, not now. She would concentrate, focus, do what she had to do to save her own life.

"Do you remember when we first met? It was at the governor's reception just after I was crowned Miss South Carolina. Remember how much we talked that night? For hours. You wanted to know everything about me. I think I fell in love with you then."

Like Scheherazade, words were the only weapon she had. Julie folded a leg beneath her and turned sideways in the seat, doing her best to draw him into the memory. The darkness outside the windows seemed to close in on the car. Huge trees flashed past on either side of the road, illuminated only briefly by the slashing headlights. Sid was driving fast, much too fast for the twists and turns of the road. Wherever they were headed, it was somewhere far off the beaten path. The knowledge was like an icy finger running down her spine.

Forcing back the fear that would turn her into a gibbering idiot if she let it, she smiled at Sid.

"You still don't have any idea, do you?" Sid's laugh was contemptuous. "We didn't just happen to meet that night. You think I usually went to receptions for beauty-contest winners? Get real. I was there that night specifically looking for you. You want to know why? Because your father, who worked for us once upon a time, stole something that belonged to my father and me, to our company, and I was trying to get it back. I had information that you knew where it was, and the reason I wanted to know all about you that night was because I thought you might slip and tell me. You didn't, but I kept on seeing you, thinking you would tell me what you knew sooner or later."

"You dated me just to get back something my father stole?" Julie's mind flashed back over her practically nonexistent relationship with her father. If he *had* stolen something, she wouldn't have known anything about it. "What was it?"

Basta made a protesting sound, and Sid glanced at him through the rearview mirror.

"You don't need to know that." His voice was rough. "It was important enough for me to come sniffing after you to get it. You were a pretty thing then—that was about twenty pounds ago, wasn't it?—and I wanted to sleep with you. But you wouldn't sleep with me, remember? Not unless I married you. That was smart. I confused lust with love like many a man before me, and I married you. I hoped you would tell me what I wanted to know about the whereabouts of the company's stolen property once you were feeling real secure in our relationship, but you didn't, and I gradually figured out you weren't telling me anything because you didn't know anything. That's the story of your life, isn't it, Julie: You don't know anything. You don't know anything, and I don't want to sleep with you anymore: that makes you disposable. Just like the trash you are."

The truth of it hit her like a slap in the face. As his words swirled around her, painting various incidents in their past in a hideous new light, Julie felt dizzy. She realized that what he was telling her explained so much: the way, at the beginning, he'd always insisted on talking about her and never himself. His inordinate interest in her father. His contemptuous attitude, which had been growing stronger over the years.

She looked at him, realized with a terrible clarity that the whole last eight years of her life had been spent living with and loving a man who was capable of arranging to have her killed, and was finally, irrevocably, forever and ever, set free of any last vestigial ties of affection or loyalty that might have still existed somewhere deep inside her.

There was a smirk to his mouth that told her he was aware of the effect his words were having on her and reveled in it. It roused her from the shock of his revelation like a bucket of cold water. Grimly she reminded herself that what was important here was her survival: any lingering psychic pain she could deal with later.

"If you're nice, though, maybe I'll let you go down on your knees for me one last time before I turn you over to Basta." His tone was malicious, taunting. Julie realized that she had been wasting her breath, trying to rekindle their connection. There never had been a connection to rekindle. Sid had never loved her.

"Oh, do you have your Viagra with you?" The words

were out before she could stop them. Julie was appalled—
so much for trying to sweet-talk her way out of this—but
not really all that sorry. She knew, deep in her heart of
hearts, that she could talk for the rest of her life, and it
wasn't going to change a thing: Sid meant to see her dead.

Time to move to Plan B. She wet her lips, casting a
surreptitious look around the interior of the car. Time
to move to Plan B—just as soon as she could come up
with it.

Sid's face flushed. Even in the dim light reflected by the
headlights, she could see it change color, see the self-
conscious glance he cast in the mirror at Basta.

"You can just shut up about that. It was for recreational
use only, to give me a buzz."

"Yeah, right. I know you used it on Amber. Did you use
it on the girls at Sweetwater's too?"

"Listen, bitch, I didn't go to Sweetwater's for the girls.
Ever since we acquired it, I've been going there several
nights a week to pick up the cash they take in. Did you
know that we own Sweetwater's now, by the way? Of course
you don't: I keep forgetting you don't know anything. The
last couple of times I went there, though, it was basically for
you: I was providing myself with an alibi so the big guy
back there could break into our house and snuff you. Only
he kept screwing it up, didn't you, Basta? You must have felt
pretty stupid when she got away from you because she bit
your nose. Then you ran over the wrong girl." He sent
another of those quick glances into the backseat, shook his
head, and laughed. "Well, never mind. You can pay her
back tonight."

"Yeah, I felt pretty stupid." It was almost the first thing
Basta had said since he'd shoved her in the car. Hearing
his voice made Julie want to cringe. Along with the smell
of onions, and the sight of his masked face staring back at

her through her bathroom mirror, the memory of it had haunted her nightmares. Now she was hearing it again in reality, and the reality was far more terrifying than any nightmare could ever be. "About as stupid as I imagine you felt when you figured out she'd been cheating on you with Daniel's little brother."

Basta meant Mac, Julie realized. Frowning, she remembered Mac saying something about Daniel. It took a second, but she came up with the context. Daniel had disappeared at the same time as her father, and Sid's first wife. . . .

"Did you kill Kelly too?" she asked Sid fiercely.

There was a laugh from the backseat.

"No, I did," Basta said. "Just like I killed Daniel. And your father. And now I'm getting ready to kill you. Sid, you want to slow down. The road's up here on the left."

Julie felt her heart lurch. The journey was coming to an end, she knew. As Sid obediently slowed, then turned left onto a bumpy dirt road that was little more than a path, Julie suddenly had to work hard to breathe. It was difficult to draw air into her suddenly constricted lungs. Her hands automatically clenched into fists as her mind swooped around like a frightened bird, trying desperately to come up with anything that seemed remotely like a plan.

"The police will be looking for me. They were there—with Mac—they'll have missed me by now. They'll know you did this."

"Ya think?" That was Basta, sounding amused.

"You stupid little slut, I sent those cops to get your boyfriend out of the way. They don't just work for the city; they're on our payroll, too. In fact, I wouldn't be surprised if McQuarry didn't have an accident on the way downtown. Maybe shot while trying to escape, or something."

"There's your car, right there," Basta said. "Pull in behind it. Then you can leave."

As Sid pulled in beside what looked like the green Lexus he'd been driving the last time she'd seen him, terror rose like bile in Julie's throat. This was it—and she had no plan. Nothing. As the car rocked to a stop, she released her seat belt. Her fingers scrabbled for the door handle, closed over it, pulled . . .

"Childproof lock," Sid said mockingly, shifting into park, as the door failed to open.

Damn those things!

From the corner of her eye, she saw Basta move. Panting with terror, heart pounding, stomach churning, she turned fully to face him. His eyes met hers, glinting like jet in the darkness. She could only watch in horror as he lifted his gun. He was going to shoot her *now*, she realized, and realized too, with a terrible sense of fatalism, that there wasn't a thing she could do about it. Closing her eyes, backpedaling against the locked, immovable door, she said every prayer she had ever heard in her life.

She was still in the act of raising her hands to cover her face when the gun exploded like point-blank thunder.

32

THE MOON WAS RISING IN THE DISTANCE, yellow and round as a tennis ball. Mac got one look as the Blazer topped a rise, then lost all view of the sky—and all light—as the SUV dipped back beneath the overhanging canopy of trees. He was running without lights, following the green blip on the global positioning unit and the red glow of the taillights not too far ahead.

Julie was in that car.

Or at least, Julie's purse with the homing device in it was in that car.

Mac's blood ran cold as, not for the first time, it occurred to him that maybe, somehow, she had become separated from her purse.

At the thought that he might have gotten it wrong, icy terror ran through his veins. He knew as well as he knew anything that Julie had only this one chance.

The idea that, at this very moment, someone might be hurting her made him homicidal. If she were killed . . . If she were killed . . .

He couldn't even finish the thought.

Earlier, when she'd cried, he had gathered her up in his arms and faced the fact that he loved her. Now he was confronting the truth of how much.

If anything happened to her, he would rip Sid and all his cohorts, past or present, real or suspected, from limb to limb. He would go insane. He would howl at the moon.

For the rest of his life.

Oh, God, he prayed. Let her be all right. Let me be right. Let me be in time.

The forest was thick and dark. The road was curvy. Staying on it without any illumination beyond the occasional patch of moonlight required all his concentration. He dared not wreck. If he did, Julie was at far greater risk than he was himself.

It occurred to him that he might have to leave the Blazer at some point, and when he did he might not wish to be observed. Driving one-handed, he hefted his Glock and used the butt to sytematically smash all of the SUV's interior bulbs.

Up ahead, the taillights vanished. The green light on the screen made a right turn. The light didn't seem to be following a road any longer, and Mac wondered if it had left the pavement. The occasional glimpses of it that he managed as it had streaked through sections of moonlight ahead of him had revealed a midsize passenger car, not an SUV.

He needed backup, bad. Knowing that he was Julie's sole hope terrified him. His cell phone had been in the Blazer, and he'd tried calling Hinkle: answering machine. Twice. Who else could he trust? The answer was stark: no one. The reach of the mob was long, and their twin weapons of money and fear were powerful: no one was immune.

In the end, before the overhanging trees had taken the signal out, he'd done what he could: he'd called the cops. They would have found Dorsey and Nichols by now; the entire police force of the state of South Carolina was undoubtedly looking for him. He wasn't their favorite person to begin with, and they sure weren't going to be liking him any better now that he had pulverized two of their own. Cops were clannish that way, as he knew from experience. By now, if they spotted him, they were likely to shoot first and ask questions later.

And a whole posse of them would be coming after him.

Among their ranks were sure to be some who had been corrupted by the mob. But only some; not all. Not even the majority. If he got enough of them together at one time, the public good would win out.

He hoped. No, he prayed.

He'd called his old captain, Greg Rice, putting the facts on the line and telling him what road he was on and which way he was headed. Then the trees had cut him off.

He trusted Greg more than most. If he was right, if Greg was solid, there were only two problems: Greg had made skeptical sounds as Mac had tersely laid the whole thing out. Mac wasn't sure Greg had believed a word he'd said. And the road he'd been on when the signal had cut out had been many twists and turns ago. He wasn't even headed in the same direction anymore.

For Julie's sake, he was willing to take his chances with his former comrades-in-arms. At this point, he didn't even care if they shot him on sight, as long as they rescued her first.

To his right, Mac caught just a glimpse of a pair of tail-lights disappearing through the trees. There was a dirt road cutting through the trees. He had almost passed it. Hanging a hard right, Mac turned off onto it. The Blazer hit the mother of all bumps, and Josephine, perched beside him, lost her balance, sliding off into the footwell.

"Sorry, Josephine."

The poodle scrambled back onto the seat, unhurt.

She'd been riding with her paws on the dashboard, seeming to peer at the road in front of them with a concentration almost equal to his own, and Mac wondered just how much she understood. The green dot slowed dramatically, then stopped. Mac glanced down at the screen, registered that, then looked up again and stood on the brake. The Blazer was at the edge of a clearing. Up ahead, in the full glare of the moonlight, a dark-colored Ford Taurus pulled to stop beside a foreign luxury car—a Lexus, he thought, although he couldn't be positive because the Taurus was between him and it.

This was it. Zero hour. If Julie was in there, this was his chance. Shoving the transmission into park, he stepped out of the car, closing the door as quietly as he could, leaving Josephine, who was watching anxiously through the windshield, behind.

Crouched low, moving fast, gun drawn, he closed on the Taurus. There were three people inside. He could just barely make out the dark shapes of them. Julie was in the front passenger seat, pressed up tight against the window. He couldn't mistake her: her black hair gleamed in the moonlight.

Thank God, thank . . .

A gunshot, muffled but unmistakeable, exploded inside the car. Julie screamed and dropped from view. Gone, just like that. Mac's heart stopped, he almost pissed his pants, and he gave a great leap forward, grabbing for the door handle, staying low. He yanked the door open just as another gunshot shook his eardrums. Julie tumbled out, falling backward, eyes and mouth wide and screaming as she hit the grass.

For a split second Julie simply lay where she had fallen, stunned. When the second shot exploded almost in her ear, she'd been curled into as tiny a ball as she could make of herself, head down, arms around her legs, pressed as far back against the hard barrier of the door as she could get. With her eyes scrunched shut, she'd felt a warm liquid spatter her legs. She'd gone all light-headed and bells had rung and lights had flashed and she'd stopped breathing. Then she had felt herself tumbling backward, falling into nothingness, into empty, open air. The thought that had run through her mind was that she'd been killed and was being sucked straight down to—heaven?

She realized she was screaming only when Mac's face intruded between her and the sky. His hand wrapped around her wrist just as another gunshot exploded right over her head. Mac dropped her wrist and staggered back, cursing. Julie scrambled to her feet, crouching near the rear tire, ducking her head and covering it with her folded arms. Her heart was pounding so hard she had to be alive, she realized. She could feel her stomach churning, feel blood pumping through her veins. Oh, God, she was alive! She was alive!

"Run!" Mac screamed at her, or maybe it was the little voice again, because she didn't think she could hear anything outside her own head. Her ears were ringing so badly she might as well have been Quasimodo in the bell tower. But run was what she wanted to do anyway, and run was what she did. Mac grabbed her wrist again and took off, and she was with him every step of the way, abject fear giving wings to her feet. Mac kept turning around to snap off shots at Basta, who, she saw with a quick, terrified look over her shoulder, had emerged from the car now and was coming after them, crouched low like they were, shooting too.

Basta dodged and ducked when one of Mac's shots kicked up turf near his feet, giving them a few extra, precious seconds. Suddenly they were out of the moonlight, running like all the hounds of hell were after them into the concealing shadow of the trees, where the Blazer loomed like a solid black box in front of them.

Julie had never been so glad to see anything in her life.

Mac let go of her wrist.

"Get in!"

This time there was no doubt the voice belonged to Mac. Julie jerked the passenger door open and dived inside, nearly crushing Josephine, who leaped nimbly into the back in the nick of time. Mac's butt hit the driver's seat at the same moment. Julie huddled in the seat, feet on the edge, fists pressed to her face, shaking and gasping, as Mac wrenched at the gearshift. She looked up just in time to see Basta coming after them, his bulky body silhouetted for a moment against the backdrop of the moonlit clearing. She screamed, the Blazer careened backward, and she was almost toppled from her perch, catching herself with a hand on the dash. When she looked again Basta was nowhere to be seen; she asssumed that he was rushing toward them through the concealing darkness beneath the trees.

"He shot Sid!" It was a near-hysterical shriek. Her voice shook with horror. The first bullet, the one she'd thought was meant for her, had blown Sid's face off. Just like that, his features had been blown away and replaced with an oozing crimson pulp that made her want to heave when she remembered it. The smell of blood—she'd never realized blood smelled like bad meat—had filled the air. Then Basta had turned the gun on her. . . .

"Who? Who shot Sid?"

Julie screamed, ducking as bullets tore through the body of the Blazer with the fierce, sharp rat-a-tat of some kind of deadly popcorn. The windshield shattered; pellets of glass pelted them like storm-driven hail. Mac cursed and drove, turned halfway around with his arm slung over the back of his seat, looking over his shoulder as the Blazer bumped and rocked and skidded backward down the little dirt road. Panting with a combination of fear and shock, Julie turned and looked that way too.

"Who shot Sid?" It was a roar.

"Basta! The hit man! The one—I bit his nose!"

Another hail of bullets hit the Blazer. Julie dove screaming for the footwell. Then the gunfire stopped. Just like that. Nothing. The sudden silence was almost as terrifying as the thunder of bullets had been.

Cautiously she lifted her head. Either they were out of range or Basta couldn't see them, but Julie knew deep in every fiber of her being that he was still giving chase. As she crawled limply back into her seat, she realized that she was shaking like a leaf; adrenaline rushed through her veins, making her jump at every bump or sound.

"This Basta—is he the one shooting at us?"

"Yes!"

The dirt road being too narrow to permit them to turn around, they were still flying backward without lights; how Mac saw to drive Julie couldn't imagine. The stockade of giant trees she had seen on the way in was rushing past on both sides, now reduced to a featureless blur. The trees melded seamlessly with the road and the night itself to her eyes. If they wrecked, Basta would catch up to them; at the thought, Julie went all light-headed, and her heart threatened to thump clean out of her chest.

Oh, God, please, she didn't want to die like Sid.

"How did you get away from the cops?"

"I managed to persuade them to see reason."

"They were dirty: they were taking bribes from Sid."

"You know, I had begun to suspect that."

Miraculously, during the course of this conversation, they somehow managed to stay on the track. When the first glimmer of approaching headlights appeared through the woods Julie thought for an instant that Mac must have succumbed to human limitations and turned on the Blazer's lights.

No such luck.

"*Shit,*" Mac said, and as Julie realized the truth she echoed the sentiment in her head. The headlights belonged to another vehicle, which was coming toward them from the direction of the road. The dirt track was too narrow to allow two vehicles to pass; trees formed a nearly impenetrable wall on both sides.

They were trapped.

"No," Julie moaned, hanging on to the edge of her seat with both hands as she stared back at the oncoming vehicle.

"Hang on."

Julie nearly bit her tongue as the Blazer veered. Mac, whose eyes were apparently a lot better than hers, sent them haring off the track to the left, somehow managing to find a space between the trees.

The good news was, they were now going forward. The bad news was, they didn't get far.

No sooner had the headlights passed them, continuing on up the track toward the clearing without pausing, which made Julie think they hadn't been seen, than the Blazer plunged nose-first into some kind of hole or ditch.

"Yow!" Julie was thrown violently forward and smacked her forehead hard on the dash. It took a couple of seconds for the stars she saw to recede. By the time they did, Mac was at her door, flinging it open and dragging her from her seat.

"We're stuck. Come on." His voice was scarcely louder

than a whisper. Head pounding, stomach churning, knees weak with fear, Julie nevertheless hit the ground running. Basta could be anywhere, near or far. He could be right behind the nearest tree. At any second he could open fire.

Against her will, Julie once again remembered Sid's destroyed face and had to fight back a wave of dizziness. Icy prickles of fear raced over her skin; gorge rose in her throat. Her hand welded to Mac's, she plunged through the forest like a frightened deer.

The next bullet might find her. Or Mac.

The realization kept her legs pumping as fast and furiously as her heart.

Seconds later Julie stepped on a rock, and nearly yelped in pain and surprise. Only the thought of Basta enabled her to bite back the sound and keep going with little more than a single, one-footed hop. It was only then that she realized she was barefoot: she had lost her shoes in the first wild rush toward the Blazer. The ground beneath her feet was slippery with leaves and sort of squishy, except for the occasional bruising rock. The humidity was thick as fog, and the smell of rotting vegetation hung heavy in the air. Under the trees, the night was so dark she could see Mac only as a dense shape plunging through the undergrowth just slightly ahead of her. All around, little glowing disks flickered on and off: fireflies. Mosquitoes were out, too. Julie could feel herself being bitten. She did not dare slap at them, for fear the sound of skin smacking skin would give them away. Although, unless Basta was right on their heels, he probably wouldn't hear. The night was alive with the whirr of insects, the eerie piping of tree frogs, the deep bass accompaniment of bullfrogs, the rustling of the forest itself. Nature's chorus was so loud that their own breathing and the soft thudding of their feet against the ground was barely audible even to herself.

As she listened, it suddenly occurred to Julie that Mac must not be in as good a shape as he looked to be, because his breathing was labored. Really labored.

In fact, he was rasping like a dying man.

"Mac . . ." Alarmed, she meant to ask him if he was all right.

At that moment he plunged forward with a splash and would have fallen on his face if Julie hadn't been slightly behind him, hanging on to his hand for dear life, her weight enough to counterbalance his forward impetus.

"Fuck," he said, just as she found it too, her foot plunging through liquid to sink ankle-deep into muddy ooze. This time it was he who kept her from going down face-first, grabbing her arm and helping her keep her balance.

Julie stopped from sheer necessity. Her feet felt like they were mired in wet concrete.

"We've got to go back," she whispered, clinging to his hand for balance and trying to turn around even as she spoke. The mud—she thought it was mud, it felt like mud, squishy, gooey mud—was reluctant to release its grip. The water that covered it was knee-deep and warm. Its smell was the rotting vegetation smell that had struck her earlier, only stronger. Julie realized that they'd stumbled into one of the swamps with which the area abounded. Rushes and foxtails grew all around them, brushing against her each time she moved, towering above her head. Tiny eyes stared at them from the trees. Raccoons? Possoms? Beyond that, Julie didn't want to speculate.

"We can't. Look."

Julie looked. Glowing disks about the size of softballs were bobbing behind them. Flashlights: she realized what they were as she saw a tree suddenly illuminated by a moving beam. They were just reaching the place where they had abandoned the Blazer, Julie calculated. . . .

"Josephine!" Horror struck through to her soul.

"She'll be all right. Nobody's after the dog. Come on, we've got to keep going. One good thing about this swamp: They won't come in here unless they have to."

Mac pulled her on, his feet making squelching noises with every step that Julie hoped, prayed, couldn't be heard much beyond their ears. She splashed after him, hanging on to his hand, moving carefully, both to minimize the sound and to keep from falling flat on her face.

By now she was way beyond terror. She was going on pure adrenaline, with Sid's fate for an impetus. If they were caught, that was what would happen to them. . . .

Without warning, Mac went down on one knee. Tethered to him by their clasped hands, Julie was nearly pulled over the top of him. He let go, and she pushed herself erect with one hand on his back, barely hearing the steady stream of under-his-breath curses that he was letting fly with.

She was too busy looking fearfully over her shoulder at the oncoming flashlights.

Until she registered that her hand on his back was covered with a warm, sticky liquid. Lifting her hand, turning it over, she saw that her palm, which should have been a pale blur, was not. It was black.

Horror struck at her heart like a blade.

"Oh, my God, Mac," she whispered. "You've been shot."

33

HIS FUTURE WAS ON THE LINE. Hell, his *life* was on the line. Basta knew it, and it was all he could do not to panic.

He had to get Julie Carlson back and send her off to join her husband. As for the man who had snatched her right out from under his nose for the second time, he was dog food. Basta knew who he was now—Daniel's little brother.

That made what was getting ready to happen almost poetic.

Sid's wife and Daniel's little brother, gone bye-bye together: talk about déjà vu all over again.

But he had other business he had to take care of first.

"How could you let this happen?" The Big Boss's face was etched with grief. Tears glinted in his eyes. He turned back from the Taurus, took a step, and had to support himself on the Lexus's trunk. He was dressed in a dark suit, and looked every inch the successful businessman he was. "My son. Oh, my son."

"He came out of nowhere, Mr. Carlson: Mac McQuarry. Dorsey and Nichols were supposed to take him out, but something must have gone wrong. Somehow he followed us out here. We never even saw him until he snatched the girl out of the car and shot your son, just like that. I got off some shots, but they escaped into the woods. They're in there somewhere. We'll get them back, I give you my word."

"Your word doesn't seem to be worth much these days. If you'd done your job properly, the little bitch would have been dead days ago and this would never have happened." John Carlson's eyes were as cold and distant as glaciers. Basta had seen that look in them before, although it had never been directed at him. The people it had been directed at were all dead.

Carlson turned to the flunky behind him. "Get some more men out here *now*. Tell them we need a heat-seeking device. Have some of them ring the perimeter of the area. I want these people found, and I don't want any more mistakes."

"Yes, sir." The flunky stepped a little apart from the group and whipped out a cell phone.

He'd made the right decision about his future, Basta thought. Before, he'd been a little unsure. If anything went wrong, his ass would be history. But that look told its own tale: He was history anyway unless he did something to save himself.

The Big Boss, the capo of capos, the mind behind the most efficient organized-crime operation on the East Coast, was done with him. And when the Big Boss turned his back, whoever he turned it on was toast.

Basta gnawed at a thumbnail, thinking.

"Excuse me, I gotta take a leak," he said to Carlson, and walked away into the dark. If he could have just kept on walking, that's what he would have done. But the Big Boss was one of the few people who knew where to find him. He would never let Basta just walk away. Fair enough, Basta thought, emptying his bladder against a tree. Walking back toward where the boss waited near the cars, he pulled the small silver silencer from his pocket and screwed it onto the end of his pistol. Ordinarily, out here, he never bothered, because the area was remote enough that no one ever heard anything.

But tonight there would be people near enough to hear. Such as the boss's flunkies. If he screwed up again, it would be the last time, literally. He would be dead.

He'd taken out Sid on his own, as part of his plan to break free of this life once and for all. He'd meant to take out Julie, too, not because he was being paid to—he didn't care about that any longer—but because Julie could identify him and was, thus, a loose end. It never paid to leave loose ends. None of them would be here tonight if they had not left a loose end dangling fifteen years ago: Mike Williams. After Daniel's unfortunate demise, Williams had cut and run. Nobody had known then that he had taken the object of their frantic search with him—Williams had been little more than a flunky, after all—but still, the very fact that Williams had taken off should have set alarm bells ringing. Somebody should have followed up on it then, found Mike Williams and taken care of him, but no one had.

As a result of that screw-up, here they all were.

He rejoined the Big Boss, putting an arm around him and walking him across the grass, listening and nodding sympathetically as the man went on and on about his son. Something the boss had once said to him popped into his mind, and the sheer appropriateness of it made him smile inwardly: Keep your friends close, but keep your enemies even closer. To John Carlson, those had been words to live by, and undoubtedly still were.

Tonight the Big Boss was his enemy, and he was going to stick to him like a burr until the job was done. To survive, he was going to have to kill the man. He'd faced it earlier, known it was the only way out. Even before the debacle with McQuarry, he'd planned to hit them all tonight: Sid and Julie, and then, on his way out of town, John Carlson.

He'd been going to make them all disappear. That was the only way to keep himself safe.

Sid had started fucking up the plan by calling him on his cell phone earlier in the day, raving mad because his wife was being unfaithful—with Daniel's little brother, yet—and insisting on being present when she bought the farm. The plan had been for Sid to be safely in Atlanta while Basta did the job, but Sid had screwed that up by coming home early, so crazy angry he wasn't thinking straight. That had actually worked out well, because Sid knew Basta's daytime identity, too—the Big Boss had been grooming Sid to take over one day, and Sid basically was in on everything—and was going to have to be taken out anyway. Basta had told him to come on, come join him, figuring on killing two birds with one stone even as he said it.

With Sid, the pissant little punk, in tow, he'd tracked Julie, even managed to get his hands on her despite complications. Then things had started going wrong. Daniel's little brother had rescued her seconds before she would have joined Sid in the great hereafter. And then, right on the heels of that disaster, the Big Boss had shown up out here without warning, complete with flunkies. According to one of the flunkies, speaking on the sly while the boss tearfully examined his son's remains, it seemed Sid had called him, apparently while Basta was in McQuarry's office building retrieving Julie, and had told him what was going down and where, and the boss had made the trip out here to make sure that this time the job he'd hired Basta to do got done. Basta suspected that his own demise was also on the agenda. This was the perfect spot, after all.

Actually, that was probably going to work out all right, too, Basta reflected, although it had been hairy there for a few minutes after the boss had arrived. Basta had been running down the dirt road in hot pursuit of his escaping prey when the boss's car had pulled up, catching him in its lights, and then he'd had to think fast.

What he'd come up with was that McQuarry had shot Sid while rescuing Julie.

Now the situation was dicey. But the plan was still in effect. The key was to keep his head. The boss's men would be loyal unto death, just as he himself had been once, and all would be armed to the teeth.

If he wanted to survive and prosper, he had to take out the Big Boss, Mac McQuarry, and Julie Carlson.

Then he would vanish into the woodwork, and be home free.

34

"I'M ALL RIGHT," MAC SAID, but it was clear that he wasn't. He got up and kept going, but it was obvious that he was finding it harder with every passing minute. The mud sucked at their feet, making each step an effort. Breathing hard, Julie clung to his hand, for his support now rather than hers, and tried not to panic as she felt his fingers growing cold where earlier they had been reassuringly warm. She was afraid he must be losing a lot of blood; when she'd put her hand on his back, it had seemed like the entire back of his shirt was covered in stickiness. Suddenly she was terribly, horribly afraid that he might lose consciousness. She couldn't carry him—but she couldn't, wouldn't, leave him, either.

She prayed he was able to stay on his feet.

Behind them, the flashlights were drawing ever closer, sweeping the darkness in what looked like a systematic search effort. There were no voices, no sounds of pursuit, but only the slashing lights. On her own, or with Mac his usual hale and hearty self, Julie realized that she probably would have been hyperventilating with fear.

But Mac was depending on her now. She had to be strong for Mac. Sloshing through the marshy water, she held to that thought like a talisman.

Keep moving, she told herself as her heart pounded with fear and exertion, her legs trembled with effort, and her feet slipped and slid on the mud that squished up between her toes. She was wet to the waist, and had been bitten by so many mosquitoes she no longer even felt the welts. The swamp was alive with splashes and plops and things that seemed to slither past her legs. Tall cypresses grew all around, their rough bark a welcome resting place for her hand as she waded past, their sturdy trunks tiptoeing out of the water on roots that were like six-feet-tall high heels.

Mac was clinging heavily to her hand for support. Julie could hear the harsh sound of his breathing, see the slump of his spine. He stumbled from time to time, although he always regained his balance before he went down; but after each near fall his movements were more ragged than before.

They weren't going to make it. Not the way they were going. The knowledge grew steadily within her until it was a certainty.

Suddenly Julie realized that the swamp itself was their best, no, their only, hope.

"We need to hide," she whispered.

"Leave me." His words tacitly confirmed her judgment of his state.

"If you think I'm going to draw them off for you, you're wrong." She strove to lighten the moment. He made a sound that could have been a groan or a laugh.

"Julie . . ."

"Don't argue." Her voice was the merest breath. "There's no way I'm leaving you. Everything else aside, do you think I'd stand a chance out here on my own?"

He didn't reply, so he must have felt that there was some truth to that. A glance over her shoulder told Julie that the flashlights were gaining on them at a terrifying rate. The glowing disks were now the size of baseballs, where before they had been the size of quarters. As she watched them arc through the darkness, her heart started beating like a drummer in a heavy metal band. Her skin prickled. Her breathing grew ragged. She took a deep, calming breath, and prayed Mac was right: their pursuers would be reluctant to wade through the swamp.

"The cypressess. We could squeeze up under the roots." The idea came to her as she touched another one.

"Good plan." His voice was so faint now she could scarcely hear it.

They had to do it almost entirely by feel, but they managed to squeeze between the fingerlike roots. Inside was a hollow dome, affording them perhaps four feet of air above the surface of the water. Julie tried not to think about what might call the cavelike place home. Her hip bumped something, and she discovered that it was a gnarled knot of roots sticking up above the surface of the water. They were able to sit on it and rest against the curved inner trunk of the tree. Mac was crowded next to her, his breathing harsh in the confined space. The trunk was close and airless. The smell was mildew to the max. Julie could see nothing beyond their small shelter.

Which was almost more terrifying than anything else, she realized. It allowed her imagination free rein. Deliberately Julie blocked out images of Basta creeping up on them, slithering through the swamp like a poisonous snake. Unless he had wings, they would know he was coming. They might not be able to see, but they could hear.

Mac was shifting around uncomfortably next to her, and Julie could sense, from the tension in his body, from his breathing, from his restless movements, that he was in pain.

"How badly are you hurt?" It was a whisper; she was ever mindful of the butchers hunting them through the night. She turned toward him, reaching out to touch his arm, his shoulder. He was wet and muddy, like she was, but his skin was cool to the touch, whereas, in the clammy heat, she was sweating buckets she was so warm. Again she worried about blood loss.

"It hurts like hell, but I think I'm going to live." His rasping voice made the words less reassuring than they might have been.

"Are you bleeding a lot?" She touched his face.

"Some."

"Okay." She wet her lips, afraid he was grossly under-stating the case. Whether he was or not, the blood loss needed to be stopped. Julie pulled off her T-shirt—the only relatively dry article of clothing either of them pos-sessed—and folded it into a tight little rectangle. "I've made my shirt into a pad. Show me where to press it."

"The right side of my back, just under my shoul-derblade."

With some difficulty—the space was tight—Julie reached around him to find the spot. It was warm and sticky with blood, impossible to mistake. She pressed the makeshift bandage over the wound. She did not dare lift his shirt—she feared it might dislodge any clotting and increase the bleeding—but she pushed down firmly to try to stop the bleeding. Mac shuddered and made a slight sound.

"Am I hurting you?"

"No."

He was clearly trying to ease her fears about his condi-tion. Determined to do what she could to keep him alive and conscious, Julie pressed harder.

"Ouch! Now you're hurting me."

"Sorry. I think it's probably really important that we get the bleeding to stop."

His reply was a grunt, which she took as acknowledgment that she was right. For a couple of moments after that they were both silent. Julie kept her hand tight over the pad, and listened for all she was worth to the sounds of the swamp. If Basta should come, or his friends with the flashlights, their only recourse would be to stay very still and quiet, like a mouse with a hawk flying overhead.

And pray they wouldn't be found.

The water lapped, warm and faintly slimy, around her legs. The tree creaked as the top of it swayed. There was a small plop nearby—a frog jumping in, she devoutly hoped—but nothing that sounded remotely human.

Julie realized her pulse was thundering, and her breathing was quick and shallow. To be able to do nothing but sit and listen for their pursuers was more nerve-racking than fleeing would have been.

"I'm so scared," she whispered, the words coming out before she could stop them. As soon as they left her mouth, she wished she could call them back. Saying it aloud didn't help; if anything, it made them both feel worse.

"We've made it this far. We'll make it the rest of the way."

He moved, and his lips brushed her mouth. The kiss was hot and sweet, and Julie closed her eyes and kissed him back and felt her fear recede a little as the familiar electricity coursed between them. Thank God for Mac, she thought. Without him, she would have been dead back there in the car with Sid. No, she would have been dead long before.

"You seem to be making a habit of saving my life."

"Maybe I think it's worth saving."

There was a loud splash out in the swamp. Julie tensed. Beside her she could feel Mac stiffen. But, though they listened intently, the sound was not repeated. Gradually they relaxed.

Mac said, "The police should be on their way. I called my old captain while I was haring around after you. They're going to get here sooner or later."

It was meant to comfort her, Julie knew. But unspoken between them lay the truth: Basta might well find them first. And even if the police came in time, could they trust whoever showed up?

Julie shivered.

"How did you find me, anyway?" She'd wondered about that.

"I put a homing device in your purse this morning." He sounded as if he were smiling. "In case you tried to give me the slip."

If she'd heard that a couple of hours earlier she would have been mad. Now she was profoundly thankful.

"Mac," she whispered after a moment, desperate to get her mind off their plight. "Did you have a brother named Daniel?"

A beat passed.

"Yeah," he said. "Why?"

"In the car, Basta said he killed him. He said he killed Daniel and Kelly and my father, too."

Another beat.

"Ah." Mac sounded as if he were expelling a breath he'd been holding for a long time. "Did he say how? Why?"

Mac's voice was expressionless. Too expressionless. Julie realized that there was a lot of emotion connected with the death of his brother. "No. Sid said my father had stolen something from him and his father. He wouldn't say what. But I got the impression my father was killed because of it."

"What else did he say?"

"Sid?" Julie gave a bitter little laugh. "Nothing much. Only that he never loved me. That he basically just married me because he thought I knew where the thing my father stole was. That he was planning to have me killed one day from the time he married me."

There was the briefest of pauses. Then Mac snorted. "Sounds like Sid. He always was the biggest idiot I ever met."

Julie smiled a little in the darkness. "You really are a sweet man, you know that? Thank you for that."

"Hey, like I said before, sweet is my middle name."

A sudden roar from just beyond the stump was followed by a high-pitched cry and a sharp snap. Julie was so startled she almost fell into the water.

"Gator," Mac, sounding as if he was speaking through gritted teeth, answered her unspoken question. "Must've caught something. Don't worry, the roots are too narrow to let one get in here."

Great. Now she didn't only have to worry about ruthless murderers, she had to worry about alligators. Julie shuddered, then deliberately forced her mind on to other things.

"How do you know Sid, anyway?"

"Sid?" Mac shifted uncomfortably, and drew a deep breath. Julie had to move, too, to keep the pad pressed to the wound. "He was Daniel's best friend. Daniel was my big brother. Our dad was a cop who was killed by a prick trying to rob a convenience store of sixty bucks. That left my mom and Daniel and me. I was only five when it happened. Daniel was thirteen, and getting ready to go to high school. On behalf of the community, John Carlson—Sid's dad—funded a scholarship for Daniel to the same expensive private school Sid went to.

Daniel was a player with the girls, a jock, a never-ending good time. Sid wanted some of Daniel's reflected glory, and they started hanging out. As a result of being pals with Richie Rich, Daniel began appreciating the finer things in life. The things Sid had and we couldn't afford. They stayed friends even after high school, and one thing led to another and Daniel ended up working for Sid. One night Daniel went to work and never came home. He was twenty-five." Mac took a deep breath, and Julie ached at the psychic pain she heard in the sound. Mac's next words were slightly uneven. "I think Daniel's disappearance killed my mom. She didn't live long after that." Another deep breath. "I always suspected—no, I always *knew*—Sid had something to do with Daniel's disappearance. With his *death*."

Mac's voice was raw, and Julie cuddled closer in a silent gesture of comfort.

"You loved Daniel a lot, didn't you?" she asked softly.

She felt rather than saw him shrug. "He was my brother."

That stark statement made a lump form in her throat. She turned her head, meaning to kiss him consolingly. Her lips brushed his cheek before moving on in search of his mouth. His head turned and his lips found hers again, and suddenly he was kissing her as though he would die if he didn't. Julie kissed him back just as desperately. With the small part of her mind capable of focusing on anything beyond the kiss, she sensed his grief and anger for his brother as well as his fear and frustration at their current situation, and realized that those were fueling the kiss along with his elemental need for her. She felt a tremendous swelling of emotion, an almost primeval urge to give him comfort. Then she knew, and pulled her mouth from his.

"I love you, Mac," she whispered against his lips.

For a moment he didn't move. She could feel his breath on her lips.

"I love you too," he said after a moment, in a deep husky whisper drawl that made her heart start to slam in her breast. "More than anything or anyone in my life."

Then he kissed her again, a soul-shaking kiss that made her forget that she was supposed to be pressing a bandage to his back, made her forget that they were hiding in a swamp from a conscienceless killer who had already murdered who knew how many people, made her forget everything in the whole world but Mac.

She wrapped her arms around his neck and kissed him back.

He broke off the kiss abruptly, stiffening and lifting his head.

"Shh," he said. "Here they come."

Julie listened, and heard it: the faint squelch, squelch of somebody walking through the swamp. It was a rhythmic sound, far different from any they had heard before. Julie broke out in a cold sweat. Her stomach clenched. Her heart began to pound.

Then, beyond the encircling roots, she saw the slashing beam of a flashlight. Suddenly Julie realized that she was about as safe as a rabbit frozen in place while the hounds close in, and began to shake.

35

In the distance Basta heard Julie screaming. His senses went on high alert. He was standing near the edge of the clearing looking out over the lake, in the high spot where they'd had to move so that the one remaining flunky who was playing bodyguard to the boss could get his cell phone to work properly. It was a beautiful sight, with the moon shining on the surface of the water and tiny twinkling stars just beginning to put in an appearance. In fact, it was just about his favorite place in the world—or, at least, his favorite killing place.

"Sounds like they found them," he said to John Carlson, who stood beside him, his face etched in grief, tears glistening in his eyes. He almost would have felt sorry for the man, had he not been absolutely sure that the next item on the Big Boss's agenda, after Basta dispatched his pesky daughter-in-law and the supposed killer of his son for him, was Basta's own demise.

The rule was as old as the playground: first one to the finish line wins. He meant to abide by it.

He had hoped to get Carlson alone, but it looked like he was out of time. The flunkies who'd been searching the swamp had obviously struck pay dirt. They'd be turning up in a few minutes with the captives, like dogs bringing their master a bone. Basta knew how it worked. He'd been a dog with a master, too. But no more.

The dog was about to bite.

"Call the rest of them in," Carlson said, his back now to the lake as he stared vindictively toward the woods. A step or so beyond him, the flunky fumbled in his pocket for his cell phone, obviously meaning to pass on the boss's order. Basta realized that Julie wasn't screaming anymore. He didn't even waste his time wondering what they'd done to shut her up. He didn't care.

"Funny how things work out," he said to the boss, as though he was just making conversation. At the same time, he took a step back. Just as quick as that, he raised his gun, aimed it—the man was still looking toward the woods—and blew a hole through the Big Boss's head. The body dropped like a felled tree, dead before it hit the ground. The bodyguard dropped his cell phone like it was suddenly red-hot, going for his gun. Basta shot him in the head, too.

Nice and easy and quiet. Couldn't ask for a hit to go down better than that.

Humming softly under his breath, Basta scooped up the fallen cell phone, stuck it in his pocket—it would never do to leave evidence like that lying around for one of the flunkies to find and wonder about—grabbed the bodies by the ankles and dragged them the few feet to the dropoff over the lake, then rolled them off. The Big Boss was still twitching as he went over the side.

"This guy's fricking heavy," the thug carrying Mac's ankles grunted. "I don't know why we couldn't just kill him back there and leave him in the swamp, instead of lugging him all this way."

"You ought to be on this end." A second thug, the one

with his hands locked under Mac's armpits, responded feelingly.

"Boss's orders." The third thug had his hand twisted in Julie's hair and his gun pressed to her neck. Walking easily over the uneven ground, he sounded unsympathetic to the others' plight. "He said bring 'em to him alive, so that's what we're gonna do."

"Quit your bitchin', Dye. We're almost there." The fourth thug was walking a few steps behind with his gun drawn and aimed at Mac, purely as a precaution, Julie thought.

Otherwise, there seemed to be no purpose in it. They'd beaten Mac unconscious. There was blood all over his face now, too. He lay limply between the two thugs, his head lolling against the one's chest, his middle sagging perilously close to the ground as they all, captives and captors, trudged across the moonlit field.

The killing field. As that thought took possession of her mind, Julie was suddenly so frightened that her legs would barely support her. She would have collapsed, she thought, except for the thug's hand twisted in her hair. She knew she was walking toward her own death, and she knew equally that there was nothing she could do to prevent it.

The instant, unwanted image of Sid's face being blown away made her queasy. Please God, she thought, please God don't let me die like that. Don't let Mac die like that. We've only just found each other. Please let us live. Please.

When the flashlight beam had hit them, shining directly through the roots of the sheltering cypress as if the thugs had known exactly where they were hiding, Mac had pushed Julie behind him and opened fire. To Julie's horror, his gun had made empty clicking sounds. Mac had said *Shit, it's wet* and stepped out with his hands up, dropping the gun on command. Then, as the two thugs had looked at Julie, squeezing out through the roots behind him, he'd launched himself at them like a missile.

Wounded and weak, he'd been beaten to a pulp.

So here they were, walking across the field, drawing closer to eternity with every step. She was wearing only her skirt and bra, with lots of bare skin on display, but she was covered with so much mud that she might as well have been fully clothed. The mud served another purpose, too: it seemed to keep the mosquitoes at bay. Not that she was going to have to worry about being bitten for very much longer.

The moonlight was beautiful, soft and white, painting the clearing with an otherworldly glow. It was a night for romance, Julie thought, for walks on the beach, for friends and laughter and love.

For Sid, and now for her and Mac, it was also a night for dying.

"Keep going."

The hand in her hair tightened painfully as she stumbled. Julie recovered, and they marched past the car where Sid's body lay. Julie averted her eyes. Her stomach churned. Gorge rose in her throat.

Sid had deserved a lot of bad things, but not to meet an end like that.

Several other cars were there, too. Julie did a double take at the big gray BMW parked beside the Lexus. That car was John's. She would recognize it anywhere. For a moment hope did its eternal thing in her breast again as the thought that her father-in-law might help her popped into her head. Then she remembered that John was part of this, too.

Did he know Sid was dead? He would grieve.

It was hard to get her mind around the fact that she

shouldn't care if Sid's father grieved. She felt as if her whole life had been turned inside out, and everything she had believed to be true suddenly—wasn't.

As they passed the cars, she saw something small and white slink out from their shadow and fall in behind them. Josephine, minus her usual happy prance. From her demeanor she was obviously aware something was amiss. Her head was down and her tail drooped. Julie felt a glimmer of joy as she spotted her, which was almost immediately superseded by fear. She would have shooed the little dog away, except she didn't want to call attention to her.

This murderous bunch might not bother with killing a dog, but she didn't want to take that chance. There was no reason for Josephine to die tonight, too.

The clearing ended in a grassy cliff overlooking a lake, Julie saw as they walked toward it. She was almost sure it was Lake Moultrie. It was north of the city, and she and Sid and Basta had been traveling in that direction.

Her father had drowned in that lake. The thought made her shiver. Until today, she'd thought it was accidental.

A man was watching them approach. The moon was big and bright behind him, making him no more than a dark shape. A bulky dark shape. A bulky dark shape with a gun in one hand.

But Julie didn't have to see his face to know who he was: Basta.

Her stomach tied itself into a pretzel. Her heart threatened to beat its way out of her chest.

"Where's the boss?" the thug bringing up the rear asked, glancing around.

"He had to take a leak," Basta said. He took a step closer, so that Julie could see his face now. The sight of that swollen, discolored nose struck terror into her soul.

Her pulse began to race; her breathing quickened. She felt light-headed suddenly, and thought she might be going to hyperventilate. Deliberately she closed her mouth, forcing herself to breathe slowly and evenly through her nose. It was impossible to breathe too hard through her nose, she had found.

"Hello, Julie." Basta smiled at her, slowly and terribly. He glanced down at Mac, who now lay sprawled on the ground, then up at the thugs. "He dead?"

"Nah, but he won't be going anywhere any time soon. Dye here got to having too much fun back there, and clobbered him over the head a couple of times too many with his gun."

"Where's Stark?" The fourth thug was still looking around.

"With the boss. What, you think he went to take a leak by himself?" Basta's eyes narrowed slightly. Julie had seen that expression before, and it made her shiver.

Stall him.

Good thought.

Basta's gun hand, which had been hanging rather negligently by his side, started to move. The moonlight glinted off the metal barrel of his gun.

"I know where the thing my father stole is." Julie almost swallowed her tongue in her haste to get the words out.

Basta's gaze swung around to her. The gun stopped its intended trajectory, which seemed to be slightly to her left. Instead it rose to point directly at her.

"You don't even know what it is," he said.

36

"I MAY NOT KNOW WHAT IT IS, but I know where it is."
Oh, God, here she was doing her Scheherazade thing
again. She hoped it worked out better this time than last.

Basta looked at her for a moment. Then he glanced at
the man holding her by the hair.

"You guys, you go wait for the boss by the cars. I need
to have a little private conversation with the lady here."

Julie realized that her hands were shaking. She clasped
them together in front of her. Her heart was racing almost
as fast as her mind. The thug holding her let go of her hair.

"You. Sit down," Basta said to her.

Julie sat. Her knees had been about to give out anyway,
so she practically dropped onto the prickly grass. She was
close to Mac, so close she could have stretched out a hand
to touch him. His face looked bad, with one eye all
swollen shut and blood trickling across his forehead from
a cut near his temple. But as she looked at him, she
thought she saw his eyelids flicker.

Wake up, she willed him. Oh, please wake up.
Although she didn't know what she thought he could do.

Josephine came up out of nowhere and crawled into
her lap, distracting her. Julie hugged her close. Making
Josephine go away was probably an impossibility, so she

wasn't even going to try. Instead she was going to take what comfort she could get. She hugged the little dog close. Josephine licked her chin.

"I don't know," the fourth thug said uneasily.

"This is stuff the boss doesn't want you to know. If you hear it, he's probably going to have to have me kill you."

The thugs looked at each other uneasily. Obviously they knew what Basta was.

"Uh. Okay."

A quick glance over her shoulder told Julie that they were moving back toward the cars. If she ran that way—they would catch or shoot her in a heartbeat.

Basta looked at Julie again. His gaze flicked down to Josephine and his mouth quirked contemptuously.

"Where'd she come from?"

"She was in the jeep when we wrecked."

He grunted, dismissing the subject. "So where is it? The thing we were discussing."

"I'd have to show you."

Basta smiled, and moved his gun in a significant way. Julie's eyes widened.

She caught her breath.

"Really. It—it's in a place that's kind of hard to describe."

Basta pursed his lips. "Maybe you better try."

Uh-oh.

"If I tell you, will you let me go?" She knew better, but she wanted to keep him talking for as long as she could. Where, oh, where, were the police? Mac had said he'd called them. Of course, if they ever arrived, they'd probably be on the bad guys' side.

Her life seemed to be working like that lately.

Basta smiled. A scary smile. Just looking at him smiling at her like that made her blood run cold.

"Sure I will. Why not? You know, I never wanted you dead, not personally. Now that Sid's dead, there's no reason you have to die. No reason at all. Sid just picked this point in time to get rid of you because he was cheating with a girl you knew and he figured you'd find out and file for divorce. Divorce is a bad thing when you're in the mob. All those nasty lawyers looking into your finances. No telling what they might find. But with Sid gone now, that reason doesn't apply."

Julie drew a breath. She suddenly felt almost calm, probably because she'd now passed so far beyond fear that she was emotionally numb. A breeze blew in off the lake, making her shiver as if it was suddenly thirty degrees out instead of eighty. All right, she thought as the shiver intensified into a full-blown case of the shakes, so maybe she wasn't as calm as she'd thought.

"Is that why Kelly was killed? Because she was going to divorce Sid?"

Basta shook his head. "Kelly did a bad thing. She thought Sid was cheating on her, too. She left a voice-activated tape recorder in his office one day. She didn't catch Sid cheating, but she did catch me and Sid and Mr. Carlson discussing something she had no business knowing about."

Julie drew in her breath. "What?"

"A dead person." His eyes hardened on her face and the gun moved again threateningly. "Just like you're going to be a dead person if you don't tell me where the damned tape is. Right now."

"It's—it's . . ." Julie stuttered, unable to get the words out past her suddenly thickened tongue. Her muscles were tense and she felt light-headed. The wind off the lake was kicking up again and she was freezing, too, so cold her teeth chattered. Or, oh yeah, she'd decided that particular reaction was attributable to fear.

She'd never been so scared in her life.

"Where is the tape?" It was a deadly growl.

"If I tell you, you'll kill me," she whispered.

"Tell me." He pointed the gun at Mac. "If you don't, I'm going to shoot little brother here."

Julie's eyes widened with alarm. She glanced over at Mac, to find that he was watching her out of eyes that were open just the tiniest slit.

Oh, God, she couldn't let him shoot Mac. But if she told him anything, he would shoot her, too.

"Last chance," Basta said.

"I—I . . ."

Out of nowhere, a cell phone began to ring, interrupting. The sound was muffled but insistent. Basta, looking startled, reached into his pocket with the hand that was not holding the gun. In Julie's lap, Josephine stiffened and began to growl. As Julie glanced down at her in surprise, the poodle leaped from her lap like she'd been launched from a catapult and threw herself with all the fury of a rabid badger across three feet of space and onto Basta's leg.

"Aiiee!" Basta jumped and howled, performing a frantic one-legged jig in an effort to shake Josephine loose. "Damn dog! Damn dog! Get off me! Get off me, you!"

For a split second, Julie watched transfixed.

Run. It was a scream inside her head.

Oh, yeah. Good plan. She leaped to her feet, tugging on Mac's bloody shirt as she did.

"Mac!"

Mac looked up, and seemed to make a tremendous effort. He surged onto all fours, then onto his feet.

Julie grabbed his hand.

Into the lake.

Her little voice was, as usual, right on. Julie saw

instantly that it was the only path of escape. She ran, and Mac ran with her, lurching and limping but nevertheless managing an amazing burst of speed considering the shape he was in.

"Bad dog!" Basta was still fighting Josephine as the land ran out beneath them. The dark waters of the lake sparkled in the moonlight what looked like a long way below. From the corner of her eye, Julie saw Basta spot them, then free himself from Josephine with a tremendous kick that sent the little dog twisting and yelping through the air. Basta turned, gun raised in a two-handed hold. . . .

And then she and Mac were leaping out into the darkness. She fell like a stone. As she did, sharp spears of sound whistled past her with a ferocity that seemed to punch holes in the air. She only realized that they were bullets when she saw them strike the water, sending up little white jets.

Mac gave a hoarse cry, and seemed to stiffen in the air. Oh, God, had he been hit? Then she struck the water and plunged beneath the surface. Mac went down beside her, and she was frantic until he grabbed her hand. At least he was alive, and conscious. . . .

When she would have surfaced, he began to swim underwater, pulling her along with him. They swam that way until they had to surface for air.

"Were you hit?" It was the first thing she asked him, voice frantic.

"Yeah. Don't worry, I'll be all right." She would have worried a lot less if his voice hadn't been tight with pain.

More bullets whistled around them. Julie's face was showered with spray. She gasped and dived, grabbing at Mac's arm as she went under. Mac was already with her, and they swam without surfacing for as long as they could. Julie hung on to his hand for dear life, terrified that he might lose consciousness. If he did, he might very well drown. She didn't know if she could keep him afloat. He was heavy, and she wasn't that strong a swimmer.

When they came up a second time, gasping, treading water, Mac was beside her and the cliff was a good distance away.

"You don't feel light-headed or anything, do you?" The darkness kept her from seeing much of his expression, so it was hard to judge the exact shape he was in. But he was breathing hard, panting really, and—was he lower in the water than he should have been?

"Don't worry, I won't faint." The faint dryness of that reassured her slightly.

"Where are you hit?"

"Left leg. Leave it till we get out of the water." He added this last and jerked the limb out of reach as she instinctively ran a hand down his leg.

They were well out from shore, probably, or so Julie hoped, beyond the reach of bullets. Plus, they had the darkness to protect them. Julie doubted that anyone could see them now from the shore. Anyway, the shooting seemed to have stopped. But their position had a major drawback: if Mac were to be incapacitated, Julie wasn't sure she could get him safely to land.

The water was cool, but not cold. Mac turned onto his back, floating, moving slowly toward the distant tree line of the eastern shore. Julie paddled anxiously beside him, listening to his breathing. It sounded labored, and his movements seemed frighteningly weak.

"I'm okay," Mac said, forcefully enough to reassure her to a certain extent. "Just stay beside me, and we'll get out of this yet."

Without warning, a helicopter swooped into view, its searchlight illuminating the lake, catching them in its beam.

In the distance, from the direction of the clearing, Julie heard sirens and slamming doors and shouts of "Freeze! Police!"

"Police!" It was shouted over a bullhorn as the chopper came in low over the lake, its blades churning the water into froth, the searchlight never leaving them. Then, seconds later, still over the bullhorn, "This is Greg Rice. Mac, is that you down there?"

"About fricking time," Mac shouted back.

Then two life preservers hit the water. As Julie snagged one, she realized that they were, finally, safe.

37

B Y THE TIME HE WAS IN THE AMBULANCE on his way to the hospital, Mac was feeling pretty rough until the pain medication kicked in. Then he felt more on the order of doped-up, which he didn't ordinarily like but, under these particular conditions, worked for him. They had hooked him up to an IV, which swayed precariously on its hook with every bump and sway of the shock-challenged vehicle. The siren blared importantly, practically deafening him.

There was, however, an upside to his present situation, he reflected. Actually, three upsides, or maybe one three-parted upside. Whatever.

The first upside was that Julie, wet and bedragggled but unharmed, dressed in a shirt loaned to her by one of the cops, was sitting beside him in the ambulance holding his hand. Josephine was huddled at her feet. How Julie had finagled that Mac couldn't even begin to guess, because animals normally were verboten in ambulances, but the dog was unharmed as well, and he supposed he now counted that as an upside, too.

Tonight Josephine had made up for all the bad things she had done since he had acquired her in spades. Never again would he think of doggy shelters in connection with her. She had earned herself a permanent place in his family.

Julie had, too. He just hadn't gotten around to mentioning it to her yet.

The second upside was that Greg Rice had told him that, thanks to his and Hinkle's work, the biggest organized-crime network in the Southeast had been cracked wide open. They could have their careers in police work back, if they wanted them—Mac was going to have to think about that; the private investigator thing had proven interesting, if nothing else—as well as apologies all around. In addition, no charges would be filed because he had beaten the bejesus out of two of the city's finest. Fortunately for him, Dorsey and Nichols were, indeed, dirty cops, and for that allowances would be made.

The third upside was that Roger Basta had been captured alive. He wasn't talking, but it was early days yet. When he saw the kind of charges he was facing, it was likely that he would sing like a bird.

Even though he now knew for certain that his brother was dead, Mac still wanted to find Daniel. Basta was the key to that. Basta knew where Daniel was. Refusing to dwell on the ache that always accompanied thoughts of his brother, Mac looked over at Julie and tightened his grip on her hand. There were lots of things he wanted to say to her, needed to say to her, but, conscious of the paramedic on his other side monitoring his vital signs on various beeping machines, he refrained.

What he said instead was, "That was good thinking, by the way, telling Basta that you knew where the tape he was looking for was hidden. Otherwise, I think he would have shot us right there on the spot. Wham, bam, thank you, ma'am."

Julie met his gaze. Her big brown eyes were tired and heavy-lidded and bloodshot, but they were still incomparably beautiful. *She* was incomparably beautiful.

"I do know where the tape's hidden. At least, I think I know. As soon as I knew it was a tape, I realized where it must be. When my father came to see me that last time, he gave me a teddy bear. It was the only present he ever gave me, and I've kept it all these years. He said it was for my birthday, and I should take real good care of it. He said he'd be back in a couple of weeks to make sure I was taking care of it. Of course, he never came back: he died before he could. But even at the time, I thought it was weird: he never visited us, but here he was, showing up on our doorstep and bringing a teddy bear as a birthday present to a grown girl. It's a soft, squishy teddy bear with a fat stomach. When I first got it, I used it as a pillow sometimes. I quit because there was something hard under all those layers of fluff. Hard and rectangular and about the size of a cassette tape, now that I think about it. At the time, I just thought it was part of the bear's innards. I'll bet anything the tape's in that teddy bear."

"Where's the teddy bear now?" Mac couldn't believe his ears. The key to this entire mess—and Julie had had it all along without knowing it? He stared at her incredulously.

"On the table beside my bed. I kept it all these years, but I never told anyone where I got it." Julie grimaced, making a face that was sad and rueful and a tad funny at the same time. "See, it was Becky's birthday, not mine. I was so jealous that he remembered her and not me that I never even told her about the bear. I just kept it for myself."

The look on her face smote him to the heart.

"Hey." Mac brought her hand to his mouth, paramedic or no paramedic, and kissed her palm. Then, because she still looked unhappy, he decided to hell with manly pride, and went for it. "Julie. I love you."

She smiled at him, a slow-dawning smile that was like the sun coming out. "I love you, too."

Ignoring the stone-faced paramedic, Mac kissed each of the slender, rose-tipped fingers he held. Then curiosity overcame him, and he looked up.

"Didn't you ever tell Sid about the bear?" If she had, Sid would have immediately suspected what was in it and taken the thing apart.

She shook her head, and a sudden spark of amusement twinkled in her eyes. "He was so nasty about my family all the time. I couldn't tell him that my father couldn't even tell me apart from Becky."

Mac laughed. All the time, Julie had held the key to the puzzle, and Sid had never been able to worm it out of her because he was such a prick. Was that poetic justice, or what?

"We've got to tell Greg." As the thought hit him, Mac tried to sit up and found himself held back by the straps around his chest.

"I already did." Julie's hand on his chest and the paramedic's sharp admonition caused him to sink back. "He's sending somebody to get the bear. He said even if the tape's in there, he'll see I get it back once the tape's removed, good as new. I guess I'll have to tell Becky about it now."

"You're something, you know that?" Mac said to her tenderly.

She smiled at him, and suddenly he was flying higher than even the pain medication had taken him. He was high as a kite—on Julie.

Then they were at the hospital, and he was taken from the ambulance and wheeled into the emergency room, and there was no more opportunity to talk.

38

THREE WEEKS LATER, Mac was once again standing on the cliff overlooking Lake Moultrie. It was a hot day, with a sky so blue it would put sapphires to shame and bright sunshine pouring down: A happy kind of day, a day for hot dogs and kites and walks on the beach. For Mac, though, it was bittersweet. A crane was lifting a rusted-out Chevy Cougar from the water. He knew that car. Daniel had bought it two months before he disappeared.

Mac's heart ached almost unbearably as he watched it rise dripping into the cerulean sky.

Basta had told them where to look. Basta, who, as it turned out, had another identity entirely: In his everyday life he was a high-level operative for the DEA. He'd worked for the agency for over thirty years, and was as dirty as they came. At first it had been garden-variety graft: He'd dealt drugs, taken bribes, fixed cases. By his own account, when he'd started busting dealers who worked for John Carlson, he'd gone over to the dark side for good. When Carlson had found out who he was and what he was up to, he had used that knowledge to get Basta under his thumb. In the end, John Carlson had owned Roger Basta. Among other things, Carlson made use of Basta's training and talents by employing him as his own private hit man, calling on his services whenever somebody got in the organization's way.

It both surprised Mac and made him proud to learn that Daniel had been a DEA agent, too. According to Basta, Daniel had been recruited right out of the military, where he'd been, like Mac, a Navy SEAL. As an old friend of Sid's, Daniel had long suspected that the Carlsons were involved in the drug trade. As a gung-ho young agent, he had gone to his boss with his suspicions. His boss had been Basta. Basta had had no choice but to let Daniel investigate; if he hadn't, he had feared that Daniel would become suspicious of him. From the moment he had started his undercover investigation of the Carlsons, Daniel had been marked for death.

Then Kelly Carlson had accidentally taped Basta, Sid, and John Carlson talking about a hit Basta had just made at their instigation. Listening to it and realizing what she was hearing, Kelly had grown frightened. She had run to Daniel, whom she had dated before she had married Sid, and told him about the tape. Daniel had told Basta. Basta, all ears, had instructed him to get the tape. Daniel had obediently gotten the tape from Kelly, and been on his way to give it to Basta when Kelly had called him, frantic. Something in the way Sid was acting toward her made her think he knew about the tape. So Daniel had hidden the tape and gone back for Kelly.

Daniel and Kelly had been killed that night.

Basta added that Mike Williams, who had also worked for the Carlsons as a gopher and nominal employee of Rand Corporation, had been instructed to follow Daniel wherever he went. Williams saw where Daniel hid the tape, retrieved it, and listened to it. Like Kelly, he got scared at what he was hearing. He knew he'd be killed if anyone found out that he knew what he knew. He ran— and took the tape with him.

But then he'd apparently gotten greedy. He had made the mistake of coming back five years later, trying to blackmail the Carlsons about the contents of the tape. For safekeeping he'd hidden it in a teddy bear, and given it to Julie. When they'd caught up with him and tried to beat the whereabouts of the tape out of him, he'd been vague, but he had told them just enough to make them suspect Julie knew where it was before he died prematurely during a further interrogation. Basta had made the death look like an accidental drowning. It had been anything but.

Then Sid had entered Julie's life in pursuit of the tape, and the rest was history.

The feds now had the tape, and it was as explosive as its billing. The hit had been on Henry Jacobs, a longtime federal judge. It was one of the most highly investigated crimes of the last two decades. It had never been solved—until the tape turned up. The recording clearly proved that Basta had done the hit, John Carlson had paid him to do it, and Sid had known everything.

When the police opened the trunk of the Cougar and found Daniel and Kelly, the story was finally ended. For Mac at least.

As the remains were lifted out and put into body bags, Mac realized that there were tears running down his cheeks, and he turned away. He leaned heavily on the crutches he was forced to use until his leg mended, and closed his eyes.

Ah, Daniel, he thought. I loved you, bro.

Seeing his distress, Julie stepped in front of him, slipped her arms around his waist, then rose up on tiptoe to kiss him. Her mouth was soft and sweet, like the rest of her, and he returned her kiss hungrily. He was surprised to find himself wanting her, even at a time like this when there were reminders of tragic death all around. It was, he supposed, an affirmation of life.

"I'm so sorry, Mac," she said softly, pulling her mouth from his at last, her eyes clouded with tears for him. He realized that he'd seen tears in her eyes too much lately: at Sid's funeral, at John Carlson's, at Carlene Squabb's. He never wanted to see tears in her eyes again, he thought, unless they were tears of joy. He made a silent vow to do his best to make sure he wouldn't.

"It's okay," he said. "I've known inside for a long time that Daniel was dead. Finding him was the last thing I could do for him. I owed him that: He was my brother."

"I wish I could have known him."

Mac managed a smile. It felt slightly crooked, but it would serve. There was no sense in dwelling on the past. The living had to move on.

"He would have liked you. Hot chicks were his hobby."

That surprised a laugh out of Julie, and hearing her laugh eased some of the pain that all his sensible cliches could not quite pry out of his heart. He looked down at her, and realized that at least some good had come out of the tragedy: he'd found Julie, the love of his life. His gaze took in the glossy black hair curling softly around her shoulders, the beautiful face, the breathtaking body. She was dressed in a short, sleeveless dress in pale yellow, and looked as delicate and lovely as a sunbeam come to earth. Beneath the dress, her long tan legs were bare.

He loved the fact that her legs were bare.

"Let's go home," he said.

They'd been living together in Mac's house, because Julie couldn't bear to so much as enter hers, and had put it up for sale. As soon as they walked through the door, Josephine greeted them with an excited yap and a wagging tail. Mac looked apprehensively around, but he couldn't see anything right off the bat that had been chewed to splinters. During a hospital visit in which Mac had made aggrieved mention of some of Josephine's less attractive traits, his grandma had looked guilty, confessed that she had totally forgotten about that, and stunned him by informing him that the dear little dog was driven into a frenzy by the sound of a ringing phone. When she had first become aware of this tendency in her beautiful Josephine she'd whisked her off to a doggy psychiatrist, who had come to the sad conclusion that, due to some unknowable trauma in Josephine's past, the dog saw the ringing phone as a threat and responded by attacking. His grandma had solved the problem by investing in a phone that, instead of ringing, played chimes.

Upon being released from the hospital, Mac had promptly done the same. He privately thought that such a simple solution was too good to be true, but Josephine, to his knowledge anyway, hadn't chewed anything since.

Relaxing as no immediate evidence of doggy mayhem met his gaze, he tossed Josephine one of the treats he'd brought in with him from the car, leaned his crutches against a wall, balanced himself carefully on his good leg, forgot about the dog, and pulled Julie into his arms.

She smiled up into his face, and lifted her lips for his kiss.

Instead he simply looked down at her. If he could only have one gift from fate for the entire rest of his life, this was the one he wanted: Julie.

"I love you," he said. "Marry me."

Her eyes widened on his face. For a moment, a heart-stopping moment, he looked down into the big brown eyes that he knew would own him for the rest of his life no matter what she said, and waited for her answer.

She frowned, and looked thoughtful. "Is Josephine part of the deal? Bad habits, rhinestone collar and all?"

He smiled. "Absolutely."

"Then, yes. Yes, I will marry you."

Mac bent his head and kissed her. Then the earth spun on its axis, and the dust motes danced and sang, and the air around them was turned to steam heat by the blaze of their passion. He made love to her with a fierce intensity that expressed without words the way she made him feel. And when she was reduced to quivering, mindless jelly in his arms, he made love to her all over again.

Whispers At Midnight

This book is dedicated as always to my husband, Doug,
and my three sons, Peter, Christopher, and Jack,
with all my love.
It is also dedicated with special love to my very own Curls,
who knows who he is.

1

"I'M NOT LIVING with no flea-bitten mutt, so you can just get it the hell out of here!"

The mutt cowered against her legs. Marsha Hughes scooped it up, then took a cautious step back, glad that Keith was standing in the doorway to the kitchen and not between her and the exit door. She knew that tone. She knew the expression on Keith's reddening face. She knew what came next after the angry tightening of his brawny arms, the clenching of his meaty fists. The dog, a small, pitiful-looking stray she had found huddled behind the Dumpster outside their run-down apartment building, seemed to know too. Looking at Keith from the shelter of her arms, it began to shake.

"Okay, okay," Marsha said to Keith placatingly, while at the same time tightening her hold on the trembling dog. It wasn't anything special, it wasn't worth making Keith mad over, but she wasn't going to let him hurt it if she could help it. There was something about it that tugged at her heart-strings. Not much bigger than a cat, it was skinny and dirty and obviously unloved, a female with liquid dark eyes in a foxlike face, big, upright ears, a short, dull black coat with a single white spot on its chest and a curling, improbably feathered tail. It wasn't pretty, but it was a sweet dog that had come to her when she had knelt and snapped her fingers at it. It had let her pick it up and carry it inside and up the stairs, licking her hand in appreciation when she had fed it a meal of baloney and cheese, which was about all they'd had in the refrigerator since this was Thursday night and neither she nor Keith got paid until Friday. In the hours between the time she'd gotten home from her job as a cashier at Winn-Dixie and had found the dog and the time Keith had come in from working the second shift at the Honda plant and started pitching a hissy fit about it, she'd kind of thought she might keep it. With Keith gone in the evenings, it would be something to come home to. Something she could talk to and fuss over and maybe even love.

When she thought about it, it was kind of sad that she was starting to have to look to a stray dog for love, but if that was the way her life was headed, then there was no point in ducking the facts. She was thirty-five years old, a redhead with a pretty good figure if she did say so herself, but a face that was starting to show some age. Men had mostly quit giving her second looks now. The other day, in the Rite-Aid, she'd sort of flirted with the hot young guy who'd filled her prescription. He'd been friendly, but when he called her "ma'am" as he told her to have a nice day she'd gotten the message: thanks, but no thanks. The plain truth was that she was slip-sliding over the hill, with two divorces behind her and not much in front of her except this good-looking but bad-tempered man and her dead-end job.

"So get it out," Keith said, his tone menacing as he gave her *the look*. The look was kind of like a storm warning, giving her a heads-up that one of their bad times was brewing. Her mouth went dry. Her stomach lurched. Keith in a good mood was sweet as moon pie. Keith in a bad mood was scary.

"Okay," she said again, and turned toward the door. Defused for the time being, Keith turned too, disappearing into the kitchen. Taking a deep, relieved breath as the door that separated the kitchen from the living room swung shut behind him, Marsha hugged the dog closer.

It licked her chin.

"Sorry, angel," she whispered regretfully in its ear. "But you see how it is: You've got to go."

The dog gave a sad little whine as if it understood and forgave her. Patting it, she felt a flicker of regret. It was a good dog.

From the kitchen, she heard Keith say *"Goddamn!"* Then, louder, *"Where the hell's the fucking baloney?"*

She almost wet her pants. Just as she had feared he would, he'd lit on an excuse to kick his bad mood up a notch. Now he was mad. Now he would take it out on her. When he got mad, it always seemed to end up being because of something she had or hadn't done. Tonight it would be about the baloney.

The refrigerator door slammed.

Galvanized, Marsha snatched her purse from under the end table beside the couch and bolted, making it out the apartment door just as he burst into the living room.

"Where the hell's the fucking baloney?" he roared. His voice boomed after her through the door that, in her haste, she'd left open behind her. By the time she reached the top of the stairs, he was already coming through it.

"I don't know." Clutching both dog and purse in her arms, she threw the answer back at him over the noise her ancient Dr. Scholl's made clattering down the metal steps.

"What do you mean, you don't know? The hell you don't. The baloney was in the refrigerator when I left for work and now it's gone. Don't tell me you don't know where it is!" He was leaning over the guardrail at the top of the stairs now, his face beet-red with rage as he glared down at her.

"I'll go to the store and get some more, all right?" Out of breath, she reached the downstairs hall. Awkwardly juggling dog and purse, she grabbed for the knob of the heavy metal door that opened onto the parking lot. The purse she had to have: her keys were in it. The dog she didn't. But if she left it behind, Keith would take his anger out on it. She knew Keith. When he was mad, he was mean as a snake.

"What'd you do with it? You don't even like baloney. *Did you feed it to that dog?*"

No, she couldn't leave the dog behind. Tightening her grip on it, glancing fearfully back as she braced herself and jerked the door wide, Marsha almost had a heart attack. Keith was no longer leaning over the guardrail but was striding with angry purpose toward the top of the stairs. Even the cloud of steamy heat that embraced her as she darted out into the night was not enough to stop an icy shiver from racing over her skin.

"You did, didn't you? *You fed my baloney to that fucking dog!*"

He was coming after her. Her heart pounded with primal fear. He was good and wound-up now. He would beat the crap out of her if he caught her.

Jesus, Jesus, please don't let him catch me.

One of her sandals came off as she ran across the parking lot toward her car, an eight-year-old junker of a Taurus with a broken air conditioner, a permanently stuck-down front passenger side window, and 127,264 miles on the odometer. Stumbling, cursing, she kicked the other sandal off too and ran on. Although it was only the twentieth of June, the summer so far had been a scorcher and the asphalt was hot as a griddle beneath her bare feet. The air was almost too thick to breathe. The single glowing yellow light atop the pole at the far end of the parking lot seemed to shimmer in the heat. Having guiltily wolfed down a McDonald's hamburger and fries on the way home from work, she'd parked next to the Dumpster so that she could dispose of the evidence before she forgot about it and Keith found it. Keith didn't like her eating fast food. He said it would make her get fat.

The Dumpster was at the very back of the lot, next to the light. She had to run through three rows of parked cars to reach her Taurus. If Keith caught her, it would be all the fault of that damned hamburger and fries.

Keith was always telling her that if she'd just do what he said, it would save her a lot of grief.

A radical thought occurred to her: Maybe she'd had just about enough of Keith.

"We're out of here, sweetie," she said breathlessly to the dog, yanking open the door and dumping the animal inside the car. It hopped into the passenger seat as she flung herself behind the wheel. The black vinyl seat was hot against the backs of her thighs, left bare by her ragged denim cutoffs. The stifling interior still carried the incriminating scent of McDonald's. Thrusting the key into the ignition, she glanced over her shoulder and saw that Keith, moving quickly now, was coming out of the building, his bodybuilder's frame looking even bigger than it was because of being backlit by the dim hall light.

"Marsha! Get back here!"

What did he think she was, dumb? No way was she going back. Pulse racing, she slammed the car into reverse. It shot backward. Braking, she looked around again to find Keith breaking into a run. Jesus, he looked like he wanted to kill her. *Keith's mad. Keith's mad.* The words pounded a crazy, panicked refrain through her head. *'Roid rage,* they called it from the steroids he used to get big. Whatever, when it got hold of him like this, it was like he was out of his mind.

He reached the third row. She shifted into drive. Cold with fear, she stomped on the gas pedal just as he emerged from between two parked cars. He was only a few feet away now. Their eyes met for one terrifying instant through the windshield. Then the Taurus rocketed past him.

"You get your ass back here, you bitch!"

Her eyes flew to the rearview mirror to find him shaking both fists after her in impotent fury. *Psycho,* she thought. Then she hung a sharp left out of the lot, and peeled rubber toward the blacktop road that led into Benton.

Praise the Lord he couldn't follow her. A friend had dropped him off; his pickup was in the shop.

It took her a few minutes to calm down. By the time her heart rate had returned to something approaching normal, she'd decided what to do: she would go to her friend Sue's for the night. It was late—a glance at the dashboard clock told her that it was nearly midnight. But Sue, who worked third shift at the Honda plant alongside Keith, would be up. Sue had a husband and three kids, and they all lived in a double-wide on the other side of town. Sue's place was filled to bursting with her own brood, but Marsha was positive that Sue would let her stay for tonight. Tomorrow, she'd see if she couldn't come up with something else.

It was a cinch she wasn't going back to Keith. Not tonight, and not tomorrow. Maybe not ever. *So you can just stick that in your bong and smoke it,* she said to her mental vision of Keith. Her uncharacteristic defiance felt good.

The dog made an anxious sound. Marsha glanced over to find that it was sitting dainty as could be in the passenger seat, its eyes fixed on her face.

"It's okay," she said, reaching out to stroke its delicate head. "Everything's gonna be all right."

The dog licked her wrist as she withdrew her hand, and Marsha suddenly felt a whole heap of a lot better. If she didn't go back to Keith, she could keep the dog. It would be tough, but if she scrounged around she could probably scrape together enough money so that she could get her own place. She even had a Plan B—a secret scheme to provide herself with a little nest egg that might or might not pan out. If it didn't, she might have to waitress or something at night to earn a little extra so she could afford to feed herself and the dog and pay the rent all in the same month, but getting rid of Keith might be worth it. No more hiding fast-food wrappers before he got home. No more waiting anxiously to see what kind of mood he was in. No more lectures, no more crap.

Possibilities as tantalizing as an empty four-lane highway suddenly seemed to open up before her.

"I'm going to do it," she said to the dog, all at once feeling almost cheerful. The dog looked at her, its eyes gleaming in the reflected glow from the instruments in the dash. Although she knew it was silly, she thought it was almost like the animal understood. "No, baby, *we're* going to do it."

She was clear on the other side of Benton now, just a few minutes away from where Sue lived. The fluorescent lights of one of Benton's two open-all-night convenience stores caught her eye. Her Visa was pretty much maxed out, but she'd sent in a fifty-dollar payment just last week, which meant that she should have at least that much credit, she calculated as she pulled into the parking lot. She could get a few things, like a toothbrush and some moisturizer, that she would need in the morning. Clothes were going to be a problem—she couldn't show up at work in what she was wearing, shorts and a tube top—but now that she thought about it, maybe calling in sick would be the best idea. By morning, Keith would probably be madder than ever because she hadn't come home all night. He would come looking for her. Where was he gonna look first? Work.

Pleased with herself for thinking things through enough to stay two steps ahead of Keith, she parked, got out and started to walk inside. Looking worried, the dog tracked her every movement with its eyes, and ended up by standing on its hind legs in the seat with its delicate front paws resting on the stuck-down window, still watching her. Its intention to follow couldn't have been more clear.

"Stay," Marsha said, stopping to shake her head forbiddingly.

The dog hopped out onto the pavement with the grace of a ballet dancer.

"Bad dog." Good thing she didn't have any kids, Marsha thought. She couldn't even sound stern enough to convince a dog. Reaching her, it abased itself at her feet. She frowned down at it for a moment, then sighed and scooped it up in defeat. It was as light as if it had hollow bones, and warm and wriggly with gratitude. There was no way she could make it stay in the car with the window stuck open as it was. If she left it outside by itself, it might wander off or get run over or something. She was surprised by how much the thought of that bothered her. Already, it was like it was her dog.

The store had a rule against dogs. It also had a rule against bare feet. She had both, and she was going in anyway. What were they going to do, she thought with another spurt of her newfound defiance, have her arrested?

She ended up getting toothpaste and Oil of Olay and a box of Puppy Chow, which was the only kind of dog food they had. On impulse, she picked up a package of Twinkies from the display by the checkout. No Keith meant she could eat whatever she liked, and she liked Twinkies. A lot. The clerk, a kid with three earrings in one ear and a silver tongue stud, took her credit card without saying a word about the dog or her feet, which, she saw as she glanced down, looked so dirty that her toes curled in embarrassment against the cold linoleum. She could only hope the woman in line behind her was too intent on scanning the tabloid headlines to notice.

"Want me to add a lottery ticket to this?" The kid, having clearly just remembered that he was supposed to ask, paused in the act of scanning her card to look at her.

"No," she said. There wasn't any point. She wouldn't win. She had never won anything in her life, not even a stuffed toy at the fair. Like the TV commercial said, somebody had to win, but as sure as God made little green apples it wouldn't be her. She had to work hard for her money.

"I heard somebody over in Macon won LottoSouth last week," the woman behind her said, reaching out to pat the dog, which wagged its tail in appreciation. "Twenty-four million."

"Yeah, I heard that too. Must be nice." Had she *ever* heard. Her friend Jeanine, whose sister lived in Macon and worked in the grocery that had sold the winning ticket, had told her. Marsha's reaction had been to hang up the phone, run to the toilet and puke. Sometimes life was so unfair it hurt, but what was new about that? She smiled at the woman, who smiled back. The clerk handed Marsha her card. Tucking it inside her purse, she scribbled her name, picked up her bag and headed back out into the overheated night. Unsurprisingly, there were only two other cars in the parking lot besides the Taurus. At this time of night, Benton was, by and large, asleep.

In that, Benton was sort of like her. She was just beginning to realize that she'd been asleep for most of her life.

"You know, maybe we could move to Atlanta," she said

to the dog as she opened the car door and slid in behind the wheel. At the thought, which had just popped into her head out of nowhere, she felt an unfamiliar glimmer of excitement.

The dog, which had settled into the passenger seat, made a soft sound and came to its feet, watching her with a sudden fixed intensity that caused her to glance at it twice. Then she realized why it was looking at her like that: she'd just fished the Twinkies out of the bag. The dog was clearly a Twinkies junkie too.

"Hang on a minute."

Holding the package one-handed, Marsha ripped it open with her teeth as she drove out of the lot. The sweetly intoxicating scent of the world's ultimate junk food filled her nostrils. She took a bite—it was so good she thought she might die—then broke off a piece and passed it to the dog. The road was deserted, a narrow ribbon of black losing itself in the deeper blackness of the rural countryside as it led out of town. Except for the red glow of the last stoplight before she got to the turnoff to Sue's, there was an almost complete absence of light. The Taurus could have been alone in the universe, she mused as she braked. This little three-stoplight town—was it really the best she could do in life? As she took another bite of the Twinkie, her head was suddenly full of thoughts of Atlanta. Marsha Hughes in the big city—wouldn't that be something? She could make a whole new—

She sensed rather than saw it, felt rather than heard it: a movement in the backseat. The dog, scuttling backward so that its tucked-in tail was pressed up against the door, began to bark hysterically, its eyes fixed on something over her shoulder. Her heart leaped. Instinctively she started to glance around—and an arm whipped across her neck from behind. Giving a scared little cry that was almost immediately choked off, she grabbed at it with both hands. Her nails clawed desperately at sweaty, hairy male flesh. The smell—the smell—she remembered that smell. . . .

The sharp point of what she guessed was a knife pricked the skin below her ear. She went abruptly still. Eyes widening, she felt the warm slide of liquid down the side of her neck and realized that he had drawn blood. Gasping for air against the brutal hold that felt like it was crushing her throat, she broke into a cold sweat.

"I told you not to tell," a hoarse voice whispered into her ear.

The hair stood up on the back of her neck. Everything—the barking dog, the changing stoplight, the night itself—receded as she realized who was in her backseat.

Horror turned her blood to ice.

2

"HERE, PUP, PUP, PUP."

The dog backed away, its white teeth showing in a near-silent snarl. The man looked at it with hate. It should be dead. When it had jumped over the front seat at him, he'd hit it hard enough to send it crashing into the rear windshield. Stunned, it had bounced off the windshield and dropped onto the seat beside him, landing on its side but struggling to get up, its feet feebly paddling the air as if it were trying to run. He had put his knife through it in a vicious downward chop even as he'd grabbed Marsha by the hair to keep her from leaping out of the car. The dog hadn't moved after that. By the time he had Marsha under control again, its bloody little body had been limp. He had pushed it down onto the floor between the seats, and hadn't thought about it again.

Until it had come flying out of the passenger side window just as he'd returned to the car after settling things up with Marsha.

For a moment, as it continued to snarl and back away, he contemplated just turning around and leaving it. Limping and dripping blood like it was, it didn't look like it had a chance of surviving for long out here in the country. If it didn't die of its injuries, likely the coyotes or some other predator would finish it off by morning. But still, it was a loose end. He'd already made up his mind that he wasn't going to leave any more loose ends around. Once upon a time he had made the biggest mistake of his life by erring on the side of restraint. He wasn't making that mistake again.

Not when all of a sudden he had so much to lose.

"Here, dog."

Trying to sound pleasant, he crouched, snapping his fingers. The dog shivered and tucked its tail between its legs, watching him but keeping a safe distance.

Giving up after a few more tries, he had a thought and went back to the car to retrieve the Twinkie Marsha had been eating. One was squashed all over the driver's seat, he discovered with a grimace as he opened the door, but there was another one still in its open package on the passenger side. Leaning in, he grabbed it. Then, Twinkie in hand, he headed back toward the dog.

"Here, dog," he said in a honeyed tone as he approached, holding out the treat.

It started to bark hysterically.

For a moment he froze. The night was dark as Hades, the nearest house was unoccupied, and the chances of anybody hearing the damned animal were slim. But still the sound grated at him, made him jumpy, had him looking all around.

"Shut up," he ordered, then as it kept barking he lost his head and lunged threateningly at it. The dog jumped away, barking even more shrilly. *This is stupid,* he thought, and threw the Twinkie at it.

Then he got into the car and floored the gas, sending showers of dirt shooting skyward as he did his best to run the ugly little thing down.

Yelping, it dodged and scuttled away, scooting under a

fence as he sent the Taurus roaring after it. He slammed on the brakes just in time to keep from hitting the fence, cursing as the dog disappeared in a sea of tall corn.

So it got away, he told himself savagely as he nosed the Taurus back onto the road a little while later. So what? It would probably be dead by morning. Anyway, it wasn't a loose end he was leaving behind, not really. It was just a damned dog.

3

"I HEAR YOU TWO had a fight."

Matt Converse watched the boyfriend's eyes. They flicked away, came back almost immediately. The guy—Keith Kenan, thirty-six years old, one divorce, employed on the line at Honda for five years and resident of Benton for that same period, clean police record except for one brawl over in Savannah two years back and a couple of old DUIs—was nervous. Nervous didn't always equal guilt, but it bore watching.

"Who told you that?"

Matt shrugged noncommittally.

"So what if we did? That don't mean anything. Everybody has fights." Kenan's tone was defensive. He was getting agitated. Matt observed the quickening of his breathing, the tightening of his jaw, the narrowing of his eyes, with clinical detachment. Kenan was a big, burly guy with a dark blond buzz cut, smallish pale blue eyes, and a tattoo of a heart pierced by a dagger on one pumped-up biceps, which was bared by the ratty tank top he was wearing with black nylon gym shorts. The two of them were standing in the combination living/dining room of the apartment Kenan shared with Marsha Hughes.

Correction: had shared. Marsha Hughes had been missing for just over a week. This was Matt's second conversation with Kenan. He'd first talked to him five days ago, after one of Marsha's friends at work had become concerned enough about her unexplained absence to report it to the sheriff's department.

"Everybody has fights," Matt conceded. Kenan started to pace. Matt took advantage of his distraction to glance around. Except for a single meal's worth of dishes on the dining-room table—apparently the previous night's supper because, upon answering the door, Kenan had complained about being rousted from bed—the apartment was neat. Furniture by Sam's Club or Wal-Mart. Worn green carpet. Gold drapes drawn against the bright morning sun. Walls painted white, hung with a few nondescript prints. As far as he could tell, nothing out of the ordinary. No telltale brown stains on the carpet. No suspicious dark spatters on the walls. No corpse sticking out from under the couch.

Matt's mouth quirked wryly. If it were only that easy.

"Look, Sheriff, I ain't stupid. I know what you're getting at," Kenan burst out, turning to face him. "I didn't lay a hand on Marsha, I swear."

"Nobody's saying you did." Matt's voice was calm, his demeanor nonconfrontational. No point in provoking Kenan by escalating the discussion into more than it needed to be at this stage of the investigation. It was still quite possible that Marsha had left on her own; she could turn up alive and well somewhere at any minute. On the other hand, he didn't like the feel of things. Call it instinct, call it applied common sense, call it whatever you wanted, but he didn't think that a woman who'd lived in the area most of her life, who'd shown up like clockwork since she'd started at the Winn-Dixie eight years ago, who had regular habits and a good number of friends, would light out to parts unknown without letting somebody know.

"She just took off," Kenan said. "She got in her car and took off. That's what happened. That's it."

Matt took his time. "Mind telling me what the fight was about?"

Kenan looked harassed. "Baloney, all right? I had some baloney in the refrigerator and it was gone when I got home from work and went to make a sandwich. Turns out she'd fed it to a damned dog." He took a deep breath. "It was stupid. Just one of those stupid things."

Over Kenan's shoulder, Matt watched his deputy, Antonio Johnson, emerge from the bathroom down the hall. Antonio would turn fifty in two weeks. He was black, a little less than six feet tall and nearly as wide, built like a linebacker gone to seed. He had a bulldog's pugnacious face, a more or less permanent scowl, and basically looked like a thug in deputy's uniform. He had asked to use the john right after Kenan had let them in, as a way of getting a look at the areas of the apartment the sheriff or his deputy were not normally allowed to see without benefit of a search warrant. It was a ploy they had used before, and would use again. Sometimes it netted them valuable information. Today, apparently, they weren't going to be so lucky. Antonio replied to his questioning look with a negative jerk of the head.

"Thanks," Antonio said to Kenan as he joined them in the living room. Kenan nodded, then glanced back at Matt.

"I didn't do nothing to her," he said, wetting his lips. "I swear to God."

Matt looked at him. Kenan held his gaze.

"You mean besides yell at her," Matt said agreeably. "And chase her down the stairs and out of the building. Isn't that what happened that night?"

Kenan didn't say anything. He didn't have to. The breath he sucked in through his teeth was as much confirmation as Matt needed this side of the courtroom.

"Might as well give it up," Antonio said, folding his arms across his massive chest and glowering at Kenan. "We *know.*"

Matt barely stopped himself from casting his deputy a wry glance. What they knew was basically what Kenan and the neighbors had already told them: Marsha Hughes had had a fight with him, had left or been chased from the apartment and had not been seen by anyone important to her since. Without any kind of solid evidence that Marsha had come to harm, what they knew didn't amount to a hill of beans. There was no case. But Antonio was an optimist. He was always thinking that if he applied enough pressure, potential suspects would crack, confessing all and saving everybody concerned a boatload of time and trouble.

Sometimes it even worked.

Kenan's expression changed. His lip curled angrily as his eyes slashed to Matt. "I saw you talking to that damned Myer woman the other day. Stayin' home all the time, claiming she hurt her back and can't work, getting her kicks butting into other people's business." His voice was tight with resentment. "She's the one who told you that, right?"

"Actually, everybody in the building who was home that night pretty much says the same thing." Matt's demeanor was still mild, still neutral, although he made a mental note to keep an eye on Audrey Myer, who had indeed been the primary source of his information, in case Kenan should live up to his hair color and try something stupid. Reaching for a brass-framed picture of Kenan with Marsha, whom he recognized from a photo he'd collected for identification purposes on his first visit to the apartment, Matt paused and glanced at Kenan before picking it up. "Do you mind?"

"Help yourself." The tension in his voice was still palpable.

Matt picked up the picture and made a show of examining it. It was a snapshot rather than a formal portrait, obviously taken at a fair or amusement park, showing the two of them dressed up in old-fashioned clothes, including a big picture hat for Marsha that hid most of her red hair. They were grinning at the camera, their arms around each other, clearly on good terms at that moment.

At another moment, had Kenan killed her?

"Good-looking woman," he said, putting the picture back down on the end table. His gaze slid to Kenan again. "You must be worried sick about her."

The point being that so far Kenan had shown no sign of being unduly concerned over Marsha's fate. Chalk up one more red flag. Of course, it was possible that Kenan was a still-waters-run-deep type, with a lot more going on beneath the surface than Matt had been able to discern. It was also possible that Kenan simply wasn't all that sorry she was gone, which still didn't make him guilty of a crime.

The thing about it was, Matt wasn't even a hundred percent sure that a crime had been committed here. His gut instinct said that Marsha Hughes's prospects for turning up unharmed did not look good, but then, his gut instinct had steered him wrong before.

"I am," Kenan said. Belligerently.

Matt took note of the tone, of the clenching of Kenan's fists, the reddening of his face.

"You've been known to hit her." Matt's voice was almost gentle. His purpose was to uncover information, not to accuse.

"Who told you that?" Kenan responded. He was breathing heavily even though he was no longer pacing.

Matt shrugged.

"Goddamned nosy-ass neighbors." A muscle in his jaw worked. His stance had shifted, become aggressive, with legs braced apart, shoulders rigid, fists clenched into tight bunches by his sides. His eyes were hard as they met Matt's. "Look, like I said, we had fights. Marsha's no angel, either. Anything I did to her, believe me, she gave as good as she got."

"Did you hit her the night she disappeared?"

"No! No. I didn't touch her. She left, all right? We had a fight and she left. She got in her car and I watched her drive away. That's the last time I saw her."

Antonio made a skeptical sound that was not quite under his breath. Kenan's gaze swung around to him. The look Kenan gave him was tense, angry. The interview was teetering on the brink of turning ugly, Matt realized. Pushing Kenan to the point of clamming up and calling a lawyer would be counterproductive. Time to hang it up for now.

"Well, thanks for your cooperation. We'll be in touch," Matt said, offering his hand before the encounter deteriorated irredeemably. After the briefest of hesitations, Kenan shook it. Antonio shook hands, too. It was clear from the expression on his face that he did so with reluctance. Making nice with those he considered bad guys was not one of Antonio's strong suits.

Antonio tended to take crime personally. Matt had spent a considerable amount of time in the two years since he'd been elected Screven County Sheriff dissuading Antonio from breaking people's arms and legs. Figuratively speaking, of course. At least, most of the time it was figurative.

Suppressing a sigh, Matt turned to the door, then glanced back over his shoulder with his hand on the knob as if he'd just remembered something.

"Just so you know: we've got an APB out on her car, and her picture and stats have been sent to every law enforcement agency in the Southeast. Plus we're still running down a few leads locally. We'll find her."

His tone was deliberately confident; if Kenan really was

WHISPERS AT MIDNIGHT — 21

concerned about his girlfriend's fate, it should provide some small degree of reassurance.

On the other hand, if he wasn't revealing any concern because he knew very well where Marsha was, having personally put her there, it should worry him.

Either way worked.

"Yeah, we'll find her." Antonio turned it into a threat as he followed Matt out into the stuffy upstairs hallway.

Kenan closed the door behind them without another word. The sound, louder than it needed to be, echoed off the concrete-block walls.

"Think you could tone the hostility down a notch?" Matt asked as they took the stairs.

"We got him. That's our man right there. The guy's an asshole."

It was hot in the stairwell; the sound of their shoes hitting the metal treads echoed around their ears.

"Last time I checked, being an asshole wasn't a crime. As for any evidence against him, we don't have diddly-squat."

"He has a history of beating up on her. She was scared enough of him the night she disappeared to run out of their apartment. He chased her outside. We've got half a dozen witnesses ready to swear to that. Nobody's seen her since. What more do you want?"

"A lot," Matt said dryly, pushing open the door and walking out into the sweltering heat. There'd been a whole string of hellishly hot days like this, nine or ten together. It was ninety-nine in the shade, and humid. He'd seen it before—the heat made people crazy. There'd been more crimes, petty and otherwise, in the last two weeks than there had been in the previous six months. His eight-man department was swamped. They were all working pretty much around the clock, himself included. Today he'd been fighting crime since five A.M., when Anson Jarboe had tried to sneak into his house after an all-night bender and been surprised by his wife, who'd been waiting in their darkened living room with a baseball bat. Anson's shrieks as she'd given him what for had roused the neighbors, and the neighbors had called the sheriff. It was now five past eleven, and he knew from experience that the day—a Friday—was just getting underway. After people got off work, the county would really start to hop.

All he wanted to do tonight was sit in his air-conditioned house in front of the TV set with a cold beer in one hand and the remote in the other; there was a baseball game he was dying to catch.

Fat chance of that.

"Well, I—" Antonio began, then broke off, a grin splitting his homely face from ear to ear. Alarmed, Matt glanced around to see what had prompted such an uncharacteristic display of glee from his typically stone-faced deputy. When his gaze lit on the cause, he barely managed to swallow a groan. He'd known it had to be bad to wrest that kind of grin out of Antonio, but this wasn't just bad—it was awful.

"Oh, Matt, there you are!" Shelby Holcomb's face brightened as she spotted him. Waving, her face wreathed in smiles, she straightened up from peering into the window of his official car and headed toward him.

"Hey, Shelby," he answered, his pace slowing.

Undeterred by his clear lack of enthusiasm, she kept on coming. Slim and attractive at thirty-two, a Benton native who had moved back to town four years before to take over the local Century 21 franchise, Shelby had twisted her honey-blond hair up in some kind of fancy-looking roll at the back of her head as her sole nod to the heat. Her makeup was on in full force, down to the bright red lipstick that gleamed as the sun hit it. She even had on a suit, for crying out loud, a powder blue number with a short skirt and elbow-length sleeves, which he guessed was no big deal for Shelby despite the soaring temperature because the woman never seemed to break a sweat. Buttoned up the front, it exposed what Shelby no doubt considered an effective but tasteful amount of cleavage. She had on hose, and heels, and was carrying that damned notebook she was using as her latest weapon in the war of conquest she was waging. Not that he was about to fall anytime soon.

She'd been chasing him for years. Last summer, in what was one of the many brain-dead episodes that continued to distinguish his existence, he'd made the mistake of letting her catch him for a while. They'd hung out, had fun, gone to some parties, the movies, Savannah for dinner a couple of times. All in all, they'd had a good time. Then Shelby had started reading magazines with titles like *June Bride* and dragging him into jewelry stores and otherwise giving off all kinds of vibes that she was starting to pair him with "forever" in her mind.

Forever gave him nightmares. Forever wasn't in his game plan. Forever and a woman? Not happening. At least, not anytime in the foreseeable future. Just the idea of being tied down to a wife and kids and a mortgage made him break out in a cold sweat.

He'd had enough responsibility in his thirty-three years to last him the rest of his life. No way was he taking on more when he was right on the brink of working his way free.

He'd come out with some lame speech in which not rushing things and her being way too good for him and his needing space had been the dominant themes. Then he'd run for the hills. She'd been gunning for him ever since.

"Matt!"

That voice was even more familiar than Shelby's, and came with its own set of worries. It belonged to Erin, the oldest of his responsibilities. He turned his head and spotted his sister as she popped out of the passenger seat of Shelby's red Honda, which was parked behind his cruiser. A recent graduate of the University of Georgia, she was twenty-two, petite and pretty with short, tousled black hair and a mischievous grin, which at the moment beamed full-wattage at him. As their eyes met over the roof of the car, he couldn't help grinning back at her, albeit a little ruefully. Erin, blast her sweet but troublemaking little hide, had gone and gotten herself engaged to Shelby's younger brother, Collin, who had set up a law practice in Benton the previous year. As Matt was paying for the wedding as well as giving the bride away and Shelby had taken upon herself the task of organizing the event, the opportunities for Shelby to hound him had multiplied exponentially. It seemed like everywhere he went lately she turned up.

"Yo, Erin," he said with a touch of reproof. His sister knew Shelby was after him, and like the rest of his family—along with half the damned county—seemed determined to do her bit to help shoo him into the trap.

"I just wanted to get your opinion before I ordered the flowers." Shelby smiled at him with determined charm. Matt obediently stopped walking as she reached him and looked down at the notebook, which she was flipping open practically under his nose. He'd been through this drill before: She showed him something—a picture, an estimate, a list—and he nodded and said, "Looks great." Then she did what she wanted—with his money.

It was expensive, but easier and safer than arguing.

This time, however, the amount in question was so high that he protested before he thought.

"Fifteen hundred dollars? For *flowers?*" He met Shelby's eyes. They smiled meltingly into his. Her lips parted. Her lashes fluttered. Alarmed, he dropped his gaze back down to the price list.

"I told her it was too much." Apology in her voice, Erin joined them. She was wearing short white shorts that showed way too much of her tanned legs, in Matt's opinion, and a lime green halter top that molded her ample breasts. Looking her up and down with a gathering frown, he made a mental note to have a chat with her sometime in the near future about the advantages of leaving something to the imagination. She apparently read his mind, or his expression, because as she met his gaze her grin returned and she gave a teasing little wriggle that set her breasts to jiggling.

He frowned at her, she wrinkled her nose at him, and they engaged in a potent but silent exchange of opinions as visions of convents filled his head. Then the sheer ridiculousness of the situation occurred to him. Somewhere, he thought, angels must be snickering at the idea that *he,* of all people, had wound up with three increasingly babelicious girls to shepherd into womanhood. It had to have been the cosmic joke of the century.

"It *is* a lot." Shelby sounded apologetic too as she curled surprisingly strong fingers around his elbow. "But I don't think the florist is being unreasonable. You have to consider that besides the bride's bouquet, we need nosegays for the bridesmaids, and boutonnieres for Collin and the groomsmen, and flowers for the church and centerpieces for the tables at the reception and—"

"Whatever you think," Matt interrupted, feeling hunted. His uniform was khaki, long pants, short-sleeved shirt, and Shelby was taking full advantage of the looseness of his shirt sleeve to slip her hand right up under there to caress his biceps. The feel of her soft, meticulously manicured hand sliding across his overheated skin was enough to make him remember that he hadn't gotten laid since he'd fled her bed at the end of March. Which was exactly what she had intended, he was pretty sure.

Antonio crossed his arms over his chest, looking thoughtful. "When Rose got married"—Rose was the younger of his two daughters—"I told her that she could choose between the flowers she wanted or the down payment on a new car. That's how much the flowers were."

"So what did she choose?" Matt asked, slightly interested.

"The flowers. Can you believe it?" Antonio shook his head at the folly of women.

"My idea is that we should just do the flowers ourselves," Erin said, giving Matt a wicked smile that told him she knew where Shelby's hand was. "We could get the cost down to five hundred dollars and still have practically the same thing."

"Whatever you think," Matt said again, desperate to end the conversation. The only thing worse than being kept abreast of every little detail of his sister's wedding plans was being stalked by Shelby at the same time. He hadn't realized it while they'd been seeing each other, but the woman had the tenacity of a bulldog; once she got her teeth into something, she never willingly let go.

More fool he for letting her sink her teeth into him in the first place.

The cell phone clipped to Matt's belt began to ring. He had a pager, but it could only be accessed by an employee of the sheriff's department. Many of his friends, neighbors, relatives and other assorted county residents preferred to bypass the whole official process and call him on his personal line. At least answering it provided an excuse for him to step away from Shelby without making his discomfort with what she was doing obvious. She looked after him in transparent disappointment as her discreetly dislodged hand dropped to her side.

Thank God Erin's wedding was only a little over three weeks away, Matt thought. He was starting to feel harassed to the max. On top of everything else, playing cat and mouse with Shelby without saying or doing something that would hurt Erin's relationship with her new family was getting old fast. It was no damn fun being the mouse.

"Got to go," Matt said as he hung up, feeling relieved and doing his best to hide it. He looked at Antonio. "Mrs. Hayden's out walking her dog down Route 1 again."

Antonio made a face.

"So what's wrong with that?" Erin looked from one to the other of them with a mystified frown.

"All she's wearing are her shoes and a big sun hat," Matt clarified. Mrs. Hayden was ninety if she was a day, and growing increasingly forgetful. Lately she had tended to forget to put on her clothes. This was the fourth time since the weather had turned nice in March that they'd gotten a call from a scandalized driver reporting that she was strolling naked alongside the road as her equally ancient shih tzu snuffled at grass clumps from the end of a leash.

"Can't somebody else deal with it?" Shelby asked with a hint of impatience, tapping her fingers against the cover of the notebook as if that were the most important thing in the world.

"She likes Matt," Antonio said, grinning again. Matt was beginning to realize that lately a great many of his deputy's rare grins were being had at his expense. "If any of the rest of us come near her, she clobbers us with her hat. She lets Matt take her home."

Erin chortled. Shelby looked disgusted.

"See ya," said Matt, taking full advantage of what he could only regard as a heaven-sent opportunity to escape.

He never would have thought it possible, but he found as he retreated in good order to his cruiser that today he was actually grateful for having been personally notified that Mrs. Hayden was having one of her more bizarre senior moments again. He'd rather deal with a naked nonagenarian than a love-thwarted thirty-something any day of the week.

With Antonio riding shotgun, he lifted a hand in farewell to his sister and his ex-girlfriend, then drove out of the parking lot.

The question of Marsha Hughes's whereabouts was temporarily put on the back burner as he sped off to make the county safe from the hazards posed by dotty old ladies.

4

On this rainy midnight, Benton was as steamy as the inside of a hot shower. It was as dark and haunted feeling as a dungeon. It was also, Carly Linton discovered as she paused to catch her breath beside the huge birch that had anchored the front yard for as long as she could remember, not quite as dead asleep as such a small town should have been at so late an hour. One person at least was awake, and she was looking right at him—or, rather, part of him.

Nice butt, was her first thought, as, muscular and tight and hugged by a pair of well-worn jeans, the butt in question moved into her line of vision. Not that she was into noticing men's butts. Not anymore. Since her divorce she'd felt more like kicking them than drooling over them, nice or not. The state of the butt was merely a fleeting observation, made in passing, as the beam of her flashlight locked onto a man on all fours backing out of the crawl space beneath the front porch of her grandmother's house. Correction, *her* house now. Her grandmother had been dead for more than three years, and the turreted Victorian mansion, which Carly had inherited, had been empty since Miss Virgie Smith, who'd been renting the place, had moved into an assisted-living home in Atlanta two months before. By all rights it should have been empty still. As in, no one living there, no one home, no one crawling out from beneath the dilapidated porch. Typical of the way her luck had been running lately that it was not.

Freezing in her tracks, her flashlight still trained on the baffling butt, Carly considered her options.

"Christ almighty, is that a *burglar?*" Sandra whispered, stopping dead beside her. Five foot ten in her bare feet, admitting to 250 pounds (which was sort of like five-foot, two-inch Carly admitting to 100, a nice lie that was quite a few pounds south of the truth), black and proud, Sandra possessed a truly formidable physical presence that should have provided some comfort under the circumstances. Unfortunately, Carly was all too well aware that beneath her employee/business partner/good friend's intimidating exterior lurked the soul of a Martha Stewart. And not a kick-ass Martha Stewart either. A soft and cuddly Martha Stewart. A Martha Stewart whose fight or flight instinct was irretrievably set on flight.

"We don't have burglars in Benton," Carly whispered back, nearly dropping the flashlight as she fumbled desperately to turn it off before the beam could give their presence away. Scant seconds after she succeeded, the man's shoulders emerged from the blackness underneath the porch, followed in due and predictable course by his head.

"Then who is he?" Sandra sounded unconvinced. The cardboard moving box full of pots and pans that she'd been carrying now rested at her feet. Carly had been so focused on the man that she hadn't even realized Sandra had set her precious cooking utensils down in the wet grass. Her own less docile cargo squirmed indignantly in her arms. Hugo hated to be carried; he considered it beneath his dignity. Carly tightened her hold on the huge Himalayan cat and prayed he wouldn't let out an untimely yowl.

"A plumber? The Orkin man? How the heck should I know?"

The night was humid and airless in the aftermath of the fierce summer storm that had just passed. A wet earthy smell that Carly always associated with rainy nights in Georgia hung in the air. Still-dripping leaves and eaves combined with the piccolo piping of a host of unseen tree frogs to cover their whispered conversation. From behind shifting clouds a pale sickle moon appeared, providing just enough light to enable Carly to see the tall form of the intruder come lithely to his feet.

In one hand, its ominous shape unmistakable despite the darkness, he held an evil-looking black pistol.

"That's it. I'm calling nine-one-one." Sandra rooted in the bright plastic tote bag that served as her purse and came up with her cell phone, which she flipped open.

"We don't have nine-one-one service in Benton."

"Shee-it." Sandra stopped punching numbers, closed the phone and rolled her eyes at Carly. "You got anything in Benton besides spooky old houses and scary men with guns?"

"We have a McDonald's. *And* a Pizza Hut." Both were recent arrivals of which her small hometown's chamber of commerce was justly proud.

"Oh, that's great. How about I just go ahead and call one of them?" Sandra shook her head in disgust. "I don't want to eat, fool. I want to be saved from the man with the gun. What about a fire department? They save cats from trees."

"In Benton if we need help we call the state police. Or the sheriff."

"Number?" Sandra flipped open her phone again.

"No clue."

They were backing away as they spoke. Carly moved carefully, mindful of lurking tree roots, her sneakers sliding a little on the slippery ground, her eyes never leaving the maybe-burglar. Clearly unaware of their presence, he stood with his back to them, seeming to focus on the huge dark shape that was the barn, which was just visible behind the house. The yard was as neglected as the rest of the property, the grass and bushes overgrown, the leaves unraked from the previous fall, which made the footing even trickier, especially since they were moving downhill. Situated at the western edge of town atop a wooded knoll some distance from its nearest neighbor, the Beadle Mansion, as the house was known thanks to its original owner, did not even possess its own driveway. Their vehicle, a bright orange U-Haul, which they had driven straight through from Chicago, was parked beside the narrow blacktop road that curled around the base of the hill. Reaching it without alerting the man to their presence should be doable. Getting inside and driving away without being spotted was a whole nother basket of bread rolls.

Sandra's cell phone snapped shut with a tiny sound that spoke of pure disgust. The man started walking away from them toward the corner of the house as if he might be headed for the barn. Carly stuck the flashlight into the front pocket of her jeans and tightened her grip on Hugo, who growled in protest. Poor cat, he hadn't liked the trip, he hadn't liked the rain, and he never liked being held against his will. He was going to like what was coming next less than all of it put together. In preparation, the fingers of her left hand locked around his front legs like kitty handcuffs, and her right forearm, on which his squirmy twenty-pound bulk rested, clamped him like a hotly contested football against her side.

Ready now, Carly glanced at Sandra. "I don't know about you, but I vote we get while the getting's good."

"I hear you."

Before they could execute the required about-face, a totally unexpected sound shattered the peace of the night. Loud as a siren, it seemed to go off right in their faces; both women jumped about three feet in the air. Under the circumstances, the shrilling tones were a little less welcome than a cloud of angry yellowjackets. Aghast, Carly realized even as her feet touched down again that the noise seemed to be coming from Sandra. Or, to be more precise, from Sandra's phone.

"Shut it up! Turn it off!" Carly instinctively grabbed for the electronic traitor even as Sandra, staring down at the shrieking thing in her hand with as much horror as if it had suddenly morphed into a writhing snake, flipped it open and started punching buttons in a frantic effort to comply. Carly's grab dislodged the phone. It somersaulted through the air to land smack at her own feet. From its new location it emitted another of its hideous blasts. Then another. And another. Frozen to the spot, she was too rattled to do anything except stare at it with dropped jaw and saucer eyes.

"Who's there?" The challenge, issued in a raised voice, held a menacing note, and it snapped Carly's appalled gaze up again. The man was no longer walking away. Though the darkness obscured much about his appearance, it was clear that he had turned around. In fact, though she and Sandra were now at least a quarter of the way back down the slope and partially concealed by soggy foliage, he seemed to be looking in their direction—damn that stupid phone anyway!—and the hand holding the gun was definitely in motion. It was rising. More to the point, the gun was rising with it—and it was turning their way.

Carly's stomach dropped like a broken elevator.

"Shit," Sandra said, summing up the situation perfectly. As one, the two of them pivoted and bolted for the U-Haul.

"Hold it right there!"

The command slowed neither Carly nor Sandra by so much as a whisker. Heart pumping a mile a minute, hanging on to a now-struggling Hugo for all she was worth, Carly ran for her life. Sandra, arms and legs moving like pistons, her black leggings and oversized black tee shirt making her little more than a rapidly vanishing blur as she tore down the hill, shot past her, opening a commanding lead.

Who knew? Carly lost focus long enough to marvel that normally indolent Sandra had it in her to move that fast. Then she thrust the thought aside, and put heart and soul into saving herself and her ungrateful cat. In other words, she tightened her death grip on writhing, clawing Hugo, put her head down, and *ran.*

Was he coming after them? Even as she ducked low-hanging branches and slithered on slimy moss, the prospect sent icy prickles down Carly's spine. Worse, was he staying put, but taking careful aim as a prelude to shooting one of them in the back? Which, given the way her life had been going lately, would be her, of course. Thanks to Sandra's unexpected burst of speed, she was closer to the prospective shooter, and in her jeans and yellow tee shirt undoubtedly a far more visible target. Carly cringed as she tried not to imagine what it would feel like to have her spine drilled by a bullet.

"You there! Stop!"

Not in this life. Gasping for breath, Carly ran faster. Her heart pounded as if it were determined to beat its way out of her chest. Blood thundered in her ears. The shout had sounded closer—hadn't it? Where was he? Were those his footsteps she heard thudding behind her now that the damned telltale phone had finally stopped ringing? Or was it her own pulse pounding?

Unable to resist a lightning glance back that showed her

exactly nothing except a whole lot of night, she stumbled over a root. She'd felt the flashlight being jarred looser and looser with every step; now it fell, hitting the ground beside her feet. It rolled, she stepped on it, and suddenly she was about as stable as a hog on ice. Hugo, taking despicable advantage of the situation, chose that moment to push off against her side with a powerful thrust of his hind legs. Thrown even more off balance, she snatched after him and came up empty. Plumy white tail waving triumphantly, he shot away from her.

"Hu—oomph!"

Windmilling, calling after Hugo, she never even heard it coming: something hit her from behind with the force of a speeding truck. Slamming nose first into the soggy ground at the foot of a stand of dripping live oaks, she realized that she had been tackled.

By the man with the gun. His arms locked around her hips, his head thudded like a dropped bowling ball into the curve of her back, and the crushing weight of his torso pinned her legs to the ground.

Carly screamed. Well, squeaked was more like it, because right at that moment she couldn't draw enough breath into her flattened lungs for an honest-to-God scream. Her flight or fight instinct, now that flight had been so rudely eliminated, switched to fight in an instant. Fueled by adrenaline, she twisted violently onto her back and in the process almost succeeded in dislodging him. Almost was the operative word, though, and it wasn't enough. A hard-breathing, featureless shadow in the dark beneath the trees, he grabbed her again before she could wriggle away. Locking one hand in her waistband, he gave an almighty yank. Thank God the metal button held; snug to begin with—she had never thought she'd live to be grateful for having gained seven pounds from the stress of the divorce—the jeans didn't budge. But she did. Her whole body slid several inches in the wrong direction, and suddenly his head was at the approximate level of her crotch. She was excruciatingly aware of his hand, warm and rough as it slid across the silky bare skin of her stomach. A wave of horror hit her; it didn't take a genius to figure out what he had in mind.

"No, no, no!" Carly went into a frenzy, beating at his head and shoulders with her fists, ramming her knees into his chest, digging her heels into the rain-softened earth. She had borne much over the last few months, but she couldn't bear this. She had to get away, had to get away, had to get away. . . .

"Let me go! You let me go! Help! Sandra! Somebody!"

The volume of her gasping cries would have shamed a cornered mouse, she realized with despair. He said something, the tone of it harsh and guttural, but she was beyond making sense of mere words. Her heart pounded so hard that it could have been playing drummer for Ozzy Osbourne. Her throat was dry as cat kibble. Terror tasted like aluminum foil in her mouth. She was facing rape, death, probably both together, and she didn't know why she was even surprised. Her life had been in the toilet for at least the last two years, and every time she thought things couldn't get worse it took a header into an even deeper, smellier part of the pit. But this—this was crossing the line. It was too much. It was the proverbial straw that broke the poor, pathetic, long-suffering camel's back. God or fate or whoever was running the circus up there was hereby put on notice: Carly Linton was mad as hell, and she wasn't going to take it anymore.

Summoning her last reserves of strength and determination, she channeled her inner Mike Tyson and contorted like a pretzel as she went for his ear with her teeth. He dodged in the nick of time, and what she got for her efforts was a head-butt to the nose. Falling back, eyes watering with pain, she changed channels but continued to fight. The slippery wetness of the ground beneath them helped her, hindered him. Wriggling like a worm on a hook, kicking at him, finally using the fortuitous contact of her foot against his shoulder as impetus, she managed to get free, and swarmed backward in a frantic belly-up crawl. He surged after her, grabbing her around the knees. At this recapture she screamed like a steam whistle—thank God her lungs were functioning at full capacity again!—and yanked one leg free, kicking him as hard as she could in the head.

"Goddammit," he roared, rearing up with a shake of his head. Before she could react he lunged forward again and dropped on top of her, flattening her beneath him. The breath went out of her with the force of a blown tire. Sprawled and winded, she bucked feebly in an effort to throw him off. Fully atop her now, he was too heavy to budge. Her right hand was pinned between their bodies—useless. Even as she tried to yank it free, she abandoned Iron Mike in favor of Catwoman and went for his eyes with her free hand, fingers curved, nails ready. She was not going to go gentle into that good night—or whatever else this thug had in mind for her.

"Scratch me, and I'll make you sorry you were ever born," he snarled, locking a hand around her wrist in midair and bringing it into forceful contact with the wet ground, where he pinned it. She was all but immobile now, but still she refused to give up. With the thumb and forefinger of her trapped hand she managed to get in a vicious pinch to the meaty part of his chest. He yelped and delved between them for her other hand. Resisting, she bucked and screamed again, right in his face.

Their battle had taken them out of the oaks' shadow into the open. The moonlight fell on his face, and as he grimaced in the wake of her air-horn-worthy blast, she got her first good look at him. Her eyes widened, her jaw dropped, and just like that the fight went out of her. Lying sprawled beneath her attacker's approximately two-hundred-pound weight, she felt oddly boneless, and realized that this was what it meant to be limp with relief.

"Matt Converse, what do you think you're doing?" she demanded furiously.

He froze. His eyes met hers, and his brows snapped together.

"Carly?" He sounded doubtful.

"Yes, Carly." There was bite to her voice. Even as she sucked in a much-needed breath, memories of the last time she'd lain beneath him like this rushed back at her, about as welcome as a rubber check.

"Jesus, you've got boobs."

His hand, with hers flattened beneath it, rested partly on top of her right one. She could feel his fingers flexing, gauging the curve of her breast. She yanked her hand free—and he copped a feel. Last time his hand had been wrapped around her breast she'd barely filled an A cup. Now she was a lush and lovely C, thanks to years of exercises and creams and good living and—all right, about five thousand dollars' worth of implants. Not that she meant to tell him *that*.

"Yeah, well, boobs happen." She glowered at him. Lucky for him his hand had slid on out from between them or she would have slapped him into next week. She *owed* him a slap. Had owed him for twelve years. She was practically itching to pay up.

"And you're blond." He was sounding mildly stupefied. His gaze was on her shoulder-length, stick-straight, stylishly choppy platinum blond hair. Its natural state was a wildly curly mouse brown, as he well knew.

"Blond happens too. Want to get off me now? At least,

I'm assuming the rape's off, since it turns out we know each other."

"Rape?" He snorted. "You've got to be kidding me. Is that what you thought?"

"You know, I don't know why, but when some guy tackles me in the dark and starts feeling me up, rape tends to be one of the possibilities that enters my mind."

Her words dripped sarcasm. His mouth quirked into the slightest of smiles.

"Curls, is that really you?" Seemingly in no hurry to move, he propped himself up on his elbows as the nickname he'd bestowed on her years before took her back to places she didn't want to go. With his dead weight still pinning her to the ground, he did a quick visual inventory of each feature. It galled her to realize that any claim to beauty she might under better circumstances have possessed had been done in by an unfortunate combination of the weather, the lateness of the hour, the marathon drive she'd just endured, and her lingering depression over the implosion of her entire, carefully constructed life. Since she'd been driving, she'd washed her face with plain old liquid rest-room soap and water at the last pit stop in an effort to keep awake, which meant she had no defenses left. What he was seeing was her face just as he no doubt remembered it: the same unadorned blue eyes, the same freckled and sure-to-be-shiny snub nose, the same too-wide, bare-except-for-Chapstick mouth. Her face, without blush to shape it, was still more round than oval, her neglected eyebrows were once again well on their way to reverting to unibrow mode, and, in a complete antithesis of the woman she'd become over the last dozen years, not a trace of tinted moisturizer remained on her face to stand between him and the unvarnished truth. This circumstance did not make her feel any more kindly toward him; in fact, it increased the vitriol factor about a hundredfold. As their eyes met again, she scowled. In response, his smile widened into a full-fledged grin.

"Baby, you've changed. And not just with the boobs and the hair. Way back when, you used to be sweet."

The teasing infuriated her all over again. If he had forgotten the most recent chapter in the history of their acquaintance, she had not.

"Way back when, I used to be a lot of things—like stupid. Very, very stupid. Now get off—"

She never finished. A copper-bottomed saucepan interrupted her as it came swooping out of the darkness like a navigation-impaired bat to crash with a sickening *thunk* into the back of his head.

5

"**D**AMN IT!" Matt yelled, grabbing his head and rolling.

"Run, Carly!" Brandishing the saucepan, Sandra was dancing around in the darkness as if someone had poured hot coals into her shoes. "Don't you move. I'll hit you again," she said threateningly to Matt as he started to sit up. "See if I don't. I'll hit you again."

"Sandra, no!" Carly shrieked as Matt, cursing, arms wrapped around his head, sat up beside her anyway and the saucepan swooped down again. Matt ducked just in time. The pan's copper bottom flashed harmlessly past his cowering shoulder. "He's a friend."

Although *friend* wasn't quite the right word to describe the role Matt had played in her life. And it certainly didn't cover her feelings for him now. The lonely little girl who had hero-worshiped the three-years-older boy was long gone. She had grown up, and in the process had painfully discovered that the swaggering black-haired youth she'd thought hung the moon was just one more in a long line of untrustworthy male rats.

"What?" Sandra looked at her, hesitating, the saucepan poised for another swing.

Matt dared an upward glance and grabbed it, yanking it away from Sandra with a disgusted sound.

"Whoops," Sandra said, backing away.

"It's okay." Carly scrambled to her feet. She felt a little shaky from the aborted battle, and her entire back side from her shoulders to her knees was damp, but as she looked down at Matt sitting on the ground with the saucepan beside him and his long fingers gingerly exploring the back of his head, a smile began to tug at the corners of her mouth. "He's stupid but harmless. Sandra, meet Matt Converse. Matt, this is Sandra Kaminski."

"Uh, pleased to meet you," Sandra said, nervously eyeing Matt.

Still feeling the back of his head, where presumably a good-sized bump was beginning to make itself felt, Matt glanced up. Carly's smile widened at the look on his face. She discovered that she really, truly liked the idea of that bump.

"Wish I could say the same." Matt's tone was sour; his hand dropped away from his head. He got to his feet, hanging on to the saucepan and grimacing. "You shouldn't go around hitting people like that. You can get yourself in a lot of trouble that way."

"Sorry," Sandra offered weakly, keeping a safe distance between them.

Carly intervened with unconcealed enjoyment. "Hey, she thought she was saving me from a rapist or murderer or something. It was really brave of her to hit you over the head. Thank you, Sandra."

"You're welcome," Sandra said, sounding happier.

Matt's gaze swung to Carly, who deliberately widened her Cheshire cat grin for his benefit.

"Think it's funny, do you?"

"Well-deserved, was more what I had in mind."

"Oh, yeah?" He considered Carly for a moment without speaking. It was too dark for her to read his eyes, but it wasn't hard to guess what was on his mind: the same thing that was on hers. The air between them all but crackled with their mutual memory of the last time they'd been together. She'd been a shy and socially backward eighteen, it had been the night of her senior prom, and he, the handsome twenty-one-year-old hell-raiser that all the other, more popular girls drooled over, had been her date. That night of glory had ended with her losing her virginity to him. She hadn't had to lose her heart, he'd owned it for years. She hadn't seen him to speak to since. The son of a bitch.

"Am I wrong, or do I detect some hostility here?"

"Ya think?" *Hostility* wasn't the word. She could feel her skin prickling with burgeoning antagonism. That whole, agonizing summer after she had given him her all, he had avoided her as if she had a communicable disease. The glimpses she'd caught of him had been rare and at a distance, like Bigfoot sightings. For years before then he'd come around almost daily, teasing her and advising her and in general treating her like a favorite little sister as he'd worked around her grandmother's house, and then, after her not-so-secret crush had found its ultimate expression in the backseat of his beat-up Chevy Impala, he'd dropped her like a wormy apple. He'd broken her heart, shattered her self-esteem, and given her her first taste of the true nature of the male beast: slimeballs, the lot of them.

"Jesus, Curls, it's been twelve years. You ever hear of forgive and forget?"

The nickname was too much. Carly gave him a huge, blatantly false smile.

"Hey, Matt?" She flipped him the bird. "Go to hell."

Matt blinked, then shook his head at her. "Ah-ah. Your grandmother's probably spinning in her grave right now.

How many times did I hear her say, *I don't care what the other girls are doing, I'm raising you to be a lady?* Too many to count. And there you go again, letting her down."

Both Carly's hands clenched into impotent fists. "Like I said, go to hell."

"I thought you said he was a friend," Sandra said uneasily, looking from one to the other.

Carly glanced at her. "I lied."

Matt gave a grunt that could have meant anything. Carly's gaze swung back to him. For a moment the two of them exchanged blistering looks. Then Matt shrugged.

"Fine. Have it your own way. You want to hold on to a twelve-year-old grudge, it's all right by me. What are you doing here, anyway?"

"I own this place now. Why shouldn't I be here? The real question is, what are *you* doing here? Don't tell me you're sleeping under porches now."

That last, uttered in the nastiest tone she could muster, was a low blow, and she knew it. It referred to his hand-to-mouth existence as a child, when he and his mother and three younger sisters had moved from trailer park to rented room to apartment to rented house with numbing frequency, depending on whether they had managed to scrape together the money to pay that month's rent. Once Matt had gotten old enough to get a job—at eleven, he'd been mowing grass and pulling weeds for her grandmother the summer she'd first met him—things had been better, and eventually the family had managed to spend a couple of years in the same small house, where, for all she knew, they lived still. Matt had always been prickly on the subject of his family's poverty, and she had always gone out of her way not to offend his sensitive male pride. He, on the other hand, had ultimately shown no such consideration for her sensitive female heart. Such one-way relationships were the story of her life, and she was sick and tired of it. The days of Carly the doormat were gone for good. A new chapter in her life had just dawned.

Call it Carly Linton: no more Mr. Nice Guy. Or girl. Or whatever. The key point was, she was sick and tired of being nice. If she had learned just one thing in her life, it was this: Nice girls get the shaft.

Matt's eyes narrowed at her. He recognized her verbal thrust for what it was, of course. He'd always been good at divining what she was thinking.

"I got a call about a possible prowler around your grandmother's house. I was checking it out." There was the briefest of pauses. "I'm the sheriff now."

For a moment Carly simply stared at him, wondering if she'd heard him aright. The Matt Converse she'd known had been a hard-partying, motorcycle-riding hellion who'd been right at the top of the town's list of native sons most likely to end up on death row. The product of the union of a tiny spitfire of a Mexican mother and a tall, blond, eye-catchingly handsome but shiftless itinerant worker who had ambled in and out of her life as the seasons and his whims dictated, Matt had been earmarked by the town as a potential troublemaker almost from the moment of his birth. His appearance, which combined his mother's Hispanic coloring with his father's height and good looks to devastating effect, had attracted attention early on. His awareness of local opinion and his defiant determination to live up to it as a boy and his increasingly bad-ass behavior as a teen and young adult had meant that too much attention flowing his way wasn't a good thing. The fact that he'd been a reliable employee, a good son and brother, and a dependable friend to Carly and a few others was known to only a limited group. The rest of the town had taken his wrong-side-of-the-tracks toughness at face value, and treated him with the kind of wary watchfulness generally reserved for a rumbling volcano.

"You're joking, right?"

"Nope."

Her eyes swept him. It was dark, but not so dark that she couldn't tell that besides the jeans, his attire consisted of a plain old white tee shirt and sneakers. She also couldn't help noting that he hadn't changed a bit in appearance. Oh, maybe his black hair was shorter and he was a little taller, certainly a whole lot broader about the shoulders and chest, but he was basically still the same old too-handsome-for-his-own-good Matt. Not that she cared. In the aftermath of that long-ago night in the steamy closeness of his backseat, she'd been inoculated against his looks but good.

"You're not wearing a uniform." Not that she actually thought he was lying or anything, but . . .

His eyes narrowed at her. "It's after midnight, in case you haven't noticed. I'm off duty. Mrs. Naylor, who you might recall is the nearest neighbor, called me at home." He reached into his back pocket and pulled out his wallet, which he flipped open. "Want to see my badge?"

His tone told her that he really had one, but still Carly looked. Sure enough, there it was, all shiny and silver and official. Unbelievable. Her gaze rose to meet his. For a moment their eyes locked and held.

Then she gave a hoot of derisive laughter. "That's hilarious."

As he returned the wallet to his pocket his lips compressed.

"Yeah, I guess it is. Just about as hilarious as you with boobs and blond hair. Anyway, I walked around the place and didn't see anything. If I missed somebody and you happen to come across him, you can always have your friend here hold him at bay with her pan while you give me a call." He handed Sandra the saucepan and turned as if to leave, then glanced back over his shoulder. "Oh, by the way, the electricity's off. A wire's down a couple miles up the road."

There was something in his voice that told Carly he really enjoyed telling her that.

"Hey, hold on just a minute. You don't want to go leaving us here all alone," Sandra called after Matt with some alarm as he started to walk away. Carly looked daggers at Sandra. Even if she'd known for sure that an anemic Count Dracula was waiting for them up at the house, Carly would have been boiled in oil before she said a word to keep Matt from leaving. Sandra turned to Carly appealingly. "Maybe we should just go to a hotel or something and come back in the morning. I don't *do* scary old houses with prowlers and no electricity. Not in the middle of the night, I don't."

"There is no hotel in Benton, remember?" Carly said through her teeth as Matt stopped walking and turned around, his body language making it as clear as a shout that in the war between personal inclination and professional duty, professional duty was winning out by just about a hair. She wasn't particularly thrilled about braving the house under the circumstances either, but they didn't have any other choice. The lack of a hotel in Benton was the whole point behind their business plan, which was to turn her grandmother's house into a bed-and-breakfast. Located near what was becoming known in touristy circles as the antebellum trail, Benton was a growing community of some 3,800 souls with a burgeoning identity as a source for quality crafts and antiques. Boutique-like shops were springing up like dandelions throughout the small downtown area. There was ample opportunity for fishing and golf nearby, a new Honda plant not ten miles to the south drew visitors, and Savannah was little more than an hour's drive away. There'd once been a run-down motel out near the expressway turnoff, but it had gone out of business a number of years before. Thanks to the recent openings of McDonald's and Pizza Hut, which Carly viewed as proof of her business plan's workability, Benton now boasted a modest selection of restaurants, but there was currently no place for a visitor to spend the night. Their proposed bed-and-breakfast was meant to fill that need.

"Oh, yeah." Sounding unhappy, Sandra clutched her pan to her chest like a scared child with a favorite teddy bear. "I knew that."

"So it's either the house, another hour or so on the road, or the U-Haul," Carly said inexorably. "And I don't know about you, but I refuse to drive any farther or sleep in the U-Haul. The air conditioner broke about the time we crossed the Georgia state line, remember? And there's only the one seat. We're better off in the house. At least we'll have beds. Besides, the electricity will come back on, and if there really was somebody prowling around, you can bet your bottom dollar it was a couple of teenagers looking for a place to get up to no good or a drunk needing a place to sleep it off. That's the only kind of prowler we ever get in Benton."

"Uh-*huh*," Sandra said, transparently unconvinced.

Exasperated, Carly glanced at Matt. The least he could do was corroborate what he knew was the truth.

"You came in a U-Haul?" Forget backing her up. Matt didn't even seem to be listening. Instead, he was looking down the slope toward the road. Following his gaze, Carly saw that the blocky orange truck was just visible through the thick foliage. The sight of it seemed to answer his question, because he glanced at her without waiting for an answer. "You moving stuff in or out?"

"In." And that was all he needed to know. She wasn't

about to share her plans with Matt. Her life was strictly not his business.

"We're going to open a bed-and-breakfast," Sandra volunteered. Carly cast her a shut up–or-die look that Sandra apparently missed completely, because she kept on talking. "We're going to call it The Inn at Beadle Mansion."

"The two of you?" Matt looked at Carly. "What about your rich lawyer husband? You leave him behind in Chicago?"

So he'd known where she was, that she was married and what John did for a living. Carly was disgusted to feel a weird little flutter in the pit of her stomach. It must be a residual thing—she was *so* over Matt. The dirty rotten son of a bitch.

"I got a divorce," she said shortly.

"Oh, yeah?"

"Yeah," Carly said in a *you-want-to-make-something-of-it?* tone.

Matt folded his arms over his chest and studied her. "You know, Curls, you've developed an attitude since you've been gone. You really ought to think about losing it. It's not attractive."

"Drop dead," Carly said. "And get lost. We don't need your help. If you get your kicks playing big bad sheriff now, go do it somewhere else. I'm not impressed."

She turned on her heel and started walking toward the house, calling Hugo as she went.

"Hey, babe, works for me." Matt turned just as abruptly and headed in the opposite direction, his long strides eating up the ground.

"Shit," Sandra said, and from the corner of her eye Carly saw that she was looking from one to the other of them as the distance between them rapidly widened. After a brief attack of apparent indecision, she hurried after Carly. Carly felt some of the tension in her shoulders ease. For a moment there she hadn't been completely sure which combatant Sandra would follow.

The truth was, she really didn't want to tackle the house alone right now.

"What did you go and do that for?" Sandra wailed as she caught up.

Carly cast her a sideways glance. "Because he's a jerk. Pond scum. Human waste. *Hugo.* Here, kitty, kitty."

It was a measure of her jazzed-up emotional state that she even bothered with the here, kitty, kitty bit. Hugo never answered to it. That was another thing he considered beneath his dignity.

"But he's the sheriff. He has a gun. And your grandma's house has me really creeped out now. Would it have killed you to have let him come up with us and check it out?"

"Yes," Carly said, not mincing matters. *"Hugo!"*

"So what do we do if we run into the prowler?"

Carly practically ground her teeth. "I already told you; we don't get prowlers in Benton. Not real ones, anyway. This is a little town, not Chicago."

Sandra snorted. "Can anyone here say, 'famous last words'?"

"If you're scared, why'd you come with me? You could have followed him back down to the road, and waited in the U-Haul. Or even gone with him. I'm sure he would have taken you anywhere you wanted to go, if for no other reason than just for the pleasure of aggravating me."

"I thought about it," Sandra admitted, sounding annoyingly guilt-free as she confessed to base thoughts of betrayal and desertion. "But there's a problem."

"What's that?"

"I've gotta pee."

Carly rolled her eyes. Traveling with Sandra, she had

learned things about her that she had previously never known, or wanted to know. Such as the fact that she always had to pee. Of course, as the owner of the Treehouse restaurant, where Sandra had worked as a cook, she'd never thought to monitor her genius of the kitchen's trips to the john. Sandra had to go approximately every fifteen minutes; if they'd missed a rest area between Chicago and Benton, it was only because Sandra hadn't seen it.

"Oh, my God. You must have a bladder the size of a walnut. *Hugo!*"

"You know what? You're starting to sound just like my ex-husband."

Great. Now Sandra was getting huffy. Carly cast her eyes heavenward. "I apologize, okay? There's a bathroom right inside the house. As soon as I get the front door open, it's all yours."

They were nearing the house now. Carly spied the box of cooking utensils Sandra had jettisoned earlier. "I'll grab these," she said, detouring to pick up the box. "Do you see your phone anywhere?"

"Nope. I dropped my purse, too." Following her, Sandra, with a gathering frown, turned to look back the way they had come.

"We'll find them in the morning." No way was she up to launching a major search and recovery effort now, not after all they'd been through. Her nerves were shot, her temper was roused, her cat was missing and she was so tired she felt like she could drop where she stood.

"Yeah." Sandra apparently felt much the same way. Beyond giving a couple of futile kicks at the tall wet grass, she made no real effort to look for her lost belongings. "Stupid phones never ring when you want them to."

"Ain't it the truth."

Conducting her own quick visual search of the area with

no result, Carly spared a moment of regret for her lost flashlight. Looking for it was an option, but given the way the thing had rolled and how dark it was, the chance of success seemed remote. Besides, she knew the inside of her grandmother's house like the back of her hand. Once she was inside, they'd have light in maybe five minutes tops. As power outages were a not infrequent problem in this largely rural part of Georgia, candles and matches always had been kept in the huge china cabinet in the dining room. It would be ridiculous to let herself be driven away by a little thing like no electricity after having traveled so far. Besides, it was starting to sprinkle, and they were a lot closer to the house than the U-Haul. All that was needed to make her night complete was to get soaked by the kind of sudden downpour that was a summer-in-Georgia staple.

And if by some chance Matt should be still hanging around, she'd be damned if she'd turn tail and give him reason to laugh at her expense.

She was *so* not afraid to go inside what was now her own house just because Matt claimed that there'd been a report of a prowler and it just happened to be after midnight and really, really dark.

A fat plop of water landed on her nose. Carly looked up, grimacing. It was official; her night was complete. Raindrops were definitely falling on her head. If she didn't get inside soon, her carefully straightened hair would start to curl into its natural state again. Until she'd learned the fine art of combining straightening gel and the blow-dryer, she'd been the victim of fat sausage ringlets that had made her look like a skinny, way-less-cute Shirley Temple and had led to Matt calling her Curls. In and of itself, she'd hated the nickname, but she had adored the boy who had bestowed it on her and thus had accepted it without protest. He'd used it teasingly, affectionately, throughout her girlhood, and she, who'd been starved for attention and affection, had hugged it to her nonexistent bosom as a sign that she was special to him.

He'd called her that on the night of the prom right before they had kissed for the first time and she had melted into a quivering bundle of crazy-in-love hormones in his arms. He'd called her that again, for the last time before their encounter tonight, on the morning after the prom, when he had walked her to the door of her grandmother's house just as the sun had begun peeping over the horizon.

"See you later, Curls," he'd said, cupping her face in his lean hands and dropping a quick but heart-stoppingly tender kiss on her mouth.

She had read all sorts of promises into that. But, mindful that her grandmother rose with the roosters and might well be marching militantly toward the porch in her housecoat at that very moment to send him on his way, she had merely smiled up at him.

" 'Night, Matt," she'd said. Then she'd turned away and gone inside the house.

Glowing. In love. Sure that he was The One, her soul mate, destined to be at her side for the rest of her life.

The no good dirty rotten son of a bitch.

Scowling at the memory, Carly thrust it forcefully from her mind and started walking again, a little faster this time, looking under bushes and up trees and behind clumps of drooping, rain-heavy flowers as she went. A pampered only pet, Hugo surely wouldn't have gone far. Although being lost was actually no more than he deserved. She could still feel the imprint of his claws in her side.

"Hugo. Damn it, get your furry buns over here. If you think I'm going to spend the rest of the night searching for you, you're sadly mistaken."

"I may have to pee a lot, but at least I don't swear at my

cat," Sandra said, falling in beside her. "Anyway, there he is."

Carly followed Sandra's gaze to find Hugo sitting high and dry on the porch. His white coat made him easy to spot. Carly heaved a sigh of relief. Losing Hugo would have fallen into the category of Too Much. Clearly unconcerned about having lost her, he was having a leisurely bath. Which, besides sleeping and eating, was basically how he spent most of his time. For cats as well as people, bright white outerwear required a lot of maintenance.

"Come on," Carly said wearily, and led the way up the steps. Trimmed in peeling gingerbread and supported by half a dozen slender posts, the porch ran the entire length of the front of the house. Hugo, with a luxurious stretch, rose to greet her. Carly cast him a withering glance and walked on past. With Hugo as well as Sandra trailing her now, she set the box down on the wicker settee that had taken pride of place against the center of the white clapboard wall for as long as she could remember, opened the creaky screen door and fumbled to fit the key into the old-fashioned lock. Beyond the small, leaded glass insert set at eye level in the ornate oak door, the house looked dark as a cave. Turning the key, Carly opened the door. The scent of the house rushed out to greet her. Stuffy from being shut up for weeks with its window units off, it nonetheless smelled just as it always had: old, with a hint of lemon furniture polish and the faintest underlying note of mustiness. Stepping inside, she wrinkled her brow and thought, *Something's missing.* Then she realized what it was: her grandmother had always kept sachets of dried verbena tucked away in every room. The smell of verbena was gone.

A wave of nostalgia hit her: She missed it. She missed her grandmother. She missed being a child in this house.

"So where's the bathroom?"

Sandra was practically breathing down her neck. Hugo darted between her legs to disappear into the darkness with a wave of his tail. Beyond the porch, rain began to fall in shining silver sheets. From deep inside the house, she could hear a faint *plop, plop*. Some things never changed: The ancient tin roof had clearly sprung yet another leak.

Forget nostalgia, Carly thought with a grimace. Present circumstances were almost more than she could handle.

Just to make sure Matt had been telling her the truth, she flipped the light switch by the door. Nothing happened.

"This way," she said to Sandra, surprised that her voice was scarcely louder than a whisper as she headed down the dark center hall. The hush of the house seemed to call for quiet. As if something inside lay sleeping and shouldn't be disturbed—which was ludicrous, of course, and could be chalked up to too much imagination coupled with too many Stephen King books. Shaking off the feeling, she continued on, but left the front door standing wide open behind them. For the light it admitted, of course, and definitely *not* as a possible escape route. Granted, the light in question was gray and meager, but it was way better than no light at all.

As for the soft roar of the rain, it was soothing, not spooky, just like the sudden rush of cool air that blew through the screen was refreshing rather than ghostly.

So there.

"The bathroom's behind that door," she said, deliberately using her normal voice and pointing. Fortunately for the health and well-being of Sandra's bladder, the door happened to be just inside the wedge of grayness cast by the open front door, because she was fairly sure that Sandra, who was edging cautiously along in her wake, would have balked at going any farther. The darkness turned black as the inside of a cauldron just a few steps beyond the bathroom door.

"*Shh!* Do you have to talk so loud?"

The house's atmosphere was clearly getting to Sandra, too. Big surprise. Sandra had freely admitted to being creeped out while they were still outside on the comparatively unatmospheric lawn. If truth were told, right at that particular moment Carly might be experiencing some of those same chickenhearted pangs herself, but as their little expedition's fearless leader she refused to give in to them. She wasn't about to allow herself to be afraid of what was now her own house.

Her own pitch-dark spooky house.

A sharp click just behind her made her jump almost out of her shoes.

"Ouch! Crap. How'm I supposed to pee in the dark? I can't even find the toilet."

Having turned into the bathroom while Carly ventured ahead, Sandra had shut the door. That was the sound she had heard, Carly realized. She sagged with relief, then caught herself up and deliberately stiffened her spine. Leaving Sandra to her own devices, she headed around the wide staircase and moved cautiously toward the dining room. It was next to the kitchen at the back of the house, through a set of pocket doors that opened off the hall. Feeling her way along, she discovered by touch that the doors were open. It was so dark, here in the bowels of the house, that she literally couldn't see her hand in front of her face. Her grandmother had favored heavy velvet draperies on all the windows. They were closed now, shutting out the faintest hope that any stray sliver of grayness might light her way.

It was the absolute darkness that was making her imagine things, Carly decided as she moved with increasingly tentative steps around the perimeter of the large dining room toward where the china cabinet had always stood against the far wall. Like the feeling that she was being watched. Like the faint, hard to place but somehow off-putting smell. Like the sudden rustling sound that seemed unnaturally loud in the darkness, as if a movement had been made by an unseen somebody or something, and quickly stilled.

Carly froze, peering blindly in the direction from which the sound had come. That part was *not* her imagination. She had definitely heard something move. For a moment she stood motionless as her heart accelerated like a race car's engine.

She was not alone. She was sure of it. Someone, *something,* was there with her in the dark.

Before she could totally hyperventilate, an imperative-sounding meow snatched her back from Jason/Freddy/Michael Myers land. With a rush of half-shamed relief, she realized just who was there in the dining room with her: Hugo, of course. His were the eyes she felt tracking her through the darkness. His fur was probably damp, accounting for the elusively familiar smell that, vaguely, she somehow associated with something unpleasant. As for the sound—perhaps he'd brushed up against something, or even batted something across the floor.

"Hugo, you scared me to death," she said. The cat didn't answer—not that she had expected him to, of course—but with the eerie feeling of another presence now explained to satisfaction Carly was reassured anyway. Just knowing that Hugo was there in the dark with her made her feel better. Taking a deep, steadying breath, she went on about her business. Another step forward, then one more, a left turn—the china cabinet should be straight ahead. The drawer she sought was on the right front side beneath the glassed-in display shelves. In just another minute or so, she'd have her hands on a candle and matches, and then there would be light.

Blessed light.

The better to see you by, my dear, she mentally cackled at Hugo in her best Big-Bad-Wolf-does-Grandma imitation, and then smiled at her own idiocy.

Still smiling, taking one more baby step forward, she stretched out a hand to make certain she didn't bump nose-first into the china cabinet, but instead of touching the smooth wood she was expecting, she felt something soft. Cloth, covering something warm and resilient. Something warm and resilient that rose slightly as she touched it.

A human chest. A living, breathing human chest.

Time seemed to stand still.

Even as it dawned on her what it was that she was touching, a hand, meaty and warm and strong, clamped around her wrist.

Carly screamed.

6

THE SCREAM OF THE CENTURY was still ripping its way out of her throat as Carly yanked her hand free and spun, ready to run like a rabbit with the dogs after it. A violent shove between her shoulder blades sent her careening into the table instead. Its sharp corner caught her hip painfully. Even as she gasped and bent double and clutched at her hip the intruder took flight. The sound of a body exploding into motion behind her was unmistakable. Something solid brushed past her protruding backside and then he—she was sure it was a he because of the size of the hand that had grabbed her wrist—was gone, feet pounding as he rushed toward the kitchen.

Another scream followed the first. Barely aware that she was the one responsible for the shattering sounds, Carly pushed away from the table and hurled herself in the opposite direction. Heart racing, cold streams of terror snaking up and down her spine, she made it into the hall in one piece, screaming all the way. Sandra, still in the bathroom, was yelling her name. Without answering, Carly torpedoed toward the open front door—and smacked into yet another warm, resilient object that grabbed her upper arms hard as she recoiled.

The scream that resulted could have deafened someone

clear on the other side of town. Galvanized by fear, she fought desperately to be free.

"Carly! Jesus, Carly, it's me!"

Matt's voice. Matt's hands. Carly quit struggling with a gasp. Her knees went weak, and she shuddered as she drew in great gulps of air. He hung on to her, his fingers digging into her soft arms. It was so dark she couldn't see him, so dark she couldn't see anything except the gray triangle that led to the open door, which beckoned like the gateway to the promised land some twenty feet away, but she would have known his voice anywhere. It was, she realized with a vague sense of chagrin, still hard-wired into the circuitry of her brain. Could it, by some miracle, have been Matt in the dining room? No. As certain as she was that it was Matt who held her now, she was equally certain that he was not the man who had grabbed her before.

"Are you all right? What the hell happened?"

"Matt. Oh, God, Matt."

She was shaking, and it was hard to get the words out. Making an indecipherable sound under his breath, he pulled her to him, wrapping his arms around her and holding her close. Carly sagged against him, grateful for his solid strength. Matt. Thank God for Matt. He might be a no good dirty rotten son of a bitch in just about every way that counted, but he wouldn't do her any physical harm. In fact, she knew as well as she knew that cinnamon rolls had calories that he would do his best to keep her safe.

"*What?*" he demanded.

Carly took a deep breath. "It must have been the prowler. He was here—in the house—in the dining room. He grabbed me." She shuddered anew at the memory. "He ran toward the kitchen."

"Stay here." Matt's voice was sharp. Grasping her wrists, he detached her sudden death-grip with laughable ease and stepped away before she could stop him—and she would have stopped him, because the idea of being left alone in the dark now scared the pants off her.

"*Matt . . .*" Under almost any other circumstances, the panicked urgency of her tone would have embarrassed her.

"Don't move." He was already out of reach. She knew because she tried to grab him. Switching on a flashlight she hadn't known he had, he was heading with swift purpose toward the dining room. She tracked his progress with instinctively held breath until the beam vanished inside the open pocket doors.

Just like that, she was on her own in the dark and terrifying hall. Exhaling, she looked warily around.

"Carly! Carly, what's wrong? What's happening?" Thumping around like a moose in a broom closet, Sandra was clearly still in the bathroom. "Ow! I can't see anything! I can't find the doorknob! Carly, can you hear me? Are you out there? Carly?"

A man yelled. Almost simultaneously, something crashed toward the back of the house, as if an object that was both big and breakable had hit the floor and shattered. Carly jumped what felt like six feet straight up, then whipped around, staring uselessly toward the kitchen, from which the sounds had seemed to come. Looking in that direction, she could see nothing at all; she might as well have been blindfolded.

Matt. Had something happened to Matt? Her heart threatened to pound its way out of her chest. Again she strained to see or hear. Nothing.

"Matt?" Calling him, her voice sounded all quavery. Matt didn't answer. She broke into a cold sweat. Had something happened to him? How would she know if something had? The downstairs was a rabbit warren of interconnecting halls and rooms. Matt could be anywhere. So, in fact, could the prowler. Having dispensed with Matt, at that very moment he could even be circling back around toward *her*. . . .

Galvanized by the thought, Carly got her rear in gear and bolted for the exit.

"Car-lee-ee!" The pitiful-sounding wail was close at hand, and it jerked her attention away from the beckoning screen door.

"Sandra!" Carly realized that she couldn't just leave her friend to the tender mercies of whatever fiend might answer her cries. Sweating, panting, she made a lightning detour to her right and yanked open the bathroom door. "Come on, come on, there's somebody in the house!"

Sandra leaped out into the hall, trusty pan in hand.

"*Somebody in the house?* What do you mean, there's somebody in the house?" Brandishing the pan, she looked wildly around.

"Come on!"

Explanations could wait. Carly took off again with Sandra, ignorant as to exactly what was going on but no fool, right on her tail. Carly shoved the screen door wide and ran out into the safer-feeling grayness of the night. Across the porch, down the steps, through the yard, into the truck, lock the doors—bingo, sounded like a plan. But before Carly could do more than barely begin to put it into motion, Sandra let out a startled cry behind her. Whirling, Carly watched through the closing screen door as Sandra went down in the hall with a crash that seemed to shake the house.

"Sandra!"

Dear God, had Sandra been shoved, shot . . . ? Pulse racing, Carly yanked the door open again, prepared to go to her friend's rescue in the teeth of the monster lurking in the dark.

"Stupid cat," Sandra groaned, rolling onto her back. As if on cue, Hugo shot through the open door in a blur of white, streaked past Carly's legs and flew across the porch to disappear over the rail into the still-falling rain.

"Hugo!" Calling uselessly after him, gaze swiveling from the place where the escapee had vanished into the night to the fallen one left behind, Carly made the obvious connection: Sandra had tripped over Hugo.

The lights came on. Just like that. One minute Carly was gaping at Sandra sprawled on the floor through the shadowy darkness, and the next she was gaping at her sprawled on the floor by the soft light of the overhead chandelier.

Hoping devoutly that all evil things knew enough to be afraid of the light, Carly edged back inside. With a quick, leery look around she crouched beside Sandra, who was focusing with rapt attention on the ceiling, her hands folded flat across her stomach so that she looked unnervingly like a laid-out corpse. The pan, abandoned now, lay upside down beside her, its copper bottom unmarred and softly gleaming in the oh-so-welcome light.

"Sandra . . ." Alarmed most of all by that fixed stare, Carly experimentally poked her in the shoulder.

Sandra's eyes rolled to meet hers.

"I just remembered why I don't like cats. Sneaky things, always getting under people's feet. You sure you wouldn't consider letting John-boy have custody?"

Carly's brows snapped together. "No."

Sandra sighed. "You're going to be hard to live with, aren't you? I was afraid of that."

Matt appeared at the top of the hall just then, expression grim, gun in one hand and flashlight in the other. He glanced their way and his eyes widened.

"What now?" Sounding thoroughly put out, he came toward them. His upper body was soaked: His black hair was plastered to his skull, his face was shiny wet and his tee shirt clung to his torso in a way that made it impossible for

Carly not to be aware of just how broad-shouldered and muscular his formerly wiry six-one frame had become.

He had changed in other ways as well. His lean, bronzed face had always been the stuff heartthrobs were made of, and it still was, but it was subtly different, too. His eyes were the same—slightly heavy-lidded and the color of coffee, set beneath thick, straight black brows—but tiny lines now radiated from their corners. His nose was the same—straight and high-bridged—and his mouth was unchanged too, except somehow he had acquired a scar, white against his tan, that bisected the left side of his upper lip. He was a grown man of thirty-three now, Carly realized with a sense of shock, and he looked it. Since she had recognized him out there in the dark, she had basically been relating to a much younger Matt, her Matt, the Matt she had grown up with: idolized friend and mentor, surrogate older brother, achingly out-of-reach dreamboat, first love and lover—and, ultimately, no good dirty rotten son of a bitch.

That Matt was still there—no doubt about it—but like a pearl he had added layers. This top layer—Matt the grown-up, gun-toting sheriff—was all new.

He was also bleeding. Carly's eyes zeroed in on a gash in his hairline. About an inch long, it poured blood, which mixed with the rain on his face to form red rivulets that ran down his temple and into the stubble that darkened his jaw.

"Are you hurt?" he asked Sandra. Reaching the fallen one's side, he frowned down at her.

"If I'm not, I should be," Sandra said, grimacing and making no visible effort to rise. "I tripped over Carly's pain-in-the-patootie cat. Just let me lay here for a minute, would you please?"

"What happened to you?" Carly asked Matt as she rose to her feet.

"Same thing." His gaze met hers, and his mouth twisted

wryly as he thrust the gun into the back waistband of his jeans and lifted a hand to the cut. Drawing back his fingers, he stared at the blood on them in disgust. "At least, that's what I'm guessing. I tripped over something, but it was too dark to see what it was. A cat sounds about right. A cat belonging to you—I'd be willing to bet on it. You know the corner cabinet in the kitchen? When I tripped my shoulder rammed into that, and the damned flowerpot on top fell off and hit me on the head."

"Oh." Feeling slightly deflated, Carly blinked at him, having expected an explanation for all that blood to involve a death-defying battle with the intruder at the very least. Then the sheer ridiculousness of what had happened to him occurred to her, and she batted her eyelashes at him and gave him a huge, razzing smile. "My hero."

"As always."

His eyes mocked her. Carly frowned.

"What are you doing here, anyway? I thought you were leaving."

"Did you really think I'd let you two come up here all by yourselves? I was walking up the porch steps when I heard you scream." He set the flashlight down on the cabinet that concealed the radiator by the door. "Good thing I didn't leave."

With that he picked up the hem of his tee shirt and swiped the wet fabric over the bloody left side of his face. Carly was rendered speechless by a surprise glimpse of six-pack abs and a buff, wide, hair-covered chest. Clamping down hard on her purely instinctive female response, she realized to her dismay that some things never change. As cynically wise to the ways of men as she had become, she was still a sucker for a hunk.

Good thing she knew this particular hunk for the skunk he was.

She wrenched her gaze away to the open dining-room doors.

"So I take it that whoever was in the dining room got away?" Glancing around, Carly shivered. The sheer horror of being grabbed in the dark was still sickeningly fresh; but the light and, as much as she hated to admit it, Matt the grown-up sheriff's reassuring presence were going a long way toward helping her to get a grip.

"He ran out the kitchen door just about the time I tripped over the cat," Matt said. The cut was still bleeding copiously, Carly saw as she looked back at him. With less moisture to dilute it, the blood was bright scarlet now, and starting to drip from his jaw. "I wasn't but a couple of yards behind him, either. That flowerpot knocked me for a loop. When I could see straight again, I chased him across the backyard, but he had too much of a start. He jumped the fence into the cornfield, and I lost him." His attention shifted back to Sandra, who was slowly, cautiously, sitting up. "Anything broken?"

"Nothing but my shoe," she said, staring dismally at the leather strap of her left sandal, which stuck straight out across her instep. "Third pair that got ruined so far this summer. Do you know how hard it is to find wide shoes?" She made a disgusted sound, and cast Carly a dark look. "See there, I told you: We should've waited 'til August. My horoscope *said* that any new venture I undertook early in the summer would turn out to be more expensive than I thought."

"Sandra's a Pisces," Carly offered with a faint rekindling of her earlier enjoyment. Matt's expression as he absorbed Sandra's gloomy acceptance of her astrological fate was priceless. He'd never had any patience with what he had called all that psycho stuff, probably because his mother, who believed in it so avidly that she kept a tarot deck beside her bed and checked her horoscope each morning, was always seeing brighter days ahead for her family that, so far as Carly knew, had never materialized. Now, as Matt extended a hand down to Sandra, he cast a derisive look Carly's way.

Carly grinned.

"The stars know what they're talking about," Sandra said, taking a good grip on the handle of her pan again before she grasped Matt's hand and let him haul her upright, which he did with impressive ease. Once on her feet, she dropped his hand, looked at him and frowned. "You know, you're bleeding."

"I think you might need stitches," Carly added, looking at Matt's cut. It was simple human decency that prompted the stab of concern she felt for him, she assured herself, and had nothing whatsoever to do with the fact that the man bleeding all over her front hall was *Matt*.

"That bad, huh?" Turning to look in the gold-framed mirror above the radiator cabinet, he grimaced at what he saw, then pulled his soaked tee shirt over his head, wadded it up, and pressed it to the cut. "Nah. Head wounds always bleed a lot. It'll stop in a few minutes."

Without any more warning than that, Carly found herself staring at a broad, muscular back. Wide and strong-looking across the shoulders, it tapered down in classic vee fashion to a lean waist and the previously noted ogle-worthy butt. The elastic of his underwear—he apparently still favored briefs over boxers—formed a narrow white band just above his hipbones. His gun, all sinister black metal, nestled in the small of his back, only partly visible above the waistband of his faded, damp, bun-loving jeans.

Yum, Carly thought, impressed by the available eye candy. Then, backtracking with alarm: *No, wait, not yum. Definitely not. No way. Nohow. Uh-uh.*

She'd gotten a bellyache's worth of that candy once already.

"You got a . . ."

As he turned from the mirror, Carly couldn't help it; she instinctively scoped out his chest. His shoulders were heavy with muscle and his pectorals were sharply defined. He was hairier than when he was younger, sporting a thicker wedge of the same fine black hair that had once felt crisp and cool beneath her exploring hands. His nipples were brown and flat; they'd puckered into hard little nubs when her fingers had brushed them. His arms had trembled as he'd wrapped them around her. They'd been hard to the touch then. She reckoned they were harder now. He'd always been strong; now his upper arms bulged, and his chest was wider even than she remembered. As she had already noted, his abs were mouthwatering. And as for—

No. Wait. Stop. She was not, not, *not* going to check out his package.

". . . Band-Aid?" he finished. Her averted gaze encountered his, and she discovered that he was regarding her with raised brows.

Thank God she hadn't looked where her baser instincts had been leading her.

"Uh, sure," she said, flustered. "I think." Realizing that she was this-close to stammering like the schoolgirl with a crush she had once been, she took a deep mental breath and got a grip and an edge. "How should I know? I haven't lived in this house for twelve years, remember?"

"I remember." His voice was dry. He started walking, holding the shirt pressed to his head, and moved past her while her gaze followed him. "I'm going out on a limb here, but I'm guessing they'd still be kept in the bathroom. Miss Virgie wasn't much for change."

Without answering, she watched him until he stepped

inside the bathroom and out of sight. Spell broken, she glanced away only to have her gaze collide with Sandra's. Their eyes held, and an unspoken message of purely feminine appreciation for a drool-worthy male was exchanged between them.

A moment later Matt reappeared with an extra-large Band-Aid plastered to his forehead. Stopping in the doorway with one arm propped against the frame, he looked at her.

"Okay, Curls, you want to walk through the house with me and see if you can tell if anything's missing?"

He still lacked a shirt, and looking at him without it was still enough to make her hot. Not that there was anything wrong with that, Carly assured herself. After all, no good dirty rotten son of a bitch or not, he was the hunkiest man she had seen in a long time, and what with the divorce and everything she hadn't had sex in—God, had it been almost two years?

She was practically re-virginized.

"Quit calling me Curls," she said through her teeth as the horror of the realization sank in. "It's a stupid nickname, I don't like it, and it no longer applies."

"Oh, yeah?" His lips twisted into a maddening smirk. Without saying anything more, he caught her by the arm and pulled her into the bathroom with him. With his hands on her shoulders, he positioned her in front of the sink. His chest was almost touching her back; although she couldn't actually feel the heat of it—her imagination was doing all the work here—just knowing that all those muscles were that close made her tingle.

The mirror was right in front of her. She had no choice but to look into it, which was probably a good thing if she wanted to get her mind off how close he was. For a moment, though, the reflection of his broad, bronzed shoulders looming above her own drew her gaze to the exclusion of everything else. Then she registered how much shorter his crow-black hair was than it had been at twenty-one; the degree of five o'clock shadow darkening his lean jaw; and how tall he was. He towered above her, just as he always had. In her flat-soled sneakers, she saw, she was still quite a few inches short of having the top of her head hit his chin.

Then something off about her own reflection caught her attention, and she refocused with a snap.

Her carefully straightened hair had given up the ghost. Instead of the stylish do she'd left Chicago with, her head was now a mass of springy blond ringlets.

Her eyes met his through the mirror.

"The more things change . . ." he said softly. And smiled one of those wickedly taunting smiles which, long ago, had been enough to infuriate her without him needing to do anything else.

Even now, at the ripe old age of thirty, it was all Carly could do to restrain her instant, childish urge to punch him in the gut as she jerked free of his grip and stomped back out into the hall.

7

"WHOA," SANDRA SAID, staring at her. "I didn't know your hair could do that."

Carly shot her a look so poisonous that it could have been used to tip blow-darts.

"So, you coming with me or not?" Matt asked, cool as lemonade as he walked past her.

For a moment Carly simply glared after him. Then, shoulders slumping in defeat, she followed, hideously aware of her Orphan Annie corkscrews bobbing with every step.

"How would I know if anything's missing?" She trailed him to the front parlor. "Unless he took a couch or something. All this is Gran's furniture, but Miss Virgie's bound to have had TVs and things of her own. That's the kind of stuff a burglar would steal."

She shivered as what had happened in the dining room replayed itself in her head. The man had been hiding there in the dark, silent and waiting. What would have happened if she'd returned to her grandmother's house alone?

Just considering the possibilities scared her anew.

"I'm pretty sure she took everything like that with her when she moved out," Matt said. "Anyway, Loren"—Loren Schuler, Miss Virgie's niece and closest relative, was a former classmate of Carly's who now worked at the bank, as Carly had discovered when she had transferred her meager account to the Benton Savings and Loan in advance of her own arrival—"spent two weeks helping her go through all her stuff beforehand. What Miss Virgie didn't want they got rid of in a yard sale."

"Still . . ."

Matt reached the doorway and turned back to look at her. Carly kept her eyes carefully fixed on his face. Letting her gaze stray to all those sexy muscles was a bad idea.

"Just do your best, okay? Think your grandmother's silver candlesticks and stuff."

"Fine." There was a welcome snap to her voice as she began to recover from the ignominy of the reversion of her hair. Hair did not equal life, she told herself firmly. Just because her hair had resumed its detested childhood form practically the second she hit Benton didn't mean the rest of her had to follow suit. She was all grown up, damn it. Captain of her own ship. Master of her own fate. Her awkward teenage years were well behind her, as was her blind adoration of the man she was now deliberately scowling at. It was all history. Vanished. *Pfft.* And so he needed to understand. But if either her expression or tone even registered with him, Matt ignored them, wrapping a hand around her elbow as casually as if they were on good terms and propelling her in the direction he wanted her to go.

"Hey, wait for me," Sandra said in alarm, pan still in hand as she made haste to bring up the rear.

Since she was decidedly *not* on good terms with him, Carly jerked her arm free. Then as Matt stood aside with an ironic expression she preceded him through the pocket doors and flipped the light switch that controlled the chandelier that was a smaller twin of the one in the hall. With the room thus illuminated, she looked around. The front parlor was one of six large, mostly rectangular rooms on the first floor. Dominated by a crimson-upholstered, intricately carved Victorian sofa, it boasted gorgeous stained-glass panels at the top of the windows, which, unfortunately, were hidden now by the heavy drapes, ornate molding, and a huge Italian marble fireplace. A rocker and a wing chair of similar vintage as the sofa, marble-topped tables, fringed lamps, a faded Oriental rug and about a thousand gewgaws completed the furnishings.

"This is nice," Sandra said from the doorway. Carly glanced over her shoulder to find Sandra looking around judiciously. Of course, Sandra was thinking in terms of their bed-and-breakfast. Carly's only thought right at that moment was a slightly disbelieving, *I'm home.* She was suddenly overwhelmed with the sights, sounds, and smells of her childhood. The grandeur of faded velvet; the rattle of the pocket doors being rolled into the wall; the scent of peppermint. Her grandmother had always kept a crystal dish full of peppermints.

A quick glance told her that the dish was there, on the table by the sofa, and the peppermints, shiny in their cellophane wrappers, were, too. Not the same ones, of course. But still, the same thing. Here in Benton, in this house, it was always the same thing.

The dour-looking portrait of her great-grandfather that had hung above the fireplace for as long as she could remember caught her eye. Looking at it, she suddenly felt about eight years old again.

That's how old she had been when she had first walked into this room and set eyes on the portrait. Her grandmother, a forbidding figure dressed all in black, had that very day fetched her away from the County Home for Innocents. Small and frightened, intimidated by the huge, silent house, the finery all around her, and most of all the grim old woman, Carly had stood in this very spot, listening to her grandmother lecture her on what, in future, she would be expected to do and how she would be expected to behave while she did it. She'd been told that she was *lucky*, and she'd known it was true.

Poor little unwanted child, lucky to be rescued.

"Well?"

Matt's voice, welcome under the circumstances, broke in on the rush of memories to pull her back to the present.

Carly took a deep breath and focused on him. He had been prowling around the room. Now he stood to one side of the sofa, casually unwrapping a peppermint as he looked at her. Carly almost had to smile. Matt had always loved those peppermints too.

"There's nothing missing that I can see," she said. "Everything looks exactly the same as it always did."

If she sounded faintly suffocated, it was because she was starting to feel that way. Her childhood seemed to be closing in on her from all sides. Maybe, she thought with a sinking feeling in the pit of her stomach, coming back here hadn't been such a good idea after all. Maybe she should have jettisoned the past entirely and tried to make a fresh start for herself somewhere new.

But having John leave her for a twenty-two-year-old law student had been the psychic equivalent of being flattened by an eighteen-wheeler. Discovering during the course of the divorce that he'd systematically had all their assets—their condominium, their cars, their bank accounts and investments, and, in fact, almost everything they owned except her most personal possessions—put into his company's name, which effectively deprived her of any claim on them, had been, in the end, even worse.

Wounded, vulnerable, and nearly broke, she'd looked at the rubble of her life post-marriage and done what many a devastated woman had done before her: hightailed it for home.

Her grandmother, whom she had grown to love dearly despite her prickly ways, was gone now. But this huge old-fashioned house, this gossipy small town where everybody knew her and she knew everybody, and the threads that had been spun together to make her who she was were still here. Life might have knocked her down, but she'd be damned if she stayed there. She was a past master at picking herself up, dusting herself off, and starting all over again. Instead of bemoaning what she had lost, she was going to go forward with what she had left: herself, and this house, this town, these people. They, all of them, were her roots; with them to build on, she was going to forge ahead.

"Uh-oh," Sandra said, having crossed the room to look through the doorway on the far side of the fireplace. "Unless the lady who was living here was one real bad housekeeper, we got trouble. Carly, Sheriff, you better take a look."

Matt and Carly exchanged glances, then started forward as one. Carly reached Sandra's side first. Looking past her into the back parlor, which her grandmother had used as her own personal sitting room, Carly gasped. Miss Virgie had apparently turned it into some kind of home office; at least, a desk, a cheap oak rolltop model that looked out of place amid the original dark Victorian furniture, had been added. It had also been trashed. The rolltop had been ripped clean off the desk; it lay in one corner of the room, looking at first glance like a discarded sheet of corrugated cardboard. Drawers had been emptied onto the worn Oriental carpet. Piles of paper lay in front of the desk in an ankle-high jumble of letters, bills, receipts, catalogues and more. Coins and odds and ends such as paper clips and rubber bands and pencils were scattered everywhere. The drawers themselves had been flung across the room. Scars in the white plaster bore mute witness that the drawers had been discarded with sufficient force to smack into the walls before crashing to the floor. What remained of the desk was empty; even the old-fashioned rotary phone dangled from the desktop by its cord.

"Looks like somebody was looking for something: money, maybe. Or a checkbook," Matt said from behind her. His hands closed around Carly's upper arms. Even as she glanced back at him, he moved her aside almost absently and walked past her into the room. "Don't touch anything."

The warning was delivered over his shoulder.

"I thought you said you didn't have burglars in Benton," Sandra said, looking at Carly accusingly. "You said the most dangerous thing that ever happened in Benton was the fireworks on the Fourth of July."

Carly shrugged. What could she say?

Matt had reached the pile of paper and was frowning down at it when an unexpected sound split the air. Carly jumped. She was, she realized, still just a *little* on edge. The shrill summons was repeated insistently.

"It's not mine," Sandra said, throwing up two empty hands as though to prove her words as Matt pulled a shrieking cell phone from his pocket, punched a button and put it to his ear.

"Matt Converse here." Carly watched his expression turn patient. "No, Mrs. Naylor, there's no need for that. I'm fine. Yes, there was a prowler, but he ran off. You really saved the day, and we sure appreciate you keeping your eyes open like that. The lights are on now because Carly Linton's moving back in. You remember Carly, Mrs. Linton's granddaughter? She just got here a little later than she meant to, is all. There'll probably be lights on in the house for a while yet.

No, there's nothing to worry about. You go on to bed. I'll tell her. You take care now. Bye."

He disconnected and his gaze met Carly's as he stuck the phone back into his pocket. "Mrs. Naylor saw lights come on in the house and got worried all over again. She wants you to come over for coffee and cake tomorrow, by the way. She said to tell you the cake's red velvet—your favorite."

Carly sighed. "Does she still spend all her time looking out her windows? It's the middle of the night, for heaven's sake. She's an old lady; she should be in bed."

A widow whose children had long since grown and gone, Mrs. Naylor had to be, by Carly's calculations, approximately older than dirt.

Matt's mouth quirked in sudden amusement. "I should warn you: she's gone high-tech. She's got binoculars now."

"Cripes."

Unspoken between them lay the memory of the numerous times over the years that Mrs. Naylor had called Carly's grandmother to report on various youthful transgressions she had observed from her windows. Like the time Carly had lain in wait on the roof of the porch to pour a bucket of paint on Matt's head in revenge for some bit of boyish teasing that she no longer remembered; or the time he had climbed up to her bedroom window to bring her a paper bag with a ham sandwich and a Coke in it, on one of the many occasions when she had been sent to bed without supper; or the time he'd given her a ride to school on the back of his motorcycle, which she'd been strictly forbidden to so much as sit on, when she'd missed the bus and had been in dire danger of being late, which would have knocked one percentage point off her grade point average and ruined her chances of being the class valedictorian, which, in the end, she hadn't been anyway.

Mrs. Naylor's eagle eyes had seen all, her flapping tongue had told all, and Carly had usually paid the price. That last peccadillo had ended up with her being grounded for three weeks.

Less than a month later, Matt had found her hunched in a little ball of misery out in the barn, crying her eyes out because the prom was two weeks away and no one had asked her. Coaxing the embarrassing secret out of her, he'd dried her eyes, chucked her under the chin, and casually offered to be her date.

Whoever had said that if something sounds too good to be true, it usually is, had hit the nail on the head. She had been more thrilled at the prospect of having Matt as her prom date than Cinderella could possibly have been at the coming of the glass slipper–bearing prince. The next few weeks, right up until a couple of days after the prom when she had first begun to suspect that her dazzling daydreams might have been just a little wide of the mark, had been among the happiest and most exciting of her life.

Of course, that was before she had begun to grasp that Matt was, at his core, a no good dirty rotten son of a bitch.

Remembering, her spine stiffened until it had the flexibility of a steel rod.

"That desk didn't belong to your grandmother." Matt's voice, seeking confirmation of something he already knew, drew her eyes to him.

"No." The single word was cold, abrupt.

He looked at her. Their gazes met and held. His eyes narrowed.

The lights went out. Total darkness, just like that.

Taken by surprise, Carly squeaked. Sandra did her one better; she let loose with a full-blown shriek. When Carly's nerves returned from orbit, she punched Sandra in the arm.

"Ow." Carly could sense rather than see Sandra rubbing her arm. "What was that for?"

"Okay," Matt said before Carly could reply. Unnerved by the sudden loss of light, she found herself reaching out for him instinctively even as his hand, reaching too, made contact with her arm and slid down to grip her wrist. "I'm going for the flashlight. You want to wait here or come with me?"

He was talking to her, Carly knew, although she couldn't see him. Couldn't, in fact, see anything. In reply, she made a sound that was the snorted equivalent of, *What do you think?*

"Yeah," Sandra said, clearly having no difficulty translating. "I hear that."

"So we'll all go." If Matt sounded a tad long-suffering, Carly discovered that she was prepared to overlook it under the circumstances. "Sandra, grab hold of Carly."

"You got it." Sandra clutched at Carly's hand.

On the other side, Matt's hand slid down to hold hers. The total inability to see was making Carly edgy all over again. She might be mad at Matt, but he was the closest thing to a port in the storm on offer. Her fingers twined with his on contact. His hand was warm and strong and reassuring as he tightened his grip.

"Ready?" he asked.

Both Carly and Sandra answered in the affirmative. Matt edged Carly aside, moved past her through the doorway, then pulled the two of them after him in a careful progression across the front parlor. Carly only stumbled once, over the edge of the rug. Considering the possibilities, she thought that was pretty good.

They made it into the hall, where the still-open door spilled its wedge of lighter darkness. Remembering her dignity as well as her grievance once she could see again, Carly pulled her hand from Matt's. If he had a problem with that, she couldn't tell. He stepped away from her without a word, picking up the flashlight from where he had left it on the radiator cover and switching it on. The bright beam was as welcome as a cold drink on a hot afternoon as he shined it around the hall.

"You know what?" Sandra said, releasing her grip on Carly's hand. "I've had it with Nowheresville, U.S.A. Give me street gangs and muggers and druggies anytime. I'm going home."

Damn, Carly thought, caught by surprise as Sandra, still hanging on to her pan, marched toward the door. The night just kept getting better and better.

"Sandra . . ." Carly trailed her out to the porch. Matt followed suit, letting the screen door bang shut behind him. The flashlight beam slid along the porch rail, slicing through the darkness like a laser. Beyond the porch, the rain had stopped. The smell of damp was as pervasive as the humidity. A chorus of frogs and insects and who knew what other kinds of revolting little creatures sang.

"You can't just turn around and go home," Carly protested. Sandra was the cook; Carly was the owner/manager/administrator/general dogsbody. The bed-and-breakfast could work without Sandra—but only if the guests who booked into The Inn at Beadle Mansion didn't object to peanut butter sandwiches.

"Oh, yeah? You just watch me." Sandra started for the stairs. Her broken sandal slapping the damp wooden floor gave extra emphasis to her militant stride. "I told you, I don't do spooky old houses and—"

"You can't go now. It's the middle of the night, and you haven't had any sleep. It took us about sixteen hours to get here, *remember?*" Carly paused before producing the clincher. "Anyway, I've got the keys."

That stopped Sandra cold at the top of the steps. Planting her fists on her hips, she turned around to fix Carly with a fulminating look. Assuming an identical stance, Carly returned that look with interest. Simmering fear leavened with bursts of terror heaped on top of utter exhaustion and added to slow-cooking despair was not a combination that encouraged calm acceptance of life's little vicissitudes, as she was in the process of discovering.

"Ladies, ladies," Matt intervened, sounding suddenly amused as he came up behind Carly. "Think you could duke it out later? This probably isn't the best time for a cat-fight."

The amusement in his voice was a mistake. The term *catfight* was a bigger one. Carly's pent-up emotions found a far more satisfying target than Sandra as they morphed into fury and focused on Matt. She swung around.

"Same old Matt," she said to him with a big faux smile. "Still the ultimate sexist pig."

Sandra stepped up to stand beside her, their disagreement forgotten in the face of this common enemy. Shoulder to shoulder, the two of them scowled at him.

"Yeah," Sandra added with relish. "Oink, oink."

The sheer anticlimactic ridiculousness of that caused Carly's eyes to roll sideways at Sandra. Her head fell forward in disbelief. For a moment Matt said nothing. Glancing up, Carly caught his gaze. A smile played around the corners of his mouth as his hand rose to flatten on the truly awesome pectoral that lay over his heart.

"Ladies, you wound me," he said, holding her gaze as his smile widened. "You really wound me."

Carly's chin snapped up. Her temper shot toward boiling. Before she could lose it entirely, Sandra once again stepped up to the plate.

"Can anybody here say *bacon?*"

Matt laughed. Sandra bridled. Her own outrage put on hold as she mentally yielded the at-bat to Sandra, Carly awaited the inevitable showdown with bated breath.

It never came. Instead, an ungodly moan filled the air. Carly's eyes widened. The sound was otherworldly, haunting—and it seemed to be coming from directly beneath their feet.

"What the hell?" Matt's brows knit as he looked down.

"That's it." Sandra did an about-face, scuttling down the steps. "Chicago, here I come."

"It's only Hugo," Carly called after Sandra, having recovered her wits enough to recognize the sound as one she had heard before. "He hates getting wet. He must be holed up under the porch. Anyway, you can't go. I've got the keys, remember?"

"Shit," Sandra said, turning to glare up at Carly. A stray moonbeam touched her face, which was already glistening from the increased humidity that the rain had left behind.

"Hugo?" Matt asked at the same time.

"My cat," Carly explained in an aside.

"Think that's going to keep me here?" Sandra was sounding belligerent. Her fists were planted on her hips again. "Hah! Not a chance. I'll just call myself a taxi, so what do you think of that, huh?"

Carly looked at her with no small degree of satisfaction. "There are no taxis in Benton."

Sandra groaned.

Another unearthly moan shivered skyward.

"Give me that." Fed up, Carly snatched the flashlight from Matt's hand and marched down the steps. Squatting beside the crawl space, she pointed the beam inside.

Bright eyes gleamed unblinkingly back at her. There was Hugo all right, huddled in a miserable-looking ball in the farthest corner of the dark, dank-smelling space. Planted directly in front of him and blocking his exit was another animal. Another *growling* animal that Carly couldn't quite see clearly because a concrete support pillar blocked her view of it. But whatever it was, it seemed to strike fear into Hugo's sheltered soul. He moaned again, clearly at bay.

"Hugo," Carly gasped, training the flashlight on him. Her cat looked at her imploringly. Then, to the other animal, which from what little she could see of it seemed to be a fox or a raccoon or, God forbid, a large skunk, she added, "You! Beat it! Shoo!" Glancing around, she spied the pea gravel that her grandmother had always used around the landscaping in lieu of mulch. Scooping up a handful, she tossed it at the predator. "Shoo!"

It didn't budge. Which wasn't much of a surprise because she missed. Hugo flinched as gravel peppered the area around him, and let loose with another of those hairraising moans.

"Are you sure that's a cat?" Matt asked dryly. Both he and Sandra were standing beside her now. Carly looked up at them.

"Something's got him trapped under there. Another animal." Her conscience smote her. She'd been so caught up in this latest series of unfolding disasters that she'd pretty much left her poor cat to fend for himself ever since they'd arrived. As a result, she was now faced with the ultimate calamity: Hugo was about to become some predator's lunch meat. Desperate to save him before the other creature could attack, she dropped to all fours and started into the crawl space.

"Shoo! Shoo!" She waved the flashlight threateningly. Hugo stared at her in alarm.

"Don't be an idiot." Matt grabbed her around the waist and dragged her back. Keeping a precautionary hold on the waistband of her jeans in case she should try again, he crouched beside her, took the flashlight out of her hand, aimed it and peered into the cavity.

"Be careful. Whatever it is might have rabies," Sandra warned.

"It's just a dog," Matt said on a note of relieved disgust. "Here, boy."

As Matt let loose with a series of idiotic dog-coaxing sounds, Carly squinched up her eyes and stared at the parts of the animal she could see. Matt was right, she decided, as it moved slightly: it was a dog. A small black dog with ears like a fox. A dog was better than a wild animal, she thought, but not by a whole heck of a lot. Hugo was a purist; he hated dogs.

"Here, boy," Matt said again. This time the dog looked around. Its eyes, dark and gleaming as the light hit them, struck Carly as being as pitiless as a wolf's. It might not be much taller than Hugo, and it was certainly skinnier, but she had little doubt that its size concealed a wiry strength. It was obviously a stray, or maybe it was even wild. She had heard tales of feral dogs that occasionally roamed Screven County in packs. They killed chickens, calves, sometimes even full-grown cows. Whatever it was, she was absolutely sure of one thing: it was more than a match for her coddled cat.

Beside her, Matt appeared to think it was harmless. Before she could clue him in to the possibilities, he made more of those ridiculous doggy-come-hither noises. In response the dog looked at him again, and gave a sharp yap.

The sound proved too much for Hugo. Fur on end, tail straight as a broomstick, he levitated, then tore toward Carly and safety so fast she was surprised his paws didn't smoke. The dog, taken by surprise, didn't recover enough to realize that its prospective snack was escaping until Hugo shot past. Then it answered the challenge with en-

thusiasm, whirling and barking its head off as it gave
chase.

Carly had the presence of mind to scramble out of the
way. Matt, who was admittedly less well acquainted with
Hugo and his hang-ups and thus understandably might not
have grasped the full extent of his peril, did not. He was
still crouched in front of the crawl space when Hugo went
over him like a freight train over a bridge. The dog, near
hysteria now, followed suit.

Matt yelled and threw up his hands, but too late. Bowled
over, he sprawled on his back in the wet grass.

The words that spilled in a steady stream from his
mouth were rude and unpleasant in tone and probably also
profane. Carly couldn't be sure, because beyond casting a
quick glance his way to make certain he wasn't dead, she
paid no further attention to him as she leaped to her feet.

"Hugo!" she cried, taking off after her pet as the yapping,
yowling midnight express tore across the lawn toward the
corner of the house. With a dreaded dog in pursuit, Hugo
might well run for miles, she knew. Even if he somehow
managed to avoid being ripped to shreds, he would have
no idea how to get home. What made the situation even
worse was that, having spent his entire well-bred life to that
point almost exclusively inside the plush confines of a luxury apartment, Hugo had very little firsthand experience of
the dangers posed by the great outdoors. Add to that the
twin facts that he was a stranger in a strange land and probably terrified out of his wits by the demon dog, and the potential for cat-astrophe loomed large.

She had lost so much, Carly thought. Basically her
whole carefully constructed life. Hugo was just about all
she had left, and she didn't think she could bear it if she
were to lose him too.

Sprinting madly after them, Carly reached the spot

where the animals had streaked out of sight around the side of the house. Glancing back, she caught just a glimpse of Sandra extending a hand down to the still supine Matt. Then, slipping and sliding on the wet grass, she pelted around the corner, and all sight of her fellow humans was abruptly lost to her.

"Hugo!"

Over her own panting calls she could still hear the dog's hysterical yaps, but she could no longer see either animal. The side yard was hugely overgrown; leafy bushes and vines and shrubberies provided an endless variety of cover. She was caught in the shadow of the house now, she realized as she sped in the direction from which the commotion seemed to be coming. The world around her was suddenly darker than before, so dark the temperature seemed to drop by a couple of degrees. The moon was a distant, fuzzy crescent playing peekaboo among enormous silver-edged clouds. Its meager light was capricious, dappling the ground in front of her one moment and then gone the next. Walnut trees grew close together in this part of the yard. Dodging between their stalwart trunks, she had to take care not to slip on the pungent husks that were all that remained of the previous fall's bounty. Thorny-leaved hollies clustered where the taller trees were not. Boxwoods pressed close against the house's pale walls; above the bushes, windows gleamed down at her like dark, all-seeing eyes.

The feeling that she was being watched flitted around the edges of her consciousness for several seconds almost unnoticed. Carly's skin prickled as she finally recognized the uncanny sensation for what it was. Glancing compulsively around, she discovered nothing to account for it. Still, her step faltered and slowed. She was not reassured by the blankness of the windows as she glanced toward the house, or the shape-shifting shadows or the ghostly columns of mist that drifted heavenward from the lowest parts of the yard. As dark as it was, she could not be sure that nothing untoward lurked in the shadows, that no one crouched behind a tree or crept her way.

Water droplets, most likely dislodged from the rain-laden canopy above, struck her face. The unexpected shower surprised a startled gasp out of her. As unnerved as if a hand had reached out of the darkness to grab her, she stopped in her tracks. Her pulse raced; her breathing came fast and shallow. And not just because she had been running, she realized. Not even primarily because she had been running. Her blood was racing and her chest was heaving from the sudden onslaught of fear.

Every sense now alert, her body almost vibrating as she sought to absorb the smallest nuance of her surroundings, she was thwarted at every turn. She saw nothing but night-dark greenery although she strained her eyes to their limit. She heard nothing beyond the sounds that she might expect to hear: the dog's war whoops, which were growing increasingly distant; foliage rustling; raindrops dripping. The choir of unseen creatures hummed louder. The scent of damp earth and walnuts and rampant vegetation was strong. Still, the feeling that she was being observed by an unseen watcher grew more intense as the night seemed to close in on her from all sides.

Only then did it occur to Carly that, under the circumstances, dashing off after Hugo was possibly not the smartest thing she had ever done.

She took a deep breath, unwilling to just abandon Hugo to his fate but knowing that, as much as she loved the cat, she was going to turn back.

"Hugo!"

But for all her concern, her voice was thin and weak-sounding. She knew she should move, should immediately turn tail and fly back to the safety that was Matt, but her feet seemed to have developed an agenda of their own and remained rooted to the spot. Breathing hard, afraid of what she might find, she slowly turned her head. The shadows took on shape and menace as she tried to make sense of them. Memories of the man in the dining room were suddenly hideously acute.

He hadn't run away after all. She was as sure of that as she was of her own name. She could feel him, out there in the dark with her, just as she had felt him in the dining room. Her eyes, now huge and scared, focused down the slope, on the most impenetrable part of the darkness near the fence where the walnuts grew thick and close. He was there; she couldn't see him but she knew it, with a hideous certainty that sent cold chills racing up and down her spine. Her heart pounded so hard now that she could hear nothing above its panicked beat. Her skin crawled.

The moon winked cruelly down at her, an uncaring witness to her distress; the singing insects crescendoed. . . .

Then, impossibly, there he was. Her first glimpse of him was caught out of the corner of her eye as he materialized not more than a few dozen yards to her right. She gasped. Her head snapped around. Frozen with horror, she watched in open-mouthed disbelief as the huge dark shape of him rushed toward her. Suddenly he was close, so close that she could feel the vibrations of his feet hitting the ground, so close that she could see the moonlight gleaming on the silver of his belt buckle, so close that she could hear the harsh rasps of his breathing.

Carly screamed like a banshee and fled.

8

THE DOG. It was the dog. When he'd heard it yapping in the dark, he'd felt a rush of hate so strong it was almost nauseating. So the damned thing hadn't died, and it hadn't left the area either. The man would recognize that high-pitched yelping anywhere. His luck had been like a world-class roller coaster lately, dishing out enormous peaks and valleys. The dog wasn't one of those valleys, not really; it wasn't that important because it was just a *dog,* but Marsha had been a definite valley and the dog was connected with her. Marsha deserved what she'd gotten. If she'd kept her mouth shut she would have been fine, but no, she couldn't do that and so she'd brought her punishment on herself. The one after Marsha, Soraya, hadn't violated their pact as far as he knew, so he felt kind of bad about her, but, hey, after Marsha's betrayal he wasn't taking any more chances. There was one more, one last girl he needed to find and permanently silence, and once that was taken care of he would be free.

The dog wasn't a danger to him, but it bugged him. The thought that it *knew,* knew who he was and what he had done, made him feel vulnerable, however stupid that might sound. He wanted it dead. A couple of times before tonight he'd come back to the cornfield where it had disappeared to look for it, but he hadn't found so much as a paw print. He'd been getting complacent about it, just like he'd gotten complacent about Marsha and the other girls, telling himself to forget them, they were part of the past and out of his life.

But then Marsha had turned up like a slug crawling out from under a rock. And now the dog had turned up, too. If it had been around earlier, when he'd popped open the Beadle Mansion's locked back door with a credit card, he hadn't seen or heard it. He'd been interrupted in the middle of his search, but not by the dog—by two women. It was just bad luck that one of them had stumbled across him in the dining room, and worse luck that the sheriff had been right there on the premises to respond to her screams. But he was still fast, still fit, and he had gotten away, using the dog's trick of hiding out in the cornfield. He'd had a bad moment when the deputies had shown up and started shining their flashlights down the rows, but he'd managed to elude them too. He had been on the other side of the fence again, jogging down toward the road and the place where his own vehicle was concealed, when all hell had broken loose behind him.

Yap, yap, yap. Yap, yap, yap, yap, yap.

The shrilly distinctive barks had come out of nowhere, making him jump, making him whirl around. It sounded like a Chihuahua on speed; there was no mistaking that it was *the dog*, or that it was in full cry after something. For a moment, near panic, he'd thought it was in full cry after him, an animal nemesis springing up out of nowhere to alert the sheriff and the deputies to his whereabouts. He had whirled around, trying to see it, trying to judge which way to run. But it was the middle of the night, and where he was standing, down under some trees, was darker than the inside of a grave. He hadn't been able to see anything but tree trunks and bushes and, up on the hill, the pale box that was the big white house that he had been chased out of just a little while earlier.

But he had been able to hear it: *Yap, yap, yap.*

"Hugo!"

A woman's voice, calling after it. He had looked toward the voice and had seen the dark shape of her silhouetted against the house. She was running, clearly chasing the dog, which just as clearly was *not* chasing him. The yaps were heading the wrong way. With his mind relieved of that worry, he had nevertheless remained motionless, watching the woman, waiting for her to be gone before he risked moving again. Was it the same woman he had encountered in the dining room? Probably—how many women could there be on the previously empty premises, after all?—but it was impossible to say for sure. Then, all of a sudden, she had stopped running. She had seemed to turn, to stare down at him. He had known he was hidden, had known he was safe from her eyes in the well-like darkness under the trees, but still he got the impression that she somehow knew where he was. He had been edging behind a thick tree trunk just as a precaution in case he was perhaps more visible than he'd thought when she suddenly shrieked like she'd been shot and started running again, back the way she had come.

Rattled now, he started running too, away from her, down toward the road. There were too many people out in the dark tonight, he wanted no part of any of them, and the last thing he needed was to be seen and maybe even recognized.

"Carly! Carly! Damn it, Carly!"

A man's voice, yelling. But it wasn't the voice that interested him. It was the name: Carly. He reached the drainage ditch that ran alongside the road, then hesitated, glancing back. No, he told himself, jumping the ditch and jogging across the road to lose himself in the strip of woods that ran alongside the old Naylor place. Not tonight. Not when Benton's finest were already on the scene searching for him. He wasn't in that big of a hurry. And he certainly wasn't that big a fool.

But soon. Soon he would be back.

Because Carly was the name of the last girl, the one he'd been hunting. He'd come up dry at a fancy apartment building in Chicago, which was the latest address he'd been able to find for her. The motive behind his visit to the Beadle Mansion tonight had been to see if he couldn't locate something more recent, an address book or a phone number or even a letter or bill that might tell him where she'd gone.

If this was her, and it almost had to be, his luck was chugging up toward one of those peaks again. Fate had deposited her right in his backyard. He would have to be careful, he had to make sure he did it right, but it would happen.

One night in the not too distant future, if this girl did indeed turn out to be the Carly he was seeking, she was going to go bye-bye just like the others and vanish without a trace.

Then he would finally be able to put the past behind him once and for all, and step out with total confidence into the bright daylight of the second chapter of his life.

9

SCREAMING, CARLY SAW MATT round the corner of the house, running full-tilt toward her.

"Matt!" She flew at him as if she had been launched from a catapult.

"He's here, he's here, he's here," she cried as the space between them closed, and then, when he was no more than a stride or so away, she threw herself at him.

The unexpected assault caused him to stagger back a step, but he caught her. His arms closed around her and he held on tight and just like that she knew she was safe. He had drawn his gun as he ran; she could feel the hard shape of it pressed flat against her hip. Shaking, panting, Carly closed her eyes and clung, burying her face against his chest, wrapping her arms around his waist. She was so terrified she couldn't even look around.

Would he shoot the man? Would the man stop at the sight of the gun?

"Jesus, you've scared ten years off my life tonight." Matt sounded breathless and exasperated and maybe just a little fond all at the same time. "What the hell are you screaming about now?"

"Behind me—" She could hardly get the words out. Did Matt not see? Had he not seen? She lifted her head to find

Matt frowning down at her. "The man in the dining room—he chased me—he's here—out here . . ."

"I didn't mean to scare her."

The deep voice was apologetic, but it made Carly start anyway. She glanced fearfully around. The man walking toward them was black, burly, and breathless. His belt buckle was silver—this was the man she'd been running from. That belt buckle eliminated all doubt. Carly sucked in her breath before she realized he knew Matt. She frowned.

He continued, "I was in the cornfield when I thought I saw somebody go over the fence into the yard. I went after him, but turns out I was chasing the lady here."

"She was never in the cornfield," Matt said. "Are you sure you saw somebody?"

His arms tightened around her. Carly realized that the tightening of his hold was probably pure reflex. In all like-lihood it had nothing to do with her at all. Still, she couldn't help herself; all at once she was acutely aware of Matt as a man rather than simply a rescuer. She absorbed the firm strength of the chest against which she rested, the hard circle of his arms holding her close, the damp warmth of his skin, the crispness of his chest hair, even the faintly musky smell of him. He was bare to the waist, and she was wrapped around him like an Ace bandage. The worst thing about it was, it felt so right.

"Pretty darn sure," the newcomer replied.

It required considerable strength of will, but Carly did it nonetheless: she de-clutched Matt's waist and pulled her-self out of his arms. No matter how right it felt, in his arms was *not* where she wanted to be.

"There was somebody down there." Her voice was still not quite steady as she mustered the inner resources to push Matt-as-man out of her mind. Taking a deep breath, she pointed down the slope to where the walnuts crowded the fence. "There, in the trees by the fence."

Both men stared in the direction she indicated. Looking too, Carly realized once again that the darkness made it impossible to distinguish anything but the barest suggestion of shapes at such a distance.

"You saw somebody?" Matt asked sharply.

It was too dark. No way could she have seen anybody. The men must be realizing that too, because they were looking at her with near-identical frowns.

"N–no." Okay, so it sounded stupid. The truth very often did. "I could just kind of—feel that he was there."

The air practically hummed with skepticism as the men exchanged glances, but neither made so much as a derisive sound.

Smart men.

"I'll check it out," the newcomer said, sounding resigned, and headed off down the slope.

"Who *is* that?" Carly asked, relieved that Matt wasn't going with him. It would have been embarrassing if she'd had to latch on to an ankle and beg him not to leave her.

"One of my deputies. When the guy I chased out of the house went over the fence, I called for backup. Antonio— that's Antonio Johnson—and Mike Toler have been searching the property ever since."

Apparently feeling that the threat was over, Matt tucked his gun away behind his back again. The moving shadow that was Antonio was now about halfway down the slope. Without warning, another shadow detached itself from the darkness to join him. Carly's eyes went wide. But there was no confrontation, no fight. Instead, a flashlight was switched on. The beam scanned the area in front of the men, then moved along the fence.

"There's Toler now," Matt said.

The other deputy. Right. Watching the flashlight's progress, Carly wondered if perhaps it had been one or both of the deputies she'd sensed watching her. It was possible—but Antonio had said he'd been in the cornfield, which was behind the house, just before he'd popped up to scare the wits out of her. Could it have been the second deputy? Maybe. But her instincts made her doubt it.

"Matt—this prowler—you don't think he could be after *me,* do you?" The question emerged spontaneously. As soon as the words left her mouth, Carly realized that they exactly expressed how she had felt both in the dining room and out here.

Matt had been looking toward where the flashlight bobbed among the trees. Now he shifted his gaze to her.

"You in particular, you mean? As in, the guy's potentially a rapist or murderer or something who for some reason has picked you out as a victim?"

Spelled out like that, even in the very reasonable tone he used, it sounded more than a little far-fetched.

"Something like that, yeah."

He looked at her thoughtfully, seeming to turn the possibility over in his mind. If nothing else, she was grateful to him for that.

"Who knew that you were going to be staying at your grandmother's house tonight?"

"Nobody. Well, hardly anybody. Sandra; a few friends."

"Anybody local?"

"No."

"You got anybody in mind as a suspect? Anybody ticked off enough at you to want to do you harm? Say, your ex-husband?"

Carly thought of John. But no, that didn't fit. *She* was ticked off at *him.* Left to enjoy all their assets plus his sexy new wife, he was happy as a clam.

"No. John doesn't have any reason to want to hurt me. There's nobody like that."

Matt was silent for a moment, then said, "Well, then, I'd say it's a pretty safe bet that whoever broke into your grandmother's house tonight was somebody who knew it was empty and was hoping to score something he could convert to easy cash. In other words, you interrupted a burglary. I'm not saying the perp wouldn't have harmed you given the opportunity, but under the circumstances I don't think it's likely that you were the target, specifically."

"Since when does Benton have burglars?" Carly asked, folding her arms over her chest in an effort to ward off a sudden, inexplicable attack of the shivers.

"We get them every now and again. Usually they're looking for things they can sell to buy drugs."

So Benton *had* changed. Still, she'd much rather be dealing with a drug-buying burglar than the alternative. Carly decided that Matt's words made sense. She might well have been in danger—the sense she'd had of that was too strong to discount—but only from being in the wrong place at the wrong time.

"Okay?" he asked.

"Okay," she said.

He nodded. "We'll dust for fingerprints, check out the word on the street, talk to Miss Virgie and Loren and see if they know anything that can help us out. Something specific the guy might have been looking for. There's definitely a criminal element in the area these days, but it's small. Identifying your burglar shouldn't be too hard."

"Wow." Carly took a deep breath and slowly let it out. "Welcome home."

"Yeah." His voice was inscrutable. It was impossible to read his expression in the dark, but the one thing she was sure of was that he was definitely *not* smiling.

"Just for the record," he added as their gazes met, "there's something I want to point out to you here. Considering that only a few minutes earlier a man had grabbed you inside your house and scared you into a flaming case of the screaming meemies before I, as you know, chased him *out*-side, for you to go haring off *out*side in the dark on your own like that was downright stupid. In fact, it was just about as stupid as it gets."

That he had a point was beside the point, Carly told herself, bristling.

"Are you by any chance calling me stupid?" It was a heck of a lot more satisfying to be mad at Matt than grateful to him. The mad went back a long way, and wasn't about to be forgotten just because tonight he'd happened to be in a position to come to her rescue. "That's rich, coming from someone who broke up with Elise Knox *three separate times* because he caught her cheating on him *three separate times*. As in, duh, you might have wanted to think about her track record before you made up with her and started dating her again." Carly snorted derisively. "Now that's what *I* call stupid."

Instead of getting mad in turn, Matt smiled reminiscently. "Maybe, but you have to admit Elise was really hot. I saw her the other day—she lives over in Milledgeville now—and she's *still* hot. When you're in high school, hot makes up for a lot of deficiencies."

Carly's anger was rock solid again.

"I need to find Hugo," she said shortly, turning away. She could no longer hear the demon dog, and she had no idea which way the chase had turned after she'd lost track of it, but anything was better than standing here listening to Matt drool over Elise Knox. "Are you coming with me or not?"

"Not." He caught her wrist, clamping onto it like a vise

and pulling her after him as he started walking toward the front of the house. "And you're not going looking for the damned cat either. Not tonight, you're not."

"I can't just leave him." Still, much as she loved Hugo and feared for him, Carly didn't really want to go careening off on her own again. She'd learned her lesson but good.

"Sure you can. He's a cat. He's probably up a tree by now. What do you plan on doing, trekking around to every tree for miles around calling 'Here, kitty, kitty'?"

Once again, he had a point. She hated it when that happened. He had always possessed the cool head dispensing nuggets of wisdom to her more impulsive self.

"He's afraid of dogs," she said with dignity, trying to make him understand what he clearly considered to be her overabundance of concern for her pet.

"Of course he's afraid of dogs. He's a *cat*."

"He's never really been outside before."

"He's never been *outside?* That enormous furball with claws has never been outside? You're kidding me. What kind of cat is that?"

"A purebred," Carly said, getting miffed at him all over again. "A blue-point Himalayan, to be precise. His mother was a show cat, a grand champion. The only reason I was able to buy Hugo was because my husband handled Hugo's mother's owner's divorce. Cats like that stay indoors."

"Pussy," Matt said scornfully.

"Hugo is not a pussy." Instinctively rushing to the defense of her really very masculine if somewhat sheltered cat, Carly said it before she thought.

Matt slanted a grin back over his shoulder at her. "Sure he is."

Carly's lips compressed. Glaring at his broad back was useless—no way could he see—but she did it anyway.

"If it will make you feel better, I'll put my deputies on cat alert. While they're searching the vicinity for the man who broke into your grandmother's house and grabbed you, they can also keep an eye out for your pussy." There was a faintly devilish note to that last word that did nothing to soothe Carly's annoyance.

"If you don't quit calling him that—" Carly broke off in mid-threat, suddenly becoming aware that they had left the house behind and were moving down the slope toward the road. "Where are we going?"

"To your U-Haul. I'm guessing your friend is there, hopefully locked inside. When you started screaming, she said 'I'll wait in the truck,' and took off like a bat out of hell. I was too busy chasing after you to watch where she went, but on the strength of our brief acquaintance I'd say she's a woman of her word."

"If she went to the U-Haul, she couldn't get in. The doors are locked and I've got the keys."

As they dodged around the dripping foliage, Matt looked back at her. "Hey, Curls, you know what? You always could cause more trouble than anyone I ever knew."

Carly gasped with indignation. Before she could decide what to object to first, the nickname or the characterization, he pulled her with him out from behind an enormous magnolia, and there was the U-Haul not a dozen feet away. Sandra was perched on the running board, cluthing the flashlight in one hand. The flashlight beam was darting hither and yon like a drunken firefly as she shined it all around. When Carly and Matt stepped out into the open, she squealed, jumped to her feet, and aimed the flashlight at them. Then she recognized them and let out a huge, relieved sigh as they approached.

"Next time I go anywhere with you," Sandra said, fixing Carly with gimlet eyes, "you can bet your sweet granny I'll be the one doing the driving."

"Fine with me. I never particularly wanted to drive in the first place. You're the one who gets nervous on the interstate. *And* on narrow country roads. *And* in traffic. *And* after dark. Which just about covers the whole spectrum of possible driving conditions, I'd say." Carly fished in the pocket of her jeans and came up with the keys. To her surprise, Matt took them out of her hand.

"This time I'm driving." He unlocked the door and held it wide. "Get in."

Sandra scrambled in with alacrity. Once inside, she turned off the flashlight and scooted to the far side of the bench seat. Carly stayed where she was.

"Look," she said to Matt. "Thanks for making like a sheriff and coming to my rescue. I really appreciate it. But I think Sandra and I can take it from here."

Matt grunted, clearly unimpressed. "I don't think so. Get in."

"I'm not going anywhere," Carly said, abandoning subtlety in favor of making her position clear. The days when Matt Converse could make a plan and she would fall slavishly in with whatever he wanted were long gone, and so he needed to understand.

"Oh, yes, you are. Your grandmother's house is now a crime scene. We're conducting an official investigation. You're hindering it. I'm going to take you two to my house, where you can spend the night. You'll be safe, and you'll be out of my way. As far as I'm concerned, life with you around just doesn't get any better than that."

Carly put her fists on her hips.

"How to put this?" she said, sugar sweet. "I don't want to go to your house. In fact, I refuse to go to your house. I'd rather sleep in the U-Haul than go to your house."

"Speak for yourself," Sandra called from inside the truck.

Both Carly and Matt ignored her.

Matt said, "Let me spell this out for you: you can spend the night at my house, or you can spend the night in jail. Your choice."

"You're bluffing." At least, Carly was reasonably certain he was bluffing.

His jaw tightened. "Try me."

"Go for it," she said, raising her chin. "Put me in jail."

"Like I said, speak for yourself." Sandra was leaning across the seat now, looking at them through the open door. She sounded alarmed.

Matt glanced at Sandra. Then he looked back at Carly.

"Curls, don't be a pain in the ass," he said softly. So softly that she was reasonably sure that only she could hear.

It was the softness of his voice that did it. The only time he employed that deceptively gentle tone was when he was on the verge of losing his temper with a vengeance. She might not have seen him in years, but she'd known him long and she'd known him well: he was perfectly capable of picking her up and stuffing her into that truck if he had to. When he talked like that, he was also perfectly capable of locking her up in the nearest cell.

"Bully," she said witheringly, and climbed into the cab.

10

PRUDENTLY SILENT in the face of victory, Matt got in behind Carly and closed the door. The cab was as hot and steamy as the inside of a sauna. Crowded up against Sandra, Carly felt sweat start to bead on her forehead. The only thing that made the stifling atmosphere even remotely bearable was the fact that Matt got to share it.

"By the way," Carly said as Matt started the truck and reached for the climate control knob, "the air conditioner's broken." Carly felt as much malicious enjoyment as he'd seemed to feel when he'd told her the power to the house was out.

A grunt was his only reply.

"Tomorrow I'm going back to Chicago, just so you know," Sandra said to Carly, effectively diverting her attention. "This place is creepier than one of those haunted houses the fire department puts on at Halloween. What made you start screaming again back there, anyway?"

"I stubbed my toe," Carly said shortly.

"Oh, yeah, *right.*"

"Ladies," Matt intervened, his voice still dangerously soft as he eased the truck off the gravel verge and onto the road. "I worked fourteen hours today. I got the call reporting the prowler just about the time I got home and fell into bed. In the last half hour, I've been hit over the head with a pan, tripped by a cat, coldcocked by a flowerpot, and screamed into next week. I've got a bump on the back of my head and a cut on the front of it. And after I get you two stowed away where you can't get into any more trouble, I have a crime scene investigation to run. I'm tired, I'm overworked, and I have the mother of all headaches. Keeping all that in mind, do you think you could, please, hold off on the bickering?"

Carly looked at him. Once again that soft voice was not lost on her. Neither was the glint in his eyes, or the grim set to his jaw. And to all those warning signs she mentally said, *Too bad.*

"Obviously you can't tell the difference between talking and bickering," she said with a sniff. "Just because we're women doesn't mean we bicker."

"You know," Sandra added in a thoughtful tone, "my horoscope said that I'd be meeting up with a handsome, dark-haired man with a bad attitude."

The glance he sent the pair of them would have silenced Oprah.

"The bottom line is, I'd appreciate it a whole heck of a lot if the two of you would just sit there and *shut up.*"

For the space of a couple of heartbeats the atmosphere in the cab seemed to sizzle.

"Fine," Carly said, folding her arms over her chest and glaring out the windshield.

"Yeah, fine," Sandra echoed, crossing her arms and glaring too.

Uneasy silence reigned while the truck bounced through a cumbersome U-turn. Wedged between Matt and Sandra, Carly was forced to learn more about the physical characteristics of her seatmates than she really cared to know. Both were far bigger than she. Both generated a considerable amount of heat. Sandra was soft and cushiony and smelled of some sort of floral perfume. Matt was firm and slick and smelled of sweat. Sandra's shirt was at least reasonably dry. Matt's bare skin was disturbingly warm and damp. Her shoulder butted into his arm. Her thigh lay alongside his. Worse, every bump and bounce—and the road suddenly seemed to be as pitted as the surface of the moon—threw her against him. She grew ever more aware that he was shirtless. Her senses were inundated with unavoidable glimpses of broad, bronzed shoulders, deep hairy chest, washboard stomach; the faintly musky scent of him; the soft sound of his breathing. She was reminded at every turn of the sleek resilience of his rib cage, the crisp texture of his chest hair, the hard strength of his arms which, incidentally, flexed as he drove.

Eventually Carly realized that she was overdosing on *Matt.*

It wasn't but a few minutes later that it occurred to her with the suddenness of a thunderclap that what she really, truly, positively wanted to do was jump his bones. Do the nasty. Right there on his lap in the cab of the truck with her butt wedged against the steering wheel. The sudden vivid fantasy made her tingle in places that had no business tingling and appalled her at the same time. *Not* happening, she told her baser self fiercely. Not again. Not in this life. Forget about it.

But still the searing image continued to flicker in taunting Technicolor around the edges of her mind. Telling herself that the man beside her was Matt, no good dirty rotten son of a bitch, was no help. No good dirty rotten son of a bitch or not, he was hot. Worse, he was making her hot, and whether she liked it or not—and she didn't!—there didn't seem to be a whole heck of a lot she could do to stop it from happening.

"Could you roll down the windows, please?" she requested faintly a few feverish minutes later. If she got any hotter, she was going to melt into a little puddle right there on the black vinyl seat.

Matt had pulled out his phone and was punching numbers into it as he drove through the center of the dark and silent town; clearly her proximity was not turning his bones to butter.

"They are down," he said absently. Sandra nodded confirmation.

Looking past them both in disbelief, Carly saw that he was telling the truth: the windows were down. Her view of the improvements proudly touted in the brochure put out by Benton's chamber of commerce—which included newly picturesque storefronts, sidewalks enhanced by strategically spaced planters overflowing with flowers and ornate iron street signs added to every corner—was largely unimpeded by bug-smeared glass. But stuck in the middle as she was, she wasn't getting so much as a whiff of fresh air.

Matt looked comfortable. The wind was ruffling his black hair and drying the sweat on his face and body. Sandra looked comfortable. Her black hair was cut too close to her head to blow in the breeze, but her dangling butterfly earrings were dancing. Carly, on the other hand, was the opposite of comfortable. Besides being tortured by graphic images of getting it on with Matt in ways she hadn't even known she knew about, she was being asphyxiated and roasted and bounced around like a baby on a clueless uncle's knee all at the same time. She was starting to feel light-headed. Her stomach was doing flip-flops. She was emotionally wrung out. She was over being scared now, but she was still shaken up by what had happened. She was depressed about her life in general. She was having grave second thoughts about the wisdom of returning to Benton at all, much less living in, and trying to make a living from, her grandmother's old and broken into house. Her friend and business partner was threatening to back out of their deal. The no good dirty rotten son of a bitch she'd been mentally hurling bricks at for years had somehow managed to once again turn up front and center in her life. After years of good behavior, her hair had reverted to its child-hood anarchy in little more than an hour. And to top things off, she was worried sick about her cat.

Talk about not having a good day. She'd gone way past that by now: plain and simple, she was not having a good life.

"Yo, I need somebody to come pick me up at my house," Matt said into the phone, interrupting the dark flow of her thoughts. "And I want you guys to keep an eye out for a miss-ing cat." Pause. "What do you mean, what does it look like? It's got four paws and a tail and weighs about a hundred fifty pounds. Think grizzly." Pause. "Jesus, it's a cat. White and fluffy. Says meow. What do you want, a composite?" Another pause. "No, they're with me. I'm taking them to my house for the night." He laughed suddenly. "Don't worry about it. I'll be fine. Yeah, I'm sure. Okay. Fifteen minutes."

He disconnected and slid the phone back into his pocket.

"Antonio's afraid that if I let you ladies sleep over at my house you might murder me during the night." A smile tugged at the corners of Matt's mouth.

"Gee, he must know you pretty well," Carly replied with a pointed faux smile of her own. She didn't know whether to be relieved that Matt had actually told someone to look for Hugo, or affronted at his description of him.

Matt didn't reply. Instead, he slowed down, then turned left into a well-established neighborhood with a mixed bag of homes. A couple of turns later, the U-Haul slowed, then swung wide, lurching up an asphalt driveway. The head-

lights swept the front of an older story-and-a-half bunga-
low with a shingle-covered facade and a pair of square ma-
sonry pillars supporting a low-hanging porch. Matt's home,
obviously. There was a car in the driveway, a small yellow
Civic, parked in front of a detached garage. Impossible to
imagine Matt at the wheel of such a vehicle.

It occurred to Carly as Matt parked behind the femi-
nine-looking thing that she was still thinking of him as the
younger Matt, the girl magnet Matt, the Matt she had
known. As she had already discovered, that kind of mistake
was fraught with pitfalls.

"I'd hate to wake your wife." Her tone was carefully neutral, absolutely noncommittal—and a total lie. She was
horrified to discover that the thought of Matt's wife—of
Matt having a wife—bothered her.

"I'm not married."

If she didn't quite sigh with relief, she came close. As she
watched Matt get out of the truck, Carly realized with chagrin that somewhere deep inside her still lurked the
teenager with the crush.

She was going to have to keep an eye on that girl.

Sliding out after Matt, who was patiently holding the
door open for her, she stood looking up at the house for a
moment as she waited for her wobbly legs to reaccustom
themselves to solid ground. Upstairs and down, the windows were uniformly dark. The house was still. She would
have thought it empty if not for that car.

"Do you mind?" Matt asked, indicating the door. Carly
obligingly stepped aside, and he closed it. As she walked
toward the front of the truck, her eyes once again found the
Civic. If he wasn't married, then who did the car belong to?

"Does your mother live with you?" she asked as he fell
into step beside her, trying her level best not to sound
hopeful. The idea pleased her. Matt at thirty-three still

making his home with his mother—there was a whole life-time's worth of retaliatory needling in that.

"My mother's dead."

"Oh." Her mood went flat. He'd loved his mother. The loss would have hurt. Instinctively Carly put a sympathetic hand on his arm. "I didn't know. I'm sorry."

She hadn't known because after she'd left Benton for college she had deliberately never asked her grandmother anything about him, and her grandmother, knowing that Matt was a sensitive topic even if she hadn't known exactly why, had not so much as once mentioned his name. At first, during Carly's infrequent, flying visits home there'd been so much to talk about that avoiding the subject of Matt had been easy. Later, as her grandmother had begun to fail, the focus had turned to the older woman's health.

"No reason you should have."

"What—when . . ." Her voice trailed off, leaving the request for details vague, so that he could tell her or not as he chose.

"A few years back. A heart attack. She was waiting tables at The Corner Café when she just collapsed." He paused and glanced down at her as her hand tightened in silent sympathy on his arm. "I was just finishing up a stint in the Marines. I came home."

Carly's throat threatened to close up. Idiot, she told herself fiercely, to be so moved by his matter-of-fact tone. But she knew him so well—too well to be deceived. That tone hid a wealth of pain. And her heart ached for him.

"What—the heck—did you pack—in this suitcase?" Panting, listing slightly to one side, Sandra rounded the front of the truck to join them. She was lugging her own small satchel in one hand and Carly's slightly larger (and obviously much heavier) gym bag in the other. Carly had thought it advisable for them each to pack an overnight bag to get them through at least their first night and day in Benton, by which time, presumably, they would have managed to get the truck unloaded. Self-conscious suddenly under Sandra's sharp-eyed gaze, Carly let her hand fall from Matt's arm.

"Oh, thanks, I forgot all about that." Without really answering she reached for her bag. The truth was that her hair dryer and brushes and shampoo and straightening gel, to say nothing of her makeup kit and clothes and various necessities for Hugo, combined for quite a lot of weight, none of which she cared to account for in front of Matt.

"Give it here." Matt beat her to it, and took Sandra's as well. If the weight of hers bothered him, he gave no sign of it, carrying both bags easily. She and Sandra followed him inside, waiting somewhat uneasily in the dark hush of the house as he put the bags down to fumble for the light switch. Seconds later he found it, and was rewarded by a burst of dazzlingly bright light followed almost immediately by a gasp and a loud thump.

"Ohmigod, Matt, you scared the life out of me! I thought you were gone for the night."

The speaker was a pretty teenage girl with thick-lashed dark eyes, a to-die-for tan, black hair that waved down to her waist, and long legs bared by a pair of tiny khaki shorts. She was sitting bolt upright on a yellow floral couch on which she'd obviously been stretched full length, clutching the edges of her unbuttoned white blouse together with both hands. Having equally obviously just fallen off the couch, a long-haired blond kid of about the same age was on the floor beside it, caught in the twin acts of trying to pull up his jeans and scramble to his feet, an almost comical deer-in-the-headlights look on his face.

It was clear to Carly, who stood just inside the door peering around Matt, that they had surprised a couple heavily engrossed in making out. It was equally clear, from the sudden tension in Matt's body as he stood regarding the pair with his hand still on the light switch, that Matt didn't like what he saw one bit.

The girl was the likely owner of the car, Carly surmised. Was she his girlfriend, caught in the act of messing around on him in his own house? Carly's mind boggled at the thought. But she looked way young for Matt—and the vibe Carly was picking up from him was off.

"You thought wrong then, didn't you?" Matt's hand dropped at last. The front door opened directly into the living room, Carly realized, which accounted for the degree to which the teenagers had been taken by surprise. The room was nicely furnished, complete with a TV and a pair of striped wing chairs and the customary lamps and tables and knickknacks. The curtains, drawn now, matched the couch. The carpet underfoot was moss green, the walls a delicate celadon. The only jarring note in the whole well-coordinated assemblage was an oversized and obviously ancient black vinyl recliner, repaired in more than one place with duct tape, which was positioned at a comfortable distance from the TV. Complete with its own floor lamp and side table, flanked by an untidy stack of newspapers and magazines, it formed an incongruously ugly island in an otherwise charmingly decorated sea.

"Time to go home, Andy." Matt moved to the center of the room to fix the kid with a disagreeable stare.

"Y–yes, sir," Andy stuttered, trying to hang on to his unfastened jeans without being obvious about it as he edged around Matt. The novelty of hearing Matt addressed as sir made Carly blink.

"Oh, for God's sake. Lighten up, will you please? I'm eighteen. I'll be going off to college next month." The girl swung her legs over the side of the couch and proceeded to button up her blouse while glaring at Matt. "Then you won't know anything about what I choose to do."

"Thank God," Matt said devoutly. He turned on a lamp and the room got even brighter.

"Uh—bye, Lissa." Andy bestowed a sickly little half smile on Carly and Sandra as he loped past them toward the door. Carly felt almost sorry for him. His face was beet red, his eyes kept darting nervously back at Matt, and his jeans kept threatening to fall down.

"See you tomorrow, Andy," Lissa called as he made it to safety and the door closed behind him. Clearly she was not as impressed by Matt's displeasure as Andy had been. Having finished with her blouse, she stood up, stretched provocatively under Matt's censorious gaze, and yawned, covering her mouth with red-tipped fingers that she tapped against her cheeks in an exaggerated display of boredom.

"Carly, Sandra, meet my sister Melissa," Matt said dryly. "Lissa, Carly Linton—you might remember Carly, she grew up here in Benton—and Sandra . . . Sandra . . ."

"Kaminski," Sandra supplied. She was standing just behind Carly, watching the action wide-eyed.

"Kaminski," Matt repeated.

"Hi," Lissa offered, wiggling her fingers at them in an airy little wave.

"Hi," they echoed in unison. Carly caught herself waving back, and felt like a fool. Luckily, no one else seemed to notice. Lissa's eyes had already swung back to Matt. She was frowning. "What happened to your head? And your shirt?"

"I got hit and it got wet." Matt disposed of her questions with curt efficiency. "I need you to look after Carly and Sandra for me. They're going to be spending the night."

"Oh, yeah?" Lissa looked interested. Her gaze returned to them, sharpened, and ran over Carly with particular care.

"Yeah." Matt's tone was as unencouraging as the look he gave her.

"Fine with me. I would never dream of saying anything about *your* private life."

"Can it, Lissa," he ordered. A horn honked from the driveway. Running both hands through his hair, Matt looked harassed. "I've got to go. Where's Erin?"

"Out."

"It's almost one-thirty."

Lissa shrugged.

"Dani?"

"Out."

"Where? Everything's clo—" Something in Lissa's expression made him break off and shake his head. "Never mind. I don't want to know."

The horn honked again.

"Damn, I need a shirt." Matt moved swiftly past them into an adjoining room, turning on the light as he went. In less than a minute he was back, pulling on a rumpled-looking Georgia Bulldogs tee shirt as he came through the doorway. He shot Lissa an exasperated look. "Can't somebody do the laundry?"

Lissa smiled. "Hello, somebody."

"Give me a break here. I've been working my butt off this week."

Lissa made a face at him. "Tell the truth: You just expect one of us to do the laundry because we're girls."

The horn sounded again. Matt swallowed whatever else he might have been going to say on the subject and turned to Carly. "Don't leave the house." He glanced at his sister. "Give one of them my room, and the other Erin's. I doubt she'll be back tonight, and when I come in, I'll sleep on the couch."

"Aye, aye, Cap'n." Lissa saluted smartly. Matt shot her a narrow-eyed look.

The horn gave a double blast.

"Later," Matt said, and took himself off.

"Be warned. He's cute, but he's bossy," Lissa said.

Carly, who'd been watching the door close behind him, glanced guiltily around to discover Lissa looking her up and down.

"Now I remember you," Lissa said suddenly, meeting her gaze. "You lived in the old Beadle Mansion and you always wore those really frilly dresses and you had like acres of curls. Didn't you used to follow Matt around everywhere?"

Carly was momentarily taken aback, but she recovered quickly enough to keep her discomfort from becoming obvious, she hoped.

"Sometimes, I guess. He did odd jobs for my grandmother." Time to take the ball into her opponent's court before Matt's baby sister dredged up any more embarrassing recollections. She hadn't seen much of the three Converse girls—her grandmother had rarely permitted her to go to Matt's house, or even to the "poor" sections of town where Matt and his family had lived—but hanging around Matt had inevitably exposed her to them from time to time. "As it happens, I remember you, too. You were little, and you wore flip-flops all the time because you couldn't tie your shoes, and you always seemed to be crying about something. Once it was because one of the neighborhood boys had stuck bubblegum in your hair. You begged Matt to get it out. So he took out his pocketknife and sawed the whole hank of hair off. He thought that would make you feel better, but when you saw that hank of hair just laying there in his hand you really bawled. He was pretty disgusted about the whole thing."

Lissa grinned. "That sounds like me—and Matt."

"Uh, excuse me," Sandra said, very polite as she shifted from one foot to the other in a way Carly knew only too well. "But would you mind if I used your bathroom?"

From the look she shot Carly, Carly realized that she was being dared to comment.

"Oh, sure. It's through here." Apparently put in a better humor by the exchange of reminiscences, Lissa started walking and beckoned them after her. "Come on, I'll show you."

They followed her into the kitchen, which was bright and cheerful with white cabinets and trellis-patterned wallpaper. A side-by-side bathroom and laundry room opened off the kitchen. The laundry room floor was piled with baskets of dirty clothes. Seeing them, Carly grinned. Somebody really did need to do the laundry.

"Do you live with Matt year-round? Or . . ." Carly had wondered if perhaps Matt's three sisters were just visiting, but she broke off as Lissa nodded. The two of them were leaning against the kitchen wall waiting for Sandra to emerge from the bathroom.

"I do, but I'm the only one of us who still does. Or at least I do until next month. Then I'm headed for the University of Georgia. My sister Dani's going to be a junior there, and Erin just graduated. Dani will be going back when I go, and Erin's getting married. So as of the middle of next month, Matt will be on his own for the first time since he came home after Mama died." Lissa grinned. "We're trying to prepare him by not doing the laundry and things. We're afraid being left on his own after having us to take care of him for so long is going to be kind of a shock."

Sandra emerged then, and Lissa took them upstairs. After showing Sandra to Erin's bedroom, a frilly affair in pink and white, Lissa took Carly along to Matt's. The rest of the house was decidedly feminine, done up in pastels and floral prints and finished off with a variety of pictures, plants and knickknacks. In contrast, Matt's room was starkly unadorned, with plain white walls, beige carpeting, the bare minimum of sturdy oak furniture, and another of those ugly recliners, this one sporting even more repairs than the one in the living room, situated for optimum viewing of a small TV.

"He won't let us touch his room," Lissa said semi-apologetically, glancing around. "He says he likes it like this. But at least it has its own bathroom." She pointed toward a door in the far wall. "It's through there."

Carly nodded as she put down her bag. By this time she was practically drooping with fatigue. The drive down from Chicago had left her exhausted. Her most pressing thought as she'd parked the U-Haul in front of her grandmother's house and started lugging Hugo up the hill had been of showers and beds. The subsequent excitement had revived her—a series of major adrenaline rushes tended to do that to people, she'd heard—but the excitement was over now and she was once again fading fast. Not even her residual worry over Hugo's fate could keep her from looking longingly at the bed.

" 'Night." Taking the hint, Lissa headed out the door, then paused with one hand on the jamb to glance back with a naughty grin.

"Wait till Shelby hears that Matt brought you home to spend the night. He *never* brings girls home. She's gonna die."

Carly's eyes widened. Before she could even begin to explain the circumstances behind her overnight stay, the girl, still grinning, gave her another of those airy little waves and went out of the room. Left standing open-mouthed in the middle of Matt's bedroom, there was nothing for Carly to do but contemplate Lissa's words—and wonder, to her eternal self-disgust, just who Shelby was and what she was to Matt.

11

IF THE DAMNED CAT had belonged to anyone except Carly, Matt thought, he would have dropped it off at the pound. No, better yet, he would have left it in the tree where Toler had found it. Or fed it to the dog that, shooed off, had still lurked hopefully beneath a nearby bush, watching as he cursed out his deputies for cowardice and then, with both Toler and Antonio grinning in the background, ascended into the branches himself to bring the spitting, clawing spawn of a saber-toothed tiger down.

But he owed Carly. Big time. Enough so that he was prepared to overlook having his arms scratched all to hell and nearly falling out of the damned tree and providing his deputies with more laughs than a Monty Python festival. Stumbling across her tonight had taken him back twelve years, to the night when the curly-haired little misfit of a teenager that he'd considered a sort of fourth sister for most of his life had morphed into a woman. A beautiful woman with big blue eyes that had openly adored him and a soft, pink-lipsticked mouth that had trembled when he looked at it and a slim, firm body hugged by a slithery satin dress that had pressed up against him tighter than his own underwear every time he'd turned around. He'd been doing her a favor, a *favor*, damn it, by taking her to her prom, and like all good deeds that favor had turned around and bitten him in the ass.

He couldn't even blame her for what had happened. She'd been a young eighteen, and she'd been so sheltered and guarded and hemmed in by her crusty old battle-ax of a grandmother that she'd never even had a date. For years he'd basked in the glow of her admiration, responding to her open hero worship like a plant to the sun, treating her in return with a careless affection that only occasionally had been jarred into real tenderness. Back then, most of the world had seen him as bad news, but not Carly. She'd thought he was wonderful, and he'd known it; had even, he saw now, been touched by it, and been motivated to be better than he actually was inclined to be because of it. When he'd stumbled across her crying because she didn't have a date to the prom, making her happy again had been easy.

But she'd surprised him. That night, his sweet little odd duck of a pal had somehow turned into a swan, and when he'd first set eyes on her as she'd walked out onto her porch to greet him he'd scarcely been able to believe what his eyes were seeing. But he'd handled it, no problem, dancing with her in her crepe paper–hung gym and making her look good in front of the other girls and assiduously keeping her away from the rum-spiked punch, which he'd imbibed just enough of himself to be able to state positively what was in it. When he'd first started getting turned on by her, he couldn't have said; but by the time they were ready to leave he'd been aroused enough to where taking her straight home no longer seemed like the only possible option.

She'd snuggled up next to him in his car, her head resting back against the top of the seat and her eyes all soft and dreamy on his face as she'd confided that most of her classmates had rented rooms in Benton's one motel, where they meant to party for what was left of the night.

Forget that, he'd said, curt because he was tempted.

But on the way home she'd said she was thirsty, and he had thought she probably was because he hadn't let her drink anything but a few sips of water from the fountain all night. So he'd stopped at the 7-Eleven to buy her a Coke and himself a beer. Then she'd begged so hard for a sip from his can that he'd finally pulled over into a graveled lay-by and let her have one. After the gulp she'd swallowed had made it safely down, she'd coughed and wrinkled up her nose with distaste and gone "Ugh." Then he'd laughed and said something like, "Curls, I don't think you're ready for beer yet."

She'd sat up straight and looked at him and said, real serious, "I'm ready for more than you think," and kissed him, hot and sweet as heavily sugared coffee, right on the mouth.

From there the situation, and his self-control with it, had gone straight to hell.

Afterward, after he'd taken her home and caught a few hours' sleep and woken up to the realization of what he'd done, he'd been literally sick to his stomach. He could hardly look at himself in the mirror. He certainly couldn't face Carly.

What could he say? I'm sorry, it was a mistake, I feel like I've fucked my sister?

Matt grimaced, remembering. In retrospect, he should have said it, or if not exactly that—surely he could have come up with something a shade more tactful—at least *something*. Avoiding her for the rest of the summer out of shame had been, as Lissa would put it, way less than cool.

So tonight he had rescued her killer cat, and was bringing it to her as a kind of penance. And he guessed that, sometime over the course of the next few days, he was going to have to work himself up to presenting her with a full-blown, heartfelt apology.

Which in her newly belligerent incarnation she would probably tell him to stuff right up there where the sun don't shine.

Smiling a little ruefully at the picture this conjured up, Matt let himself into his dark house—meeting with no unwelcome surprises this time, thank God—and started up the stairs, the razor-clawed behemoth crouched silently at the bottom of a canvas duffel bag (courtesy of Toler), which he carried out in front of him as carefully as if it held a bomb.

It was now just after four A.M. Carly's grandmother's house had been searched, photographed, and dusted for fingerprints. The grounds and outbuildings had been searched. The damned cat had been rescued. Just as he'd been battling to bag the beast, his phone had rung. On the other end had been Cindy Nichols, reporting ghostly knockings in her bedroom that were scaring her to death. As Mrs. Nichols had been growing increasingly paranoid about the supposed poltergeist in her house, and he'd already personally made several calls to check it out, he didn't feel obliged to answer this one. Instead, after ascertaining the woman's location—she'd locked herself in her bedroom closet and was whispering to him on her cell phone so as not to alert the poltergeist to her location—he'd dispatched Antonio, who'd been laughing so hard over his superior's struggles with the cat that he'd had to sit down on the ground, to do the honors.

His only hope was that this time the poltergeist was ready, willing and able to terrorize someone besides Mrs. Nichols. Antonio, for example.

Then he'd called it a day and, complete with his bagged peace offering, headed for home. He'd been on the job since seven that—no, make it the previous—morning, and he was dead beat. The county council was either going to have to break down and cough up the funds for an additional deputy or two, or they were going to have to start pulling shifts themselves.

Reaching the top of the stairs, he paused, recollected that he wasn't sure where Carly was sleeping, and mentally shrugged. Whatever choice he made—his room or Erin's—he had a fifty percent chance of being right. In any case, as long as *he* didn't have to sleep within claws' reach of the cat from hell, it didn't matter. He knew for a fact that his room had a strong door and a sturdy latch, which were all that the situation required. He'd shut his prisoner in good and tight, check to make sure Dani was home, and if she was, head downstairs to sleep. If she wasn't . . .

Hell, she was twenty years old. Nine months out of the year she was away at college and he had no idea how she spent her nights. If she wasn't in her bedroom he would head downstairs and collapse on the couch and go to sleep anyway.

He opened the door to his bedroom quietly, not wanting to wake whoever was sleeping inside. Blocking the exit with his body so the damned cat couldn't get past him, being as quiet as possible, he upended the duffel bag and shook the monster out—not without a certain degree of satisfaction as it landed with a *thump,* then stayed put, lashing its tail but looking dazed. He was still looking down at the cat when he realized that he could actually *see* it, that the visibility in his bedroom was significantly better than in the rest of the dark house. Glancing up, he saw why: the light had been left on in his bathroom. The door was open no more than a crack, but it was enough. He looked at the bed, curious to know if it was occupied by Carly or her friend. His brow knit as he realized that it was empty. The pillows were in disarray, the covers had been thrown back, but nobody was in it.

He was just making the obvious connection—whoever had been in his bed was now in the bathroom—when his gaze, for some obscure reason that was forever lost to him, was drawn to the far corner of the room. There, in his comfy old BarcaLounger, sat Carly. She was huddled in a little ball with her knees drawn up to her chin, looking impossibly small and lost.

She was looking at him. Shrouded in shadows, dwarfed by his chair, sitting silent and motionless in what he guessed was the hope that he wouldn't notice her, she was watching his every move. For the space of a couple of heartbeats he felt an unfamiliar combination of nervous and guilty as he recollected his lack of tender loving care in connection with the delivery of her pet.

Then he realized something else. With a fist pressed against her mouth, she was fighting to hold back sobs, and doing a piss-poor job of it, too.

Shit. He didn't want to know. He really didn't. For the past seven years he'd been drowning in a sea of pink. Ever since his mother's death when he'd turned his back on a promising career in the Marine Corps to come home and raise his young sisters, he'd been dealing on a daily basis with a whole spectrum of generally incomprehensible female emotions. Now, when he was finally seeing light at the end of the tunnel, did he want to add yet another freak-out prone female to his problem pool?

No. Hell, no. No way.

But this was Carly. He'd been looking out for her since she was eight years old. To his own disgust, he was discovering that his protective instincts where she was concerned were still strong. Their friendship might have hit kind of a pothole there in the backseat of his car, but the infrastructure was still intact. He was beginning to realize that a long-standing relationship like theirs was kind of like riding a bicycle—once you'd learned how it worked, it was forever imprinted in your brain. He couldn't just walk away and leave her sitting there all alone in the dark, crying.

Damn it to hell and back anyway.

"Hey," he said, striving for a light note. "What's up?"

"Go away." There was a detectable thickness to her voice—from bitter experience he extrapolated from it that she'd been crying for a good little while—but her tone was definitely hostile.

Good, he told himself. She didn't want him around. He was off the hook. He could just turn tail and . . .

She sniffed. Not a delicate little sniff, either. A good, solid, haul-it-all-back-up-inside-there sniff.

"Damn," he muttered, resigning himself to his fate as he stepped inside his bedroom and closed the door behind him. The cat, no friend, hissed at him as he moved toward it and scrambled away to hide under the bed. Matt paid scant attention. Crossing the room to Carly's side, cursing the luck that had caused him to open her door at just that moment, he stopped in front of the chair to look down at her. Sliding his hands into his pockets and rocking back on his heels, he considered her silently through the wealth of shadows that shrouded the chair. Her eyes rose to meet his, gleaming as they reflected the light from his bathroom back at him.

If anything, he thought, she looked even smaller and more vulnerable than before from this angle, with her body as closely wound together as a paper clip and her head full of curls thrown back to expose the pale column of her throat. She was wearing long pajama pants and a tiny little knit top that exposed part of her midriff, and her feet were bare. Except for the change in hair color and the newly womanly curves that he couldn't help but notice, she looked exactly as he remembered her from when she was about sixteen years old.

Shit.

"I found your cat."

If that was her problem, he was in luck; it was already solved.

"Yippee. Thanks a lot. Now go away."

So when had his luck ever been that good? Besides being thick, her voice had a noticeable catch in it. From her tone it was clear that he had not saved the day. Knowing women, she could be crying over anything. But whatever had turned on her faucets, she'd clearly been going at it pretty hard. With her face tilted up to his he had no problem telling that her eyes were swollen and her nose was red. Her cheeks were marred by tear tracks so wet they were shiny, too.

Shit.

"Okay, Curls, give it up. What's the problem?" So he was not exactly coming off like Sympathy Central. He was practically out on his feet and a weeping woman—any weeping woman—was the last thing in the world he wanted to deal with at the moment. But he was dealing, which in his opinion counted for a lot.

Her eyes narrowed at him.

"Exactly what part of *go away* did you not understand?"

Her antagonism had exactly the opposite effect to what she apparently intended. It touched him. The thing about Carly was, she was about as big as a mosquito and as girly-looking as she could be with her big blue eyes and head full of curls, but she'd always had plenty of fight. Even more than he had, she'd experienced a world full of hurt in her life, and yet here she was, still coming out swinging. He admired that in a person, male or female.

"Right now I'll take a pass on the whole concept. I want to know why you're crying, and I'm not going to go away until you tell me."

"So stand there all night and see if I care."

Matt sighed. At this rate he wasn't going to be hitting the sack anytime soon. "You know you're being childish as hell, right?"

"So what? You're being nosy as hell, so I'd say that makes us even. Anyway, it's none of your damned business why I'm crying."

"Sure it's my business. Hey, I'm practically your oldest friend." Sometimes, with women, cajolery worked. As late as it was, and as tired as he was, anything was worth a try.

"Here's a news flash for you: We're not friends. We don't even know each other anymore."

So much for cajolery. She sniffed again, as disgustingly as before. Matt mentally abandoned all hope of catching any sleep before dawn and dropped into a crouch in front of her.

"What's the matter, baby?" There was so much tenderness in his voice that it even surprised him.

She glared at him. It would have been a real good glare except her lips trembled at the same time.

"I had a bad dream, okay? It woke me up, but I'm fine now. Or at least, I would be if you'd run along and mind your own business and leave me to mind mine."

"Want to tell me about it?"

"No."

"Was it about your mother?" Her mother had been a neglectful, man-loving drunk who'd left her only child in the care of neighbors for days at a time while she went off somewhere to party. Finally, one day, she simply hadn't come back; later Carly had found out that she'd lit out for California and a new life with her latest boyfriend. After a while, when the neighbor caring for Carly realized that she'd been left holding the bag, she had called social workers to come and get the child. They did, and Carly had ended up in an institution for what the state called children in crisis. And there she had stayed until her grandmother, whom Carly had never before in her life even met, had come to fetch her away. All this Matt knew because everybody in Benton knew it. That for years afterward she'd had nightmares about her mother's abandonment of her was his own private piece of information. He knew it because Carly had told him about the nightmares herself, whimpering like a little wounded animal in his awkward and reluctant arms. In his experience, recalling her mother was the only thing that had ever made Carly cry.

"No!" There was outrage in her face now. Clearly she didn't like being reminded that he knew what pushed her buttons.

"It wasn't?"

"No! It was about the Home, okay?"

"Ah." The Home, he knew, referred to the institution where the state had parked her before her grandmother had shown up. "It must have been pretty bad, to make you cry."

"It was—horrible." Her voice trembled, and he realized that she was talking about the experience itself rather than the dream. It occurred to him that she'd never really said anything before about the time she'd spent there. She hadn't been there long—not more than a week or two, he was pretty sure. Too brief an interlude to have made much of an impression, he'd thought until now. Anyway, one of her grandmother's favorite expressions had been, no use crying over spilled milk. Carly hadn't gotten much encouragement to dwell on past hurts from that stern old woman.

"So tell me."

"I haven't even thought about it in years," she said, her voice so low and husky that he had to strain to hear. "I don't know what made me . . . Tonight, for some reason, I dreamed I was back there. There were—these old iron bunk beds that creaked every time you moved. In the dream, I heard one of them creak." She paused, took a deep breath. "I was so scared."

Her voice shook. Pressing her fist to her mouth again as though she was determined not to cry, she looked at him over it as if daring him to comment. Then all that courage was undermined by physiology as tears overflowed her eyes to gush down her cheeks.

Those tears hit him like a blow to the heart.

"Hey," he said, and stood up. She didn't even try to resist when he scooped her up as easily as if she'd still been a little girl and sat down in his chair with her on his lap. Instead, she wrapped her arms around his neck and burrowed her face into his shoulder and wept out what seemed like a whole ocean's worth of tears there in his arms. He didn't say much beyond murmuring *shh* and *it's okay* at appropriate intervals, but he held her close and listened to her largely incomprehensible murmurings and was simply there, which he had figured out by trial and error over the years was pretty much all that occasions like this called for.

Eventually she got herself all cried out. She lay limp and spent against his chest, her arms curled around his neck still but slackened off some from the stranglehold she had first put on him. Her breathing was ragged—he could feel the uneven rise and fall of her chest—but the sobs had ceased.

"Better?" He smoothed her hair away from the ear closest to his mouth. The springy curls wrapped around his fingers, cool and faintly coarse, just as they had always done whenever he'd touched them. His cheek brushed hers as he spoke. Her skin was damp. And silky soft. She smelled faintly, familiarly of Irish Spring—he realized she must have taken a shower with *his* soap—and some kind of fruity shampoo.

She nodded. He couldn't see the nod, but he felt it.

"I feel like an idiot," she said, her voice unsteady, her face still buried out of sight. "I never cry. Well, not very often."

"I know." His fingers played with her curls.

"You should have just left me alone. I would have been fine."

"I know."

"It's *you*. You're the only person I ever cry around. You bring it out in me."

"Glad to be of service."

She took a deep, ragged breath, sat up and looked at him.

"I don't believe this." She dashed tears from her cheeks with both hands.

"What?" He watched her idly. She was sitting upright on his lap now with her feet dangling a few inches above the floor and his arms looped loosely around her waist. She felt soft and warm and very female, and for some time now he had been acutely conscious of the firm curve of her butt sitting on top of his thighs. Every time she shifted positions his awareness increased. Which was not necessarily a bad thing, but it was probably something she didn't need to know.

"You. Me. This."

She made a gesture that encompassed the two of them and the chair. Then she sniffed again, and swiped the back of her hand across her nose. Matt smiled at the homely gesture, which reminded him irresistibly of the dauntless little girl she had been. Watching him, she stiffened. The look she gave him was suddenly stark with dislike.

"Asshole," she said.

Smiling had clearly been an error.

He was so tired that he felt boneless, at one with the chair, as if the slightest movement would require a major effort. His head rested back against the padded vinyl seat. His linked hands were brushing the bare part of her back, and he would have been a liar if he'd claimed not to be enjoying that slight contact with her skin. He was warm and comfortable and growing ever so slightly horny, and the woman on his lap was one that he would have been more than happy to take to bed except for the fact that she was *Carly*, and this was a mistake that he had made before.

Still, he could enjoy the view: pretty face, barely marred at all by swollen eyes, reddened nose, or even the scowl she was directing at him; narrow shoulders left almost completely naked by a pair of tiny straps that seemed to be composed, ridiculously, of a chain of crocheted daisies; soft round breasts that had improved out of all recognition since he'd last had occasion to ogle them swelling lushly against the thin, pale knit of her abbreviated top; slender, shapely midsection, lightly tanned. The rest of her he couldn't really assess, since she was covered from just below the waist by the baggy pajama pants, but then he didn't need to look to conclude that what was concealed under there was all one hundred percent prime female flesh. He remembered with more clarity than was probably good for him the smooth flatness of her belly, the slender curves of her legs, her bush with its thicket of tiny curls even tighter than the ones on her head. And her butt—he definitely remembered her butt. Cute and round and sexy as hell, even before he'd peeled away the prim white cotton grandma panties she'd been wearing under her prom dress.

His body stirred in unmistakable response. Under the circumstances, revisiting that particular memory had probably been a mistake.

"Did you hear what I said?" She was sounding good and ticked off at him now. He forced his mind off of the interesting way she was wriggling around in his lap and did his best to focus on what she was saying. "I called you an asshole."

"I heard you," he said mildly. He was really too tired to fight, and anyway she had a point. "I'm not arguing."

"*What?*"

Ah. That was more of a bounce than a wriggle, but it was damned effective.

"You're right," he clarified. "I'm an asshole."

The look she gave him should have singed his eyeballs. Wasn't that just like a woman? Agree with them, and they get madder than ever.

He remembered then that he'd always thought Carly looked really cute when she got mad.

"Do you even know what I'm talking about?" she demanded, incensed.

She was sitting still now, but in a really good spot. His hands opened and flattened across her back. Beneath them, her skin felt like warm satin. They started to slide south . . .

No. Been there, done that. Pull up; bail out; error. *Danger, Will Robinson.*

His hands clenched behind her back.

"Sure I know what you're talking about. You're still mad at me twelve years later because I busted your cherry, then didn't call you."

He said it on purpose to make her mad, partly because he wanted see if her eyes still shot sparks and her cheeks still got all rosy like he remembered, and partly aiming to rile her up enough so that she would jump off his lap and end the torture before he lost the strength to resist. Pushing her away physically would have been simpler, maybe, but he didn't think he had enough willpower left for that. No, he decided, as her muscles went so rigid he feared her now-hard little butt might be going to break something—like his most vital personal part—he definitely didn't have enough willpower left for that.

Just as he'd expected, her eyes widened and shot sparks. Her cheeks darkened as color rushed into her face. Her lips parted as she sucked air in through them. Then, without any more warning than that, she swung at him.

Tired as he was, he was just quick enough to catch her fist before it connected with his jaw. Hanging on to it, he responded reflexively to the unexpected attack. His body twisted, throwing her over his hip. Their combined momentum caused them both to slam sideways into the back of the chair. For a moment after they landed she lay still, panting, pressed right up against him, chest to chest, with her legs still draped over his but at a different angle than before and his left arm around her, pinning her so that she couldn't move, while he kept careful hold of her fist.

Their eyes met.

"Son of a bitch," she said, quivering with anger. Their faces were just inches apart. He had no trouble discerning the fury blazing in her eyes or the grim set to her lips. She wasn't struggling but she was breathing hard, from rage more than exertion, he thought. He could feel her breasts heaving against his chest, feel her softness, feel her heat. He inhaled the scent of fruit and Irish Spring, and was suddenly assaulted by a vivid mental picture of her in his shower, naked except for suds.

"Dirty rotten son of a bitch. No good dirty . . ."

Hell, she was right again. He was a son of a bitch. More of one than she had any way of knowing. Right now, despite everything, despite the deep affection he still felt for her and his clear and present memory of the debacle that had resulted the last time he'd given into his baser impulses where she was concerned and her righteous fury and his well-deserved shame, he wanted her so much that his desire was, literally, a physical ache.

"... rotten son of a bitch," she concluded, breathing fire.

"I'm sorry," he said, meaning it. The apology was long overdue, and he no longer felt like trying to provoke her. Anyway, he was experiencing a kind of sinking feeling that told him that anything he could manage in the way of making her mad enough to stomp away from him before he got too turned on to resist his baser impulses would now be pretty much a case of too little, too late. "I shouldn't have let things get out of hand like they did the night of your prom. Afterward, I shouldn't have disappeared on you. The thing was, I never expected things between us to get hot like that. We were buddies, pals. Friends. When I woke up the next morning and realized what I had done, I felt like I had betrayed your trust, and I was ashamed. So I stayed away."

As apologies went, that one was handsome, comprehensive, and had the additional virtue of being absolutely sincere. He released his grip on her fist and waited fatalistically. If she still felt like punching him out, he was prepared to take it like a man. She said nothing, just looked at him and breathed as her freed fingers flexed against his chest. But he thought some of the rigidity had left her body. He could feel the sudden pliability of her spine, the lessening of tension in her arms. And her heat. Slow rolling waves of heat.

"I was a kid," he continued, his eyes locking with hers, determined to get it all out and over with so he could get up and get the hell out of Dodge before he did anything he was pretty sure he would later regret. "A stupid kid. And that's what I acted like—a stupid kid. Forgive me. Please."

Her lashes fluttered down. Her hands slid up his chest to rest on his shoulders. Her body shifted so that she was lying full against him, chest to chest, thigh to thigh, all soft curves and dizzying heat. He could feel her heart slamming against her breastbone. He could feel her breasts pressing against his chest. He could smell Irish Spring.

This is a mistake. Get up. Get out, he told himself.

But he didn't. Instead, he tightened his hold on her waist, all too conscious that his hands were pressing into bare skin as they once again fought the urge to head south.

Her lids lifted and their gazes met.

"I—" she began. But whatever she'd meant to say was lost as she broke off abruptly to wet her lips with the tip of her tongue. Watching with fascination, he figured that the feel of his fingers slipping inside the waistband of her pants just above her butt had something to do with her loss of concentration. He had lost all control of his hands now; they were doing precisely what they wanted. He couldn't seem to find within himself the resolve necessary to even try to pull them back.

"Matt," she said, then broke off again to breathe. He knew just exactly how deep and shaky the breath she took was because he felt her breasts flattening against his chest as her rib cage expanded—and because he watched her lips open and tremble. Suddenly he was remembering just how soft those lips were, and how sweet and hot . . .

Her eyes closed; for whatever reason, her face lifted toward his. And then, God help him, he suffered another one of those brain-dead episodes of his, totally forgetting all the reasons why this was a really bad idea. Intoxicated by the improbable but potent combination of the scent of Irish Spring soap and the feel of her soft warm curves, he bent his head and kissed her.

12

TWELVE YEARS, one husband and several boyfriends later, and she was still a sucker for Matt's kisses, Carly reflected ruefully. No, face it, she was still a sucker for Matt, period. She'd been yearning and burning for him tonight as much as she ever had as a lovesick teenager with an oversized crush. More, probably. Because now she was old enough to know just exactly what she was yearning and burning for.

And he was old enough to give it to her.

Carly realized that from the moment their lips touched. His mouth did no more than sample hers at first, kissing her softly, barely there. His lips were firm, and dry, and tantalizingly gentle. He was so much bigger than she was, so much taller and broader and stronger, muscular where she was soft, firm where she was yielding. She liked the difference in their sizes, liked his easy strength, liked his muscularity. She always had.

And she liked his kisses, too.

His hands, which had been stroking her bare back just inside the waistband of her baggy pants, slid even lower, then flattened against her lower back and pulled her closer. The evidence of his desire was suddenly right there between them, unmistakably hard, impossible to miss. Her mind, which had been busy shouting out all the reasons why being like this with Matt was so wrong, went a little fuzzy. Deep inside her body, something tightened and began to throb.

It had been a long, long time since she'd felt like this.

"Say you forgive me," he whispered, his mouth scant millimeters above hers so that she could feel the warmth of his breath feathering her lips. Concentrating fiercely, she opened her eyes; she opened her mouth too, determined to say something on the order of, not in this life.

He kissed her again, soft and coaxing.

What he had learned in twelve years, she decided, willing herself not to respond and failing miserably, was the fine art of finesse. Digging her nails into his shoulders, determined not to make the final concession of sliding her arms around his neck, she surrendered to temptation and kissed him back.

Just a kiss. Only a kiss. God, he was good at this.

"Carly—" He broke contact first, lifting his mouth away. His voice was rougher, lower, thicker than before.

She forced her eyes open. His black hair was tousled, unruly, cut short like it hadn't been when they'd been kids but still long enough to succumb to its own slight tendency to wave. The Band-Aid was still there on his forehead, reminding her that things had changed, that there were burglars in Benton now and Matt, however crazy it seemed, was the sheriff and he and she were all grown up and, to all intents and purposes, strangers. But then her gaze drifted down and she discovered that he was looking at her, too. His eyes hadn't changed. They were still dark, sleepy-lidded pools promising her untold carnal delights. His mouth, long and masculine, hadn't changed either, and it had such a sensuous curve to it that it was hard for her to drag her eyes away.

Looking at him, which she had counted on to shock her

back to good sense, was unfortunately having the opposite effect, she realized. What she'd hoped would be the solution was, instead, the very core of her problem: Yes, indeed, he was still the same old Matt. But instead of thinking *no good dirty rotten son of a bitch* when she looked at him, what she thought was, *it's Matt,* almost with wonder. *It's Matt,* still handsomer than he had any right to be and still sexier than hell and still seeming to know more about how to please a woman than any man she had ever met. *It's Matt,* so achingly familiar that lying in his arms like this just somehow seemed right.

"I forgive you," she managed, caving in sheer self-defense, knowing that what she was on the verge of doing was the absolute wrong thing to do and digging deep to try to summon the strength to pull herself out of his arms before she did it. They were almost nose to nose in the big chair, lying sideways, wedged tightly together. He was holding her, his hands on her back pressing her close, but it would have been an easy hold to break. Sitting up, standing up, walking away—nothing could have been simpler.

She couldn't do it, she realized glumly. Soon, maybe, but not—quite—yet.

"Ah," he said, and smiled at her. Watching the slow curve of his lips, Carly felt her blood heat. She inhaled, met his gaze. His eyes flared, and he kissed her again, still soft, still gentle, but so thoroughly that she was dazzled. Dimly she realized that his restraint was probably deliberate, that she was being tantalized right past the roadblocks her good judgment would normally throw in his way, but by then she simply didn't care. The stubble on his jaw felt rawly masculine as it brushed against her cheeks and chin. His body against hers felt firm and hot and unmistakably masculine too. And good—he felt so good. She quivered a little at the sheer goodness of it.

He must have felt the tiny tremor that went through her limbs, because all of a sudden he stiffened and his breath seemed to catch. Then, without any more warning than that, he was kissing her like she wanted to be kissed, like she needed to be kissed, like she had dreamed of being kissed over years of lonely nights. His tongue invaded her mouth, hot and wet and hungry, filling it, moving against hers, stroking the roof of her mouth and the inside of her cheeks and lips, provoking a mind-blowing response. The heat that was already smoldering inside her blazed up like grease on a griddle. Sliding her arms around his neck, she closed her eyes and curled her toes and kissed him back and *enjoyed,* promising herself that she would call a halt right—after—this.

But then his hands moved again, sliding right on down inside her pants until his fingertips reached the first gentle upward curve of her cheeks. There they stopped.

Oh, God. Her heart pounded. Her breathing suspended. Her nether regions, already well aware of what was going on, segued in an instant from a pleasant throbbing into a full-blown, gotta-have-it kind of quake. His hands were long-fingered, broad-palmed, strong, searing their imprint into her flesh. *She wanted them cupping her butt.* She wanted it so badly that it was all she could do not to reach around and guide them to the right place. Tightening her arms around his neck, she kissed him with feverish intensity, moving against him, rocking with new-found abandon against the swollen hardness at the front of his jeans.

He lifted his head, breaking the kiss. Feeling almost drugged by desire, Carly opened her eyes to discover that he was watching her. He was breathing heavily, his eyes were hot, his chest heaved against her breasts, and his arms as they curved around her had grown hard. His entire body seemed to pulse with a kind of hungry urgency that left her in no doubt about just how aroused he was.

"Probably this isn't such a good idea," he said. His voice was hoarse, raspy. Despite his words his eyes blazed at her, and he showed no inclination to let her go.

Just looking at him looking at her like that got her so turned on that she had to take a breath before she could talk.

"Probably not."

"We should just—" He broke off as his arms tightened, pulling her closer yet in a silent contradiction of his words.

She tried not to pant. "Yes, we should."

Even before she finished speaking, his hands were on the move again, sliding down over her butt cheeks at last. Carly gasped, trembling with pleasure. The hot abrasion of those long-fingered hands molding her curves sent pure fire licking out along her nerve endings and reduced her bones to Jell-O.

"Oh, God, Matt." It was all she could do not to come right there and then from the sheer intensity of the sensations that were rocketing through her. But she fought the good fight, holding off, not wanting the most mind-blowing Big O that had hovered on her horizon in years to be over with so soon. Beneath her passion-weighted lids she saw that he was watching her with eyes that suddenly glittered. She remembered that he'd always had a pretty good idea about what was running through her mind. At the idea that he knew exactly just how turned on she was, she felt a thrill shoot clear down to her toes.

"You're not wearing panties," he said. It didn't sound like his voice at all.

Carly breathed. She was too far gone now to talk, to explain that she never wore panties with pajamas. She just shook her head.

His jaw tightened, and his hands tightened too, gripping a smooth, round cheek in each one as he pulled her slowly and deliberately up against him.

Carly gasped and trembled and closed her eyes. She was on fire, weak with need, burning up with it. Every last scrap of reason she possessed was lost, blocked out by a tsunami of good, old-fashioned lust. Tightening her arms around his neck, she lifted her face and met his mouth as it descended and kissed him as if she'd die if she didn't.

He kissed her senseless, kissed her until her muscles dissolved and her head was whirling and her body was flaming and throbbing and absolutely his for the taking. Then all of a sudden he stopped kissing her, for no earthly reason that she could fathom, just pulled his mouth away from hers and lifted his head. His hands let go of her butt and slid out of her pants and his arms, which had been hard and tight around her, loosened so that they no longer even seemed to be holding her.

Bereft, bewildered, and breathless, Carly opened her eyes to see what he was doing. It took a moment—she was so turned on it was hard to focus—but she saw that he was looking down at their entwined bodies with a frown. She followed suit, and discovered that his hands were on the outside of her pants now, tugging at them, trying to pull them off, wanting to make her naked. She wanted that too, she realized with a swift upsurge of heat, wanted to be naked with him, wanted him naked and on her and in her. . . .

Their eyes met as she reached down to help. His were narrow and as black and glittery as onyx. He was breathing like he'd run for miles, and his face was dark with passion. Just looking at him like that made her melt, made her want him more than she had ever wanted anything in her life. He must have seen something of what she was feeling in her expression because even as she fumbled between them he shifted positions, moving her with him, lifting her on top of him, yanking urgently at her pants. Thrown off balance, she slithered down his other side. He grabbed at her to steady her and then somehow, just like that, they rolled out of the chair and crashed down onto the floor.

It wasn't much of a fall, and she landed on top of him, no harm done. Still, it was slightly disorienting to say the least, and it took her a minute to recover and get her bearings. When she did, she lifted her head and looked at him. He lay flat on his back on the carpet with her sprawled chest-down on top of him, her chin at the approximate level of his breastbone, his hands resting on her waist. His eyes were open, too, she discovered. He was looking at her and breathing hard, but he made no effort to take up where they had left off.

"It's a drawstring," Carly murmured helpfully as she wriggled up his body, glad to have suddenly recollected the underlying cause of the fall. His hands moved then, closing over her hipbones, hard and purposeful as he arrested her upward journey. When he didn't answer but continued to look at her with what she assumed was passion- or fall-induced incomprehension, she elucidated. "My pants. They're tied with a drawstring. You just need to untie them and—"

She broke off as he frowned, clearly still not back with the program, and reached down to untie the drawstring herself on the theory that just doing it was worth a thousand words. Besides, the idea of kicking off her pants and lying on top of him naked from the waist down while he was still fully dressed was kind of exciting. In fact, as she considered it she discovered that it excited her more than any erotic thought she'd had in years. She would—

"Wait. Stop. No." His protest was slightly disjointed but

forceful. He caught her hands even as they found the draw-string, imprisoning them in his, holding them immobile. Carly looked at him in surprise. He met her gaze. His eyes were dark with passion. His face was flushed with it. His hands tightened on hers—and then he rolled with her so that all of a sudden she was no longer lying on top of him. She was sliding—and then she was on the rug, lying on her side facing him, close still but with their linked hands the only points of actual contact.

Carly had a funny feeling that this might not be a pre-lude to some sexy new position.

"Matt?"

To her dismay she discovered that he was grimacing. His brows met over his nose in a pained-looking frown, and his lips were drawn back to reveal clenched teeth.

"We're not doing this," he said after a second, sounding strained but also sounding as if he really, truly meant it. "We—are—not—doing—this."

With that he let go of her hands, jackknifed into a sitting position and got to his feet. Too surprised to even try to stop him, Carly sat up, gaping at him, her hands resting on the smooth flat wool on either side of her thighs, her legs stretched straight out in front of her.

"Matt . . ." She had to look a long way up to meet his gaze. He moved restlessly, as if her uncomprehending re-gard made him uncomfortable, then jammed his hands into his pockets and took a step backward.

"Look, we already made this mistake once." His expres-sion as he looked at her was as wary as if he'd suddenly dis-covered that she was stuffed full of explosives. Disbelieving, she realized that he was continuing to back away. "We're not making it again. We're friends, Curls. *Friends.* This isn't us."

"What?" She still didn't understand.

"Hell, you've been mad at me for twelve years over the

last time." Talking faster now, he reached the door and felt behind him for the knob. "I care too much about you for this. There are lots of girls I can fuck. You're my only girl *friend.*"

"*What?*" Now she understood. He was leaving her high and dry, the no good dirty rotten son of a bitch.

"I want to keep it like that," he said, opening the door. "You will too, once you think about it." Then, backing out into the cave-dark hall, he tacked on a soft, "Later," and closed the door in the teeth of her sputters.

Just like that. *Click.* No more Matt.

Carly couldn't believe it. He was gone, leaving her all on her lonesome in his dark bedroom, sitting stunned in the middle of his ugly beige carpet, her body still throbbing with need, her cat peering out at her from under the bed. It took several minutes for the shock to subside enough so that she could even start to get mad.

13

By the time Carly headed downstairs the next morning, mad didn't even begin to cover how she felt. The good news was, being dumped like that had almost completely erased from her mind the night's assorted other traumas. The bad news was, she was so furious at Matt that she had spent the rest of the night fuming instead of sleeping. It didn't help that poor shell-shocked Hugo had persisted in curling up right on top of her every time she'd stretched out on the bed, seeking to soothe his inner kitten by kneading her with needle-sharp claws whenever she was just about to nod off. It also didn't help that her clueless body still tingled and throbbed, hankering after Matt. To make matters worse, she was almost as mad at herself as she was at Matt. She'd *known* he was a handsome skunk, a sexy jackass, a no good dirty rotten son of a bitch. What had she been thinking?

The depressing, embarrassing, infuriating answer was that she hadn't been thinking at all. She'd been too busy feeling. Which was, she supposed, the all-too-predictable result of letting herself get into a state where she was practically re-virginized again.

Along about eight A.M., when she'd all but given up trying to get any more sleep, it occurred to her that she was in

Matt's house. It stood to reason that she could therefore expect to see Matt when she went downstairs. At first the idea horrified her. Her bottom line was, she never wanted to see the no good dirty rotten son of a bitch again as long as she lived. But the more she thought about it, the more she decided that that was a crock. Never again was she going to simply stew in silence while catching occasional distant glimpses of the object of her ire. Oh, no. That was a different Carly. This Carly, this new mad-as-hell, not-going-to-take-it-anymore Carly, was going in a whole nother direction. She was going to be up front, in your face, visibly, verbally, violently mad.

And she could already tell that it was going to feel good.

Still, looking in the mirror as she painstakingly blow-dried her hair straight again, she experienced a moment when the new Carly almost wimped out on her. Discovering that she looked like hell was definitely *not* a confidence booster. The new Carly she saw in her head was prettier, younger, sexier-looking than the woman in the mirror. It took her a while to argue herself around to believing that the new Carly was about how she felt inside, and not about how she looked, but she did it. Finally she accepted the slightly depressing truth: This was how the new Carly looked, same as how the old Carly looked, especially when she'd had a total of about three hours of sleep. As always, lack of sleep gave her dark circles and bloodshot eyes and dull skin, to say nothing of an extra dollop of crankiness. But the crankiness might pay off, especially today, when she was hoping to be at her new Carly best while she had one final conversation with Matt, which she planned to begin by suggesting he go do unmentionable things to himself and end by ordering him to stay the hell away from her because she never wanted to see him again as long as she lived.

If he wanted *friends,* he could watch TV.

On that bright note, she headed downstairs. Descending with head held high and one hand carefully clutching the rail—no point in taking a chance on ruining the cool, confident, and in-control image she was trying to project by tumbling head over heels down the stairs—she scanned the living room for her quarry. No luck. The room was empty. Her shoulders slumped—she'd been psyched for the kill—but then she bucked herself up and headed for the kitchen, which she could tell from the chattering voices and breakfasty smells was where a significant number of the occupants of the house had gathered. The prospect of telling Matt where to go in front of an audience was tempting—the old Carly would never have done that—but then, she really didn't want anybody except herself and Matt to know just why she wanted him to take a long walk on a short pier. Therefore, her best course of action would be to ask him if she might, please, have a word with him in private.

Pinning a pleasant smile on her carefully glossed lips in anticipation of making just that request as soon as she set eyes on him, clamping firmly down on the vain wish that she had packed something with a little more of a va-va-voom quotient than white capris and an orange tee shirt with a pair of big red kissy lips on the front, Carly walked into the kitchen.

A cheerful mix of sounds greeted her that included water bubbling on the stove and cutlery clanking against dishes and people talking a mile a minute. The smell of breakfast—pancakes and syrup, eggs, bacon, coffee—filled the air. Ordinarily it would have made her stomach rumble. This morning it left her unmoved. She was, she realized, too keyed up at the prospect of finally facing Matt down to feel the least bit hungry.

The room was positively packed with people, she saw as

she hesitated on the threshold, glancing around for him. Which was, she decided after an instant's consideration, probably a good thing. At least they could have some privacy elsewhere in the house while she bade Matt a not-so-sweet farewell.

Sandra was at the stove with her back to the door, wearing black pants and a tunic-length black tee shirt, looking comfortable as a duck in water as she stirred a spoon around in a steaming pot, with nary a sign of the previous night's bad attitude to be seen. Lissa, wearing a bright green sundress with her long hair streaming over one shoulder, was hanging over the back of a wooden chair in which sat another girl who looked so much like her that she had to be another of Matt's sisters. This girl, who was perhaps a little taller and slimmer than Lissa, had her black hair styled in a smooth shoulder-length bob and was wearing a black knit top. She was frowning over what appeared to be a book of material swatches that was spread open on the big round kitchen table in front of her. Seated beside her and pointing to a particular swatch was a woman of about Carly's age in a sleeveless white silk blouse and pearls, with carefully upswept honey-blond hair, delicate, slightly sharp features and a slim build. Next to her was a man in a white shirt and a red tie with features and coloring so similar to hers that they almost had to be related. Rounding out the table were a couple of Matt's uniformed deputies—big, burly Antonio from last night, who was digging into a plate of pancakes with gusto, and another, much younger man with a bristly russet-colored buzz cut who appeared to be finished and was pushing his empty plate away. A third girl with short black hair—undoubtedly Matt's final sister— was just turning away from the refrigerator, a carton of orange juice in her hand. She was wearing a knee-skimming turquoise shift.

It struck Carly that it was Sunday morning, and Sunday mornings in Benton, at least in her experience, meant church. Everyone except the deputies seemed dressed to attend. A pang of residual guilt reminded her that Sunday mornings in Benton had once meant church for her, too. Her grandmother, a pillar of the First Baptist Church of Benton, had never permitted her to miss a single Sunday unless she was really, truly (as in running a high temperature) ill. Since leaving for college, she had gotten out of the habit, and the only times she and John had gone inside a church had been to attend weddings and funerals.

She was all grown up now, she reminded the shadow of her younger self who still lurked uneasily inside. She might have come home to Benton, but that didn't mean she had to totally revert. She could still do any damned thing she wanted to do.

Like not go to church. Today, at least. Darn it all, her clothes weren't even unpacked, and she just had too much to do.

As she continued to look around, she was forced to conclude that her first impression had been right on target: Matt was not in the room.

"This is the best darned breakfast I've had in years," Antonio said to Sandra, popping a forkful of pancakes into his mouth and chewing happily.

"No way am I wearing a bubblegum pink bridesmaid's dress," the girl with the black bob said with revulsion. "The dress I tried on was dark green."

"I wouldn't call it *bubblegum*." The blond woman sounded slightly affronted. "And dark green's more suited to fall than summer. It's the same dress, just a more summery color."

"Hey, Dani, why not give it a chance? Maybe bubblegum pink's your color," Lissa put in with a grin.

Dani—Carly remembered she was Matt's middle sister—scowled up at Lissa. "You're going to be wearing it too."

"Thanks for the breakfast, Miss Kaminski. It sure was good," the second deputy said, chugging along on the original conversational track.

"Sandra," Sandra said to him. Then, to Antonio in a honeyed tone, "Would you like another egg? Or some more pancakes?"

Carly's antennae went up. Sounded like Sandra had Antonio in her sights. If so, talking her out of heading home to Chicago might be less of a battle than Carly had been prepared to wage. Which was good news for the success of their bed-and-breakfast, but probably bad news for Antonio's waistline. Those whom Sandra cared about, she fed.

"Can't do it," Antonio replied, patting his stomach and looking regretful. "It's going to be all I can do to finish this. I sure would like to, though."

"What, are you finally getting full?" the other deputy asked. "I don't believe it."

"Shut your trap, Toler," Antonio said, scowling at him. "Or next time I'll let *you* run the raccoon out of Miz Nichols's attic."

"Erin, could I get some more juice here?" the blond woman's male clone asked.

"Sure, honey." The girl with short black hair smiled and crossed to his side, carton in hand. Erin was the oldest of Matt's three sisters. Carly sort of recognized her now, although the petitely pretty woman in front of her certainly looked different from the dirty-faced, smart-mouthed little girl she vaguely remembered.

"Weren't you planning to match the men's ties and cummerbunds to the bridesmaids' dresses?" Lissa asked, looking at Erin.

"That's usually how it's done," the blond woman answered before Erin, who was busy pouring juice, could reply.

Lissa and Dani exchanged looks.

"Matt is going to look *so* fantastic in bubblegum pink," Lissa said solemnly, and the two of them burst out laughing.

"Hey, Collin's wearing it too," Erin said, shooting her sister a reproving look.

"Collin would," the second deputy muttered. He probably meant the sour-toned observation to go unheard, but he'd spoken into a lull in the conversation. All eyes swung to him—and in the process Carly was discovered standing just inside the doorway.

"Oh, hi." It was Lissa who spotted her. She grinned, her eyes sparkling wickedly. "Want some breakfast?"

It was now all eyes on Carly.

"Uh, no thanks," Carly said, feeling suddenly awkward. Matt was clearly nowhere in the vicinity, and the rest of these people, with the exception of Sandra of course, were virtual strangers. For her part, Sandra waved her spoon vaguely in greeting, then turned back to her cooking. Reminding herself of her mission, Carly moved on into the room and added in a more purposeful tone, "Is Matt around?"

"No, and he probably won't be until sometime tonight," Erin said, making no bones about looking her up and down. At the news, Carly felt both relieved and let down. Her inner No More Ms. Nice Girl had been ready, willing, and able, but she wasn't all that sorry to be put on hold, either. Carly had never been confrontational by nature, and she was discovering that girding herself up for battle and then staying in attack mode until the enemy could be located required a lot more psychic energy than she would have thought. "He went into work early."

"Yeah, real early. Like around five A.M. He was on his way

out when I was coming in," Dani said with a grimace. "He was in a lousy mood, too."

There, at least, was some good news, Carly thought.

Having finished checking out the newcomer, Dani exchanged a significant look with Lissa.

"If you were just coming in at five in the morning, I can see why. Five in the morning's no time for a young girl to be getting home," Antonio said, pointing his fork censoriously at Dani, who made a face at him.

"Hey, I did better than Erin. She didn't come home at all. At least, not until just about an hour ago, and then only because she had to get dressed for church," Dani said.

Erin looked self-conscious. The two younger men at the table looked less than happy at the revelation. The blond one shot Dani a dirty look. The red-haired deputy glared at Erin. Watching, Carly thought, *uh-oh, something's up.* But, thankfully, if there was a problem, it wasn't hers to solve.

"Shut up, Dani," Erin said, glaring at her sister.

The blond woman, meanwhile, was looking hard at Carly, who felt her gaze and glanced over to meet it.

"I know you," the blond woman said suddenly. Carly realized that she was right. The reason she realized this was because, now that she took a good close look at the blonde, she recognized her too.

"You're Carly Linton," the other woman said.

"And you're Shelby Holcomb," Carly replied.

Shelby had been two years ahead of her in school. Head cheerleader. Homecoming queen. Voted Most Popular Girl. Perfect hair. Perfect clothes. Perfect teeth. Studious, curly-haired little Carly hadn't even been on her radar screen. The only reason Carly knew who Shelby was, as someone other than one of those high school superstars the rank-and-file students could only watch with envy from a distance, was because Shelby had had a huge thing for Matt.

The year Carly had been a freshman, Shelby had been a junior and Matt had been a senior; Shelby had chased Matt relentlessly. Probably the only thing that had kept her from catching him had been Elise Knox.

Carly had never, ever thought that she might feel grateful to Elise Knox, but now, suddenly, she did. At least Matt's involvement with Elise had kept him out of Shelby's hands.

But Elise was no longer in the picture to run interference, and Shelby had obviously caught Matt at last. Because here she was early on a Sunday morning in Matt's house, eating breakfast at Matt's table, on the most informal of terms with Matt's sisters. Last night Lissa had said that Matt never brought girls home, and Shelby was going to die because he had. Carly hadn't realized that Lissa was talking about *this* Shelby, Miss Queen of Everything.

If, in Matt's immortal words, Carly was his only girl *friend*, then Shelby was obviously one of the girls—or *the* girl—he fucked.

The realization burst upon her like an exploding firework lighting up an inky night sky.

Carly's first instinctive thought was, *I'll kill him.*

It made her beyond furious to think that Matt had been cheating on her with Shelby. Then she realized: no, wait, it was the other way around. Appalled, Carly faced the hideous truth: she had only reentered the picture last night. If Matt belonged to Shelby now, then Matt had been cheating on Shelby with *her.*

I'll kill him, Carly thought again. *I am going to kill him.*

That she'd already pretty much intended to do that was beside the point. Now that the true extent of his perfidy had become clear, she felt like killing him *twice.*

"How long are you back in town for?" Shelby asked, looking her over with the slightest of frowns.

"Permanently, I hope." Carly managed a small, polite (she hoped) smile.

"We're opening a bed-and-breakfast," Sandra piped up. This evidence that Sandra had apparently abandoned her intention to run back to Chicago should have cheered Carly up. It didn't. The way she felt at the moment, nothing short of Matt's disembowelment in front of her eyes could make her feel chipper.

"You can count me in for the breakfast part," Antonio said, putting down his fork at last. Sandra beamed at him.

"Oops, I guess we forgot about introductions," Lissa said to Carly. The teenager was looking pleased about something, but Carly had a sneaking suspicion that she was better off not knowing what that something was. "Since you know Shelby, and you know us, then that just leaves Matt's deputies, Antonio Johnson and Mike Toler, and Shelby's brother Collin, who's also Erin's fiancé—oh, I guess if you know Shelby, you probably know Collin too."

"I met Antonio last night," Carly said, not mentioning that Antonio had practically scared her to death. Antonio nodded at her. With his contented expression and bulging stomach, today he looked about as scary as Santa Claus. Carly smiled at Mike Toler, who murmured *Pleased to meet you.* Then she said to Collin, "I *think* I remember you."

"Don't feel bad if you don't," Collin said. "I'm seven years younger than Shelby, actually, so . . ."

"If we're going to make it to church on time, we'd better be on our way," Shelby trilled, shooting her brother a silencing look as she got to her feet. Interpreting that look to mean that Shelby didn't care to have everyone reminded of her age, and remembering that she herself was two years younger than Shelby, Carly smiled. It was good to know that there was at least one area in which she had Miss Queen of Everything bested.

There was a chorus of agreement to Shelby's reminder. Suddenly everyone was standing, moving about, bustling as they got ready to leave. In the midst of the quick kitchen cleanup that ensued, Carly noted that Shelby was tall and thin, even thinner than she'd been in high school, and elegant in the simple black skirt and heels she'd paired with her white blouse. This eliminated any last lingering remnant of her earlier spurt of pleasure at her own two-year age advantage. In fact, she found it more than mildly annoying, although she refused to acknowledge the feeling even to herself. After all, she told herself, if Matt chose to keep company with a tall, thin woman who looked like she'd cornered the market on hair spray, it was certainly no concern of hers.

To know that her own small and curvy self had about as much chance of looking elegant on a typical day as Hugo did of sprouting wings and flying did not, however, make Carly feel any less annoyed. By the time she schlepped down the stairs with Hugo tucked under one arm and her heavy-as-lead bag practically dragging the floor in her other hand, her annoyance had grown too pronounced to deny. She was many things, she was forced to acknowledge, but elegant wasn't one of them.

Elegant was Shelby.

The thought irritated her so much that it was all she could do to wave a polite good-bye as, after clambering less than gracefully into the driver's seat of the U-Haul, blocking Hugo's attempted panicked exit with a (loving) swat, and waiting with a fixed smile and sweat pouring down her face while Sandra finished a low-voiced conversation with Antonio through the window, she finally was able to start the damned truck and back down the driveway. It didn't help at all that, while she was waving cheerily at the three lissome and lovely Converse sisters, chic Shelby and her handsome brother as the quintet piled into an imposing black sedan, she cut her exit from the driveway too close and clipped Matt's mailbox.

All right, she didn't clip it, she knocked it down.

"Christ," Sandra said as the metal cylinder scraped noisily along the side of the truck before the wooden pole it was mounted on surrendered to *force majeure* with a dismal crack and toppled to the ground. "You can't drive."

"Well, neither can you," Carly snapped, relieved to no longer have to pretend that everything in her life was just all hunky-dory. "And you can just keep quiet about the mailbox, okay?"

A quick glance in her side and rearview mirrors told Carly that neither the church party in the black sedan, which had pulled out and was heading down the street, or the two deputies, who'd insisted on accompanying them back to Carly's grandmother's house and were waiting ahead of them in their official sheriff's department car, had seen her little oopsy because the U-Haul's bulk was blocking their view of it. Had the mailbox belonged to anyone but Matt, Carly would have gone looking for the homeowner to confess all and offer to pay for the mailbox's repair. At the very least, she would have left a note with her name and address. Since the mailbox was Matt's, she didn't do either of those things. Instead, as she pulled on down the street leaving the broken mailbox in her wake, she decided that if she'd had two free hands she would have given herself a high five.

14

"I THINK THAT'S CALLED leaving the scene of an accident," Sandra said uneasily. "And that's the *sheriff's* mailbox, too. Killing the sheriff's mailbox like that and then just driving away is probably a bad thing."

"Screw the sheriff," Carly said, continuing to drive away.

"Woo-ee, did somebody get up on the wrong side of the bed this morning or what?" Sandra gave her a sideways look. "Or does somebody have the hots for that hunky sheriff?"

The fact that Sandra then had to grab on to the overhead strap as the truck bounced and jounced out of the subdivision and onto the main road at about twice the speed it should have was purely coincidental. It in no way reflected Carly's reaction to the question.

"I thought you were heading back to Chicago this morning. What happened to, *I don't do spooky old houses* and *forget Nowheresville, U.S.A.?*" Carly's voice held more than a suggestion of bite.

"I decided to give Benton one more chance." Sandra's expression was innocent. Her tone was demure. And Carly believed her like she believed Publishers' Clearinghouse was going to show up on her doorstep with her big sweepstakes win the next time they came through town.

Carly snorted. "Or could it be that somebody has the hots for that *hunky* deputy?"

With Sandra hanging on to the strap and Hugo hunkered down behind Carly's head, his claws digging into the vinyl for all he was worth, Carly sent the U-Haul careening into Benton's small downtown, which, luckily for all concerned, was deserted, with everybody either being at church or pretending to be at church.

Instead of getting annoyed in turn, Sandra grinned. "You mean *hungry* deputy, don't you? Hey, I'm not proud. We each got to go with what works. You chase after the hunky ones, I'll chase after the hungry ones, and maybe we'll both bag somebody."

"I don't want to *bag* anybody."

"Well, I do. Whoa, can anybody say *stop?*"

The warning was unnecessary. Carly was already stomping on the brake. She would have done it sooner, but she had only realized that Benton had added a new stoplight at the last minute, and then only because the deputies' car was sitting beneath it, waiting in blissful ignorance of what was speeding up behind it.

"Are you in bad mood or what?" Sandra's eyes widened with alarm as the U-Haul plowed to a quivering halt just inches from the car's bumper. "You know, there's not any traffic, and it's not raining, and it's not dark. Maybe I should drive."

"Next time I have a death wish I'll think about letting you. And I am not in a bad mood. I'm just really, really ready to get out of this damned truck."

It wasn't even a lie. With the air conditioner broken and the bright sunlight pouring in, it was swelteringly hot in the cab. Unable to open the windows more than a few inches because of Hugo's clear intention to exit the truck at the first opportunity, Carly was already sweating like an ice cube in July. It didn't help that Hugo, unhappy and agitated and *shedding,* kept swiping his hairy tail across her damp face.

"I hear you."

The light changed, and the deputies' car proceeded on-ward as if it had no clue that only minutes ago disaster had stopped inches short of its back bumper. It took Carly a beat or so to follow suit.

"You know, that cat sheds. You don't think . . ." Sandra said as the U-Haul bounced through the green light and picked up speed again.

"No." Carly cut her off before she could finish. They'd had this discussion before, when they'd been making their plans for the bed-and-breakfast. Sandra had an aversion to cats. Carly had a cat. On that point, Carly wasn't giving an inch. Sandra just had to deal.

"Fine. But just so you know, you're the one who's going to be doing the vacuuming."

"Fine."

The First Baptist Church was coming up on the left. It was a small brick building with a tall steeple and a parking lot large enough to accommodate most sports stadiums. The parking lot was full. As Carly passed it, she had a sudden mental vision of little devils coming after her with pitchforks because she wasn't inside. She stepped on the gas.

"You ever want to get married again, that cat might be a problem. A lot of men don't like cats."

"Too bad. The way I feel about it is, love me, love my cat." Carly paused to bat Hugo's tail away from her lips. "Anyway, I don't want to get married again. Ever. Been there, done that."

"Yeah."

Sandra's gloomy agreement stemmed from her own late, unlamented marriage, Carly knew. Sandra had been Carly's first hire when she'd opened the Treehouse four years before. Thirty-two at the time, in the process of getting a divorce, Sandra had been bad-humored, beaten down, and broke. Carly had hired her to wait tables. Sandra had been the waitress from hell, prone to such public-relations no-no's as telling a customer who complained about a sauce smelling a little off that the only thing that smelled *off* in the Treehouse was him, and if he left and went home and took a shower, then nothing would smell *off.* Carly had been on the verge of firing her when her ruinously expensive, cordon bleu–trained chef threw a hissy fit in the kitchen one hectic Saturday night and walked out. Doing her best to rally the remainder of the kitchen staff, all of whom had seemed to be in various stages of meltdown too, Carly had been frantically trying to fill the remaining orders when Sandra, repulsed by a plate of Stroganoff that she said looked like dog barf, had thrown down her pad and pencil, elbowed the overwhelmed *sous*-chef aside, and proceeded to cook like an angel from heaven. Openmouthed, Carly had observed plate after plate of scrumptious food served up to table after table of satisfied diners, and had realized that she was in the presence of a true culinary genius. At the end of the evening, she'd put Sandra in charge of the kitchen. Since then, she'd nursed Sandra through a divorce, Sandra had nursed her through a divorce, they'd operated a restaurant together, lost their livelihoods together, and set their feet on a whole new path together. Two days ago, Carly had moved out of the dumpy little apartment she'd moved into when her plush condominium had been sold out from under her as a result of the divorce, Sandra had moved out of the dumpy little house she'd been sharing with an aunt and a cousin for the last three years, and, along with Hugo and all their worldly goods, they'd loaded up the U-Haul and headed for Benton, Georgia.

Now Carly was getting the feeling that they were going

to rival Oscar and Felix in the I-love-my-roommate department.

Sandra continued after a moment's rumination, "Okay, so maybe we don't want to get married. That doesn't mean we have to swear off men. Men are fun. At least, they're more fun than vibrators."

"Says who?"

"You ever have a vibrator give you a present? Or massage your feet? Anyway, don't tell me you wouldn't like to play patty-cake with that sheriff. I saw the way you were looking at him."

"Damn it, Sandra—" Realizing that outright denial would be useless, Carly took a deep breath and opted for semi-truth. "All right, so he's cute. So I noticed. So what? In his case, looks are deceiving. Believe me, I know."

"Whatever." Clearly unconvinced, Sandra grabbed hold of the strap again as the U-Haul rocked around a bend. "Anyway, as far as I'm concerned, men are like shoes. It's not all that easy to find a good fit. When you do, I say, grab 'em quick before somebody else does."

"Good philosophy." If men were shoes, then Matt was a pair of six-inch stilettos, great-looking and sexy as all get-out but murder on the feet. Not that Matt had come to mind because she was thinking about him as a possible good fit, because she wasn't. Ever again.

"Now, Antonio, he's a Leo. I asked him. Pisces and Leo together—that combination's supposed to generate sparks. I don't know about you, but I could sure use some sparks." Sandra glanced sideways at Carly. "You know the sheriff's birthday?"

Of course Carly did. November 16. For years, what present to get him had been one of the major concerns of her life.

"Nope," she said. "By the way, while you were asking

Antonio his birth date, did you by any chance bother to ask him if he was married?"

Sandra's jaw dropped. "I forgot to ask him that. I can't believe I forgot to ask him that."

"Great. Nice sense of priorities."

The U-Haul made it around another bend, and all of a sudden, up there on the hill to her right, was her grand-mother's house—no, *her* house; Carly could see she was going to have trouble remembering that. With the brilliant sunshine banishing all but the most inviting of shadows, the big white house in its setting of leafy old trees looked picturesque and homey rather than spooky. Carly had a troubling moment as she remembered the burglar and how frightened she had actually been the previous night, but then she saw the deputies' car pulling over at the base of the hill and reminded herself that Matt and his department had investigated and apparently had found nothing particularly alarming to report. Whatever faults he might have, and she wasn't even going to go there because if she did she'd be there for the rest of the day and on into the night, Matt would let her know in a heartbeat if he thought there was any reason at all why she wouldn't be safe in the house. As things stood, she certainly wasn't going to let having been the victim of a garden-variety break-in stand in the way of her and her new life.

As she pulled in behind the car, the deputies got out and started walking toward the U-Haul. Broad as the back side of a barn, dark-skinned and blunt-featured, Antonio was squinting at the truck as if something pained him. Mike had one hand raised to keep the sun out of his eyes. Well-built and actually quite handsome aside from the awful russet crew cut, Mike was staring at the truck too.

"Is it just my imagination, or do they not look too happy?" Carly asked, shifting into park.

"Maybe they know about the mailbox." Sandra sounded uneasy as she watched them approach.

"How could they—" Carly began, only to break off with a yelp as Sandra opened the door. But it was too late. Glimpsing freedom, Hugo went for it, streaking for blue skies with the deadly accuracy of a missile.

Carly grabbed for him, missed, and slumped in defeat.

"Sorry," Sandra said, grimacing apologetically as she got out of the truck.

Carly straightened and took a deep breath. "No big deal."

As long as there was no demon dog to give chase, Hugo would probably be fine.

"Was that that cat?" Mike asked in a tone of deep foreboding.

"Yep," Sandra said, rolling her eyes.

"Oh, man, I remember that thing." Mike started to grin. "You should have seen Matt—"

He broke off abruptly as Antonio elbowed him in the side. Clutching his ribs, he cast Antonio a reproachful look. Then his grin came back.

"You want us to try to catch it?" Antonio asked, looking in at Carly. Mike's grin vanished. The expression that took its place was pure alarm. Although why that should be so, Carly had no clue.

She sighed. "No, he should be fine."

After all, Hugo was in much the same boat as she was herself, Carly thought. Life as he had known it before was over. He was going to have to adapt to this new one as best he could.

"Just so you know, there's a speed limit of twenty-five going through town," Antonio said, his tone carefully neutral now. "We figured you didn't see the signs."

Sandra made an indecipherable sound.

"No, I didn't." Carly was being perfectly truthful. One unfortunate side effect of complete and utter aggravation was that it had a tendency to blind one to little things like road signs, as she had just discovered.

Antonio nodded and switched his attention to Sandra. Carly slid out of the truck.

Running her fingers through her hair, lifting the clingy little tendrils up off her face and neck for a moment in the hope that it might make her feel cooler, Carly walked around the front of the cab. She couldn't help but look for Hugo. He was nowhere in sight. This time yesterday that would have made her anxious; she was still anxious, she realized, but also resigned. She and Hugo had been thrown into the deep end; now it was time to see if they could swim. Although the drastic alteration in their circumstances certainly wasn't anything she would have wished for, the change was probably going to be good for both of them. If nothing else, it was sure to be one of those growth experiences they were always talking about on the TV talk shows she'd had way too much time to watch since the Treehouse had closed down.

Grimacing, Carly allowed herself a little personal pity time to acknowledge that she missed her restaurant, she missed her condominium, she missed her car, and she really missed her bank accounts. But as she thought about it she realized with some surprise that she didn't miss John, or their life together. Not one bit. With the clarity of hindsight, she saw that her life with John had at its center boiled down to the two of them endlessly striving to get ahead. It had been all about achieving security, success, and status rather than love or any real sense of being a couple, of belonging together. Her life without him? She lifted her chin and straightened her spine as she made a promise to herself: her life without him was going to be about being the person she had always wanted to be.

The possibilities suddenly seemed endless, and fascinating.

Carly rounded the cab just in time to hear Sandra say to the men, "That sure is nice of you. How about you bring your wives around to dinner sometime this week as a sort of thank-you?"

Listening to Sandra's uncharacteristically molasses-coated tone, it was all Carly could do not to roll her eyes.

"I'm not married," Mike said. "But I could sure do with dinner."

"Me neither," Antonio said. "I mean, me too. I mean, I'm a widower, but I'd sure appreciate coming to dinner. You sure are one fine cook."

"Thank you." Sandra beamed at him, and flashed Carly, who'd just walked up beside her, a glinting look that was the eye-contact equivalent of a thumbs-up. Carly had to hand it to Sandra; she knew what she wanted, and she was going after it.

"These nice men," Sandra said to her, all but batting her lashes at Antonio, "are going to help us unload the truck."

"That *is* nice," Carly said, then glanced from one to the other of the deputies. "But should you? I mean, I don't want you to get into trouble. If you're supposed to be working . . ."

Her voice trailed off. Not that their help wouldn't be welcome, but she thought there was probably some kind of rule about people on public payrolls performing any but public duties while they were on the clock.

"We're off duty," Mike assured her. "Anyway, Matt said we should help you unload."

Carly's eyes narrowed.

"Which it is our pleasure to do," Antonio added with some haste, clearly misinterpreting the reason for her sour-ing expression. "By the way, speaking of Matt, he was just on the radio asking if we knew anything about his mailbox being knocked down. Seems one of his neighbors called him to say it was lying in his yard, broken clean in half. It was still standing when we left his house, I'm pretty sure. At least, I think we would have noticed if it was lying in his yard. You don't happen to remember seeing it when you were pulling out, do you? It was standing right up beside his driveway."

Sandra looked as if she'd swallowed a bug.

"I'm sure we would have noticed if it had been knocked down," Carly said, sliding her hand around Sandra's elbow and smiling innocently as her fingers tightened in a warning squeeze. It was always a good feeling to know one was telling the truth, she reflected. When Matt's mailbox was knocked down, she and Sandra certainly *had* noticed, no doubt about it. She just wasn't admitting to doing it, on the theory that anything that added an extra dollop of grief to Matt's life was a small price for him to pay in exchange for the truly enormous amount of aggravation he had dumped in hers.

"That's what I think, too." Antonio shrugged. "If you want to unlock the back, we can start unloading."

Carly took a breath, ready to reject any help that had been prompted by Matt no matter how welcome it might be, only to have Sandra step on her foot.

"Ow!" Carly jerked her poor injured toes out of harm's way.

"Oh, sorry." That was so blatantly insincere that Carly couldn't believe it. Sandra took the keys from Carly and handed them to Antonio with another of those melting smiles. "We really appreciate this. Thanks so much."

"Sure." Keys jingling, Antonio and Mike headed around to the back of the truck.

"Are you crazy? Don't you dare tell them we don't need any help," Sandra hissed at Carly the moment they were alone. "It's hotter than a pizza oven out here and that's one big hill. You want to go around cutting off your nose to spite your face, that's fine with me, but only as long as you leave me out of it. What did that sheriff do to you to make you so mad at him, anyway?"

"I don't know what you're talking about."

"Yeah, right." Sandra turned away, reaching into the cab and dragging out Carly's overnight bag, her own overnight bag, and the pan she'd wielded for most of the previous night. "Come on, let's get going with this before they figure out how hot it is and take off."

Carly grimaced but had to admit Sandra had a point as she picked up her bag. It still felt like it was loaded down with an anvil or two. With Sandra right behind her and Mike, juggling an armload of brooms and mops along with a vacuum cleaner, and Antonio, carrying a stack of boxes, following, she began staggering up the hill.

Besides being hot, the day was already so humid that the earth itself seemed to be sweating. As she trudged upward, Carly could practically feel drops of moisture hanging in the air. The sky was a fresh-washed, cloudless blue. Birds sang, crickets chirped, cicadas whirred, and mosquitoes launched their assaults in waves. The dense canopy of trees kept the worst of the sun's rays at bay, and the deep shade it provided was welcome for that reason, but it also kept the heat and the bugs and the residual moisture from the previous day's rain down close to the ground. By the time Carly was within spitting distance of the porch she would have traded the whole somnolent Southern summer for a single breath of one of Lake Michigan's brisk breezes. She'd forgotten just how hot July in Georgia could be.

She'd forgotten just how itchy July in Georgia could be.

"Found my phone," Sandra announced triumphantly. Carly glanced around to see Sandra holding up her cell phone. Her bright plastic tote, already recovered, hung from her arm, and as Carly watched, Sandra slid the phone inside it. Huffing and puffing like the little engine that could, glistening with sweat, surrounded by a cloud of gnats, Sandra looked as happy as Carly had ever seen her. It didn't take a rocket scientist to figure out why: Antonio had picked up the pace until he was walking beside her.

Lust was a many-splendored thing.

"Yay," Carly said. Pretending she was waiting for the others to catch up to her, she put her leaden bag down and stretched her back as unobtrusively as possible, looking up at the house. With its peaked roof and octagonal turret, its wide front porch and shuttered windows, it had a nine-teenth-century charm that should translate beautifully into a bed-and-breakfast. But the paint was peeling, several of the shutters hung at drunken angles, and the porch roof sagged at one end. Remembering the *plop, plop* she had heard inside the house last night, Carly had little doubt that the roof needed attention too. To say nothing of the plumbing, and the electricity, and . . .

An explosion of barking rent the air. Even as Carly watched in jaw-dropping dismay, Hugo tore out from under the porch with the demon dog on his tail. Hugo swarmed up the steps to the porch. The dog leaped after him. After a single frozen moment, Carly whirled. Snatching a broom from Mike, who was slow on the uptake, she emitted a war whoop that would have done credit to Geronimo at his finest and charged to the defense of her cat.

"Hugo!"

Brandishing the broom, she reached the top of the steps in time to see Hugo racing toward her across the back of the settee. The dog, unable to attain such a lofty perch, yipped and yapped and leaped as it gave chase from the floor. Its nails skittered and slid on the wood. Its high-pitched battle cry echoed from the rafters.

"Bad dog," Carly cried, and plunged forward, bringing the broom down with a resounding *slap* on the floor in front of the dog. It yelped and Hugo leaped, rocketing through the air toward her like a football with a grudge. The broom went flying as the cat hit her in the shoulder in what was clearly a misguided attempt to seek safety in her arms. Staggering backward, she tried to catch him, to steady him—and went down. The stairs, to be precise.

Tumbling head over heels like laundry in a dryer, she got a brief, kaleidoscopic glimpse of what the world looked like to a soccer ball before she fetched up with a thud in the thick grass at the base of the steps. For a moment she lay there, flat on her back, watching as stars and little birdies twirled in a gossamer cloud of dislodged cat hair overhead.

Then she felt something warm and wet on her cheek. Casting her gaze sideways, she found herself eyeball to eyeball with the demon dog.

15

IT WAS LICKING HER. Carly registered that, registered anxious dark eyes in a small, triangular face and big pointed ears and a body so thin she could see its ribs through its coarse black coat. Then it turned tail and ran, and as Carly tuned in to the whole wide world around her again she understood why.

"Carly!"

Having jettisoned their cargo, Sandra and Antonio and Mike were rushing toward her like stampeding cattle, shouting her name. If she'd been capable of moving more than her eyeballs, Carly would have scrambled to safety, too.

"Are you okay?" Sandra stopped just short of trampling her. Antonio and Mike were right behind her. All three were breathing hard, their faces creased with concern as they looked down at her.

Carly looked up, up past the trio of frowning faces, up at the soothing vista of gnarled limbs and sun-dappled leaves and soft blue sky, and breathed, slowly and experimentally. She smelled damp earth, damp grass and damp shoes. The fall had knocked the wind out of her, she realized. But her lungs worked now, and as they filled with air she tried an experimental wiggle of her fingers and toes. They worked too, and so did her arms and legs and even her neck.

Okay, so maybe she was going to live.

To a chorus of *be careful*s and *you might want to take it easy for a few minutes,* Carly slowly sat up. The broom she'd commandeered for the abortive rescue attempt lay nearby. More brooms and mops and the vacuum cleaner and assorted boxes and bags littered the spot from which she had launched her ill-fated invasion of the porch. A quick scan of her surroundings revealed that neither Hugo nor the dog were anywhere in sight. She didn't hear any barking either. Clearly the dog had abandoned the chase.

Poor little dog, it had looked half-starved.

Of course, that didn't excuse it for trying to eat her cat.

"Did you see where Hugo went?" Deciding to go for it, she struggled to her feet. Hands grabbed her arms and helped her get safely upright. She wasn't hurt, but she was grateful for the support. She was, she discovered, just a little unsteady on her feet. Good thing it had been so long since the yard had seen a lawn mower. The long grass had cushioned her fall.

"He's up there." Antonio's voice was dry as he jerked his head toward the huge birch. Carly looked up, way up, way, way up, into the tree's leafy dome and sure enough there was Hugo, crouched on a branch, staring down at her.

"Hugo! Come down here!"

Hugo's tail twitched disdainfully. It was the only sign he gave of having heard.

"Damned cat," Carly muttered under her breath.

"Amen to that," Sandra said.

Carly shot her a dirty look.

"Listen, how about if we wait a little bit to see if your cat comes down on its own?" Mike asked, having just finished exchanging alarmed glances with Antonio.

Carly frowned. Something in the atmosphere told her that the men really, truly didn't want to go up that tree after

Hugo. But then, there really wasn't any need for them to. Unlike last night, she knew where he was, and he was hardly likely to come to harm in a tree. If he didn't come down by himself within a reasonable period of time, *then* she would worry. After all, Hugo's days of lazily surveying the world through a high-rise apartment's picture window were over. The good news was, now he got to live life rather than just watch it. The bad news was the same as the good news.

"Yes, fine, I—"

She broke off as the front door opened. Carly caught the movement from the corner of her eye, and then her head turned and she watched with surprise as a white-haired, sixtyish man stepped out onto the porch. He was neatly dressed in a blue short-sleeved shirt and dark pants. A leather tool belt was buckled around his waist. A moment later he was joined by a younger man, fair-haired, stockily built and dressed in jeans.

Carly stared at them in surprise. Who were they, and what were they doing in her house?

"Almost done," the older man called to them with a cheery wave, then crouched down and started doing something to her front door. Steadying the door, the younger man lifted a hand in greeting, too.

"Hey, Walter, Barry." Antonio waved back. He glanced at Carly. "Why don't you go on inside and sit down? That was some fall you took."

"I'm okay," Carly said, although she could already feel a few twinges that told her she was going to have some aches and pains later. "Walter and Barry?"

"Walter and Barry Hindley," Antonio said, as he and Sandra and Mike shepherded her up the stairs.

Walter and Barry Hindley, Carly thought. She remembered them both. Walter owned—or at least he used to own—Hindley's Hardware Store in town. Besides selling nails and hammers and all that other good hardware stuff, he had also sold candy and comic books. Every kid in town had been a regular in Mr. Hindley's store. Barry was the Hindleys' only son. He'd been a year ahead of Carly in high school. A jock, he hadn't been anyone she'd known well. She'd never been on any of the high school boys' lists of top ten hot chicks.

Once she was close enough, she recognized them both.

"Hello, Mr. Hindley, Barry," she said, conscious of a few more twinges as she crossed the porch. The *who* had been answered, but she still had to find out what they were doing in her house.

"Carly? Hi," Barry said, looking her up and down with transparent surprise as she stopped beside him. He'd put on a little weight, but otherwise had hardly changed at all.

"Well, hello there, Carly." Mr. Hindley glanced up with a smile. Beyond adding a few pounds and a few wrinkles, he had not, she thought, changed much at all either, except that today he held a screwdriver in one hand and in the other her dismembered doorknob. "Good to have you back home."

"It's good to be back home." She smiled at them both, but could contain her curiosity no longer. "What are you guys doing?"

Barry looked surprised. "Didn't Matt tell you? He asked us to come around today and change your locks. He said you needed some new ones bad."

"I would've waited till later, but Ellen and I've got the grandkids coming this afternoon," Mr. Hindley said. "So I just decided to go ahead and miss church and drag Barry over here with me and get it done."

"No, Matt didn't tell me." Since Barry was holding the door open, Carly went on ahead and stepped inside. Somebody had turned on the window units, she was glad to notice. The air inside the house was twenty degrees cooler than the air outside. "But I sure appreciate your missing church." She looked at Barry. "And I appreciate you taking time away from your family."

He shook his head and smiled slowly at her. "I'm not married. The grandkids Dad's talking about belong to my sister."

"Oh," Carly said. From his smile, she had little doubt that Barry had a reason for telling her that. But she had zero interest in him. And the reason for her lack of interest, she realized with chagrin, stood about six-one, with black hair.

"Put you on some nice deadbolts," Mr. Hindley said. "And fixed your windows so nobody's going to be coming in that way. Ron Graves'll be by later to put your security system in for you. Once that's done, I don't see how old Harry Houdini himself could get in your house."

"Security system?" Carly asked, annoyed with herself for *not* being interested in Barry. Her three nursemaids were in the hall with her now, making the area around the door feel a little crowded. "What security system?"

Mr. Hindley adjusted the position of the door and gripped it with his knees. Eyeballing a pencil mark he'd apparently made earlier, he scored it into the wood with the screwdriver. Barry handed him a drill.

"The one Matt said you had to have installed today so you'd feel safe tonight sleeping in your granny's house," Barry said.

Mr. Hindley added, "He called Ron early this morning and asked him to do it. On account of the break-in. Matt said it was urgent, so Ron said he would."

Matt said. As far as Carly was concerned, the too-often repeated words were by now the verbal equivalent of waving a red flag at a bull. She looked at Barry with determinedly fresh eyes. He was a perfectly nice guy, as far as she could recall. It was good to know that Benton's eligible males did not begin and end with Matt. But any chance Carly might have had to offer verbal encouragement to Barry was drowned out as Mr. Hindley turned on the drill. Then Barry winked at her.

Okay, he might be a perfectly nice guy but she wasn't feeling it at the moment, she decided. Probably because she was still so mad at Matt.

"If you don't want the security system, I guess you could call Ron Graves and tell him not to come," Antonio said doubtfully after taking one look at Carly's face. His voice was raised to be heard over the sound of the drill. "Matt said you'd want it, though."

"We want it," Sandra said before Carly could reply. Giving her a *don't-you-dare* look, Sandra dragged Carly away.

It wasn't so much that she didn't want the system, Carly reflected indignantly, although paying for it was certainly an issue. But *Matt said* didn't mean *Matt got*. Not with her it didn't. Not anymore. Anyway, it was his sheer high-handedness in arranging to have the thing installed without bothering to so much as mention it to her first that annoyed the stuffing out of her. Same thing with the new locks. And with asking his deputies to help her move in. It was her house, they were her doors and it was her move. And none of them were any of Matt's business. Her *life* was none of Matt's business, and so she meant to make clear to him the minute she laid eyes on him again. And when that was taken care of, then maybe she'd be ready to start taking advantage of Benton's singles scene.

In the process of being towed into the parlor, Carly caught a glimpse of herself in the mirror over the radiator. Her gaze was already moving on when she did a double-take and stopped dead, dislodging Sandra's hand from her arm in the process.

In the teeth of her best efforts, her years of blow-dryer expertise, and the wonders of modern chemistry, her curls were back. Just like nearly everything else in her life since she had returned to Benton, her hair seemed determined to turn back the clock.

"No," she whispered despairingly as she stared at her reflection in disbelief. Twisting spirals of hair clustered on her forehead, around her ears, down her neck.

"Uh, we'll just get back to unloading that truck," Antonio called over the whirr of the drill.

"That would be great," Sandra replied, her tone artificially bright. "I'll be right out to help. Just let me get Carly settled."

"No rush on that." Antonio waved a hand dismissively. "You take your time."

The deputies went back out the door, which was still open as Barry and Mr. Hindley worked. As soon as they were out of sight, Sandra grabbed Carly's arm again and hauled her bodily into the front parlor.

"Don't even *think* about telling somebody not to put in that security system," Sandra said, crossing her arms over her chest and fixing Carly with a forbidding stare as, sapped of her last bit of strength by the horror in the mirror, Carly sank bonelessly down on the sofa. "I don't care what that hunky sheriff did to make you mad, I want that security system. You get to have a cat, I get to have a security system."

Visions of her culinary better half cutting and running back to Chicago trumped Carly's determination to symbolically thumb her nose at Matt. Sandra in a snit was nothing to mess with. Sandra scared and in a snit—the havoc that could result was too much to contemplate.

"Fine," Carly said, crossing her arms too and glaring at Sandra even as she tried to make herself comfortable on the sofa. Even if she hadn't had a bruised tailbone and achy muscles it would have been impossible, as she should have remembered from childhood. The thing was stuffed with horsehair and, despite its magnificent velvet upholstery, hard as a rock. Pair the unforgiving piece of furniture with her banged-up body, and comfort wasn't even a possibility.

"Damn right, fine," Sandra said with satisfaction, then turned to smile meltingly at Antonio as he carried the boxes he'd dropped earlier into the house.

Carly stuck her tongue out at Sandra's back. Then, in the interests of doing what she could to soothe her battered body, mind, and soul, she reached instinctively for the elixir that had never failed to make her feel better as a little girl in this house: she picked up a peppermint, unwrapped it, and popped it into her mouth.

By the time suppertime rolled around, the truck was unloaded. Boxes in various stages of being emptied were strewn all over the house. Clothes were tucked away in chests and closets. Towels, soap and various assorted toiletries were in the bathrooms. With the worst of her discomfort eased by megadoses of Tylenol, Carly was feeling almost as good as new. She had unpacked most of her belongings and had even made up the bed in her childhood bedroom, which she had elected to keep as her own. The practical reason for her choice was that it was one of the smaller rear bedrooms, and the larger front bedrooms would better please paying guests. The real reason for her choice was, it just felt right. Sandra had settled on another of the smaller rooms—not coincidentally the one right next to Carly's—which left four bedchambers that they could rent out. She had reacquainted herself with the house, which, besides the six downstairs rooms plus bath, consisted of six bedrooms plus two baths on the second floor and the entire third floor, which was basically one huge room. At some point, Carly hoped that the business would be doing well enough so that it became both necessary and desirable to turn the third floor into additional guest quarters. For now, it was going to be all their budget could handle just to refurbish the two lower floors. The mess the burglar had made of the back parlor had been cleaned up as well as possible, but the dents in the plaster walls would require repair. Other than that, the downstairs was in decent shape. With a good scrubbing and a couple of coats of fresh paint, the front and back parlors, the music room, which was directly across the hall from the front parlor, the dining room, which adjoined the music room, and the kitchen and breakfast room, which adjoined the dining room, were good to go. New, commercial grade appliances would have to be purchased for the kitchen, of course, but most of the available money would have to go to refurbishing the newly designated guest rooms and such essentials as upgrading the wiring.

The house, which had felt dark and closed-in for as long as Carly could remember, was already starting to take on a whole new ambience. To Carly it felt like it was waking up after a long sleep. She wasn't sure how it had happened, exactly, but by suppertime it was bursting to the seams with people, all of whom seemed to be intent on one thing: food. Sandra's food, to be precise. Never happier than when she had a crowd to cook for, Sandra was at the stove, concocting a delectable-smelling shrimp scampi out of ingredients she had scavenged from the pantry and deep freeze. Carly herself was standing at one of the long counters making a salad, which was one of the few cooking-related tasks Sandra was willing to delegate to her. The salad consisted of tomatoes and onions donated by Mrs. Naylor, who, along with her daughter, Martha Highcamp, and an elderly friend had stepped across the road at around four P.M. to bring Carly a welcome-home present of her famous Red Velvet cake. By some process that escaped Carly, the three had ended up deciding to stay for dinner, with Mrs. Naylor's garden's bounty having been placed at Sandra's disposal and her cake as the prospective dessert. Antonio and Mike were still there, obviously tired but hanging on in the lip-smacking expectation of eating soon. Ron Graves, having just finished wrapping up the installation of the security system, had made a number of appreciative comments about the aroma and had accepted with alacrity the subsequent invitation to stay and eat. Loren Schuler had dropped in to see about removing her aunt's damaged desk, gotten into a discussion with Martha Highcamp about a Fourth of July committee they were both on, and decided that she could eat, too. Rounding out the party, Matt's sister Erin had stopped by to return an earring Sandra had left behind. She was still there, perched on a kitchen counter shooting the breeze, giving no indication that she meant to go anywhere else anytime soon. Observing her laughing with Mike, Carly concluded that she was hanging around largely because he was present. Certainly Sandra's food did not appear to be the motivating force for her that it was for the others. Given that Erin was engaged to Collin Holcomb, her apparent pleasure in the deputy's company set off little warning bells in Carly's mind. But Erin's doings were none of her business, Carly reminded herself, deliberately focusing her attention instead on slicing the onions thin enough to suit Sandra's requirements. Just because everybody in this little town continually meddled in the affairs of everyone else, did not mean that she had to follow suit. She might have returned to Benton, but she had not been repossessed by it.

While their dinner guests were certainly welcome, they were unexpected. The one person that Carly, in her secret heart of hearts, *did* expect, especially given that his sister and deputies were present, was Matt. Without acknowledging to herself that she was waiting to hear his voice, she had been on edge throughout the afternoon and on into the evening as she anticipated his appearance and planned how she would react. Even as she sliced and spiced at Sandra's direction, she found herself listening for him. When the meal was served up in the dining room, which had a custom-made table large enough to accommodate such a crowd, she had caught herself glancing toward the door more than once, expecting to see Matt standing there.

Not that she *wanted* to see him. She just expected to. Which, she assured herself, was quite a different thing.

With the lights all on and a roomful of people present, the dining room bore little resemblance to the previous night's pitch-black chamber of horrors. In recounting, at everyone's urging, her close encounter with the burglar, Carly even managed to find a few elements of the tale almost funny. The reality of the heart-stopping terror she had experienced at the time receded, and became, in her own mind and in her retelling, something of an overreaction. The corner of the room where the intruder had lurked was no longer sinister; it was simply an ordinary corner where an unlucky burglar had tried to hide and been discovered. Everyone laughed heartily at the role Hugo had played, at the role Sandra had played, at the role Matt had played. Then Mike launched into a truly hilarious description of Matt's struggle to get Hugo down from the tree. Everyone laughed some more, and the conversation moved on from there.

Except Carly kept getting stuck on a series of related, recurring images: herself frightened out of her mind, running through the dark, running to Matt. Herself shaken and scared, crying in the dark, crying on Matt. Matt holding her close, keeping her safe, comforting her, kissing her . . .

And then walking out. Because they were *friends,* and he didn't want to mess with that.

Every time she remembered, her temper heated all over again.

Accidentally knocking his mailbox down was small potatoes compared to what he deserved, she told herself, fuming. He deserved—he deserved . . .

She couldn't think of anything bad enough. But when she did, he better watch out.

"I'll go cut the cake," she said to the table in general, and, picking up her dishes, fled the general merriment for the peace and quiet of the kitchen. She was so furious with Matt, so *through* with Matt, and yet the fact that he hadn't shown up to help them move in or to eat or even to check on how they were doing was driving her nuts. She told herself that it was because she was all revved up to tell him off and had no place to go with her crushing speech. She told herself that since he'd had the last word, both literally and figuratively, at their last encounter, she was in dire need of the kind of closure she could only get by telling him that *she* did not want *him.*

She was standing over the sink getting ready to scrape what remained of her shrimp scampi down the disposal when she noticed that Hugo, who had, indeed, gotten in touch with his inner alley cat for long enough to get out of the tree on his own, was perched on top of the refrigerator staring fixedly through the nearest window. Her first thought was that Hugo was indulging in one of his favorite pastimes: bird-watching. But his demeanor wasn't quite right for that. For one thing, his fur had the Mohawk thing going on down the middle of his back, which he only got when he was alarmed. For another, he was perfectly still.

Carly glanced out the window too. She could see across the considerable expanse of the backyard to the imposing, black-painted barn, which was empty now except for miscellaneous items that had been stored in it over the years, and the cornfield beside it. A slight breeze had sprung up; she could see it ruffling the silky tops of the tall cornstalks in the field next to the barn. It was about eight P.M., some two hours before it would be fully night. But the baking heat of the afternoon had mellowed into something more closely resembling a warming oven than a broiler, and long shadows slanted across the grass. A small black creature was moving toward the house from the cornfield, slinking across the lawn, disappearing under bushes and then reappearing again, keeping to the shadows as much as possible. As Carly watched, it stopped in the open to look toward the house, lifting its head, sniffing at the air.

The demon dog was being drawn from its hiding place by the smell of shrimp scampi.

It was probably hungry. Carly remembered how skinny it was, how anxious its dark eyes had been as it had stood over her after she had fallen down the stairs. She remembered how it had licked her cheek.

She still had her barely-touched plate of shrimp in her hand. She'd been so busy trying not to listen for Matt that she hadn't managed to eat more than a couple of bites. Now her supper could be put to a better, more noble use than dulling the disposal blade.

"Just because it chased you doesn't mean we should let it starve," she said to Hugo, who replied with a disdainful glance and a twitch of his tail. Then, carrying her plate, she opened the back door and stepped out onto the small rear porch.

As soon as Carly stepped outside, the dog ran under a bush. Clearly it held no very great opinion of human beings. She'd never had a dog herself, but unlike Hugo, she had nothing against them as a species. It was just that her grandmother had not permitted her to have any pets, and when she'd gotten into a position to please herself, she'd acquired Hugo.

And Hugo harbored a definite prejudice against dogs.

She walked down the steps and crossed the yard to the bush under which the dog had disappeared. It was a snowball bush, taller than she was, green and round and bursting with the tennis ball–sized white blossoms that gave it its name. Crouching, she peered beneath it. For a moment she thought that somehow the dog had managed to dart away without her seeing it. Then she spotted it, huddled against the trunk, watching her out of big scared eyes.

"Are you hungry?" Carly asked softly. "I brought you some food."

Staring at her, it seemed to sink even closer to the ground. Carly set the plate down. She saw its nostrils flare, saw it sniff the air.

"Come here," she said. Then, remembering Matt and the ridiculous sounds he had made, she clicked her tongue against the roof of her mouth.

Incredibly, it came. Slinking on its belly, its tail tucked between its legs, it crawled toward her. She kept making encouraging sounds, and it kept coming until it was right at the edge of the bush. Then it hesitated, looking from her to the plate of food, clearly trying to make up its mind if she could be trusted.

"I won't hurt you," she said. "I promise."

And she moved the plate of food fractionally closer to it.

With a last long look at her, the dog crept out from under the bush. When it reached the plate, it began to eat voraciously, gulping down the food as if it hadn't had a meal for weeks.

Watching it, Carly felt her heart contract. It was so skinny that it was practically skeletal. It was a little taller than Hugo but not much, although she guessed her cat outweighed it by a good six or seven pounds. Hugo's aristocratic pedigree was evident at a glance. This dog's ancestry was evident at a glance, too: strictly Heinz 57. It was a homely little dog, with eyes and ears way too big for its heart-shaped face, stalklike legs, and a long, bedraggled tail. Its coat was dull and matted, black with a small whitish patch on its chest.

The sensible thing to do for it was take it to the pound. Watching it inhale the spicy shrimp, Carly already knew she wasn't going to be able to do that.

She reached out to pat it. Her touch was tentative, because clearly the animal was a stray, not somebody's pet, and she already knew that it was not a friend to cats, and it might just bite. It glanced at her when she touched it, lifting its head away from the plate it was now licking clean of every last trace of sauce with a suddenness that made her pull her hand back. For a moment their eyes met. The dog's eyes were big and dark and sad, as if it knew the world was a hard place for small unwanted dogs and accepted that fact. Then, the movement barely perceptible at first, it began to wag its tail.

That was when Carly decided to take a chance.

"Good dog," Carly whispered, easing closer to it. It had gone back to licking the plate, but as she patted it more firmly this time it lifted its head to look at her again and its tail beat the air. It was a female, she saw as her hand slid around its rib cage. It trembled but didn't resist as she picked it up, gathered it close and stood up with it.

"Good dog," Carly said again, holding it carefully. It was warm and wriggly and ridiculously light in her arms. She could feel the tremors that racked its slight body, see the doubt in its eyes as it looked at her. It was not accustomed to kindness, that much was clear. There was a hard, raised line on its belly that felt like some sort of scabbed-over cut, its coat was crusted with a substance that made it feel almost brittle to the touch, and it undoubtedly had fleas, if nothing worse.

For some ridiculous reason, it reminded her of herself. Oh, not of herself as she was now, but of herself as she had been as a little girl, before her grandmother had entered her life. She too had been unloved and unfed, dirty and neglected, slow to trust and wary of people. She knew how it felt to be small and helpless and scared and alone.

"Don't worry," she said, looking down into its anxious eyes. "Everything's going to be all right."

It gave a soft little whimper, almost like it understood. More moved than she could remember being for a long time, she hugged it close. Lifting its head, it licked her chin.

Carly realized that the two of them had just bonded for life. Sandra was going to kill her. Hugo was going to die. They were just going to have to deal, the pair of them. She was going to keep the dog.

Once upon a time, she, too, had been rescued from a hard-knock life. Just like she was going to rescue this dog.

"You need a name," she said, and suddenly she knew what it had to be. "How does Annie sound to you?"

Annie, seeming to realize that something good had just happened to her for once in her life, wagged her tail as if to say that Carly could call her anything she liked and that would be fine with her.

"Good girl," Carly said. "Good girl, Annie."

And she carried the dog inside.

16

It was the Fourth of July, a beautiful, starry night, and Carly and Sandra were sitting on a quilt in the middle of the laughing, partying crowd that had gathered in the town square waiting for the fireworks to begin. Sandra was just polishing off a ham sandwich. Carly was savoring mouthfuls of a thick, sweet/tart concoction of lemon and sugar and shaved ice and water that she and Sandra had come up with for the Treehouse and called Lemon Crush. Along with her usual basic black, Sandra had on long, dangly earrings that spelled out USA in tiny flashing lights. Carly, too, had dressed for the occasion in navy shorts, a red tee shirt festooned with white stars, and a denim baseball cap with an American flag on the front. The baseball cap served a triple purpose: besides acting as a mini-billboard for her patriotism, and being just plain cute, the hat did a really good job of hiding her curls, which were pulled back into a ponytail.

"Uh, you know, I think the sheriff might kind of know who knocked over his mailbox." Sandra's voice was low; clearly she didn't want to be overheard. She glanced at Carly, then looked away.

"What makes you think so?" Carly asked. Sandra's innocent expression was a dead giveaway. Carly lowered her cup and looked at her suspiciously. "You told Antonio, didn't you?"

During the three days since he had helped them move in, Antonio had become nearly as much a fixture around the place as the front porch. When he wasn't working or sleeping, he could basically be found in her kitchen. Not that Carly really minded. She liked the deputy, he was quite a bit of help. He had, for example, brought his mower over and cut the grass for them—and she was glad that Sandra's love life was keeping her mind off certain domestic sore points like the addition of Annie to their household. But through no fault of his own, Antonio had one major draw-back: he was a constant reminder of Matt.

"Okay, so it might have sort of slipped out when he was talking about helping the sheriff pour concrete around the pole for the new mailbox." Sandra sounded a little guilty, as well she might. "I thought I ought to let you know, because, um, he told the sheriff."

"What?" Despite her best intentions, Carly couldn't help herself. She had to ask. "What did he say? Matt, I mean."

Sandra glanced at her again. She seemed to hesitate. Carly waited.

"He said, 'That girl's been nothing but a pain in the ass since the moment I first laid eyes on her.' "

Carly sucked in her breath.

"Oh, he did, did he?" Swelling with indignation, Carly glared in the direction of the sheriff's office, a long, low brick building that was located beside the firehouse just on the other side of the square. Not that Matt was in it. He was here, somewhere in the crowd. She had already seen him once, at a distance, although she didn't think he'd seen her. Yet. But he was going to.

Her inner No More Ms. Nice Girl was practically chomping at the bit.

Before her fleeting glimpse of him a little while earlier, she hadn't set eyes on him since that night in his bedroom. While Antonio had been conspicuous by his presence, Matt had been conspicuous by his absence.

He hadn't stopped by, called, or sent a message via Antonio, his sisters (all of whom had dropped in), or anyone or anything else, including the local florist, e-mail, or even that oldie but goodie, the United States Postal Service.

But that was okay.

Not.

Radio silence might be his modus operandi after a hot and heavy session such as the one they'd shared, but it just wasn't working for her. Ever since he had closed the bedroom door in her disbelieving face, anger had been building inside her like pressure in a volcano. If she didn't get a chance to vent soon, she was going to explode.

In fact, one very important side benefit she'd hoped to reap from attending Benton's annual display of fireworks tonight was the opportunity to tell off her local sheriff.

Just thinking about it got her all excited.

But by the time the first firework rocketed into the sky, Carly wasn't any closer to expressing her feelings to Matt than she had been when he'd left her high and dry in his bedroom. Oh, she could definitely see Matt. In full sheriff mode—khaki uniform, badge, holstered gun at his side—he was everywhere. Everywhere, that is, but near her. He and his deputies were working the crowd, which as far as Carly could tell consisted of pretty much everyone in Benton and the surrounding countryside. As brilliant explosions of red, white, and blue lit up the night, they wove through the islands of people sprawled on quilts and the thickets of people clustered in lawn chairs and the forests of people standing around the periphery of the crowd, all with their faces turned toward the sky, with systematic efficiency.

Besides Sandra, Carly's particular quilt cluster included Mrs. Naylor, who had hailed Carly and Sandra on sight, her daughter, Martha, and Martha's family, plus Loren Schuler and Bets Haskell, who was another friend from high school, and their families. Their group attracted more than its fair share of visitors as a good portion of the town, having heard that Carly was back and intending to open a bed-and-breakfast in her grandmother's house, stopped by to welcome her home as well as give her their opinions on the viability of such a plan. Barry Hindley stopped by, making his interest in her very clear, and Carly once again thought what a shame it was that she couldn't seem to get past being mad at Matt for long enough to focus on any other man. Hal Reynolds, another high school friend, also came over to renew old ties, but Carly couldn't get excited about him either. Sandra had her own particular visitor in Antonio who, despite being on duty, still managed to find time to grab a snack and stand around chatting with her for some time. Even after he was gone, Sandra glowed.

The good news was, at least one of them was well on her way to finding a replacement for her vibrator. The bad news was, the other wasn't.

After Antonio left, it wasn't long before the other deputies began heading their way. Singly and in pairs, every single deputy found time to stop by. That those visits were motivated to a large extent by the ample cooler full of goodies Sandra had packed, Carly had little doubt. Antonio had clearly spread the word among his fellow sheriff's department employees as to where good eats could be found. That, plus the fact that Martha's teenage daughter Heather was a friend of Lissa Converse, who, along with boyfriend Andy, had plopped down on a corner of Carly's quilt and munched lemon cookies for a while, led Carly to expect that at some point during the evening their little group would be favored by a visit from the high-and-mighty sheriff him-self—unless he was deliberately avoiding her, of course.

Which, it grew ever more apparent, was just what he was doing. Steaming, Carly found herself watching Matt more than the fireworks. The town's onetime favorite can-didate for Face Most Likely to Be Seen on a Wanted Poster now seemed to be respected by all, liked by most, and chased by quite a few—females, that is. The more he walked around, the more he seemed to trail women like a comet trailed dust. Not that Carly was surprised. For as long as she had known him, Matt had always had to fight girls off with a stick. The fact that he was now thirty-three, single, gainfully employed, and so damned handsome that he even managed to look hot in a sheriff's uniform was bound to make him as attractive to the town's distaff popu-lation as catnip was to Hugo.

It also served to kick her anger at him up a few more notches. A pain in the ass, was she? She'd show him pain in the ass.

He didn't even have the grace to wave. Oh, he knew where she was sitting. The head honcho was bound to know, if the rest of his department knew, where to come for treats. He did the meet-and-greet, the backslap, the hand-shake, the frowning buddy-I-think-you've-had-too-much-beer thing all over the whole blessed square. The only area he didn't honor with his presence? The twenty or so square yards around where she sat.

Her opinion of that was, *coincidence? I think not.*

It occurred to Carly then that the no good dirty rotten son of a bitch might actually think she *wanted* him. That she did, or had, was beside the point: it was his thinking that she did that made her want to kill him. The idea that he thought she wanted him when he didn't want *her*, or at least not as anything but a *friend*, made her so mad she saw red—and not just because a brilliant scarlet starburst was exploding overhead just at that moment, either. It made her crazy to think that he imagined that she was as pathetically eager to be on the receiving end of his attentions as the rest of the single female population of Benton seemed to be. She watched one woman in a tiny pair of white shorts stand up as he passed and felt physically ill when he stopped to put an arm around her and bend his head close to talk to her. She was just registering the churning in her stomach when she realized that the woman was his sister Erin, and that what she was observing was a quick brother-sister conversation conducted in the teeth of the booming explosions overhead. But the churning didn't even have a chance to subside before another woman in white shorts stood up to hug him even as Erin flopped back down on her blanket. More fireworks burst overhead, and by their light Carly saw that this woman was tall and thin with upswept blond hair—Shelby.

Who unlike Carly belonged to the category of girls he fucked.

Suddenly Carly wasn't sick to her stomach any longer. Instead, visions of murder weapons danced in her head. Because it had just occurred to her that what she was experiencing at his hands was no more or less than déjà vu.

This was exactly how he had treated her in the days and weeks and months following her prom.

Her jaw clenched as suddenly the whole pattern became crystal clear.

He was dealing with his discomfort over the addition of a sexual component to their relationship by staying away from her—again. A neon sign flashing *Baby, I don't want to know* over his head couldn't have made his feelings about what had happened between them the other night any clearer.

Just like the last time, he didn't want to know that she had a jones for him.

Not that she did. At least, not when she was wide-awake and in full possession of her senses.

Anyway, he'd been hot as hell for her too. He could run as far and fast as he liked, he could deny it as much as he wanted, but she wasn't a shy and besotted eighteen-year-old anymore. She was a thirty-year-old grown woman and she now knew one end of a hard-on from the other, thank you very much. And the bottom line was, he had wanted her, too.

Only he couldn't handle it. Because, he said, he cared too much about her. He wanted them to be *friends*.

In other words, think Bert and Ernie, rather than J. Lo and Ben.

That was so insulting that just picturing it made her hair curl—no, wait, it did that anyway. It made her *toes* curl.

At that moment, the fireworks climaxed in a spectacular display. Even Carly's fuming meditation on the merits and methods of murdering Matt couldn't compete against the huge, noisy spectacle. To the accompaniment of near-deafening booms and the Screven County High School marching band's rousing rendition of "America the Beautiful," the night sky was lit up by a glorious American flag. By the time it faded away, along with the appreciative clapping and yelling that followed, the scent of gunpowder-tinged smoke wafting over the assembly was almost as strong as the smell of beer.

Then the celebration was over. As people began to pack up their gear on all sides, Carly realized that any hope she'd harbored that Matt might be going to come her way was over too. He was the one who kept insisting they were *friends*. Well, for a friend, his behavior was mighty peculiar, to say the least. He hadn't acknowledged her presence in any way. He hadn't even waved.

She was perfectly willing to be friends. What she wasn't perfectly willing to be was ignored.

"Oh, my, would you look at that." Mrs. Naylor was standing, bracing herself on her daughter's arm as she strained to see over the crowd. Carly wasn't sure whether it was because she had grown up or her neighbor had aged, but Mrs. Naylor seemed much less daunting now than when Carly had been a girl. But she was still plump and gray-haired, and as nosy as ever.

"Who is that?" Martha asked, craning her neck right along with her mother. She was a big, loose-limbed, handsome rather than pretty woman with short brown hair and a hearty laugh, who had been captain of the field hockey team in high school.

Carly couldn't see anything except a wall of backs, although she looked in the same direction as everyone else. At her height, this was always a problem.

"The sheriff's arresting somebody," Sandra informed her from her superior vantage point, seeing Carly's dilemma. She looked again, pretended to shiver, and glanced at Carly with a wicked little glint. "He sure is looking fine, too. Don't you just love a man in uniform?"

Beyond casting Sandra a sour look, Carly ignored all but the first part of that. She knew when she was being teased. But she became bound and determined to see what was going on. A quick glance around provided the solution. She hopped up on the cooler, and from there she had a perfect view.

Matt was standing in the middle of the street. Since she had noticed that he did indeed look fine in his uniform much earlier in the evening, Carly saw no need to reacknowledge that fact even to herself. Instead, she focused on what was happening: seemingly unperturbed by the exiting crowd that was starting to stream around him, he was holding the arm of a scrawny little man who had his hands cuffed behind his back, and shaking his head warningly at an equally tiny woman who was practically vibrating with fury as she yelled at the man. Carly wasn't close enough to hear what was being said, but Matt's stance told her that the arrest was nothing serious. The man was more a nuisance than a threat.

"Oh, that's just Anson Jarboe," Mrs. Naylor said, seeming to lose interest once she had made the identification. "Probably drunk as usual. Ida's right to give him what for."

With nothing in the proceedings apparently deemed worth watching any longer, they all turned away and went back to gathering up their belongings. All, that is, except Carly, who was so focused on Matt that she remained unaware of the others' shift in attention. She didn't stand there long, because it was just a matter of minutes before Matt propelled the offender across the street and into the sheriff's office, at which time the door shut behind the two of them and there was nothing but the brick building itself to look at.

Carly blinked, looked around, and quickly stepped down from her perch, glad to see that no one else seemed to have noticed that she'd watched longer than the rest. Feeling conspicuous anyway, she looked around for something to do and snatched up the quilt they'd been sitting on. Shaking it out, folding it on top of the cooler, Carly was just bending over to retrieve the big plastic cup that held what was left of her Lemon Crush when Sandra caught her eye.

"You know," she said, just loud enough for Carly to hear. "I'd take that hunky sheriff over a vibrator any day. Even if he had called me a pain in the ass."

Obviously, Sandra had noticed her overlong observation

of the incident—all right, of Matt—in the street. "Yeah, well," she said, picking up her cup. "The thing about me is, *I* have standards."

A few minutes later, she and Sandra were saying their good-byes as their little island of quilts broke up. With one of them on either side of the cooler, they headed down toward where their new van—well, their new used van, a '98 Windstar Carly had purchased for three thousand dollars cash just after turning the U-Haul in—was parked behind the bank.

"Uh, Carly."

"What?" Carly almost jumped. They were part of the crowd surging down the sidewalk, and at that precise moment they'd just happened to draw even with the sheriff's office. Carly had just happened to be looking to see what she could see through the windows—which was precisely nothing because the blinds were drawn—when Sandra spoke.

"I've gotta pee."

Carly looked at Sandra, and her step slowed. Her eyes widened as, for once in her life when she heard opportunity knock, she actually listened.

"No, I can't hold it until we get home." Sandra sounded testy, obviously in response to her interpretation of the expression on Carly's face. The cooler bumped against Carly's shin as Sandra, who'd gotten ahead of her when Carly had slowed, was jostled by a passerby. It was semi-painful, but Carly barely noticed. Having come to a full stop by now, she was too busy listening to the little devil that was whispering in her ear.

"Did I say you should hold it?" Carly suddenly felt so supportive of Sandra's affliction that she just wanted to hug herself. "You definitely should not hold it. Holding it will probably do bad things to your bladder. And are you ever in luck. See, I just happen to know right where a bathroom is."

"Where?" Mystified but eager, Sandra was looking all around even as Carly, plowing through the crowd with the ruthlessness of a baseball player headed for first, led the way across the street.

The local chamber of commerce had done its best to render the one-story brick building attractive. Flower-filled window boxes had been affixed to the one large picture window and the two smaller barred windows on either side of the gray metal door. The purple petunias and pink nasturtiums and trailing vines that crowded the boxes definitely added something to the building's ambience. Carly just wasn't certain what that something was. By the soft yellow light of ye olde corner streetlamp, Carly read the legend painted in black script on the door: SCREVEN COUNTY SHERIFF'S DEPARTMENT.

Carly smiled with satisfaction. Her heartbroken eighteen-year-old self might have thought she had no choice but to put up with Matt's bad behavior. Her cool, calm, in control, mad as hell, not going to take it anymore thirty-year-old self knew differently: she could always go to Plan B.

As in, hunt the dirty rotten son of a bitch down.

"There's a bathroom in here." Giving Sandra a big, supportive smile, struggling to hang on to both cup and cooler handle at the same time, Carly nevertheless managed to get a good grip on the knob and pull open the Screven County Sheriff's Department's door.

17

"I REALLY APPRECIATE THIS, Matt," Anson Jarboe said earnestly as Matt closed the cell door on him.

Matt looked at him standing on the other side of the long iron bars and shook his head. Bony, undersized, with untidy white hair and bloodshot blue eyes, Anson was wearing his usual attire of an undershirt and overalls. His face was its usual color too: a deep, flushed, boozy red.

"You ever thought it might be easier just to quit drinking?" Matt reattached the cuffs he'd used on Anson to his belt and headed for his desk, from which vantage point he could keep an eye on both his prisoner and the front door, and still check his messages. With everyone else out on crowd control, he and Anson were the only people in the office.

"I have quit. Ten, twenty times. It never took. Anyway, yelling at me gives Ida something to do." He shook his head. "That woman sure can get mad. Sometimes she's enough to put the fear of God right down deep inside me."

"Like tonight." Matt's voice was dry. There were special-delivery packages on his desk, but not, he saw as he picked up the envelopes and looked through them, the particular one he'd been waiting for. Marsha Hughes had not turned up, alive and well or otherwise, and he'd been doing some digging into both her and her boyfriend's background.

Marsha had two in-state ex-husbands and a sister in Tennessee, none of whom had so far responded to his phone messages. Kenan had previously lived in Clearwater, Florida. In the past there'd been some visits by the police to his residence there to check out reports of possible domestic violence. Kenan hadn't been arrested, but Matt was interested anyway. He wanted to see what Clearwater had, and they'd promised to overnight him a copy of their file.

So far, it hadn't come.

"It's a national holiday! I was celebrating! Crazy old woman, she just wants me to sit around the house with her and watch TV." Grumbling, Anson kicked off his shoes and stretched out on the bunk. There were three cells, side by side along the building's east wall. Another cinder-block wall, painted off-white like the rest of the interior, stood between the cells and the front door and extended three-quarters of the way up the room, shielding the prisoners from the view of anyone coming into or leaving the building. "If you hadn't been there, I don't know what I would have done. Like I said, I sure appreciate you arresting me."

"The jail isn't a hotel." Matt sat down behind his desk and started opening his mail. It was common knowledge around Benton that Anson and Ida Jarboe had been fighting for the entire forty-some years they'd been married. Usually it was over his drinking, but they were the type to fight over anything. The milder-tempered of the two, Anson usually got the worst of it. Lots of times when he'd been drinking he didn't even bother to go home. He just stopped by the jail and got himself arrested. That way he didn't have to face his wife until he'd slept it off.

"Makes a good one, though." Anson chuckled, pulled the blanket over himself, and turned on his side. "Wake me up in time for breakfast, would you?"

Matt grunted by way of a reply. If ever there was a poster

couple for not getting married, he thought, scanning an advertisement for Take 'Em Down, touted as a new, *professional-strength* pepper spray, Anson and Ida Jarboe were it.

The door opened. Matt glanced up.

Carly's friend Sandra sort of backed in over the threshold. He frowned. He'd been hearing a lot about Sandra lately—Antonio kept raving about how the lady could cook—but he wouldn't have expected to see her in the sheriff's office, of all places, especially at this time of night. Then he saw that she was lugging a large cooler, or, rather, half a large cooler, and the other shoe dropped. Sure enough, hanging on to the south end of that cooler was Carly. Her head was down, her cute little backside was thrust out, and she was quick-stepping as she played beat the door with the self-closing mechanism that always propelled it firmly shut.

Watching her, he had to smile.

Without warning she looked up and their gazes collided. The rush of familiarity, of homecoming, he experienced while his eyes were locked with those baby-doll blues almost shocked him, until he remembered that he'd looked into those eyes thousands of times before. They were part and parcel of his boyhood, of his wild, carefree, happily misspent youth, of his earliest forays into manhood. For the space of about a heartbeat, he was warmed by the sense of ease and comfort he took from her gaze, warmed enough to forget that he'd been keeping well away from her over the last four days for a reason, to forget that he couldn't even take a shower now with the Irish Spring soap he'd been using for years because the smell conjured up instant, erotic visions of how she'd felt in his arms, to forget how close he had come to toppling into the tiger pit dug by the needs of a woman he cared about enough not to want to hurt.

Then he remembered, and his senses went on red alert.

Quicker than a fly could dodge a swat, Matt realized that he was looking at trouble.

Carly smiled at him, sweet as sugar. "You don't mind if Sandra uses your bathroom, do you?"

Make that trouble with a capital T. He knew Carly. The sweeter she smiled, the madder she was.

Shit. This he did not need.

"Help yourself. It's right down there," he said to Sandra, pointing to the hall on his right. There were rest rooms down there, and a break room, and the deputies' cubicles. The evidence room and the room where the guns were stored were down there too, kept locked up tight.

"Thanks," Sandra said. She was indeed a big woman, Matt saw, reconfirming his previous impression, possibly bigger even than she appeared because of what his sisters had assured him were the slenderizing virtues of solid black, which she was wearing, but she was attractive nonetheless. He could see what Antonio saw in her. What he saw in her besides her cooking, that is, which, to Antonio at the moment, seemed to reign supreme. She and Carly set the cooler down just inside the door, then Sandra headed off toward the bathroom. Carly, on the other hand, headed toward him.

His first instinct was to stand up. She was a woman, after all, and his manners, having been drummed into him by a household full of women over the years, were relatively good where that kind of thing was concerned. But she was also Carly, his pal, and he wanted to keep it that way. If he started standing up when she walked into a room, then that put her in another category altogether, out of the friend column and into the other one, and he had already discovered that getting his columns mixed like that opened up a real can of worms. So he didn't stand, settling back into his chair instead, stretching out his legs and linking his hands across his stomach in a deliberate assumption of ease as he watched her approach.

Pal or not, she had definitely grown up. She was small and curved in all the right places, and her legs were tanned and slender beneath her mid-thigh-length shorts. Where most women of his acquaintance would have worn heels to make their legs look sexier, she wore tennis shoes—and her legs were plenty sexy enough to make his blood start to heat if he let himself think about them, which he didn't. Her hips in the dark blue shorts were slim, her waist was narrow and her tomato-red tee shirt did great things for her breasts. That soft wide mouth of hers that had been his downfall twice before was stretched into the extremely insincere sweet smile he'd previously noticed. Her cute little nose had been sunburned since he'd last seen her, and the color extended on out across her cheeks so that she looked all rosy and flushed. Her eyes, ordinarily a restful blue, a wide, baby-doll blue, were narrowed and glinting dangerously. Her outrageous hair—he didn't think he'd ever known anyone with such a crop of curls, or such an aversion to them—was tucked up beneath a denim baseball cap. But a number of spiraling tendrils had escaped to frame her face, and the result was—she looked pretty. Real pretty. She was blond now where she had been a soft light brown before, and stacked where she had been skinny. Maybe that accounted for the way he was having trouble keeping her firmly planted in his friend column. She looked like Carly, his pal, but better. Prettier. Sexier. In fact, way too sexy for his peace of mind.

To get his thoughts off just how much he'd like to take her to bed if only it wasn't such a bad idea, he focused on the storm that was getting ready to break over his head. It was clear from her gait, from her smile, from the sparks in her eyes—hell, from everything about her—that she was meaning to tear a strip off his hide.

"Nice hat," he said lazily, knowing that he was heaping coals on the fire but having too much fun watching her sizzle to be able to stop himself.

"Screw you."

She had reached his desk and was marching around it. Since his chair had wheels, he rolled himself back a little so he had room to dodge if he had to, but kept the same relaxed posture because he could tell it annoyed the hell out of her.

"I hear you knocked down my mailbox."

"I hear you called me a pain in the ass."

She stopped in the general vicinity of his knees to glare at him. Still leaning back in his chair, Matt found that he was looking up into her face. This was a new position for them. He discovered that he kind of enjoyed it.

"Maybe you shouldn't listen to gossip," he said. She was so close to him now that her sexy bare leg brushed his thigh. If he wanted to, it would be the easiest thing in the world to reach out and grab her hipbones and pull her down so that she was straddling him and—

Jesus, what was he doing? No way did he want to go there even in his mind. Sleeping with Carly was the last thing he wanted to do. He knew she wasn't the one-night-stand type. She wasn't even the three- or four-month, red-hot love affair type. She was the sex leads to commitment type, and that was dangerous to his plans.

"You," she said, pointing an accusing finger at him even as she fixed him with those glinting blue eyes, "have issues. You have problems. You have hang-ups."

"Don't we all."

"This thing you do—this kiss-and-run thing—it really doesn't work for me."

"You make it sound like we had a car accident." A little humor to defuse the situation—now what was there in that to make her eyes flash so?

"You've been deliberately avoiding me."

Obviously humor hadn't worked as a defusing device.

"Just like you deliberately avoided me that entire summer after . . ." Here she hesitated. He knew where she was going; the only question was, how graphic was she going to be? ". . . after my prom."

Not graphic at all. This was the Carly he knew, all right. Just blond and stacked and sexy as hell and all grown-up.

"Hey, give me a break. I apologized for that." Which had turned out really well. So well, in fact, that they'd gone through pretty much the same rigmarole again, and she'd ended up here, chewing him out.

"The point I'm trying to make is that you might really want to think about working on your romantic technique."

"Now, wait—" He'd never had any complaints. Except, now that he thought about it, about the tendency he'd exhibited over the years to, uh, kiss and run.

"Because it sucks. It really, truly sucks."

Then, before he had any inkling of what she meant to do, she took her big plastic cup and upended it over his head.

The sheer iciness of it hit him first. "What the hell?" he roared, leaping to his feet and brushing his hands over his head. His hair was wet, cold, sticky. Frigid droplets flew everywhere, and a squeezed shapeless lemon half hit the floor. He looked at it in disbelief.

"Have a nice life," she said, giving him another of those saccharine smiles, apparently not one whit discomposed by his rocketing fury. Then, while he swore and stomped and shook his head and splattered icy droplets all over the place, she set her now-empty cup down on his desk and turned her back, clearly intent on marching right out the door.

"I don't think so."

He grabbed her by the waist, not sure what he meant to do but knowing that he was not just going to let her walk out with that smug little smirk while he stood there like a cold, dripping, lemon-scented fool. But she solved his problem for him by suddenly swinging around in his hold, no longer smiling that maddening smile but now as furious as he was, her eyes blazing, that soft wide mouth tense and thinner than he could ever remember seeing it as she stretched herself up to her full sixty-two inches of height and matched him glare for glare.

"Did I say your romantic technique sucks?" She started out low but by the last word she was yelling at him, so mad that she was practically jumping up off the floor as she sought to get in his face. His hands were on her hipbones and to keep her down he had to tighten his grip and put a little weight into it. "That's not the only thing that sucks. You suck, Matt Converse. Did you hear me? *You* suck."

Suddenly it struck him as almost funny, Carly so small and cute and madder than he had ever seen her, shooting sparks all over the place and grabbing hold of his shirtfront and screaming at him, while he, almost twice her weight and a foot taller and a uniformed officer of the law, for God's sake, stood there with his head soaked in lemonade doing his best to hold her off.

God, he'd missed her. God, he wanted her. Wet and cold and sticky as he was, furious as he'd been until just a second or so before, he was suddenly consumed by an attack of lust so fierce that the sheer ache of it was almost enough to bend him double. What he wanted to do right at that moment more than he had ever wanted to do anything in his life was kiss her senseless and sweep his arm across the top of his desk and lay her down on it and—

"Who do you think you are, that you can treat people like that? That you can treat *me* like that? I—"

She was in full spiel, and he cut her off by the simple expedient of kissing her.

She tasted like lemonade, but the inside of her mouth was hot so it was hot lemonade, hot and sweet lemonade and he couldn't seem to get enough of it, so he slanted his mouth across hers and thrust his tongue deep, taking her mouth as his body wanted to take hers. His arms closed around her, and he pulled her so tight up against him that he could feel her nipples poking into his chest even through the layers of their clothes. He could feel the soft curve of her mound pressing against him, the whole intoxicating female shape of her, the heat of her, the sudden shivery yieldingness of her as she let go of his shirt and wrapped her arms around his neck and melted against him and started kissing him back.

His heart pounded. His blood turned to pure steam. He was on fire for her, burned for her, had to have her. She wouldn't stop him, he knew, knew she was his for the taking, that all he had to do was . . .

Kissing her greedily, he bent her back over his arm, ready to sweep her up and carry her to his desk and lay her down and damn the consequences.

A collective gasp made him open his eyes at just about the same instant as her ridiculous cap fell off.

Matt found himself looking at all three of his sisters, as well as Antonio, Shelby, Collin, the Andy kid he'd kicked out of his house only a couple of nights before, and the Craig guy that Dani had been dating. They were crowded around the open doorway, some of them inside, some of them still outside in the street with passersby thronging past behind them. To a person their eyes were wide and their mouths were agape.

Shit.

Carly obviously realized that something was amiss, because she went all tense and quit kissing him just about a nanosecond before he straightened both of them back up, pulled his mouth from hers and lifted his head. His instinct was to shield her, to protect her from the curiosity and amusement and in one case at least outright hostility of their audience, but she was already looking around and it was too late for that and anyway, short of trying to stuff her up under his shirt, there wasn't much of anything he could do. The lights were bright, the room was open, and there was no possible way to mistake who was who and what was what.

"Sorry," Erin offered weakly just as, from the corner of his eye, Matt became aware that their largest audience was not their only one. Anson was sitting bolt upright in his bunk observing them with evident amazement. Glancing around even farther, he found Sandra watching with what looked very much like awe.

Matt couldn't remember the last time he'd felt embarrassed. It was so long ago that he couldn't immediately pull the occasion to the forefront of his mind. But being caught passionately kissing a woman while lemonade dripped from his hair and his clothes was enough to make him recall with perfect clarity how it felt.

Carly discovered their audience and said, "Oh, hi," with what he considered really admirable aplomb. Of course, being fair-skinned, her embarrassment was less easy to conceal than his. The degree of mortification she felt was easy to gauge as her face turned almost the color of her shirt. She let go of his neck and pushed at his chest in a discreet but imperative signal that she wanted him to let her go.

He would have. He really would have. He agreed with her one hundred percent that stepping away from each other at this moment was the correct thing to do. Unfortunately, he had a problem. There in that open room with the fluorescent overhead fixtures providing merciless light, without her to shield him it was going to be obvious to even the most casual observer just how turned-on he was.

Which should ratchet up the embarrassment quotient considerably for all concerned.

"Want to give us a minute here?" Matt asked with as much ease as he could muster.

At just about that same time Carly shoved harder against his chest in a silent demand to be released and Erin said, "Uh, we'll just come back."

Matt's appreciation for his sister increased tenfold as she managed to shepherd the largest part of his audience back out through the door. Of course, that still left Anson and Sandra as interested onlookers, but there wasn't much he could do about them. He therefore elected to ignore them.

"Curls, look," he began seconds after the door clicked shut, gazing down at the woman he still held in his arms. She was glaring fiercely up at him, he saw with some surprise, notwithstanding the hot, heavy and absolutely, without a doubt, totally mutual kiss they had so recently shared.

"Jackass," she said, kicking him in the shin. Then she pulled herself out of his arms and stomped off toward the door.

"Ow!" That hurt. Matt hopped backward, grabbing at his leg. Seeing where she was headed, he straightened and went after her, limp and all. "Carly, what the *hell?*"

"I never want to see you again as long as I live. Just stay away from me, do you hear?" She threw a nasty look over her shoulder at him.

"What?"

She answered with her feet, and he was too slow to catch her before she whisked herself out the door. Remembering the audience that probably still lurked on the sidewalk and not wanting to make any more of a fool of himself than he had already, he stopped short and watched as the door shut in his face.

"Goddammit," he said bitterly, hobbling back toward his

desk. His leg hurt, his self-respect hurt, and he was wet and sticky and suddenly aware of how very cold the air-conditioning really was. Without realizing it he put his foot down on the lemon half and slid precariously, recovered without quite going down, then kicked the offending thing into a wall. When it bounced and ended up on top of a pile of very important papers on his desk, he faced the fact that the night had somehow gone to hell on a slide and let loose with a string of curses the likes of which he hadn't put together in years.

"Thanks for letting me use the bathroom," Sandra said. Damn, he'd forgotten all about her, Matt realized, and Anson too. She sidled on past him, eyeing him as if she feared he was losing it, and cast a single, assessing glance at the cooler before apparently deciding it wasn't worth it. Then she, too, was out the door.

"And I thought *I* had woman trouble," Anson said as Matt turned to grimly eye the mess Carly had left behind. Glancing around, Matt discovered that his prisoner was shaking his head at him. "My woman trouble is nothing compared to the woman trouble you got, believe me."

"Shut up, Anson," Matt said. "Or I'll take you home to your wife."

Spying Carly's cap lying upside down on the floor, he scooped it up, walked over to his desk, deposited it beside Carly's now empty cup and surveyed the damage to his documents. The lemon half rested on top of an arrest warrant scheduled to be served first thing in the morning. On such a document, the dried remains of a wet, citrusy circle should be barely even noticeable. Or at least, if it was noticed, no one would know what the hell it was. With that comforting thought, Matt gingerly picked up the offending piece of squashed and sticky fruit and dropped it into the trash. Then he headed into the back for a mop.

18

WAS THE DAMNED WOMAN never alone? The man stayed back, in the dark, watching as Carly Linton came around the front of the van she'd been driving. His heart pounded, his breathing quickened, and his palms grew moist. From adrenaline, he knew. He felt like a hunter catching sight of his prey. He was primed, ready to take her down—but then that other woman, that big black woman, slid out of the passenger seat to join her.

He gritted his teeth in frustration. Two was too many. Even if the other woman had been as petite as Carly, he still would have made himself hold off. Grab one, the other would run off screaming. Of course, this place was isolated, and it was late at night and dark, except for right up there around the house. If he attacked now, while they were still down near the road . . .

But no. That would be stupid. All the other obstacles in his path had been removed. Carly was the last one.

He would remove her too. When the time was right. When luck turned his way again, as it was bound to do.

But in the meantime he would have to be careful. The last thing he wanted to do was scare her, so that she would start looking over her shoulder. He had already scared her into getting new locks and an alarm system for her house, although that had been a complete accident on his part. At the time he hadn't even known she was anywhere around. The amusing thing was, he hadn't even had to attempt another break-in to find out about the new security precautions. He couldn't help but laugh. He had come by the knowledge in a far simpler way.

But his new knowledge left him with a problem. If breaking into the house was no longer an option—at least, not an easy one—he would have to catch her unawares outside the house.

He'd suspected that she would go to the fireworks display. Most of the town usually did. So he'd gone to it himself, and had actually seen her there. He'd thought about following her on the off chance that she would wander off somewhere on her own, but then he'd realized that there were too many people; the chance that he would be seen was too high.

Instead he'd left early and taken up position in her yard. It would be much easier, much safer to grab her when she came home.

If she came home alone.

Which she hadn't, of course.

On a positive note, the dog didn't seem to be anywhere around. At least, he hadn't seen it, and he hadn't heard it barking. Maybe it had wandered away. Or maybe the coyotes had finally picked it off.

Maybe that was a sign that his luck was turning up again.

Maybe, if he really applied himself, he'd be able to spirit Carly away from a locked-up-tight house without setting off the alarm system.

If he could pull that off, Benton would really have something to talk about.

19

"LISTEN, I KNOW what I saw, and what I saw was *hot*."
Sandra made a big production out of pretending to fan herself with her hand. "I practically melted where I stood."

"Give it a rest, Sandra, will you please?" Carly asked tiredly.

"Then you went and kicked him. Honey, men in general don't like that. Not unless they're kinky, that is. Is that hunky sheriff kinky? 'Cause I want him if he is."

"Sandra . . ."

Having been forced to listen to variations on the same theme from practically the moment Sandra had slid into the van beside her, Carly was deathly sick of the whole subject. She'd already had to endure the burning humiliation of walking past the madly gossiping group of Matt's friends, relatives and supporters as soon as she had hit the sidewalk after escaping from Matt himself. They'd quit talking as soon as they had spotted her, of course; it didn't take a genius to deduce what the subject of all that intense conversation was. To a self-conscious chorus of *Hi, Carly*'s she had managed to smile, and reply in kind. Then, thank you, God, she had had to turn the corner to reach her van. She'd never been so glad to be swallowed up by darkness in all her life.

Sandra, agog, had joined her in the van just about the

time Carly had been getting her mind around what had just occurred. It was unbelievable that, when she had finally let loose her newfound No More Ms. Nice Girl and told Matt exactly what she thought of him, thereby getting off her chest in masterly fashion—if she did say so herself—the hurt and anger that had been festering inside her for twelve years, to say nothing of the far more recent hurt and anger he had caused her, he had turned right around and kissed her, thus starting the whole blessed cycle up again. And she, of course, unprepared and unguarded and unable to control her inner slut, had reacted just like the old Carly had always reacted to any physical overture of Matt's and practically liquefied right there in his arms, thus sending her attempts at achieving closure for herself where Matt was concerned all the way back to square one. Fortunately, the kiss had been interrupted.

In any case, she had taken advantage of one last opportunity to go for closure when she had kicked Matt in the leg and told him what she thought of him.

The ride home had been consumed by Sandra's apparent inability to put the incident out of her head. Carly's attempt to gloss things over by claiming that what Sandra had witnessed was really nothing more than a kiss between old friends had been met with loud skepticism, and worse, a blow-by-blow recital of everything Sandra had seen, and deduced from what she had seen.

"The thing I don't get is, why'd you tell him you never wanted to see him again? If he was kissing me like that, the last thing I'd ever do is tell him I never wanted to see him again." Sandra grinned, her teeth a pale flash in the darkness. "I'd get him into bed so fast he wouldn't know what hit him, is what I'd do."

The two of them were, just at that moment, trudging up the front lawn toward the house. The smell of fresh-cut grass was strong. The serenading tree frogs were loud. Carly's level of annoyance was high, and getting higher by the moment.

"I don't notice you getting Antonio into bed." Desperate, Carly fell back on the old standby about the best defense being a good offense.

"Hey, give it time." Sandra grinned again. "I don't want him to think I'm easy."

It was getting close to midnight, dark as pitch, humid as a greenhouse and buggy as a swamp. The van was parked behind them on the shoulder of the road; up ahead, every light in the house was on, as, in a mutual, *damn-the-electricity-bill* nod to the lingering trauma of their first night in Benton, they had decided that coming home to a dark house was not going to work for either of them. The security system was worth every penny it had cost; in fact, Carly didn't think she would be able to sleep without knowing that it was standing silent guard over the windows and doors, but it didn't do them much good when they were outside. As a result, they were both walking fast in the teeth of the incline and the heat, and Carly at least was casting furtive glances around her with every other step.

Loath as she was to admit it, she was half-afraid to be there, at what was now her very own house. At least, she was once day turned to night. Even with Sandra in the house with her, and Hugo and now Annie too, she would find herself waking, sometimes at two A.M., sometimes at three, to lie with her heart pounding for no earthly reason that she could think of, just listening. For what? She didn't know. She only knew that she was absolutely gripped by fear.

Night terrors. She remembered them. When she'd first come to live with her grandmother, she'd suffered from terrible screaming nightmares that had shaken the walls of the house. The pediatrician that her grandmother had taken her to for all her medical needs had called them night terrors, said they were fairly common in young children, nothing to worry about, and were, in Carly's case, probably caused by the change in her living arrangements and the fact that she was still sorely missing her mother. They would go away, he promised.

It had taken a couple of years, during which their frequency had gradually decreased, but finally the night terrors had gone away. She hadn't suffered from more than the occasional garden-variety bad dream in years—until that night in Matt's bedroom. Until her first night back in Benton.

Carly shivered, just thinking about it. Were the night terrors coming back? Aside from that one nightmare in Matt's house in which she'd been a little girl again, frightened and missing her mother and back in the Home, she couldn't even remember dreaming on the nights when she woke up afraid. But maybe she was. Maybe what was waking her was a deeply experienced, forgotten-on-waking bad dream.

At least, she thought with a spurt of black humor, she didn't still scream.

But whatever woke her, eventually her heartbeat would calm and her fright would recede and she would fall back asleep, and in the bright morning light her fear seemed far away and childish and even faintly ridiculous. Certainly she wasn't going to tell anybody that she woke up in the middle of the night frightened half out of her wits. Anyway, who was there to tell? She didn't want to spook Sandra any more than Sandra, a city girl through and through, was already spooked just by her new rural environment; the fear that Sandra might hightail it back to Chicago continued to lurk at the back of her mind. And until just a little while earlier she hadn't seen Matt to confide in—not that she would have confided in him anyway.

Except, of course, he already knew about her bad dreams. But she wasn't going to confide in him *again*. She'd stood up for herself at last, and that was the end of that. Finis. Closure. The past coming full circle in a final, neat, appropriate ending.

Only it wasn't, because he had kissed her. And that kiss had seared its way down to her heart.

"Antonio was standing there on the sidewalk when I left the sheriff's office. He walked me partway to the van. Know what he said about you and the sheriff?" Sandra chuckled as she followed Carly up onto the porch. *"Hubba-hubba."* This she said in a deep and salacious voice, presumably mimicking Antonio.

Carly groaned. She really, truly, did not want to know.

Sandra continued in a more serious tone: "What I don't understand is why you just don't go ahead and sleep with the man. You know you want to."

The porch light was on, wrapping them in a comforting yellow glow that felt a whole lot safer than the shrouded darkness of the heavily treed yard. Still, the pervasive uneasiness that rarely left her when she was at home after dark meant that Carly was in such a hurry to get the key into the lock that she fumbled and almost dropped the entire key ring. It was stupid, she knew, and it was almost certainly all on account of that blasted burglar, but she couldn't get over the feeling that there were eyes out there in the dark watching her every move.

"I do *not* want to sleep with Matt," Carly said shortly as the key went home at last. "Believe me, he's got issues."

She got the door open and stepped into the hall with a feeling of relief. The tinny sound of the alarm system warning that whoever had opened the door had forty-five seconds to turn it off before it started shrieking was music to her ears. That meant there was nobody in the house.

"What kind of issues?" Sandra walked in behind her.

"He can't get it up, okay?" Carly snapped. Sandra's reaction made the spur-of-the-moment slander worth it. Round eyes, round mouth—and stilled tongue.

"You are lying in your teeth," Sandra said, recovering.

Carly didn't reply as she closed and locked the door. The smell of fresh paint—she'd already finished painting the front parlor and had gotten a good start on the rear one—made her wrinkle her nose. Hugo was sitting on the radiator cover, and he got up and stretched in greeting, then jumped to the floor, making a solid-sounding *thump* as he landed. Annie came flying in from the kitchen, toenails scrabbling over the hardwood, tail wagging madly.

Hugo jumped at this sudden onslaught of *dog,* spat, and shot off through the front parlor, while Annie, with a joyous yap, took off in hot and deliriously happy pursuit.

"Hugo! Annie! No! Stop that!"

Carly looked after them in defeat. Like that was going to work. The makers of mayhem didn't even slow down. Carly listened to the two of them tearing through the downstairs with a weary sigh.

"Welcome to the Inn at Beadle Zoo," Sandra said dryly. Carly shot her a look—Sandra had made her feelings concerning the addition of Annie to their little household very clear—and then followed her ears as she went to Hugo's rescue for the umpteenth time. Sandra, meanwhile, headed toward the kitchen.

"Annie, hush! Hugo, don't be such a—" the word *pussy* came to mind, bringing with it an unwelcome memory of Matt using the exact same word for the exact same reason, but Carly dismissed both firmly "—baby."

Rescuing Hugo from atop the tall mantel in the rear parlor, shushing Annie who danced deliriously beneath him, Carly carried the cat toward the kitchen, scolding both him and Annie, who didn't yap anymore but looked longingly up at Hugo as she trotted at Carly's heels. Like siblings, Carly thought, the two of them were simply going to have to learn to live together.

"You *are* lying, right?" Sandra asked as Carly entered the kitchen and set Hugo down on the counter.

"About what?"

"You know. The sheriff."

Carly now dropped to one knee, and Annie wagged her tail and put her front paws on Carly's leg and licked her cheek.

"Carly . . ."

"Okay." As much as Matt deserved the calumny, Carly found that she couldn't utter such a whopper twice. So she shrugged. "You're right. I am lying. Absolutely."

Sandra frowned.

"Good girl," Carly said to the dog. Picking up Annie, she hugged her warm body close and scratched behind her ears, which Annie loved. Annie expressed that love by opening her mouth in a doggy grin and panting in delight. Sandra, still with that thoughtful frown on her face, glanced at the two of them, then opened the refrigerator and reached inside, emerging with a piece of ham, which she tossed to Annie. Annie caught the treat in midair, gobbling it down with delight.

"See there," Carly said. "You love her. You know you do."

Sandra grimaced. "Let's see, why didn't I mention when we were talking about this bed-and-breakfast thing way back in Chicago that I don't do dogs? Because nobody said anything to me about a dog. If *some*body," she emphasized it pointedly, "had said, I want a dog, I would have said, I don't do dogs. But nobody did. They—meaning you—just found us a dog."

This was a continuation of a conversation they'd been having over the last few days. Sandra's complaints would have carried more weight if she hadn't then tossed another piece of ham to Annie, and then, with a quick look at her chief ally in the we-don't-need-a-dog department, handed one off to Hugo, who'd been watching the feeding of his rival with at first astonishment and then tail-lashing disbelief.

"Now that was nice," Carly said, her eyes twinkling. "See, you love Hugo too."

Sandra turned back to the refrigerator with a grunt. Carly looked down at Annie, who was wagging her tail hopefully as she watched Sandra. The dog had still not totally adapted to her new life, but, of course, it was early days yet and Carly was confident that she would. She was still timid, shying away from unfamiliar people and slinking around on her belly if someone spoke to her in other than a loving tone, but she was gentle and affectionate (except with Hugo, of course) and, Carly was convinced, grateful to finally have been saved from her hard-knock life. Sandra pooh-poohed the whole notion that a dog could be grateful, but Carly was persuaded that grateful was exactly how Annie felt: grateful for the home, grateful for the food, but most of all grateful for the love. She had taken Annie to the vet, who had examined her, given her a slew of shots, and estimated her to be about five years old. He'd said that she had most likely been a stray for a long time, but that she had no real health problems beyond being malnourished, which regular meals would fix, and a fairly recent injury: a nasty cut to the stomach just behind her front legs that, fortunately, had scabbed over without getting infected and was already, thanks to her assiduous licking of it, well on its way to being healed. The dark substance matting her coat he had identified as Annie's own blood, almost certainly from the healing cut. Carly had been horrified to think that the dog had bled so badly, but the blood had washed away easily enough, leaving her coat soft, black, and just slightly wavy, and the gash didn't seem to bother her. Now bathed, brushed and de-fleaed, Annie was quite a different dog.

Almost, even, a pretty dog. Certainly a sweet one.

"What a good girl, Annie," Carly said approvingly as, without letting loose with so much as a whine, Annie watched Hugo, who was more deliberate about these things, lick his piece of ham all over before consuming it in front of the dog's envious eyes. When it was gone, the eyes of both animals immediately swung back to Sandra, who was still rooting through the refrigerator.

Sandra straightened and shut the refrigerator door after extracting nothing more exciting than a soda.

Annie drooped with disappointment. Hugo swished his tail, sat down, and began to wash a paw.

Buoyed by the animals' calm acceptance of each other's consumption of the coveted ham, Carly decided to see if she couldn't help the relationship stabilize on this new, tolerant plateau. She carried Annie over to visit Hugo.

"See?" she said to them both, reaching out to stroke Hugo (and also, subtly, hold him in place) while she brought Annie closer—but not quite so close that a strategic swipe could reach the dog's moist black nose. "You two can be friends. You just—"

Annie yapped. Hugo hissed and bolted. Annie struggled, clearly eager to give chase, prevented only by the fact that Carly refused to let her go.

"You know, I don't think we're bonding here," Sandra observed, heading out of the kitchen with her drink.

"They will," Carly said.

By the time Carly finished bathing in the old-fashioned claw-footed tub that made up in sheer size for what it lacked in modern convenience, it was already close to one A.M. Pulling on her pajamas, trailed as usual by Annie, whose nails clicked on the hardwood floor with every step, she passed Sandra's already closed door and went into her own bedroom. It had changed very little since she'd lived in it as a child. The lavender-sprigged wallpaper and airy white curtains she'd been allowed to choose as a fifteenth birthday present from her grandmother were the same, as was the pastel braided rug at the foot of her bed and even the bed itself, a brass double that had only been altered by the substitution of a white chenille spread for the lavender, unicorn-strewn comforter of her teen years. As a child she'd always felt safe in this room. It bothered her that she no longer truly did. But tonight, with the security system on and Hugo curled up fast asleep on the bed and Annie, after a single longing glance at Hugo's clearly superior spot, stretching out to snooze on the rug, Carly felt as secure as she had since she'd come back to Benton. It helped that she was dead tired, too tired, hopefully, for any kind of bad dream to disturb her rest. It also helped that the images that crowded into her mind as soon as she crawled into bed and turned off the light all had to do with Matt. Matt saying *nice hat* with that provocative drawl of his and Matt's face after she had dumped what was left of her Lemon Crush on his head and Matt kissing her—

No, no, no. That wasn't helping. She absolutely, positively refused to go down that road either. Or to think about anything at all to do with Matt.

Ironically enough, it was on that thought, which was accompanied by swirling visions of dozens of memories of

Matt, each rejected one after the other so that the effect was almost like counting sheep, that Carly fell asleep.

And stayed asleep until something jolted her awake. Blinking groggily in the grayed darkness, Carly realized that the jolt had come from Hugo, who had used her body as a springboard to leap to the top of the tall wardrobe next to the bed. He crouched on it, tail swishing, eyes gleaming as he looked down at her.

Then Carly realized something else: the reason Hugo had decided to go trampolining in the middle of the night was because Annie was standing with her front paws on the sill of the long window that opened onto the roof of the back porch. Even as Carly spotted her, she started barking in frantic warning.

The curtains were thin, almost sheer, and didn't quite meet in the middle. Even before Annie had parted them more with her body, Carly had been able to see a sliver of starlit night. Only now, she realized to her horror, she wasn't seeing any stars.

Not a single one.

Something—some*one?*—was outside the window blocking her view of the night.

20

THE DOG. The dog. The damned dog. It was there in the house.

The man ran lightly to the edge of the porch, squatted, grasped the edge and jumped over the side. It was a low porch, a one-story porch that covered only a portion of the back of the house. Earlier, he'd been about to leave the yard when he'd looked up and there she was, framed by a window: Carly, with her curly blond hair—funny he didn't remember that about her, but then, he didn't remember much about those days—wearing pajamas. He couldn't see much through the barely parted curtains, just a slice of a lamplit room. But he could see enough to know that it was a bedroom. Her bedroom. She was going to bed.

One of the windows of her bedroom was directly over the small back porch.

There it was again, he'd thought: luck. Lately his had been almost all good.

She had turned off the light, and he hadn't seen anything more of her. But still, he'd hung around. Maybe this was his chance. Maybe he could just creep in there and bring her out.

He knew how security systems worked. They were only wired to the windows on the ground floor.

Another stroke of luck: he had a glass cutter in his car.

He'd given her an hour to fall asleep. Then he had climbed up on the porch roof—the rain spout beside it made the feat ridiculously easy—and eased on over, checking for wires that might indicate that the security system had been installed up here after all. But there weren't any; he checked the shutters, the window frame, the glass, growing increasingly confident that he was right. Through the parted curtain, he could just see a sliver of white that was the bed—her bed.

And a lump curving through the middle of that sliver of white that was *her*.

The way his luck was going, he thought as he pulled the glass cutter out of his pocket, he would be able to get the whole thing taken care of tonight.

Then it would be, *Hello, brave new world.*

He'd just been putting the glass cutter to the glass when the curtain had fluttered. Reflexively he'd glanced down—and there it was, looking at him through the window: the dog.

The damned, damned dog.

He was already running for the edge of the roof as it started to bark.

Yap, yap, yap. Yap, yap, yap, yap, yap.

21

HUGO PRANCED toward her in the afternoon sunlight like a high-bred show horse, lifting each paw high and shaking it with disbelief before putting it back down and repeating the process. Carly had to smile. He gave the phrase *cat on a hot tin roof* a whole new meaning.

Because he was, literally, a cat on a hot tin roof.

"How did you get up here, anyway?" she asked him, crawling carefully to his rescue. Scooping him up, she scooted backward until she reached the patch of shade she'd been working in. When she set him back on his feet again, he looked apprehensive until he realized that the surface beneath his feet was relatively cool. Then, with a twitch of his tail and a level look at her to make sure that she understood that, despite his recent brief lapse in temperature judgment his dignity was still very much intact, he sat down in the lee of the chimney and started giving himself a bath.

Carly wasn't offended. She had realized long since that being a cat meant never having to say thank you.

She picked up her hammer and went back to work. It was late in the afternoon of July fifth, and she was up on top of the house repairing the red tin roof. The task involved nailing the loose parts of the roof down, then painting over the nails with a red-tinted, tar-like substance that would keep moisture from creeping down the holes. The work was more tedious than difficult, and as long as she remembered where she was and didn't back over the edge it wasn't dangerous, but the suffocating heat rendered it fairly miserable. No fool, she had been working in the patch of shade cast by the huge walnut tree nearest the house, but at some point she was going to have to leave its protection and venture out into the broiling sun. She was hoping to time it so that the patch of shade moved with her. It was either that, or finish the repairs after the sun went down. And seeing as how at its peak the roof was some forty feet off the ground, working on it after dark was probably not a good idea. Falling might very well prove fatal.

Anyway, she wasn't planning on doing *any*thing outside the house after dark anytime soon. Wild horses couldn't drag her guilty secret from her, but she was now thoroughly scared of the place once night fell. That this might prove to be a problem at some point, she was well aware. Being afraid in one's home after dark probably was not conducive to a peaceful life. Maybe it was just a matter of getting used to the rural setting again, after so many years spent living in big cities. Maybe the eyes she felt watching her through the dark belonged to nothing more terrifying than tree frogs. Maybe the cold feeling that sometimes stole over her when she looked into the shadowy recesses of the yard was simply a reaction to sweat drying on her skin.

Maybe. And maybe not.

Could the burglar still be hanging around, hoping for a second go?

Just thinking about the possibility sent cold chills racing up and down her spine.

Last night, when she had turned on the lamp beside her bed and peered, with heart-thumping bravado, outside her window, there had been nothing there. Just the silent trees, and the twinkling stars, and the night. Even as she had watched, with Annie quivering beside her, a cloud had blown across the sky, blocking the stars from view, taking the night from gray to black. Had it been nothing more than a cloud blowing past that had made her think someone stood in front of the window, blocking the sky? It was possible. It was even probable.

It was also possible that Annie had been roused by something like a raccoon or even a squirrel running across the porch roof. After all, she loved barking at Hugo; it was quite likely that another running animal would evoke a similar response. Or maybe she'd been startled by a falling limb.

Who knew? Certainly the return of the burglar was the least likely possibility.

Still, Carly hadn't been able to go back to sleep. She'd spent the rest of the night huddled in a pitiful little ball in her bed while her eyes stayed trained on the window. A few times the window had indeed darkened, which she'd had no difficulty in ascribing to a passing cloud. But Annie and Hugo, both of whom had soon dozed off again, had not wakened. In fact, neither animal had stirred for the rest of the night.

In the morning, Carly had gone outside to discover that a branch had, indeed, fallen onto the roof of the back porch.

See there? she told herself. *That's what all the commotion was about.*

The sound of it hitting probably freaked Annie out.

She knew it was almost certainly so. But still, when the electrician she'd hired to update the wiring to accommodate commercial appliances understood exactly what she wanted and had made a good start, which meant that she didn't need to supervise him, and Sandra went into town for groceries, Carly had donned her oldest jeans, a faded green camp shirt and tied a bandanna around her head before pulling out her hammer and nails and making short work of her bedroom windows, security system or not.

If the burglar was still lurking around, he wasn't getting in that way: she nailed the damned windows shut.

Not that she didn't have confidence in the security system, of course. But as her grandmother had often said, *Praise the Lord and pass the ammunition.*

To which she now said, *Amen.*

While she was at it, she nailed shut practically every window in the house. The only ones she didn't touch were the ones downstairs. She was tempted, but the woodwork was too beautiful to mar by driving nails through it. Anyway, there was always the security system. It was state of the art. It was reliable. It could be trusted to keep her—her and Sandra and Annie and Hugo—safe.

She had been counting the downstairs windows to see how many brooms she needed to buy so that she could saw off their heads and wedge the sticks in the tracks, thus thwarting any possible entry by any possible burglar without harming the wood, when Sandra came home with the groceries.

Caught red-handed, hammer in hand and nails in a pouch slung around her waist, Carly had thought fast. Last night Sandra had slept through Annie's barking. Sandra had no idea that Carly was growing increasingly paranoid about the things that went bump in the night—especially the things that went bump in the night outside her bedroom window. Sandra was pursuing Antonio with the single-mindedness of a hunter after a twelve-point buck. Sandra was also the biggest coward on the planet.

If, for Sandra, it came down to a choice between true

lust and chickenheartedness, Carly didn't want to find out which would win. It was better to skirt the whole issue by keeping the fear factor from entering into Sandra's calculations.

So she had replied to Sandra's question about the hammer and nails by saying that she was just on her way up to fix the roof.

Which needed doing anyway, so she did it. Or at least, she got started.

"So what brings you up here?" she said to Hugo, on the theory that a little friendly conversation might help pass the time.

Hugo, unfortunately, did not seem to be in the mood to be scintillating company. He gave her a baleful stare, then went right back to his grooming as if it were the most important thing on earth.

But she knew her cat well. That was his way of saying that all was not catnip and tuna fish in his world.

"Okay, I know you have a problem with Annie," she said, hammering another nail home and then dabbing it with the roof goop. "I know you wish you were back in our nice condominium with the nice central air and the nice view of the lake. I know it's hot here and you're shedding and you're probably picking up fleas from being outside and now we've got a dog. But maybe what you need to do is think of this whole thing as a growth experience."

"Who on earth are you talking to?" The voice—Matt's voice—coming at her seemingly out of nowhere almost made Carly, who was in the act of driving another nail, whop her thumb with the hammer. Snatching her hand out of harm's way in the nick of time, she scowled and looked around to find Matt regarding her quizzically. He was standing on the narrow ladder she had propped against the side of the house to gain access to the roof. His head and shoulders were the only parts of him visible above the roofline.

"Hugo." Now that she had ascertained where he was, Carly repositioned the nail he'd made her miss and this time hammered it home. Then she sank back on her haunches and looked at him again, her scowl firmly in place.

"Catch my burglar yet?" Hostility simmered in her voice.

"Working on it."

"Great. I take it you're not calling on official business, then. So what are you doing here?"

"I brought back your cooler. And your cap."

He didn't seem one bit discomposed by the obvious fact that she was not happy to see him. As Carly, on all fours now, deliberately ignored him in favor of clobbering another nail, he climbed onto the roof. He was wearing a gray tee shirt that said ATLANTA BRAVES across the front of it, scruffy jeans, and decrepit-looking sneakers. Dressed like a bum, with the faintest suggestion of stubble darkening his jaw and his black hair waving from the heat and his eyes narrowed against the glare bouncing off the roof, he still managed to look so handsome that her scowl deepened into a full-blown glower.

If they were being cast in some kind of Southern-fried version of *Beauty and the Beast,* she knew which one of them would get to play the Beast.

"You know, you seem to have real trouble following directions. I thought I told you that I never wanted to see you again."

"Was that before or after you kicked me in the leg?" Having repaired the roof many times himself when he was a teenager, Matt knew enough to respect its pitch. Moving carefully, he eased into the patch of shade where she was working, and spotted Hugo by the chimney. "Hey, Pussy."

"After. And don't call him that."

"He likes it. He . . ." Matt's voice trailed off as Hugo, after giving him a disdainful look, stood up and walked away with a haughty swish of his tail. "All right, so maybe he doesn't like it."

"Maybe he just doesn't like *you*." Her memory of Mike and Antonio's tale of Matt fetching Hugo down from the tree was still vivid.

"That's always a possibility."

Matt grinned and sat down on the spot—just about the only flat spot on that section of the roof—that Hugo had just vacated.

Carly drove another nail. "Okay, you brought back my cap and the cooler. You even climbed all the way up here to tell me you brought back my cap and cooler. I'm impressed. I'm grateful. So now how about you go away?"

Matt looked at her for a moment. His expression was impossible to read. At least, with her on her hands and knees looking at him over her shoulder while holding in place another nail she'd just positioned for driving, it was impossible to read.

"Did I ever happen to mention that you've got a really great ass?"

For just a second, Carly had to run that through her auditory sensors one more time to make sure that what she'd heard was what he'd actually said. It was. Outraged—and only then realizing that her position had afforded him an excellent view of her butt—she sank back on her haunches and glared at him.

"Okay, that's it. Now leave."

He grinned at her without budging. "I hear I need a prescription for Viagra."

Carly remembered that Sandra had been in town.

"Maybe you shouldn't listen to gossip," she said, and,

taking care not to present her backside to him this time, hammered in her nail.

"Maybe you shouldn't tell lies."

"How do you know that came from me? I'm sure there are lots of women ready, willing and able to gossip about you and your need—or not—for Viagra." She broke off to bestow one more flattening whack on the head of the nail she'd just driven. Pretending it was Matt's head helped her to give it a really satisfactory blow.

"Actually, not that many, not lately. In fact, none lately."

"Yeah, right." Carly threw him a look while she fished in her pouch for another nail. "What about . . ." she almost said Miss Queen of Everything, "Shelby?"

He shrugged, watching her. "We went out for a few months. We broke up in March."

"Oh, sure. You broke up in March, but she's over at your house early on a Sunday morning and your sisters seem to think she has a claim on you and she looked at me like she wanted to hit me over the head with an ax after . . . after—"

"She caught us kissing in my office?" His voice, filling in the blank for her when she couldn't quite say the words, was silky smooth. Carly felt a rush of heat to her face as an explicit memory of that kiss took momentary possession of her senses. Mentally shoving it away, hoping that he would credit any deepening in her color to the heat, she positioned the nail and whacked it with an extra degree of savagery.

"Erin is engaged to Shelby's brother. Since I'm the closest thing to a mother Erin has now and I'm not much help as far as flower arrangements and bridesmaids' dresses and things like that are concerned, Shelby is helping to plan the wedding. That's basically why she's still hanging around."

Carly positioned another nail. "And that explains why she looked at me like she wanted to kill me."

Matt quirked an eyebrow at her. "Jealous, Curls?"

This time she did hit her thumb. "Ouch!" Dropping the hammer, she shook her injured hand.

"No, I'm not jealous," she said, glaring at him. "I can't believe you'd even ask me that."

Matt grinned at her. On the verge of losing her temper, Carly decided that doing so right at that point might make it look like she was, indeed, jealous, which was the last thing she wanted him to think, especially since it absolutely, positively, was not true. Taking a deep breath, she opted for dignity instead. Shaking her hand one more time, she decided that her thumb was going to live and picked up her hammer again.

"Look, I'm trying to fix a roof here. Don't you have somewhere else you need to be?"

"Nope." He reached over and plucked the hammer from her grasp. "I took the afternoon off."

That would explain his clothes.

"So why don't you go fishing or something?" The question was tart. "Or bird-watching? Or butterfly-chasing? Or whatever it is you do for fun nowadays."

Sinking back on her haunches again, she surveyed him with disfavor. Grappling with Matt over her hammer would be undignified—and also useless. From many years' experience in dealing with him, she knew the score: if he didn't want to give it to her, she wasn't going to get it back. Instead she reached for her roof goop. Taking the high road in the certainty that it would annoy the dickens out of him, she started slopping sticky red stuff over the nails she'd already put in place.

"Actually, I am out having fun; I'm on my motorcycle."

Carly stopped slopping goop to look at him.

"You still have a motorcycle?" She hooted. "Let's see, I seem to remember somebody saying, *The more things change . . .*"

"Hey, I've moved up in the world. This one's a Harley."

"Whoa. I'm impressed. A Harley. That is moving up. So why don't you go ride your Harley and let me finish fixing the roof?"

"Besides bringing back your cap and your cooler, I stopped by to see if you wanted to go for a ride with me."

That caught Carly by surprise. She let a couple of heartbeats pass before she replied.

"What?"

"I came by to see if you wanted to go for a motorcycle ride with me. Maybe we could grab supper somewhere."

Carly slowly put the brush back into the can of goop. She looked at him narrow-eyed. "Matt Converse, are you by any chance asking me out?"

His eyes met hers.

"Yeah, I think I am."

For a moment Carly simply looked at him without replying. She had been so furious at him—was that just the night before? And so hurt and wary, too. And she still was; at least, part of her was. But another part of her, her heart, she guessed, kept whispering: *It's Matt.* A whole lifetime's worth of memories chased one another through her head. Wasn't there some song that said something like, *how do you repay someone who has taken you from crayons to perfume?* For her, that someone was Matt.

"Wait a minute," she said, aware that her heart was already starting to beat faster. "You're not going to pull that kiss-and-run thing again, are you?"

His smile was slow, crooked, and devastatingly attractive. It took a long time to reach his eyes. By the time it did, Carly was breathless—annoyed at herself for being such a sucker for Matt's smile, but definitely breathless anyway.

"That would imply that you think I'm planning to kiss you."

"Well, are you?"

"Maybe."

"Not good enough, Sheriff." Carly reached for her brush, and slopped more goop on the roof without even caring if she actually got anywhere near the nails or not. Her heart was pounding so hard now that she could actually feel her blood thudding against her eardrums. Butterflies were taking wing in her stomach. Going out with Matt, getting involved with Matt, kissing Matt—God help her, the very thought of that made her dizzy—was a mistake. She knew it was a mistake. She knew it with every fiber of her being. But she wanted to make that mistake so badly that she already knew, too, that she was going to do it; she was going to leap right out of the frying pan into the fire. The worst thing about it was, she was doing it with her eyes wide open. If she got burned again, she had no one to blame this time but herself.

Carly sank back on her heels and glared ferociously at him. "I'm warning you right now that if you pull that *friend* crap on me again, I'm going to cut off your balls with a butter knife."

Matt looked at her for a moment, his eyes widening with slow-dawning delight. Then he chuckled. Reaching over, he grabbed her arm and hauled her toward him, goop-filled brush and all.

"You're scaring me, Curls," he said, and kissed her.

22

H IS KISS WAS EVERY BIT as mind-blowing as the last one had been. Carly closed her eyes and was lost. When he lifted her onto his lap, she wrapped her arms around his neck. His lips were firm, dry, and warm as toast. When he touched her lips with his tongue, she parted them helplessly. Her body was quaking, on fire, hungry. This was Matt and she wanted him. Pressing her breasts up against his chest, she kissed him back.

He tasted faintly musky. His tongue was hot, strong, demanding. It filled her mouth and she felt dizzy, almost as if she were floating, as if he were the only solid thing in the world and if she let go she would whirl away like a leaf in the wind. She touched his tongue with hers, stroked it, explored his mouth as he was exploring hers. When he turned her so that her head was resting back against his broad, hard shoulder, she felt small and helpless and ravished, and because it was Matt, she loved the feeling. Drawing a deep, shaken breath, she started to caress the warm skin at the nape of his neck, realized that she was still holding the paintbrush, and dropped it. It hit the roof with a soft clatter, and she didn't think about it again.

Her fingers threaded into his hair; the strands just above the nape were short and silky. He was bending over her, bending her back so that she was almost reclining with her head pillowed on his shoulder, running his mouth across her cheek and the line of her jaw, trailing tiny kisses down her neck, nibbling her earlobe, then kissing her senseless again. His arms were taut around her, flattening her breasts against his chest. She could feel the need in him, the urgency, the tension in his shoulders and back. She could feel the telltale hardness of him pressing against her thigh. Her heart threatened to pound out of her chest.

Then his hand was on her breast, covering it, squeezing, and it felt so good, so wonderful, that Carly made a tiny sound deep in her throat and quivered with pleasure.

He lifted his head, breaking the kiss. Carly opened her eyes a slit, looking dazedly up at him. Dark color suffused his face. His eyes were blazing. He was breathing hard.

He wanted her. Badly. There was no mistaking that.

His hand was still on her breast. She looked down at it, at that long-fingered, tan, utterly masculine and utterly beautiful hand splayed across the front of her faded green shirt, and caught her breath. It was Matt's hand, she'd had a million dreams about that hand, she would know it anywhere, and it was warm and strong and cupping her breast. Her nipple hardened into his palm. Pure heat shot through her and her loins pulsed with need and she had to work to suck in air.

"Matt . . ." she whispered in abject surrender as her insides quaked and quivered with passion, absolutely his for the taking now. Closing her eyes, suffused with the sweetness of surrender, she lifted her mouth to his.

"Carly." There was a husky undertone to his voice—and a note of semi-amused ruefulness as well. The semi-amused ruefulness part was just beginning to fully register when he continued with unmistakable regret. "Baby, I don't think this is such a good idea."

He didn't think this was such a good idea?

Her eyes popped open.

"What?" she growled, glaring at him, struggling to sit up. He was still leaning over her, still holding her, but she shoved against his shoulder and sat bolt upright even as he grabbed her around the waist to prevent her from leaping to her feet and met her gaze with a twinkle.

She was going to kill him, she was really going to kill him; this time she was going to do it for sure. . . .

"We're on the roof," he said, and despite the twinkle she saw that his eyes were dark with passion and hot color stained his cheekbones and his breathing was not quite steady. "One wrong move and it's like forty feet down. Not a good place for where this is going."

She eyed him narrowly. He grinned.

"You're beautiful," he said, tracing a finger down the bridge of her nose. For a moment she simply looked at him suspiciously, because no one had ever called her that, not John, not Matt ever before, not anyone, and anyway she knew it wasn't true.

"That would be you," she said.

He shook his head at her. "No, that would be you." She thought she saw a sudden wealth of tenderness for her in his eyes. "Trust me on this, Curls: that would be you."

Sliding his hand beneath her jaw, he tilted her face up to his and kissed her. It was a soft kiss, a gentle kiss, but thorough nevertheless. Its effect on Carly was devastating. She melted against him, turned absolutely boneless, wrapping her arms around his neck and kissing him back with a neediness that shook her when she realized it for what it was.

"Okay, off the roof." He broke the kiss and lifted her off his lap before she had quite recovered her wits. "Think you can make it back to terra firma without killing yourself?"

He got to his feet and stood looking down at her. For a

moment longer she sat in a near daze with her shoulder pressed up against the chimney, dreamily aware of the heat in the bricks against which she leaned and in the tin panel on which she sat and in the air. She realized that it was still full daylight, with the late afternoon sun slanting through the branches of the walnut tree to make intricate patterns in light and shadow on the roof. The sky was a soft cerulean blue and the clouds were like cotton candy and a pair of noisy blue jays flitted around in the tree and a bushy-tailed squirrel scampered along a branch not far above their heads—and the tarry smell of roof goop wafted beneath her nose.

Okay, so it wasn't quite perfect. It was still a beautiful day, a glorious day, and she had a date with Matt.

Was her life looking up or what?

"Did you hear what I said?" Matt asked dryly, holding his hand out for her to grab.

Carly's gaze snapped to his face. Not for anything was she going to let Matt know just how very dazzled she was. Not that he probably didn't already have a pretty good idea.

"Yes, of course I heard what you said. You're not *that* great a kisser, Matt Converse."

She put her hand in his, and he pulled her upright.

"Later I'm going to make you eat those words," he said, and lifted her hand to his mouth.

Carly watched him press his lips to her knuckles and her pulse went crazy. His lips were warm on her skin and his eyes were hot as he met her gaze over her bent fingers. The gesture was totally disarming, totally romantic, totally unlike any aspect of Matt she knew, and she'd thought she knew every aspect of Matt there was. This one was . . . Matt the lover. Like Matt the grown-up sheriff, it was part of the man he was now, not the boy he had been. As she realized the seismic shift in their relationship his kissing of her fingers signified, her stomach lurched and her knees went weak.

Boy or man, he was still Matt, and she still wanted him so much she burned with it.

"Come on," he said, lowering their joined hands and starting to head toward the ladder, moving carefully, pulling her after him.

"Wait, I've got to get my things." Her scattered senses suddenly came together in a concentrated whole, and she tugged her hand free. She couldn't just leave her work materials behind. Her hammer, a single loose nail and the can of roof goop lay forgotten about a yard away. Her paintbrush, still loaded with goop, was near Matt's feet. Bending, she reached for the paintbrush.

He took it from her, stuck it into the goop can, and hung the can over his arm. Then, stowing the hammer and nail in his front pocket, he caught her hand again and pulled her after him toward the ladder.

Holding the ends of the ladder to steady it as she stepped onto it, he made her go first. Climbing down, Carly couldn't help but glance up to admire his long, powerful leg muscles and the cute roundness of his butt in the washed-thin jeans as he followed her. He was Matt, he was gorgeous, and he was soon to be hers. At the thought she almost missed a rung.

Tumbling thirty feet to her probable death would not be a good way to start what promised to be the most amazing evening of her life, Carly thought, focusing on her own hands and feet as she climbed down.

They were nearly on the ground when Carly realized that they were being watched. By multiple pairs of eyes, as it happened. Hugo lay almost even with them on one of the big walnut tree's lower branches, at ease, looking comfortable, his tail barely moving as he tracked their descent. It said much for Matt's effect on her that she had forgotten all about her coddled cat until that moment. Clearly Hugo had gone native to a far greater degree than she had realized if he could get himself on and off the roof via the walnut.

Benton had wrought great changes in both her and her cat, Carly thought, glancing up at Matt again. In fact, Carly realized with a flicker of surprise, she had hardly thought of John or anything concerning her divorce since she'd first slid out of that U-Haul. Her life as Mrs. John Grunwald— not that she'd ever used that name, preferring to keep her own—seemed far away, distant, as if it had belonged to someone else. *This* was her real life. She glanced up again, and her heart skipped a beat. Matt was her real life.

At the thought Carly almost missed another rung.

Recovering, her gaze fell on Annie, who waited at the base of the ladder, her tail wagging as she looked up at them. Behind Annie, Antonio, Mike and Sandra were gathered, watching too, their turned-up faces reflecting various degrees of surprise, interest and speculation. Glancing sideways, her attention drawn by a movement caught from the corner of her eye, Carly saw Erin getting out of the passenger seat of a red Honda that had just parked in front of the house. Even at such a distance Carly was able to tell when Erin spotted her brother coming down the ladder. Erin froze, staring up the hill toward them.

Hail, hail, the gang's all here, Carly thought wryly.

That their audience was speculating wildly on just exactly what was going on between the two of them was impossible to miss. She didn't think she could have felt more self-conscious if she'd been climbing down the ladder naked.

"So, did you get the roof fixed?" Sandra asked in a slightly too hearty tone as Carly stepped onto the grass.

"Most of it." Carly wiped her sweaty palms on the back of her jeans, proud of how composed she sounded, and bent to give Annie a pat. She was also proud that she managed *not* to look at Matt, who was just now reaching the ground beside her. Still, she was so conscious of him as she straightened again that she could practically feel him breathe. She was also so conscious of having just made out with him on the roof that she was positive her face was a bright telltale red.

"Who's this?" Matt asked, setting the bucket of roof goop on the ground and sweeping the assembled company with a comprehensive glance before his gaze fixed on Annie, who was sniffing rather suspiciously at his feet. Unlike herself, Matt looked and sounded perfectly relaxed, perfectly himself.

Their eyes met. Carly couldn't help herself. She smiled at him, and her heart missed a beat as he smiled slowly back. A slight shuffling sound reminded her of their audience, and, self-conscious again, she focused on his question and glanced down at the little dog.

"This is Annie. You remember the dog that chased Hugo that first night? We decided to adopt her."

Sandra snorted. "Speak for yourself," she said.

Carly ignored her comment, but noticed Sandra glancing with interest from her face to Matt's.

"Annie's a sweetheart," Carly told Matt.

"I bet." If his tone was dry, still he held out his hand so that Annie could sniff his fingers and then scratched behind her ears before straightening to look at Antonio and Mike.

"So what's up?" Matt asked them.

The deputies were in uniform, and, Carly presumed from the question and the tone in which it was asked, on duty.

Up until that moment they, like Sandra, had been casting covert glances from Matt to Carly and looking slyly amused as they did it. Their expressions quickly altered as they met their boss's level gaze. Mike shuffled his feet and glanced away. Antonio crossed his arms over his chest and cleared his throat.

"There was a radio call for you about ten minutes ago," Antonio said. "Dispatch said a caller was trying to get through to your cell phone, but it was turned off. Seems Mrs. Hayden's out walking her dog again."

There seemed to be some special significance to that, because Matt looked faintly vexed while Antonio and Mike both appeared to be trying hard to suppress grins.

"My phone's off for a reason." Matt started to put his hands into his pockets, encountered the hammer, pulled it out, fished for the nail and handed both to Carly. "And the reason is, I'm off duty. Somebody else is going to have to take care of Mrs. Hayden."

"I'll tell 'em to send Knight. He could use a little seasoning," Antonio said.

"Good call." Matt grinned then, apparently finding considerable humor in whatever picture this conjured up. "Anything else?"

Listening to Matt being large and in charge had a surprising effect on Carly. She thought back to the boy he had been, to the youth he had been, to the young man he had been, and felt a surge of pride. The boy the town would have voted Most Likely to Become an Ax Murderer had turned out pretty well after all. *You've come a long way, baby,* were the words that popped into her mind, and at the sheer ridiculousness of them as applied to Matt, she smiled.

"Thompson broke his leg falling down his back steps, and Brooks called in with a stomach virus," Antonio said.

"You've got to be kidding me." Matt looked harassed. "We're understaffed as it is. That brings us down to six. When's their next shift?"

"Both on at eleven tonight."

"Christ," Matt said. "Who's covering?"

"Everybody's already pulled a double shift within the last twenty-four hours. We don't get some more people hired, we're all gonna turn into zombies."

"The funding's not there." Matt grimaced. "All right, fine. To hell with it. I'll cover for Thompson, you cover for Brooks."

"I was afraid you were going to say that," Antonio said gloomily.

"Hey, you put in for Chief Deputy."

"Yeah, I know." Antonio sounded depressed as he glanced at Sandra. "I just kind of thought rank would have a little more privilege."

Matt snorted, and reached for Carly's hand. Immediately Sandra, Antonio, and Mike homed in on their entwined fingers like missiles seeking heat. Under the weight of their stares Carly couldn't have felt more conspicuous if someone had suddenly pasted a scarlet A on her forehead.

"Ready?" he said. Carly nodded, and he tightened his hold on her hand as he glanced back at their audience.

"Is that it?" he asked his deputies. "Because we're out of here."

"We're going to hang around for supper." Antonio met Matt's gaze and shrugged defensively. "Hey, we get an hour, and we gotta eat."

"Hi, everybody."

With that cheerful greeting Erin joined them. She was wearing a denim miniskirt and white tank, and with her tan and tousled black hair looked fresh and glowing—and faintly worried. Mike's eyes lit up when he saw her, but she wasn't looking at him. She glanced from Matt to Carly, then down at their linked hands. She then focused on her brother, her expression guarded. "Uh, Matt, could I talk to you for a minute?"

"What now?" Matt asked, sounding resigned. His hand tightened briefly on Carly's, and then he let go and allowed his sister to pull him aside.

"I'm just going to run inside and get my purse," Carly said brightly, glad of the distraction. She had suddenly recollected that she was wearing her oldest undies and a ratty bra and she needed a shower and her makeup was nonexistent and . . .

If sleeping with Matt was on the agenda, and it might very well be, she had to make some massive changes fast.

By the time she was inside, she was practically running, stripping off the bandanna and then unbuttoning her shirt as she went. She was unzipping her jeans as she stepped over the bathroom threshold. Throwing off her clothes, she took the world's fastest shower, shaved her legs and underarms with a haste that gave razor burn a whole new meaning, and stared in dismay at the nest of blond curls tangling around her face before deciding that trying to tame them was a waste of time and effort. Running—all right, yanking—a brush through them, she fluffed them with her fingers and left them to do their own thing. She smoothed tinted moisturizer into her skin for that lovely glow promised on the packaging, added the barest suggestions of blush and eyeshadow, treated her lashes to a quick coat of mascara and her lips to a slick of watermelon lip gloss, and approved her appearance in the mirror—had Matt really said she was beautiful? Just thinking about it made her feel all warm and squishy inside. She wrapped a towel around herself and sprinted for her bedroom.

She'd accomplished a minor miracle in ten minutes, tops. Matt would hardly have had time to miss her yet.

If he were to figure out that she was showering and primping and changing her undies and in general making herself as attractive as possible in anticipation of having sex with him, she would be mortified. Of course, knowing Matt, he might very well guess. But if she hurried, and got back downstairs before he had really had time to wonder what the heck she was doing, she hoped it might not even enter his mind.

"Just so you know, the sheriff had to leave."

Sandra was sitting on the edge of Carly's bed as Carly flew through the door. She was wearing her favorite attire of black leggings with an oversized black tee shirt, which made her absolutely impossible to miss against the white spread. This particular tee shirt had Mini-Me's likeness on the front. Her earrings were dangling silver smiley faces; in contrast, she was looking uncharacteristically serious as she watched Carly's frantic progress.

"What?" Carly froze in the act of rushing toward her dresser to swing her gaze around to Sandra.

Sandra nodded. "He said to tell you he'd pick you up in half an hour. On the motorcycle, so wear jeans."

Carly's heart started beating again. For a moment there, she'd been terrified that she'd been the victim of another patented Matt Converse kiss-and-run.

In which case he would have died a slow and agonizing death.

"Where did he go?"

Moving at a dignified pace now, she continued toward her dresser. When she reached it, she opened her lingerie drawer and started searching through the contents. Luckily she still had some really nice things left over from when she'd still been having sex what seemed like a whole lifetime ago. A black lace demi-cup bra caught her eye. Somewhere in the drawer should be tiny matching panties. . . .

Just the thought of Matt seeing her in such sexy scanties was enough to weaken her knees. The last time he'd seen her undies, she'd been wearing white cotton panties that covered her from her navel to the tops of her thighs. Fortunately, she'd been too flat-chested to have to worry about a bra, because if she'd been wearing one it would have been equally white and cotton and lacking in sex appeal.

Kind of like she had been.

"You sure you want to hear this?" Sandra asked.

The way Sandra said it, Carly was pretty sure she didn't. Still, she nodded.

"Apparently that Shelby woman gave his sister a ride over here. She was waiting in her car. That was what the sister pulled him aside to tell him. The sheriff went down to talk to her. He called a few minutes later on his cell phone to say that he was taking her home and would be back to pick you up."

Carly's hand tightened into a fist on the panties, and she didn't even realize it until she glanced down. It was almost embarrassing to admit even to herself how much she really, truly didn't like the idea of Matt's being with Shelby. Then she remembered how, up on the roof, he'd asked her if she was jealous.

If she'd been telling the truth, she would have had to say yes. But not nearly as jealous as she was right now.

"You know, the sheriff's a real hunk, and Antonio seems to think he's a good guy," Sandra said, sounding worried as Carly stared unseeingly down at the panties crumpled in her hand. "But you might just want to rethink this. He's got a reputation as a love 'em and leave 'em kind of guy. Antonio says that he goes through girlfriends as fast as he goes through socks because he's allergic to any kind of long-term relationship. He's a Scorpio, you know—I asked Antonio when his birthday is—and Scorpios are all about sex. Well, look at him, anybody can tell that. As long as you're just wanting to have a good time, that's great. But you're just now starting to feel like climbing back in the saddle where sex is concerned, and that makes you kind of vulnerable. And honey, you sure look to me like you're getting ready to do something real stupid like fall in love."

Sandra had comforted and counseled and cursed and cried with her through the whole rocky road that had been her divorce. She knew how badly Carly had been hurt, and Carly had no doubt that her warning sprang from a deep well of caring and concern. In fact, she knew that listening to what Sandra was trying to tell her was probably the wisest thing she could do. Accordingly, Carly took a deep breath and mentally turned her emotions over for careful review. *Was* she getting ready to fall in love with Matt? Now that she thought about it, she decided, that was almost funny.

She turned around and leaned back against the dresser as she met Sandra's gaze.

"Actually," she said dismally, "I think I've been in love with Matt almost my whole life."

"That's bad." Sandra's expression turned sympathetic. "That's real bad. Last thing you need is to get your heart stomped again. What are you going to do?"

"I don't know," Carly said slowly, thinking about it. "If he—"

"Sandra! Carly!" The bellowing voice belonged to Antonio, Carly realized a second or so after it reached her ears. The urgency of the summons was impossible to mistake. She and Sandra exchanged alarmed glances. Carly straightened away from the dresser. Sandra jumped off the bed. "Get down here quick! There's something wrong with this dog!"

23

It was a little more than an hour later when Carly, with Sandra, Erin, Antonio and Mike behind her, walked out of the veterinarian's examining room and into his waiting room. The bright fluorescent lights combined with the air-conditioning to make the place seem almost deathly cold. The smell—a medicinal, antiseptic-type smell with undertones of urine and fear—was nauseating. Shivering in her tee shirt and jeans, Carly wrapped her arms around herself and rubbed her upper arms in a vain attempt to warm herself. She felt drained, exhausted, and heartsick. To see Annie suffering so had been almost more than she could bear.

"Yo," Matt said. At least, she was pretty sure that was what he'd said, although she couldn't really hear him. He was standing outside the glass door, which was locked, peering in. Carly crossed to the door and fumbled with the lock. But Antonio had to reach around her and actually unfasten it, because her fingers didn't quite seem to want to work properly. She felt almost as if she were underwater, as if she were seeing—and feeling—things through a rippling veil.

Matt pushed the door open, took one look at Carly's face and pulled her against him. His arms wrapped around her, gentle and strong and protective, holding her close. Too spent to even remember all the reasons why depending on him so utterly was probably a mistake, she rested her forehead against his chest and clutched the front of his tee shirt and let him take most of her weight. He was warm and solid, and his chest was firm with muscle and his arms were hard with it, and it felt so good to be held by him that it didn't even occur to her that they had an interested audience or that she should maybe pull away. This was Matt, and there was more comfort for her in his arms than anywhere else in the world. The knowledge would have worried her if she'd had enough strength left to worry about anything.

"So what happened with the dog?" Matt was asking the others, talking over her head, but it was Carly who replied, lifting her head to look up at him.

"She was poisoned." Remembering the ordeal Annie had gone through, Carly shuddered. She kept seeing Annie's eyes, darkly luminous and terror-filled, seeming to say *Help me, help me* as she writhed in torment in the grass. Terrified herself, Carly had scooped her up and run. . . .

"*Poisoned?* What kind of poison?" Matt's voice was sharp.

"Could have been anything. Rat poison, weed killer, even antifreeze." It was Antonio who answered. "Bart—" Bart Lindsey was the vet "—said he won't know for sure until he runs some tests."

"It was an accident though, right?" Matt sounded like he was frowning.

"Probably." The door between the waiting and examining rooms had swung open in time to permit the veterinarian to hear Matt's question. Bart Lindsey was a small, round-faced man with rimless spectacles and a soft stomach that protruded slightly over his belt. With his blue lab coat unbuttoned and his gray hair untidy, he looked rumpled and a little tired. "It's impossible to know, but I'd say the chances are slim that it was anything else. Oh, by the way, good to see you, Matt. I just wish the circumstances were a little more pleasant. You remember my brother Hiram, don't you?" He nodded at the burly, white-haired man in khaki slacks and a blue lab coat like his own who followed him into the reception area. "Hiram used to own this clinic, but he sold out to me twenty years ago and moved to Macon. He would have been the vet here when you were a kid."

"Sure I remember Hiram," Matt said, nodding.

"I'd be willing to give you odds it was nothing but plain old rat poison," Hiram Lindsey said. "The symptoms are classic."

Carly shuddered, and Matt's hold on her tightened.

"It was a good thing we saw her." Erin's voice was soft and low, but something about its husky timbre reminded Carly of Matt's. "Everybody else had either gone in or gone, but Mike and I were still standing out in the yard talking when the poor little dog started trembling and foaming at the mouth and throwing up. Then she just kind of fell over." Erin sounded as if she were shuddering too. "Bart said that if we hadn't gotten her in here right away she would have died."

"You mean she's not dead?" Matt sounded mildly flabbergasted, as if their reactions had led him to expect a different conclusion to the day's tragedy.

"No," Carly said, resting her forehead against his chest again. "Dr. Lindsey said she's going to be all right."

Then she closed her eyes and clung tighter to his shirt and just breathed, terrified that she was going to burst into tears right there in front of them all.

"Christ." Matt tightened his hold on her, hugging her close. As usual, he seemed able to divine what she was feeling. "Can we get out of here or does somebody need to wait for the dog or something?" This he said in a louder voice and was presumably addressed to the vet.

"She'll need to stay at least overnight, and possibly a little longer," Bart Lindsey answered. "Poor little dog, she's been through a lot. I had to put her under in order to treat her, and I pumped her stomach, so it'll be at least twenty-four hours before I feel comfortable about letting her go."

"We really appreciate what you did for her." Sandra had been shaken by the degree of Annie's suffering, too. She still sounded subdued. "Do you want us to go ahead and pay now, or when we come to take her home?"

At least Sandra was now thinking of their house as Annie's home. Even such a hideously dark cloud as this one seemed to have the slenderest of silver linings.

"When you come to pick her up will be fine," Bart Lindsey answered.

"Okay, let's go. Thanks, Bart," Matt said. "Good to see you again, Hiram."

"Have a good one," Bart replied, while his brother added, "Good to see you too. Sorry it wasn't under happier circumstances."

Matt's arm, heavy with muscle, stayed looped around Carly's shoulders as he ushered her outside. Carly was grateful for his strength because she had precious little left herself. The wall of heat she walked into when she stepped outside helped some. It wrapped around her like a warm blanket, embracing her, slowly leaching away the worst of the chill. The vet's office was located on the very edge of downtown, which meant, in practical terms, that it was about four blocks from the town square, although the chamber of commerce's beautification efforts had not extended out quite this far yet. The four-way intersection beside which it was located was also home to a 7-Eleven store, a Rite-Aid pharmacy and Benton Liquors.

Standing on the sidewalk that ran between the strip of medical offices and the parking lot, Carly took a deep breath, inhaling with real gratitude the not particularly pleasant odors of sun-softened asphalt and exhaust from the few passing vehicles. Something about the smells' ordinariness made the nausea that had threatened her in the vet's office recede. The roar of an idling, muffler-impaired pickup and a honking horn accompanied by a hollered "Hey, Matt!" caused her to look toward the street. A gnarled hand was waving out the open window of a dark blue, rusted-out Ford. Matt waved back, the engine revved sharply as the light turned green and the truck was gone.

Now that she was outside, away from the sights and sounds and scents that had made the horror of what had befallen Annie so hideously real, Carly was starting to feel stronger, better, more capable of standing on her own two feet.

But she continued to lean against Matt. Matt made her feel better. Matt made her feel safe.

Although what she needed to be made safe from Carly couldn't have said.

"Carly!" A white panel van rolled through the intersection, and a man yelled at her through the window he quickly opened. Glancing up, Carly saw that it was Barry Hindley. "I heard about your dog. Is it okay?"

"She's going to be fine," Sandra called back when it became obvious that Carly was having trouble drawing enough breath into her lungs for a reply. Barry waved again and drove on.

"So what's the plan?" Erin asked, her eyes flicking from her brother to Carly and back. The curiosity and speculation with which Erin had earlier regarded their togetherness had given way to a kind of interested acceptance of the two of them as a couple, Carly realized, then added in a little addendum to her own thoughts: if indeed a couple was what she and Matt were. At this point, she wasn't sure. She wasn't sure of anything, least of all anything to do with herself and Matt.

But thinking of couples caused Carly to notice that Mike stood close behind Erin, while Antonio was closer to Sandra. The first of those pairings was particularly interesting, or at least it would have been if she'd been feeling more herself. But she was still a little light-headed, still a little nauseous, still a lot upset about Annie. Speculating about the state of others' relationships would have to wait for another time. Heck, she thought, she wasn't even up to speculating about the state of her own relationship, or whether or not what she had going with Matt could even properly be termed a relationship. It was, she realized with some dismay, actually more like a need, at least on her part. She needed to be with him. She needed his arm around her, needed him beside her, needed his warmth, needed his strength. She flat-out needed Matt.

Which, in light of what she knew about his predilection for *friends* and others, might not be such a good thing.

"Carly's going with me," Matt said, without bothering to ask Carly whether she had other plans or thoughts on the subject. Not that she did, of course. Basically, anything Matt wanted her to do she was willing to do, at least while she was feeling so drained and dependent and *needy*. It was just that making such a unilateral statement without consulting her wishes or preferences was high-handed, but it was also typically Matt. Good thing she wasn't shy about protesting when and if she needed to. "Antonio and Mike will take you and Sandra home, and then they've got to get back on the job. Right at this moment, we've only got three men working."

"I'm supposed to meet Collin at seven at The Corner

Café. He's bringing his law school roommate and his wife. You know, Tim Bernard. The best man. From Atlanta." Erin gave her obviously un-knowing brother a disgusted look, then glanced down at her watch. "It's only six-fifteen, but I've got to go home and change first."

"I'll give you a ride," Mike volunteered.

"That suit?" Matt asked Erin. She nodded. He looked at Mike. "You're in your cruiser?"

Mike nodded. There were now two official sheriff's department cars in the parking lot, Carly saw, plus her and Sandra's van. She, Sandra, Erin and Antonio had rushed Annie here in the van, with Sandra driving and Carly holding Annie's limp little body in her arms while Antonio rode, white-knuckled, in the back. Mike had led the way, lights flashing, siren wailing, in his cruiser.

The other cruiser in the parking lot, which had the words SCREVEN COUNTY SHERIFF painted on the driver's door, obviously belonged to Matt.

"Okay, you take Sandra home," Matt said to Antonio. He then looked at Mike. "Then after you drop Erin off you can head over to the Beadle Mansion and pick Antonio up. If things get slow, swing by the office. There's a whole pile of warrants to serve."

"Get slow?" Antonio snorted. "You're kidding me, right?"

"You never know," Matt said, and glanced up at the clear blue sky. "Hell, maybe it'll snow."

"I'll be there in about half an hour," Mike said to Antonio, and then he and Erin headed out across the parking lot.

"Uh, if you want to give me the keys, I'd sure be pleased to drive," Antonio said to Sandra, holding out his hand. Carly remembered their wild ride to the vet's office, and couldn't blame him. Sandra behind the wheel was not anything you wanted to experience twice.

For just a moment, as she watched Sandra's expression, Carly thought Antonio might be in for a pretty pithy reply. But then Sandra appeared to remember just who it was who had insulted her driving. She summoned a smile, fished in her tote and came up with the keys, which she dropped into his palm.

"Get on the radio and tell everybody to be at the office at eleven," Matt said to Antonio. "We're going to have about a fifteen-minute staff meeting and see if we can't figure out how to apportion some of this extra work."

Antonio nodded. Then he cupped a hand around Sandra's elbow.

"Meet you at home," Sandra said to Carly over her shoulder as Antonio escorted her away. Carly nodded, then watched the flirtatious way Sandra looked at him, watched the deliberately dancing earrings and the sexy little extra sway Sandra put into her walk and felt a spurt of envy. Good, old-fashioned lust uncomplicated by a yearning, burning heart was something she could only wish she was experiencing.

"Feeling better?" Matt looked down at her. Carly nodded and managed a smile for him. No, she thought then, meeting his eyes, which were dark and warm and full of concern for her, she had to take her previous wish back. Lust on its own couldn't begin to compare with this. To get a rush like she was experiencing just from looking at someone, there had to be something more.

Something like love.

Facing the horrible truth, it was all she could do not to groan.

Another honk sounded as Matt, his arm still around her shoulders, steered her across the parking lot. Another hand waved from the window of a vehicle stopped at the stoplight. This time the vehicle in question was a tan car.

"Hey, Matt, thanks for speaking at the school assembly last week," a white-haired man yelled. Carly stared, then gaped. Was that . . . ?

"Glad to," Matt yelled back.

" 'Preciate it." The man waved again and was gone as the light changed.

"Oh, my God. Was that *Mr. Simmons?*" Carly gasped.

"Yep." Matt grinned down at her, clearly as fully cognizant of the hilarious irony of the situation as she was. Mr. Simmons was—or at least, he had been—the high school principal when she and Matt had attended. He'd busted Matt so many times on so many different violations that Matt had basically spent every lunch hour of his entire senior year in Mr. Simmons's office.

"That's funny," Carly said.

"I have to say, I never in my wildest dreams thought I'd wind up being best buds with Simple Simon."

The name the teenage Matt had always called the principal behind his back made Carly laugh, and laughing made her feel better.

"You're good at this, aren't you?" she asked, looking up at him as they reached the car.

"What?"

"Being sheriff."

"I try." His mouth quirked. "It's not anything I want to do long-term though, believe me."

"You don't? Why not?" Carly frowned as Matt opened the passenger door for her and waited for her to get in. The vinyl seat was hot; the interior of the car was stifling. Carly realized that she still had not quite recovered from the shock of what had happened to Annie, because even such an overabundance of heat was welcome. Sinking down into the soft bucket seat, pulling on her seat belt, she finally started to feel warm enough again as the buildup of heat inside the car baked away the last of the chill that had held her in thrall. Knowing that Annie was likely going to be all right helped her return to something approaching normal, too.

Taking a deep breath, she was able to slowly let go of the sense of dread and fear that had roiled her stomach ever since she had first run outside to discover her poor little dog convulsing in the grass. Thinking about Matt as sheriff provided a welcome distraction as well. It occurred to her that she knew him so well, knew him on a level that felt almost biological, almost cellular, but there was a large chunk of his life that she had no factual knowledge of: the years between the time she had left, and the time she had come home again.

Matt slid in behind the steering wheel.

"Why not?" she asked again, resting her head back against the seat and savoring the heat on her neck as she looked at him.

He glanced at her as he started the car and pulled out of the parking lot. "I feel like I've been responsible for somebody or something practically since the day I was born. I got away once, joined the Marines—" he slanted a grin her way, "—still can't believe that, can you?—and thought I was all set. Oh, I sent money back to Mom, kinda kept tabs on her and the girls, but I was free and living my own life and having a pretty good time. Then Mom died, and what are you gonna do? There wasn't anybody else to take the girls. They would have had to go to a foster home. They're my sisters, for Christ's sake. The foster home was not happening. So I came home. The sheriff's department needed deputies—hell, we always need deputies; that's the sheriff's department in a nutshell. Anyway, I got hired on, worked as a deputy for a while, then when Sheriff Beatty retired he backed me and I got elected sheriff. It's been a good gig; I've been able to take care of the girls, but let's just say it's not what I ever thought I'd be doing with my life. Lissa's off to college next month. I'll hang around here until I'm sure she's settled, sure they're all settled, which should be just about the time my term as sheriff expires. Then I'm out of here. I'm gone. I'm hopping on my Harley and riding off into the sunset with nobody to look out for but me."

There was humor in his words, and he smiled a little crookedly as he said that last, but Carly knew that what she was hearing was, more or less, the sound of her heart cracking in two. She wanted him; he wanted his freedom. The two were incompatible. Was that the story of her life or what?

Not that she was about to let him know that he had just dealt her budding hopes of happily-ever-after a death blow.

"Speaking of Harleys," she said, keeping things casual while she worked at replacing her pretty pipe dreams with gritty reality, "where's your motorcycle?"

"It's parked in front of your house. When I had to . . . uh—" he broke off, grimacing.

"When you had to drive Shelby home?" Carly finished for him, sweet as pie. The sheriff's office flashed by outside the window, and she realized that they were heading toward her house. Was he taking her straight home? She didn't want to ask, not until she had sorted out exactly how she felt about things. Like love. And sex. And Matt.

He slanted a look at her. "Yeah. Who told you that, anyway?"

"Does it matter?" she asked, her eyes fixed on his face. The sun's rays slanted through the windshield to gild his lean cheeks. His expression was faintly wary as he glanced her way again. With his elegantly carved features and dark, slumberous eyes, with his black hair waving back away from his brow and the faintest suggestion of stubble roughening his jaw, he looked so sexy that she almost couldn't breathe. He was her Matt, her too-handsome-for-his-own-good Matt, her best friend turned dream lover Matt, and yet, she realized with a sharp little stab of pain, he wasn't. At least, he wasn't really *hers,* no matter how much she might wish it were otherwise. If she had fallen in love with him way back when they were kids and the emotion had stuck, that was her problem, not his. He had made no bones about how he felt about her. He loved her. Just not that way.

Not the way she loved him.

Which pretty much sucked. For her, anyway.

"No. Hell, no. Of course it doesn't matter. Could have been any one of dozens of people. Everybody knows every step everybody else takes around this place." There was disgust in his voice. "Okay, yeah, when I had to drive Shelby home we went in her car. I made sure she was okay, then got a ride to my house and picked up my cruiser, drove back to your house, found your place deserted, called in to see if anybody knew what had happened to make a whole group of people I care about disappear, and heard about your dog."

"And came right away." She looked at him meditatively. He was handsome and sexy and she loved him and she wanted him and . . .

"Yep."

"Why?" . . . she might not be able to have everything she wanted, she might not be able to have her happily-ever-after . . .

"What do you mean, why? Why do you think? I thought your dog was probably dead. I thought you'd be upset. I thought you'd be glad to see me." He glanced at her, frowning. "I thought you might need me."

"I did, yeah." . . . but she could have some of what she

wanted. He was hers for the taking, if she was willing to accept that it was just a short-term thing. "Thank you for coming, by the way."

Half a loaf is better than no bread. She could almost hear her grandmother saying it. But was it really? Or did it just leave you hungrier than ever for the half you didn't get?

"Matt?"

"Hmm?"

"Why, exactly, did you feel like you had to drive Shelby home?"

The look he sent her was unreadable. "She was upset, all right?"

"How upset?"

He sighed. "Crying. She was crying. She's been having a hard time dealing with the fact that she and I as a couple are over, and she was sitting out there in her car crying because she thinks I've found someone new. Which, in case you're wondering, would be you."

Carly winced. She'd never thought she could possibly feel sorry for Miss Queen of Everything, but suddenly she did. "What kind of promises did you make her? Before you broke up with her, I mean?"

Matt looked outraged. "None. Hey, I never make promises. Anything she thought to the contrary was all in her head."

The sad thing was, she had no doubt that he absolutely believed every word of that. Such male obtuseness made her feel like smacking him upside the head. "You slept with her, didn't you? Listen, you lunkhead, to a woman that's a promise right there."

"No, it isn't. She wanted to get married and I didn't. She knew how I felt about marriage going in. I never promised her anything. I never did anything to make her think I wanted to marry her."

Except have sex with her. Carly didn't say it aloud, but the words were there in her head, a neon sign flashing caution.

"There, you see: You did it again. That kiss-and-run thing. Admit it. That's what you do. That's what I meant when I said you have issues."

"Since when does not wanting to get married mean that somebody has issues?" He sounded exasperated.

"Since every time you start getting too involved with somebody you get scared and just cut and run."

"I do not get scared."

"Yes, you do. You pulled it on Shelby. You've pulled it on me twice. No telling how many other poor, unsuspecting women you've pulled it on." She scowled at him. "So let me ask you something. What, exactly, did you envision happening between us when you asked me to go for a motorcycle ride with you today?"

"I was going to take you out to dinner." He glanced at her, then smiled a little ruefully. "Okay, I was going to take you out to dinner and then I was going to take you to bed. Now that I think about it though, I see that it was a really bad idea. At least, the bed part was."

There was a pause in which neither of them spoke. Carly turned the facts of the situation over in her mind. The man had issues, all right. He had problems. He had hang-ups. Only a masochistic idiot would enter into any kind of a romantic relationship with him. He needed a big DANGER sign to wear around his neck to warn off the unwary. All he had to offer any woman was half a loaf.

Sex. Probably great sex. But nothing beyond that.

Wham, bam, thank you, ma'am. *Next.*

But he was Matt, and she had loved him for most of her life, and wanted him for nearly as long as she'd loved him. With anyone else, she would have said, take your half a loaf and shove it. But with Matt, she was starting to think that her grandmother had known what she was talking about.

"Just out of curiosity," Carly asked politely, "*why* is dinner and bed a bad idea? At least, why is it a bad idea now, when it wasn't a bad idea earlier? I mean, *you* climbed three stories up a ladder to my roof and kissed me and asked me out. Nobody was holding a gun to your head."

He was still heading due west, toward her house. The last stoplight before they left town behind turned red in front of them, and he braked to wait it out. The sun was shining directly in at them. Matt flipped down his visor to shield his eyes, and Carly did the same. The protection was welcome, and probably even needed, but Carly got the feeling that he did it at least partially to stall for time. She also got the impression that he was weighing just how honest to be.

"Look, Curls," he said finally. She could tell that he had opted for total frankness, and wished, as she had on numerous previous occasions, that they didn't know each other well enough to make that an option. Sometimes being allowed to maintain a few of one's illusions was a plus. "Here's the thing: Sometimes men think with their dicks. If you'd stayed away from me, we would have been fine, the just-friends thing would have been fine, but you didn't, you dumped lemonade all over my head and I kissed you and now we aren't fine. Specifically, I'm not fine. I want to sleep with you so badly that I've pretty much been walking around with a woody ever since you kicked me and ran out of my office. And you want me too. I know you do. So there it is: I want you and you want me. When I asked you out, I thought maybe we could go with that, just have dinner and maybe sex and see how it went from there. But I've got to admit that you've got a point with the kiss-and-run thing. Whenever I get the feeling a woman is after a commitment,

I tend to get the hell out. And the woman tends to end up getting hurt." He glanced at her. "And I don't want that for you. Which makes the bed thing a bad idea. Because, basically, you and I want two different things."

"We do?" Carly watched the play of light and shadow over his face as the car started moving forward again, and made up her mind. She was going to go with half a loaf, and damn the torpedoes.

"Yeah, we do. The bottom line is, I want sex, you want love and a husband and babies and forever." He glanced her way again and must have seen something in her expression that made him suspect that she was about to disagree, because he shook his head at her. "Don't even try to mess with me. I know how you think." He gave an unamused-sounding snort. "I love you like one of my sisters, and I want you so much that at least half of me thinks I'm a damned fool for telling you this, but I don't do forever. Not even for you, I don't."

"Did I ask you to?" Carly tried not to wince as the "sister" thing went home. Determinedly she embraced her inner slut. "I'm with you: forever sucks. Been there, done that. You keep forgetting that I'm older and wiser than I used to be. I'm all grown up. I've been married and divorced. And what I want now is basically the same thing you do: great sex, no strings."

And if she crossed her fingers behind her back, well, he didn't have to know.

24

"Bullshit."

Matt said it without heat. The lack of heat was an indication of how little he believed her, Carly realized. She also realized that deceiving a man who knew her as well as Matt did was going to be something less than a piece of cake.

"Try me."

He shot her a skeptical glance.

"Not happening, Curls."

Carly could not believe that she was having to practically con this man into making love to her. Somebody's priorities were not in the right place.

"For goodness' sake, Matt, use your brain. I've only been officially divorced for a few months. Why on earth would I want to even think about getting married again? The first time was enough to permanently turn me off the whole institution, believe me."

This time there was a glimmer of interest in the look he sent her.

"Oh, yeah?"

"Yeah," Carly said, watching the First Baptist Church go by on the left. If she didn't think fast, she'd be home in less than five minutes. "You know, I'm starving. You could still take me out to dinner, and I could tell you all about my horrible, no-good, very bad marriage while we eat."

"No," he said.

"*No?*" Carly repeated, starting to get annoyed. "What do you mean, no?"

"Baby, you think I haven't been on the receiving end of enough come-ons that I don't know when somebody's trying to talk me into bed?"

Carly glared at him.

"You're not conceited or anything, are you, Matt Converse?"

"Are you trying to make me believe that you're *not* trying to talk me into bed?"

Carly's lips pursed. Blast the man, he knew her too well.

"Okay, so maybe I am," she conceded. Then she took a deep breath and came out with the clincher, "Dammit, Matt, I haven't had sex in *two whole years.*"

He glanced swiftly at her, then just as swiftly returned his attention to the road, which had grown both bumpier and curvier over the last few miles. She watched as his jaw tightened, and as he shifted his foot from the gas to the brake. The car slowed, and Carly tried not to let any trace of the thumbs-up she mentally gave herself show as he pulled over on the grassy verge.

"Okay," he said, putting the transmission in park and releasing his seat belt and turning a little sideways in his seat so that he could look at her. The quality of the light was golden now, gilding the tops of the tall corn that grew on one side of the road and the sparse grass of the cow-cropped pasture on the other, gilding the black fences and the road itself and Matt's face. His eyes narrowed as they ran over her; his mouth thinned and lengthened mistrustfully. But there was a restless gleam in the depths of his eyes, and she knew him well enough to recognize that gleam for what it was: desire.

He could fight it all he wanted, but he wanted her, too.

Her heart started to beat a little faster.

"You want to run that by me one more time?"

"You know, this is embarrassing."

His brows twitched closer together. "If it embarrasses you, you shouldn't have brought it up. How come you haven't had sex in two years?"

"More than two years, actually," Carly said, scrupulously honest.

"Curls . . ." His voice held a note of warning.

Carly glanced away, out at the narrow black ribbon of road winding off through the fields and trees and hills, and rubbed her hands down her jeans-clad thighs because her palms were suddenly a little sweaty. Talking about sex wasn't something she usually did with men, and getting down to the nitty-gritty of such a personal topic really did make her feel kind of embarrassed, even if the man was Matt and she didn't have a whole lot of secrets that he didn't know. But the goal was a worthy one, she thought, and with that in mind she crossed her arms over her chest and looked back at him.

"Why do you think? I haven't had anybody to have sex *with*."

The look he gave her spoke volumes.

Carly was outraged. "Believe it or not, I don't sleep around."

His eyes softened slightly. "Okay, that I believe."

He reached out to tug on a wayward lock of her hair. As the curl twined around his finger, Carly reflexively jerked her head out of his reach, and he smiled. They'd been playing variations on that same scenario since she was eight, Carly realized, and glared at him.

"What about your husband? Like you said, you've only been divorced a few months."

"He had a girlfriend." Carly's voice went flat. "It took me a while to figure out what was going on. We didn't make love, but I thought he was busy, or stressed, or, well, something. Whatever men get when they don't want to get you in bed three times a day. And I was busy with my restaurant—you know I owned a restaurant, the Treehouse." Matt nodded; Carly was too familiar with the jungle-drums quality of gossip in Benton to be surprised. "Well, running a restaurant is a lot of work, and . . . and I didn't really feel like having sex anyway. I didn't have time for it, I was stressed, the whole bit. The truth is, I was so busy with work that the state of our marriage just kind of got away from me. Even when I realized something was wrong, I never guessed he was cheating. I didn't figure that out until I came home early from work one day and caught him with his girlfriend in our bed."

"Sounds bad." There was sympathy for her in his eyes.

"It *was* bad." Carly took a deep breath. "Actually, it was awful."

"Want me to go to Chicago and punch the bastard in the nose for you?" The offer was made in an almost negligent tone. Carly saw that he was only partly joking. Looking at him, at his broad shoulders lounging back against the window and his strong neck and the bulging muscles of his arms, all set off most attractively by the clinginess of his decrepit tee shirt, Carly had a sudden mental vision of slender, bespectacled *I'm-so-proud-of-my-intellect* John and realized that any physical confrontation between the two of them wouldn't even be a contest. A slight smile still lurked around Matt's mouth, but his eyes were serious. Carly knew that if she really wanted him to punch John out for her, she had only to say the word.

"You really would, wouldn't you?" Her tone mixed admiration and scolding.

"You bet."

"My hero," she said as she had many times before while they were growing up, trying to keep it light, batting her lashes at him in exaggerated adoration. Usually the words were a joke between them. This time she meant every syllable.

"As always." His voice was dry. The words were his stock response too, but the look in his eyes for her—it was all new.

Her breath caught.

There was an invisible tension in the air between them suddenly, a sense of connection, a blast of heat. He was still on his side of the car and she was still on hers, but the space in which they were confined all at once seemed much smaller, the distance between them reduced as though something, the moisture, the molecules keeping them apart, something, had just evaporated.

"Just for the record," he said, still fixing her with that dark, level gaze. "I think your ex-husband is a fucking idiot."

"Well," she said, smiling at him a little because this, too, was familiar. He'd always stood up for her whenever anyone had tried to bully her at school or elsewhere until all her less-than-pleasant schoolmates and acquaintances had been made forcefully aware that bothering Carly meant taking on Matt and had consequently left her alone. It felt strange and a little wonderful to have him taking up for her again, and she realized that she'd gotten used, maybe too used, to fighting all her battles alone. "I think so too."

He looked at her for a long moment without speaking, then said, "To hell with it" in a voice grown suddenly husky and reached for her. She met him halfway, twining her arms around his neck and meeting his gaze with what she was sure could be nothing short of bedazzlement in her eyes as he cupped her face with his hands and sought her mouth with his. Then she shut her eyes as his lips closed over hers, hard and sure. As his tongue staked its claim to her mouth, she kissed him back with hungry abandon and felt fire shoot clear down to her toes.

Two quick blasts from a horn broke them apart. Breathing hard, still dazed and tingly and not even sure exactly what it was she'd heard, Carly glanced around in time to spot another sheriff's department cruiser speeding past. Just before it disappeared around the nearest bend, she saw the driver waving jauntily at them.

"Shit," Matt said, looking after the car.

He was breathing hard, too. His hands still cupped her face and her arms were still looped around his neck. His eyes looked almost black in the golden light, she saw, and his skin looked very bronze. The light revealed every tiny line around his eyes and emphasized the small scar on his lip. Carly caught her breath as she remembered that the Matt who was kissing her now was all grown up. The boy she had known so well was still there, but he had added layers upon layers of experiences that she knew nothing about. The thought with all its various implications was so erotic that her mouth went dry and her loins clutched and her breasts tightened and swelled against the satiny confines of her bra. She must have made some slight sound, because his gaze came back to her, and then he kissed her again, hard and hot and so thoroughly that she was lost. She responded with fiery hunger, uncaring that anyone who just might happen to drive by could, and would, certainly see, that they would be the subject of town gossip for months if not years, that if they didn't stop, soon, being charged with public indecency became a real possibility, or at least it would have been if he hadn't been the sheriff, which in itself would add a whole other dimension to the explosion of gossip.

"Okay, enough," he said in a low, thick voice, as without warning he freed his mouth from hers and pulled her arms from around his neck and put her firmly back in her seat.

"Matt . . ." Impossible to disguise that her voice was unsteady.

"We're not teenagers and it's not dark. And we're sure as hell not doing it beside the road in a damned marked car." He took a deep breath, settled back into his seat and gripped the steering wheel with both hands as he rested his forehead against it. "We might as well sell tickets."

He was right and she knew he was right, but still that didn't stop her from wanting him so much that she was dizzy with it.

"Put your seat belt on," he said after a moment, lifting his head to look at her. His eyes were still hot and dark, but she could tell from the set of his mouth and jaw that he once again had himself well under control.

Conscious of a little pang of disappointment—she liked the idea that she could make Matt lose control—Carly complied as he started the car and pulled out onto the road, then executed a quick, neat and wildly illegal U-turn before heading back toward town. Dry-mouthed, she felt her heart start to pump faster from just thinking about what *doing it* with Matt would be like. The last time she'd gone all the way with him she'd been a clueless virgin and he'd been all of twenty-one. And the earth had still rocked and the sky had still exploded and her heart had been stolen away and her body had been branded as his forevermore.

Because he was Matt, and because she'd loved him then every bit as fiercely as she loved him now.

Not that she meant to tell him that. Not now, and maybe not ever.

"You hungry?" He shot her a narrow-eyed look. Knowing that he meant hungry for food, she shook her head. His eyes still had that hot, dark gleam that made her quake, but she managed to preserve the outward appearance of cool, or at least she hoped she did. Not that Matt was likely to be fooled. He knew how much she wanted him.

"Just sex, no strings," he said, looking at her hard.

"Absolutely," she said, while her fingers mentally crossed again and her heart threatened to pound through her chest.

Looking almost grim, he gave a curt nod.

"Where are we going?" she asked after a couple of minutes, when he turned down a road that did not lead back to town. She was pleased at how steady her voice sounded, particularly considering the fact that her senses were going haywire at the imminent prospect of sleeping with Matt. Now that she thought about it, though, where *could* they go? Her house was Grand Central Station. His was no better. The sheriff's office was definitely out, and he had just nixed the car.

A hotel? There wasn't one in Benton. Even if there had been, she could just see herself and Matt, the well-known and clearly popular county sheriff, checking in. The whole town would probably be standing outside with binoculars before they'd even gotten the door to their room closed.

She had never really realized it before, but she now saw it for the self-evident truth it was: little towns were hell on a person's sex life.

Matt glanced at her. "I happen to own a boat. I also happen to rent a garage to keep it in. The garage happens to have a small apartment above it that's included in the rent."

The cautious way he phrased this coupled with her memory of Lissa saying that Matt never brought girls home provided Carly with a burst of enlightenment: Matt had already figured out that a decent sex life for a single small-town sheriff saddled with live-in sisters could be problematic, and

had taken steps to deal with the problem. The garage apartment was that step.

She didn't begrudge him the sex life, she discovered,
thinking the matter over. As long as from now on, it included her.

"How convenient," she said, just to let him know that he
was not the only person who could read minds.

He glanced at her and grinned.

The garage was located in an area of apartments and
storage buildings and mini-warehouses scattered across
barren acres punctuated by Dumpsters and rusty chain-
link fences. As Matt pointed it out and then turned up the
short gravel driveway that culminated in a small, story-
and-a-half building sheathed in gray aluminum siding,
Carly saw that their destination was just that, a garage,
looking as if it might have been constructed as a detached
appurtenance to a house that was no longer there. Whatever had happened to the house, the garage, still set in a
weedy little lot, remained. Apparently not having had the
foresight to provide himself with the remote control that
generally operated the type of overhead garage door that
confronted them when they stopped, Matt got out and
rolled open the door by hand. As she waited, a quick glance
around showed Carly that, while there was a pickup truck
parked in front of a cluster of mini-warehouses farther
down the street, no one was in sight. If they were lucky, the
town would never know that Matt had driven her to a remote garage for purposes that the gossip mill would have a
field day speculating about.

Then Matt got back inside the car and drove into the
garage. As he parked and got out, walking back to pull the
door down behind them, Carly got out too, and discovered, to her own surprise, that she was suddenly, absurdly
nervous about what they were about to do.

At least, if they'd gotten it on in the car while they were both so hot, she wouldn't have to keep hearing Sandra's warning about getting her heart stomped repeating itself over and over in her brain.

Despite all kinds of expert advice to the contrary, giving oneself lots of time to think important decisions through was not, she was discovering, always the best thing.

The door rattled as Matt closed it. He had flipped the light on, so that even when the door was closed Carly was able to see that what she was standing in was crude even by garage standards. It was hot in the stifling way of little-used buildings in the summertime, and it smelled faintly of gasoline. The cement floor was cracked and uneven in places. The walls were unpainted boards. The ceiling was supported by exposed beams that ran the width of it, and electrical lines and white PVC pipes ran alongside the beams. A single overhead bulb provided illumination. Unpainted wooden steps mounted one wall, disappearing into an opening in the ceiling. These, Carly assumed, led to Matt's apartment.

She hoped it was in somewhat better shape than the garage itself. Not that it really mattered, of course. They were only going to be using it for a little while, just long enough to . . .

At the thought of what they were going to be using it to do, Carly felt butterflies do loop-de-loops in her stomach.

"How do you like my boat?"

Matt had come up behind her, and at the sound of his voice she jumped. Turning around, glancing at the fifteen-foot runabout he was eyeing with such pride, she hardly saw it.

"It's lovely," she said, having noticed almost nothing about it except that it was a boat and painted white.

He looked at her closely, and she was reminded again

that he knew her well enough to be able to guess a lot of what passed through her head.

"Okay, Curls, spit it out." His voice was dry.

He was not, Carly noticed, touching her. Instead he hooked his hands in his pockets and rocked back on his heels a little as he studied her face. He was standing close enough to her so that she was once again aware that the top of her head didn't quite reach his chin and his shoulders were twice the breadth of hers and he could probably tuck her under one arm and run off with her if he felt so inclined.

"What?" If her tone was defensive, it was because she couldn't help it. Her mouth was dry and her heart was pounding and the butterflies in her stomach could have put the Blue Angels to shame with all the aerial acrobatics they were doing.

"If you want to chicken out, feel free. This is one hundred percent your call."

"Of course I don't want to chicken out."

When she'd worked so hard to get him here? Not a chance. It was just that she was, most unexpectedly, a little nervous, that's all.

"Then quit looking at me like I'm a serial killer and you're a Cheerio."

That was such a bad joke that Carly groaned. He grinned and picked up her hand and kissed it, and looked at her over it in that sexy way that she had already discovered made her knees go weak, and suddenly she wasn't nervous anymore. At least, she was, but now it was in a good way. A delicious, anticipatory way.

Just in time, too, because he was heading for the stairs, holding her hand, pulling her up after him. Trying to ignore her shaky knees and pounding heart, she followed him up to a tiny, rickety landing where a railing of roughly nailed together two-by-fours was all that kept unwary souls from taking a step sideways and plunging back down to the concrete garage floor. It was dark and dusty and hotter than blazes up there and she couldn't help it, she was nervous. Still, scared he might be going to have second thoughts if he guessed how really utterly discomposed she felt, she managed a smile for him as he let go of her hand to feel above the door.

Whatever came of it, she wanted to do this, she told herself stoutly. She was going to do this. She was going to have great sex with Matt.

The no-strings part they could work on later.

Retrieving the key, he opened the door and stood back to allow her to step inside.

Taking a deep breath, Carly did.

25

THE APARTMENT WAS SMALL, consisting of one large rectangular room, a bathroom and a tiny galley kitchen. All this Carly saw as soon as she stepped over the threshold and Matt closed the door behind her. He didn't turn on the light, although the switch was right there beside him. This omission was deliberate, Carly had no doubt, and at the implications her knees threatened to give out. Still, she managed to hold it together, pretending not to notice that they were standing there in the hushed twilight with only the light filtering in between closed curtains for illumination. The air was pleasantly cool, courtesy of a hotel type heating/air-conditioning unit installed directly in the back wall. A nondescript beige carpet covered the floor. The furnishings were of the functional variety, with a recliner that looked like the ugly stepsister of the two at Matt's house and a worn brown tweed couch plus a table, lamp and TV grouped in the half of the room nearest the door. The other half of the room was given over to a queen-sized bed. Spotting it, Carly was almost afraid to look any closer. Would it have a fur spread? Rubber sheets? Handcuffs attached to the dark wood headboard?

Hey, it was a bachelor pad. Sin Central. *The* place to come for a hot time in the old town tonight. Who knew what he got up to in it?

It occurred to Carly with equal parts dismay and fascination that she didn't have the slightest idea what Matt the grown-up sheriff liked to do in bed.

"Shoot, I knew I was forgetting something," Matt said. He was still behind her, and she turned to look at him almost thankfully, glad to have anything to look at besides that bed. At least, she was until she realized that he was looking really amazingly sexy, and his dark eyes were tinged with humor and something else—heat. For her.

"What?"

"I left my whips and chains at home."

It took Carly a second. Then she narrowed her eyes at him.

"You are so not funny."

But she had to smile. And with that smile a great deal of her nervousness left her. He might be the kind of tall, dark, and handsome stud muffin that women dreamed about, but he was also Matt. Matt of the protective instincts and corny jokes and ability to read her like a book. Her Matt.

If it turned out he was kinky in bed, she would just learn to deal.

He gave her a wry half-smile and reached for her hand. His hand was warm and strong and familiar, and Carly held on to it like a dying woman to a lifeline as she went with the flow and let him lead her across the room toward the bed. By the time they stopped at its foot and he turned to face her, her fingers were twined with his and her heart was thudding and she was hot from just thinking about what his next move might be. Also, face it, she was nervous as hell all over again.

This was the part where they got naked and—

"Look up," he ordered.

—kinky, apparently. But okay, she was up for it. If he wanted to jump her bones while she was looking up, she could do that.

She looked up and waited. Textured white ceiling tiles, a little dingy, met her gaze. There was a cobweb in the corner where the two walls met. No spider, she was thankful to see. When nothing happened, she got fed up with waiting and looked at him again. He was watching her with that wry little smile still on his face. The bed, covered in a perfectly ordinary looking comforter in a kind of earth-tone Aztec print, loomed like the proverbial elephant in the room. It was there, right there, so close her leg practically brushed it, but she was doing her best to ignore it.

"So?" she said.

"No mirror. No camera. No peepholes. Nothing deviant." He grinned at her and shook his head. "Jesus, you've got a dirty mind."

Carly felt instantly self-conscious. "I never thought—"

"Oh, yes you did." His eyes twinkled. He took her other hand so that he was holding both of them now. "Just for the record, what I basically do here is watch sports on TV. I can never get the remote at home."

Carly eyed him. "Yeah, right."

It was a nice lie, a gentlemanly lie, but—pay for a garage with an apartment over it just so that he could watch sports?

"Anyway," he said, "I haven't been here in a while."

Now *that* she believed. She'd already detected a fine layer of dust on the wood surfaces.

"Good," she said, before she quite thought through how that might sound. Did expressing satisfaction with an apparent lull in his sex life before they got together mesh with her great sex, no-strings pledge? Who knew? And who was clearheaded enough at the moment to try to figure it out?

Not she, that was for sure. That bed was getting under her skin. Any second now, he was going to throw her on it and— At the thought of what the *and* might entail, her body tightened deep inside and began to quake.

"Okay," she said, desperate to get on with this before she gave herself away, or he decided to run, or the roof caved in, or something else happened to mess this up. "So how do you want to do this?"

He'd been in the act of raising her hand to his mouth. He paused, looked at her, then grinned a slow-dawning grin before kissing, not the backs of her fingers, but her palm this time. Carly watched in fascination as he turned her hand over and pressed his mouth to her skin. She could feel the whisper of his breath, the prickle of the five o'clock shadow that darkened his jaw, the moist heat of his mouth all the way through to her solar plexus.

She took a deep breath as the quake intensified.

"I don't know," he said as if he were giving the matter serious consideration, lifting both her hands to his shoulders and then reaching down to lightly clasp her waist and pull her a step closer to him. There was humor in his eyes still, Carly saw, but a flame had ignited in their depths and his mouth had a sensuous curve to it now that made her heart skip a beat as she looked at it. "I thought maybe I could take your shirt off, and then you could take mine off, and then I could take your pants off, and you could take mine off . . . something like that."

Her loins clenched, her breasts swelled, her breathing grew erratic.

"Sounds good," she said, her voice unsteady. And thought, *is that the understatement of the year or what?* Sounds good didn't even begin to cover it.

"Just out of curiosity," he said as his fingers slid up under the hem of her shirt and he started inching it upward, "want to tell me why your shirt's on inside out?"

"Oh, God." Carly looked down at herself, barely able to think with his warm hands gliding up over her stomach, up the sides of her rib cage, heading slowly and tan-

278 — KAREN ROBARDS

talizingly north toward her swelling breasts and taking her shirt with them. Sure enough, her tee shirt was inside out. Instead of seeing embroidered butterflies on the navy blue background, she saw lots of little red and pink and green threads hanging from it. Like the rest of her clothes, she had put it on so fast that she hadn't even noticed, or cared, because . . . "Annie. I was in a rush to get to Annie."

"Hey, you heard Bart. She's going to be all right." His voice was low and thick, and as she looked up she saw the hot dark glitter in his eyes and her mouth went dry.

"I know."

His hands found her breasts beneath her tee shirt then, covered them, caressed and squeezed them. Even with the gossamer layer of her bra between them, the sensation was unbelievable. Her nipples went rigid. Her breasts swelled into his hands. She gasped and trembled. At her response his eyes flared, and he leaned over, kissing her softly but thoroughly while she dug her nails into his shoulders and his hands played with her breasts. If his purpose was to distract her from the bad memory, and Carly was fairly sure that was at least part of what he had in mind, it worked. It definitely worked. When he broke the kiss and the contact to pull her shirt off over her head, she was dazed and breathless and weak-kneed. So dazed and breathless and weak-kneed that it took the sight of him staring at her chest to make her realize that she was now standing in front of him in nothing but her jeans and bra.

It was the black lace one she'd planned to wear for just this purpose. Underneath her jeans were the tiny matching panties that she'd been holding in her hand when Antonio had started yelling. Throwing on her clothes as fast as she could, she'd grabbed the first things that had come to hand—and by sheer luck they had turned out to be the sexy scanties she'd been scoping out for the express purpose of dazzling Matt.

Her bra, at least, seemed to be doing the trick.

"Nice," he said, running his index finger along the deep décolletage of the cups. His eyes were hot as they followed the path his finger traced. Lips parted, breathing unevenly, Carly watched too. The plump white curves of her breasts filled the provocative bra to overflowing. His finger was long and deeply tan and unmistakably masculine against her skin. The entire effect was erotic, and Carly was visited by a moment of extreme thankfulness that, in an effort to please hypercritical John, she'd had her breasts enhanced. The last time Matt had seen them, they hadn't been much to look at. Now, they were soft and round and sexy and beautiful. And sensitive. So exquisitely sensitive that she seemed to feel the touch of Matt's finger with every nerve ending she possessed.

Oh, God, she wanted him. She wanted to drop the rest of her clothes and yank off his and . . . But no. It was better to take it slow, spin it out, make it Great Sex. The problem was, just getting it on with Matt fell under the heading of Great Sex for her. She had no idea what it did for him.

"My turn." She didn't know why she was surprised to find that her voice was unsteady, given the fact her insides were quivering like Jell-O.

"Okay." His hand dropped to his side. His fingers flexed for a moment as if he were having trouble keeping them there as his eyes blazed down at her. Breathless at the thought of what she was about to do, she slipped her hands up under his tee shirt and started sliding them up his chest, mimicking him, inching his shirt up while she slid her hands over him just as he had done moments before to her. His skin was warm, and smooth, and faintly damp over a layer of firm, resilient muscles that seemed to expand as he breathed in and out. His chest hair was silky, growing thicker and more luxuriant as her hands moved up his body. His nipples were flat round nubs that hardened as her fingers found them. At that instant telltale response, Carly felt her nether regions tighten as the quake that had been pulsing through her entire body homed in and solidified and began to pulse in a series of quick rhythmic contractions that made her shudder. She had his shirt pushed up under his armpits now, and she rubbed her fingers over his nipples again, deliberately sensuous, looking up to see what he thought of that.

"Jesus." His jaw was hard; his eyes were so dark they were almost black. From that, and the uneven tenor of his breathing, she deduced that he liked it. Very much.

She took a deep, steadying breath, then tugged his shirt up higher, struggling to get it over his head. In the end, because he was so much taller, he had to pull it off himself. As he dropped it to the floor, Carly's gaze went to his chest. His shoulders were heavy with muscle. His upper arms bulged. His chest was broad and solid-looking, with a triangle of thick black hair that tapered down over the six-pack abs to disappear beneath the waistband of his jeans. His hips were narrow compared to the width of his shoulders. Shirtless, he was bronzed and muscular and so sexy that she got wet just looking at him.

"Nice," she said when she could speak again, flicking a glance up at his eyes. There was a definite glitter in them now, a hot, dangerous, predatory glitter. Carly's heart skipped a beat as she realized that never before in the history of their relationship had Matt looked at her precisely like that.

"Think so, huh?" He was already reaching for her, hooking a hand in the waistband of her jeans, pulling her just that little bit closer, his fingers warm and hard against her stomach as he opened the metal button that fastened them. She could feel the heat of him, smell soap and man, and it was the most amazing aphrodisiac, more of a turn-on than any fancy shaving lotion or expensive cologne or anything else she had ever smelled. Her hands were on his waist, holding on tight because watching him slowly pull her zipper down was making her dizzy; her fingers pressed into his skin; she loved the warmth of it, and the steely strength of the muscles beneath. She loved it that he was honed and hard and hungry and *hers*.

A black lace triangle that was her panties appeared in the widening opening. They were tiny, sexy, barely covering her. Her breathing went fast and erratic as she watched him look, watched his eyes get all heavy-lidded and smoldering and sensual. She tried to control it, tried not to let him know just how very turned-on she was—but then he trailed his finger down the front of her panties, down to where the zipper stopped, touching nothing but black lace yet arousing her so much that she gasped aloud. It was the lightest of touches, but it burned through the thin lace like a brand.

"Matt."

He glanced up.

"Hmm?" It was a husky murmur. His eyes smoldered at her. His hand slid inside her zipper, covering the lace, squeezing her mound.

"Nothing. Oh, God." If she hadn't been holding on to him she would have slithered to the ground.

His fingers pushed between her legs, rubbing her through her panties, and she couldn't help it, she leaned forward so that her forehead rested against his chest, barely managing to stifle a groan.

"Just so you know, sexy underwear really does it for me." His mouth was at her ear, murmuring in it before pressing hot and wet against the soft sensitive spot just below it. "And yours is sexy as hell."

"I'll—try to keep that in mind."

It was all she could do to think, much less talk as his hand withdrew to slide flat-palmed across her stomach even while his mouth slid slowly down the side of her neck. She wanted to tell him that this slow striptease thing they were doing was too much, that she was on fire, roused to a fever pitch already, ready to get naked and get it on and slake her burgeoning lust before she melted into an embarrassing little puddle right there at his feet. But if this was a game of sexual chicken she wasn't going to be the first to cave, she wasn't going to be the one to pull him down on the bed and jump his bones, she wasn't going to let him know how very much she wanted it. No, wanted him.

What she was going to do was turn the tables a little. She pressed her mouth to his chest, kissed it, slid her lips along the firm contours. It was warm and damp and hairy and his skin tasted faintly of salt, and her heart slammed like a jackhammer in her breast and she could hardly breathe.

Then she reached his nipple and drew it into her mouth, licking and nibbling even as her hand slid over the hard bulge at the front of his jeans.

He stiffened and went still. She could feel the thudding of his heart, feel the sudden steely quality of his chest muscles beneath her lips and another, more personal muscle beneath her hand, feel the tension in him, the surge of heat.

He moved, catching her face in his hands, turning it up to his.

"Baby, you've grown up," he said, thick and low, and bent his head and took her mouth. Carly's blood superheated in an instant, and she wrapped her arms around his neck in urgent response. Sliding his arms around her waist, he pulled her close. His kiss was slow, sensual, drugging. He was naked to the waist and she was nearly so and he felt so good, so big and strong and hard against her, that she crowded closer still, greedy for contact. Her breasts in their flimsy lace covering pressed against his chest. Her nipples were so stiff that the sensation became almost an ache, and she moaned into his mouth in a response she no longer even cared to hide. The small sound seemed to electrify him. His kiss turned hard and fierce. His tongue was scalding hot as it thrust deep into her mouth, and his lips were hot too and unbelievably erotic as they slanted across hers. She trembled and clung and kissed him back, loving the way he felt against her, the taste and heat of his mouth, the hard insistence of his body. Then his hands slid down inside her loosened waistband, down inside her jeans, down inside her panties, and he was cupping her cheeks as he had once before and pulling her hard up against the stiffness in the front of his jeans. He held a cheek in each hand, palms flat, fingers spread, gently squeezing the soft, rounded flesh, moving her against him, letting her feel the strength of his desire. Her whole body responded with a cataclysmic shudder and she wanted to die, just absolutely die, from the sheer wonder of what he was making her feel.

He slid his mouth down her neck and then, while she was still pulsing and burning with need, lifted his head and pulled his hands out of her pants and stepped back.

"Matt—" It was a protest, uttered as she blinked at him out of passion-drugged eyes.

"Let's go to bed," he said, and picked her up, scooping her high up against his chest and kissing her hard and then, even as she clung to him and kissed him back, depositing her in the middle of that earth-toned comforter. Straightening, he pulled off her sneakers and her jeans in a series of quick efficient movements and tossed them aside, then stood for a moment beside the bed looking down at her.

For an instant she saw herself as he must be seeing her, slender and petite but curvy where it counted, her skin creamy in the dim light, naked except for the delicate black lace undergarments that barely kept her decent. She was leaning back on her elbows in the middle of the bed, sinking a little into the thick softness of the comforter, one knee bent. Her head was thrown back far enough so that she could feel her curls just touching her back, her lips were parted and her eyes were luminous with wanting as they met his.

"You're beautiful." He was unfastening his jeans, unzipping them, and the passion that blazed in his eyes shook Carly to the core. He shucked his jeans and she watched, dry-mouthed, as they went south along with his briefs. Then he straightened, and she looked and looked without even realizing she was staring.

He was the one who was beautiful, there was no doubt about it, broad-shouldered and narrow-hipped and muscular, with long, strong, powerful legs. But she had known that. Beautiful was Matt, and had been forever, for as long as she'd known him. What held her fascinated gaze was something else, something that she hadn't known, or at least hadn't remembered.

"Oh, my God," she said, riveted. "You're huge."

He made a sound that was partway between a laugh and a groan. His eyes were hot and dark with the promise of secret, unspeakable deeds and delights as they moved over her. Everywhere they touched, Carly seemed to burn. Her fingers curled into the comforter. Her lips parted as she sucked in air.

"It's your fault," he said, thick and low but with the merest thread of humor too, and came down on the bed beside her, his weight rolling her against him.

26

SHE WASN'T the most beautiful woman he'd ever seen. Hell, she wasn't even the most beautiful woman he'd ever fucked. But she was Carly, and that made all the difference. She was soft and sexy and sweet as she rolled against him, and he wanted her more than he had ever wanted a woman in his life.

Hell, he didn't have a woody anymore. He had a god-damned giant sequoia.

Which she had, of course, felt she just had to mention. That was Carly, irrepressible to the end.

Normally, in his experience at least, humor and hard-ons didn't mix, but he was still smiling a little as he kissed her.

She wrapped herself around him, and suddenly he wasn't smiling at all as he rolled her onto her back and pressed himself down on top of her and took her mouth. He was consumed with lust, on fire with lust, burning up with the need to push himself inside her and thrust and thrust and thrust until he exploded, until he achieved the blessed Nirvana that was the best thing he knew, better than football, better than boating, better than being astride his Harley with an open road in front of him and nothing to hold him back.

He slid a hand beneath her thigh, pulled it up so that her knee was bent and he was lying between her legs, pressed up hard against her, just shove that little bitty bit of lace aside and in he'd go . . .

Which was pretty much what he had done the last time he'd done her.

It was embarrassing to think that at thirty-three he didn't have any more control than he'd had as a horny twenty-one-year-old kid.

Ordinarily he did. Ordinarily, if he did say so himself, he was pretty damned good in bed. He'd been making women come for years.

He didn't doubt he could make Carly come. She was already breathing hard, trembling, clinging to him, her thighs all soft and parted for him, her nipples in that scratchy lace bra poking up against his chest. She was hot and wet and ready and he was hot and hard and ready and this could be a good thing if he just followed his instincts and dove in.

But this was Carly. He wanted to take his time. When he finished with her, he wanted her to be sated, exhausted, bedazzled. In other words, he wanted her to know that she'd been well and truly fucked.

He reached around between her shoulder blades and unclipped her bra with a deftness born of practice. The little moan of protest she made as he lifted his mouth from hers and tugged her bra off and slid his lips down her neck all at the same time almost made him change his mind. But then he saw her breasts, her succulent ripe breasts with the nipples round and rosy as raspberries. He had to taste them, had to take them into his mouth and suckle them, had to lave the nipple with his tongue and test it with his teeth and feel her gasp and squirm beneath him and clasp the back of his head while he slid his hands inside those sexy little panties and gave himself the worst case of blue balls he'd had since he'd first started scoring more home runs than strikeouts with girls at age fifteen.

By the time he licked his way south her fingers were digging into the bed and she was moaning and moving her hips in a way that anyone but a masochist would consider evidence of a pump well and truly primed. But he wasn't finished with her, not yet, the feel of her all hot and wet and slick against his fingers wasn't enough, he wanted more.

He pulled her panties down her legs and threw them over the side. Then, on all fours as he prepared to move back up her body, he paused to look at her. Naked, with her breasts all flushed and pointy from his ministrations and her legs parted in quivering surrender, she was as erotic as any sight he had ever seen. She was all lush curves and softness and sex, and he wanted her so much that he burned.

He moved back up her body and slid his hands beneath her butt, filling his hands with her firm round cheeks as he shifted her for optimum access. Then he pressed his mouth to the cleft between her legs and tasted her.

She gasped, stiffened, and tried to close her legs against him in instinctive defense, he thought, against the breaching of this last frontier. He squeezed her butt, lifted her closer, kissed the quivering little nub that was the center of her pleasure, licked it, slid his tongue inside her. By then her fingers were threading through his hair and holding him to her and her hips were coming off the bed as he took her with his mouth.

"Matt."

At that he glanced up to find that she had lifted her lids and was blinking down at him, her eyes all cloudy and dazed with passion. He found himself looking into those sex-drugged baby-doll blues and thinking that they could belong to no one else in the world but Carly. Knowing that it was Carly spread out naked before him, Carly who was watching him go down on her, Carly he was getting ready to fuck into next week, took erotic to a whole new level. It was the most carnal experience he had ever had in his life.

"Please." She tugged at his hair.

To hell with it. He couldn't hold out anymore. He knew what she wanted, and it was what he wanted too, so much that he was throbbing and aching with the pain of denial, so much that he couldn't slide up her body fast enough. He kissed her and his arms went around her and her arms and legs wrapped around him too and he pushed inside her, all at just about the same time. Her sheath was so hot, so scaldingly hot and so wet and so tight as it closed around him, that he groaned into her mouth and then took her hard and fierce, plunging deep, taking and taking and taking mindlessly because it felt so damned good that he was never going to stop.

Great sex? Oh, yeah.

But he couldn't go on forever. The heat of her and the way she squirmed beneath him and her soft little cries were pushing him over the edge. He knew it, knew he was on the brink of losing it and slid his hand down between her legs to touch her in a way that could pretty much be counted on to make her come too.

She came all right, convulsing around him, shuddering and shaking and digging her nails into his back and crying out her pleasure: "Oh God Matt oh God Matt oh God oh Matt I love you I love you oh God *I love you, Matt.*"

He thrust one last time and exploded, holding himself inside her, holding her tight while he rocketed through the universe and she rode her own wave.

It felt so good, so goddamned good. . . .

Still, his last thought before he collapsed atop her, spent, was a surprisingly coherent *oh, shit.*

It took a few minutes of near catatonia and a not-so-gentle shove on his arm before he was able to summon the energy to roll off her. Flopping onto his back, Matt rested his head on a bent arm and reluctantly contemplated what had just happened. Actually, he suspected that he had stayed where he was for so long because he didn't want to face the awful truth: in another one of those patented brain-dead episodes of his, he'd gone and fallen right into the tiger pit he'd spent most of the last seven years avoiding.

That it was Carly's tiger pit made it a little better, but not much.

He cast his eyes cautiously sideways to find that she was curled on her side with her head resting on a bent arm too and her face tilted so that she was looking at him. She was naked, but he couldn't see much. Her knees were drawn up in such a way as to hide the sweet little nest of curls that he was already putting on his list of favorite sites to re-explore. Her arm lay across her breasts, deliberately shielding them from his view. He knew that it was deliberate because he knew Carly. Carly would be feeling shy about now, self-conscious about being naked, embarrassed at having just been so thoroughly done.

She was shy and sexy and naked and his for the taking. He could go back for a double-dip, he thought, and felt his body begin to stir.

Then he remembered why fucking her in the first place had been such a bad idea. Under the circumstances, fucking her a second time would be even worse, but he suddenly wanted to do it so much that the sheer effort required to resist caused his muscles to tense and his teeth to clench.

Don't panic, he told himself, but panic was already clawing at his gut. *You can still get out of this.*

Just about that time his cute little cuddle-bunny rolled

away from him, making for the edge of the bed without so much as a word or a nuzzle.

"Hold it," he said, grabbing her wrist. He might have only had sex with her once before, in the back of a car when she was eighteen, but he knew Carly: silent flight was not her normal postcoital behavior.

Having made it all the way to the edge of the bed, she turned her head to look at him even as he noted with absent interest how very slender and fine-boned her wrist felt beneath his hand. She was sitting there with her legs already swung over the side, affording him a really nice view of her back and the sweet curve of her ass. He'd been ticked at her, a little, thinking that while he certainly deserved a large share of the blame for the situation in which they found themselves, she couldn't be considered innocent of wrongdoing by any means, but the wary, defensive look she cast him went a long way toward dissipating his anger. He realized with a spurt of self-disgust that getting mad at Carly for being what nature had made her was kind of like getting mad at Bambi for being a deer.

"What?" she said.

He eyed her. She was still all flushed with sex, and her mouth was full and a little swollen from his kisses and the tip of her breast that kept jiggling into his view as she looked around at him was rosy and swollen-looking from his kisses too, and that plus the sight of her butt, which he really hadn't gotten as thoroughly acquainted with as he might like, and the tangle of corkscrew curls and the big blue eyes and the soft wide mouth that equaled Carly in his mind were beginning to do a real number on him.

Wasn't there a quote that said something like, *mighty sequoias from little acorns grow?* Or anyway, close enough. And it was happening again.

Not to put too fine a point on it, he was beginning to grow seriously fond of the idea of doing her again.

But wait, stop, no, that would be just about as stupid as deliberately wading deeper into quicksand. He was so close to getting his life back, so close to earning his freedom, so close to having all the females in his life in a place where they were able to function happily without him, that the thought of screwing it up (and if ever there was an appropriate expression, that was it) here in the home stretch scared him to death.

"Great sex, no strings, huh?"

If there was a sardonic note to his voice, well, he couldn't help it. Damn it, this would have been easy to avoid; all she'd had to do was just let him stick to his original plan of staying the hell away from her.

"Hey, don't feel bad. I know you tried your best," she said.

It took him about half a beat to get that. Mighty mouth. He remembered calling her that more than once when they were kids because she was so small and girly-looking and basically physically defenseless and yet so completely unable to keep her mouth shut even when staying silent was all she had to do to save her skin. All grown up and she was still at it, pretending to commiserate with him about his sexual performance when she knew as well as he did what he was talking about.

"Damn it, Carly—" he began, and she said "Let go!" and gave her hand a yank.

They weren't going to play tug of war with the arm; he knew how that went, she'd start squeaking *you're hurting me* when his grip wouldn't hurt a gnat and then the whole situation would go downhill and he would end up being in the wrong and apologizing (which was the object of the exercise, he'd learned over the years) while she walked off with her nose in the air and a moral victory and he never even got to speak his piece.

To nip that whole scenario in the bud, he sat up, hooked an arm around her waist, and hauled her kicking and squealing across him, depositing her back in bed beside him, trapping her between his body and the wall and holding her in place.

"You can't manhandle me!"

"Looks like I can."

They were lying on their sides, practically nose to nose and eyeball to eyeball with his arms around her waist while she braced her hands against his chest to keep some space between them and glared ferociously at him.

"Listen, baby, I'm not blaming you for this. I knew better. I knew the 'no strings' bit was a crock going in."

"I don't know what you're talking about," she said, taut with indignation.

Her nipples moved against his chest as she spoke. He could feel them like twin points of fire. Her thighs moved too. He was consumed by the thought of just how really, really easy it would be to just kind of shift his leg and slide his knee between them—

"Oh, yes, you do. Hey, Curls, I was there. Tell me how *I love you, Matt* fits in with no strings."

Her lips compressed. "I always say that when I come. Well, not the Matt part, but the other."

"You do not."

"How do you know?"

"I know."

She moved restlessly, pushing against his chest a little, but somehow managing to settle herself closer to him where it counted. The heat of her, the brushing of her nipples against his chest, the sliding of her thighs against his, the soft prickle of the curls between her legs pressed against his stomach, was driving him crazy.

"What's your problem, anyway? Just because I said *I love you, Matt* when I was getting off doesn't mean I really do. And even if I did, which I don't, except like, as a really good friend, I don't see why it creates a problem for *you.*"

She didn't see why it created a problem for him? She ought to try looking at things from his point of view. She was flushed and big-eyed and tousle-haired and so pretty, and she felt so good in his arms, so hot and soft and sexy, that the panic he knew he should be feeling, would be feeling if he was in his right mind, was being overcome by sheer heat.

"Because I don't want you to get hurt. Because I care about you. Because doing you and then taking off into the sunset makes me feel like a fucking heel."

And if he kept reminding himself of all that, maybe he would manage to get off this bed without doing her again. Or maybe not.

Carly stiffened in his arms, clearly less than pleased by what she had heard. Her eyes widened and shot sparks at him. She pushed against his chest again, which had the ultimate effect of getting her breasts just far enough away so that her nipples could joggle against him while shifting her lower body closer yet. Or maybe he was doing that by tightening his arms around her. Yeah, he was probably doing that by tightening his arms around her.

"News flash, sweet cheeks. You couldn't hurt me if you tried," she said. "How to put this so you'll understand? The only thing I want from you is your hot hunky body."

The word *bullshit* occurred to him, and he knew that was exactly what he was hearing, but he was so far gone now that he didn't even feel like arguing about it. Lust was attacking him in waves, completely sweeping away any and all rational thoughts, fears, plans for the future. He seemed to recall telling her that men basically think with their dicks. If they'd been having that conversation now, he could have offered himself up as Exhibit A.

"Sweet cheeks?" He should have said it with a chuckle, but chuckling was beyond him. Even smiling was beyond him. Actually, anything much removed from fucking was beyond him. She was pressed up against him now, and he could feel every soft, sweet, seductive inch, and she kept moving too, almost wriggling really, which made it worse. His knee bent, touched her legs, probed . . .

"Yeah, sweet cheeks." The look she gave him was nothing short of truculent. "Baby, did I ever happen to mention that you've got a really great ass?"

He could smile after all. He did, at just about the same time as he got his knee between her legs and wrapped a hand around the nearest breast and kissed her. She went perfectly still for a minute, but as his thumb found her nipple and he pressed his thigh all the way up between her legs until he could feel her all hot and wet against him, she moaned into his mouth and wrapped her arms around his neck and kissed him too.

Then he rolled her onto her back and did her, great sex one more time, and then rolled onto his back and pulled her on top of him and did her that way too.

Finally, as she lay atop him, sated and exhausted and hopefully bedazzled just as he had planned, it occurred to him that she had come twice more.

Both times she'd gasped out some variation of *oh God, oh God, oh God, oh God.*

Not one *I love you.* Not one *Matt.*

Which pretty much told the tale right there.

"Shit," he said tiredly.

She stirred and looked up at him, propping her chin on

her hands. It was almost dark outside now, and the light that had earlier filtered through the curtains was gone. Still, it was not so dark that he couldn't see her, and for that he didn't know whether to be glad or sorry. There could be no doubt that the woman lying on top of him was Carly: Kewpie-doll cute, with her twists of blond curls and big blue eyes and soft, kissed-pink lips. All warm curves and silky, naked skin. She looked sleepy and wanton and vaguely blissed-out, and she smelled of shampoo and sex and him. She was Carly, the only girl he'd always liked too much to fuck, and now he'd taken a header down that slippery slope he'd first started sliding on twelve years ago and fucked her big-time. She made him hot as hell and he loved her like a sister—no, not a sister now, perish the thought— but *like* that, but Carly was all about forever and forever just wasn't in his game plan.

I love you, Matt.

"What?" she asked.

He could just walk away but he knew he couldn't, he'd want her again and not be able to keep himself from taking what he wanted any more than he'd been able to keep her out of his bed today. They could just have a red-hot affair until he was ready to leave town, but he knew she couldn't, she just wasn't made that way. The idea of forever scared him. It made him nauseous. It made him break out in a cold sweat.

I love you, Matt.

Tough titty, he told himself, he'd known going in that this was a bad idea and now he got to reap the whirlwind he had sown. He knew Carly. She didn't say *I love you* lightly. She'd always been a tough-talking, big-mouthed brat with a marshmallow center, and it was the marshmallow center part that worried him now. She hadn't had that many people in her life to love, a crappy childhood with no family besides her stiff-necked old grandmother, and then a husband who'd cheated on her in the cruelest possible way before walking out on her for another woman. She was a good girl, a great girl; she didn't deserve the hand she'd been dealt, but she'd played it with a lot of courage. He was crazy about her really, loved her without being *in love,* whatever that meant, with her, and he'd cut off his left nut before he'd leave her all crumpled and crying like Shelby had been in her car today. And that was where this was headed. No doubt at all, just as he'd foreseen going in.

I love you, Matt.

If she said it she meant it, and he was basically screwed. It was either go with forever or give up Carly altogether, just get up, get dressed, drive her home and walk away, with the comforting reflection that sooner or later she'd get over it.

Yeah, and on the way out the door he'd kick a kitten and a puppy or two.

He couldn't do it. She was sweet and vulnerable and *Carly,* and he couldn't do it. Anyway, he could already tell that he was going to want to fuck her again. Soon, and frequently. A good guess was several times a day until the urge wore off.

"What?" she asked again, frowning a little at him because it was taking him so long to answer.

"I give up," he said. "You win. You want forever? Fine. You got it. Marry me."

27

Had Matt really just asked her to marry him? Carly stared at him, hardly able to believe her ears. He looked big and dark and just about good enough to eat lying flat on his back on the white fitted sheet that was the only piece of bedclothes that still remained on the bed, one hand tucked beneath his head, the other warm and relaxed as it nestled in the small of her back. His hair was tousled, his eyes had a dark secret gleam that made her think of sex, and his mouth was twisted into a resigned-looking grimace.

A resigned-looking grimace? When he was *proposing*, for God's sake?

"You're joking, right?" she asked, giving a pseudo-playful tweak to a strand of silky black chest hair that just happened to lie beneath her fingers.

"Ouch." He flattened her hand against his chest, presumably to keep it from inflicting any more pain. "No, I'm not joking."

"You're asking me to marry you?"

"Sounded like it, didn't it? Yeah, I'm asking you to marry me." With his tone, and expression, he could have been a poster boy for Testy-R-Us.

"You ever hear of candlelight, flowers, bended knee?"

"Hey, I'm asking, all right?"

And thereby doing her a big favor. Because he felt guilty. He couldn't have made the subtext any more clear if he'd said it aloud. She couldn't believe she'd gotten herself into this position, it was all because she'd lost control of her mouth and gasped out *I love you* when she'd only meant to think it. With anybody else, she could have pretended that she hadn't meant it, that it was one of those things that just came out during sex, but not with Matt. He knew her too well.

She'd heard of pity fucks, but pity proposals? This was new.

"You *jackass*." She punched him in the ribs and rolled off him.

"Ouch! What the hell was that for?" Rubbing his side, he glared at her as she came to her feet beside the bed and stood arms akimbo annihilating him with her eyes.

"Listen, sweet cheeks, what is it about 'no strings' that you don't understand?" Carly said through her teeth, spotting her clothes and bending to snatch them up, then catching the appreciative widening of his eyes and turning so that she was facing him and snapping her arm across her bosom at the same time as she realized that bending was probably not the most modest move she could make.

"Give it a rest, Curls." Matt turned on his side and propped his head up with a hand as he watched her with every evidence of continuing interest. With a fulminating eye on her audience, she managed to kneel in a very-ladylike-despite-being-naked manner in order to recover her clothes.

He continued, "You're dying to say yes, and we both know it. Say it, get over it, and come back here. We don't have to get up for another—" he cocked an eye at the bed-side clock "—hell, almost an hour."

"Hey, Matt?" Carly picked up his jeans too, straightened, and threw them at him. "Screw you."

"That's the idea," he said with a slow-dawning grin, neatly fielding her missile. "There's time."

Without another word Carly stomped off into the bathroom.

By the time she came back out, showered and dressed and looking as presentable as she could manage under the circumstances, he had turned on the overhead light and was dressed too and standing in the middle of the room talking on his cell phone. He was frowning as he spoke, and running a hand through his hair as though what he was hearing frustrated the heck out of him. He looked so damned handsome and sexy and sure of himself that she wanted to kill him.

She would have stomped straight out the door, but he stepped neatly in front of her, blocking her path. For a moment Carly contemplated decking him. The problem was, she didn't think she could do it. No, she knew she couldn't do it. He was too damned big. But she wanted to.

Her eyes must have told him something of the sort, because he grinned mockingly at her.

He said good-bye and clicked his phone shut and slid it into his pocket. Then he took her hand—actually wrested her hand toward him when she initially resisted—went down on one knee in front of her, and pressed her hand to his heart. She could feel the warmth and strength of his chest through his tee shirt.

Too astonished to speak, Carly quit trying to get her hand back and gaped at him.

Her brows started to contract.

"I'm short on candlelight and flowers at the moment, but bended knee I can do: Carly, baby, darling, angel, will you marry me?"

"No," she said, snatching her hand back. His phone rang while he was getting to his feet, and she took advantage of his momentary distraction to walk past him and out the door.

The garage was pitch dark and as hot and airless as Death Valley after the air-conditioned apartment. Probably going down those rickety stairs without being able to see so much as her hand in front of her was a mistake.

If it would get her away from Matt, though, it was a mistake she was willing to make.

The light came on just in time to keep her from breaking her neck, and Carly realized that Matt was coming down behind her. She didn't even look back.

"What do you mean, *no?*" he said to her back. Having reached the bottom of the stairs, she turned to glare up at him. He was about halfway down, and he was looking thoroughly exasperated.

Had he really expected her to say yes? Had he really thought that she was so crazy about him that she would jump on an offer of marriage like a dog on a bone just because he felt guilty enough to toss one her way?

"Do you want me to spell it out? Write it down for you? What? N–O. No. How hard is that?" She stalked toward his car. "Take me home."

"You're the one who threatened to cut my balls off if I did another—what was it you called it? Oh, yeah, a kiss-and-run—on you." He followed her across the garage. "So you should be happy. This time I'm not kissing and running. I'm *proposing,* for God's sake."

"Yeah, well, you know what you can do with your proposal."

"Come on, Curls, get real. You know forever is what you want."

Whoever it was who said the truth hurts had gotten it wrong. In Carly's case at least, what the truth did was infuriate. Sizzling inside like sausage on a grill, she turned with one hand on the door handle and launched napalm at him with her eyes.

"Listen, you, just so you know. Forever is a heck of a long time. You're not *that* good in bed."

Opening the car door, she slid inside and pulled on her seat belt. It was even hotter and stuffier in the car, but she didn't care. Anything that would get her away from Matt she was ready to embrace with open arms.

The garage door rattled up, the overhead light went out so that it was suddenly dark in the garage, and then he opened the door and got behind the wheel.

"Now let me get this straight." He started the car, turned on the lights and began backing out. She could see him now. The reflected glow from the headlights touched his face. He was frowning, his brow furrowed, his eyes narrowed. "You're mad at me."

Typical Matt, exquisitely perceptive. Carly gave a little snort of laughter. "Ya think?"

"Want to let me in on why?"

Because you're stomping on my heart here? But she couldn't say that. No, she wouldn't say that. She had some pride.

"Because you're a jackass?" she suggested sweetly.

He gave her a look before stopping the car, getting out and closing the garage door. The dashboard clock said ten-twenty-five. He had to be at work in thirty-five minutes. Good. The sooner she was rid of him the better. He got back behind the wheel, reversed out of the driveway and then shifted the car into drive and headed toward the main road before he said another word.

"Look," he said in the measured tone of a reasonable man forced to deal with the unreasonable—which in this case would be her. "We've been tight since we were kids, I care about you, you care about me, there's a lot of history there. Add sex to that, and it was bound to happen. This whole love thing should not be a surprise."

"There is no—" Carly began hotly, glad of the darkness to cover the sudden heat in her face as she sought for any weapon—lies would do; anger wasn't bad either—to deflect the humiliating certainty that Matt suspected—no, *knew*, get real—that she was in love with him.

"Let me finish here," Matt interrupted, holding up a warning hand. Gritting her teeth, Carly crossed her arms over her chest and stared stonily out the windshield. The headlights arced over a half-empty parking lot and a small apartment complex as the car paused at the intersection and then turned right. "Like it or not, we have a relationship here that neither one of us is going to be able to just walk away from very easily. The thing is, I could do the 'great sex, no strings' thing, but you can't. I know it. I accept it. Hell, there's even an upside to it. If we get married, we can do it as much as we want. And we completely undercut the whole town gossip network."

There was the faintest undertone of humor to that last.

Carly seethed. He was stomping all over her heart, and he thought it was amusing? She didn't know why she was even surprised. After all, it wasn't like she hadn't known the score going in. She'd even been warned.

"You know, it's kind of you to think of me and my needs, but contrary to what you seem to think, I'm not really in the market for a *second* husband." If her tone got any sweeter, she was going to need insulin. "In fact, the more I think about it, the more I think I like you better as a one-night stand."

Matt rolled his eyes skyward. "I don't believe this. The only time in my life I ever ask a woman to marry me, and she gets all bent out of shape about it."

All bent out of shape didn't even begin to cover it. Try furious.

"Like I told you before, sweet cheeks, your romantic technique needs work."

He shot her a look, but before he could say anything more his phone rang. Cursing under his breath, he fished it out of his pocket.

"What?" he barked into it. He was sounding pretty ticked off himself by this time. Which made her feel a little better. Anything was better than his sounding amused, resigned, prepared to shoulder the burden of one more responsibility.

She was many things, but *not* one of Matt's responsibilities. And she never wanted to be as long as she lived. What she wanted, she realized dismally, was for him to be as madly in love with her as, to her everlasting regret, she seemed to be with him. Which, given the fiasco the "great sex" thing had turned into, didn't look like it was going to happen anytime soon.

"You've got to be kidding me." He listened, focusing on the road ahead while the night flew by outside the windows. "Okay, I'm on my way. Twenty minutes, max."

He hung up, then glanced her way.

"Antonio just backed his car up and ran over Knight's foot, which means we're short another deputy." He shook his head and glanced at her. "I don't have time for this."

He was pulling up before her house as he spoke. The headlight beams touched on his motorcycle, parked right where he had left it. Carly looked up the hill, up at the softly illuminated windows of the big white house that was once again her home, and was suddenly so glad to see it that she could feel incipient tears burning at the backs of her eyes.

Or maybe tears were burning at the backs of her eyes because of Matt.

She was head over heels in love with him, and he "cared"

about her. How humiliating, infuriating, heartbreaking was that?

"You know what? I think you were right about the bed thing being a really bad idea for us," she said, already opening her door as he slid the transmission into park. "So why don't we just agree not to do it anymore?"

Getting out, she slammed the door behind her with a considerable amount of force, and started tramping up the dark and shadowy slope toward the house. The tree frogs piped a welcome. The insect chorus joined in. A pale moon waxed high overhead. The sky was aswarm with stars. It was hot and steamy, and the scent of magnolia and cut grass and rotting walnuts hung in the air.

"Like either one of us is going to be able to stick to that." Matt fell into step beside her.

Carly cast him an evil look. "*I* don't see a problem."

"Well, I do."

"How to put this? In that case, it sucks to be you."

"Not to be ungentlemanly here, but if you care to cast your mind back you might recall that *you* were the one who practically begged me to take you to bed, not the other way around. Of course I could be mistaken, but it *was* you who said something about not having had sex in two years, wasn't it?"

"Well," Carly said, "*now* I remember why I let it go so long."

"Don't give me that. I made you come. Multiple times."

Carly curled her lip and wished him dead. "Think that makes you special? So does my vibrator."

Matt stopped dead. Carly could feel his eyes boring into her back as she marched on. *Hah,* she thought, *chew on that.*

He caught up with her. "All right, I've had it with this crap. This is your last chance. Do you want to marry me or not?" He sounded fed up to his back teeth now. Carly could go him one better. She was mad enough to chew nails.

"Not." Her legs were still rubbery, Carly discovered, and the discovery made her madder.

"Okay, fine, I asked. Don't ever say I didn't. I don't ever want to hear that kiss-and-run malarkey come out of your mouth again."

"Don't worry, you won't."

"Meaning?"

"Figure it out."

He didn't reply. The two of them stalked upward in silence for a moment.

Fuming, Carly cast him a sideways glance. "I thought you had to be somewhere."

"I do. I'm walking you to your door first."

"I don't want you to walk me to my door. I want you to leave."

"Too bad."

"You know, I'm getting pretty sick of this whole king-of-the-world thing you do."

"Gosh almighty, are you really? What can I say? How about, deal with it."

They had reached the steps now. Carly stomped up them. Matt followed. Not stomping. But he was scowling, and for Matt that was something.

The soft yellow porch light was warm and welcoming. The house itself seemed to glow invitingly. Sandra had left the curtains open, and Carly noted that, seen from the porch, the front parlor looked both elegant and serene. Viewed through the wavery prism of century-old glass, even the portrait of Great-grandfather over the fireplace looked charming rather than dour. From the looks of things, Sandra had turned every lamp in the house on, and no wonder, Carly thought, as it occurred to her for the first time that her prolonged absence had meant that Sandra had probably been home all alone when darkness fell.

She fished her keys out of her pocket, and he took them from her without so much as a raised eyebrow asking permission and found the right one, fitting it into the lock with no difficulty. As he opened the door and stood back for her to enter, the tinny buzz of the alarm sounded in the distance.

Okay, so Matt had been right about the security alarm. Its reassuring presence did make her feel safer.

Just like the nails in the upstairs windows.

Hugo was crouched on the radiator, his tale twitching. Carly scooped him up and turned to face Matt as he stepped in behind her.

"Good ni-ight," Carly said, the last word stretched into two falsetto syllables.

Frowning now, with the soft light of the hall chandelier spilling down on him so that she could see the angry glint in his eyes, Matt was looking tall and dark and dangerous. He loomed over her, his eyes narrowed, his mouth unsmiling. His stance might almost have been described as intimidating—except she knew him too well to be intimidated. *Nice try though,* she thought, as his gaze flicked to her mouth.

"Go for a good-night kiss and die," Carly said.

"Know what, Curls? You're being a real pain in the ass." Matt's eyes were hard. His voice was soft.

She knew that expression and that voice. He was on the verge of losing his temper. Well, goody-goody. She'd lost hers about half an hour back.

"Then I guess that makes you a—"

His phone started to ring.

"Dammit to hell and back." He pulled it out, opened it, answered, listened, said, "On my way," and closed it again.

"I don't have time for this," he said again, glowering at her. "Not tonight. I'll see you tomorrow."

"Not if I see you first," Carly said, knowing that it was childish and not caring. Matt gave her a look, then turned on his heel and walked out the door. She closed it behind him, locked it, and watched him stride across the porch. Then, still clutching Hugo, she hurried toward the kitchen. She didn't know how long that last little exchange with Matt had taken, but she couldn't have very much time left before the alarm went off.

She made it just in time, putting Hugo down and keying in the code. The warning buzz went silent. She reset the alarm and glanced around. There were a couple of dishes in the sink, but otherwise everything was tidy. The back door was locked. The curtains were drawn. For a moment she just stood there, gripping the counter and taking deep breaths as she tried to block all memories of the night's debacle from her mind before Sandra saw her and knew immediately that something big had occurred with Matt.

God, had she blown it or what?

The great sex thing had seemed like a good idea at the time. Unfortunately, it had backfired on her with a vengeance. In the heat of the moment, *I love you, Matt* had just kind of popped out, and now he knew. And felt *sorry* for her. How pathetic was that?

Carly groaned and pushed away from the counter. She couldn't stand to think about it. She *refused* to think about it. Crossing to the refrigerator, she opened the door and peered inside. It occurred to her that she hadn't had supper. She'd had sex instead. But she wasn't going to think about that, she reminded herself fiercely. The contents of the refrigerator, tempting just seconds before, were suddenly unappealing. She wasn't hungry anyway. What she was was rubbery-legged, weak-kneed, drained. Sex—at least sex with Matt—was exhausting.

Exciting. Explosive.

Block it out, she ordered herself, grabbing the carton of premium orange juice. Pouring herself a glass, she swallowed a mouthful even as she returned the carton to the refrigerator. What she needed here was blood sugar. Then, maybe, she'd start to feel normal again.

The sooner her body stopped feeling like it had been flattened by a Mack truck, the sooner she could put Matt out of her mind.

"Sandra! I'm home," she called, taking her glass with her as she walked determinedly toward the rear parlor. They used it as a sitting room, and she could hear the television. She needed a distraction, and Sandra and the TV were that, even if Sandra was going to immediately want to know every little detail of what had happened with Matt.

Sandra didn't answer. She wasn't in the rear parlor, although clearly she had been earlier. There was a magazine on the floor beside the chair she favored, and an open can of Diet Mountain Dew—Sandra's new favorite tipple—on the table beside the chair. Carly turned off the TV and frowned. Hugo had vanished, and the house seemed quiet—almost too quiet. Annie would have been prancing at her feet about now, being cute and distracting. She missed the little dog, Carly realized, a truly enormous amount considering how brief a time Annie had been a part of her life. Whereas Hugo had a tendency to do his own thing, Annie was a faithful companion. Impossible to believe that she'd somehow gotten into poison. Thank God she was going to be all right. Tomorrow, Carly told herself, she would start looking around to see if she could discover the source. Perhaps Miss Virgie had put out something to kill mice.

"Sandra?" Carly was walking toward the front parlor when she heard it: the rush and rattle of the plumbing. Immediately her brow cleared. The sound was unmistakable. Sandra was filling the tub. Of course, it was nearly eleven o'clock. Sandra, who usually showered in the mornings, must tonight have decided to have a bath before going to bed.

Swallowing another gulp of juice, Carly reflected that it was a good thing she'd already showered. The hot water heater was old—it was something else that needed to be replaced—and it had a limited output. Generally it didn't stretch to two baths in a row.

Hugo was back again, weaving around her feet as Carly walked through the downstairs turning off the lights. Ever since she had surprised the burglar in the dining room she had tended to scuttle through it as quickly as she could whenever she had to go in there alone, and tonight was no exception. Even knowing that Sandra was upstairs didn't erase the willies that plunging that particular room into darkness gave her. But electricity was expensive, and they couldn't afford to leave the house lit up like a Christmas tree all night, every night, no matter how secretly chicken she might be. Which was why they had the security system, after all. Its comforting red eye told her that it was armed and on guard when she passed through the kitchen again on the way to turn off the last of the downstairs lights.

With the first floor now dark and full of shadows (and her heart now beating ridiculously fast in consequence), Carly hurried up the wide, old-fashioned staircase. Hugo swarmed up the polished oak treads in front of her, seeming as intent on reaching the second floor as she was. It wasn't particularly bright up there, but the small lamp that hung at the top of the stairs was on, and the rear bathroom light was on too, of course, because Sandra was in there.

And as soon as she got to her bedroom, Carly reminded herself in an attempt to quiet the annoying little quiver of trepidation that just would not go away, she could shut and lock her door.

With her door locked, her windows nailed shut, and the security system on, her bedroom was about as safe as a bedroom could get.

It was silly, she knew, and she would never confess it to another living soul, but since returning to this house to live she had developed an increasingly intense fear of the night.

Carly sent that acknowledgment to the same mental perdition to which she had banished (okay, tried to banish) thoughts of Matt. Taking a deep breath and a restorative sip of juice and feeling better now that she was once again in the presence of light, she headed toward the back of the house and her jury-rigged sanctuary. Hugo, knowing the routine by now, led the way. The bathroom Sandra was using was located between their bedrooms. Light shone beneath the door, just as Carly had expected. Sandra's bedroom door was closed. Hers was just as she'd left it, partially ajar. Both bedrooms were dark. Besides the hall light, and the bathroom light spilling out under the door, the whole house was dark.

And that was for no more sinister reason than that she herself, in preparation for bed, had just turned off the lights, she reminded herself firmly, and took another deep breath and another sip of juice.

"Sandra, I'm home!" she called again.

No answer. Probably Sandra couldn't hear her over the rush of the water.

Hugo reached the bathroom door and stopped, looked back over his shoulder at her, and meowed. There was something about that meow. . . .

Carly's step slowed. The water had been running for a

long time, more than long enough to fill the tub. Long enough that by now all the hot water should have run out . . .

"Sandra?"

Hugo pawed at the bathroom door. It opened a few inches, just far enough to let Carly see that the shower curtain had been pulled around the tub. It was an old-fashioned curtain of white canvas suspended from the ceiling on an oval rod that completely surrounded the equally old-fashioned huge cast-iron claw-foot tub. The curtain didn't quite meet at the edges. The gap was about an inch wide. Through it, Carly could see Sandra's head lying back against the lip of the tub. There was no mistaking even such a narrow sliver of her close-cropped black hair.

Sandra was taking a bath with the water running and the shower curtain closed?

Hugo, no respecter of privacy, walked right up to the tub and meowed.

"Sandra?"

Sandra didn't budge.

"Sandra?" Carly pushed the door wide. The sound of running water was suddenly loud as it echoed off the tile floor, tile walls. Steam clouded the bathroom mirror and hung in the air. Whatever the state of the hot water now, it was obvious that it had worked for some time.

"Sandra?"

Nothing. No movement. No response. Had Sandra fallen in the tub? Or—?

On that thought Carly rushed to the tub, jerked the curtain back, and froze, gasping. Her breathing suspended. Her heart skipped a beat. Sandra lay in the tub, all right. Fully clothed except for her shoes, she lay with her knees bent and her head lolling limply against the rolled cast-iron edge. Rope bound her ankles. Her hands were out of sight behind her back. From the position of her arms, Carly had no doubt that they were bound, too. She was soaking wet and there was blood everywhere, on her face, her neck, dripping down into the scarlet-tinged water that swirled ankle deep around her before disappearing down the open drain. A strip of silver duct tape covered her mouth.

Carly sucked in air with a horrified little squeak. Sandra's eyes opened. They were blinking, unfocused.

"Sandra! Oh, my God, Sandra, what happened? Oh, my God, oh, my God."

Carly was babbling, bending over the tub, reaching for the tape covering Sandra's mouth, when Sandra's eyes, which had been fixed groggily on her face, moved beyond her and seemed to focus. Suddenly they widened and filled with terror.

Something—someone—was behind her. Carly knew it with the kind of icy certainty that left no room for doubt.

The hair rose on the back of her neck. Shooting upright, she whirled around.

28

CARLY'S HEARTBEAT EXPLODED as a man, all in black with a hood of some sort pulled over his face, lunged toward her. He'd been behind the door when she had entered, watching her, waiting, Carly realized in that split second before she reacted.

She screamed, an earsplitting shriek that bounced off ceiling, walls and floor, and leaped away. Hugo skittered out of the way, disappearing under the tub. The glass she'd been holding hit the floor with a crash and shattered, sending orange juice and glass flying in every direction. His dead white hand snatched at her arm, missed by scant millimeters. Carly screamed again, stepping back, ducking behind the other end of the tub, barely eluding his grabbing arms, dodging the flying silver blade of the knife he clutched in one hand.

"Come back here."

His voice was hoarse, raspy, muffled by the hood so that it came out as a hideous whisper barely audible over the rushing water and Carly's own echoing screams. Sandra, horribly mute, eyes rolling, face shiny with water and blood, was flopping around in the tub like a landed fish. Sandra's movements seemed to attract his attention; with a sound like a snarl he sent the knife plunging down toward her even as he came charging after Carly. Carly shrieked and leaped toward him, shoving him with all her might. The knife missed its target, striking the porcelain with a terrible metallic ring just inches from Sandra's shoulder. Caught by surprise, he took a step backward, almost falling on the slippery floor.

"*Bitch.*"

He recovered his balance and came after Carly before she had time to even so much as think about making a break for the door. Carly slipped behind the tub, for once thanking God for her small size as she was able to wedge through the few inches between the tub and the wall. He couldn't, he was too big, thick muscular legs in black sweatpants, she saw as he tried. Thick arms and torso in a loose black coat, black executioner-style hood that looked homemade, not much more than medium height but *big,* huge, in fact, in this enclosed space, all of which she registered in the space of a panicked heartbeat as he lunged forward, bending at the waist, grabbing at her, *catching her.*

Carly screamed like a banshee and hit at him as his fingers, weirdly plastic-feeling fingers, dug hurtfully into her bare upper arm and yanked her toward him. No match for his strength, she almost catapulted headfirst into his grasp but managed to save herself at the last possible second by grabbing the lip of the tub. The forward impetus caused by his pull coupled with her resistance cost her her balance. She fell on top of Sandra, landing on her side then rolling willy-nilly onto her back. Sandra's body gave beneath her, and she felt the rush of tepid water on her hips and rear and the slipperiness of the tub beneath her fingers as she scrabbled uselessly at its sides, kicking and clawing as she tried to pull herself up and out.

He had lost his grip on her arm as she fell, but it didn't help her because, she realized with a surge of utter terror as she struggled to right herself, she was as helpless as a turtle on its back now. Kicking wildly, her hands sliding on the slick wet porcelain, she couldn't seem to get a good enough grip to heave herself up and over in time to get out of the way. She could only stare up with a galloping pulse and a wildly pounding heart as he lifted the knife high and sent it plunging down toward her chest.

Shrieking, she tried to dodge, but it was a mighty heave of Sandra's body that saved her. It sent her rolling over the side of the tub, tumbling, falling. The knife just missed, glancing off the porcelain again with another of those awful metallic screams, and Carly screamed again too as she hit the floor on hands and knees. Water sloshed out of the tub with her, turning the tile into a slimy, treacherous pool of water and orange juice and glass and blood. Carly realized that some of that blood was coming from her now because she was cut, cut by glass, she thought, one of the big sharp shards of glass that lay on the floor, or his knife. Blood poured from her left palm, she saw with a single terrified glance down, a lot of blood, but she hadn't felt the cut and didn't feel any pain.

Shock. She was in shock. She heard a hoarse cry. She glanced up to see him slip and almost fall on the wet tile.

She scrambled for the door—she was closer to it than he was now—but she couldn't seem to make any headway, couldn't seem to get any traction. Her hands and tennis shoes slipped and slithered on the slick tile. Carly could hear the wet squeak of his shoes, hear the harsh rasp of his breathing, hear the rustle of his clothes as he charged. She could smell orange juice and soap and her own fear and something else—a hideous sweetish something else that gave her a sensation almost of vertigo, making her stomach revolt and the room seem to tilt and her head spin. A cloth clamped against her cheek, cold, wet, permeated with the horrible sweetish smell. The smell . . .

Pure horror broke over her like a wave. Night threatened to swirl her away. The smell . . .

He was upon her, trying to clamp that horrible wet cloth over her nose and mouth. Batting it away, she threw herself to one side, falling onto her hip and shoulder on the hard tile, sliding through the sloshing mess on the floor and crunchy broken glass . . .

The cloth—white, nondescript, folded into a square—hit the tile in front of her face. The smell . . .

The water on the floor soaked through it immediately. The smell was gone.

"Got you."

A terrified glance up, and then he pounced on her like a cat on a baby bird, bending over her, grabbing her by the hair and wrenching her head back even as she scrambled up onto her hands and knees, her nails scrabbling over the slippery tile as she fought to get away.

Fearfully she looked up at the black executioner's hood and found that she was able to see, through rough-edged holes that looked like they had been cut out with scissors, his eyes. They were a curiously light blue, bloodshot, almost lashless, their pupils small black pinpricks, inhuman in their lack of emotion, their coldness. They told her that he would butcher her without remorse.

This can't be happening, was the thought that pounded through her mind in sync with the terrified racing of her pulse. He didn't even strike her as human, just a horror-film monster garbed in black, Jason/Freddy/Michael Myers in surgical gloves—those white hands were surgical gloves, she knew now—and with a knife. She was so frightened that she couldn't seem to breathe, couldn't seem to move, her arms and legs seemed weighted with lead, and the whole nightmarish sequence seemed to be happening in hideous slow motion.

"Now I remember you," he said, in that horrible raspy whisper through the mouth-slit in his mask. His head was bent over hers, and he seemed to be staring down at her. Eyes wide, whimpering with fear, Carly could look at nothing but the glinting knife as he slowly lifted it. It was poised, she realized in another of those instants of icy clarity, to cut her throat.

She could hear the rushing water and her own rapid, shallow breathing and his deeper, harsher-sounding breaths. She could feel the grip of his hand in her hair and the cold slipperiness of the tile beneath her fingers and the terrified pounding of her own heart. The one thought in her mind was, *I'm going to die.*

If the cut on her hand was any indication, it wouldn't hurt. She wouldn't feel a thing. The blade would cut deep and she would be in shock and the warm blood would gush out but she wouldn't feel it, wouldn't know anything except a horrible awareness of her own puny mortality and then nothing at all. . . .

She didn't want to die.

"No!" she screamed, so loud she shocked herself back to reality, so loud the word drowned out the drumming of her pulse in her ears and the rushing water and her breathing and his and everything else in the universe except the primal need to survive.

Screaming, she lunged to the left as the blade swooped like a silver, death-dealing hawk toward the vulnerable curve of her throat, feeling the sting of hair being ripped from her scalp as the knife missed its target and slid across the top of her shoulder. She felt a sharp pain as her flesh was pierced and then the icy burn of a cut.

He cursed and twined his hand in her hair and hauled her head back for a second go and she screamed again, despairingly this time. Her heart was beating so fast she could feel it pounding in her chest. She broke out in a cold sweat as she faced the certainty of her own imminent death.

His hold was unbreakable now. She would not be able to dodge eternity a second time. Panting with terror, she thought it again: she didn't want to die. *Please God please God please God . . .*

Her fingers scrabbling desperately over the floor encountered something hard, something sharp, and she realized that it was a long, jagged shard of glass.

The knife was already arcing toward her throat again when she jammed the piece of glass back behind her into his knee.

He shrieked and dropped the knife with a clatter and let go of her hair. Just like that, she was free.

Screaming, Carly shot through the door like a runner off the mark, heart racing, cold sweat pouring over her like someone had turned on a faucet, her shoes sliding on the hardwood floor as she gained the hall and bolted for the stairs. A terrified glance over her shoulder told her that he was coming after her, lurching wildly as blood poured from the wound she had inflicted in his leg, cursing and sobbing but coming, and then she was flying down the stairs, her feet barely touching the treads.

He'd taken time to pick up the knife. It glinted in his hand.

"You're dead. You're dead. You're dead." That hoarse, raspy whisper sent a finger of pure terror racing down her spine.

Galvanized by fear, Carly leaped down the last remaining stairs. She landed in the hall on the balls of both feet and tore toward the door.

But he was close, really close, too close. Even as she felt the cold metal of the knob beneath her hand, she knew that she wasn't going to make it, that if she stopped long enough to unlock the deadbolt and pull the door open he would catch her before she could get through it. Her blood ran cold as she realized that she wasn't going to be able to get out the door, wasn't going to be able to pick up the phone and call for help or even hit the panic button on the alarm because all those things took too much time, precious seconds she didn't have, precious seconds that would allow him to catch her. Even diving for the light switch would take time—and it might backfire. She would be able to see him, but then, he would also be able to see her.

"You're dead." He was in the hall now, breathing hard, lumbering after her, a limping, lopsided gait, but fast. Even injured, he was so terrifyingly fast.

Carly screamed and fled into the shadowy darkness of the front parlor, slip-sliding on her wet soles, thankful that she knew the house well enough so that the lack of light gave her the tiniest of advantages. She knew how the rooms connected and the angle of the halls and . . .

So did he.

The burglar. The burglar. He was her burglar. She was as sure of that as she was that Christmas was in December.

He'd come back. For her? At the thought her blood turned to ice.

It hit her then what she had to do. It was her only hope, an outside chance, maybe it would work and maybe it wouldn't but . . .

She dived for the table by the sofa, snatched the crystal peppermint dish from it and hurled it with all her might through the window. The sound of shattering glass was almost instantly followed by the shrill wail of the alarm system's siren.

"Bitch."

It worked. It worked. The security system worked. *The perimeter has been breached. Send the marines.*

But he was still coming. He was in the parlor now, she

could see him as a dark hellish shape rushing toward her. The wailing alarm notwithstanding, he was not going to let her go.

If he caught her he would kill her. . . .

Shrieking loudly enough to be heard all the way to Atlanta, her fight or flight response in full bore, adrenaline-fueled flight mode, Carly darted for the rear parlor. Her feet barely touched the ground as she flew through it and burst out into the back hall and pounded toward the kitchen, into the kitchen—and stopped dead.

She didn't know how she knew, but she knew. He had somehow circled back around on her. He was still now, silent, waiting for her there in the dark kitchen.

Waiting for her to walk into his trap.

Her breathing stopped. Her heart skipped a beat.

A furious pounding sounded over the screeching alarm. Someone was beating on the front door, rattling the knob, pounding with a flat hand on the glass.

The marines had arrived at last.

Carly turned and ran like a bat out of hell. By the time she reached the front door, she was gasping for breath. Her blood was drumming so hard in her ears that she could barely hear anything over it, not the wailing alarm, not the pounding on the door, not anything. Certainly no sounds of pursuit. Where was he? He could leap out of the darkness at any second, bringing that razor-honed knife plunging down into her back. Seconds from being saved, she would be dead.

Screaming, glancing fearfully over her shoulder, Carly fumbled at the door. Her hands were slippery with sweat; she could barely turn the lock, turn the knob—

"Carly!" It was Matt. As soon as she unlocked the door he burst through it, big and tough and yelling her name and armed with a drawn gun, and she threw herself against him and clung and felt her legs turn to limp spaghetti and her head spin as she collapsed in his arms.

"What is it? What happened? Damn it to hell—" He let loose with a string of curses as he thrust his gun into his holster and wrapped his arms around her before she could totally lose it and slide bonelessly to the floor.

He felt so solid, so strong, so warm, so safe. Now that Matt was here, it was over. She wasn't going to die. She was safe.

"Sandra . . . Matt, oh, Matt, he's here in the house . . . in the kitchen . . . the burglar . . . Sandra's in the bathroom . . . she's hurt . . . Oh, Matt. Oh, Matt." Carly's legs gave out.

"Check the house." Matt gave the harsh-voiced order over his shoulder even as he scooped her up in his arms, and Carly realized that at least two men were with him. They rushed by, one of them turning on the hall light. By its bright and nearly blinding light Carly recognized them, Antonio and Mike, moving fast, with drawn guns.

"Sandra—in the bathroom by my bedroom. He hurt her . . ."

This time Matt seemed to absorb what she was saying.

"Antonio," Matt bellowed after his men. "Sandra's in the back upstairs bathroom. Hurt, Carly says. Mike, check out the kitchen."

Antonio doubled back, bounded up the stairs.

Exhausted, Carly let her head fall back against Matt's shoulder. She felt alarmingly light-headed. Her stomach was churning, and she was shaking and freezing cold and the room was tilting and she was starting to feel almost weightless, like her body didn't exist. She had never fainted in her life. She had a feeling that this just might be getting ready to be the first time.

"Jesus H. Christ!" Matt was carrying her toward the front parlor when he stopped dead. Carly managed to focus long enough to discover that he was looking down at her in horror. So weak she could hardly lift her head now, she nevertheless glanced down at herself, spurred by the stark fear in his eyes. Held against his chest, his brawny brown arms curled around her shoulders and knees, she was deathly pale, shaking, slender in her wet, smeared jeans and navy tee shirt, only it wasn't navy now, it was red. . . .

"You're covered in blood. You're bleeding. The bastard cut you. Goddamnit to *hell*. Carly, *stay with me*."

This last, uttered in an urgent tone, just reached her ears as the last of her strength gave out. She didn't faint but she rested, closed her eyes and went limp in his arms and rested as he tightened his grip and cursed a blue streak and rushed somewhere with her.

She knew it was only a rest and not a faint because in the distance she could hear Antonio shout, "Call an ambulance!"

29

IF ANYONE HAD SEEN HIM, the man would have looked like a hunchback as he half-ran, half-hopped through the night-dark woods. He was bent over, clutching his bleeding leg, sweating with exertion and pain.

He was hurt, he was hurt, damn the bitch, she'd stabbed him with broken glass. The jagged edges had done more damage to his knee than any knife, he was going to be months recovering from this and she was *dead*.

What had started as an impersonal quest to ensure his own safety was now personal. She'd turned the tables and wounded him and escaped, and when he caught her again she was *dead*.

They were after him, the sheriff and his deputies, at least one of them was, out in the dark with a flashlight and a pistol, moving cautiously as he searched the grounds behind the house. More would come, he had little doubt. It was just minutes after he had fled the house, the damned alarm was still going off, and lights had just gone on in the old lady's house that was just up the hill from him now as he plunged through the woods on his way to his truck. More deputies would be speeding down the road soon with sirens blaring. He would be long gone by then. They weren't going to catch him, not tonight, not ever. He wasn't stupid, and he wasn't careless. Tonight's failure could be put down to plain old bad luck.

His was like a seesaw lately: sometimes up, sometimes down.

He'd gotten rid of the dog. A sprinkle of rat poison on a plate of scraps set out under a bush in the backyard. The dog had wolfed the whole thing right down. He'd been watching as they had found it, watching as they'd gathered it up and rushed down to their van and sped off toward—he presumed—their local vet.

All gone. House empty. And—he'd checked—no one had thought to either lock up or set the alarm.

There was his luck going up again. Leaving the house unsecured was a bonus he hadn't expected, but then, life was like that: full of surprises.

In the immortal words of Forrest Gump, you never know what you're going to get.

He'd left and taken care of some rather urgent business, then returned and made himself at home, taking a quick look through the closets and drawers and coming up with a gem in the kitchen—the code to the security system, no need to worry about that anymore—and in general famil-iarizing himself with the house. It was a nice house, old but big and well-furnished, and picking out a good place to hide in comfort for hours if he needed to had been easy. He had a new plan, brilliant in its simplicity, handed to him on a platter as a result of his success in getting rid of the dog. He would wait in the house until Carly was home and asleep and then just carry her out. He had nowhere he had to be tonight. He had all the time in the world. Any other loose ends he needed to finish off—like the dog if it wasn't dead—could just as well wait for morning.

He'd heard the friend come in—Sandra, he'd learned her name was—along with her deputy boyfriend. Knowing that he was hidden away upstairs while an armed officer of the law lounged around downstairs all unsuspecting had provided him with considerable amusement. Then the deputy had left—from an upstairs window, he'd watched him walk down the front lawn to his car—and he and Sandra had been alone in the house.

For the next hour or so he had camped out in an unused upstairs bedroom. Later, because of the lock he had discovered on her bedroom door that might make getting to her more of a hassle than he cared to deal with, his plan was to slide under Carly's bed and wait there until she was asleep. But that was a position he'd rather not assume until he had to; it would grow uncomfortable if he was forced to stay under there for any length of time. The closet—more comfortable than beneath the bed but not exactly where he would choose to spend a number of hours—he had ruled out after a cursory inspection. It was small and, anyway, who knew if she was neat? She might hang up her clothes at night.

Saying *boo* when she opened her closet door might be fun, but chasing her down would be a lot of trouble, and the probability of something going wrong was greatly increased if she actually got a chance to scream and run.

He'd been right about that, he reflected sourly now as he reached his truck. Wincing as he pulled himself up inside it, he stretched his leg out on the seat in front of him and rooted around in his bag for something he could use to stop the bleeding until he got home. A brief shine of a flashlight over the bag's contents—he didn't want to risk anything more than a few seconds of light in case it should bring his pursuers down on him—told him that the hole was every bit as deep and ugly as he'd first thought. His pants leg was already soaked with blood. More blood welled from the wound.

It was all the fault of that damned cat.

He'd been on his way back to his hidey-hole after a quiet reconnoiter of the back bedrooms just to make sure that Carly had not somehow managed to sneak home on him without him being aware of it when he had heard Sandra coming up the stairs. She'd been talking to someone—the cat, he figured out later—and he had melted away quickly, ducking back into Carly's bedroom, hiding behind the door because the stairs came up in the middle of the hall and he never could have made it back to the front bedroom without her seeing him. He'd trusted to luck that Sandra was headed for her bedroom, or maybe the bathroom, but just in case, he'd zipped up the coat he always wore for this kind of thing and pulled his hood down over his head on the off-chance she should spot him and somehow manage to get away. Not that he was really worried. There was no reason for her to come into Carly's room that he could see, and she wouldn't have—except for the cat.

It had walked in and stared at him concealed behind the door and twitched its tail and meowed.

"What are you looking at, cat?" he'd heard Sandra say, and then there she'd been, just as quick as that, standing behind the cat, staring right at him, her eyes widening with horror.

He hadn't come to kill her, didn't have a thing against her in the world except she kept interfering in his plans for Carly, but there she was, staring at him. What could he do?

Take care of her, too, of course.

He'd been in the midst of doing just that when he'd heard Carly calling to her and realized that she was coming up the stairs.

Then there'd been that damned cat again, pushing open the door, walking into the room, bringing Carly with it.

He was beginning to think there was something about

him and animals, some kind of karma, something weird. They kept messing up his perfectly good life.

He'd gotten to where he hated the damned things.

Now, binding his bleeding leg up with duct tape because he didn't have anything else, he wished vainly that he'd had the foresight to do something about the cat.

Then he realized something, and froze in the act of slicing through the duct tape with his knife.

His handkerchief, his neat white handkerchief that he'd pressed into use tonight because it had been in his pocket and handy when he'd needed to chloroform Sandra into submission, was missing. A quick check of his pockets and bag confirmed it: the handkerchief was gone.

Now that he thought about it, he remembered trying to use it on the bitch and then dropping it when she pushed his hand away.

Just an ordinary handkerchief, not a big loss—except that it had his initials embroidered on it.

30

HOSPITALS WERE DEFINITELY *not* Carly's favorite places in the world. Not even when Matt slept in the chair beside her bed with his arms crossed over his chest and his feet propped up on her mattress. Not even when he awoke grumpy and unshaven, and growled at everybody who crossed his path while eating her breakfast.

Not even when he showed every indication that he planned to follow her into the bathroom.

"Look, give me a break here. I'm going to take a shower," she said, shutting the door firmly in his face.

His evident devotion *did* act as a balm of sorts for her bruised and battered heart, until she reflected that, as one of his responsibilities, she could probably expect no less of him. She had no doubt that he would look after one of his sisters in the exact same way if they'd been attacked and hospitalized.

Which was really kind of depressing.

When she emerged he was out in the hall talking to Antonio, who looked just about as tired and bent out of shape as Matt did. She was wearing fresh clothes—gingham shorts and a pale blue tee shirt—which someone had fetched from the house during the night along with her purse, which meant she'd also had access to some makeup and a brush. She had three stitches in her shoulder and a bandage around her left hand, and except for a little stinging and burning at the sites of the cuts, she essentially felt normal.

As long as she didn't think about the black-hooded monster. Last night, after the doctor had finished stitching her up, she'd had an attack of what felt almost like vertigo, dizziness and nausea and sweating, and it had caused the doctor to insist that she be kept overnight and watched for shock.

So she blocked the monster out, just blocked him out as she had learned long ago to do to unpleasant things, which seemed to work. The problem was that the only thoughts strong enough to keep the horror-movie images at bay were connected with Matt. Considering the state of her heart, he probably wasn't too safe to think about either, but anything, even the specter of a thoroughly stomped heart, was preferable to a single mental glimpse of that black-hooded face, or that flashing knife. . . .

So she thought about Matt, about the sex, which had been great, and the no strings, which had been pretty much a disaster, and about how her heart had clutched in those few seconds after he'd first asked her to marry him and she hadn't had time to think it through, when she'd thought maybe he meant it.

And about how absolutely heart-stoppingly irresistible he'd looked proposing on bended knee.

Or at least, how absolutely heart-stoppingly irresistible she would have thought he looked if she hadn't known she was on the receiving end of one of the world's first pity proposals.

Which was approximately where her thoughts had been last night when the doctor had finished examining her.

Then they'd given her a shot, and she'd slept dreamlessly until she'd been awakened around nine A.M. by the nurse popping a thermometer into her mouth and Matt snoring in the chair beside the bed.

She hadn't known he snored, and she hadn't known he was grumpy in the mornings, and she hadn't known he liked ketchup on his (her) eggs. Actually, that last bit of knowledge she could have done without.

Unfortunately, even those three bits of negative information did not seem to change the fact that she was as crazy in love with him when she woke up as she had been last night when the doctor had conked her out. But at least the deep, dreamless hours of drugged sleep had given her her common sense back.

She was not going to pine for a man who loved her like a friend or a sister, a man who liked sleeping with her but felt uneasy about it, a man who hated the very idea of spending forever with her but proposed anyway out of guilt.

Not even if that man was Matt.

She was many things, but not a masochist. She loved him; he "cared" about her. She wasn't taking another step down that path. Real heartbreak lay that way.

"Where are you going?" Matt asked her as she stepped into the hall, breaking off his conversation with Antonio. Both men wore sleep-rumpled uniforms. Antonio simply looked tired and rumpled. Matt—blast him—looked tired and rumpled and sexy and macho and good enough to eat.

"To talk to Sandra," she said shortly. Matt nodded. She could feel his eyes following her as she went.

West County Hospital was a three-story brick building with two wings, gray linoleum, pastel walls and most of the basics, such as X-ray capabilities and an emergency room. For anything major, patients were sent to Atlanta. The fact that both she and Sandra had been admitted here was a silent testament to their injuries' relative lack of seriousness.

She'd needed stitches, a bandage, treatment for shock, and a night's dreamless sleep. Sandra had fared worse. She had a concussion, a stab wound in the thigh, and possible bruised ribs.

Like her own, Sandra's room was a tiny gray cubicle, a dozen or so of which opened off the nurses' station like spokes extending out from a wheel. Clad in the same kind of unflattering green hospital gown that Carly had just discarded, Sandra had her bed raised so that she was in a semi-sitting position. A white bandage formed a turban around her head, an IV was in her arm, and her leg, the thigh wrapped in a thick layer of bandages, was outside the blue blanket and elevated. She had the remote in one hand, and she was flipping channels on the TV.

"Hi," Carly greeted her. They'd spoken the night before, in the hall of the house when Sandra had been brought down and in the ambulance and the emergency room. In those disjointed, emotional conversations they'd relived the horror of the attack for each other and for Matt and his deputies as well, who had also taken official statements from them. Last night they'd been variously shocked, scared, shaken and weepy. This morning, aside from the bandages and hospital gown, Sandra looked almost back to normal.

"Aren't you looking better? Are you outta here?" Sandra turned the TV off.

"Soon. Do you want me to bring you anything?"

"Decent food. Those eggs were *nasty*. A decent night-gown—this thing's not fit to be seen in. I had to ask Antonio to leave the room before I could get up and go to the bathroom. No point in flashing the poor guy at this point. A sight like that could scare him off. Oh, and a *TV Guide*."

"Will do." Carly came and sat down beside the bed. "How are you feeling?"

Sandra shrugged and winced. "Like I got hit over the head and stabbed and drugged with something and beat up. Otherwise not so bad."

Carly grinned. During their respective divorces, she and Sandra had both learned the value of the old saying, *might as well laugh as cry.* Crying served no earthly purpose except to stop up your nose. At least if you laughed you felt better.

"Hey, I can relate. You know, I think you saved my life last night. Remember when I fell on you in the tub? If you hadn't thrown me back out, I think I would have been toast. Or hamburger. That knife was coming down at me."

" 'Course I threw you off. You landed on my cracked ribs. Think that didn't hurt?" Sandra winced, rubbed her ribs and grinned. "You're not that much of a lightweight, you know. Anyway, you saved mine first. I couldn't believe you shoved that Darth Vader–looking dude like that, but I'm sure glad you did. He almost skewered me in the throat that time."

Suddenly the memories were impossible to hold at bay. Carly saw that black-hooded face, that white, plastic-looking hand, the flashing knife slamming into the side of the tub just inches from Sandra . . .

Her stomach churned. Her blood ran cold. Her—

"Time to change your IV," the nurse said, interrupting. Carly struggled to push the horrible images away as the nurse switched one bag of IV fluids for another. By the time the nurse left, the vivid mental pictures were once again banished to the murky realm of things she refused to re-member.

"I'm so sorry you had to go through all this. I get sick thinking of you in the house all alone with that monster," Carly said quietly, suddenly serious. "I feel responsible in a weird kind of way, because you wouldn't even be here in Benton if it wasn't for me."

"No, I'd still be a waitress with a bad attitude in Chicago." Sandra gave her a wry little smile, then shuddered. "Let's not talk about it, okay? It gives me the willies. I don't ever want to think about last night again if I don't have to." Her mouth trembled, and she instantly firmed it up by pressing her lips together. She drew a deep breath in through her nose and fixed Carly with a reprimanding look. "Next time I tell you I don't *do* spooky old houses and want to go home to the big city where it's safe, maybe you'll listen."

Carly made a face. "If I'd known what was coming down the pike, I would have been right back in that U-Haul beside you, believe me." Her expression changed, and she looked at Sandra a little hesitantly. "If you want to move back to Chicago after this, I'll understand."

Sandra met her gaze, started to speak, and paused to cast a crafty glance behind Carly at the door.

"Antonio's been in here three times already this morning. He was sitting in that very same chair you're sitting in now when I woke up," Sandra said in a near-whisper, keeping one eye on the door. "He's *worried* about me. Do you have any idea how long it's been since a man was worried about me? No way am I letting some Darth Vader dude mess this up."

"Are those wedding bells I'm hearing?" Carly asked, teasing.

"I couldn't get so lucky." Sandra sounded glum. Knowing that Sandra's ex-husband had done a real number on Sandra's estimation of her own attractiveness to men, Carly felt a surge of protective affection for her.

"Antonio's the one who would be lucky to get you," Carly said fiercely, although like Sandra she kept her voice low. "You're amazing, Sandra. Did you know that? Really amazing."

Sandra grinned. "What's more to the point, I can cook. Whoever said that's the way to a man's heart must have known Antonio." She cast another cautious look over Carly's shoulder. "Speaking of wedding bells, I hear that the hunky sheriff about had a heart attack over you. I hear that after he did his crime scene thing he came back here and slept in your room."

"Matt takes his responsibilities very seriously," Carly said sourly. "And he's decided that I'm one of his responsibilities."

"Did he *say* that?" Sandra asked, sounding both appalled and fascinated.

Carly nodded, and tried hard not to look as depressed as she suddenly felt.

Sandra shook her head. "Honey, you need to do something to wake that man up. Like take him to bed and pull out all the stops."

Carly didn't say anything.

Sandra looked at her closely. "You've gone and done it with him, haven't you? When? Last night? You mean while I was being attacked by the sicko psycho you were getting it on with the sheriff? That's the story of my life right there. I'm getting murdered and you're getting off." Sandra shook her head in disgust, and then her eyes sharpened on Carly's face. "And he *still* thinks you're a responsibility?"

Carly nodded glumly.

Sandra grimaced. "That's not so good."

"Yeah, it's not."

"What are you going to—"

"Oh, there you are, Miss Linton. If you'll just sign these papers, you're free to go." Another nurse appeared in the doorway with a clipboard.

"I'll be back later with the nightgown and things," Carly said to Sandra, and went to sign the papers.

Matt was waiting for her in the hall. They said very little as they rode down the elevator. Carly had nothing to take away with her except her purse—the clothes she'd been wearing the previous night were ruined, and anyway she never wanted to see them again as long as she lived—and as they reached the revolving doors that opened onto the parking lot, she realized that she was holding on to the purse so tightly that her knuckles were white. It had just occurred to her that she was going home—home to her house—her house where she had been violently attacked the night before. Even thinking about spending another night in that house made her heart race.

With Sandra in the hospital, she would be sleeping in the house alone.

With the man who had attacked them still on the loose.

"Matt," she said in a small voice when he put her into his cruiser and then came around to slide behind the wheel, "I don't think I can go home. Not to stay. Not by myself. Not even with the security system. Not while that man is still out there."

There was a humiliating little tremor in her voice as she said that last.

Matt slid a hand behind her neck, leaned over and kissed her, a quick comforting kiss that, despite its clearly nonsexual intent, made Carly's heart miss a beat. She was just clutching at his shirt front and reflecting on how much better she already felt when he let her go and started the car.

"You think I'd let you? You're going to be staying at my house until we catch this guy." He cast an unsmiling glance her way as he pulled out of the parking lot. "Your killer cat's already there, and we can pick up your dog on the way. You didn't really think I'd leave you on your own in your grandmother's house after last night, did you?"

Carly looked at him and shook her head. That is, she hadn't really thought about it until this minute. She just had been instinctively terrified at the idea of going home again. But now that she did think about it, she knew that Matt would never have left her there on her own. As she'd told Sandra, he took his responsibilities very seriously.

Suddenly being one of his responsibilities didn't seem so bad.

"I know I've asked you this before, but I want you to really think about it now. Is there anyone, anyone at all, who might want to hurt you?" They were approaching town now, and there was actually quite a bit of traffic, both vehicular and pedestrian. The revamped storefronts on Main Street looked solid and prosperous, and the flower-filled planters and ye olde street signs added picturesque touches to what was basically the same little town she'd known since childhood. But what struck Carly most was how normal everything seemed. Her world had changed overnight, grown dark and scary around the edges. But the sun still shone and flowers still bloomed and people still went about their business.

She was going to get back to normal, too.

Carly shook her head. "I can't think of anyone. You've known me practically my whole life. Why would anyone want to hurt me? Who?"

"Just so you know, I'm having your ex-husband checked out." Matt's voice was grim.

"O—kay." At this point Carly was willing to have Santa Claus investigated if it would help find the attacker. "But it certainly wasn't John himself, and he doesn't have any reason to hire someone to hurt me. I'm sure he isn't behind it."

"Then who else could it be?" His voice was impatient, a little fierce.

"You don't think it was just some random psycho, then?"

If it was a random psycho, he might just go away. She really, really wanted to think he might just go away.

"Do you?"

Carly took a deep breath and faced what her senses had been telling her all along. "No. I think it was the burglar. I think he—came back. I told you—he said, *Now I remember you.* Who else could it be?"

There was the tiniest of breaks in her voice. Matt's jaw tightened.

"That's what I think too. I think he's been stalking you, waiting his chance. He made no move that would lead me to think he's a rapist. What we have here is a would-be killer. And I think it's you he's after, specifically, not Sandra. He had plenty of time alone in the house with Sandra last night, but he didn't go after her until she stumbled across him. He waited for you. You're damned lucky I had Antonio and Mike drop me off to pick up my motorcycle last night. If I hadn't been right there when you threw that dish through the window, he might still have had time to do what he came to do before we could get a car out there."

Remembering the horrible moment when she had stood in the kitchen, sure that her attacker was only a few feet away ready to pounce even while the alarm wailed overhead, Carly shivered. Matt knew about that, of course. He knew the whole story from beginning to end. On the way to the hospital last night Carly had told him everything, about her conviction that someone had been watching her in the dark and about the night she'd been sure someone had been at her bedroom window and about how she'd been so scared she'd nailed the upstairs windows shut— not that it had done any good in the end.

Matt's response? A harsh, why didn't you tell me all this before?

Because there hadn't been anything tangible until last

night. Because she'd felt foolish. Because she hadn't trusted her instincts. . . .

Carly gasped. "Oh, my God, do you think he poisoned Annie?"

Matt looked grimmer than ever. "I'd say it's a good possibility. Without the dog, I'm betting he would have come after you that night. He got rid of Annie so her barking wouldn't alert you when he tried again." He braked at the light and looked at her. His eyes were hard as stones. "What we have here is a planned, premeditated attempt to kill you."

"Who would do such a thing?" There was despair in her voice. "Matt, it isn't John, I'm sure it's not. But who else is there?"

"We'll find out. Don't worry, Curls, we're going to find out. And I'm going to make sure you're safe until we do."

He pulled into the strip mall where the vet's office was located, and they went in to get Annie.

"Did you by any chance keep the contents of her stomach when you pumped them out?" Matt asked Bart Lindsey when Annie was brought to them in the examining room.

"I'm afraid not. There didn't seem to be any reason to." The vet shook his head apologetically as he handed Annie to Carly. "I feel pretty confident in saying that it was rat poison, though. She had all the classic symptoms."

"No way to tell if somebody gave it to her deliberately?"

The vet shrugged. "It's possible. With dogs, it's hard to say. A lot of them will eat just about anything."

"Do I need to do anything special for her? Give her medicine or anything?" Carly asked worriedly as she held Annie close. The little dog's tail was drooping, and she seemed slightly groggy. She felt frailer than ever in Carly's arms, practically skin and bones now after her ordeal. At the sound of her voice, Annie gave a little whimper.

"Poor Annie," Carly said, caressing her ears.

"She's still slightly sedated. She'll be more herself when it wears all the way off." Bart Lindsey met Carly's gaze. "I heard about what happened to you and your friend last night. That's just horrible. I can't believe, in our little town . . ." His voice trailed off and his gaze returned to Matt. "You think it was another burglary gone bad?"

"I don't know what I think." Matt held the door open so that Carly could precede him into the waiting room. There was someone else there. Carly recognized him at once: Hiram Lindsey.

"Hiram!" Dr. Lindsey greeted him with pleasure as he followed them into the waiting room. "You back, or haven't you gone home yet?"

"I'm back," Hiram Lindsey said, then looked at Carly. "How's the dog?"

"Better," Carly said. Annie, as though in confirmation, whimpered.

"She should make a full recovery," Bart Lindsey said, just as the door swung open and a woman carrying a placid-looking tabby cat came in.

Annie gave a small, sad-sounding yap. She might be recovering from a horrible experience, but Annie was still not a fan of cats.

"Hullo, Alice. Muffy ready for her shots?" Bart Lindsey greeted the newcomer cordially as Carly hurried out the door.

"So you have a dog that doesn't like cats and a cat that doesn't like dogs," Matt said, sounding resigned when they were in the car. "And they're both going to be living together in my house. This is going to be interesting."

"Hey, I can always stay somewhere else." Carly patted Annie, who was curled up in her lap, in the certain expectation that Matt wouldn't take her up on it. "With my dog and my cat."

Matt's mouth twisted wryly. "Curls, for you I'm even willing to put up with the zoo."

And that was saying a lot, Carly knew.

The rest of the day passed in surprisingly pleasant fashion. Matt went back to work—Carly suspected he was headed back for her house, although she didn't ask and he didn't say so—and left her in the care of one of his deputies, Sammy Brooks, a stocky, balding, amiable man who looked to be around forty, giving them both explicit instructions that Carly was not to be left alone. If she went out, he was to go with her. If she stayed in, he was to be there in the house. Fixing Carly with a stern gaze, he told her that this was the way it was going to be until the man who had attacked her was caught. This was Matt in his best king-of-the-world mode, but Carly wasn't arguing. In this case, under these circumstances, she was perfectly willing to do as he said.

"Told you he was bossy," Lissa said to Carly with a grin when Matt left at last.

"I hope you don't mind me staying here for a while," Carly said to her apologetically. Having watched Carly's installation in Matt's bedroom with great interest—although she had at first demurred, Matt had ordered her to take it, declaring his intention of sleeping on the couch—Lissa was now on her way to work. She, Carly, and Dani were all in the kitchen. Sammy was already camped out on the living-room couch watching the sports channel. Carly leaned against the kitchen counter, having just finished waving Matt off. Dani sat at the table polishing off a salad. Lissa stood on one foot near the door, pulling on a high-heeled sandal. "I just couldn't stay at my house after . . ."

"Of course we don't mind if you stay. Anyway, I don't blame you a bit." Lissa got her shoe on and shuddered dramatically. "Everybody's talking about what happened, you know. That must have been so scary."

"It's Matt's house," Dani said, taking another bite of salad. "He can invite whoever he wants to stay here. But he never has. Until you and your friend spent the night the other night, he's never even had a woman over here for more than like an hour before."

"That's very significant," Lissa told Carly with a twinkle as she reached for her purse. "At least, we think it is. We think big brother's smitten."

Carly made a wry face. It was a nice thought. Too bad it wasn't exactly accurate. "He thinks of me as kind of another sister."

Lissa hooted. Dani shook her head.

"He doesn't look at us like that. And he doesn't treat us like we're made of eggshells, either. If something horrible like what happened to you happened to one of us, he'd be mad as hell and he'd do his best to make sure we were safe. But he wouldn't . . . hover." Dani's tone was precise.

"Good word." Lissa nodded at her approvingly. "That's just what he does." She looked at Carly again. "Usually it's the girls who are all over him. He doesn't hover."

"For a while there I thought Shelby might actually be going to get him." Dani finished her salad and stood up. "I'm glad she's not."

The phone rang then, with someone calling to ask if it was true that Carly Linton was staying with them because a madman had attacked her in her house, and the conversation was dropped. The rest of the day passed surprisingly swiftly. Mike Toler had stopped by with a haphazard collection of clothes pulled from their closets and drawers for both her and Sandra, which fortunately included a nightgown and robe which would be suitable for Sandra to wear in the hospital. Carly took them to her along with the other things Sandra had asked for and then ran errands. Finally she went back to see Sandra again with a stack of magazines and a supply of Sandra's favorite malted milk balls, and found Antonio with her again and Sandra happy as a clam. Everywhere Carly went people had heard what had happened and flocked around her, exclaiming over her injuries, her courage, the unbelievability of it all. Finally, supper was very much a party-type affair, with all three of Matt's sisters present and several deputies, including Sammy, who was relieved by Mike Toler, but who stayed to eat anyway. Matt himself would not be in until later. He was . . . busy, Mike said.

Given the way Mike said it, Carly took that to mean that he was doing something concerning the investigation into what had happened at her house, but no one got specific and she didn't ask. She didn't want to know. It was getting dark outside now, and she didn't even want to think about the previous night.

By the time Carly went upstairs to bed around ten—she made sure to go up early, while the house was still full of people and light and laughter—she was feeling almost cheerful. Matt wasn't home yet, but that was probably a good thing too. She needed a night, just one night, to sleep and clear her head, and then tomorrow she would start facing her problems again one by one.

Including the problem of what to do about Matt.

She took a shower, taking care not to get her stitches or bandage wet. The stitches felt a little tight and the cut beneath the bandages a little sore, but the worst thing about her injuries was that they served as a constant reminder of the previous night's horror. She refused to think about it, refused to allow the nightmare images in, and so she sang all the cheerful songs she could remember as she went about her usual nightly routine. Then she took one of the sleeping pills the doctor had given her for the first few nights to help her, as he put it, cope with the shock, and put on her candy-striped pajama pants and pink top. She chose them deliberately because the color was cheerful, coated her lips with cherry-flavored Chap Stick because the taste made her feel cheerful, turned Matt's TV to *Nick at Night* to watch reruns of *Cheers* and *The Cosby Show* because they were cheerful. She was tucked in bed with Hugo curled beside her and Annie on the rug beside the bed, watching Dr. Cosby having a fatherly chat with Theo and reflecting on just how really cheerful she really, truly was feeling when sleep hit her like a giant black wave.

She didn't know how long she slept. She only knew that her sleep was deep, but not restful. There were things in her sleep. Things she didn't want to see. Things that grabbed her even though she fought against them. Things that were too big, too strong, too terrifying to escape.

Things with eyes. Light blue, lashless eyes. Coming closer and closer and closer until they were just inches away from her face. Monster eyes . . .

Then she was back in the Home.

31

THE LIVING ROOM COUCH was long. It was wide. It was comfortable.

Not.

Matt threw his pillow to the floor in disgust and gave up trying to get comfortable. It didn't matter. He couldn't sleep anyway, even though he knew he needed sleep badly. He'd had all of—what?—maybe two hours of shut-eye in the last twenty-four? But sleep was proving as elusive as the identity of the bastard who had attacked Carly. The really terrifying part about it was that he felt pretty sure that the guy was going to keep coming after her until he either got her or was caught. And catching the bastard was going to be up to him and his department. The state police had been out to the scene, but had basically given him to understand that the heat wave was doing bad things to their workload, too, and that this assault on two women at home that had not resulted in rape, grievous bodily harm, or death to either, was not a top priority for them. The FBI had no jurisdiction and less interest, although an agent friend had offered to run some of the blood recovered at the scene that Matt had been able to identify as belonging to the perp through their computers to check on a possible DNA match. Matt didn't have much hope of that panning out—DNA matches only happened if the perp's DNA happened to already be on file—and so he was pinning his hopes on less high-tech methods, like piecing together the clues. Flopping onto his back, he stared up into the darkness and ran through what he knew, or thought he knew.

First, what he had by way of a physical description: the bastard was an inch or so taller than Sandra, which made him five-eleven to six feet; stocky build; light blue, nearly lashless eyes. The lashless part meant that he was probably fair-haired: Blonds or near-blonds tended to have fewer hairs, and their eyelashes, sans makeup, which most guys tended not to wear, were generally pale, which would make them hard to see, ergo, Carly's lashless description.

Second, the perp was wearing a coat and a full-face mask in ninety-seven–degree heat. What did that tell him? Maybe the guy was trying to terrify, in which case he might have been expected to want to torture his victims to prolong the vicarious thrill he got from their fear. But that hadn't happened; as soon as he'd gotten hold of Carly, the bastard had tried to cut her throat. Which pretty much ruled out the infliction of fear as a motive for the freak-wear.

Maybe the guy was simply a lunatic who got off on dressing up like a cartoon ninja. But a lunatic who specifically targeted Carly? It was possible, but in his opinion not probable.

Maybe the guy didn't want to be recognized. A coat and a full-face mask could be used to conceal his identity in case someone besides the victim (it was easier to think of her as the victim; it helped him contain the white-hot anger that threatened to cloud his reason when he thought of *Carly* at the mercy of the murderous bastard) saw him or in case the victim herself survived to tell the tale, as had happened in this case. To add weight to this possibility, the guy had said *Now I remember you* to Carly. Remembered her from where was the million-dollar question. Of course, it was always possible that he remembered her from having grabbed her in the dining room. That the burglar and the murderous attacker were one and the same was so likely that he considered it almost a certainty.

For his money, he was going with the last scenario. Another point in its favor was that statistically people were usually murdered by people they knew.

So what he had was a stocky, fair-haired guy with light blue eyes who was around six feet tall that Carly—or Sandra, or some chance passerby—would recognize without the disguise.

His next clue was, of course, the wound itself and the blood that the attacker had shed copiously at the scene. (And bravo to Carly for that. She'd always had more fight in her than any three men he knew.) Area hospitals were being checked to see if any had treated a man with the kind of leg cut that might be the result of being slashed with a piece of jagged glass. As for the blood itself, the house had been awash in it. He'd already had it typed: It was O, like about half the population. Not much help in winnowing out suspects. Of course, it was always possible that there'd be a DNA match. Following the trail of blood (courtesy of Billy Tynan's dogs) had also led him to where the perp's vehicle had been parked. He suspected that it was some kind of four-wheel-drive truck because the hiding place had been off-road and fairly inaccessible. But again, in these parts, that didn't rule many people out. So far, efforts to recover a tire print or any other kind of forensic evidence from that locale had been fruitless.

His fourth clue was a footprint. The perp had run out the back door when Matt had burst in through the front, but he had run around toward the front of the house before disappearing, and in his haste had knocked over the can of tarry red paint Carly had been using on the roof. He had then stepped in it, leaving behind a beauty of a shoeprint. Matt had had a plaster cast made of the print today, and was having it analyzed at that very moment.

And last but not least was a handkerchief. A plain white man's handkerchief that had apparently been soaked in some kind of soporific liquid and applied to Sandra's face to keep her quiet after she'd been initially knocked unconscious. The perp had tried that tactic on Carly too, but with a less successful result. The bastard had dropped it when she'd fought back.

He was having the handkerchief analyzed too, to see if they could identify the liquid the perp had used. Matt had his suspicions, but it was better to wait for the lab results to be sure.

But the best thing about that handkerchief was—

A scream ripped through the night, a terrified scream, a woman's scream, echoing off the walls, electrifying every nerve ending Matt possessed. *Carly.* He knew who the screamer was even before he launched himself off the couch and took the stairs two at a time. Stark fear lent wings to his feet. His heart pounded. His mouth went dry.

The dog was barking now, wild hysterical yaps which lent even more impetus to his headlong rush.

Surely to God the bastard hadn't managed to get to her here.

It occurred to Matt that he wasn't carrying his pistol. It also occurred to him that he wasn't going to need it. If the murderous bastard was in there with Carly, he was going to take him apart with his bare hands.

And enjoy every minute of it.

Matt burst through his bedroom door like a running back carrying the ball that last yard to the goal. The door slammed back on its hinges. He saw Carly, sitting bolt upright in the middle of his bed, still screaming, her eyes huge and glinting in the dim light from the cracked-open bathroom door. The damned dog, barking hysterically, charged him, going for his bare ankle. Matt dodged, hit the light switch, yelled, "Annie! No!" and watched the cat perform aerial gymnastics before it landed on the back of his recliner.

The last echoes of the scream still hung in the air as he determined that there was no one in the room besides Carly and himself.

"Quiet, Annie," he said to the dog, which had backed off but continued to bark. To his surprise, she shut up, apparently having finally recognized him as a friend.

Standing in the middle of the room, his chest heaving, his heartbeat just starting to slow down, Matt watched awareness come into Carly's face and realized what he was dealing with.

"Matt . . ." she said in a quavery little voice at just about the same time as his gaggle of girls piled into the doorway behind him, gasping and exclaiming.

"Matt, what happened?"

"Carly, are you all right?"

"Did somebody try to break in?"

Matt turned around, shaking his head at his sisters. They were in their usual summer night gear, shorty nightgowns and big tee shirts and pajamas, Lissa with her hair tied up in rags so it would be curly in the morning, Dani with hers pulled back in a ponytail so it would be smooth, Erin's face shiny with cream.

They gaped at him, their faces studies in surprise and speculation and amusement. He realized then that he was standing there in nothing but his underwear, and scowled at them.

"I'm sorry. I had a nightmare," Carly said in a small voice behind him. She was talking to his sisters, he knew.

"Okay, I'll handle this. Out," he said to them, walking purposefully toward them. The cheeky things grinned at him. Matt ignored those grins and the three pairs of eyes twinkling up at him even as he backed them up a step and closed the door in their faces. And locked it for good measure.

God save him from his sisters.

Then he turned back to Carly. She was as white as the walls, no color to her at all, and he could tell that she was still badly shaken. Her hair was a tumbled mass of blond corkscrews, wild as a lion's mane around her face. Those baby-doll blue eyes were huge. Her lips trembled. She was still sitting bolt upright in the middle of the mattress, looking small and vulnerable and very female in her tiny pink top that was all that he could see of her attire, given the fact that the covers were pooled around her waist. There was a large flesh-colored Band-Aid on her shoulder, and white bandages wrapped the palm of her left hand.

These reminders of how close she had come to dying made his stomach clench.

Padding across the carpet, he turned off the overhead light, tensed instinctively at the soft involuntary gasp she gave as darkness wrapped around them, walked to the bathroom and turned off that light too, then moved to the side of the bed, pulled the covers back and got in.

She moved against him with a small wordless whimper that made his heart contract. He pulled the pillow beneath his head and lay on his back and wrapped his arms around her as she snuggled close. By the time they were settled, her head rested on his chest and her arm was draped across him.

She smelled like his soap again. Not Irish Spring. He'd already had to switch brands once because getting a hard-on every time he took a shower could be inconvenient, to say the least. Now she smelled like his new soap, Zest. He supposed he'd be getting rid of that brand, too.

"Want to tell me about it?" he said into the darkness.

She shuddered.

"Okay," he said, supremely conscious of the soft warm curves pressed up against him. But this was Carly, and she was hurt and scared and needed him, and no way was he going to even so much as think about sex, not tonight. "We can play twenty questions. Was it one of the old bad dreams, or an all-new one?"

"Eyes," she said, shuddering again. "I dreamed about his eyes. They were looking at me. And then I dreamed about the Home."

Matt had no trouble understanding that the eyes she referred to belonged to the bastard who had attacked her. He tightened his hold on her fractionally, a purely reflexive gesture in response to how close he had actually come to losing her, and she snuggled closer still. He always forgot how petite she was, but with her pressed up against him like this her size was pretty hard to miss. Her feet reached about halfway down his calves and her bones felt delicate and there was really no weight to her at all, just a sensation of roundness and heat and lush femininity . . .

Don't go there.

"You've never told me much about the Home. You weren't there long, were you? A week? Two?" He asked about the Home because he figured it would be easier for her to think about that than the bastard who had attacked her. Just the thought of Carly being helpless and scared and at the mercy of somebody bigger and stronger than she was made him feel homicidal. If he had anything to say about it, she wasn't going to go back there again even in her mind.

"Eight days."

"So what was it about it that gives you nightmares all these years later? Were they bad to you there? Abusive?"

He could feel the negative movement of Carly's head, the tightening of her fingers on his flesh. Her hand lay up near his shoulder with her arm curved across his chest, but not by the wildest stretch of the imagination could her grip be termed an embrace. It felt more like she was hanging on to him for dear life.

"Curls?" he prompted. He called her that deliberately, hoping the childhood nickname would remind him that this was his friend, his pal, the little girl with the acres of hair who'd followed him around everywhere when they were kids, yakking a blue streak all the while. In the beginning he'd considered her a giant pain in the ass, and even after he'd grown to like the little nuisance and finally regard her almost as another sister he'd never in his wildest dreams thought that one day he'd be lying in bed beside her like this, turned-on to his back teeth.

"They were nice to me," she said in a shaky little voice, and pressed closer. "But I was scared. I was only eight years old, and I really, really missed my mother, and I didn't have any idea why they'd taken me away from our neighbor who was supposed to be watching me until my mother came back and dropped me off at what kind of looked like a school. And nobody bothered to explain it. I guess they thought I was too young to understand. But it wasn't a bad place, it was actually okay, there was enough to eat and we all had our own beds and a locker for our things—not that I had very many things—and we could go outside. There was a big area in back, and a barn, and some animals. They even had a donkey. He was funny, hee-hawing all the time."

She paused and took a deep breath.

"Then I got sick and they put me in the infirmary. The nightmares are about when I was in the infirmary."

She paused again. Matt felt her shiver.

"Hey," he said, patting the soft bare skin between her shoulder blades comfortingly. At least, he meant it to be comforting. There was no doing anything about the fact that the silkiness beneath his fingers reminded him of other, even silkier parts of her body. "I'm right here. You're safe. As safe as you've ever been in your life. Tell me about the infirmary."

She rubbed her cheek against his chest. Matt felt the moist heat of her breath flutter across his nipple and gritted his teeth. Carly needed him right now, and not for sex. She needed somebody she could count on to make her feel safe. That would be him. It struck him that she really had nobody else.

"It was kind of like a dorm room, a little bigger than that but not really big. There were four of us in it. The others were all older than I was and a couple of the girls were really kind of tough and I was afraid of them, a little. They didn't pay much attention to me, I was too young, but they'd talk to each other and I would lie up in my bunk and listen. Oh, there were bunk beds, white iron bunk beds with metal springs that creaked every time anybody moved. I had one of the top bunks."

She stopped talking. Matt gave her a minute, then said, "Okay, you're in the top bunk. Then what?"

Carly took a deep breath. "I don't really know. I just remember lying up there in the dark and hearing the beds creak. That's what the dream is, you know, the one about the Home. Just me lying there in the dark with my eyes open, and I hear a bed creak." She shivered. "I don't know why that scares me so. Maybe because that was about the time I started getting really afraid that my mother wasn't ever coming back. When you're eight years old, that's the scariest thing in the world."

Her mother hadn't come back, Matt reflected grimly. As far as Matt knew, Carly had never seen her again. She'd died out in California when Carly was a teenager. Matt remembered Carly and her grandmother flying out for the funeral, and Carly coming back and being really quiet and withdrawn for a couple of weeks. It had been summer, and he had been so bothered by little Mighty Mouth's unnatural silence that he'd started climbing up to her room in the middle of the night and coaxing her out on midnight adventures to cheer her up. If her grandmother had ever found out, she would have skinned Carly alive. But by the time school started again, Carly had been back to her old self.

"Hey," he said, to get her in a happier frame of mind. "Remember when you fell out of that big tree down by the creek and broke your wrist?"

"Because you told me there was a snake in it and if I didn't get down really fast it was going to slither up my shirt because snakes are attracted to heat? Yeah, I remember." Her voice held both humor and reproach.

"I was thirteen," he protested. "I had a fort in that tree, and you were a pesky little girl. Thirteen-year-old boys do not want pesky little girls near their forts."

"You also walked me home and told my grandmother I broke my wrist by tripping over a root in the backyard."

Matt smiled faintly. "She didn't think much of you being in the woods with me, did she? And she didn't like you climbing trees. I thought the least I could do, after I made you fall out of that tree, was keep you from getting in trouble for being in it in the first place, if I could."

She was smiling. Matt could feel the movement of her facial muscles against his chest. She felt relaxed now, all pliant and yielding, radiating heat. He was all too aware that he was next door to naked and she wasn't much more fully dressed and she was a woman and . . .

She yawned. "I feel so incredibly sleepy."

So much for the effect he was having on her. "So go to sleep."

"Matt." She stirred against him, her hand sliding down over his chest to rest just above his waist, trailing pure fire as it went.

"Hmm?"

"Thank you."

"For?"

"For saving for my life last night. And for this. For being here. I don't feel scared with you here, and I'm so tired of feeling scared."

"Not a problem." Although, actually, it kind of was. Because he wanted to do her, so much that he kept having to picture little-girl Carly to keep from rolling over with her and—

"You're not going to go away, are you? Can you just sleep here for the rest of the night?" She was sounding really drowsy now.

"Yeah, I can sleep here for the rest of the night." If his voice was a shade dry as well as being gruff, well, he couldn't help it. Sleeping wasn't really exactly what he had in mind, but for her . . . "Just think of me as your own personal teddy bear."

He felt her smile again.

"I like that." Then she gave another mighty yawn. " 'Night, Matt."

" 'Night."

Seconds later he heard the softest of snores and realized that she had fallen asleep. He grimaced ruefully up at the ceiling. This was kind of like taking a little kid into a candy store and then telling him he couldn't buy any. Downright cruel. But at least his bed was roomier than the couch. Even with Carly draped across him and the mother of all hard-ons he was more comfortable than he had been all night. He was just about to drift off himself when the damned cat jumped up on the bed and curled up near his head. He pushed it off. It came back. He pushed it off again. It came back. This went on until he gave up and the cat won. When he finally fell asleep, it was to the tune of Carly's gentle snores tickling one ear and the cat's rumbling purrs torturing the other.

His last waking thought was, *Welcome to domesticity.* Then he realized that someone way up there in the cosmos must be having a whole truckload of fun at his expense.

When he went downstairs the next morning the fun just kept on coming. All three of his sisters were seated around the table in the kitchen, where he'd instinctively headed, drawn both by habit and the alluring smell of fresh coffee. He'd showered, shaved, and put on his uniform without disturbing either Carly or the cat, which still slumbered by his pillow. The dog, though, came down with him. Grunting a good morning while the girls broke off their chatter to look at him in such a way that he knew just exactly what they'd been talking about, he crossed the kitchen to let Annie out into the backyard. Then, resigned, he turned around to face the battery of mascaraed eyes.

Erin started. "Did you have a good sleep?" she asked brightly.

"Okay," he said, shooting a quelling glance at the three of them as he crossed to the counter where the coffeemaker hummed away. "Carly had a nightmare. She was scared. I stayed with her. End of story."

Yeah, right. Not if he knew these three.

"What does that do to your 'no sex under my roof' rule?" That was Lissa, grinning at him.

"We did not have—wait a minute, I'm not about to discuss my sex life with my sisters." Matt cast Lissa a grim look and poured himself a cup of coffee. "Anyway, the rule stands."

"She's cute, Matt," Dani said. "Actually, you two are cute together."

"Give me a break," Matt said, revolted. "She's a friend."

"Face facts, big bro: You're in love." Now Erin was grinning at him too. At the thought, Matt felt his blood run cold. No way. No how. Not happening.

"About time, too," Dani said.

"You want to drop the subject?" If he sounded a little testy, it was because they were, as usual, making a whole lot of something out of nothing. What did they know about him and love? Nothing. They were girls: they saw love in every kiss. With that comforting reflection, Matt took a gulp of coffee and almost choked because it had something totally disgusting like vanilla in it. "Jesus, who made this?"

"I did," Erin said. "It's a specialty blend. Collin likes gourmet coffees."

All three of her siblings rolled their eyes simultaneously.

"Hey, Matt, you look really hot in your skivvies," Lissa said, and snickered. The other two nodded and grinned.

"Okay," Matt said, putting down his cup and fixing his tormentors with a level look. "Give it a rest."

"Just so you know," Dani was trying to look grave while her eyes sparkled wickedly at him. "Girls really go for boxers more."

"Don't you three have somewhere you need to be?" Matt emptied the contents of his cup down the sink.

"It's Sunday. Church."

"Oh, yeah." Now that Matt thought about it, he saw that they were wearing dresses and heels, which for them either meant a hot Saturday night or a sober Sunday morning. No, given the demureness of the dresses, it was definitely Sunday morning. He glanced at Erin. "So where's loverboy?"

"If you mean Collin, he'll be here shortly," Erin said with dignity.

"What about Thing One and Thing Two?"

"He's talking about Andy and Craig," Dani informed Lissa. She did not, Matt noticed, sound particularly insulted. Probably because the descriptions were apt. If pushed, he could have come up with an even more flattering one for loverboy.

"He's just trying to change the subject. But it's not working," Lissa replied, then focused on Matt again. "We want to talk about you and Carly."

"Not your business." Matt dumped the entire contents of the coffeepot down the sink.

"Hey, that was for Collin," Erin protested. "He'll be here in a minute."

"He can thank me later."

"We took a vote," Dani said. "You and Carly: we approve."

"Well, now I can die happy," Matt said, and turned on the faucet to rinse out the pot and, not incidentally, drown out the chorus.

"You do realize you have just a teensy little problem," Erin said when he turned the water off. "Shelby's going to be here any minute. She's going to church with us."

"Shit," Matt said, setting down the pot as he had a lively vision of Carly coming down just in time to join this sure-to-be-happy gathering. "Can't you find somebody besides Shelby's brother to marry?"

"I could," Erin said as Matt crossed to the door and opened it, whistling for Annie. To his relief, the dog came bounding in. "But why?"

"Because Collin's pretty much a prick?" Dani suggested sweetly.

"He is not!" Erin was hot.

"Yeah," Lissa concurred with a grimace. "He is."

"Matt . . ." Erin looked at him appealingly.

"I'm outta this, ladies. As long as I don't have to wear a pink bow tie to the ceremony, Erin can marry Collin if she wants to." He spotted Mike Toler, who'd drawn the morning's Carly watch, and waved him in. "Even if he is a prick."

"Who?" Mike said, sounding interested.

"The girls will explain." Matt grinned mockingly at Erin, lifted a hand in farewell, and went to work.

And spent the whole day trying to get the theme song to a stupid old sitcom out of his head. The one that coupled love and marriage—and horse and carriage . . .

32

THE NEXT WEEK passed quickly. Not wanting to make a fool of herself in front of the whole house again, Carly had started doubling up on the sleeping pills so at least she'd be spared the embarrassment of screaming nightmares, and that seemed to work. Sandra got out of the hospital and moved into Matt's room with Carly, sleeping on a rollaway bed lent by a neighbor. Matt seemed to feel that the attack on Sandra fell under the heading of collateral damage. In other words, the attacker would not be coming after her again. But, as Sandra put it, there was no way in hell she was staying in that spooky old house by herself after what had happened. Anyway, Matt was still treating the house as a crime scene, which basically meant that it was off-limits to everyone except law enforcement types. Thus Sandra and Carly became roommates, literally this time. This was a good thing, Carly assured herself, as it meant that (a) sleeping with Matt was no longer an option and so she didn't have to worry about whether or not it was a good idea; (b) she and Sandra got to bond like a fly and flypaper; and (c) she was never alone. Never, ever, ever, unless she was in the bathroom with the door locked.

As grateful as she was for having been placed in protective custody, as Matt officially described it, as sorry as she would have been to find herself on her own in this situation, Carly was starting to feel like the whole *save me, save me, I'm afraid for my life* ride she'd been on since the monster had invaded her house was getting old. One could only be terrified for so long, and then life had to start getting back to normal or a person would go nuts, she discovered. To begin with, the lack of privacy was getting really irksome. She had little doubt that it was fraying everyone else's nerves as well; the whole group, herself included, was starting to get a little frazzled. Matt's sisters were great, she liked them a lot, but having two strange women living in their house with them when they had jobs and boyfriends and Erin's imminent wedding to prepare for had to be a strain. Add to that the facts that one of the deputies was in the house whenever Carly was, Sandra's cooking drew the others whenever they weren't actively on duty elsewhere, and Hugo and Annie played chase the kitty at least once a day and the place was a circus pretty much around the clock. The good news was, it was impossible to feel terrified, or even a little scared, in the midst of such chaotic surroundings; the bad new was, it was crazy-making.

Matt himself was not really an integral part of the tumult. He showed up basically to sleep, passing out on the couch around midnight most nights and leaving again around six in the morning. He was, Mike Toler confided on one of his house shifts, working like a dog. They all were. They had a backload of cases up the yahoo, the usual laundry list of crimes was still being committed even as files on the old ones were piling up in their in baskets, and Matt was spending every minute he could spare running down leads about the identity of the man who had attacked Carly and Sandra. Without notable success so far, as Antonio confided with a grimace when it was his turn to Carly-sit. One of their most promising clues was the handkerchief the perp had dropped. It had been soaked with chloroform—which accounted for the sweetish smell Carly had noticed—and it had three initials embroidered on it. A monogram, almost certainly. The problem was that the handkerchief was so old and worn and the embroidery was so stylized that the tiny letters could be BLH or RIH or RLH or BIH. It was even possible that the last H was not an H at all but an A. They were trying to run down the manufacturer to see if they could get a handle on the script; they were also having a computer analysis done to see if the initials couldn't be made clearer. In any case, none of the letter combinations they'd come up with so far meant anything to Carly or anyone else. Without that clue, they pretty much had the suspect list narrowed down to about one-fourth the male population of Georgia, plus or minus a few random stalkers from Carly's married years who might have decided to head south.

None of which, as far as getting all of them off the circus train and back to something resembling normal life, sounded particularly promising.

On Thursday, Carly made up her mind that the situation could not go on as it was indefinitely and decided to talk to Matt about it. On Friday, she was still waiting to talk to Matt about it. On Saturday, she was *still* waiting, and none too happily either. Short of getting up at two A.M. and creeping downstairs to shake him awake on the couch, it didn't look like anything in the nature of private conversation was going to happen between them anytime soon. All things considered, she had no real objection to rousing Matt in the middle of the night for this really very important chat, but the chances of her actually getting downstairs without Sandra waking and wanting to know where she was going, or having a conversation with Matt without being interrupted by one or another of his sisters coming home with her boyfriend, or all four of the other women in the house gathering together at the top of the stairs to listen to every blessed word that was said, seemed slim. Still, Carly was hoping that Saturday night, when the girls went out and Antonio took Sandra to dinner as, he said, his way of saying a little *thank you* for all the truly outstanding meals she had fixed for them, might provide her with an opportunity.

No such luck. Matt did not come home all day. By eight P.M., Carly was stuck on the couch with Hugo shedding on her lap, Annie dreaming at her feet and a uniformed Mike Toler in full guard-dog mode beside her, watching reruns as first Sandra left with Antonio, then Lissa left with Andy, then Dani left with Craig. Erin came down last to wait for Collin, who was picking her up but was late, as Carly had learned was usual for him.

Pacing the living room impatiently, Erin finally stopped, hands on hips, to survey Carly and Mike sitting side by side on the couch. Carly followed her gaze to Mike, who was sitting with his arms crossed over his chest and a frown marring his face as he stared fixedly at the TV. His entire attitude told Carly that he had approximately the same degree of enthusiasm for spending the evening with her as she did with him.

"You two look gloomy." Cute in a short denim halter dress and heels, Erin shook her head at them. Sometimes her mannerisms were so much like Matt's that Carly just wanted to close her eyes and block them out. "Where the heck is Matt? Carly, you ought to chase him down and make him take you out somewhere. And as for you," Erin's gaze met Mike's, "don't you know any pretty girls? I mean, any who aren't already taken?"

"I'm working," Mike said. His tone bordered on curt, and he kept his eyes glued to the TV. Erin frowned at him. Carly observed this little byplay with a flicker of interest, then tried to erase all indication of guilty knowledge from her face as Erin then looked at her with lifted brows, clearly waiting for a response.

"Matt's working too," Carly said. "Not that he would

take me out if he wasn't. I keep telling you, Matt's not my boyfriend. We don't have that kind of relationship."

Erin and Mike both gave her skeptical looks.

"Anyway, he's busy," Carly said defensively.

"He's staying away from you on purpose," Erin said. "Lissa and Dani and I teased him the other day about being in love with you. I think we scared him."

"Matt's not in love with me," Carly said flatly. She thought about it for a second, then looked up at Erin, who, she had come to realize, knew her big brother pretty darn well. "Is he?"

Erin shrugged. "Actually, it's kind of hard to tell with Matt. We think he is. He's different around you. Protective. Bossy, of course, but in a sweet kind of way. And he slept with you up in his bedroom with us in the house. *That's* never happened before."

"Uh, I don't think I should be hearing this," Mike said, shifting uneasily. Both women ignored him.

Carly was still focused on Erin. "I had a nightmare. Nothing happened."

"But see, that's significant right there. How many women do you think he's slept with and nothing happened? The problem is, he's got this thing about commitment. If he really thought he was falling in love, he'd run for the hills."

"Just because he runs for the hills doesn't mean he thinks he's falling in love," Carly said tartly. "It's just something he does. I call it a kiss-and-run."

Erin laughed. "Did you tell him that?"

Carly nodded.

"Was that before or after he kissed you in his office?"

A smile curved Carly's mouth. "Right about that same time, I think."

"See, that's great. That's what he needs. Somebody who

stands up to him. Matt's the best brother on earth, I mean he's practically sacrificed his whole life to take care of us, but he tends to be a little, uh, masterful. Plus he's never had to work to get a girl in his life. He just has to stand there and breathe, and girls swarm all over him. Mm, I don't mean you."

"I swarmed just like everybody else," Carly confessed. "Starting about twenty years ago."

Erin grinned and shrugged. "Well, there you go, then. See what I mean? But in your case, it doesn't seem to be such a bad thing. I mean, it seems to have worked. He's different with you than he is with anyone else he's been involved with, truly. With you, it's not just all about sex."

"I *really* don't think I should be hearing this," Mike said. Neither Carly nor Erin so much as glanced at him.

"That's because I'm his only girl *friend*," Carly said dismally. "Two words. Not girlfriend. Girl slash friend."

Erin grimaced. "Did he actually tell you that?"

"Oh, yeah."

A horn tooted from the driveway.

"Oh, that'll be Collin, I've got to go." Erin started moving toward the door. Then she glanced back at Carly. "So do something to shake him up a little. I take it you've tried the sex thing . . ."

"I don't want to know," Mike said.

Carly nodded at Erin.

"Hmm. Well, I can see that for Matt that might be nothing new. How about the no-sex thing? Believe me, for him, *that* would be new."

"There's a thought," Carly said.

"Sheesh." Mike put his hands over his ears. "If Matt knew you all were talking like this in front of me, he'd kill you. If he knew I was just sitting here listening, he'd kill me."

The horn honked again, a double toot that bespoke impatience.

"Oh, hush," Erin said to the horn. Then, to Mike, she added: "Unless you tell him, he won't ever know, will he?" She looked at Carly again. "You know we're all leaving soon, Lissa and Dani and me? We really don't like the idea of Matt being left all alone. We've talked, and we all think you're perfect for him. So we're prepared to help any way we can."

"That's nice, but I don't think—" Carly began.

The car horn blared.

"Oh, I'm *coming*," Erin threw over her shoulder, as though Collin could actually hear her. Then she turned back to Carly. "Let me think about this. There's bound to be something—"

The horn blared and kept blaring, as though Collin was holding his hand down on it now.

"Got to go," Erin said, giving up and moving quickly toward the door. "We'll talk later."

Then with a waggle of her fingers, she left.

The horn stopped blaring as she stepped outside. Both Carly and Mike were left staring at the closed door. They were still seated side by side on the couch, alone again except for the snoozing animals and the blaring TV.

Just another one of her patented hot Saturday nights, Carly thought.

"You tell me why she puts up with that guy," Mike said a moment later. Carly looked at him. She had suspected that he was interested in Erin all along, and now here was confirmation.

"She's marrying him next weekend," Carly said by way of a reminder.

"Yeah, I know."

"Does she know how you feel about her?"

He shrugged. In man-speak, Carly decided, that meant a qualified "yes."

"How does she feel about you?"

He cast her a disgruntled look. "She wants to be friends."

Did that sound familiar or what? The "friends" thing must run in the family.

"I have an idea," Carly said slowly. "We're stuck with each other until about midnight or so, right?"

"Actually, my shift ends at eleven." Mike cast her a sideways look. "Not that I feel like I'm stuck with you or anything."

"You're stuck with me," she said firmly. Mike didn't argue.

Carly thought for a moment. Going out at night was probably a big no-no as far as her personal safety was concerned—at least, she hadn't been outside after dark since the attack—but then, she would have an armed deputy with her. How safe was that? And as she had noted before, said deputy was a good-looking man, if one liked the type. Her own particular preference tended to be for tall, well-built, way too handsome men with crow-black hair, coffee-brown eyes and a maddening my-way-or-the-highway style, but then, there was no accounting for tastes, and under the circumstances a shorter, stockier, perfectly attractive hazel-eyed redhead would do.

"You know, the Converses aren't the only game in town," Carly said. "I think we should go out. You and I. We can have dinner, and maybe go listen to some music somewhere or something, and not get back until really late. Unless you have plans for later?"

"Are you asking me out on a date?" The look he gave her was mildly horrified. He seemed to scrunch closer to his end of the couch.

Instead of being offended, Carly chuckled. "Don't panic. Listen . . ."

In the end, dinner was easy. They went to The Corner Café, which was packed, since it was Saturday night. In the course of waiting for a table and then settling into a small, dark alcove in the back (which Carly had to tell Mike he needed to specifically ask for) they talked to at least half the town. The general reaction at seeing them together was amazement, both of the wide-eyed variety and the more politely concealed kind. Carly got a few pointed *How's the sheriff 's?* and *Where's Matt's?* Mike got more than a few reproving looks.

"You're getting me in trouble here," he muttered as she tucked her hand in his arm and waved at people right and left when they finally finished and exited through the evergrowing crowd. "By tomorrow morning this is going to be all over town."

"That's the *point,* remember." Carly barely managed to keep from sounding exasperated. Mike was a nice guy, but as a thrilling date he lacked a major requirement—like thrill. If Erin wanted him, she could have him. "Okay, now what?"

"Hey, this was your idea."

Masterful the man was not. Carly sighed.

"Okay, pretend I'm Erin," she said. "If you really wanted to razzle-dazzle me, where would you take me?"

He looked dubious. "You're going to get me fired, you know. Matt is going to be so pissed about this."

"If you're lucky, Erin will be too. From what I've seen, the two of them seem to think a lot alike."

"They do, don't they?" Mike said, brightening up a bit at the thought. "If you were Erin, I'd take you to Savannah."

Now that had promise. Matt usually got home around midnight, and she'd heard Erin tell Dani that she would be home around then too, because she had to be at church early the next morning to go over something about her wedding music with the organist. The reflection that Erin would know how late he had kept Carly out seemed to clinch the matter for Mike. They drove to Savannah, went

to a bar, listened to music—they didn't dance, because neither of them felt the slightest inclination to dance with the
other—and drove back to Benton. As far as dates went, it
didn't even rate. But in the end, it was almost two A.M.
when Mike pulled back up Matt's driveway, and that made
it a success.

Matt's cruiser was already there. Seeing it, and the faint
glow through the curtains that meant somebody was in the
living room, Carly smiled with anticipation.

She had no doubt at all who that somebody was.

"Matt's gonna kill me," Mike said, nervous again now
that D-Day was at hand. He lagged behind Carly as she
walked toward the door. In this case, letting her go first was
not so much courtesy as cowardice, Carly thought.

"No, he isn't. Matt and I aren't even a couple, for God's
sake. And you and I had a good time, remember? Try to act
like it," Carly hissed, fishing in her purse for the key. She
was wearing a short black knit skirt and a black tee shirt
that ordinarily, if she'd had access to her full wardrobe, she
never would have dreamed of pairing because, in her opinion, the solid black along with the clinginess of the knit
made the outfit just a little tarty. However, for this occasion
tartiness worked. Some black heels she had "borrowed"
from Erin, who wore the same size she did, and a pair of
Sandra's dangly earrings completed the ensemble. She
smoothed her skirt, adjusted her tee shirt to make sure no
skin was showing, and took a deep breath. Then she in-
serted the key into the lock.

As she pushed the door open, a cacophony of sound
filled the air. Before they had even had time to step inside,
there was dead silence except for Annie, who rushed the
door, her tail wagging madly, and the TV. Suddenly she and
Mike were the cynosure of what felt like a hundred pairs of
eyes. Carly crouched to pat and silence Annie even as she

glanced around in surprise. She had expected to find Matt. She had not expected to find all three of his sisters, their boyfriends, and Sandra and Antonio as well, lounging on every available piece of furniture. From the various drinks and snacks sitting around, it was clear they'd been making quite a party of it. Matt was sitting in his recliner with a bottle of Heineken's in his hand. He'd obviously been home for some time, because he'd changed out of his uniform into jeans and a tee shirt and a discarded and obviously read newspaper was on the floor beside him. He didn't get to his feet, but, like everyone else, he looked at them. His face was carefully expressionless at first, but as his gaze ran over her his mouth thinned. Then his eyes moved on to poor Mike, whom Carly could practically feel shrinking behind her.

"Hi, everyone," she said with a little wave, thinking as she straightened that she sounded as brightly chipper as vintage Kathie Lee Gifford.

There was a chorus of answering *hi*'s.

"Have a good time?" Matt's voice was deceptively casual. Deceptively *soft* and casual.

"Wonderful," she said, and turned to smile with dazzling brilliance at Mike, who looked hunted.

"Wow, you look really hot." Lissa looked Carly up and down in transparent surprise. Carly realized that it was the first time Lissa—or any of them, except Sandra and Matt years ago—had seen her in anything but the most casual of clothes.

"Where'd you go?" Dani asked. She sounded almost fascinated by this new turn of events.

"Savannah." Mike found his voice at last. Casting a covert glance at Erin, Carly saw that she was looking ever so slightly annoyed. That, along with her silence, indicated that Mike's feelings for her weren't entirely unreciprocated, Carly thought. Of course, one had to subtract from that the fact that Collin was seated beside her holding her hand. "We danced."

Liar, liar, pants on fire. Carly barely managed not to betray any surprise. Mike had taken the bit between his teeth, clearly determined to go for it. Matt was lounging back in his chair now, his head resting against the rolled seat back, his lids at about half mast, his eyes agleam. Only the slight tightening of his hands on the chair arms revealed his true state of mind.

"Mike's a really good dancer," Carly said enthusiastically, with an eye toward helping his cause along as well as her own. Matt's eyes narrowed at her, then slid to Mike's face.

"You know, next time you pull protective custody duty, you might want to let me know before you take the subject out on a date. If I hadn't heard through the grapevine what was going down with you two, I might have been just a little worried when I got home and found the house empty and the subject nowhere around," Matt said to Mike. His tone was perfectly pleasant with only the most barely perceptible of steely undertones.

"Sorry." Mike shifted his feet nervously. "It just kind of happened."

"I'm sure it did."

"Gee, I guess I didn't realize I was supposed to be under house arrest, too," Carly said. Matt smiled at her.

"Uh, well, I think I'll just be shoving off now," Mike said.

"Yeah, it's late." That was Matt again.

Carly smiled brightly at Mike. "I'll walk you out."

"Don't go any farther than the porch," Matt called after her as she suited the action to the words. "Mike, you make sure she gets back in before you leave."

"Will do," Mike said, and went out the door with Carly right behind him.

"That went well," Carly said with an impish smile when

the door was closed behind them. Matt's reminder that he didn't consider it safe for her to be outside alone at night had made her a little nervous, and she stood closer to Mike than she otherwise might have done.

"For you, maybe. I'm going to be pulling grunt duty for the next six months," Mike said. "That is, if I don't get fired tomorrow. Matt was mad."

"He was, wasn't he?" Carly glanced around at the dark shadows crowding close to the porch. There was nothing there, she told herself firmly. No one there. This was the county sheriff's house, for crying out loud, and it was practically bursting to the seams with people. "Erin didn't like it, either."

"She didn't say a word, did you notice?" Mike sounded a little more cheerful.

The porch light came on. It was white and hazy and a definite hint. Carly had no doubt at all about who had flipped the switch. Not that she was willing to admit it to anyone except herself, but she was grateful for the light.

"Okay, I'm gone. You can go back in now." Mike was regarding her warily. Carly suspected that he was afraid she was going to insist on a good-night kiss. Which wasn't happening. He was a nice guy, she liked him, and he'd been a big help tonight, but he just wasn't her type. And she wasn't *that* mad at Matt.

When she went inside, secretly relieved to be out of the night, Matt was standing near the door talking to Antonio, who was standing too. The other men were in the process of getting to their feet, and Carly saw that the party was breaking up. She suspected that its sole, although probably unstated, purpose had been to wait for her and Mike, and witness Matt's reaction to their return.

If you didn't know him, it had been deceptively mild. But then, she did know him. Very well.

"Well, I'm going to say good night now," she said to the room in general.

Various versions of good night, including a very dry one from Matt, answered her. Carly could feel his gaze on her back as she went up the stairs. However good a face he might be trying to put on it, he hadn't liked her going out with Mike, that much was certain. Not one bit. At the thought of Matt being jealous, she felt a little thrill.

Could he be in love with her? Her heart went into triple time at the thought.

One way or another, she was determined to find out.

The entire female population of the house followed her upstairs.

"The whole town's talking about you going out with Mike," Lissa whispered at the top of the stairs. "One of my friends came up and asked me if you and Matt had broken up."

"It made for an interesting evening," Dani said. "Especially after we got home."

"So just how did you and Mike decide to go out?" Erin asked carefully.

"Ladies," Matt called up the stairs. "If you're going to gossip, do you think you could do it somewhere where I can't overhear?"

Lissa giggled, Dani called down, "You shouldn't listen," and Erin just gave Carly a quick, slightly uncertain smile before they all went their separate ways to bed.

Sandra waited until she and Carly, plus Annie and Hugo, of course, were alone in the bedroom they shared before turning to her with a huge grin.

"Woo-ee, that woke him up, all right. He didn't like that."

"Was he really mad?" Carly slipped out of Erin's shoes—she'd return them tomorrow—and grinned back at Sandra.

"The first time he called Antonio to see if he knew where

you and Mike were, he was real worried. The next couple of times, he was hotter than a firecracker on the Fourth of July." Sandra shook her head. "Mike must have turned his phone and his radio off"—Carly had practically had to twist his arm to get him to do it—"and Matt was *ticked* because he couldn't get hold of either of you. He did some fancy cussing. By the time we got back to the house, people had been talking to him and he knew where you were—well, he knew you were somewhere on a date with Mike. Lissa and her boyfriend were here with him and he'd pretty much cooled down. Guess he didn't want everybody thinking he was jealous."

"Was he jealous, do you think?" Carly realized she sounded just a little wistful.

"Oh, yeah. No doubt about that. He didn't want to make a fool of himself in front of the company, but I imagine you'll be hearing more about that."

"I hope so." Carly slid the earrings out of her ears, and held them out to Sandra. "Thanks for these, by the way. How was your night?"

"Let's just say that Antonio now appreciates me for something besides my cooking," Sandra said with a naughty twinkle as she accepted the earrings and moved across the room to drop them back into the drawer from which Carly had taken them. The slight limp as she moved was now the only visible reminder of the injuries she had suffered.

"Oh, yeah? How was it?"

Sandra smiled a tantalizing smile.

"That good, huh?" Carly felt a twinge of jealousy as she headed for the bathroom. *Matt . . .*

"Hey, wait a minute, if you're planning on one of those hour-long soaks of yours, I need to get in there first," Sandra said as Carly reached the door.

Carly sighed. What she needed, besides Matt, was her life back.

33

CARLY DIDN'T SEE MATT again until late the following afternoon. Dressed in a short, stretchy white piqué shift and flip-flops, she was sitting on the back stoop beside her escort of the day, Sammy Brooks, watching Annie making mad dashes after birds and butterflies and anything else that moved. It was Sunday—she'd finally surrendered to years of conditioning and gone to church, and was thankful just to have survived the gossip gauntlet afterward—and the house, as usual, was full of people. No, correction, it was even more full of people than usual. Sandra was cooking a sumptuous feast, and news of it had apparently gone out far and wide and drawn a crowd.

Since it appeared that the opening of her bed-and-breakfast had suffered at the very least a not inconsiderable delay, maybe she should think about starting a restaurant, Carly reflected. With every meal, it seemed like they were feeding more of the town.

Then she glanced sideways and there was Matt, leaning on the chain-link fence that surrounded the backyard. Dressed in full sheriff mode with a sheaf of papers in one hand, he was looking at her, not quite smiling, so handsome in the bright sunlight that her heart skipped a beat.

She was glad to see him, she realized, really, really glad,

and smiled at him before she remembered that maybe acting a little cooler toward him might serve her purpose better. But he had taken her by surprise, and anyway he was
already letting himself in through the fence and quite possibly hadn't even noticed.

"Hey," he said as he reached the stoop, and from the look
in his eyes she knew that he *had* noticed, that he was perfectly well aware that her heartbeat was suddenly as erratic as
one of those yellow butterflies Annie had been chasing before spying Matt and rushing over to be patted. But it was so
hot, the humidity was so enervating, and she was so tired,
mentally and physically, from everything that had happened,
that at the moment she just didn't have the energy to sort out
what kind of attitude would best serve her purpose.

Besides, she'd already won a victory of sorts, she realized.
The kiss-and-run was over for the moment. He was here.

And good luck to you too, Mike.

"I'll take over the baby-sitting detail," Matt said after
greeting Sammy. "You can go serve these."

Sammy nodded, already on his feet, and Matt passed
him the papers he was holding. Then Matt looked at Carly.

"Want to go for a ride?"

Her stomach was behaving as erratically as her heart.

She nodded, and he held out his hand to her. She put
hers into his—just feeling his hand close around hers
caused her pulse to skip—and he pulled her to her feet.
With a quick glance at the closed back door, which muffled
most of the laughter and chatter in the kitchen but not all of
it, he steered her back toward the gate, still holding her
hand. He was clearly of the same mind she was. No point in
facing a battery of curious eyes and tongues unless it was
absolutely necessary.

But their stealth getaway was almost thwarted. When
the gate shut behind them, Annie, who'd been following on

their heels, was still inside. She started up with an indignant yapping.

They stopped and looked back. Annie was bouncing up and down like a kid on a pogo stick, barking all the while.

"Bring her," Matt said in disgust.

Carly opened the gate and Annie, happy now, bounded through. Not another word was said until all three of them were in Matt's cruiser. Matt picked Annie up off Carly's lap and deposited her firmly in the rear. Then he leaned over and kissed Carly hard.

Caught by surprise, her lips fluttered and flattened beneath his. Then her hand came up to clutch the back of his head and she kissed him back.

"Now that we've got that straight," Matt said after he'd let her go, "why don't you tell me how you talked Mike into taking you out?"

As he spoke, he started the car and reversed it down the driveway without coming anywhere near the restored mailbox, Carly noted.

"What makes you think I talked him into it?" Carly hedged. Her pulse was still pounding from that kiss and she was still breathing too quickly.

Matt's mouth twisted wryly. "I know him, and I know you."

"Maybe I like him." Carly was rallying a little, trying her best not to appear too besotted. Like Erin had said, Matt had had girls swarming over him his entire life. One thing she did not want to be was just part of the swarm.

"I'm sure you do. He's a nice guy. What's not to like?" They were turning out of the subdivision, heading toward town.

"Maybe I *really* like him. He's cute, have you noticed? And sweet. And thoughtful. And—"

Matt glanced at her. "Give it a rest, Curls. You went out with him to get a rise out of me."

Carly looked at him meditatively. As she had noted before, there were numerous disadvantages to trying to have a relationship with a man who knew her so well. "To make you jealous, you mean?"

"That's what I mean."

"So did it work?"

He grinned. "Okay. It worked—until I saw you two together. Mike looked like he had a tiger by the tail. You looked like the tiger. Then I remembered something."

Carly was cautious. "What?"

"That you're crazy in love with me."

That home truth hit her like a body blow. She sucked in air, realized that he was enjoying her reaction, and frantically tried to regroup. "Listen, sweet cheeks, I wouldn't get cocky. Maybe I just want your body."

He was smiling now as he watched the road. "There's that, too."

They braked at a stoplight. Desperate for something to look at besides him, Carly glanced around. By the golden glow of the late summer sun she could see beautiful downtown Benton unfolding around her in all its refurbished glory. Theirs wasn't the only vehicle on the road—Sunday afternoon drives were a favorite activity—but most of the other cars were clustered in the parking lot that served The Corner Café. Sunday supper out was a popular activity too.

"Where are we going?" Carly asked as the light changed.

"Well, we can go for a drive, maybe revisit scenic childhood haunts and walk down a memory lane or two. Or we can grab a bite at The Corner Café and give our friends and neighbors the chance to see that I'm back in your good graces again. Or we could forget about the preliminaries and just cut to the chase and go have great sex."

Carly's heart started to pound. She pretended to think it over. "If we have great sex, are you going to propose?"

She thought his jaw tightened fractionally. He glanced at her, his expression faintly wary. "Do you want me to?"

Not if he didn't want to. Never if he didn't want to.

"Just so you know—if you do you're dead."

"I take it that's a 'yes' to the great sex option?" The heat in the look he sent her way made her quake.

"Yes."

It was probably stupid, Carly thought, she should hold out, she vividly remembered Erin recommending "no sex" as a way of getting Matt, but suddenly she was far more interested in doing Matt than getting him and anyway at the moment stratagems were pretty much beyond her. At the thought of him on her and in her, she was dizzy, melting, ready to rip off all her clothes and jump his bones and—

"If you don't quit looking at me like that, I'm liable to end up wrecking the car."

The drawl in his voice was pronounced; the heat in his eyes was palpable; the electricity in the car was as potent as summer lightning.

It was all Carly could do to breathe.

"The county wouldn't like that," she said, striving to keep him from guessing that it was all she could do not to pant, that she was so hot and hungry for him that she could practically come from just looking at him, from just thinking about what they were going to do. But of course he knew her so well. He knew how turned-on she was. She could tell from the dark color creeping up into his cheekbones and the sudden tension in his body and the hot secret gleam in his eyes that he knew.

And she knew how turned-on he was, too.

The car stopped, and she managed to focus enough on something beyond the two of them to discover that they were in front of his rented garage. Reaching past her, he opened the glove compartment and extracted a homely blue garage door opener. He pressed the button, the door went up, and they drove into the dusty shadows. Then he pressed the button again, and put the transmission in park and turned off the key as the door rattled its way back down, enclosing them in the cave-like interior.

It was cool in the car, and dark, and Annie was napping in the backseat. Carly just sat where she was for a second, dizzy with wanting him, willing herself to ignore her weakened knees and trembling muscles and dry mouth and get out. Matt looked at her as he undid his seat belt, then reached over and undid hers, too. She stroked his arm, sliding her fingers right up under his short sleeve to caress the hard warm bulge of his biceps, and he turned his head and pressed his mouth into the curve between her shoulder and her neck. She caught her breath, clutching at him, and he lifted his head and looked at her. Then he gathered her up and lifted her right across the console onto his lap, tilting her back against his arm and the door, and kissed her. His lips molded themselves to hers, his tongue was hot and fierce and demanding, and his hand was on her breast, closing over it, squeezing. She wrapped her arms around his neck and kissed him back with abandon, wanting him so much she could die. She was in an awkward position, cradled on his lap with her hip pressed into the steering wheel and her bare legs (she'd stripped off her pantyhose and shoes as soon as she got home from church) bent over the console so that her feet, wearing only one flip-flop now as the other had fallen off, were in her seat. But it didn't feel awkward, it felt wonderful, *he* felt wonderful, so warm and strong and good that he made her head spin. Kicking off the other flip-flop, toes curling, she threaded her fingers into his hair, holding his head for her kiss, taking his mouth with her tongue. Her heart was pounding and she was breathing hard and the quickening deep inside her was already fast and close and urgent.

"You've been using my soap again, Curls," he murmured as he slid his mouth down her throat.

That made no sense, or maybe she was just too fuzzy-headed to sort it out, so she kind of opened her eyes to find him watching her. He was breathing hard too and looming over her so that his wide shoulders blocked out her view of the rest of the front seat, looking dark and sexy and turned-on as hell. She forgot why she was looking at him then and just looked and breathed, and his eyes turned obsidian on her and he kissed her with a fierce hunger that made her moan into his mouth. His hand was on her breasts, caressing and squeezing, and she arched her back like a cat being petted, letting her head fall back against his arm and reveling in his touch and kissing him back until she was trembling and dizzy and so hot she thought she'd catch fire. Then his hand moved down her body, down between her legs, and slid warm and hard over the soft smooth skin of her thigh. He pushed her skirt up and touched her through the thin pink nylon of her panties, pressing against her, rubbing her until she was on fire and gasping into his mouth and moving mindlessly beneath his hand. Then he slipped his hand beneath the elastic of one of the leg openings and touched her that way too, and his fingers felt so good on her that she couldn't stand it, she was slick and hot and wet for him and so ready that when they slid inside her she moaned and moved and couldn't wait . . .

Do me, Matt.

He made a sound like a growl against her lips and she realized that she might have said it aloud, no, she *had* said it aloud, and then she stopped thinking at all as in a fierce, urgent burst of need he pulled her panties off and scooted the seat back and unzipped his pants and lifted her astride him and thrust into her. He was big and hot and huge with desire and the sensation as he drove into her was mind-blowing.

"Ride me," he said, his voice thick and guttural, and she did, closing her eyes and clinging to his shoulders as he grasped her hips and surged up into her again and again and again. He kissed and sucked and bit at her breasts through her clothes and then finally yanked her dress up over her head and pulled her bra off too. Then he kissed and sucked at her breasts some more so that the hot dampness of his mouth on her bare skin drove her wild and she pressed his head against her breasts and arched her back and moved with mindless pleasure and gasped out *yes, oh yes, oh yes.*

"Carly," he said then, groaning, and thrust hard, grinding himself into her, pushing her butt back up against the steering wheel, making her cry out, making her shudder, making her clench and convulse inside and then come so hard and fast that she was screaming, mindless, blown away—and utterly his.

I love you, Matt.

This time, when those damning little words came out of her mouth, it wasn't in the heat of passion. It was in the drugged aftermath, when she lay limply against him, naked and damp with sweat and utterly spent. For a moment after she heard them, she hoped they were part of her inner dialogue, that she hadn't actually said them aloud, but no such luck. When had she ever had that kind of luck?

"Yeah, Curls, I know you do," he said, sounding as tired as she felt.

Oh, the romance of it.

She lifted her head to look him in the eye. It was not a loving look. She was draped across him, her arms looped around his neck, her body plastered to his so tightly that she could feel the entire outline of his metal badge pressed into her breast. Totally, unmistakably, indisputably his, and he clearly realized it too. Her spine stiffened at the thought, and she sat up in his lap.

"Sweet cheeks, just so you know, I say that to all the guys."

One corner of his mouth tilted up fractionally. His gaze was moving down her body now, his eyes gleaming appreciatively as he drank everything in, and she realized that while she was naked he was still fully dressed, although his shirt was halfway unbuttoned and wildly askew and his pants were somewhere down around his thighs. Still, he had a distinct advantage in the dignity department, especially considering the fact that she was straddling him and whenever she moved, her butt hit the steering wheel and her breasts brushed his chest.

"Your nose just grew," he said, flicking it.

Goaded, she scowled at him. Before she could say anything else he laughed and leaned up and kissed her, primarily, she thought, to shut her up. Then he let her go and lay back in the seat and slid his hands up her rib cage until they rested just below her breasts and smiled lazily at her.

"Just so you know, Curls: I love you too."

Carly felt as if every one of her senses had been suddenly suspended. *"What?"*

"Yeah," he said, a little ruefully but she would take it, she could see it in his eyes, he meant it. "I do."

She breathed in and her heart expanded and her world suddenly seemed to pulse and shimmer and glow with a kaleidoscope of colors it had never possessed before.

Matt had said he loved her. Matt—loved—her.

"Oh, my God," she said.

He grinned at that. "Yeah, well, that's kind of how I feel about it, too."

She punched him in the arm. Then she kissed him and the whole great-sex thing started up one more time and he would have done her again right there in the car except her leg got a cramp. They had to get out and she pulled on her dress in the teeth of his protests as he massaged her leg for her—no way was she standing around in the garage naked while he, having fastened his pants, was more or less dressed—and then Annie yapped because they'd forgotten she was in the car and they let her out and then all three of them went upstairs.

And two of them played undress your local sheriff and went to bed.

Not to surface again until an urgent ringing sent Matt searching groggily for his cell phone.

"Yeah," he said into it, and listened. "No, everything's fine; I just forgot about the time. Yes. Yes. Not your business. *Really* not your business. Probably sometime tomorrow. Yeah, okay. 'Bye."

Carly rolled onto her back and clutched the sheet to her bosom and turned on the bedside lamp just as Matt disconnected.

"Who—?"

"Erin. She wanted to make sure we were okay. It's almost two A.M. I told her we probably wouldn't be back until tomorrow. Then she wanted to know if you'd gotten me into bed."

"She did not!" Actually, knowing Erin, that was probably just exactly what she'd asked. "What did you say?"

She remembered those *yes*es.

"I said I'd been fucked to within an inch of my life, but I was recovering."

"You did not." Having heard his end of the conversation, she didn't even bother to put any heat into that.

"Okay, maybe I didn't. But I could have."

He was standing there smiling at her as he put the phone down on the table, casually naked, dark and muscular and so hot that just looking at him made her sizzle, and, best of all, he was *Matt*.

No, best of all, he was hers.

At the thought, Carly smiled a beatific smile.

"You look like the cat who swallowed the canary." Matt was surveying her with a meaningful little smile of his own. Considering the number and variety of their activities since they had come upstairs, Carly realized she had to be looking well and truly *had*.

"In that case, come here, Tweety." Looking him over with a naughty little twinkle, she beckoned suggestively. He laughed and crawled back into bed.

Later, he propped himself up on an elbow, frowning down at her. Drowsy and sated and warm with happiness, she smiled sleepily at him.

"What?" she asked when he continued to look at her without saying anything.

He picked up a lock of her hair and twined it around his fingers. "We're sticking with the no-strings thing, huh? You sure?"

Carly considered. "Maybe one or two strings. Like, you can't just drop off the face of the earth tomorrow. And you might want to think about taking me out from time to time, so I don't have to wrangle dinner out of nice guys like Mike. But other than that, no strings."

He still frowned. "No strings doesn't sound like something you do, Curls."

She loved him so much she ached with it, loved him so much that just looking at him made her glow, loved him so much that no matter how this thing between them worked out he would always be branded into her heart—but she also loved him so much that she didn't want him if, ultimately, what he wanted was to be free. He'd said he loved her—several times now—and she knew him well enough to know that he did. But she could see the shadow at the backs of his eyes when he said it, and she knew that what put it there was fear. Fear that love meant chains, holding him back, holding him down, locking him to responsibility and this little town and her forever.

Despite the fear, she knew that he was ready, willing, and able to offer her forever. But she was never going to take it while she could still see that fear.

"No strings," she said firmly, and kissed him. The distraction that presented kept them both occupied for most of what was left of the night.

It was ninety-two degrees at seven-thirty the following morning. Carly knew, because she was in Matt's car listening to the radio as they pulled out of the garage. It was going to be a little embarrassing if she ran into anyone who had seen her leave Matt's house the afternoon before in the same white shift and flip-flops that she was wearing once again, but the thought was not enough to affect the sense of well-being that filled her. She was happy and sleepy and just a little sore in interesting places, and despite the fact that she knew that there were monsters in the world, and one in particular who wanted to kill her, she could not bring herself to *believe* it, not this morning when the sun was rising lazily to steam the mist from the ground and there was a steady stream of cars on the road as people headed to work and Matt sat beside her, clean-shaven and smelling of soap and her.

Her was the best part.

Then she realized that he was taking her back to his house. The circus the past week had turned into was getting ready to start up all over again, and the knowledge depressed her high spirits, to say the least. While her love life had just improved from nonexistent to excellent, the rest of her life just kept diving deeper into the toilet, she realized glumly. Then she thought, *no,* and summoned up the shade of her late, unlamented No More Ms. Nice Girl as she decided that she wasn't going to take it anymore.

"Matt," she said firmly. "I want my life back."

They were at the intersection, waiting patiently for the light to change.

"Sounds ominous," he said, casting a smiling glance her way. "What did I do?"

She gave him a look, then when the light changed and he would have headed for town said, "Turn right."

He did, and glanced at her again with raised brows. "Where to?"

"My house," she said.

He frowned. "Why?"

"Because I can't live like this. Who knows how long it's going to be before you catch the guy who attacked me? What if you never do? I can't spend my whole life at your house, under virtual house arrest. I have a living to earn, and a business to get off the ground, and a house that's *mine*. I can't just put all that aside for an indefinite period of time. I don't want to."

"Carly," he said, and the look on his face and his tone told her that he was suddenly dead serious. "Somebody tried to kill you. He's still out there. My best assessment is that he's going to keep coming. Until we figure out why, or who he is, or something, I'm leaving you in that house alone, or anywhere alone, over my dead body."

"Matt—"

"Don't *Matt* me. I mean what I say."

"For your information, Mr. King of the World, just because you're sleeping with me does not make you my boss."

"No, but my being the sheriff and your being a subject in protective custody does."

Carly scowled at him. He frowned right back at her. Then he sighed.

"I know this is tough on you. It would be tough on anybody, but it's the best arrangement I can come up with to keep you safe. I could move into your house with you, but I can't be there twenty-four/seven. Anyway, it's a big house. You're safer in my house, which is relatively small and which has a ton of people in it all the time. People with un-predictable schedules. So this guy can't plan anything."

"Do you really think he's going to try again? Why would anyone want to kill me?" It was a cry straight from the heart.

"Baby, when we figure out the 'why' I'm pretty sure we'll know the 'who.' But in the meantime, please, to make me happy, to keep me from having a nervous breakdown or a heart attack or something, will you just cooperate with what I tell you to do?"

The idea of Matt caring enough about her to have a ner-vous breakdown or a heart attack or something, to say nothing of coaxing rather than attempting to order her into compliance, was irresistible. She looked at him and melted, realizing that she was practically putty in his hands at this point and that it was probably not a good thing to let him know it. He was cocky enough already.

"Okay. For now. But if this drags on, all bets are off." She gave him a militant look, just to cover up how marshmal-lowy she was feeling inside. They came around a bend, and there was her house, looking so normal, just as it always looked, that she sighed. "Since we're here, can we stop? I'd like to at least get some more clothes."

"Sure." Matt glanced at her. "We've done everything we need to do here. It's all cleaned up, even. Only—stay close to me, will you?"

Carly stared at him as a tiny *frisson* of fear snaked down her spine. For Matt to be so worried about her scared her anew. It made the threat seem close again, and suddenly all too real. "Do you think he's *following* us or something?"

Matt shook his head, and pulled off onto the grassy verge in front of the house. "No one followed us here; I've been keeping an eye out. Still, better safe than sorry."

After that, Carly was only too glad to cling to his hand as they walked up the hill. Leaving Annie outside, running in circles, obviously elated at being back on familiar ground, they went in. Carly was surprised at the violence of her own reaction as soon as she stepped over the threshold. As the gloom of the house enveloped her, her stomach tensed; her breathing quickened; her heart raced.

"Oh, my God, Matt," she said, and stopped while a wave of dizziness hit her and the walls seemed to tilt around her.

"You okay?" He slid an arm around her and pulled her close to his side. She noticed that he unsnapped the top of his holster for easier access to his gun. That steadied her. Matt was with her. He would keep her safe. "I didn't think this was a good idea."

"No, it's—I'm fine." And she was better. The dizziness was already passing. Taking a deep breath and leaning against Matt, she reminded herself that this was *her* house. No murderous creep was going to ruin it for her. She straightened. "This is the place I've thought of as home for the last twenty-two years. I'm not about to let one bad memory wipe that out."

"That's my Curls." Matt tightened his grip and smiled down at her. "A fighter through and through."

Carly leaned against him and gazed up at him with her heart, she feared, in her eyes. "I love you," she said, then pushed away from him before he could reply and stood on her own two feet. "Let's get this over with."

Moving determinedly, she walked through every room downstairs, remembering how she had fled through them with blood pouring from her hand and shoulder. She remembered the gleam of the attacker's knife and the sound of his raspy voice saying *you're dead* and the way he had lurched from the wound she had inflicted. She remembered how terrified she had been, the cold shock of the knife slicing through her shoulder, the despair she had felt when she had realized that she wasn't going to be able to get out the door. Then she remembered that she had survived, that she had outwitted the monster and Matt had come in time. And now she was going to take back her house.

Jaw set, head held high, she went up the stairs, then walked through the entire second floor, paying particular attention to where the attacker had lain in wait and to the bathroom, which was pristine again with not so much as a drop of blood staining the grout. Then she went into her bedroom and gathered up a few more clothes and folded them neatly into her overnight bag. Finally, feeling drained and relieved and somehow almost at peace, she walked back down the stairs and through the front hall and out onto the porch.

Where her knees finally betrayed her. They trembled and threatened to give out. She made it to the stairs, then gave up the attempt, sinking down rather abruptly on the top step. Taking a deep breath, she looked out at the grassy yard and the big silver birch and the oaks and the road below where Matt's cruiser was parked, and let the heat and sunlight bake away the last of the chill the house had left her with.

"What's up?" Matt was behind her, carrying the bag she had packed. He put it down and sat beside her.

"I just needed to catch my breath." She glanced at him and smiled.

"Oh, yeah?" The glance he gave her was skeptical.

"Okay, so my knees gave out." She made a face at him.

"That's better." He tweaked a curl. "Walking through the house made you feel better, though, didn't it?"

Carly took a deep breath and nodded. "It's my house. I couldn't let that monster ruin it for me."

Matt picked up her hand, the one with the nearly healed gash across her palm, and pressed the back of it to his mouth. Carly looked at him and smiled. She was just about to say something when Annie caught her eye. Annie, backing out from under the porch and dragging something with her teeth. Something that was black and kind of round with a strap and heavy enough to make her have to work to move it.

"Looks like she's got a woman's purse," Matt said on a note of mild surprise, watching the dog too.

"Oh, gosh, I wonder whose." As much to test the reliability of her knees as for any other reason, Carly stood up and walked down the remaining stairs. Her knees were stronger, and she was stronger, and she knew that the next time she walked inside her house it would be easier, and the time after that easier still. The memory of the attack would always be there, but it would be her house once more, and once her attacker was caught she could start to live in it again and the horror would fade away.

"Annie, let me see that." Annie had the strap in her teeth but she dropped it when Carly bent to pick the purse up. It was a cheap purse, Carly saw, vinyl rather than leather and cold and dirty from being, presumably, beneath the porch for some time. She didn't recognize it, it wasn't hers or Sandra's, and so she unzipped it and looked inside and then reached for the wallet.

"Belong to anybody I know?" Matt was standing beside her with her bag slung over his shoulder.

Carly opened the wallet and looked at the driver's license. An attractive red-haired woman stared back at her from the tiny photo.

"Marsha Mary Hughes," she read.

The effect on Matt was immediate and electric.

"*What?*" he said, and took the wallet from her, looking down at the driver's license in its plastic case as if he couldn't believe his eyes.

34

"I'VE GOT A COUPLE of questions for you," Matt said when Keith Kenan opened the door to his apartment in response to Matt's knock. "Mind if I come in?"

Kenan looked less than happy, but he stepped back in silent acquiescence. It was a little after two P.M. on Monday, some six hours after Annie had refocused Matt's attention on Marsha Hughes's disappearance in a big way. At the moment, men and dogs were scouring the grounds around the Beadle Mansion for any trace of Marsha's body. Carly was safe at his house in the care of Sammy Brooks. And Annie—well, Annie still had a role to play.

"I don't know nothing about Marsha," Kenan said, already belligerent as he closed the door behind Matt. The man was wearing long, baggy gym shorts and a black tee shirt with the sleeves ripped off, the better, Matt judged, to show off his pumped arms. A quick glance around showed Matt that the apartment was maybe a little dirtier than the last time he had visited, but essentially unchanged. The gold drapes were open this time, allowing daylight in. As far as he could tell, Kenan was alone.

"You haven't heard from her?" Matt asked, keeping his tone conversational. Butting heads with Kenan at this point would be the worst thing he could do.

"Not a squeak since the night she left. Look, I gotta go in to work early today, and I've got stuff I gotta do first. Can you make this quick?"

"I'll do my best."

Kenan was approximately the right height, the right build, the right coloring. Matt focused on his eyes: pale blue; lashes blond like his hair and possibly difficult to see under certain lighting conditions—such as those in an old-fashioned bathroom. Could two of the letters on the hand-kerchief possibly have been KK?

"I thought you said you were going to find her. You were sending out flyers and shit."

"We've been trying. She hasn't touched a penny in her bank account, and she hasn't used any of her credit cards. I have to tell you, things in that department aren't looking good." Matt crossed the room toward the table, which was clear of dishes but dusty.

Kenan tracked his progress, folding his arms over his chest and turning his head to keep Matt in sight. "So what do you want to ask me?"

"Why don't you have a seat?"

Kenan's lips compressed, but he pulled out one of the dining chairs and sat. Matt got a good look at both knees. No marks that he could see. The guy couldn't have healed this fast. Had Carly been mistaken about the part of the anatomy she hit? A possibility.

"So," Kenan asked.

"I want you to look at something for me. Mind if I put this down here?" *This* referred to the briefcase he was carrying. At Kenan's gesture telling him to go ahead, Matt put the case on the table and opened it. Kenan frowned as he watched Matt lift out Marsha's purse, which was carefully preserved in a Ziploc bag and destined to be exhaustively examined for forensic evidence after being delivered to the state crime lab later that day. Showing what was potentially a major piece of evidence to a subject of an investigation before sending it to the lab was slightly unorthodox, but Matt wanted to see what Kenan had to say about its discovery—and he wanted to watch Kenan's eyes while he said it.

"Ever seen this before?" He held the purse up so that Kenan could get a good look at it.

Kenan looked and shrugged. "It's a purse. Maybe. I don't know."

"It's got Marsha's identification in it."

Kenan's eyes widened. "Are you saying that's Marsha's purse?" He looked more closely, leaning in and peering through the clear plastic bag at the grimy black vinyl. "Yeah, I guess it could be. I guess it is."

As a man himself, Matt didn't find anything amiss in Kenan's failure to recognize his former live-in lady's purse. Purses were not part of the landscape most men saw. But Kenan's failure to be alarmed at the discovery of the purse told him something: either Kenan was a heck of an actor, or he had no reason to worry because the purse had been found.

"Did she take her purse with her the night she left?" Matt asked, restoring the bagged purse to the briefcase and closing it.

Kenan grimaced, looking as if he were trying to remember. "Yeah. Yeah, she did. She grabbed it and—"

"Ran like hell out of here," Matt finished dryly when Kenan broke off with the air of a man who had just realized he was about to shoot himself in the foot. "We've already been over that part, remember?"

"I didn't touch her," Kenan said, running both hands over his head. "Not that night. If something's happened to her it wasn't me who done it. Sheriff, I swear—"

There was a knock on the door. Kenan frowned and glanced at it almost hesitantly. Matt wondered who Kenan was expecting that he didn't want the law to see, or vice versa. Not that he particularly cared, at the moment. What he cared about was getting information about Marsha Hughes. If her purse was under Carly's porch, then her body was very likely somewhere in the same vicinity. If her body was there, then the chances were high that it had been put there, and the chances that she had not died a natural death were even higher.

What they were dealing with in that case was a murderer operating on the grounds of the Beadle Mansion. And the odds that there were two separate killers—or, rather, a successful killer and a failed killer—both doing their thing on the same property within such a short span of time were so slim as to be practically nonexistent. Ergo, whoever had killed Marsha Hughes had tried to kill Carly.

What was the connection?

"That should be one of my deputies at the door," Matt said when it seemed Kenan wasn't going to answer the knock. He had wanted to wait to introduce this new line of questioning until after he had seen Kenan's reaction to the purse. "You want to let him in?"

"If you found the purse," Kenan said slowly, moving to the door, "does that mean you found Marsha?"

It had taken him a little while, but Kenan had finally heard the other shoe drop.

"Not yet," Matt said.

Kenan opened the door. Antonio stood in the hall with Annie in his arms.

"Kenan," Antonio said curtly in greeting, and then his gaze went past him to find Matt. Behind Kenan's back, Matt gave a slight, negative shake of his head.

"You care if Deputy Johnson comes in?" Matt asked.

Kenan's face tightened, but he stood back, and Antonio walked past him.

"Is that some kind of drug-sniffing dog?" Kenan asked suspiciously, staring at Annie. The little dog seemed to quail at the sound of his voice.

Matt now knew with almost one hundred percent certainty that Kenan was engaged in at least one type of illegal activity. The guy had, indeed, shot himself in the foot with his mouth. Obviously he was not the sharpest tack on the board. But at the moment Matt wasn't interested in what kind of drugs Kenan was scoring.

Antonio stopped and put Annie down. Looking at her, Matt almost felt sorry for the poor little thing. She stood shivering and glancing around, looking nervous as hell.

"What's with the dog?" Kenan asked, frowning down at Annie with no recognition that Matt could see. "It's not getting ready to pee on my rug, is it?"

Annie seemed to shiver more than ever at the sound of his voice. Her head lowered, and her tail curled between her legs.

"You ever seen her before?"

Kenan frowned.

Matt continued with hard-won patience: "Last time I was here, you said that the fight you and Marsha had was over her feeding baloney to a dog. Is this the dog?"

Kenan looked at Annie more closely. The dog cringed, pressing her belly to the rug.

"It might be. It was an ugly little black mutt, all right. Yeah, I think it is."

Matt felt his stomach tighten. He was on the right track here. He'd known it from the time he'd seen the ID in the wallet.

"Here, Annie." Now that the identification had been made, he couldn't stand to see Carly's dog looking so cowed. He bent, scooped her up and patted her. She trembled still in his hold, but wagged her tail feebly to show that she appreciated being picked up by someone she recognized as a friend. Matt looked at Kenan. "So Marsha fed your baloney to the dog. Where? Here in this apartment? Then what happened?"

Kenan hesitated.

Matt had to work to curb his impatience. "Look, for what it's worth, I don't think you had anything to do with Marsha's disappearance. But I think you have information that can help us find her—and if we find her and you had nothing to do with it, we leave you alone, so there's a benefit in this for you, too. Just tell me what happened, and I'll ignore anything that doesn't relate to the big picture, okay? Stuff like you threatening her, or chasing her, that kind of thing."

Kenan looked from him to Antonio—who, thank God, managed to look relatively benign standing there with an impassive expression on his face and his arms crossed over his chest—and grimaced.

"Start with the dog," Matt said.

"She had it here in the apartment when I came home from work. She was always picking up strays, and I was getting sick of it. Anyway, I told her we couldn't keep it, then went into the kitchen to grab something to eat. What I wanted was a baloney sandwich, but the baloney was gone. I knew right then that she'd fed it to the damned dog. So I said something to her, and by the time I came out of the kitchen she was heading out the apartment door."

"Did she have the dog with her?"

"She was carrying it."

"What about her purse?"

"Yeah, she would have had to have her purse. She always kept her keys in it, and she got in her car and drove off."

"Okay, let's back up a little. She ran out of here with the dog and her purse, and you chased her down to the parking lot, is that right?"

Kenan looked uncomfortable.

"Like I said the last time we were here," Antonio said, his stare intimidating now, "we *know*."

"Okay," Kenan said, wetting his lips and looking from one to the other of them. "I chased her into the parking lot. I was mad, okay? But I didn't hurt her. I didn't catch her. She hopped in her car and peeled rubber right past me and drove out of the parking lot. That's the last time I ever saw her. I swear."

"Did she have the dog with her in the car?" Matt asked.

"Yeah, she did. I could see the stupid little mutt in the passenger seat as she drove past."

Yes. Bingo. The dog was in the car. That meant the dog was probably with Marsha when she was killed. The dog had been at the Beadle Mansion the night Carly had arrived. The dog had dragged out the purse.

The dog was the key.

"Marsha have any enemies? Anyone who'd want to hurt her?"

"You asked me that before, and I answered before. No. Not that I know of." Kenan was starting to sound agitated. He paced toward the window, casting a quick, surreptitious glance at the clock as he passed it. "Can you hurry this up? I got things to do."

"You can talk to us here, or we can take you in and you can talk to us there," Antonio said.

Kenan shot him a quick, resentful look.

"We're almost done here," Matt said in his role of good cop. "Can you fill me in on Marsha's background a little? I've been trying to get in touch with her sister and her ex-husbands, but so far I'm not having any luck."

Kenan snorted. "The husbands are a pair of losers, and Marsha never saw the sister. They didn't grow up together. Their mom was a druggie, and they spent most of their time in foster homes. Different foster homes. Marsha said some of the places were pretty bad."

Matt thought about that, about what happened to a child when the parents were missing or irresponsible and the impact it had on the child's life. Carly, abandoned by her mother as a little girl, had been rescued by her grandmother before any real damage could be done to her, but the experience had left her scrappy, feisty—and also a little unsure of herself inside. She still had nightmares. . . .

Matt felt as if a lightbulb had suddenly been turned on in his head. He looked at Kenan with dawning excitement.

"Did Marsha ever mention anything about the County Home for Innocents? Do you know if she ever stayed there?"

"Yeah, she did," Keith said. "I remember her telling me about some donkey they had. I told you, she liked animals. She never said much else about it, though, except that it was kind of a weird place."

There it was: the connection. He'd known there had to be one. Marsha and Carly had both stayed at the Home as children. Marsha was dead, somebody wanted Carly dead, and all these years later Carly still had nightmares about the brief time she'd spent there. If he had learned anything in his years in law enforcement, it was this: in criminal investigations, there was no such thing as coincidence.

He'd be willing to bet a year's pay that the perp had some connection to that Home.

By the time they left the apartment, Matt had ascertained that as far as Kenan knew, Marsha had not kept in touch with anyone from the Home, had never been contacted by anyone who'd stayed at the Home, and had only received the occasional mass mailing from the Home itself as part of what sounded like a perpetual fund solicitation effort aimed at the general public.

He had also obtained permission to search Marsha's computer after Kenan had mentioned in passing that Marsha had been spending more time than usual on it in the last few days before she had disappeared. Maybe somebody had been in touch with her by e-mail. Or maybe she'd been in touch with somebody. Maybe she'd visited a telltale site. Who knew?

"*We're* gonna search this computer?" Antonio asked skeptically, holding the bulky, old model in his arms as they trudged down the stairs. After the air-conditioned apartment the concrete stairwell felt like a furnace. It smelled faintly musty, like mold was growing somewhere. The metal stair treads were almost slick beneath their feet, a result, Matt knew, of the prolonged humidity. He'd just about given up hope that they were going to see a break in the heat anytime soon.

"Yeah, we are," Matt said, bearing his own twin burdens of Annie and the briefcase. The heat might not break, but the case was about to, he was almost sure, their combined departmental lack of computer expertise notwithstanding. "If worse comes to worst, that Andy kid Lissa dates is a computer freak. Antonio, the connection between Marsha Hughes and Carly is the County Home for the Innocents. They both were there as kids. The perp has to have some kind of connection to it. It's the only link between them that I can see."

"I saw you picking up on something in there that I wasn't quite getting. So Carly was at the Home? I didn't know that. I thought she grew up in well-off circumstances with her grandmother."

"That was later. As a little girl she had it kind of rough."

They reached the bottom of the stairs. A slim young blond in a red halter top and shorts so tiny there wasn't much point pulled open the door from the parking lot at about that time. She stepped inside and headed toward them, blinking as her eyes adjusted to the relative gloom of the hall, then all but stopped dead as she saw Matt and Antonio and took in the uniforms. It took her just an instant to collect herself again and keep on coming with a nervous little *hi* for them as she passed, but the damage had been done. If they'd been looking for an easy bust, Matt had little doubt they would have found it right there.

"Wonder where she's got it stashed?" Antonio asked dryly as Matt pulled open the door and they stepped out into the blinding sunlight.

"The possibilities boggle the mind." Squinting against the glare, hitching Annie higher up under his arm, Matt headed toward the cruiser which, thanks to some asphalt resurfacing being done up close to the building, was parked near the back of the lot.

Antonio kept pace beside him. "Carly doing okay? Sandra says that a couple of times since they've been sharing a room she's woken her up crying out from nightmares."

"She has nightmares," Matt said grimly. "But otherwise she's okay. Well, as okay as about five foot two inches of nothing can be when she knows that there's some man out there trying to kill her."

"I really want to catch this creep," Antonio said as they reached the car. "He sliced my woman up. That makes it personal."

"Yeah," Matt said, walking around to the driver's side and meeting Antonio's gaze over the top of the car. "That does kind of make it personal."

35

WHEN THE MAN SAW the men with dogs and the men with metal detectors and the men with long metal poles moving systematically over the grounds of the Beadle Mansion, he almost ran off the road. There were sheriff's department vehicles parked along the front, too, and down by the road the old woman who lived across the street stood talking a mile a minute to one of the deputies.

That they were searching for something he had no doubt. The question was, what? But much as he hated to face it he had little doubt about the answer to that, too. They had to be searching for a body. Or bodies. The only question was, whose?

Marsha's? Or Soraya's? Or both?

How the hell had they found out?

Cool as a creek in summer, he drove right on past, even honked and waved at the old lady and the deputy as country people were wont to do. Then he turned at the next intersection and made his way back to town and got to The Corner Café at just about supper time.

He didn't even have to ask. The place was abuzz with the news.

Forking down his meat loaf and mashed potatoes, he just kind of guided the conversation.

No, they hadn't found a body yet. They were sure looking, though. The sheriff had been out to the Beadle Mansion this morning with Carly Linton—it was her grandma's house—and they'd found something that made them think that the cashier at the Winn-Dixie who'd gone missing a few weeks back might be buried up there. Marsha something. Marsha Hughes.

So they'd found something that would eventually lead them to Marsha. If they found Marsha, unless they were totally inept, they were going to find Soraya, too. If they found Soraya it shouldn't take long to trace the connection with Carly, and once they did that it was only a matter of time before they came looking for him.

He started sweating at the thought. Carly knew who he was. She had been there that night, too.

She'd been a little girl, he didn't know how old exactly, but almost certainly less than ten. Younger than the others. Maybe she hadn't realized what was happening. Maybe she didn't know, or didn't remember, or at least didn't know or remember enough to put it all together.

But maybe she did.

He realized that he was faced with a choice. He could cut his losses and walk away, leave her alone and trust to luck that they wouldn't somehow goad her into remembering, that either she really hadn't seen or she'd been too young and didn't understand or that she had somehow repressed the memory as he'd heard trauma sometimes caused people to do. Or that she'd be too afraid to say anything if she did remember.

He'd chosen that last route before, and almost gotten burned.

Or he could go for it, go for the gold, for the score, for the slam dunk that won the game. Without Carly, who was the only one left alive to tell, he didn't think there was any way that anyone would ever find out the truth of what had happened, much less manage to link it to him. They might find Marsha and Soraya, they might even manage to link them back to the County Home and to Carly, but there were no records of him there, no records of what had happened, nothing at all to fill in the dots for them.

Except Carly.

As he thought about it, he realized that he really didn't have much choice after all. Once they found those bodies—and they would eventually, if they were that close—it was all going to come out if Carly had any memory of what had happened. With the wisdom of hindsight, he realized that it had been boneheaded of him to have concealed them on her property. But of course he couldn't know how things would go down, or even that she had any plan to return to her childhood home. It was one of those things that had seemed like a good idea at the time. He'd been doing his homework on his three victims-to-be, finding out where they lived and watching them, when he had gone by Carly's childhood home and discovered that it was deserted. Empty. No one lived there. All that acreage on top of that hill well away from neighbors, well away from the road—who could ask for a better killing ground? Or burying ground.

Of course, if he'd known Carly was going to come back like that and take up residence there again, he wouldn't have used it as he had, but he hadn't known. You make the best choices you can at the time, and you live with them.

Which was what he was doing now. Making the best choice he could. And it wasn't even a difficult one. To keep himself safe, he had to get rid of her.

The fact that Carly was now under the sheriff's protective wing, living in his house with what seemed to be most of the population of the county, trailing a deputy behind her everywhere she went, made things harder.

But not impossible. If he thought about it, if he watched and waited and stayed nearby, luck would hand him an opportunity.

Luck was going against him right now, but it would turn his way again. It always did.

And when it did, just like he had promised her after she had stabbed him in the leg in her house, Carly Linton was dead.

36

BY MIDNIGHT WEDNESDAY, Carly was starting to get just a tad annoyed. Not angry, mind you. Just the teeniest little bit bent out of shape. After professing his love and vowing that his kiss-and-run deal was a thing of the past, Matt had once again done just that. She had not seen him since he had brought her home on Monday morning, walked her into the house, dropped a quick, hard but unmistakably preoccupied kiss on her lips, and vanished back out the door.

He was working flat-out, she knew, following up on hot leads meant to link the body he was sure was buried somewhere on her property, even though it had not yet been found, to the monster who had attacked her. Doing that would somehow identify the attacker—both Sammy and Mike, who had also pulled baby-sitting detail and were the sources of her information, were unsure as to precisely how—so that was a good thing for her.

Except she really, really missed Matt.

The only thing that made her feel any better was that Sandra was similarly bereft. Even Lissa's Andy had basically disappeared for two days, having been roped in to help out with a computer that had somehow become part of the in-vestigation. During that time period Carly had endured endless teasing over the night she had spent with Matt, done what work she could in connection with her bed-and-breakfast—comparing insurance rates, going over ads that were due to start running in September, when they were scheduled to be open for business, arranging for regular deliveries of the premium foodstuffs they would need if Sandra's genius was to be allowed full rein—and had helped out as much as she could with the hundred and one last-minute things that needed to be done to get ready for Erin's wedding on Saturday. It was to be a small, intimate affair (this was Lissa's description) for approximately three hundred guests, so there were lots of small but important chores.

Good thing the wedding presents were being stored at Erin's new house, Lissa said. Otherwise they'd all have to move out.

When Matt unexpectedly walked in the front door followed by Antonio, Carly had given up all hope of seeing him that night. She was in the living room along with Sandra, Lissa, Erin, Dani and Mike, who was on guard duty, and Annie, on the floor, and Hugo, stretched out in Matt's empty recliner. At Erin's request, the women were tying birdseed up in little white tulle bags for throwing at the new couple on Saturday. Mike, having declined the chore, was leaning back on the couch in the midst of the chaos, watching TV with his arms crossed over his chest and a disgruntled expression on his face that told Carly at least that he was not being as successful at ignoring the activity going on around him as he pretended.

Considering that Erin was being almost too cheerfully vivacious, Carly could not help but think that getting under Mike's skin was the primary point of the activity.

"What is this, party central?" Matt asked as he stopped just inside the door to survey the scene. Dressed in cutoffs and a tee shirt, Carly was sitting cross-legged on the floor with a length of curling silver ribbon between her teeth. He looked tired and a little irritable, and her heart leaped at the sight of him. She had to finish off her bow before she could smile at him. By the time she did, he had exchanged greetings with everybody else and was standing over her, looking down with the smallest of smiles.

"I'm starving," he said. "Want to come out in the kitchen with me while I grab something to eat?"

Aware that they were being watched, covertly and not so covertly, on all sides, Carly nodded and let him pull her to her feet. He kept her hand in his as he led her off toward the kitchen.

"So what's going on with—?" She started to ask him about the investigation, but he cut her off with a shake of his head.

"I don't want to talk about it right now. I'm dead beat, and I want—" He broke off to pull her through the kitchen door.

"What?" she asked as the door closed behind them.

"Guess," he said, and backed her up against the refrigerator and kissed her. By the time he lifted his head, Carly was dizzy and breathing fast and quite ready to forgive and forget that she hadn't had so much as a word from him in more than forty-eight hours.

"I thought you were hungry," she said, leaning back against the refrigerator and looking up at him. From the little self-satisfied smile that curved his lips she was sure he was able to see everything she was feeling in her eyes, but there wasn't much point in worrying about it—he could pretty much always tell what she was thinking anyway.

"I am, but not for food. Antonio and I grabbed McDonald's on the way home." He kissed her again, so hotly that Carly practically melted where she stood.

"Carly?" Sandra opened the door and poked her head through. Still plastered against Matt with her arms around his neck, Carly felt slightly self-conscious. But, though she turned her head to look at Sandra, she didn't let go.

"Hm?"

Sandra was looking slightly self-conscious too. "I'm going to be spending the night out. I just wanted to let you know."

"Oh, yeah?" Carly looked at Sandra with interest. A dozen unspoken thoughts flashed between them. With Matt present, though, the conversation was left unsaid. "Okay. Fine. See you tomorrow."

"Have a good night," Sandra said with the slightest of naughty twinkles, and withdrew.

"Wow," Carly said thoughtfully, leaning against Matt but still staring at the closed door. "That worked out."

Then as she realized all that her words had implied she looked up at Matt. He was smiling, his eyes dark and gleaming wickedly as he met her gaze.

"Why do you think I brought Antonio home with me? He needed his woman, I need my woman, and we both need a decent night's sleep. This way it works out for everybody."

She surveyed him a little severely. "Your woman, huh?"

"You got a problem with that?" He was nudging her back against the refrigerator as he spoke, leaning into her, rocking against her.

"It sounds a little sexist, don't you think?" She was way too conscious of how good he felt.

"Oh, yeah?" He nudged a little harder. His hands were sliding down over her butt now, pulling her up against him.

"Yeah." Then she gave up. "Otherwise, I have no problem with it at all."

He smiled down into her eyes. "Let's go to bed."

That brought her out of it. She immediately thought of all the interested pairs of eyes in the living room.

"This is going to be embarrassing," she said.

The kitchen door opened, and Erin and Mike Toler walked in. They both stopped short, looking at Matt and Carly with undisguised interest.

"You're right, this is embarrassing," Matt said in her ear, then as her arms dropped from around his neck he stepped away from her and looked at Mike, who shifted uncomfortably. "I thought you were going home."

"We're going to have a sandwich first," Erin said, then added with a twinkle, "How was the roast?"

"Great. I recommend it." Matt caught Carly's hand and pulled her out of the kitchen. To Carly's great relief, they ran into no one else on the way to the stairs. Sandra and Antonio were apparently already gone, and Dani and Lissa were nowhere in sight.

"Hurry," she urged him, already a good two steps ahead and tugging on his hand as he climbed at his normal pace. If there was any chance to avoid another embarrassing encounter, she was ready, willing and able to take it.

"Mike's not making a nuisance of himself, is he?" Apparently unaware of her concern, Matt was frowning over something entirely different as they reached the upstairs hall.

"With Erin, you mean?" So he'd finally noticed. Well, that prospective little pow-wow in the kitchen had been hard to miss.

"Erin?" He sounded genuinely surprised. "I meant with you."

Carly stopped dead and looked over her shoulder at him. One glance, and she realized that he genuinely hadn't a clue. Honestly, men.

"You," she said, shaking her head at him, "are obtuse."

He pushed her on into his bedroom and closed the door.

Wrapping his arms around her, he kissed her, then lifted his head to say, "You want to explain that remark to me?"

"Later," she said, and pressed her mouth to his. Annie broke them apart by scratching on the door. Matt cursed and reached around with one hand to open it, and the little dog trotted in. Behind her came Hugo, who crossed the room and leaped onto the bed with the air of one who owned it.

"Do you have to come complete with your own zoo?" He sounded mildly disgusted as he and Hugo exchanged measuring stares.

"Love me, love my—" She broke off to grin at him.

"Yeah, I know. Lucky for the furball there that I do."

He would have kissed her again but Carly, reminded of certain urgent personal needs, pulled herself out of his arms.

"I'll be right back," she promised.

She went into the bathroom and closed the door. While she was in there, she took a second to brush her teeth and hair and apply a little lip gloss. By the time she was satisfied with what she saw in the mirror, her insides were melting and her heart was beating like a bunny's.

It was unsettling and fun and *wicked* to get so hot from just thinking about sex.

Ripe with anticipation, she walked back into the bedroom and stopped dead. Matt was lying on his back in the middle of his big bed, fully dressed except for his shoes, with Hugo curled up purring near his head. His eyes were closed and he looked completely limp. As Carly drew closer, gaping at him disbelievingly, a snore issued from between those chiseled masculine lips.

Was that the way her life worked or what? Forget all dressed up and no place to go. This was way worse: she was all revved up and no way to come.

Sandra's rollaway bed was made up in the corner, but

Carly barely spared it a glance. If she couldn't have sex, she could at least sleep with Matt. It wasn't quite what she'd had in mind, but it would do. Yes, it would definitely do.

Sound asleep, Matt looked sweet and boyish and endearing in addition to being his usual handsome and sexy self, of course. Grinning a little as she thought how little he would relish the first part of that description, she put on her pajamas, pulled back the covers—he was on top of the blanket, and she knew from experience that she had no hope of shifting him even if she tried with all her strength—and climbed between the sheets.

Then she turned off the bedside lamp and snuggled close, planting a kiss on his stubbled cheek. On his other side, Hugo purred like a motor.

"Catch you in the morning, sweet cheeks," she whispered in Matt's ear.

And she did.

Afterward, Matt showered and dressed and then went on downstairs while she finished dressing, ostensibly to let Annie out but really, Carly knew, to take the edge off the gauntlet for her if he could. It was early, but the chances that no one would be around downstairs were so slim as to be nonexistent. This was a major embarrassment opportunity, and fate wasn't going to let her miss it, she knew. Her life just didn't work like that.

As she headed toward the kitchen, she could hear snatches of conversation. Good God, it sounded as if all three of his sisters were in there. She almost turned tail and went back upstairs, but that would be cowardly. Anyway, the situation had to be faced sometime. Might as well get it over with.

As Carly approached the door she heard Lissa say, "So I guess that just about kills your 'no sex under my roof' rule, huh?"

"There's something I forgot to tell you about that rule." Matt sounded completely unruffled. "See, it applies to everyone in this house—but me."

"No *fair*," Lissa said, and then Carly walked into the kitchen. Lissa, Dani, and Erin were sitting around the table, and Matt was leaning against the counter drinking a cup of coffee. Four pairs of nearly identical coffee-brown eyes immediately focused on her, one rueful, the others amused.

"Good morning," Carly said, and hoped like hell that her face wasn't turning red.

"Good morning," they answered in chorus. Lissa grinned openly at her. Erin and Dani twinkled.

"Want some coffee?" Matt said.

"Thanks."

As he turned around to pour it for her, Erin grinned and gave her a thumbs-up.

Twenty minutes later, she and Matt were in his car. By way of pillow talk earlier, Matt had told her something of how the investigation was going. He'd told her about how Marsha had spent nearly a month in the home as a girl; he'd discovered that, according to their records, she and Carly had been there at the same time. They had been in the *infirmary* at the same time, along with two other girls: Genny Auden and Soraya Smith. He was having somebody try to track down those girls—women now, they were all four to six years older than Carly—as they spoke.

"I think something happened in that infirmary," he'd said. "That's the only connection I can find between you and Marsha. You were eight years old. You don't remember consciously. But I think it's there in your nightmares." He had looked at her and seemed to hesitate. "How do you feel about driving out to the Home with me and looking around and seeing if anything jogs your memory?"

She had agreed. So now here they were in his car, entering the gates of the Home, having driven all the way up to the northernmost tip of the county to reach it.

Funny to think that she hadn't been back here since the morning when her grandmother had arrived to pick her up, Carly reflected. She'd lived in Rocky Ford, a smaller town even than Benton, until the social worker had come to take her away. She and her mother had been dirt poor and her mother had had a drinking problem—all right, she'd heard a neighbor describe her mother as a "stinking drunk"—although her mother hadn't been raised that way. But Carly hadn't known that then; she'd learned the facts later, when she'd been grown, from her grandmother. Apparently her mother had been wild to a fault as a teenager, capping a tumultuous few years by climbing on the back of an even wilder boy's motorcycle and eloping with him in the teeth of being warned that if she left like that she could never come back. Subsequently, Carly had been born, the boy had run off with someone else and eventually been killed in a car accident in Tennessee, and her grandmother had, as promised, refused to take her daughter back. But when the social workers had tracked her down and notified her that Carly had been abandoned and was being kept in the County Home for Innocents, her grandmother had agreed to take Carly in. And eventually she'd grown to love Carly, and Carly had grown to love her.

But those eight days before her grandmother had come to take her away had been among the loneliest and most frightening in her life.

Looking at the low brick buildings now, as she walked toward them from the parking lot with Matt beside her, Carly thought they looked pleasant, bathed in sunshine and surrounded by acres of green grass with a playground and a basketball court off to one side. There were children outside—*poor little children*—and more children inside, most of them young teens, a few sitting around the common room watching TV, more walking the halls, one boy with a buzzed head glimpsed through an open door sitting on a twin bed in a tiny room.

Matt spoke to an older woman who came out to greet them. Carly caught fragments of the conversation: *Hello, Sheriff* and *I called* and *it's through here.* But she wasn't really listening; she was too busy taking it all in, absorbing it through her skin, reliving rather than just remembering it.

She'd been so scared.

"Are you okay?" Matt asked in a low voice as he took her arm to follow the woman, and for a minute she was, because he was there, his hand warm and strong against her skin, his eyes concerned for her. She nodded, and then there it was in front of her, the waiting room with the scarred wood counter where the children who had needed medication had come for their doses, and beyond the counter a door: some kind of gray metal, with a small square glass window. It was open.

There was only one, he just had an allergic reaction. I put him in another room.

Thanks, I appreciate it.

Carly heard Matt and the woman talking as if from a long way away as she pulled free of Matt's hand and walked into the room, which was unoccupied. It was small, with a good-sized window that looked out over—not a barn, but a shelter—a rickety-looking shelter in an area surrounded by a board fence. That pen had held a donkey once, and some chickens, and a couple of baby goats and a little pig. She had loved the animals. . . .

They were still there, the bunk beds. White painted iron, twin-sized, one on each wall. She had slept in the top bunk on the left. Carly looked at it. It was the same: metal springs, a thin mattress made up with a blue blanket and a

flat pillow. At the time it had seemed an awfully long way
off the ground. It still did. Carly saw that the edge of the top
mattress was even higher than the top of her head. She'd
had to climb a ladder to get up there.

The ladder was still there, attached to the far end of the
bunk. Carly walked around to it and climbed up. She was
wearing white capris and a black linen shirt that buttoned
up the front and tennis shoes, and climbing up was easy,
and so was crawling out onto the bunk.

Creak. Creak. The sound was the same. *Be careful not to
fall off*—she heard the warning again in her head. There
had been an older woman working here then, too, a nice
woman who'd watched over them all day and warned her
not to fall. She *had* been careful, sleeping with her back
pressed up against the wall, scared she'd roll.

Trying to remember how it had felt, she stretched out on
the bunk on her side with her back to the wall.

"Carly."

She heard him: it was Matt. He stepped into the room
quickly, looking around for her and then seeing her up
there on the bunk.

"You okay?" He walked right up to the side of the bunk
and looked at her across the mattress, and all she could see
of him was about three-quarters of his face, not his chin but
his mouth and nose and eyes.

His eyes. Looking at her. His eyes.

Carly began to shake.

37

She was white as a sheet of paper, her eyes huge and unfocused, her lips parted as she breathed. Her back was against the wall and her arm was folded beneath her head so that her curls cascaded over it and she was—God, she was trembling.

"Okay, forget it," Matt said, reaching out to clasp her arm and draw her toward him because he couldn't stand to see her like this no matter how good the cause. It was warm in the room, the air-conditioning wasn't much, but her skin was cold as he slid his hand around her bare arm. "You don't have to do this. Carly. . . ."

"I remember." Her voice was unsteady. She looked at him out of those lost little girl eyes, and Matt felt his heart turn over. "It was the eyes. When I saw you looking at me across the mattress I remembered the eyes. They're the eyes I see in my nightmares, Matt. His eyes—light blue. No lashes. The same eyes as the monster who attacked me. He said 'Now I remember you.' " She took a deep, shaky breath. "Well, now I remember him."

"So tell me." He was as tense as if he were being forced to observe her being tortured before his eyes, which, in a sense, he was. But if she remembered, if she could tell him who the perp was, it would all be over and she would be safe. He rubbed her arm once, a small gesture of comfort, then kept his hand on her as she started talking.

"It was at night. Always late at night. I got to where I was afraid to go to sleep, because then I might not see him coming. He would open the door, and I would see him standing there in the opening—it was dark in here and light in the room beyond, so what I saw was this big black silhouette—and then he would come in and close the door and . . . and start."

She was trembling like a leaf beneath his hand now. Matt gritted his teeth, wanting to pull her off that bunk and into his arms so badly that it was all he could do to resist, afraid of what he was going to hear, of what it was going to do to her to remember.

But he'd opened the floodgates and now he couldn't hold back the water. Even as he was wondering if he shouldn't just cut this off, just end it and take her out of here and go at this from another angle, she continued.

"He would go from bed to bed. He usually liked to start over there"—she nodded at the bunk against the opposite wall—"and go from bottom to top. I was last." She was shaking so badly that she was almost shuddering. "He'd get to me, and look at me, and I would be pressed up against the wall just like this and what I remember seeing are his eyes." She breathed in and it sounded almost like a gasp. "I would pretend to be asleep and he would put this rag over my face—it was cold and wet and smelled awful, kind of sweet—and whisper *'Nighty-night, princess.'* I was afraid to fight, afraid to do anything, and he would put this rag over my face and I would just go to sleep."

The bastard had chloroformed her. Matt realized it instantly. The bastard had come in here to a room full of little girls and *chloroformed them.* He was sick at his stomach. His free hand clenched into a fist.

"Only it didn't always work. After the first night I learned to turn my head, just a little, and not to breathe, and he didn't really seem to care all that much about me anyway. He was more interested in the other girls, they were older, developed, you know, so I was a little woozy but not *asleep,* and I would hear him get into bed with them. I could hear the springs."

Carly shuddered so hard that she shook the bed, and he could hear the springs, too.

Creak. Creak.

"Carly . . ." That was it, he couldn't stand it. He couldn't listen to another minute of this. If that bastard had touched her, it was going to tear his heart out, rip his guts in two, drive him insane with grief and rage.

"I remember, Matt," she said in a voice so small it was almost piteous, while she looked at him with an expression in her eyes that he knew was going to haunt him forever. "On the last night before my grandmother came, one of them—it was Genny, I remember Genny, she was around thirteen I think and kind of tough and I was half scared of her—woke up while he was in bed with her and she started to yell and he hit her. He hit her with his fist and then with something else and I could hear the *thunk* and then he got up out of the bunk and picked her up and carried her out of the room."

She finished in a rush and sucked in another one of those gasping breaths. "My grandmother came the next morning. Genny hadn't come back by the time I left."

Matt had already dug far enough into this to know that Genny Auden, age thirteen, had supposedly run away from the Home twenty-two years ago, on the night of August 13. They were doing a trace. Last time he'd checked in, there'd been nothing at all on her after that date.

Now he figured they were looking for a corpse.

"Who was it, baby? Who did it? Do you remember a name?" Thinking of her having to go through that was killing him, his voice was hoarse and his heart was racing and he was having trouble keeping his anger under wraps enough to be gentle for her now while she needed him.

Carly gave a tiny little nod. "The Donkeyman. We called him the Donkeyman."

Donkeyman. A name? A kids' version of a name? A physical description? Someone who had brought the donkey to the Home, cared for the donkey, had some connection with the donkey? What?

"At the time I just thought Genny had gone away, maybe somewhere safe like I had when my grandmother came. I just didn't think about it, it was bad and I just didn't think about it, it was over and I didn't see any reason to think about it. But now . . ." she paused and breathed, "Now I think he might have killed her."

"Yeah, I think so too." He had what he'd come for. No need to put her through any more of this. Deliberately he made his voice crisp. "Okay, come on, get down from there. We're going."

"Matt . . ."

"Come on. You heard me." When she seemed to be having trouble moving, he hauled her toward him and to hell with the neatly made bunk. Then she sat up at his urging and he put his hands on either side of her waist and lifted her down. Even fully grown, Carly weighed about as much as your average preteen; as an eight-year-old she wouldn't have been much bigger than a gnat. The thought of this guy—this big, burly guy—preying on her was driving him around the bend.

I'm coming for you, you bastard, he promised him there and then.

Her knees gave out. If he hadn't been holding on to her,

she would have crumpled to the linoleum. He scooped her up and headed for the door.

"Matt, no. Wait." She moved in his arms. Her hands were on his shoulders, and her fingers tightened protestingly.

"What?" He stopped and looked down at her. She was breathing slowly and deliberately, trying, he saw, to get herself back under control. Her face was still pale, but her mouth no longer shook and her eyes were back in focus.

"You can't walk out of here with me like this. Put me down."

"If I put you down, you're going to end up in a little puddle on the floor."

"No, I won't." She pushed against his shoulder now. "All these kids . . . Put me down. Please."

Against his better judgment he let her slide to her feet, keeping an arm around her in case her knees gave way again. She leaned against him for a moment, an arm draped over his shoulder, letting him take her weight. Then she straightened and pushed away from him—carefully, so he knew she wasn't sure about what her knees were going to do, either—and stood on her own two feet.

He looked at her, felt a rush of protective tenderness so strong it amazed him, and tugged at a lock of her hair to cover up.

"You're something, Curls, you know that?"

She smiled at him, and then the matron came to the door and he had to make polite conversation while getting them out of there.

In the car on the way back to town she looked over at him. Her head rested against the seat and she looked tired and a little pale and he would have pulled over and kissed the color back into her face if he hadn't had so damned much to do. This guy was within reach now, ready to be identified and pulled in and made to pay. All Matt had to do was connect a few more dots, just a few more, and they had him. Then he could turn his attention to Carly again.

"Matt."

"Hmm?"

"Just so you know. Except to put that cloth over my face, he never touched me. He was interested in the older girls."

His lips compressed and he stared unseeingly out through the windshield. It was near noon now, one more blazing hot day with heat chimeras rising up in front of the car and everything from the kids to the insects seeking to spend the worst of it in the air-conditioned indoors. Cornfields and cow pastures and small houses covered in aluminum siding flashed by. He was aware of none of them. All he could think about was Carly, helpless and eight years old and at the mercy of a hideously twisted man.

"What makes you think that was even on my mind?"

She gave him a wry little smile. "Well, for one thing, you've been clenching your jaw ever since we got into the car. For another, I know you."

He glanced at her, aware for the first time that his jaw *was* clenched. Deliberately he tried to relax it. "Okay. So I want to kill the guy. So sue me."

"My hero," she said, those baby-doll blue eyes going all soft on his face. Then, "I love you."

What do you say to that? He pulled over and kissed her rosy, then got back on the road and drove her back to town.

It was around one P.M. when he turned her over to Mike—there was something up with that guy—he would get to the bottom of it when he had the bastard who preyed on women and girls securely behind bars—refusing even to stop for lunch. He nodded at Carly's reminder that Erin's wedding rehearsal was tonight because the church was booked for the following night, with dinner to follow at

The Corner Café, and he absolutely, positively, had to be at the church in a suit at eight. The information promptly was buried by an avalanche of more urgent thoughts—weddings, even his sister's, weren't his top priority at the moment—as he headed out toward the Beadle Mansion. So far they were drawing a blank on finding Marsha's body despite employing cadaver-sniffing dogs and metal detectors and such low-tech methods as prodding the ground for soft spots, but it was there, he knew it was there, and they would find it. In this case, however, sooner was better than later. Poor little Genny Auden's corpse was going to have to wait in line. After twenty-two years, it would be able to tell them far less than Marsha's far fresher corpse. Anyway, they knew approximately where Marsha was; with Genny the search area was wide open. The perp would have to be stupid to have buried her there at the Home, and whatever else this guy was he wasn't stupid.

He'd just caught sight of Carly's house when Doris Moorman's voice crackled at him over the radio, summoning him back to the office.

Their computer search had been delayed by the ridiculously arduous process involved in securing Marsha's password—Kenan hadn't known it—from AOL. Now, apparently, the password had come through and Andy was in.

Matt walked into the sheriff's office to find his sister's boyfriend seated behind his desk with the computer glowing in front of him and Antonio, Doris, and Anson Jarboe, who'd checked himself into the jail for one of his little mini-vacations the night before, hanging over Andy's shoulders staring at the screen.

"Get your nose out of there. This is a criminal investigation," he said to Anson even as he came around behind Andy to look at the screen too.

"Come on, Matt," Anson protested. "I won't tell nobody."

Matt shook his head and pointed at the door. "You're released. Out."

He looked at the screen but refrained from saying anything while Anson grudgingly complied. This investigation was too important to compromise by having the details spread all over town before he had the perp behind bars. He'd temporarily deputized Andy and sworn him to secrecy, but he'd be damned if he was going to let Anson into the loop too.

They were so close now he could feel his palms itching in anticipation of making the bust.

"So what've you got?" he said.

"Look at this." Andy clicked the mouse, and Marsha's electronic mailbox popped up on the screen. Then he clicked *Mail you've sent* and lit on a particular piece, and Matt found himself staring at an e-mail message Marsha had sent—he checked the date—a little less than a week before she disappeared.

It was addressed to Silverado42.

Heard about your good luck. I'm down on mine right now. Maybe you could share. If you do, I won't tell.

The next one, from later that same night, read: *Don't worry, I've kept my mouth shut all these years* and *I'll keep it shut till I die. But it's going to cost you. Say—a million dollars.*

And a third one from that night: *See, you do remember. So do I. Everything. Genny was my friend.*

"Jesus. She was trying to blackmail him."

There were more in that same vein. Matt read them with grim triumph. Everything he had suspected was true. Then he looked at the e-mail address they were sent to. It told him approximately nothing that was of any use at all in the real world. "Who? Who is it? Who?"

Somebody who could afford to pay out a million dollars. Hell, that let out everybody he knew.

"Silverado42," Antonio mused. "Sounds like an older guy. See, his birthday could be 1942, and he could have silver—gray—hair."

"Or he could have a Ford Silverado, like my husband," Doris said. Then she looked horrified at what that implied. "Oh, mercy, Matt, you know it isn't him."

Matt, who was pretty sure that Doris's scrawny husband could be safely crossed off the list, said, "Don't worry, Doris, I think Frank's in the clear," then looked at Andy.

"Any kind of electronic trick you can pull to find out who this guy is?"

" 'Fraid not. We'll have to go through AOL again," Andy said. "You want to see his replies?"

Matt felt like kissing the kid. "Yes. Yes, I do."

The first one read, *Who are you? What are you talking about?*

Then, *Is this Marsha? Or Soraya? Or Carly?*

Then, *Marsha? I know it's you.*

Talk about setting yourself up to be murdered. Marsha had tried to blackmail the kind of man who preyed on helpless little girls. The man who had killed one of them. He'd come after her to shut her up—and then he'd come after Carly, too. And almost certainly Soraya as well.

So far, they hadn't been able to find Soraya, although they were checking all known addresses and trying to run down people who had known her. Matt had a feeling they might well be looking for her corpse, too. If so, then out of four little girls who had just happened to have the bad luck to get sick at a particular time while in the county's protective care, three were now dead. Carly, his Carly, was the lone survivor.

At the thought, Matt's blood ran cold.

"This is our guy. Find out who he is. Get on the phone to AOL right now, and tell them it's a police emergency or whatever you have to do." He looked at Antonio. "Like I told you, it's the Home. Carly remembered what happened there." He would go into the details later, when Andy and Doris weren't listening. There was no point in broadcasting every little detail of Carly's personal business to anyone who didn't need to know. "The name she came up with was the Donkeyman. Could be a name, or some kind of kids' variation thereof, could be something about the way he looked, could be somebody who took care of a donkey they had on the premises at the time. I want you to go over the Home's records one more time for anybody who might have been called that by four scared little girls."

Antonio nodded. "Will do."

When Matt left the office about an hour later to head for the Beadle Mansion, he noticed that the quality of light was different. There was a cool hint of silver beneath all that brilliant gold. The sun still shone, it was still hotter than Hades, but there was a kind of stillness in the air, an edge of portentousness.

Portentousness, indeed, he thought, glancing up. Black clouds were gathering on the horizon.

For the first time in more than a month, it looked like it was going to rain.

38

MATT ALMOST MISSED the wedding rehearsal. At Erin's urging, Carly, as Matt's date, had gone on to the church with Erin, Lissa, and Dani—and Mike, of course—and was sitting in a back pew when Matt rushed in about fifteen minutes late. Craig was there, having shown up a few minutes before to escort Dani to the rehearsal dinner afterward. Shelby was standing near the front, looking elegant in a black satin suit that made Carly glad she had gone for its polar opposite, a flame red sleeveless dress with a flounce around the hem. Its modest cut was belied by the curve-hugging properties of the silky knit.

All right, elegant was beyond her. But she could still (she hoped) look good. She had put the morning's horrors firmly behind her, resolving not to rain on Erin's parade by sharing them with anyone or even thinking of them again if she could help it. Accordingly, she'd lent a hand to some last minute details that Erin had requested her help with, chatted with Sandra (who had returned from Antonio's aglow, and would, along with Antonio, be joining them at the restaurant for dinner), admired Lissa's bridesmaid's dress and in general kept busy until it was time to go upstairs and dress. By the time they left for the church, it was almost as though the morning had never happened.

At Matt's entrance the entire wedding party, which was standing in front of Reverend Musselman as he went over the ceremony with them, turned to look at him. He was wearing a charcoal suit that looked fantastic on his tall athletic frame, and when she saw him walk in Carly caught her breath. His eyes sought her out, and he grinned at her before looking toward the others. Besides Erin, in pistachio silk, Dani and Lissa stood in front of the altar too, both in pastels, along with two of Erin's friends and a little girl belonging to one of them who was the flower girl. They were grouped behind Erin, while Collin stood beside his prospective bride holding her hand with four of his friends and his little nephew, as ring bearer, behind him. As an emergency stopgap, Mike had been filling in for Matt, walking Erin down the aisle in time to the organist enthusiastically playing "Here Comes the Bride" and passing her hand to Collin with so much barely concealed ill-will that Carly had been watching with the kind of horrified fascination usually reserved for train wrecks.

"About time," Erin called to Matt accusingly.

"Sorry. I got tied up." He tweaked Carly's hair in passing—the man was a master at the romantic gesture—as he strode up the aisle.

"Where's Andy?" Lissa glared at him, clearly blaming him for the absence of her date.

"He's doing something for me. He'll be at the restaurant, don't worry."

To Carly's relief, as Matt took his place beside Erin, Mike retreated to sit beside her.

"You're scowling," Carly informed him in a whisper.

"I feel like punching him in the nose."

Carly had no doubt that Mike was referring to Collin. "It's her choice."

The look on Mike's face told her his opinion of that.

"The wedding's day after tomorrow," she reminded him, still whispering.

"Yeah, I know. What do you suppose her reaction would be if I stood up at the place where they ask for objections and say I have one?"

"I hope that's a joke."

"Not cool, huh?" He sounded glum.

Carly shook her head, picturing the scene that would result. "If you've got an objection, I suggest you put it to Erin before she starts walking down the aisle. Way before. Like, today would be good."

"She knows I have an objection." There was so much dejection in his voice that Carly patted his leg. He gave her a rather wan smile. "I'm glad things worked out for you with Matt, anyway."

"Me too. Listen, Erin can't be totally indifferent to you. She was in the kitchen with you last night."

"Yeah," Mike said gloomily. "We ate roast beef sandwiches."

He sounded so disgusted that Carly giggled. She couldn't help it. He shot her an unamused look.

To her surprise, when the adults' part of the rehearsal was over (the flower girl and ring bearer were being put through their paces a few more times under the watchful eyes of their mothers and Reverend Musselman), Matt pulled her into the vestibule, which was a small and intimate space paneled in beautifully aged dark wood that rose to the ceiling. Light filtering through a pair of stained glass windows on either side of the doors spilled rainbows over the hardwood floor, and discreetly recessed doors on either side led to small retiring rooms used by brides and their attendants for last-minute primping and to await their cues, and rest rooms.

Once he had her alone, Matt brought up the subject of his deputy.

"So what's the deal with you and Mike?" he asked.

To say that caught her by surprise was an understatement. Carly looked at him—it wasn't quite as far as usual because she was wearing extremely high heels—and was amazed by something she saw in his eyes.

"You *are* jealous," she said, and at the idea of Matt—gorgeous Matt, whom she had loved all her life and who definitely knew how to put the thrill in thrilling—being jealous of Mike the Stolid, she chuckled. "That's hilarious."

The look he gave her told her that he didn't think so.

"There's something up with him. He's always hanging around the house even after he's done working, he's weird with me lately—and then he sits beside you and you two whisper and you giggle and pat his leg. I *know* you're not interested in him, but . . . is he coming on to you? Are you somehow encouraging him? Tell me I'm imagining this."

"I love you being jealous." She grinned hugely at him and curled her hands around his lapels and, after a glance around to make sure they weren't being observed, rose up on tiptoe to press a quick kiss to his mouth. "You're cute when you're jealous. Actually, you're just cute anyway."

"You're better than cute. You're beautiful. And you're mine." He slid his hands around her upper arms and pulled her against him. His lips curved in the slightest of rueful smiles as he looked down at her. "Okay, so I'm jealous. A little. Not much. So go ahead and laugh. You'll pay for it when I get you in bed tonight."

"Now you're scaring me." She made big eyes at him. What he was actually doing was exciting her madly. If he was going to make her pay in bed, she could hardly wait. "Just for the record though, Mike isn't after me. He's after your sister."

"What?" Matt looked startled. "Which one?"

Carly shook her head at him. "I cannot believe you have missed this: Erin."

"She's getting married on Saturday." Sounding dumbfounded, he looked back inside the sanctuary to discover the others coming toward them en masse. "Does she know?"

"I think so," Carly said dryly, freeing her arms and stepping back from him because this was, after all, a church. "How do you think I was able to talk Mike into taking me out that night? He wanted to make Erin jealous. No way in the world he would have done it otherwise."

"Jesus." Matt looked back at her and shook his head. "I don't believe this. Women. You think Erin's interested in him back?"

Before Carly could reply, they were surrounded by people. Everyone except the still-rehearsing children crowded into the vestibule, talking at once, then spilled out onto the sidewalk and parking lot. It was only about nine-thirty, which ordinarily in July meant that the sun was a little less hot than at noon, but was still bright. This evening, though, for the first time in weeks the sky was clouded over. There was a heaviness to the air that warned of coming rain.

Life was like that. Take a shower and the phone rings. Plan a wedding and it rains.

While they waited for the children to finish, the rest of them stood around talking. Matt had his hand curved negligently around Carly's arm just above her elbow as they stood with Dani and Craig and two of Collin's groomsmen and their dates. All of a sudden Carly had the sensation that she was being watched. Startled, feeling as though a cold trickle of water had suddenly run down her spine, she glanced around—and met Shelby's gaze.

Shelby was far better than the alternative. For a moment it had almost felt like the monster's eyes had been on her again.

But they weren't, of course. Not here at the church, when Matt was with her and it was still full daylight and she was positively surrounded by people. She was still feeling a little vulnerable from her experience of the morning—which she absolutely, positively, was not going to think about. If she did, she would get upset, and Matt would know, and he would get upset and take her home, and Erin's rehearsal dinner would be spoiled.

She was going to think about anything else instead. Even Shelby.

The other woman was definitely attractive. Cool and a little haughty in that fitted black suit. And, dammit, elegant.

Three things Carly knew she would never be.

Knowing that Shelby had slept with Matt bothered her a little, but then, Carly reflected, Matt's ex-girlfriends were practically legion. If she was going to let herself get bent out of shape every time she ran into one, she was going to spend a lot of time feeling like a pretzel.

And Matt *had* slept with Shelby, then panicked when Shelby started letting him see that she thought their relationship was getting serious and done his kiss-and-run thing and left her high and dry. If Shelby was upset over that, Carly couldn't really blame her. She hadn't been a happy camper herself when Matt had pulled that same stunt on her.

She wasn't going to be a happy camper if he did it again.

A profession of love and a lot of great sex didn't add up to forever. Even that growled *You're mine* that had made her heart go pitter-pat didn't equal forever. She could deny it all she wanted, to him and herself, but forever with Matt was what she was hoping for. No, it was what she was praying for.

But Matt was clearly perfectly happy with great sex, no strings. As far as she was concerned, though, the problem with that was, once the great sex burned itself out, what they were left with was no strings.

If he opted out then, her heart was going to break.

He'd made no promises to her either, and she'd be wise to remember that. She could very easily find herself in Shelby's shoes one day.

With that in mind, Carly pulled her arm free of Matt's hold, murmured a polite "excuse me" to the others and went over to speak to Shelby, who was standing with her brother and Erin just outside the church's arched doors.

"The wedding's going to be beautiful," she said to Erin. Then she smiled at Shelby. "Erin said you basically planned it. You've done a great job."

"Thank you," Shelby said. Her gaze ran over Carly. "It's been fun. A lot of work, but fun."

"You know, you two might be able to do some business together," Erin said, clearly hoping to help ease an awkward situation. "Shelby's a realtor. Carly's opening a bed-and-breakfast." She looked at Shelby. "If you have people come to town looking for a house, you could probably arrange to have them stay at Carly's place."

"That's an idea," Shelby said, and smiled at Carly.

Matt came toward them, talking on his cell phone, bringing Mike with him. He closed the phone as he reached them and put it into his pocket.

"Hey, Shelby. Collin." He nodded at them by way of greeting, then looked at Carly.

"Something's come up," he said, and glanced at Erin. "I've got to go in to the office for a while. I won't be any longer than I can help."

"You're always working," Erin said in disgust.

"The better to pay for your wedding, sweetie," Matt said, and glanced at Shelby. "I dropped that check off by your office, by the way."

"The one for the photographer? Thank you."

Matt's gaze shifted to Carly, and his eyes softened fractionally on her face. "I'll meet you at the restaurant. Mike's back on duty. Good thing he didn't leave, isn't it?"

There was the faintest hint of dryness to that. Carly realized that discovering that Mike's apparent lovesickness was directed at his sister rather than herself didn't really please Matt either.

Could anyone say overprotective? She loved that about him, but he did sometimes carry it to extremes.

"I won't be longer than an hour, tops," Matt promised, then tugged one of Carly's curls in an affectionate gesture and departed.

Watching him reverse his cruiser out of the parking lot, Carly reflected that she'd rather have Matt's hair tugs than any other man's kisses.

In other words, she had it bad.

"Could I talk to you for just a minute? In private?" Shelby asked in a lowered tone. While Carly had been watching Matt leave, Collin had moved off to say something to one of his groomsmen. Mike had taken advantage of the opportunity to talk to Erin. They were standing right there next to Carly and Shelby, but Mike had angled his body in such a way that he and Erin were able to talk more or less privately.

"Sure," Carly said. Shelby pushed open the church door and stepped back inside the vestibule. With it open, Carly could clearly hear the strains of the wedding march. Those poor children must be trudging up the aisle one more time. She touched Mike's arm, and he glanced at her. "I'm just going right here with Shelby." She indicated the vestibule.

"Okay. Yell if you need me."

Shelby was standing just inside the door. Carly glanced past her to see, at the front of the church, Reverend Musselman bent over talking to the children. The children's mothers stood nearby, while the organist sat at her instrument with her fingers resting on the keys.

"Matt's crazy about you, isn't he?" Shelby said as Carly joined her. "It's so easy to see."

Carly looked at her rather cautiously. "We've been friends practically our whole lives."

Shelby snorted. Such a homely sound from such an elegant woman was a surprise. "I just wish he'd been friends like that with me."

"I'm sorry your relationship ended badly."

"I am too. He's by far the best catch in town, and I won't hide that I wish I could have reeled him in. But you've clearly got him. Which brings me to what I wanted to tell you: As far as I'm concerned, he's strictly off-limits now. I won't be going after him anymore." Shelby smiled, and Carly found herself almost liking her for the first time in her life. "Unless and until you break up, that is. Then I might."

"*Then* you're welcome," Carly said, and smiled back.

"I wasn't very nice to you in high school, was I?" Shelby grimaced. "I'm sorry."

"That's okay. That was then, this is now, and we've both grown up."

"Well," Shelby said as the organist started to play again. "Now that I've said my piece, I think I'll just nip into the rest room."

She smiled and did, and Carly turned to go back outside. As her hand curled around the heavy brass door handle, the wedding march filled the church. Reverend Musselman beat time in the air as the children lockstepped up the aisle.

"Carly."

Carly turned inquiringly at the sound of her name.

There was a man behind her. He'd just stepped out of the door on the other side of the vestibule from the one Shelby had disappeared through. The men's side, Carly realized. He moved toward her, smiling, neatly dressed in khakis and a navy sport shirt. She smiled instinctively. She was still smiling when he grabbed her arm and clamped a chloroform-soaked rag over her face.

39

"**Y**OU'RE NOT GOING to believe this," Andy said as Matt strode into the sheriff's office. Antonio was still there—or he was back, rather, because he'd headed for the Home at the same time that Matt had left for the Beadle Mansion earlier. "I think this guy won the lottery."

"What?" Matt glanced in surprise at Antonio.

"Not me," Antonio said. "I wish. Him." He pointed at the computer. "Nice threads, by the way."

"Who?" Matt asked, ignoring that last. He moved to stand behind Andy and looked down at the screen.

"Silverado42. Look at this. It's an e-mail to Marsha from Jeanini8."

The message on the screen said: *Ohmigod, you'll never guess who won the lottery. That guy, you know—that creep from when you were a kid. You know, the one who comes into the grocery in Macon where my sister works.*

Matt looked at the date: approximately two weeks before Marsha disappeared.

"Now look at Marsha's reply." Andy clicked the mouse, and another message popped up.

You mean DingDong the Donkeyman? Get outta here!

Matt started to feel a bubble of excitement.

"Here's Jeanini8 again." Another click.

It's true. I swear to God. He won LottoSouth—24 million!!!!

"Back to Marsha." Click.

How do you know?

"And Jeanini8." Click.

You know he's been living in Macon forever, and he's been coming into the grocery where she works every week. He's been playing the same numbers for the last five years. My sister knows them by heart. He hasn't come forward to claim his prize yet, but the store gets 100 grand for selling the winning ticket and they're going to give my sister a bonus because she's the one who sold it.

"And Marsha."

Do you happen to know his e-mail address?

"And Jeanini8."

I got it from my sister, who got it from the frequent shopper card he filled out. Here it is: Silverado42@aol.com. What, do you want to say congratulations?

"And Marsha."

Something like that.

"And Jeanini8."

You're bad. By the way, don't tell anybody I told you. The store told my sister not to say anything until he comes forward because of his privacy or something. I don't want her to get in trouble.

"And Marsha again."

Don't worry, I won't tell.

"That's basically it for the important stuff," Andy said.

"Jesus Christ." Matt's hands tightened on the back of the chair—his chair—that Andy was sitting in. "There it is right there. The whole thing. I was wondering why Marsha decided to start blackmailing him now, after leaving him alone all these years. The bastard won the lottery. Once Marsha started blackmailing him, he must have been afraid they all would. So he decided to eliminate the problem."

"Can you believe that?" Antonio said with disgust. "I

play that damned thing every week, and I've never won so much as a dollar."

"So we've basically got it all figured out," Matt said, ignoring Antonio in favor of turning various bits and pieces of information over in his head. "The only thing we still don't know is who the bastard is. Any luck getting the name out of AOL?"

"Not yet," Andy said. "I'm working on it, though. But I think I may have found a quicker way. I found Jeanini8's phone number. She e-mailed Marsha her new one."

"Shit," Matt said as Andy handed him a piece of paper with a phone number on it. "You are shitting me." He looked at Andy. "Anytime you want to marry my sister, just let me know. She's yours."

Andy looked alarmed. "Well, uh—"

"Or not." Matt grinned at him, recognizing a fellow commitment-phobe, even if the kid was just barely old enough to shave.

"Want me to call?" Antonio reached for the phone.

Matt shook his head. "I will."

This was one call he really wanted to make. Jeanini8, whoever she was, knew who the bastard was. As soon as he got the name, the perp was going down. Not even Erin's party was going to stand in his way.

The phone started to ring. Antonio, who was closer, answered it. After the initial, crisp, "Sheriff's Department," he just listened for a minute, a look of growing horror on his face.

"Oh, crap. Oh, no. Oh, man. Hold on." Antonio's face was gray by the time he put a hand over the mouthpiece and looked at Matt.

Matt was already rigid with alarm. He knew Antonio, had known him for years. He'd never seen that particular look on his face.

"What?" he demanded.

"Carly's disappeared. From the church. She went back inside to talk to Shelby and Shelby went to the bathroom and Carly vanished. They've looked all over. Mike's shitting bricks."

Matt's blood turned to ice. He felt as if all his internal organs had suddenly seized up. For a minute he went all light-headed and had to put a hand down on his desk to steady himself. He knew what had happened, knew it as well as if he'd been an eyewitness: the bastard had grabbed Carly.

At the thought of what he might be doing to her right that very minute, Matt broke into a cold sweat.

"Fuck," he said. "Fuck, fuck, fuck, fuck, fuck." It was more prayer than curse.

Then he got a grip and looked at Antonio.

"Get some roadblocks set up," he said hoarsely. "Call the state police. I want men, I want helicopters, I want infrared equipment. And I want Billy Tynan's dogs over at that church pronto. Tell him I'll be there in ten minutes."

Then he picked up the phone and punched in the number for Jeanini8.

40

"Hello, Carly." He was leaning over her, whispering almost tenderly. Carly blinked, staring up at him. He was all blurry. She felt woozy, dizzy, sick at her stomach. Where was she?

"What happened?" she started to say, only to find she couldn't. There was something over her mouth. Something preventing her from speaking, from opening it, from drawing air in through it. She moved her head from side to side. Something, carpet, cheap, scratchy nylon carpet, abraded her cheek. She was lying all curled up on carpet. Whatever was over her mouth stayed in place. She managed to get her tongue between her smashed-together lips. Slightly bitter, sticky, plastic—duct tape. At the realization her eyes widened. Slowly his face came into focus.

Round, pale, plump, unremarkable. Blue eyes. Pale blue. Lashless.

Looking at her.

Carly's heart exploded into what felt like a thousand beats a minute. Her blood ran cold. Her stomach knotted. She wanted to scream, but all that emerged was a strangled squeak.

The Donkeyman. And also . . . also . . . She knew him,

not well but vaguely, knew his name—but she was so sick, so terrified, she couldn't think.

"I see you're awake." His voice was low and pleasant, with an unmistakably southern intonation. It made Carly's skin crawl. She struggled to move. Her arms were pulled uncomfortably behind her back and secured at the wrists with—it felt like more duct tape. Her ankles were similarly bound. Her arms tingled, that pins and needles sensation that means they've fallen asleep. Her legs were better. They didn't hurt. He leaned closer, bending over her, and she realized that he was leaning in through the door of a vehicle, a truck, a pickup truck, realized that she was on the floor, in the front passenger footwell, wedged in, and he was trying to get her out. She struggled frantically, but it didn't help. He wrapped his arms around her waist, and heaved her up and out, then let her slump to the ground while he closed the door of the truck.

Rain hit her face, her hair, her skin. Big fat drops. It was raining. Warm rain, and it was dark, night, moonless, and she was lying in short grass, the smell of wet grass filled her nostrils, there was gravel in the grass, she could feel it digging into her cheek and arm. She was lying in short grass near a gravel driveway, the truck was white, there was a small house nearby, a cabin really, some kind of dark wood.

Carly realized that she was still feeling the effects of the chloroform he had used on her. Her head whirled. Her thoughts were fuzzy. Her limbs felt leaden, heavy.

It was then that terror, true icy terror, flooded her veins. Her stomach cramped. Her chest heaved as she fought to breathe.

She was going to die. He had brought her to this place to kill her.

He was a big man, stocky, strong. He bent over her, wrapping his arms around her middle, trying to pick her up. He should have been able to do it easily, but she resisted. Heart racing with fear, almost suffocating in her desperate effort to breathe, Carly struggled frantically, writhing and thrashing until he cursed and fumbled with something and thrust that cool wet cloth over her face again. She gagged, smelling it, smothered by it, that hideous sweet scent that had haunted her dreams for years, the scent of terror; the scent of horrible drugged sleep; for her, tonight, the scent of death.

When she regained consciousness again, she was slung over his shoulder, blood pounding in her temples as she hung upside down, her head bobbing against his back, his arms clamped around her legs. He was walking downstairs, carrying her down into what looked like a basement, gray concrete walls, a single bare lightbulb in the center of the room, dark shadows crowding the walls. She could feel his hand, meaty and warm, through the fragile nylon of her pantyhose, pressing against her thigh. She was wet, wet with rain and cold. Her dress had ridden up. She realized that she was wearing her red dress, the sexy one, that she was still dressed for Erin's rehearsal dinner, except her shoes were missing.

Matt. Matt. She wanted Matt.

She was shivering, trembling, her bones had turned to jelly. Her stomach cramped from fear. Her heart thudded in her chest.

"Well, now, here we are." He reached the bottom of the stairs and took the few steps necessary to cross the room. There he lowered her to the ground, quite gently really, considering that he was going to kill her so it shouldn't matter if he banged her up a little first. She thought about struggling, but she was so sick, so woozy, all she really wanted to do was close her eyes and sleep, and anyway, what was the point? There was no possible way she was going to escape.

She was helpless. At his mercy. And he had no mercy, none at all. Not for her.

She was going to die.

And he was looking forward to it. She could tell from his smug little smile.

Her worst nightmare had come true: the Donkeyman had her. Carly shuddered in horror. Cold sweat poured over her in waves.

Please God Please God Please God I don't want to die.

"I've been thinking about this," he said as he moved to stand in front of a big white metal chest, really big, about the size of two washing machines pushed together. He lifted the lid and she realized that she was looking at a freezer.

Another burst of terror, fresh and sharp and new, raced down her spine like an icy finger.

"We've got a couple of options here." He turned toward her, walked toward her, stood over her, put his fists on his hips as if he were considering. Looking up at him, Carly knew that he was toying with her, he already knew how he was going to do it, how he was going to kill her, and that it was going to happen soon, within minutes, *now*.

He bent over her, and she saw that he had a knife in his hand.

Her eyes went wide. Panic almost overwhelmed her. God, she had felt that knife. She cringed as he waggled it in front of her face, remembering the quick surprising pain of its cold blade slicing through her skin.

"I could cut your throat." He touched the tip of the knife, oh so delicately, to the soft spot just below her ear, then stroked it very softly across the front of her neck. Carly held very still and closed her eyes. Her heart slammed painfully against her breastbone. She held her breath. Any second now, she was going to feel the blade going deep—

"But that's too messy," he said, sounding cheerful. "I'd have to clean up afterwards. Anyway, I like the second option better."

He bent down and scooped her up. Carly cringed and shuddered, but he picked her up and held her in his arms and looked down at her and smiled.

Then he carried her to the freezer and lowered her inside. There were packages of frozen food on the bottom. They were hard and cold and uncomfortable against her back. The sides of the freezer were thick with frost.

She could feel the cold blast of it caressing her skin.

Then he straightened. Carly's breathing suspended as she realized what he meant to do.

"At your size, there's probably enough air for you to survive about forty-five minutes. And I've turned the temperature down to zero. So the question is, will you suffocate or freeze to death first? It will be interesting to find out, don't you think?"

Carly whimpered, a small terrified sound, and his smile broadened. Then he shut the lid.

She was left all alone in the icy, nearly airless dark.

41

"Is this it?" Matt swung around in the front seat to glare at the passenger in the back. *"I said, is this it?"*

"Yes, yes. For God's sake, Matt." Bart Lindsey was nervous, shaky, intimidated, as well he should be. Matt had grabbed him by the scruff of his neck and practically thrown him into the back of the cruiser as soon as the vet had admitted that, although his brother had lived a hundred miles away in Macon for the last twenty years, he did still own a house relatively nearby, a hunting cabin he rarely if ever used, nestled in the thick piney woods about fifteen miles west of town. Jeanini8—Marsha's friend Jeanine LeMaster— had known instantly who DingDong the Donkeyman was when Matt got her on the phone: Hiram Lindsay, who twenty-two years ago had owned the vet practice that his brother now operated and had gone out to the County Home for Innocents one blazing August to tend a sick donkey.

Hiram Lindsey had Carly. She'd been missing for over an hour now. Matt's driving fear was that she was already dead.

He was out of the door and running through the pouring rain toward the cabin with his gun drawn before Antonio, who was driving, had done more than pull off the road. A light was on inside, glowing feebly through the small square front window. There was a truck in the driveway—a white Silverado. Raindrops sounded like BB's as they rattled off its roof.

"Open up! Sheriff's department! Lindsey, I know you're in there! Open this goddamn door!" Heart pounding, the metallic taste of fear in his mouth, Matt hammered on the flimsy wooden door as two more cruisers pulled up behind his and his deputies jumped out, guns drawn.

They raced toward him, backing him up as he got tired of waiting and kicked in the damned door.

"*Carly!*"

There he was, the bastard, scuttling toward a back room like a frightened crab, looking over his shoulder as Matt came after him.

"What . . . what . . . ?" he sputtered, face white, eyes wide, still trying to run.

"Where is she? You sick bastard, where is she? If you've hurt her . . ." Matt collared him, literally wrapped his hand in his collar and spun him around, spun him against the slick plastic paneling covering the wall. Lindsey didn't even try to resist. He leaned against the wall, panting, sweating, while Matt dug his fingers into the back of his neck and cuffed him. Behind him, his men had already spread out, searching the place.

"Carly!"

Nothing. No answer.

"What's the meaning of this? What are you doing?" Lindsey's pathetic bleats were a bad waste of good air.

"*Where's Carly?*" Police brutality be damned. Matt slammed the flat of his hand down on the side of the bastard's head and ground his cheek into the wall. He was pumped with terror, fueled by it, practically jumping out of his skin with it. The bastard was here. Carly was not.

That was enough to make cold sweat break out all over him.

"I don't know what you're talking about. Carly who? Sheriff, whoever you think you're looking for, you've got the wrong man."

"Like hell." Matt was panting. He could hear his deputies taking the house apart. They weren't finding her. "Listen, you slimeball, it's over. I know about Marsha, Soraya, poor little Genny. I know about the lottery. I know about Marsha blackmailing you. I know *everything,* do you hear me? What I don't know is where Carly is. And you're going to tell me."

"I don't know what you're talking about."

Matt could feel and see and even smell Lindsey's sweat. The man was lying. He did know. He had her. Oh, God, was he too late? Was she dead?

"Matt, look at this." Antonio ran in from outside, through the door that hung on broken hinges now letting in the sound and smell of rain. Matt glanced around to see what he'd found. His heart almost stopped. Antonio was dangling one of Carly's spiky red shoes from one hand.

"Where is she?" he roared, slamming his shoulder into Lindsey's back. "Damn you, you . . . *Where is she?"*

"I don't know what you're talking about," Lindsey said again, sounding less frightened now.

Icy calm suddenly possessed Matt. He drew his pistol out of the holster and wedged it nice and tight against Lindsey's temple. Then he got right up in the bastard's face.

Behind him, he could see Antonio's horrified expression. Mike came in from the back of the house and stopped dead.

Neither of them even tried to interfere.

"Here's how this works," Matt said through his teeth, barely able to speak through the panic that was welling like gorge in his throat. He ground the pistol in a little harder. His grip on it was so tight that his knuckles showed white.

"You tell me where she is, or I blow you to hell. I'm going to give you to the count of three. *One.*"

"I don't know what you're talking about."

"*Two.*"

"You're an officer of the law. You can't do this." Fear sharpened Lindsey's voice.

"Watch me. *Thr—*"

"Hiram, if you know where Carly is, you'd better tell him," Bart Lindsey said softly. Matt felt the bastard sag.

"She's in the freezer in the basement," Lindsey said, and closed his eyes.

Matt pulled his pistol back and thrust the bastard toward Antonio.

"Get him out of here," he said. Then, heart pounding, he raced for the basement.

By the time he reached the freezer, he was sweating buckets. His deputies were still pounding down the stairs in his wake when he threw up the lid.

Looking down, he felt cold stark terror grab him by the throat. There she was, bound hand and foot, huddled in a little ball, a strip of duct tape covering her mouth. She was white as death and unmoving. Frost had already started to rim her nose and mouth.

Jesus, Jesus, was he too late?

"*Carly.*"

He snatched her out of there, reached down and grabbed her up and into the warmth, and Mike reached in and pulled the duct tape off her mouth even as he put her down and knelt beside her so that he could start CPR.

She was so cold, so limp, had been so cold and limp in his arms.

"Carly." His voice broke. Behind him he could hear somebody radioing for an ambulance.

Then, miracle of miracles, he felt her stir. Her chest expanded and her lids fluttered up and she looked up at him, dazed and disoriented, but alive.

"Matt," she said.

Matt drew in a great, shaking breath and let his head fall to his chest in profound thanks for an answered prayer. Then he gathered her up in his arms.

42

Twenty-four hours later, Carly was sitting up in bed in Matt's bedroom waiting a little less than patiently for him to get home from work. It was just after midnight, and she was more or less back to normal, although she'd spent most of the previous night—after she'd gotten out of the freezer—in the hospital emergency room being treated for what was basically shock. While she was still at the hospital, Hiram Lindsey had told his brother where to find Marsha and Soraya and Genny. Genny was buried out behind his cabin. Marsha and Soraya were in an old freezer in the basement of Carly's house.

Knowing that she and Sandra had lived there with those bodies in the basement was almost the worst thing of all.

But she wasn't going to think about that. She was going to concentrate on the positive. And the positive was that the monster who had haunted her dreams for almost all of her life was now behind bars. It was the most liberating thing in the world, she discovered, to finally be free of fear.

At the moment, she was warm and comfortable, dressed in a sexy little shorty nightgown that she had decided was more appropriate for her planned evening's activities than the pajamas she usually wore, sitting up in bed with a book open on her lap, Hugo purring like a motor beside her and Annie asleep on the rug at the foot of the bed. All would be right with her world if Matt would ever get his hot bod home from work.

The killer was caught, the case was closed, and the heat wave had finally broken. One would think that, under that combination of positive circumstances, the sheriff could get home at a decent hour. But no. He had things to catch up on, he'd said.

Carly was just beginning to seriously entertain the idea of turning off the light and going to sleep without him when the bedroom door opened without warning and Matt walked into the room.

He was in full sheriff mode, with raindrops gleaming on his black hair and a slight, and slightly wry, smile curving his lips.

In his hand was a huge bouquet of red roses. In his other hand was—something. Carly was too fixated on the roses to take the time to ascertain what.

The scent of the flowers reached her all the way across the room.

"I can't believe you brought me roses," Carly said, charmed by the gesture. She had a thought and narrowed her eyes at him. "What did you do?"

He laughed and crossed the room to put the roses on the bedside table. She was leaning over them to inhale when she noticed the tiny votive candle he put down next to them. Her eyes widening, she watched as he extracted a lighter from his pocket and proceeded to flick his Bic. Touching the flame to the wick, he lit the candle.

Carly's heart started to pound.

He was watching her watch him with a crooked little smile on his face.

"Matt . . ." she began.

He reached for her book and tossed it aside, picked Hugo up and moved him too, receiving a nasty cat look for his pains, and then caught her hands.

"Get up," he said.

Perfectly willing under these conditions to have the chance to show off her hot little nightie, and more than anxious to see just exactly what he had in mind, she let him pull her to her feet.

Holding her hands, he dropped down on one knee in front of her.

The romantic effect was slightly skewed by the rueful twinkle in his eyes, but she didn't care, she would take it, she had waited all her life for this. Carly took a deep breath, knowing for sure now what was coming. Her heart raced and her breathing got all out of whack and her knees went weak.

"Candlelight, flowers, and bended knee," he said, and the twinkle vanished to be replaced by a dark hot gleam that started her insides to melting. "I love you. Marry me?"

Carly was temporarily bereft of speech as most of her major muscle groups turned to jelly. Her eyes stayed locked to his. With the air of one patiently waiting, Matt carried her left hand to his mouth, kissed her knuckles, then turned her hand over to press his lips to her still healing palm. Carly felt the touch of those warm, firm lips all the way down to her toes.

This time, he meant it. She could see it in his eyes. He was offering her forever, and he meant it.

"Yes," she said, and her voice shook. "Yes, yes, yes."

Then he stood up and she threw herself into his arms and they didn't say anything else for a very long time.

Finally, when they were both up for conversation again, Matt turned on the bedside lamp and slid out of bed.

"What are you doing?" she asked curiously as he picked up his pants, which had been discarded in the near vicinity of the bed.

"I forgot," he said, feeling in his pocket and extracting a small black box. "I got you something."

Carly stared agog at the box as he brought it to her in bed.

She knew what it was: a jeweler's box.

When she opened it, she was more agog than ever.

"Oh, my God," she said, looking from it to him and back. "It's huge. It's beautiful. Matt . . ."

"Hmm?" He picked up the box, extracted the ring from it, and put it on her finger.

Her voice started to shake. "I love you."

"I love you, too," he said, and climbed back into bed.

It must have been around two A.M. when Matt heard it: something out in the hall. Footsteps. Footsteps that definitely did not belong to any of his three sisters, whose step he had learned to recognize long since.

"What is it?" Carly asked sleepily as he slid out of bed.

"Shh," he said, and reached for his pants. "There's somebody in the house."

Decent now, moving quietly, he padded to the door and eased it open. Looking down the hall, he saw that he was right. There was a man moving almost silently away from him.

"Hold it right there," he said, and flipped on the light.

The man whirled. And he found himself looking at Mike. His deputy, Mike.

Dressed in a pair of boxers and nothing else.

Looking so guilty and alarmed that Matt didn't even have to wonder if he was up to no good. He knew.

"What the hell," he said in a soft and dangerous tone,

"are you doing in my house dressed like that at this time of night?"

"I . . . I . . ." Mike stuttered.

Matt felt Carly behind him, leaning against him, peering around him. At the same time Erin's door opened. She looked out, saw what was happening and came out into the hall in her short little slip of a nightgown.

"He's visiting," Erin said, taking Mike's hand. If possible, Mike looked even more alarmed than before.

"Like hell." Matt must have said it louder than he intended, because within just about a minute Dani's door popped open and she stuck her head out. Lissa did the same thing approximately three seconds later. Their wide eyes as they looked from him to Mike told Matt that they had a tolerable understanding of the situation.

"Don't be mad, Matt," Erin said coaxingly, twining her fingers in Mike's. Matt knew what she meant. She didn't care if he got mad at her. She meant, don't be mad at Mike.

"You're getting married tomorrow." He couldn't help it. His voice was set on that same muted roar. "And not to him."

He pilloried Mike with a you-are-going-to-die look.

"Well," Erin said guiltily, "as to that—"

"Oh, my God, Carly's got a ring!" That was Lissa, who happened to be nearest to Carly and must have seen the light catch on the ring Matt had given her approximately two hours before. "Matt, did you *propose*?"

"Yes, I did, but—"

His sisters weren't paying the least bit of attention to him. They skittered right on past him like he wasn't even there, surrounding Carly and exclaiming over her ring and holding her hand up and twisting it this way and that.

Matt gave Mike another of those prepare-to-die looks and turned to focus on the chaos behind him.

"What do you mean, *as to that?*" he asked Erin in a suitably awful tone.

Erin looked guilty. "I don't think I want to marry Collin after all."

"You've got to be kidding me."

Mike looked triumphant. Matt saw his face out of the corner of his eye and glanced back over his shoulder threateningly.

Erin smiled her most beguiling smile at him. "I'm really sorry, Matt. I know it's cost you a fortune and we're going to lose most of the deposits and it's going to be a huge hassle for you to tell everybody the wedding's off—"

"Me?" Matt asked.

"But you wouldn't want me to marry somebody just because of that, would you?"

She had him there.

"No," he said sourly after a moment. "I wouldn't."

Lissa looked at him, her eyes suddenly wide. "Matt," she said in a hushed tone, "I've got the best idea. Instead of canceling the wedding, why don't we just switch couples? You and Carly can get married tomorrow—er, today."

"*What?*" He didn't believe this. They were all chattering among themselves now and making plans, and only glancing occasionally at him. He just did not believe any of it. This was his life in a nutshell. One long series of problems with crazy-making women.

"What do you think?" Carly asked him almost hesitantly. His eyes softened. For her, he did forever. Anytime, anyplace, anywhere. He said so, and the group—except for Mike, who was still in major doo-doo with him over this—erupted into shrill little feminine cries of excitement.

Watching the four of them with their heads together hatching plans, it occurred to Matt that his life was as infested with women as a junkyard dog was with fleas.

Good thing he was starting to kind of like the itch.

In fact, he liked it so well that he married one of the pesky little things later that day.